BEACHAM'S
POPULAR FICTION

BEACHAM'S POPULAR FICTION 1950–Present

Volume 4
Q-Z
Appendices I, II, III
Index

Edited By
Walton Beacham

Assistant Editor
Suzanne Niemeyer

Beacham Publishing

Library of Congress
Cataloging in Publication Data

Beacham's Popular Fiction in America/ edited by Walton Beacham—
Washington, D.C.: Beacham Publishing.
4 v.; 24 cm.

Bibliography.
Includes index in v. 4

Publishing and critical history of best-selling fiction writers; critical
evaluations of selected titles.

1. American fiction—20th century—History and criticism. 2. Popular
literature—United States—History and criticism. 3. English fiction—20th
century—History and criticism. 4. Popular literature—Great Britain—History
and criticism. I. Beacham, Walton, 1943-

PS374.P63B43   813'.5'09   86-25857

Library of Congress Catalog Card Number: 86-25857

ISBN: 0-933833-10-5

Printed in the United States of America
First Printing, November 1986
Second Printing, August 1987

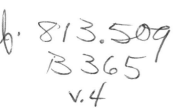
PREFACE

From its earliest beginnings, fiction has been designed to reach a "popular" audience, and to designate any work of fiction as "popular" is a reflection of critical attitudes which have developed about the genre. It is not the intention of this series to make any critical judgments or to categorize any author according to the arguments of "popular" versus "literary" works. The criteria for including an author here is that he was a best-selling author and that his works reflect social concerns.

Our underlying thesis is that fiction which becomes enormously popular contains elements which touch on deep-rooted social attitudes, concerns, fears, or desires. In the eighteenth and nineteenth centuries, art was thought to be a mirror of nature; in the twentieth century popular fiction is a mirror of society, and is often a barometer of social and psychological change.

Each of these articles attempts to illustrate how the writer was perceived by the critics, the extent of his popular acceptance, and the elements which caused his books to become best sellers. By understanding the undercurrents behind the plot, it is possible to see how popular fiction measures societal needs.

The response of the contributors to this series suggests changing critical opinions about "popular" fiction. Many of the contributors are professors whose specialties are traditional literature, from Renaissance to Victorian, and their enthusiasm for the novels they've examined, combined with the parallels they see to the literary tradition, indicate an important acceptance of a genre which has been considered light-headed by many critics and scholars.

A second series, which covers popular fiction writers from 1900–1950, contemporary writers not included here, and writers whose works have been translated into English and became best sellers, was published in 1987. We are also planning a series on fiction writers and dramatists who have achieved wide critical attention but whose works have not yet reached popular success.

As always, Beacham Publishing is interested in producing books which are devoted to improving the research capabilities of students. We welcome any suggestions for revising this title or ideas for other types of books. Write to: Beacham Publishing, 2100 "S" Street, NW, Washington, D.C. 20008.

Walton Beacham

CONTRIBUTORS

Carol Nevin Abromaitis
Loyola College of Baltimore

Timothy Dow Adams
West Virginia University

Janet P. Alwang
Pennsylvania State University

Kwaku Amoabeng
SUNY, Stony Brook

Stephen C.B. Atkinson
Hofstra University

Karl Avery

Margaret Ann Baker
Iowa State University

Jane L. Ball
Wilberforce University

Janet Ball

Carol M. Barnum
Southern Technical Institute

Richard Beckham
University of Wisconsin-River Falls

Sue Bridwell Beckham
University of Wisconsin-Stout

Kirk H. Beetz
National University, Sacramento

Kate Begnal
Utah State University

Anthony J. Bernardo, Jr.

Mary G. Bernath
Bloomsburg University

Charles Berryman
University of Southern California

Winifred Farrant Bevilacqua
University of Turin-Italy

George Bishop
Daemen College

Franz Blaha
University of Nebraska-Lincoln

Harold Branam

Dudley C. Brown
Allegany Community College

Carl W. Brucker
Arkansas Tech University

Mitzi M. Brunsdale
Mayville State College

Elizabeth Buckmaster
Pennsylvania State University

Leonard Casper
Boston College

Edgar L. Chapman
Bradley University

John R. Clark
University of South Florida

William Condon
Arkansas State University

Fred D. Crawford
University of Oregon

Alan Davis
Moorhead State University

J. Madison Davis
Pennsylvania State University/
Behrend College

Joan F. Dean
University of Missouri-Kansas City

Roger E. Dendinger
Francis Marion College

Thomas F. Dillingham
Stephens College

Robert DiYanni
Pace University

David C. Dougherty
Loyola College of Baltimore

William Ryland Drennan
University of Wisconsin-Baraboo/
  Sauk

Douglas Dunson
Arkansas State University

Ann W. Engar
University of Utah

Steven H. Gale
Missouri Southern State College

Richard Gardner
University of Wisconsin-Stout

Keith Garebian

Wesley C. Gibson

Kenneth B. Grant
University of Wisconsin-Baraboo/
  Sauk

Lyman B. Hagen
Arkansas State University

Jay L. Halio
University of Delaware

Gertrude K. Hamilton
Marymount College

Judith L. Hardin
Western Illinois University

Terry Heller
Coe College

Barbara Horwitz
C.W. Post Campus, Long Island
  University

James M. Hutchisson
University of Delaware

John L. Idol, Jr.
Clemson University

B.R. Johnson
New Mexico Highlands University

Sister Irma M. Kashuba, S.S.J.
Chestnut Hill College

Steven G. Kellman
University of Texas at San Antonio

Rebecca Kelly
Southern Technical Institute

Pamela Kay Kett
Moorhead State University

Peter Klovan
University of Alberta

Joy Kuropatwa
Brescia College

Carrol Lasker
SUNY, Stony Brook

Michael M. Levy
University of Wisconsin-Stout

Leon Lewis
Appalachian State University

James Maloney
Humber College

Laurence W. Mazzeno
U.S. Naval Academy

Michael McCully
Bloomsburg University

Richard E. Meyer
Western Oregon State College

Edmund Miller
C.W. Post Campus, Long Island
  University

Ray Miller, Jr.
Wilmington College

Amy B. Millstone
University of South Carolina

Sally Mitchell
Temple University

Claire Clements Morton
Huntingdon College

Kevin P. Mulcahy
Rutgers University

John Mulryan
St. Bonaventure University

Suzanne M. Munich
University of California, Davis

Suzanne Niemeyer

Leslie O'Dell
Wilfrid Laurier University

Robert M. Otten
Indiana University-Purdue University
    at Fort Wayne

Alice Hall Petry
Rhode Island School of Design

Bonnie C. Plummer
Eastern Kentucky University

Janet Polansky
University of Wisconsin-Stout

Elizabeth M. Rajec
City College of New York

Edward C. Reilly
Arkansas State University

Danny L. Robinson
Bloomsburg University

Kay Kinsella Rout
Michigan State University

Wanda La Faye Seay
Oklahoma State University

Barbara Kitt Seidman
Linfield College

Steve Serafin
Hunter College

Lynne P. Shackelford
Furman University

Jack Shreve
Allegany Community College

Charles L.P. Silet
Iowa State University

Nelson C. Smith
University of Victoria, Canada

Ira Smolensky
Monmouth College

Marjorie Smolensky
Augustana College

Katherine Snipes
Eastern Washington University

Charlotte Spivack
University of Massachusetts

Eve Walsh Stoddard
St. Lawrence University

Gerald H. Strauss
Bloomsburg University

Paul Stuewe

William F. Touponce
Indiana University at Indianapolis

Nancy Walker
Stephens College

Tomasz Warchol
Georgia Southern College

Susan J. Warwick
York University, Toronto

Mark A. Weinstein
University of Nevada, Las Vegas

Mark I. West
University of North Carolina at
  Charlotte

Robert F. Willson, Jr.
University of Missouri-Kansas City

Stephen F. Wolfe
Linfield College

Bruce W. Young
Brigham Young University

BEACHAM'S
POPULAR FICTION

ELLERY QUEEN
Daniel Nathan (1905-1982)
and Manford Lepofsky (1905-1971)

Publishing History

Ellery Queen began his multi-faceted career in 1929 with the publication of *The Roman Hat Mystery* for which he was assigned the dual role of author and detective-hero by his creators, Frederic Dannay, born Daniel Nathan (1905-1982) and his cousin Manfred Bennington Lee, born Manford Lepofsky (1905-1971). Dannay and Lee's entry into the world of detective fiction was prompted by the announcement of a $7500 prize contest co-sponsored by *McClure's* magazine and Frederick A. Stokes Publishing. The two cousins spent three months of evenings and weekends collaboratively writing *The Roman Hat Mystery* which they then submitted to the judges. Although they received unofficial notice that they were the contest winners, before they could claim their prize *McClure's* went into bankruptcy and those who took over the magazine chose Isabel Briggs Myers' submission as the winner. However, Stokes decided to publish Dannay and Lee's novel independent of the contest, and thus began Ellery Queen's long and varied history as author and detective.

It was not until 1936, after the release of nine novels under the pseudonym of Ellery Queen, that Dannay and Lee were revealed as the true authors of these works. At the same time it was disclosed that in 1932 Dannay and Lee has created another pseudonym, Barnaby Ross, for their collaborative efforts, under which they had published four novels featuring the amateur detective Drury Lane. During the 1929-1935 period, Dannay and Lee also published, under the Queen name, a collection of short stories titled *The Adventures of Ellery Queen,* a number of other stories in various periodicals, and *Mystery League* appeared before its collapse in 1934, but the editorial experience gained during its existence was to serve Queen well in the years to come.

If the 1929-1935 period was a busy one for Queen's creators, the three and a half decades that followed would have to be described as hectic. Twenty-six more Queen novels appeared between 1936 and 1971, as well as countless short stories, omnibuses, anthologies and other works bearing the Queen name. To many, Ellery Queen is known best as an editor, anthologist and scholar. In 1938 Queen published the first of at least eighty anthologies, *Challenge to the Reader,* in which he presented twenty-five stories by well-known mystery writers. The reader's "challenge" here was to identify the true author and detective of each item, for Queen had altered all their names prior to publication. In 1941 the inaugural issue of *Ellery Queen's Mystery Magazine* appeared featuring works by Dashiell Hammett, Margery Allingham, and Cornell Woolrich among others. In 1945 Queen instituted an annual contest for the best new work appearing in the magazine, and in 1946 an anthology series, *The Queen's Awards,* containing the best from the pages of *Ellery Queen's Mystery Magazine.* After 1957 *The Queen's Awards* series was discontinued and replaced by *Ellery Queen's Mystery Annual,* the *Ellery Queen's Anthology* series, and other collections bearing individualized titles, all presenting the best new crime fiction to the public.

Other anthologies edited by Queen served different purposes. *101 Years' Entertainment: The Great Detective Stories, 1841-1941* presented stories by the most distinguished figures in the field of crime fiction, from Poe and Doyle, Chesterton and Leblanc to Christie and Sayers, Hammett and Queen himself. In *Sporting Blood* (1942) Queen collected twenty sports detective stories, in *The Female of the Species* (1943) he presented the great women detectives and criminals, in *The Literature of Crime* (1950) the work on Hemingway, Faulkner, Steinbeck and Dickens appeared, and in *Poetic Justice* (1967) Queen anthologized the work of poets such as Chaucer, Byron, Whitman and Dylan Thomas on the subject of crime. It should be noted that although the Queen name appeared as editor for *Ellery Queen's Mystery Magazine* and the anthologies, their production was the work of Dannay alone. Taken together, the pages of the magazine and the anthologies reveal a virtually complete catalogue of the major writers in the field of crime literature.

Over the years, other Queen endeavors included the painstaking assembly of one of the world's largest collections of short crime fiction, the writing of a number of scholarly and bibliographic books treating these collected works, the most noteworthy being *Queen's Quorum: A History of the Detective-Crime Short Story as Revealed by the 100 Most Important Books Published in this Field Since 1845,* and the radio drama, *The Adventures of Ellery Queen,* which aired on CBS from 1939 to 1948.

Given the range and diversity of Queen's work, not to mention its quantity, it is not surprising that his name is one of the most well-known among readers of crime and mystery fiction. Over the forty-two years during which Dannay and Lee presented their work in print, 120 million readers were drawn into the Queenian world of mystery and detection. Many more came to know Ellery Queen, detective, on radio, television and film so that Queen's overall popularity is difficult to measure. Suffice it to say that Ellery Queen, author and detective, is one of the most significant figures in the history of detective fiction.

Critical Reception, Honors, and Popularity

Despite his reputation and popularity among readers of detective novels, Queen's fiction has not received the same degree of critical scrutiny as the work of other American writers of detective fiction, such as Dashiell Hammett, Raymond Chandler, and Robert B. Parker. One reason for this lack of attention is that many critics regard Queen's work as a throwback to an earlier form of detective fiction, that popularized in the 1920s by the writers of the Golden Age of detective novels, most notably Agatha Christie, Dorothy Sayers, Anthony Berkeley in England, and S.S.

Van Dine in the United States. Variously labelled the formal detective novel, the classic whodunit, the puzzle novel, the work of these writers placed primary emphasis upon order, social decorum, and human reason. The setting of their novels was usually a remote and isolated one, their characters were largely drawn from the upper levels of society, and their plots centered on the collection, elaboration, and piecing together of a complex set of clues. The detective-hero of these works was often an amateur, but always a gentleman well-versed in the accomplishments of the social milieu in which he worked.

Much of this description can be applied to Queen's work, particularily to the first nine novels. Although Queen left behind some of the elements of the formal detective novel in his later work, his fiction never became part of the dominant American tradition of the "hard-boiled" detective novel. The year that *The Roman Hat Mystery* was published also saw the release of Hammett's first two novels, *Red Harvest* and *The Dain Curse,* works far removed from the tradition of the Golden Age. While Hammett was laying bare the seamy side of urban life in America in the 1920s and 1930s through the eyes of his cynical, tough-talking, hard-drinking private eyes, Queen continued in the field of the formal detective story, focussing primary attention on the close and logical analysis of clues to the mystery. So committed to the puzzle element in the detective story was Queen that in the first group of novels there appeared a brief section titled "Challenge to the Reader" advising that all the clues needed to solve the case had been presented and that "a diligent study of what has gone before should educe a clear understanding of what is to come." Although Queen discarded the "Challenge" in his later works, its presence could still be felt for the emphasis continued to be placed on the rational explication of accumulated evidence, and not on characterization or social commentary. While Queen as detective became less intellectual, more emotional, and his cases brought him into closer contact than before with "real" life in America, the work in which he appeared never wholly abandoned the pattern of "adventures in deduction."

Although he continued to be read by millions, Queen as novelist was regarded by most critics as a formula writer whose works, unlike those of his contemporaries, Hammett, Chandler, Ross Macdonald, were remote from the mainstream of American life with respect to characterization, theme, and language. Yet praise for Queen's accomplishments was not entirely absent. Accepting Queen's dedication to the puzzle format, many reviewers, evaluating the first nine novels as classic whodunits, regard them as among the best of their kind. Particular respect is accorded Queen's strict adherence to the principles of fair play in these novels. Others maintain that a number of Queen's later works, most notably *Calamity Town, The Murderer is a Fox,* and *Cat of Many Tails,* successfully combine elements of the puzzle format and a naturalistic treatment of American life. In addition, two of the four Drury Lane novels, *The Tragedy of X* and *The Tragedy of Y,* were well received by the critics who felt that Dannay and Lee, unencumbered by Ellery, succeeded in blending deduction and careful characterization.

Regardless of their own personal response to Queen's fiction, nearly all critics acknowledge his popularity among readers of detective fiction, and his importance as a key figure in the history of American mystery writing. By far the most laudatory evaluations of Queen's work focus on his accomplishments as an editor and anthologist. Many consider *Ellery Queen's Mystery Magazine* the most significant periodical in the field of crime literature ever published, and his anthologies as central to the history of the genre.

Queen has received numerous awards and honors, including five Edgars, the most important award in the field of mystery writing. He was given an Edgar for the radio program of Queen's adventures, his contribution to the popularity of crime fiction, his critical writing in the field of detective literature, his work as editor of *Ellery Queen's Mystery Magazine*, and The Grand Master for his overall achievement. He was also awarded the Silver Gertrude for selling over a million copies of a book, and the Golden Gertrude for selling over five million copies of his work as a whole. Other honors include the Mystery Writers of Japan award and Iona College's Columbia Mystery Prize.

Analysis of Selected Titles

THE FRENCH POWDER MYSTERY
The French Powder Mystery, 1930, novel.

Social Concerns
The French Powder Mystery, the second Queen novel, is an excellent example of the formal detective novel. Given its form, it is not surprising that, on the surface, the work seems to concern itself little with significant social issues for the formal detective novel is, by nature, dominated by the action of solving a mystery through the elaboration and intensely analytical study of clues and evidence. Yet such works are not without social concerns, and *The French Powder Mystery* is no exception.

The plot of the novel centers on Ellery Queen's attempt to discover who murdered Winifred Marchbanks French, and the solution to the puzzle involves Queen and company in the world of the narcotics trade. Although the novel offers some insight into the illegal drug trade of the 1920s and the effects of narcotics upon users, it can hardly be said to reflect a strongly realistic view of these topics. What makes *The French Powder Mystery* interesting in terms of social issues is its treatment of the twin themes of order and disorder. Although these themes may not seem readily apparent on the surface, they are central to an understanding of all formal detective novels. In these works the reader encounters a group of characters, usually wealthy and well-bred, frequently in an isolated locale. Their usually peaceful, well-ordered world has been disrupted by a criminal action, most often murder. The police are called in, but they are baffled by the case, and it is only with the arrival of an unofficial investigator, the gentleman amateur detective, that the pieces of the puzzle begin to fall into place.

In *The French Powder Mystery* the date is Tuesday, May 24, and the scene, French's Department Store where, in a display window's concealed wall bed, the murdered body of Winifred Marchbanks French, second wife of Cyrus French, the store's owner, is discovered. Inspector Richard Queen of the New York City Police Department is called in to investigate, and along with him and his associates comes his son Ellery, writer of detective stories, amateur sleuth, and student of culture. All involved with the case, family members, the store's directors and employees, are assembled, and the slow process of establishing motives, opportunity and alibis is begun. Simultaneously the collection of evidence and clues commences. As the sorting out of this complex wealth of material proceeds, the reader is drawn into the world of those involved in and affected by the murder of Mrs. French. Their superficially harmonious society has been rendered chaotic by the murderer's action, and it is the function of the amateur detective to restore order to it. To accomplish this he must uncover the roots of the discord that threatens the social order.

In *The French Powder Mystery* Ellery learns that Bernice Carmody, daughter of Mrs. French by her previous marriage to Vincent Carmody, is a habitual drug-user, and that her mother, having become aware of this fact, arranged to meet the man who was supplying her daughter with the drugs on Monday evening at the family's store. Her murder is then ordered by the key figures in the drug ring for she knows too much about the organization to be allowed to live. In the final pages of the novel Ellery leads the reader and the cast of characters through a detailed account of his investigation, and finally presents the solution to the case. The drug ring is smashed, the murderer exposed, and all others involved released from suspicion. Within a larger frame, the social and moral code broken by both the victim's and the culprit's actions has been restored to wholeness. The appeal of works like *The French Powder Mystery* rests largely upon a belief in social order and decorum. Those who challenge and threaten the established order must be expelled so that harmony may be regained. Underlying the maze of clues and alibis in *The French Powder Mystery* is a clear commitment to the upholding of social and ethical code of existence.

Themes

In a general sense, *The French Powder Mystery* is primarily concerned with good and evil. Evil, in the form of narcotics and murder, has intruded into the self-contained world of the French family and business. As in other formula literature, such as the fairy tale and the western, good and evil are painted with broad strokes in the detective story. *The French Powder Mystery* is no exception to this pattern. Characters are not allowed complex emotions or motives for their behavior. They either uphold the rules of decency and goodness, or they do not. The appeal of this black and white presentation of virtue and vice rests upon shared assumptions of author and reader about good and evil. The typical reader desires that those who are honest, faithful to friends and family, and hard-working will be rewarded, and that those who are dishonest, disloyal, and lacking in industry will be punished. The detective story does not disappoint in this regard. While it is undoubtedly true that the simple resolution of the forces of good and evil in *The French Powder Mystery* presents a naive and artificial view of existence, it is also true that the simplicity of its vision provides both diversion and reassurance for its many readers.

Characters

The most important personality in all of the Queen works is, of course, Ellery Queen, amateur detective. In *The French Powder Mystery* and the other early formal detective works, Queen is presented as an almost pure logician, relentlessly examining pieces of evidence, from the small traces of powder on a bookend to the large details of complex social interactions. A descendant of Poe's Dupin and Conan Doyle's Holmes he is something of an eccentric, has a unique appearance, and is in possession of a vast and esoteric body of knowledge. In the preface to *The French Powder Mystery* the reader learns that Ellery, along with his wife, son, and father, Inspector Richard Queen, retired member of the New York Police Department, is now living in a tiny mountain-home in Italy, having given up his old profession. (Ellery's wife and son mysteriously disappear in subsequent works.) The novel itself goes back to the time when Ellery and his father lived together in a West 87th Street apartment in New York City, "a veritable fairyland of easy bachelordom." Ellery, a Harvard graduate, places great store in the values of the past, and has an independent income which allows him the opportunity to pursue a dilettante's study of culture. Given to wearing smoking jackets, a pince-nez, carrying a walking stick, and speaking abtrusely, many commentators regard Queen as a snobbish prig, especially in the early works. Yet rigorously analytical and emotionally detached, Ellery is capable of penetrating mysteries that all others find beyond comprehension. In doing so, he restores the world to order, and it is within this role as problem-solver that his true character emerges. He is fundamentally a comic hero whose intelligence and imagination enable him to solve a complex problem, and thereby bring about the reintegration of the social community.

The other characters in *The French Powder Mystery* are, by and large, stereotypes, fulfilling certain needs within the plot's development. The Cast of Characters appearing at the outset of the novel makes clear their representative natures and functions. Cyrus French is "a common American avatar-merchant prince and Puritan," his daughter Marion, "a silken Cinderella," and her fiancé, Westley Weaver, "an amanuensis and lover—and friend to the author." More important and interesting than these supporting characters are the figures of the victim and the villain.

Although they too are necessities of the plot, and in most respects, stereotypes, an understanding of their roles and characteristics is essential for an appreciation of the comic texture of the work.

The victim, in this instance the two victims Bernice and Winifred, while members of the community threatened by the villain's action, are slowly revealed to be, to some extent, worthy of their fates. Their behavior, though less reprehensible than the culprit's, has made them social offenders. Bernice in her involvement with narcotics, and Winifred in her semi-adulterous actions have violated accepted morality, and thus are not entirely unworthy of their suffering. Only those who are perceived to be socially unacceptable in some way experience the fate of the victim, for participation in the happiness of the comic work's conclusion is restricted to those truly "good" individuals. The villain is, of course, excluded from this happiness for he has broken the laws of God and man. His actions are more inherently evil than those of his victims, yet he is often more interesting than they. His breach of the social and legal code makes it necessary that he be removed from society, yet he gains a certain esteem in that his intelligence has allowed him to commit a clever crime and to escape discovery for most of the novel by presenting himself as one of the innocent. His pretense of innocence must be uncovered by the detective-hero, and his true nature revealed in order that the truly innocent be released from chaos and suspicion.

Techniques

The French Powder Mystery is a classic example of the detective novel as pure puzzle. The first piece of the puzzle is the discovery of Mrs. French's murdered body in the display window. From here the novel proceeds through a lengthy collection and examination of clues, alibis, and motives until the final solution is presented by Queen. While this novel, like so many other classic whodunits, has its fair share of red herrings, confusion, and deception, its central technical achievement is its strict adherence to the principles of fair play. With sufficient attention paid, by the conclusion of Queen's deductive puzzles the reader is always in a position to solve the mystery himself, for Queen presents all clues fairly and clearly as the case unfolds. Abiding by the rules of fair play, Queen invites the reader to match his wits against those of Ellery, and the appeal of works like *The French Powder Mystery* rests, in part, on this exercise.

Many critics have approvingly noted that Queen's claim, that all necessary clues to the mystery are presented before the solution and that only one solution is possible, is consistently accurate. The same could not be said of all detective stories. While many readers may not have the patience to solve the crime themselves, their enjoyment of the novel's building suspense is undiminished, for instead of matching their wits against Queen's they are content to follow and admire his brilliant and rational methods of deduction. One of Queen's major achievements is his ability to delay the presentation of the mystery's solution for as long as possible. In *The French Powder Mystery,* this ability is clearly evident for the culprit is not named until the novel's final two words.

Other notable technical features of the early Queen's works, including *The French Powder Mystery,* are the use of the same name for author and detective, a device used in all Queen's work; the creation of a narrator, J.J. McC., to present some of Ellery's cases in written form to the public; and meticulous plotting. The construction of plot in *The French Powder Mystery* leads unerringly to the final proof which is achieved by the exercise of reason. Queen's stress on the rational faculty is revealed in his detailed analysis of tangible evidence, his use of diagrams, maps, plans, and the avoidance of violence as a tool for uncovering criminal activity.

Literary Precedents

Queen's literary ancestors include Poe, Conan Doyle, E.C. Bentley, and closer to home, S.S. Van Dine. Like these writers, Queen emphasizes the principles of rational deduction, and creates a detective-hero who is intelligent, eccentric, and infallible. Like Poe's Dupin and Conan Doyle's Holmes, Queen possesses extraordinary deductive abilities and a creative imagination which, in concert, enable him to penetrate almost insoluble mysteries. Yet Queen is less anti-social than either of these figures, less sardonic in his response to the world. He is, like E.C. Bentley's Philip Trent, a gentleman accepted by the upper levels of the society in which he moves. However, it is to Van Dine's Philo Vance that the early Ellery Queen bears the closest resemblance. S.S. Van Dine, the pseudonym of the journalist and art critic Willard Huntington Wright, wrote eleven novels featuring his detective-hero Vance. These novels reveal the basic structure of the formal deductive puzzle, and are noted for their ingenious and complex plots. Like Vance, Ellery Queen is a refined, cultivated, and learned young man. Both inherited money from a relative, Vance from an aunt, Queen from an uncle, which removed them from "the class of social parasite" and allowed them to lead the "ideal intellectual life." Vance is drawn into the world of crime and murder through his acquaintance with District Attorney John F.X. Markham, while Queen's contact with this world is through his father, Inspector Richard Queen of the NYPD. Like Van Dine, Queen creates in the early works intricate plots at the expense of detailed characterization. Queen departed from the Van Dine model in his decision to make author and sleuth identical where Van Dine had made his author identical with his sleuth's assistant, and in his insistence upon fair play. Many critics regard Van Dine's work, while logical, as obscurely intellectual, making the reader's task of following his deductions almost impossible. Queen's puzzles, on the other hand, require far less arcane knowledge on the part of his readers for their solutions.

Other literary precedents for Queen's early work outside the field of crime literature include the novel of manners and Restoration comedies of manners. While Queen's work clearly suffers in comparison with that of writers like Austen, Congreve, and Sheridan, there is in his novels a similar presentation of a stable and closed society which places the highest value upon the observance of custom and convention. Queen's work lacks the satiric tone of many comedies of manners, yet it does resemble them in its belief in a secure and benevolent universe. Violations of the social code may occur, crimes may be committed, but the fabric of this genteel world is never seriously threatened. Order is always restored at the end. Like many comedies of manners, Queen's formal detective novels seem distant from actual experience. Written in the 1930s, they make virtually no reference to the political, economic or social disturbances of the time. Instead they provide a vision of existence which, like that of comedy, reassures the reader that the wicked will be punished, the virtuous rewarded, and that truth will always triumph. In their avoidance of extremes, complex emotion, and violence they serve as reminders of a world of innocence and simplicity, a world unlike that occupied by most of their readers. Naive and escapist they may be, but like other non-realistic literary forms such as the Elizabethan pastoral they answered certain needs of the readers of their time.

Related Titles

The other novels bearing the sub-title "A Problem in Deduction" are *The Roman Hat Mystery* (1929), *The Dutch Shoe Mystery* (1931), *The Greek Coffin Mystery* (1932), *The Egyptian Cross Mystery* (1932), *The American Gun Mystery* (1933), *The Siamese Twin Mystery* (1933), *The Chinese Orange Mystery* (1934), *The Spanish Cape Mystery* (1935), *Halfway House* (1936), *The Door Between* (1937), *The Devil to Pay* (1938), *The Four of Hearts* (1938), and *The Dragon's Teeth* (1939). They resemble *The French Powder Mystery* in their emphasis upon the puzzle, upon order and social decorum, and upon the importance of plot rather than character.

THE MURDERER IS A FOX
The Murderer is a Fox, 1945, novel.

Social Concerns/Themes

The Murderer is a Fox belongs to the middle period of Queen's detective fiction. Beginning with *Halfway House* (1936) Queen abandoned his use of a nationality in the title of his works, and began to lessen his emphasis on the puzzle element in his novels, But it was not until 1942 and the publication of *Calamity Town* that a clear change in Queen's work was apparent. *Calamity Town* is subtitled a "novel," not "a problem in deduction" as had been the earlier works, and this fact alone signals Queen's movement away from the restrictions of the pure puzzle format. *Calamity Town* is also the first Queen novel set in Wrightsville, a small new England town which serves as a microcosm of middle American society. While *Calamity Town* does contain a puzzle to be solved, this element is downplayed sufficiently to allow for commentary on other issues such as marital discord and the insularity of the small town.

The Murderer is a Fox is the second Queen work set in Wrightsville and as such bears a certain resemblance to *Calamity Town* in its exploration of the surfaces and depths of American small town existence. The time is the summer of 1944, and the action begins with Captain Davy Fox's return to his hometown after his participation in World War Two. Davy, the reader soon learns, is a tormented man, emotionally troubled by his experience of death and dying. Not only has he witnessed the deaths of fellow servicemen during his service as a fighter pilot in the China-Burma-India theater, but twelve years earlier his mother, Jessica Fox, had died of an overdose of digitalis administered, according to the verdict in her murder trial, by her husband and Davy's father, Bayard Fox. The result of these experiences, coupled with the suspicion of his wife Linda's infidelity, a suspicion fostered by the receipt of letters while overseas from an unknown sender hinting at her unfaithfulness, is the creation within Davy of a compulsion to kill his wife. Linda, informed by Davy of his fear that he will kill her, decides to enlist the aid of Ellery Queen. the man who had been instrumental in solving the Wright murder case several years earlier, the case recounted in *Calamity Town.*

After assessing the situation, Queen determines that the only way to help Davy is to re-open his mother's murder case in the hope of proving that Davy's father was not responsible for her death, and by extension that Davy is not the son of a murderer. If this could be proven, then Davy would no longer believe that his inheritance from his father was "tainted blood" and the "killer instinct." While much of the novel is devoted to Queen's investigation of the twelve-year-old murder, the work departs from a strict adherence to the "whodunit" pattern to examine material other than clues and evidence. This material includes the psychological impact of the war experience upon individuals, the underside of the superficially harmonious small town, and the theme of the sins of the father being visited upon the child. Although Queen does not delve into these issues in great depth, their presence makes *The Murderer is a Fox* a more socially relevant work than his earlier "problems in deduction." As a consequence, the reader is more involved with the outcome of the investigation, for the characters and their situations have been presented in more than a stereotypic and one-dimensional fashion.

As in all Queen's work, and most detective fiction, the dominant theme concerns the restoration of wholeness and order to a community or family torn apart by the intrusion of violence and anti-social action into their world. What makes *The Murderer is a Fox* more interesting in this regard than many of Queen's earlier pieces is that the detective-hero is permitted to accomplish only so much in his role as problem-solver. While Ellery does succeed in removing the stigma of being a murderer's son from Davy Fox, he can do little but reflect upon the operation of the forces of good and evil in the world at large. At the conclusion of the novel, the members of the Fox family are happily reunited, but to the unknown future are left such questions as how Wrightsville will receive the now-innocent Bayard, and how Davy and Linda will deal with the legacy of his war experiences.

Characters

The central character in *The Murderer is a Fox* is once again Ellery Queen. Although he remains relentlessly analytical, he is less emotionally detached here than in many previous works. His involvement in the affairs of the Fox family affect him as a human being, and his attempt to solve the mystery is prompted not so much by his fascination with puzzle decipherment as by his desire to help Davy and Linda Fox discover happiness. Ellery, having abandoned his pince-nez and walking stick, has ceased to be the pure logician and the snobbish prig. Significantly, along with Ellery's growth into a rounded character came the creation of three-dimensional supporting figures in his adventures. The portraits of the death-obsessed Davy Fox, the caring wife Linda, and the falsely convicted Bayard while not flawless, reveal an important development in Queen's abilities in the field of characterization. Rather than serving as mere plot facilitators, they exist as individuals caught up in real human dilemmas. Other noteworthy characters in the novel include Alvin Cain, the malicious young man determined to destroy Davy and Linda's marriage, and Emmy DuPré, the town gossip. Together the cast of characters in *The Murderer is a Fox* present a reasonably satisfying picture of the complexity underlying all human communities.

Techniques

At the heart of *The Murderer is a Fox* lies a puzzle to be solved, and as in all Queen's work the solution to the puzzle necessitates the development of a complex plot. The plot in this novel involves Queen in a detailed reconstruction of the events of the day, twelve years earlier, that Jessica Fox died. Still true to the tradition of empirical thought, Ellery conscientiously considers all the evidence, both the remaining physical evidence and the testimony of those present at the time of Jessica's death in order to arrive at the solution to the case. Given that the crime under investigation occurred twelve years earlier, the novel, to be successful, requires that the past be convincingly recreated. Such a recreation demands a fair measure of skill, for should the characters remember the past too clearly and precisely, the reader will feel that the novel lacks credibility. Queen avoids this danger by giving all the individuals involved with Jessica's death incomplete and sometimes contradictory memories.

Although the analysis of clues and evidence plays an important role in the case's solution, in this novel intuition is given a certain measure of authority. This moves *The Murderer is a Fox* away from the pure puzzle format, for Ellery's resolution of the case requires the exercise of both reason and emotion. Also interesting in this regard is the fact that the final solution, presented after an earlier false solution is established, remains unverifiable.

Literary Precedents

Queen's departure from the pure puzzle format in *Calamity Town* and *The Murderer is a Fox* suggests the influence of writers outside the field of the formal detective novel. Also suggestive of other influences is Queen's depiction of the small town of Wrightsville. Given that Queen in his magazine, had been publishing the work of writers such as Hammett, it is possible that their treatment of American life had an impact upon his writing. While Queen can never be considered a member of the hard-boiled tradition of detective fiction, his post-1940s work, including *The Murderer is a Fox* reveals an attempt to broaden his social vision beyond the confines of the enclosed world of the upper class.

The town of Wrightsville, named perhaps in tribute to S.S. Van Dine, the pseudonym of Willard Huntington Wright, serves as an example of typical middle American life. Superficially placid and orderly, beneath its surface it reveals the same measure of unhappiness and discord as any other human community. A number of commentators have suggested that Queen's movement away from the restricted scene of a small group of people in an isolated locale into the larger world reveals the influence of the naturalistic school of American fiction as practiced by Frank Norris, Jack London, and Theodore Dreiser. Clearly none of Queen's novels can be considered entirely naturalistic, but in their examination of the social forces at work upon man, and in their view of human action as explicable in cause and effect terms they display elements of this school of fiction. Less artificial works that are more representative of the human condition suggest that Queen was attempting to present, within the framework of the detective novel, a more serious approach to the world at large than he had before.

Related Titles

Other Queen works set in the town of Wrightsville and exploring the same milieu include *Calamity Town* (1942), *Ten Days' Wonder* (1948), *Double, Double* (1950), *The Last Woman in his Life* (1970), and the short stories "The Robber of Wrightsville," "The Gamblers' Club," "Death of Don Juan," "The Wrightsville Heirs," "Mum is the Word," and "Eve of the Wedding."

THE LAST WOMAN IN HIS LIFE

The Last Woman in his Life, 1970, novel.

Social Concerns/Themes

While few critics have lavished praise on Queen's post-1950s works, a number remain interesting in their attempts to treat contemporary social issues. *And on the Eighth Day* is considered by some to be a protest novel, examining the failures of twentieth-century society by means of a contrast with the religious-socialist community which serves as the novel's setting. In *The Last Woman in his Life* Queen deals with the topic of homosexuality, albeit in a rather dated fashion. The plot centers upon the investigation of the murder of John Levering Benedict III, a Harvard classmate of Ellery's. After meeting Ellery and his father at the airport, Johnny offers them the use of a cabin on his country estate near Wrightsville for some rest and relaxation. The Queens' escape from the cares of the world in Wrightsville, still a "viable Shangri-La" for Ellery, is soon interrupted by the arrival of Johnny, his attorney and best friend Al Marsh, and Johnny's three ex-wives for a financial discussion as Johnny intends to change his will. That evening Johnny is murdered, but not before he has provided Queen with a holographic will, and a "dying message." Discovered near his body are three pieces of clothing, one each from the closets of the three ex-wives. As the case unfolds much suspicion is cast on these three women and their associates before the true culprit is revealed.

While the solving of the puzzle is central to *The Last Woman in his Life,* Queen focuses much of his attention in this novel on the themes of love, money, and power. Benedict had intended to leave his fortune to his soon-to-be fourth wife Laura, his "true love," but if he were not married at the time of his death it was to go to his only living relative, Leslie Carpenter. Leslie, unlike the majority of the other characters, is neither greedy nor power hungry. Her commitment in life is to helping the poor. Leslie and Ellery provide the novel with its moral focus, arguing in the way they live their lives that love cannot be bought, that money must be used wisely and for the social good, and that the exercise of power requires discretion and compassion.

Characters

While the individuals in *The Last Woman in his Life* are essentially stereotypes, they are interesting as representative of certain human behavior. The primary force driving most of the characters to action is greed. The three ex-wives, Audrey the actress, Marcia the show-girl, Alice the nurse, along with Sanford Effing the lawyer, Foxy Faulks the gambler, and the many women trying to establish themselves as Laura, Johnny's "true love," are motivated only by their desire for wealth. As a result they are accorded little respect or admiration. Interestingly, the novel's villain, Al Marsh, is presented much more sympathetically, for his crime was not the result of a desire for money or power, but is perceived as a crime of passion. Having revealed himself to Johnny as a homosexual and confessed his love for him, he is subjected to Johnny's horror and disgust. Fearing exposure of his homosexuality and distraught at Johnny's rejection, he murders him. As in many of Queen's early works, the victim in this novel is presented as, to some extent, worthy of his fate. Johnny, incapable of lasting relationships with women, careless in the use of is money and power, and lacking compassion for his friend's situation, violates the social code on many levels. For this reason his murder is not entirely unfitting. At the end of the novel the good, in this case Leslie Carpenter, are rewarded, and the social virtues of honesty, compassion, and hard work are upheld.

Techniques
While *The Last Woman in his Life* combines the solving of a puzzle and commentary on social issues such as money-madness and homosexuality, it lacks the unity of much of Queen's previous work. One reason for this lack of unity is that the plot displays numerous clichés and failings in the exercise of logic. The presence of the holographic will, the "dying message," the red herrings of the women's clothing, and the "missing woman" make the work seem rather tired and hackneyed on the level of plot. As well, the hints at the true identity of the murderer throughout the text are so clear that the reader wonders why the usually logical Queen takes so long to solve the case. Despite these weaknesses, *The Last Woman in his Life* is noteworthy for Queen's attempt to treat the subject of homosexuality objectively, and for its depiction of a society consumed by materialism.

Adaptations
The radio series of Queen's adventures which ran from 1939 to 1948 was well-received by critics and public alike, but Queen's transition to the film medium was far less successful. In 1935 Republic Studios released the first Queen movie, *The Spanish Cape Mystery,* and followed in 1936 with *The Mandarin Mystery,* adapted from *The Chinese Orange Mystery.* Reviewers liked neither, commenting that the careful plotting of Queen's novels was largely absent from the film versions. In 1940 Columbia began a new series of Queen films featuring Ralph Bellamy as Ellery. Some of these were based on Queen novels, albeit loosely, while others had no connection with published Queen material. *Ellery Queen, Master Detective* (1940) was based on *The Door Between*, *Ellery Queen and the Perfect Crime* (1941) on *The Devil to Pay,* and *Ellery Queen and the Murder Ring* (1941) on *The Dutch Shoe Mystery.* Those films not derived from Queen work include *Ellery Queen's Penthouse Mystery* (1941), *A Close Call for Ellery Queen* (1942), *A Desperate Chance for Ellery Queen* (1942), and *Enemy Agents Meet Ellery Queen* (1942). Although both Dannay and Lee worked as screenwriters for Columbia, Paramount and MGM from 1936 to 1940, they were not involved with the screen versions of Queen's adventures.
Television viewers came to know Ellery Queen beginning in 1950 with the series starring Richard Hart as the master detective. In 1955 a second series, featuring Hugh Marlowe as Ellery, aired, and the 1958-1959 season saw yet another version

of Queen's adventures, *The Further Adventures of Ellery Queen*, starring George Nader. In 1971 a pilot film for a new Queen television series appeared. Titled *Ellery Queen: Don't Look Behind You*, it was based on *Cat of Many Tails* and starred Peter Lawford as an English Ellery. The series it was intended to introduce was never produced. Also in 1971 Claude Chabrol directed a film version of *Ten Days' Wonder* starring Orson Welles and Anthony Perkins. Chabrol resituated the action from Wrightsville to an estate in Alsace, but preserved much of Queen's plot. However, most critics were unimpressed by the film calling it "an absurd mess," "a travesty," and more kindly, a failure that was still "fascinating to watch."

Other Titles

Novels: *There was an Old Woman*, 1943; *Cat of Many Tails*, 1949; *The Origin of Evil*, 1951; *The King is Dead*, 1952; *The Scarlet Letters*, 1953; *The Glass Village*, 1954; *Inspector Queen's Own Case*, 1956; *The Finishing Stroke*, 1958; *The Player on the Other Side*, 1963; *And on the Eighth Day*, 1964; *The Fourth Side of the Triangle*, 1965; *A Study in Terror*, 1966; *Face to Face*, 1967; *The House of Brass*, 1968; *Cop Out*, 1969; *A Fine and Private Place*, 1971. Works published under the pseudonym Barnaby Ross are: *The Tragedy of X*, 1932; *The Tragedy of Y*, 1932; *The Tragedy of Z*, 1933; *Drury Lane's Last Case*, 1933.

Short Story Collections: *The Adventures of Ellery Queen*, 1934; *The New Adventures of Ellery Queen*, 1940; *The Case Book of Ellery Queen*, 1945; *Calendar of Crime*, 1952; *QBI: Queen's Bureau of Investigation*, 1955; *Queen's Full*, 1965; *QED: Queen's Experiments in Detection*, 1968.

Additional Sources

Boucher, Anthony, *Ellery Queen: A Double Profile*. Boston: Little, Brown & Co., 1951. Outlines Queen's career up to the publication of *The Origin of Evil*.

Haycraft, Howard, *Murder for Pleasure: The Life and Times of the Detective Story*. New York: Biblo and Tannen, 1968, pp. 173-177. Discusses Queen's place within the history of mystery fiction.

Nevins, Francis M., *Royal Bloodline: Ellery Queen, Author and Detective*. Bowling Green, OH: Bowling Green University Popular Press, 1974. An indispensable discussion of all of Queen's work. Includes biographical, critical, and bibliographic information.

Symons, Julian, *Bloody Murder; From the Detective Story to the Crime Novel: A History*. New York: Viking, 1985, pp. 111-112, 139-140. Discusses Queen's work within the context of the Golden Age of detective fiction.

Susan J. Warwick
York University, Toronto

MARY RENAULT
Mary Challans
1905-1983

Publishing History

At the age of eight, Mary Challans determined that she would be an author, and after taking an Honours degree in English literature at Oxford, she trained as a nurse because "my experience of life was largely derived from other people's books, which were good because their writers had got it first-hand." Her first five novels, published in Britain by Longmans and in the United States by Morrow, appeared, like all of her work, under the pseudonym Mary Renault. These contemporary novels derive from her experience before and during World War II, when she worked as a neurosurgical nurse at Oxford's Radcliffe Infirmary, and they were reissued in England in 1976 by Queens House. Because of its sympathetic treatment of homosexuality, unusual for its time, *The Charioteer*, published in England in 1953, did not appear in America until 1959, reprinted by Bantam in 1974.

Of the Mediterranean lands Renault visited after the war, she "found Greece incomparably the most moving and memorable," and she spent the rest of her life on eight superbly realized fictional evocations of Greek Classical history, all published in New York by Pantheon and reissued by Bantam. Gilbert Highet, in the *Book-of-the-Month Club News*, 1966, recommended *The Mask of Apollo* "with complete confidence to all those tens of thousands of readers who were moved by *The King Must Die* and *The Bull From the Sea*," Book-of-the-Month selections in 1958 and 1962 respectively, as was *Fire From Heaven*, 1969. *The Praise Singer* was a Literary Guild Alternate in 1978.

Critical Reception, Honors, and Popularity

Even before her Greek novels, both the public and reviewers accepted Renault's work enthusiastically, although she herself deprecated her early books. The *New York Times* praised *Promise of Love*, 1939, as "an unusually excellent first novel." *Return to Night*, 1947, received the $150,000 MGM Award, the largest financial prize then offered in the field of literature, though it was never filmed, like *The King Must Die*, which was on best seller lists for nearly a year and was purchased by Twentieth Century Fox in 1958. *Return to Night* gave Renault an extensive American audience which her Greek novels later expanded.

Renault's popular success has never been matched by critical attention to her work, often dismissed as "historical fiction," a genre usually hag-ridden with devotees of formulaic sex-and-sensationalism. Although nothing could be farther from Renault's austerely conceived yet glowingly evocative scenes of ancient Greece, the pejorative "historical" label attached to her work by critics seems to have largely prevented serious critical examinations of it. No exhaustive critical treatment of

Mary Renault's work yet exists.

An accompanying difficulty in dealing with Renault's Greek novels today is a general lack of knowledge about and interest in the Classical world. Only a few American readers and scholars are equipped to understand Athenian history. Nevertheless, as her large sales and the revival of her earlier works indicate, the highly disciplined artistry of Renault's best sellers has made her one of the foremost historical novelists of our time.

Renault was a past president of the P.E.N. Club of South Africa; a Fellow of the Royal Society of Literature; and recipient of the National Association of Independent Schools Award, 1963, and the Silver Pen Award, 1971, for *Fire From Heaven*.

Analysis of Selected Titles

THE LAST OF THE WINE
The Last of the Wine, 1956, novel.

Social Concerns

Mary Renault explained her refusal to use the past as a metaphor for the present in a 1973 essay, "History in Fiction": ". . . if what you are really talking about is Nazi Germany or Vietnam or Texas, why not say so instead of misleading your readers about Nero or Caesar or Troy?" Beginning with *The Last of the Wine*, considered her masterpiece, Renault scrupulously followed Herakleitos' maxim *You cannot step twice into the same river,* recreating ancient Greece and bringing her readers to it, not it to them, as Bernard Dick has noted.

In Athens' fall to Sparta in the Peloponnesian Wars, the setting of *The Last of the Wine*, Renault offers historical perspectives on problems still bedevilling Western society: the seemingly inevitable linkage of corruption with power in charismatic political leaders like Alkibiades; the nature of democracy and the responsibility of the gifted individual to it; the ambivalent potential of the homosexual relationship. *The Last of the Wine* illuminates such complexities, and more, in the unforgettably clear light of the Greece of Socrates and Plato.

Themes

Just as the search for individual *arete,* the inward thirst for achievement knowingly made beautiful, formed the basis for the society of the Athenian Golden Age, the chief theme of *The Last of the Wine* is Alexias' growth to manhood through his profound relation with Lysis, who was himself the historical subject of Plato's dialogue on Friendship. Together Alexias and Lysis progress toward perception of the Absolute Good, Absolute Beauty, Absolute Truth delineated in Plato's *Symposium.* Plato espouses the nature of Love, in which physical expression is only the first step to the ennoblement of the human soul.

As Lysis guides Alexias' development, both men illustrate the Classical pursuit of truth, goodness, and beauty won by overcoming physical and spiritual suffering. The scene of Lysis' beating during Renault's parody of an athletic contest reveals the perversion of Athens' ideals that lead to the decline of its Golden Age. Alexias, however, by selling himself to feed Lysis, achieves his own maturity. *To philotimo,* the outward striving for honor, brings both Lysis and Alexias the inward beauty of moral victory, the kind W. B. Yeats called "Not natural to an age like this, being high and solitary and most stern."

Characters

In the Greek custom to which the title *The Last of the Wine* refers, a lover tosses out the dregs of his wine to form the initial of his beloved's name. This is a constant symbol, according to Landon Burns, of "the depth and brevity of love." Alexias and Lysis humanize the power of love, as Socrates taught, each drinking life to its lees in honor of the other. The Greeks knew, and Renault shows, that not all men can do so. The greater or lesser capacity to love, as well as the outright failure or rejection of love, motivates all of the principal characters of *The Last of the Wine,* perhaps most tragically with Alkibiades, the magnetic but flawed leader-turned-traitor who cost Athens so dearly for its infatuation with him. Like Dion in *The Mask of Apollo,* who led Athens into its disastrous Syracusan adventure, Alkibiades is afflicted grievously by the power forced on him "by the mediocrity, or even the downright moral weakness of his associates." Alkibiades, whose downfall parallels Athens' in *The Last of the Wine,* proves incapable of the love of honor and freedom and truth over the seduction of cold-eyed, cold-hearted politicians whose love of self blocks their rise. Alkibiades cannot rise to the redeeming self-sacrifice necessary to scale Plato's ladder of love.

Techniques

Mary Renault learned well from the master sculptors of the Parthenon, who worked with both Greece's incomparable light and the deep shadows it casts, carving their immortal reliefs to be viewed in the context of the monument as a whole. Landon Casson has pointed out that as Renault shaped the "very special and precious relationship that could exist between men who were lovers" in *The Last of the Wine,* she simultaneously revealed "the pathetic lot of Athenian women of good family . . . the role of housekeeper and brood mare." Renault's unfailing good taste and Classical restraint also illuminates such sobering Greek practices as infanticide, bringing them into convincing perspective.

As well as adapting material from Platonic dialogues in *The Last of the Wine* and fleshing out the historical account of the Peloponnesian Wars, Renault adopted the first-person memoir style Classical writers loved and used so often. Renault employed this narrative device in all of her Greek novels except *Fire From Heaven,* achieving an immediacy and freshness that strongly involves her readers in actions which seem familiar, because of their quintessentially human qualities. Her characters bridge the gulfs of time and culture between their lives and the readers'.

Literary Precedents

Bernard Dick traces Renault's novelistic technique to Herodotus, the fifth century B.C. military historian, chronicler, and ethnographer, who called his *History* "presentations of research." Like Herodotus, Alexias and Renault's other narrators reconstruct their past in terms of their nation's history, reminiscing, digressing, and philosophizing, often passing aphoristic judgement on vital human issues, as does Lysis in *The Last of the Wine:* "A man who thinks himself as good as everyone else will be at no pains to grow better . . . Must we forsake the love of excellence, then, till every citizen feels it alike?"

Renault's love of excellence animates all of her Greek novels, perhaps most pervasively *The Last of the Wine,* and helps explain why so few historical novels can match its quality. That trap of historical novelists summed up by E.M. Forster's dismissal of Sir Walter Scott—"a trivial mind and a heavy style"—can only be avoided by scholarly devotion, meticulous attention to detail, and an unerring, even Classical, sense of proportion, evidences of literary quality generally lacking in the genre. To make novels like *The Last of the Wine* more real than history also demands the artistic integrity Renault explained in 1970: "I think one has a duty to the uninformed reader to tell him when one is giving him authentic history and when one is making it up . . . one *must* aim at enlightening the reader rather than obfuscating him; and nothing pleases me so much as to hear from a reader (as I often have) that I have caused him or her to seek out the actual sources."

THE KING MUST DIE
The King Must Die, 1958, novel. Sequel: *The Bull From the Sea,* 1962, novel.

Social Concerns/Themes

D.H. Lawrence, no stranger to artistic integrity and its price, called myth an attempt to explain that which goes too deep in the blood and soul for rational analysis. With *The King Must Die* and its sequel *The Bull From the Sea,* Renault explores the myth of Theseus, Athens' greatest hero, in legends predating the Trojan War.

Renault's re-presentation of Theseus' myth again treats what Virginia Woolf called "the sadness back of things" the Greeks knew so well. Renault focuses on the issue of kingship, so she shapes her tragic theme of the king's willing consent to *moira,* his destiny, to which even Zeus must bow. *The King Must Die* presents the bright aspect of kingship generally assumed at the outset of the old tragedies, which is the development of a hero worthy to lead his people; while the more somber *The Bull From the Sea* examines the *hybris* (pride) which Theseus' success inexorably engenders in his personality, and which brings about his tragic fall.

Renault also develops several secondary themes connected to Theseus' kingship: the hidden son's need to prove his heritage and claim his throne; the father-king's fear of being supplanted; the slaying of a monster to save the nation; male blood-brotherhood; marital infidelity in thought or deed and its grievous consequences. Renault binds these together through the religious and socio-political role of the king in the ancient patriarchal societies of northern Greece. The king was the embodiment of the Sky God's will on earth as well as the figure primarily responsi-ble for appeasing the gods so that the nation might prosper. Renault points out in her Author's Note to *The Bull From the Sea*, "On the king devolved the noble responsibility of offering his own life as supreme sacrifice when, in times of great crisis, the auguries demand it." She saw Theseus' entire life as a "tension and conflict" between the patriarchal Sky God of the North and the cult of the Earth Mother worshipped by the Pelasgian Shore Folk of southern Greece, as well as the Minoans of Crete who built the civilization Theseus helped overthrow. The worship of both principles, as Renault tells Theseus' story, resounds with rich archetypal overtones still fascinating today, as the immense popularity of both novels indi-cates.

Characters

Theseus, as the protagonist of Renault's tragedy, passes through five stages of his tragic development in *The King Must Die,* each connected, as Landon Burns has demonstrated, with the consenting death of a king. In Troizen, the King Horse is sacrificed by Theseus' grandfather Pittheus, who sounds the keynote for Renault's recurrent theme: "It is not the sacrifice . . . it is not the blood-letting that calls down the power. It is the consenting, Theseus. The readiness is all." In Eleusis, Kerkyon, king-for-a-year, perishes, and in Athens, young Theseus voluntarily re-linquishes his royalty to join the victims sent to Crete for Minos' tribute; Minos himself succumbs in Knossos, and Aigeus, Theseus' father, answers the god's call, leaving Theseus to assume the throne. Renault clearly demonstrates that it is the king's duty "to fulfill the appointed end with pride, with honor, and with humility." With each death, as in an episode of a Classical tragedy, Theseus learns more about himself, travelling one step closer to his own consenting destiny.

Techniques

Theseus grows from child to man in *The King Must Die,* and Renault adapts the style of his first-person narration to reveal the successive stages of his grcwth. The mature Theseus speaks with archaically elevated diction, Homeric in its simplicity and its reliance on the everyday to suggest the eternal. Renault has an extraordinary ability to convey realistic explanations of supernatural events through Theseus' matter-of-fact descriptions of his adventures. She consistently allows elements of mystery in its religious, as well as in its denotative, sense to exist at the heart of things too deep in the blood and soul to explain away entirely. Theseus' *hybris* prevents him from remembering much of the past in the sequel, *The Bull From the Sea:* "A bound is set to our knowing, and wisdom is not to search beyond it. Men are only men."

Related Titles

Even though Renault's Theseus novels have often been called legendary romances rather than historical fiction, *The Bull From the Sea,* shadowed by Theseus' fatal *atē,* the Greeks' name for the madness that forces men into acts outside their will and honor, fulfills Theseus' tragedy in fictional form. Its four episodes also speak about the deaths of kings: Oedipus' end in Marathon; Hippolyta's death in battle in place of Theseus at Pontos; Theseus' lethal curse on his son Hippolytus; and Theseus' own plunge into the arms of Poseidon, his symbolic father. Theseus learns through grief and loss that "readiness," the king's intellectual and spiritual maturity, is all.

FIRE FROM HEAVEN

Fire From Heaven, 1969, novel. Sequels: *The Persian Boy,* 1972, novel; *Funeral Games,* 1981, novel. Associated work: *The Nature of Alexander,* 1975, biography.

Social Concerns/Themes

An even greater human mystery than mythic kingship lights Renault's *Fire From Heaven,* her fictionalized portrait of young Alexander of Macedon, Theseus' spiritual heir. Achilles' touchstone for a man was, "Theseus would have done it," and eight hundred years later, Alexander celebrated Achilles as his own ideal, saying, "It is a lovely thing to live with courage, and die leaving an everlasting fame."

Renault chronicles the simultaneous conflicts Alexander experienced through international and emotional growing pains. The rise of Macedon under Alexander's powerful father Philip accompanied the self-defeat of the "politically bankrupt, spiritually dying, eternally quarreling" Greek city states, incapable of uniting to defend themselves against Macedonian military might. At the same time, Alexander and Philip were locked in a psychologically complex power struggle between a gifted father and son of surpassing genius; their battle was ended, but not resolved, by an assassin's knife at Aigai. Greece had been Philip's, but the rest of the world had to be Alexander's conquest.

Characters

Renault positioned a wealth of scrupulously drawn figures around the already magnetic youth Alexander, based firmly on ancient sources and often confirmed by modern archaeology: the fearsome Philip; Alexander's terrifying half-mad mother Olympias; Leonidas the Spartan, Alexander's tutor; Alexander's companion Hephaistion. Down to the last Macedonian warrior and the least servant at a princely feast, Renault builds each character solidly out of an exhaustive self-taught knowledge of the world of ancient Greece.

To modern eyes, one of the questionable aspects of Alexander's society is its easy acceptance of bisexuality as a norm of male behavior. Renault points out that Alexander's "three state marriages qualified him for normality," and "for [his] contemporaries, his most striking peculiarity was his refusal to exploit defenseless victims like captive women and slave-boys, a practice then universal." She leaves her readers free to decide the nature of Alexander's bond with his beloved Hephaistion, for no physical relationship has been proved; all that is certain is that Alexander described Hephaistion to the conquered Persian Queen Mother Sisygambis as "Alexander, too."

Techniques

Fire From Heaven is Renault's only novel of ancient Greece told in the third person, keeping more distance between Alexander and her audience than her usual first person narration allows. By doing so, she is able to show all of Alexander's many gifts—his political shrewdness, his organizational genius, his physical beauty and his intellectual power. She never forgets, however, that Alexander, like Achilles before him, was a consummate soldier. The Macedonian army elected their king, and the sense of honor, his and theirs, that made him their only choice, made all the rest possible.

Related Titles

Renault reveals the last seven years of Alexander's meteoric career through the eyes of *The Persian Boy,* Alexander's handsome eunuch Bagoas, with her most precarious treatment of homosexuality in fiction. Some commentators find Bagoas' view of the convoluted politics of Alexander's reign inconsistent with Bagoas' relatively minor position as a household slave, albeit a favored and talented one. Other critics find that the homoerotic aura which usually heightens Renault's creative insights into the remote past somewhat obscures the story of Alexander's achievements. In any case, *The Persian Boy* exhibits tragedy as well as glory, for Hephaistion, who Renault feels is "the most underrated man in history," appears throughout as "Alexander, too," the better self that Alexander loved and lost.

At his death, Alexander named no heir, and his lieutenants tore his empire asunder. *Funeral Games* is the fictional memoir of Alexander's one steadfast general, his half-brother Ptolemy, later King of Egypt, and it records the last flickering shadows of the heavenly light born at Macedon. *Funeral Games* closes Renault's career as well as Alexander's, leaving her readers to ponder the mystery he left behind.

Other Titles

Promise of Love, 1939, rpt. 1976 (novel); *Kind Are Her Answers,* 1940, rpt. 1976 (novel); *The Middle Mist,* 1945, rpt. 1976 (novel); *Return to Night,* 1947, rpt. 1976 (novel); *North Face,* 1948, rpt. 1976 (novel); *The Charioteer,* 1959, rpt. 1974 (novel); *The Lion in the Gateway,* 1964 (juvenile); *The Mask of Apollo,* 1966 (novel); *The Praise Singer,* 1978 (novel).

Additional Sources

Brunsdale, Mitzi M., "Mary Renault," *Critical Survey of Long Fiction.* Englewood Cliffs, NJ: Salem Press, 1983. Overview and analysis of Renault's Greek novels.

Burns, Landon C., Jr., "Men Are Only Men: The Novels of Mary Renault," *Critique* 6 (Winter 1963): 102-121. A discussion of *The Last of the Wine, The King Must Die,* and *The Bull From the Sea* as historical fiction.

Dick, Bernard F., *The Hellenism of Mary Renault.* Carbondale: Southern Illinois University Press, 1972. An analysis of Renault's re-creation of ancient Greek life and a justification for historical fiction.

———. "The Herodotean Novelist," *Sewanee Review* 81 (Autumn 1973): 864-869. A discussion of *Fire From Heaven* and *The Persian Boy* in the context of "Herodotean" historical fiction-as-memoir.

Wolfe, Peter, *Mary Renault.* New York: Twayne, 1969. An introductory study of Renault's first ten novels, emphasizing their derivation from the cultural milieu of the 1930's.

Mitzi M. Brunsdale
Mayville State College

ANNE RICE
1941

Publishing History

Anne Rice has written four novels and several short stories under her own name and, as Ann Rampling, she has written two novels. Her first novel, *Interview with the Vampire* (1979), was a popular success and has become the first book of a series, *Chronicles of the Vampires*. She published her second novel, *The Feast of All Saints*, in 1981 and her third, *Cry to Heaven*, in 1982. Her fourth novel, *The Vampire Lestat* (1985), is the sequel to *Interview with the Vampire*. As Ann Rampling she has written *Exit to Eden* (1985) and *Belinda* (1986).

Critical Reception, Honors, and Popularity

The first two books of Rice's *Chronicles of the Vampires* were extolled and excoriated, sometimes both in the same review. Critics gave Rice mixed reviews because although her prose is rich and captivating, both books contain long, motionless passages and metaphysical soliloquies which do not march to the Gothic drummer. One reviewer suggested that Rice needed to see more horror movies, while another praised her unique departure from the typical vampire story. Regardless of the critics, *Interview with the Vampire* has had huge paperback sales, garnered a film option, been selected by the Book-of-the-Month-Club, and been translated into several languages. *The Vampire Lestat* was also a Book-of-the-Month-Club selection.

Analysis of Selected Titles

INTERVIEW WITH THE VAMPIRE

Interview with the Vampire, 1979, novel. Sequel: *The Vampire Lestat*, 1985, novel.

Social Concerns

In *Interview with the Vampire*, Anne Rice mates the old Gothic tradition with a late twentieth-century perspective. Her vampire hero, Louis, bears only a faint resemblance to the Vladimirs and Draculas of old, who were powerful, nefarious beings. Louis belongs to the narcissistic 1970s. He mirrors the self-probing "me-generation" of the past few decades.

Louis constantly questions his morality, his priorities, his feelings, and continues to react like a "sensitive" human being long after his change from life to undeath. Gradually, as the novel unfolds, he realizes that his traffic in blood and violence has totally depleted his treasury of human compassion. He has become a moral cipher who tries to retain a semblance of sensitivity by brooding upon himself and by imitating the extravagant gestures of a man in anguish. Louis' desperate imposture may be an accurate portrait of our self-conscious, self-indulgent times.

Like all vampires, Louis is alienated from society, whether it be eighteenth-century New Orleans where he began his new "life" or twentieth-century San Francisco where the interview takes place. He is aware of his alienation and of his victimization by Lestat, the vampire who "made" him. Every vampire in the book is both predator and victim, a point that Rice makes repeatedly. Like grotesque children of abusive parents, the vampires keep the wheel of victimization turning: Louis, who vowed he wouldn't, turns five-year-old Claudia into a vampire.

A question arises concerning Rice's vampires: do we dare blame the victims? As predators (murderers, rapists, torturers), the vampires deserve the stake. But Rice also portrays her vampires as victims—lost exiles from all humanity. In the latter case, therapy, not capital punishment, would be appropriate. The image of a vampire on a psychiatrist's couch may be ludicrous, but Rice has touched on a hair-trigger issue of our times. The ambivalence in our society about crime and victimization is a strong undercurrent in Rice's otherwise patently Gothic novel.

Themes

Other themes in the book, such as immortality and loss of innocence, are perhaps more obvious. Immortality is a curse to Louis. Although he has reached the pinnacle of human desire, eternal life, he has done so through the veins of youth. Like young Werther he contemplates suicide but nevertheless he clings to his immortal half-life, damned though it be. Self-preservation is far more powerful force than morality.

Rice also treats the theme of lost innocence. In fact, the entire book is about Louis' coming of age, vampire style. Louis learns that he really is inhuman, that he really does enjoy blood, that he really is undead. He loses his human innocence and, eventually, his human guilt as well.

Characters

The three main characters of *Interview with the Vampire*, Louis, Lestat, and Claudia, are primarily plot facilitators. There is a certain flacidity of character development in the book. Most of the time Louis seems sensitive, introverted, almost tender, but when necessary, he can also appear cold, savage, or indifferent. Likewise Lestat, cynical and barbarous, can also act in a well-educated and thoughtful manner. Claudia, the changeling monster-child, has practically no personality at all. The characters are simply vampires, weird creatures that Rice pulls and twists along Parisienne boulevards and mountain crags. They are like markers in a board game. Although they articulate the themes of the novel and act out scenes of uncanny violence, in reality they do not have lives of their own.

Techniques

Anne Rice uses the flashback technique in both *Interview with the Vampire* and *Vampire Lestat*. Besides grounding the books in the present while visiting the past, the flashback technique also allows Louis (who is being interviewed) to speak in the first person. Rice also plays with tempo. A scene which may be ponderous and still is juxtaposed with a scene of quick passion and violence. The resulting tension, particularly in *Interview with the Vampire*, is extremely unsettling.

Literary Precedents

If Bram Stoker could have read this book, he might have had trouble appreciating Louis' vacillating, self-absorbed character. But he would have had no trouble recognizing the desolate Transylvanian landscape that Louis and Claudia visit in search of their roots. The moldy tower, terrified peasantry, black capes and carriage in this scene are direct descendants of Gothic tradition. In the midst of these melodramatic elements, however, Rice develops a psychology of vampirism. Her exploration of the fictional world of vampiric emotions, sexuality, spirituality and society is unique.

Related Titles

In *The Vampire Lestat* the villain tells his side of the story. Lestat, an insensitive Philistine in *Interview with the Vampire*, relates his personal history as a counterbalance to Louis' tale. This sequel includes more detailed accounts of ancient vampire cults of Egypt and Greece. But on the whole, *The Vampire Lestat* continues to explore the inner workings of vampires' souls and societies while shining an uncanny light on human society as well.

Additional Sources

"Anne Rice," *Contemporary Authors*, Jane Bowden, ed. Detroit: Gale Research, 1977. A brief biographical sketch of Rice's education, interests and goals.

Reviews of *Interview with a Vampire* can be found in the following sources:

New York Times Book Review (2 May 1976): 7, 14.

National Review (3 September 1976): 966.

New Republic (8 May 1976): 29-30.

Newsweek (10 May 1976): 108-109.

Reviews of *Vampire Lestat:*

Library Journal (1 October 1985): 114.

New York Times Book Review (27 October 1985): 15.

Playboy (December 1985): 42.

People (25 November 1985): 21-22.

Vogue (November 1985): 282.

Janet M. Ball

HAROLD ROBBINS
Francis Kane
1916

Publishing History

Harold Robbins (originally Francis Kane, adopted as Harold Rubin or Rubins) has led a life as adventurous as any described in one of his books. Supporting himself with odd jobs from the time he was ten, he became a millionaire in the food business by the time he was twenty but then lost everything in one bad speculation. He began life anew as a shipping clerk and rose to the position of executive director of budget and planning at the New York office of Universal Pictures. To win a hundred dollar bet with a studio vice president, he wrote *Never Love a Stranger* during the three hours each evening he had to wait for the California office to close. In doing so, he found a new profession and made himself a millionaire all over again. His particular appeal is to lower middle class readers. He happened upon the publishing scene at an opportune moment since the paperback revolution made it possible for his works to reach this audience in a way that hardcover books do not, and in fact Robbins tends to sell only modestly in hardcover although all of his novels remain in print in paperback, and each sells at least 600,000 copies a year, year after year. Robbins still publishes new books regularly, but the continuing sales of reprints and subsidiary rights provide most of his enormous income. In 1986 Robbins turned himself into a publishing industry officially with the inauguration of a series of novels under the imprint "Harold Robbins Presents." The first three novels in this series are *At the Top* (1986) by Michael Donovan, *Blue Sky* (1986) by Sam Stewart, and *The White Knight* by Carl F. Furst.

Critical Reception, Honors, and Popularity

Robbins' first novel was the autobiographical *Never Love a Stranger.* This book was praised for its truthful picture of growing up the hard way in New York, but it was banned as obscene in Philadelphia. In his next novel, *The Dream Merchants,* Robbins won praise from the critics for his realistic insider's picture of Hollywood. Robbins returned to urban life in the Depression for this third novel, *A Stone for Danny Fisher,* in which the critics still found much to praise, but thereafter his popularity grew so great and so out of proportion to his merit that it was hard to find a critic with a kind word for him. The general verdict is that he took a raw talent in need of nothing more than nurturing and polishing and sold out to the lowest common denominator of popular taste. Since he was going to sell millions of copies regardless, reviewers felt free to condemn his faults in the roundest terms, often without mentioning his virtues. Typical is W. F. Gavin's hyperbolic condemnation of *The Adventurers*: "Only once in a generation does a writer display such a complete lack of taste with such a total lack of talent."

Robbins' work is undeniably laced with scenes of gratuitous sex and explicit violence, and he is something of an anti-intellectual as charged, but these facts alone cannot account for his appeal and his abiding popularity, for they are the commonplaces of pulp fiction. His lasting success can be attributed to a combination of three factors. In the first place, he is an excellent writer. That is, he knows how to plot a story in true Victorian fashion with dozens of characters pursuing interlocking obsessions across five hundred pages in a way that is all neatly disentangled in the last chapter. He is as good at keeping secrets as Dickens and not so sentimental in using them to explain away the loose ends of a story. He claims to be concerned with people and not with plot, but when he says this he is describing his methodology of composition and not the books as they finally exist. Not without reason is he billed as "The World's Best Storyteller" on the covers of the paperback editions of his books. Robbins also knows how to write in the sense that he can compose literate, sophisticated prose that encourages the reader to go on by the rhythm of the language independent of the material.

The second reason for his success he has pointed to himself: each of his novels is a clear moral fable; indeed it is always the same moral fable, the story of the great decision when the protagonist has to "choose his morality and live with it," as Robbins has expressed it. Again his methods are the same as those of Dickens and the great Victorian popular novelists. Many another contemporary writer attempting to emulate the success of Robbins has failed to see through the surface details of sex and violence to the simple moral imperative behind the work.

There is, however, one final key to the success of Robbins, and here he parts company with Dickens and perhaps earns the scorn that has been leveled at him by reviewers. He does pander; however, he knows exactly how to do this. Publishers, reviewers, readers, and jealous rivals alike seem to think that it is the quantity and explicitness of the sex and violence that distinguish Robbins from his fellows, and this fact has probably led to the enormous growth in the number and explicitness of sex scenes in American popular fiction of the last thirty years. But it is the quality of the sex and violence that distinguishes Robbins from his fellows. He can make violence more painful, and he can make sex disgusting, and this fact, and not the explicitness of his descriptions, has earned him his popular following. Indeed, he is not even uniform in the way he treats taboo subjects. *A Stone for Danny Fisher* is full of explicit violence; however, although seething with sexuality, it has no explicit descriptions of sex. *The Carpetbaggers* is notorious for the freedom with which it uses four-letter words, but it was followed immediately with *Where Love Has Gone,* which uses no such language. Although Robbins is unabashedly pornographic when he feels it appropriate, he is careful to tailor his pornography to his plot. This is the real key to his success.

There have been numerous movie adaptations of his books, among these *Where Love Has Gone* (1964), *Stiletto* (1969), *The Adventurers* (1970), *The Betsy,* (1979), and *The Lonely Lady* (1983). *The Pirate* was a television movie in 1978.

Analysis of Selected Titles

THE CARPETBAGGERS

The Dream Merchants, 1949, novel; *The Carpetbaggers,* 1961, novel; *The Inheritors,* 1969, novel.

Social Concerns

Social significance is probably not something that any one of its millions of readers has picked up *The Carpetbaggers* expecting to find; however, in common with many of Robbins' other books, this one fulfills an important social purpose by providing readers with vicarious access to a world of power and yet suggesting that it is not worth the effort necessary for reaching it. Lower middle class readers would remain unconvinced by a conventional moralizing that suggested the price was too high because the hero had to lie, cheat, and kill his way to the top. But Robbins' message is more subtle: he takes no moral stand against the lying and the cheating and the killing. In fact he goes out of his way to find contexts in which these can be viewed sympathetically. What member of the lower classes would, for example, begrudge Nevada Smith the opportunity to take revenge on the men who had murdered his parents? The fact that his methods are peculiarly sadistic only endears him to Robbins' readers: sadism practiced in a good cause absolves the guilt. The problem with life at the top is not any moral price paid in getting there. The problem as Robbins presents it is that, despite its apparent glamour, life at the top is nevertheless empty and unsatisfactory. This recurring motif enables readers to congratulate themselves for not having wasted their efforts on success.

There is a practical corollary to this pervasive attitude toward societal success. Such a view of the nature of success is an illustration of the psychology of immaturity. In this context, the lurid sexuality of *The Carpetbaggers* is not only explicable; it is inevitable. As John Sutherland has pointed out, Robbins recreates an adolescent view of the adult world, defining the parameters of power in the imagery of sexuality that is the only arena of power the adolescent mentality can understand. Robbins is a master at ambivalent presentation of the attractions of power and its hollow ring. In *The Carpetbaggers* he is particularly masterful in using scenes of explicit sex and violence to present this ambivalence.

Themes

If *The Carpetbaggers* has a specific theme it is that only by the most Herculean efforts can an individual overcome the circumstances of his upbringing and lift the dead weight of the past from his shoulders. *The Carpetbaggers* is, however, the fourth most read book of all time for reasons that transcend theme. It is certainly a well told story, but it reached its extraordinarily large audience because of a combination of circumstances. It satisfies both normal curiosity about behind the scenes in Hollywood and prurient curiosity about the reclusive Howard Hughes. In addition, the extensive use of four-letter words and the scenes of graphic sex and violence certainly gave the work special fascination to its original readers. *The Carpetbaggers* is, in fact, the best illustration of the Robbins technique of entertaining the lower middle class with tales of the lurid sex lives of the rich and famous, showing his readers just how revolting life can be in the fast lane. Readers get a chance to enjoy pornography without having to admit that they do or that it has anything to do with their own uneventful lives.

Characters

The Carpetbaggers is a *roman à clef,* and the main character Jonas Cord is an obvious portrait of eccentric billionaire Howard Hughes—in his earlier, more active years. Robbins is a master of the *roman à clef* mode, giving his readers more than enough information to make the connection but then improving on prurient curiosity with a fictional closure that explains (and explains away) just how Cord became such a hard-driving and hard-driven character. The real Howard Hughes had no daughter to disown mistakenly, but Cord's discovery of his mistake provides effective closure for this complex narrative. Robbins never settles for reminding the reader of a real person; he always follows this created character through to his logical development in a clearly orchestrated plot.

After Jonas, the most striking character in the book is perhaps Rina Marlowe, a conflation of Jean Harlow (for the unfortunate sex life) and Jane Russell (for the film career and the curious relationship with Hughes). The character of Monica Winthrop owes something to Jean Peters, and the character of Nevada Smith owes a great deal to the cowboy star Ken Maynard. The character of Jennie Denton, a prostitute who becomes first a movie star and then a nun, is a conflation of various real people.

Techniques

The Carpetbaggers is divided into nine books. The odd-numbered books are narrated in the first person by Jonas Cord. Each of the even-numbered books is a third-person narration focusing on a person whose life Cord changes: Nevada Smith, Rina Marlowe, David Woolf, and Jennie Denton. Book Two tells "The Story of Nevada Smith" with so much detail concerning this character's early life that it is virtually a self-contained novel.

Literary Precedents

The *roman à clef* was introduced to a wide audience in the novels of Benjamin Disraeli during the Victorian period. W. Somerset Maugham, Evelyn Waugh, and Ernest Hemingway have written in this mode, but it has become a particular vogue during the last few decades, in part at least because of the success of *The Carpet-baggers*. Other Robbins novels including major characters who are transparently derived from real people include *Where Love Has Gone* (Lana Turner), *The Adventurers* (Porfirio Rubirosa and Barbara Hutton), *The Pirate* (a conflation of Adnan Khashoggi and Abdlatif al-Hamad), *The Lonely Lady* (Jacqueline Susann), *Dreams Die First* (Hugh Hefner), and *Spellbinder* (Billy Graham).

Related Titles

Together with *The Dream Merchants* and *The Inheritors*, *The Carpetbaggers* is part of Robbins' Hollywood Trilogy. As in the case of The Depression in New York Trilogy described below, the novels deal with unrelated characters but create a panorama when read in conjunction. Whereas *The Carpetbaggers* concerns Hollywood in the heyday of the studio system, *The Dream Merchants* concerns the early years of independent entrepreneurship, and *The Inheritors* concerns the new world of television.

At the time of original publication, *The Saturday Review* called *The Dream Merchants* "by far the most ambitious novel ever to be fashioned around the American motion-picture industry." Johnny Edge is a small-time hustler who helps nickelodeon owner Peter Kessler rise to be a major Hollywood producer of quality films. At first seduced by the glamour of movie star Dulcie Warren, Johnny in the end reciprocates the love of Kessler's daughter Doris. The book is strong on characterization, and F. S. Nugent, the reviewer for the New York *Times,* particularly praised the book for avoiding the sort of caricature common in Hollywood novels. *The Dream Merchants* is framed by Johnny's first-person narration in the present, but he is interrupted by a number of third-person narrations from the past. This ingenious point of view is effectively maintained.

The Inheritors concerns the new generation in Hollywood. Stephen Gaunt brings a magic touch to the world of television programming, but the main interest of the book is what happens in the bedroom, not the board room. Gaunt is an unsympathetic character who knows sex but not love. His affairs are numerous, but he never acknowledges his women by name; they are just a sum of their physical characteristics to him.

Adaptations

In 1964 *The Carpetbaggers* was given a lavish movie production under the direction of Edward Dmytryk. It stars George Peppard as Jonas Cord, Carroll Baker as Rina Marlowe, and Alan Ladd (in his last role) as Nevada Smith. The huge supporting cast features Bob Cummings, Martha Hyer, Elizabeth Ashley, Lew Ayres, and Martin Balsam. Since *The Carpetbaggers* had been so recently published at the time and so widely read, the movie had to be reasonably faithful to the book, and despite the vast range of material, it is. Although it has no special artistic distinction, it is clearly plotted and well paced. The cast is excellent and manages to be convincing even at the most melodramatic moments in the plot. The movie was a huge financial success.

In 1966 Henry Hathaway directed a movie western called *Nevada Smith* about the early life of this character and based on portions of *The Carpetbaggers* that had not been used in the movie version of that novel. This effective, lean revenge melodrama stars Steve McQueen, Karl Malden, Brian Keith, and Suzanne Pleshette. *Nevada Smith* was remade as a television movie starring Cliff Potts, Lorne Greene, and Adam West in 1975 under the direction of Gordon Douglas. This was the pilot for a projected series never made.

The Dream Merchants was a 1980 miniseries under the direction of Victor Sherman. It starred Mark Harmon as Johnny Edge, Vincent Gardinia as Peter Kessler, and Morgan Fairchild as Dulcie Warren. Also in the cast were Brianne Leary, Robert Picardo, Eve Arden, Kaye Ballard, Morgan Brittany, Red Buttons, Robert Culp, Howard Duff, José Ferrer, Robert Goulet, David Groh, Carolyn Jones, Fernando Lamas, Ray Milland, and Jan Murray. The production evoked the atmosphere of the evolving film industry very effectively, and the large cast performed well.

When *The Inheritors* was first published, Joseph E. Levine bought the screen rights and announced that a movie could be expected shortly. Later the project was to be a television series, but as yet nothing has come of either plan.

A STONE FOR DANNY FISHER

Never Love a Stranger, 1948, novel; *A Stone for Danny Fisher,* 1952, novel; *79 Park Avenue,* 1955, novel.

Social Concerns

When Danny returns to New York after failing to throw a fight for bookie Maxie Fields, Robbins saves him from the consequences of his earlier action quite arbitrarily. In much the same way, Robbins later kills off Danny's daughter—and with the same purpose—to show that it is an unreasoning fate that guides "life among the lowly" (as Harriet Beecher Stowe subtitled *Uncle Tom's Cabin*). Of course, Danny is just a teenager at the time of the fight and only about twenty when his daughter dies; however, Robbins' portrait of Danny's world is effective and realistic just because the character of Danny can tell the whole of his own life story without pausing for one moment of serious self-reflection. His shady dealings escalate from shoplifting, mugging, agreeing to fix a fight, and cheating the Department of Welfare to blackmail, blackmarketeering, and arranging to have his brother-in-law killed by a hit man, but he never considers the moral or even the practical implications of what he is doing. The hit goes wrong in the same way that the fixed fight does. Danny learns too late that he does not have the facts straight. This time the mistake kills him.

At another level the book illustrates lower middle class striving for the security and protection of a home of one's own. Danny's anger at his father begins when the family home is lost, and he finally resolves this anger on the day when he moves back into the house but can do so only because his father reaches out to him saying, "We've all come home again."

Themes

The social issue of the effect of fate on the aspirations of the lower middle class and the reciprocal concern for the security of a home are important thematic motifs in the book, but from Danny's point of the view, the theme of his life is probably "Without a buck, you're nothin' but crap." Although the novel is autobiographical, for Robbins the theme of the book as a whole is not so simple, but it is perhaps summed up in this observation of Danny's: "Someone you know all your life tries to kick your teeth in, and a man you never saw before and will never see again comes along and saves your life." Logically enough the book ends with a hymn to the "ordinary man."

Characters

Danny Fisher is a "jerk" in search of a picaresque adventure in which he might have been a rogue. Danny has the reader's full sympathy throughout because of the point of view (see the discussion of techniques below), but by any objective standard he misses his chance again and again simply because he fails to consider his options. He agrees to throw the Golden Gloves championship fight to enable his father to start his own business again, but he fails to realize that losing the fight will end the professional boxing career that was to be his ticket out of the slums. To make matters worse, his father throws him out of the house on the night of the fight for wasting his life in pursuit of a dangerous boxing career, but it never occurs to Danny to explain that this amateur fight is to be his last. Then he allows his boxing skill to overwhelm the logic of the bad deal he has made and goes on to win the fight, leaving himself hunted for years by the gambler with whom he had made his dirty deal and a disappointment to the high school coach who had invested thousands of dollars in his potential as a fighter. When he returns to New York, he takes no precautions to avoid his old enemies. Danny is totally lacking in introspection, and he does not change in the course of the work. This fact is not a flaw in the book's characterization but a necessary condition of the theme that fate is beyond man's control and understanding.

There are a large number of minor characters, all etched with an almost Dickensian eye for the significant characterizing detail. Nellie Petito is the good girl Danny marries. She domesticates him. She also has an irrational premonition that Danny is in danger on the day they are moving back to his childhood home. With no good reason for her fears, she nevertheless turns out to be right, for Robbins is using her to illustrate his fatalistic theme. Sarah Dorfman (professional name Ronnie) is the whore with a heart of gold who saves Danny when he fails to throw the fight and barters away her own chance for happiness to support her disabled brother. Sam Gottkin (later Gordon) is a person from this world who makes it—for a while. He is already a high school coach at the beginning of the book, but he becomes a summer entrepreneur and then a major businessman. But he too is a product and a victim of the urban scene, and he never really adopts middle class values. As a coach, he lets, indeed requires, squabbling boys to fight out their antagonisms. He is also carrying on an adulterous affair. And as a businessman he makes deals with gangsters on their own level and cuts what corners can be cut. Mimi, Danny's sister, sells herself into a loveless marriage with Sam as her way out of the slums.

Perhaps the most interesting characters in the book are Danny's parents, who strike the appropriate postures for lower middle class domesticity and fail to see when and how their dreams slip away from them. Danny's father is cold and rejecting and unwilling to listen to reason, but Danny never recognizes that he has adopted the very same stereotypic male attitudes, not only when he slugs the welfare investigator but even when, especially when, he is blaming his father for the death of his dog or for the loss of their home in the paradise that is Brooklyn.

Techniques

Danny Fisher narrates his own story in the first person, but by the ingenious device of a prologue spoken by Danny from the grave to the son he never knew, Robbins is able not only to maintain the verisimilitude of a first-person narration but even to describe plausibly incidents Danny had not witnessed in his life, for example the reactions of his mother on the morning she discovers that the milk service has been stopped for non-payment. Such passages are clearly marked "I WASN'T THERE WHEN," making the shifts of focus easy to follow and helping to maintain overall consistency of mood.

Although Robbins is more a writer of incident than image, he can be wonderfully effective at important turning points in the story by presenting a minor detail of life in a way that suggests the whole direction of the story. For example, when Danny's mother does learn that milk service will be discontinued, she sits down in front of the open icebox. "Whatever cold was left in it would escape," Robbins writes, "but somehow it didn't matter. She didn't have the strength to get up and close the door. . . . She stared into the almost empty icebox until it seemed to grow larger and larger and she was lost in its half-empty, half-cold world."

To use Phyllis Bentley's terms, *A Stone for Danny Fisher* is almost all scene and no summary; that is to say, numerous episodes from Danny's life are presented to the reader, but there are no narrative links connecting these episodes. This technique gives a graphic urgency to the story and allows a long book to move very rapidly. The character Danny is also able to give the impression that he is neither self-centered nor self-justifying (although he is both) because he never comments on what he was doing but merely describes what he said and did. Thus the book avoids a possible sentimentality, and the technique helps the reader to focus on the theme that the evils of urban life and of the Depression have conspired to destroy what chance there might have been for happiness in the lower middle class.

Although liberally seasoned with explicit violence, *A Stone for Danny Fisher* stops the sex scenes just short of the graphic. In doing so in this book Robbins shows himself to be a remarkably astute judge of the threshold of reader arousal. This technique also suits the material well because Danny lives so naturally in a world of eroticism (and violence). The image of the girl next door purposely walking around naked in her bedroom to tease him is an emblem for the life he leads when he grows up—the pleasures of life are always just within sight, daring him to risk the disappointment of actually reaching for them.

A Stone for Danny Fisher is written in a racy, colloquial style, but it is written with such a sure control of the idiomatic that the father's occasional Yiddishisms seem a bit jarring; however, this fact may have increased the book's appeal by making the milieu seem only superficially and accidentally Jewish. The problems of Danny are, after all, the problems of all working class ethnics during the Depression.

Literary Precedents

A Stone for Danny Fisher is a *Bildungsroman* (or novel of growing up) in the picaresque tradition that goes back at least to *Don Quixote* by Miguel de Cervantes. More immediate ancestors include the nineteenth-century moral tales of Horatio Alger, turn-of-the-century muckracking novels of low life like *The Jungle* (1906) by Upton Sinclair, and proletarian novels of the 1930s like *Studs Lonigan* (1932-35) by James T. Farrell. James Lane has also suggested a specific relationship between *A Stone for Danny Fisher* and *A Tree Grows in Brooklyn* (1943) by Betty Smith and *Knock on Any Door* (1947) by Willard Motley. In particular, Smith's Francie Nolan symbolizes the aspirations of those determined to overcome the dehumanizing effects of the modern urban experience through hard work. Danny Fisher illustrates how easy it is to be destroyed by this world.

Related Titles

After he had written the three novels *Never Love a Stranger, A Stone for Danny Fisher,* and *79 Park Avenue,* Robbins came to see them as forming a trilogy which he calls The Depression in New York. These are parallel stories involving different characters but all illustrating the struggle for survival of the lower middle classes during the Depression.

Never Love a Stranger is, with regard to incident and characterization, an intensely autobiographical novel. Even the name of the hero is Frankie Kane, the name Robbins received when he was, like his hero, a foundling, but Robbins imposes his fine sense of plot closure on the materials of his life up to this time (many of them reused, of course, in *A Stone for Danny Fisher*). The point of view of this novel is of interest because it has the same advantages for storytelling as the point of view adopted in *A Stone for Danny Fisher*. Frankie Kane narrates most of his own story in the first person, but the main narration is interrupted in places for first-person reminiscences by his friends. This allows Robbins to include the death of his hero—or anti-hero, for Frankie Kane is a stoic victim of social conditions just like Danny Fisher. *Never Love a Stranger* puts considerable emphasis on sex in a way that alienated reviewers, but Robbins was praised for his handling of religious misunderstandings and for his characterization. Some reviewers complained that the hero lacked introspection, leaving readers uncertain of his motivation; however, as in the case of Danny Fisher, this lack of introspection is the key to the social theme of the book.

79 Park Avenue is a rare use by Robbins of a female central character (*The Lonely Lady* is another). It is essentially the same story as *A Stone for Danny Fisher* and *Never Love a Stranger,* but Marja Fuldicki survives by turning to prostitution rather than gangsterism. The book was an early use by Robbins of the *roman à clef* since it is based in part on the Jelke trial.

Adaptations

Michael Curtis directed a movie version of *A Stone for Danny Fisher* called *King Creole* (1958). In order to tailor the material to star Elvis Presley, the locale was changed from New York to New Orleans, and the hero was made a Cajun rather than a Jew and given a talent for singing rather than boxing. Despite these major changes, the movie is faithful to the seedy atmosphere of the book and leaves many important character relationships intact. It shows an imaginative integration of the musical numbers into the dramatic story and includes what is probably Presley's best film performance. The supporting cast includes Walter Matthau, Vic Morrow, Carolyn Jones, Dean Jagger, Jan Shepherd, Paul Stewart, and Dolores Hart.

Never Love a Stranger was filmed in 1958 from a screenplay written by Robbins in collaboration with Richard Day. The director was Robert Stevens, and the movie stars John Drew Barrymore and Steve McQueen. In 1977, *79 Park Avenue* was a six-hour television movie directed by Paul Wendkos. It starred Lesley Ann Warren (fatally miscast), Marc Singer, and David Dukes and featured a huge supporting cast of name players. This movie was cut to four hours for rebroadcast. Neither of these adaptations was a critical or a popular success.

Other Titles

Never Leave Me, 1953 (novel); *Stiletto,* 1960 (novel); *Where Love Has Gone,*

1962 (novel); *The Adventurers,* 1966 (novel—Robbins adapted this as a film script the following year, but his version was not the one used); "The Survivors," 1969 (television series—Robbins provided the concept for the series, but his initial script was not used); *The Betsy,* 1971 (novel); *The Pirate,* 1974 (novel); *The Lonely Lady,* 1976 (novel); *Dreams Die First,* 1977 (novel); *Memories of Another Day,* 1979 (novel); *Goodbye, Janette,* 1981 (novel); *Spellbinder,* 1982 (novel); *Descent from Xanadu,* 1984 (novel).

Additional Sources

Contemporary Authors vol. 73-76. Detroit: Gale Research, 1978, pp. 533-534. Brief survey of Robbins' publishing history with pithy quotations from reviews.

Contemporary Literary Criticism vol. 5. Detroit: Gale Research, 1976, pp. 378-380. Excerpts from reviews.

Current Biography Yearbook. New York: H.W. Wilson, 1970, pp. 355-357. Survey of Robbins' career to 1970.

Lane, James B., "Violence and Sex in the Post-War Popular Urban Novel: With a Consideration of Harold Robbins' *A Stone for Danny Fisher* and Hubert Selby's *Last Exit to Brooklyn,*" *Journal of Popular Culture* 8 (1974): 295-308. Sensitive reading of Robbins as a representative of lower middle class values.

Sutherland, John, "Harold Robbins: The *Roman à Clef* I," *Bestsellers: Popular Fiction of the 1970s.* London: Routledge & Kegan Paul, 1981, pp. 122-29. Short chapter illustrating the adolescent voyeurism of Robbins' appeal.

Thompson, Thomas, "Close-Up: The Man Who Turns Sex and Adventure into Cash: The World's Best-paid Writer: A Tour Through the Harold Robbins Industry," *Life* 63 (8 December 1967): 49-63. Racy use of interview material in which Robbins sees himself as the greatest writer in history.

Edmund Miller
Long Island University
C. W. Post Campus

TOM ROBBINS
1936

Publishing History

At 24, after completing an enlistment in the U. S. Air Force including a tour in Korea, Tom Robbins accepted his first professional writing job as copy editor for the Richmond, Virginia *Times-Dispatch*. Fired from the Richmond newspaper for running photographs of black celebrities, Robbins moved to the Seattle area where he accepted a position as art critic for the *Seattle Times*. In 1964, he temporarily left Seattle for New York where he began research on a still-unpublished book on Jackson Pollack. Back in Seattle, Robbins worked for *Seattle Magazine* until he gave up his column to devote his attention full-time to writing his first novel.

That first novel, *Another Roadside Attraction*, did not sell well in the hard cover market. Only when the twice-rejected novel was published in paperback did it become a financial success. In fact, hard cover sales for all of Robbins's novels have been modest in direct contrast to the large number of paperbacks sold. Because of his great popularity in the soft cover market, Robbins has been called the "Prince of the Paperback Literati" by at least one critic. According to Bantam, over three million copies of his novels have been sold in the United States; worldwide, his work has been translated into ten languages.

Critical Reception, Honors, and Popularity

Generally considered a counterculture novelist, Robbins has been virtually ignored by scholars and literary critics. Indeed, his status as cult novelist almost guarantees that he would not be the recipient of any mainstream awards or prizes and that any attention to his work would be given only grudgingly. Still, Robbins is immensely popular, especially with high school and college students who appreciate his gentle criticism of American society and his outlandish humor.

Critics seem unable to classify Robbins's novels; he has been categorized as a Mark Twain humorist, a Western writer, a California novelist, a hack grinding out formula novels, and an experimental writer of the freshest sort. With the exception of *Still Life with Woodpecker*, reviewers in most newspapers and magazines have greeted Robbins's work with pleasure, though not necessarily with much understanding. These positive initial receptions have not been followed by many critical commentaries and evaluations.

It is too early to gauge Robbins's literary reputation. With two of his novels published during the 1980s, any assertion of Robbins's ability as social critic must carry with it certain reservations. Though Robbins has not yet won critical recognition, the fact that his four novels continue in print and that his latest novel, *Jitterbug Perfume,* served as a book club featured selection speak well of his large and still growing popularity.

Tom Robbins

Analysis of Selected Titles

ANOTHER ROADSIDE ATTRACTION
Another Roadside Attraction, 1971, novel.

Social Concerns/Themes

The setting for much of Robbins's first novel is Captain Kendrick's Memorial Hot Dog Wildlife Preserve, the roadside attraction to which the body of Jesus Christ is temporarily brought before John Paul Ziller and Plucky Purcell flee the FBI, steal a solar balloon, and attempt to melt the dead body of Christ and the living body of John Paul Ziller in the sun's radiation. All of this is recorded by Marx Marvelous, skeptic researcher, who in the course of the novel comes to learn about lifestyle, nature, and personal freedom from Amanda, Robbins's central character and heroine. These improbable events and unlikely characters provide Robbins with a vehicle through which he can comment on American culture and the possibility of a new, healthier and happier lifestyle.

Robbins argues that contemporary religion, as represented by the body of Christ, is dead and that mankind needs a different set of beliefs which will help individuals to live in greater harmony with nature. Arguing that the western Christian tradition incorrectly places mankind in the center of the universe, Robbins posits an alternate spiritual system which places humankind appropriately in its own tiny corner of the universe. Amanda, the prime exponent of this alternate outlook in the novel, advances the cause of magic over reason, love over indifference, personal development and freedom over social action. Through Amanda and her articulation of Zen philosophy, Robbins educates Marx Marvelous. Rather than offering the reader a pessimistic vision of the twentieth century with its dead Christ, *Another Roadside Attraction* optimistically presents what Robbins sees as a naturally harmonious lifestyle designed to permit individual freedom and development. Significantly, at the heart of the action in this novel is Plucky Purcell, dope dealing outlaw, whose theft of the body of Christ exposes the hoax of the resurrection. The outlaw willing to challenge society's rules appears in each of Robbins's later novels.

Characters

Amanda casts her magic over all of *Another Roadside Attraction.* In the novel's opening pages the reader learns that Amanda likes five things: butterflies, cacti, mushrooms, motorcycles, and the Infinite Goof. Shortly thereafter the reader learns that she also believes in five things: birth, copulation, death, magic, and freedom. The combined list of ten provides the material through which Robbins presents his criticism of Christianity and the tenets of his new spiritual viewpoint. Amanda serves as the teacher of this new philosophy. And if Amanda is the teacher, Marx Marvelous, who narrates the events in the novel and represents

Robbins, is the willing student.

Each of Robbins's characters lives at odds with society. Amanda and John Paul Ziller exist at society's very fringe; Marx Marvelous holds it in contempt, and Plucky Purcell moves outside it altogether, a wanted man, alternatively sought by police, the FBI and the Pope's hitmen.

Techniques

The most distinctive aspect of Robbins's novel is its exuberant prose style. *Another Roadside Attraction* gains much of its effect from the author's wit and his conscious manipulation of language. The novel is filled with word play: bizarre descriptions, outlandish metaphors, and frequent authorial intrusions abound. Robbins jokes with the reader throughout the novel, and the puns and linguistic slapstick produce the novel's comic texture. This playful style masks the serious issues Robbins presents and makes acceptable much bitter didactic debate. On a larger level, Robbins uses numerous short anecdotes, exchanges, digressions, letters, and biographical notes to structure the novel.

Literary Precedents

Reviewers have consistently linked Robbins with Thomas Pynchon, John Barth, Kurt Vonnegut, and Richard Brautigan. Robbins, like these authors, writes metafiction, fiction in which the nature of writing itself is explored. Both stylistically and thematically, Robbins seems to be most closely connected with Pynchon. Clearly, there is documentation of Pynchon's familiarity with Robbins; Pynchon has written quite warmly of Robbins's ability as storyteller. Additionally, readers have noted similarities between Pynchon and Robbins in their mutual devotion to uncertainty and their delight in absurdity. Indeed, *The Crying of Lot 49* and *Another Roadside Attraction* have much in common in their presentation of America's west coast lifestyles and their implementation of non-Newtonian physics as metaphor material.

EVEN COWGIRLS GET THE BLUES
Even Cowgirls Get the Blues, 1976, novel.

Social Concerns/Themes

Like *Another Roadside Attraction, Even Cowgirls Get the Blues* expresses its social concern through the theme of personal freedom. One of the main plotlines involves the takeover of the Rubber Rose ranch, a women's health farm owned by a cosmetic and feminine hygiene company. Bonanza Jellybean and a group of cowgirls intend to turn the dude ranch into a working one. Their action is a form of social protest against a society which allows girls to wear cowgirl outfits only until they reach puberty, against a society which limits the roles available to women. In the course of the novel, Sissy Hankshaw arrives at the Rubber Rose. Sissy, who works as a model for the same cosmetic concern, was born with huge thumbs which she uses for hitching rides across the country. Like the dissident cowgirls, Sissy's deviation from the norm has resulted in unhappiness, as she has been pressured by society to conform completely even in her physical features. Robbins further heightens the conflict between individual freedom and social conformity by introducing the last remaining flock of whooping cranes into the plot of the novel. These cranes, like Sissy and Bonanza Jellybean, risk their survival rather than limit their freedom.

At the same time Robbins contrasts personal freedom with social conformity, he presents a satire of militancy. His targets are all those who sacrifice themselves to their causes, whether they be the militant feminists at the Rubber Rose or militant proponents of counterculture lifestyles. This satire once again reinforces Robbins' belief that the individual is more important than the group and that social action is less important than the perfection of the individual. In addition, he finds fault with religions, both eastern and western, which cannot provide the spiritual direction necessary for individual human fulfillment. Robbins turns to the classical god Pan and fertility goddesses as a more sensible spiritual center to counter the repressive nature of most western religions.

Once again, Robbins investigates the nature of fiction in his novel. Dr. Robbins, the narrator in *Even Cowgirls Get the Blues,* like Marx Marvelous in *Another Roadside Attraction,* undertakes the writing of the novel only after falling in love with the heroine. In the course of his novel, Robbins considers the modern novel in America, alluding to Capote, Barth, Updike, Vonnegut, Oates, Kerouac, and Kesey.

Characters

Even Cowgirls Get the Blues is filled with characters who do not fit the mold dictated by normal society. From Sissy Hankshaw, with her large thumbs which provide freedom of movement, to the Chink who lives in a cave and discourses on the Clockpeople, Robbins's novels are peopled by unusual characters with large sexual appetites. Robbins generates interest by placing his dissenting characters in situations in which society attempts to command conformity. Like Bonanza Jellybean who dies rather than allow society to dictate the appropriateness of her role, each character helps Robbins advance his theme of individual freedom.

Techniques

Robbins divides his novel in 121 short sections which contain an assortment of jokes, puns, metaphors, and word play, designed to amuse the reader on each page.

His ability as a humorist is widely acknowledged. The novel itself is picaresque, Sissy and the whooping cranes serving as the greatest exponents of the freedom of movement Robbins professes. At the end of the novel, Robbins presents a special bonus parable in which Confucius, Buddha, and Christ fail to find sweetness in a jar of vinegar, the emblem of life, but Pan and his fertile woman accomplice find sweetness—offering a final clear example of the failure of both eastern and western religion to bring mankind happiness.

STILL LIFE WITH WOODPECKER: A SORT OF A LOVE STORY
Still Life With Woodpecker, 1980, novel.

Social Concerns/Themes

Clearly the most accessible of his novels, *Still Life With Woodpecker* is the least well received by critics who have charged Robbins with selling out by writing a purely commercial fiction intended solely to climb the best seller lists. The novel is a love story of a princess and an outlaw: the princess, Princess Leigh-Cheri Fursenberg-Barcalona and the outlaw, escaped anarchist Bernard Mickey Wrangle. Both the princess and the outlaw seek to change society, the Princess as an environmentalist who attends the Geo-Therapy Care Fest on Maui, the outlaw as an anarchist who attends the same conference committed to blowing it up. Robbins's fairy tale love story returns to a favored theme, that romantic love is more important than social concern. At the end of the novel, both princess and outlaw live happily ever after, having retired from active social commitment and chosen to dedicate themselves to personal development and love.

Characters

Missing from the opening pages of *Still Life With Woodpecker* is the standard disclaimer that any resemblance by the characters in the novel to actual persons, either alive or dead, is purely coincidental. In this case, Bernard Mickey Wrangle, the Woodpecker of the novel's title, is a thinly disguised Dwight Armstrong who was convicted for his part in the bombing of Sterling Hall on the University of Wisconsin-Madison campus. Even with the actions of Dwight Armstrong resonating in the background of the novel, both Bernard Mickey Wrangle and Princess Leigh-Cheri lack the complexity of Robbins's other lovers and offer less to engage the interest of the readers.

Techniques

Once again displaying his interest in the process of writing, Robbins opens *Still Life With Woodpecker* by praising his newly purchased Remington SL3 typewriter which he feels certain contains the novel he intends to write. Remington SL3 unplugged, the exasperated author ends the novel in a scrawled message about the mystery of the connection and love. Between the typeset Prologue and hand written final remarks, Robbins provides 106 sections on the main plot as well as a number of Interludes and an Epilogue which trace the author's progress as he engages in the writing process.

Literary Precedents

Robbins combines fable and romance, traditional literary forms. Structurally and stylistically, *Still Life With Woodpecker* resembles Vonnegut's *Slaughterhouse-Five*. The two novels employ a short episodic structure which promotes the authors' use of humor and word play, and both gain much from the repetition of catch phrases for stylistic effect; in Vonnegut, "So it goes," in Robbins, "Oh-Oh, spaghetti-o." The accusation by some critics that Robbins has sold out to achieve commercial success with *Still Life With Woodpecker* seems paradoxical since Robbins, like Vonnegut, has always appealed to the popular, commercial market.

Other Titles

Guy Anderson, 1965 (biography); *Jitterbug Perfume,* 1984 (novel).

Additional Sources

Contemporary Literary Criticism, vol. 32. Jean C. Stine and Daniel G. Marowski, eds. Detroit: Gale Research, 1985, pp. 365-374. Provides extensive excerpts from book reviews and scholarly examinations of Robbins' novels.

Karl, Frederick R., *American Fictions 1940-1980.* New York: Harper & Row, 1983, pp. 173-174. Places Robbins's *Even Cowgirls Get the Blues* in the tradition of "Growing Up in America" fiction.

Nadeau, Robert L., "Physics and Cosmology in the Fiction of Tom Robbins," *Critique* 20 (1978): 63-74. Points out Robbins's use of non-Newtonian physics in his fiction.

Siegel, Mark, *Tom Robbins* (Western Writers Series 42). Boise: Boise State University, 1980. Views Robbins as a Western writer and provides analyses of his first three novels.

Kenneth B. Grant
University of Wisconsin Center
Baraboo/Sauk County

JUDITH (PERELMAN) ROSSNER
1935

Publishing History

Judith Rossner always wanted to be a writer. Encouraged by her mother, she wrote as a child. She began with short stories and then published a book for children in 1963 entitled *What Kind of Feet Does a Bear Have?* Before her highly successful *Looking for Mr. Goodbar* in 1975, she published three other novels—*To the Precipice* (1967), *Nine Months in the Life of an Old Maid* (1969), and *Any Minute I Can Split* (1972)—all of which were favorably reviewed. She is identified primarily with *Looking for Mr. Goodbar,* which was translated into fourteen languages, including Japanese, Hebrew, and Serbo-Croatian, was chosen as a Literary Guild Alternate and a Women Today Selection, and was made into a movie. She has mixed feelings about being known primarily as the author of *Looking for Mr. Goodbar,* wishing to be identified instead as the author of a "whole bunch of good books." Three other successful novels have followed, though none has enjoyed the commercial success of *Looking for Mr. Goodbar. Attachments* (1977) has been translated into five languages, *Emmeline* (1980) was chosen as a Literary Guild Alternate, and *August* (1983) has been translated into nine languages. She is currently working on a new novel.

Critical Reception, Honors, and Popularity

Judith Rossner's novels have all been well received by critics, though the later reviews have been less overwhelmingly favorable than the early ones. Her three novels published prior to *Looking for Mr. Goodbar* were all praised for their marvelous dialogue, fully realized characterization, and subtlety. This praise of her writing reached its height with *Looking for Mr. Goodbar,* which was admired for its great sensitivity and skill. C.E. Rinzler's review in the *New York Times Book Review* is representative: "The sureness of Rossner's writing and her almost flawless sense of timing create a complex and chilling portrait of a woman's descent into hell that gives this book considerable literary merit. . . . If there is a genre into which [this book] falls, it is a genre of uncommonly well-written and well-constructed fiction, easily accessible, but full of insight and intelligence and illumination. It is a noble genre." *Attachments,* with its rather bizarre focus on the marriage of two women to Siamese twins, was called "funny, sexy, and sad," but also labeled "a mawkish fantasy" and "soft-core pornography." *Emmeline* fared better with the critics. M.M. Leber in *Library Journal* wrote, "Rossner has never been better: a stunning, haunting book," and Walter Clemons said in *Newsweek* that the novel is "built to last." Other critics, however, labeled it "dull," and lacking in poise and imagination. A similarly mixed reception greeted *August,* her most recent book, about the relationship between a psychiatrist and her patient.

Called "healthy meat and potatoes prose" by Jeffrey Schaire in *Harper's*, it was praised for characters that are "solid, believable, and engaging." Others said it "reeks of real life" and that it reproduces the hesitations, repetitions, and Freudian slips of real conversation with "exact fidelity." These same critics, however, noted occasional lapses in the style, inconsistencies in tone, and flaws in the pacing of the book. Even Rossner's characterization received some criticism. According to Laurie Stone in *The Village Voice*, "Disappointingly when Lulu and Dawn are not thinking interesting psychoanalytic thoughts, their thoughts aren't very interesting. Rossner has imagined engrossing inner lives for her characters, but she hasn't matched them with equally sympathetic or compelling outer lives." *August* does, however, according to Walter Kindrick, deserve praise for "convey[ing] the exact feel of analysis—its tensions and relaxations, its insights achieved or evaded and also, at times, its *longueurs*."

Analysis of Selected Titles

LOOKING FOR MR. GOODBAR

Looking for Mr. Goodbar, 1975, novel.

Social Concerns

Looking for Mr. Goodbar is a novel of its times. It was based on an actual event, the 1973 murder of a school teacher named Roseann Quinn by a man she met in a Manhattan singles bar and took back to her apartment. On one level it deals with the modern singles lifestyle and its dangers, a focus picked up by a reviewer in *Ms.* who called the book "a haunting, compelling thriller, guaranteed to make any woman terrified of the next strange man she meets."

Its relevance is far broader than that, however. When Judith Rossner says the book "struck a nerve," she is referring to its concern with the sexual revolution, the women's movement, the widespread lack of self-esteem, and the difficulties in today's society of getting to know others, resulting in overwhelming loneliness.

Feminists took up the heroine as a victim in the male-oriented world, but the blame is not so easily assigned. The men in the book are victims, too, especially Terry's would-be fiance James and even her murderer, who is only exhausted and kills her out of frustration and then panic. Martha Duffy, in *Time*, declared Theresa "a giant step forward in the long-term interests of sexual détente." The book deals frankly with sex and with the difficulties of women in learning to like their bodies and admit openly their need for sex. Through a vignette describing the marriage of one of Terry's casual bed partners, Ali (Eli), a Hassidic Jew, Rossner depicts the tragedy of women conditioned to hate sex and distrust pleasure. Yet sensual satisfaction and a relationship with a man are hardly enough to fulfill a woman. "Why is it that if you ask a woman how she is, the first thing she tells you is about her husband or boyfriend?" one of Theresa's friends from school laments. A major concern in this book is the need for women to have an identity deeper than their relationship to a man, to have "real lives of their own." Yet Theresa is hesitant to join Evelyn's discussion groups, lacking the self confidence she needs to become the independent woman she would like to be.

This lack of self-esteem, which is a major theme of the book, relates not to women only but to everyone. Theresa clearly doesn't like herself and feels what is inside her is best kept hidden there. An idle comment by her father during her childhood about "opening a can of worms" has stayed with her, and she always imagines people that way—"bright, neat-looking on the outside, but . . . pink and slimy and . . . more like intestines . . . if you turned yourself inside out." She associates the wormlike scar on her back with these worms and shudders when she sees it. Permanently marked by her childhood scoliosis and year-long hospitalization, she is overly sensitive about her scar, her limp, her weight, and her overall appearance. Her would-be fiance James defines—correctly—her sleeping around as a "lack of self regard." This phenomenon of the person who doesn't like herself and treats herself carelessly, even to the point of committing suicide through this passivity toward life, abounds in the present high-pressured society. Another by-product of this society is a difficulty in getting to know others, resulting in overwhelming loneliness. Theresa, with her inability to really listen to others and her reticence in initiating friendships, substitutes casual sex partners for real friends and is eventually destroyed by that choice.

Themes

The major theme of this book is the need for love and companionship. Paradoxically, this need is often accompanied by a reluctance to form a permanent attachment, to truly love someone and accept his love in return. The book suggests that Theresa's refusal stems from the lack of self regard (no one could really love me once he knows me) and the fear of loss. The result is a painful loneliness, which Theresa fills indiscriminately by having sex with the nearest available warm body.

Theresa's first and best companion was her brother Thomas, who visited and read to her throughout her illness, but he was killed in a training-camp gun accident at the age of eighteen, devastating her entire family. She spends her life, unconsciously, trying to replace him and realizes, only at the very end but is unable to express the thought, that James could and does fill that role. "I love you so much, James," she thinks to herself in their last conversation. "I wish you were my brother. I wish Thomas were alive." But she can't express that love aloud and rejects James, only to go to Mr. Goodbar and be murdered the next day.

Her life has been a series of rejections and rebuffs, many of her own making. She doesn't believe her parents love her, but only her beautiful sister Katherine. She knows her grandmother loved her, but she died while Theresa was in the hospital, and her parents told Theresa only that Grandmother Theresa Maria had gone to live in California, so for years afterward she'd strain for a glimpse of her grandmother on every live TV broadcast from California. She told Martin Engle, her college English professor, "I love you so much, Martin," but he replied with irony and cynicism, "Ah, yes . . . . Love." But he fulfilled the one criterion most important to Theresa in a relationship—he talked to her. Brooks, one of her sister Katherine's husbands, and James Morrisey, her would-be fiance, also talk to her. To James she can confess her love for teaching, something she has never said to anyone outside of school. "She was more herself, the real Theresa, . . . with James, than she'd ever been with anyone." Yet she has no sexual attraction for him even though, when they eventually make love, she admits to herself that he makes her feel beautiful, "languorous and graceful, as though she were in an underwater ballet." But he is too decent, he takes precautions so she won't become pregnant, and their lovemaking is dry and painful.

Disillusioned by "love," Theresa turns to sex. She invites casual one-night flings with an assortment of men: Brooks' friend Carter; Ali, the Hassidic Jew who sleeps in a warehouse; Victor, a businessman she met in a bar and spent a hotel weekend with; and several whose names she never bothered to ask, including one who'd been castrated. The most satisfying and most durable of these sex partners is Tony Lopanto, whom she regards as a "delightful, tender, and energetic lover." Their relationship is one of pure sensual pleasure. They never talk, they never go out, they only strip and leap into bed to the blare of rock music on the radio. The one time they do go out, to a birthday party for Tony's mother, he insults both his mother and Theresa, and he is thrown out of the party. Theresa's coldness toward him later that night angers him, and the relationship is essentially over. Once Tony is gone and James and she become closer, she is reluctant to return to the bars, even though she longs for the momentary pleasure offered by such encounters.

Theresa is unable to commit herself to James because she feels he sees her as a princess and she could never live up to his image of her. He assures her that his view of her is much closer to reality than her own. He admits his love helps him see her virtues more readily, but insists the virtues are truly there.

When he gives her a ring as a Christmas present, she has difficulty breathing, "as though she were putting something around her neck instead of her finger," and slips it on her right hand instead of her left. She resents the ring as a token of ownership and rebels against it, yet once when she thinks James has left for good, she becomes distraught and admits to herself that "if James disappeared from her life he would leave an enormous gap that couldn't easily be filled, something she could not honestly say about any of the others."

That realization still does not make it possible to accept his love, though, and at the end she returns to Mr. Goodbar in search of a good lay, of someone who will give her pleasure, keep her warm for a time, and leave when she asks. Her loneliness the night of her murder is tremendous. It is Christmas vacation, so she is not seeing the children she loves or her friends from school; James has decided not to see her until she makes up her mind; Tony is gone; and even Katherine is away. She resolves to begin a diary, hoping words will help make order out of her life. "She felt as though she were walking a tightrope and certain moves would send her plunging, but she had no way of knowing exactly what they were." In the end she makes the wrong choice and loses her life just as she seemed about to take charge of her own destiny, to treat herself as a person of some worth. Her temporary relapse into her old ways as a cure for the loneliness makes a permanent recovery totally out of her reach. In those last moments she calls out to James, to Mommy and Daddy, but none of them can reach her.

Characters

Judith Rossner creates in Theresa Dunn a tangible embodiment of all the themes and concerns of the book. She is a lonely person, a person torn between two very different images of herself, neither of which she wishes to abandon. "Actually, when she thought about it at all, she didn't really feel that she *had* a life, one life, that is, belonging to a person, Theresa Dunn. There was a Miss Dunn who taught a bunch of children who adored her . . . and there was someone named Terry who whored around in bars when she couldn't sleep at night. But the only thing these two people had in common was the body they inhabited. If one died, the other would never miss her—although she herself, Theresa, the person who thought and felt but had no life, would miss either one."

Theresa's divided self illustrates two of the main thrusts of women's liberation. Miss Dunn, the teacher, is a person in her own right, though she is too self-conscious to join a women's group which might have helped her recognize that fact and freed her from her dependence on men. Her strong desire for an education, inspired by her childhood teacher Sister Rosalie, along with her present reputation as a gifted teacher, are ample evidence of the strength of her career commitment. But it is not enough. Her alter-ego, Terry, the sexual being who frequents bars, is representative of another aspect of the women's movement, of the new openness toward sex and admission of a woman's need for satisfaction in sex.

Theresa, the person who includes both, has a tremendous capacity to love, as shown by her devotion to her children at school, yet she denies it. When James brings up marriage the first time, he is puzzled by her declaration, "I can't see any reason to get married unless you want to have children and I can't stand children." Later she admits it is only when they're sick that she doesn't love them. Again it comes back to the pain of her own childhood illness and the fear of losing those she loves. She also avoids her father once he becomes ill with cancer.

This reluctance to make a commitment without a guarantee of perfection is the main obstacle to real love, yet Theresa's need for love and its warmth are what drive her to the temporary sexual relationships that keep her going and eventually destroy her. Those relationships fail to satisfy not only because they don't engage her mind, as a true love relationship would, but also because her Catholic school upbringing nags at her about the immorality of her actions. "It was one thing to sin and another to enjoy it so thoroughly." Besides, her behavior is incompatible with her professional image as a teacher. Even Tony is shocked to discover, well into their relationship, that truth about her. "What the hell you doin' fucking around in bars if you're a teacher?" he asks. Her lack of respect for herself troubles everyone who knows about it, including herself, but she can't stop acting the way she does.

The other characters in the book—her parents, her sisters, James, Tony, her friends at school, the men she knows, her murderer—are all stereotypes, necessary to help reveal Rossner's themes through Theresa. The reader can sympathize with James and even with the murderer, but only Theresa really matters.

Techniques

Looking for Mr. Goodbar begins with the end, the aftermath of the murder. Rossner introduces the murderer, Gary Cooper White, and develops some sympathy for him before launching into the narrative about Theresa's life. The effect of this is to know Theresa is doomed from the start; the only suspense that remains is what will precipitate the murder and how much of her life will precede her death. Still, ignoring Rossner's warning, the reader gets involved with Theresa in spite of himself and hopes she will free herself from the trap she has set. The proportions are just right, with the murderer getting the first word, though brief, and Theresa getting the balance of the book. Readers find themselves rereading the first section when they reach the end to bring the story full circle.

The novel is a psychological one, and Rossner gives a clear look into Theresa's mind through dreams, which highlight and reveal her subconscious desires and fears. The other technique for getting into Theresa's mind is the use of italicized statements for imagined conversations or thoughts she can't express. These often contradict the words she speaks aloud, highlighting her reluctance to let her real self out.

Literary Precedents

Looking for Mr. Goodbar, according to Carol Eisen Rinzler in the *New York Times Book Review,* might be placed in a number of literary genres. It might be considered a modern passion play, or perhaps a feminist treatise, with Theresa a political victim of rape. Theresa Dunn, according to Rinzler, "takes her place beside Henry James's Isabel Archer and Scott Fitzgerald's Nicole Diver as another victim of the American Dream, a woman who never roused herself enough to wake up from the nightmare."

Among modern writers, Rossner is most often compared with Joyce Carol Oates. In *Looking for Mr. Goodbar,* according to Roger Sale, "Rossner is good the way Oates can be, and is more efficient too, so that without resorting to a pressurized cabin atmosphere she can locate the tangles of her heroine's Bronx family and the gradual wastedness of her obvious intelligence."

Related Titles

Looking for Mr. Goodbar, like all of Rossner's novels, deals with the theme of attachments, which was to become the title of the novel to follow. In an interview with Liz Driven of CBS News in 1977, Judith Rossner stated her belief that the fear of being attached and not being attached are the same, and not opposites as some people would believe. She says Terry is afraid to be attached because of her fear of loss. She considers her major theme to be "people coming together and coming apart, sometimes from houses, sometimes from other people."

The books prior to *Looking for Mr. Goodbar* each dealt with this theme of attachments. Ruth Kossoff, the bright Jewish heroine of *To the Precipice,* has a number of relationships with men during her life. The attachment between two sisters is the focus in *Nine Months in the Life of an Old Maid. Any Minute I Can Split* deals with the painful attachment and separation of Margaret McDonough Adams from her father and husband, one of whom rejected her and the other of whom abused her. Prior to writing *Looking for Mr. Goodbar,* Rossner became interested in Siamese twins as an obvious case of non-separation, and she began *Attachments* quite a bit before *Looking for Mr. Goodbar,* then set it aside. In *Attachments,* Rossner continues *Looking for Mr. Goodbar*'s concern with the women's movement, especially its support of a woman's need to have a life of her own, with loneliness, and with the inability of people to accept love.

Adaptations

Looking for Mr. Goodbar was sold to the movies for $225,000, and the 1977 film starred Diane Keaton and Richard Gere. The screenplay was based only loosely on the book. Judith Rossner, who said she "counted three lines of dialogue from the book in the movie," did not like the production and felt Hollywood had "cheapened" the story.

ATTACHMENTS

Attachments, 1977, novel.

Social Concerns

The major social issue developed in *Attachments* is the need for a woman to have a meaningful life of her own. While in college, Nadine, the heroine, admires her boyfriend Schlomo's mother for her career as a dentist and is ashamed of her own mother's inactivity. As an adult, although she freely chooses the role of housewife for herself, she eventually becomes frustrated and unfulfilled by it. "How could I have longed to be a housewife and mother when I grew up," she wonders, "when I'd grown up knowing that my housewife-mother was the loneliest of women?" She becomes jealous of Dianne's law career and angry "at still being stuffed into a role

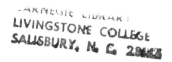

[she'd] partly outgrown." She regrets having never completed her degree and becomes insecure about her intelligence. Eventually she becomes convinced that "marriage is a weight that pulls me down" and she feels compelled to leave Amos "to make a life for myself."

Attachments also addresses the sexual revolution of the 1970s, presenting it in relatively negative terms as having assumed too much importance. In describing her sexual fumbling with Schlomo in college, for example, she is pleased with their lack of anxiety over their performance, free of "that sense that seems to pervade so many sexual transactions of the seventies, that our entire selves were at stake."

Themes

Loneliness is again a major theme in *Attachments,* as it was in *Looking for Mr. Goodbar.* Nadine's life is governed by trying to avoid loneliness, which is represented for her by the image of falling. In the early pages she admits that "during the first twenty-five or thirty years of my life I was too agitated to learn much. Too busy trying to keep myself from falling." The death of her parents in a freak swimming accident is a blow from which she never fully recovers. Periodically she wishes to be a little girl again, watching her parents swimming together, though that memory evokes also the loneliness of returning to a bed no longer cozy but now "a cold and lonely place."

The belief throughout *Attachments* is that each person has room for only one attachment at a time. The Siamese twins, Amos and Eddie, have each other and, though they like the companionship of Dianne and Nadine, such relationships are not essential to their emotional well-being. Once separated, however, Amos turns to Nadine for the support he previously got from his brother. When Dianne is pregnant with Carly, Nadine is intensely jealous and feels the "baby was making love to her." She feels terribly alone—Dianne has the baby and the twins have each other. Then closeness with Dianne's baby Carlotta fills her emptiness and she no longer needs the others. When Nadine herself has a baby, Dianne's Carly is pushed out, and so it goes throughout the book. The loneliness after rejection is a terrible thing, whether experienced by Nadine, by Carly, or by Amos.

Nadine was first attracted to the Siamese twins because they had achieved her dream of "being permanently attached to someone else so I could never fall." They were not freaks to her, having been "born to a condition I was spending my life trying to achieve." She imagines herself in the space between them, absorbing their togetherness, just as she had desired as a child to be in the pool with her parents, swimming between them. The twins didn't have to talk to communicate. Only after separation would they get some conception of what loneliness is, as evidenced by Amos' sometimes grabbing Nadine in the night "as though to break a fall." Amos is strong, though, and will survive after Nadine leaves him. Ironically, Nadine may not, for clearly loneliness is a way of life for her.

While *Attachments* presents loneliness as a natural enough feeling, to be so fixated on it as Nadine is not the norm. Rossner presents her terror of being alone and her inability to accept love as a deficiency. Once in the book, when Carly fits her Raggedy Ann with a "Tachment" like her daddy's, Nadine herself is appalled and throws it away. "If she has not yet considered the dangers of attaching oneself to others out of sheer terror at the alternative," Rossner writes, "she has at least absorbed the reality principle insofar as Carlotta must live with it."

Nadine has distrusted love all her life, beginning with her inability to accept her first boyfriend Schlomo's kindness, deliberately hurting and then losing him by rushing out for sex with every available male on campus. She also deliberately alienates Alex, her next boyfriend, even though she loves him, when she feels his love doesn't match hers in intensity. After a brief marriage to Joe Tumulty and his kids, she hesitates to marry again, finding it "far worse to have a wonderful man and lose him than never to have him at all." With the twins, there is no risk. They have each other; her bond to them is merely symbiosis. When they are separated and become their own persons, even though Amos needs her more and is a more tender husband, he has lost his attractiveness for her. He has become ordinary, and their four-way marriage begins to come unglued.

That marriage foursome highlights still another of the themes of *Attachments,* the importance of friendships between women. Nadine always looked to Dianne for her intelligence, her stability, and her sense of right and wrong. She is special to Nadine, too, because she knew Nadine's parents and, through her, Nadine's roots remain alive. Their friendship cools and intensifies depending on how full their lives are otherwise, but Nadine needs for her to be always available. The attachment of the men binds Nadine and Dianne as well. Nadine fears sometimes that "our friendship had gotten lost in our marriage" but realizes too, on the eve of the operation, that "Dianne is too precious to let out of my sight for five minutes."

Judith Rossner has said in an interview that she has always been particularly interested in friendships between women because they are "more often very, very deep than between men and women." She feels it is "almost as though sex, heterosexuality, enables one not to get deeper." Sex serves as a substitute for putting feelings into words, she finds, and women understand each other better. That belief gets substance in the friendship here between Nadine and Dianne, who understand each other perfectly, even when in intense competition.

Characters

Judith Rossner uses Nadine as the embodiment of the neurosis that can be produced by an intense fear of loneliness. She is the narrator, so readers sympathize with her to a point, but clearly normalcy resides in the more self-sufficient characters, such as Dianne. Amos and Eddie function only as symbol until the separation but afterwards, although Eddie remains flat, Amos matures into a real character. Always intelligent, he goes from a nasty man to a loving one, capable of giving and receiving affection. He comes to rely on Nadine, who lets him down "just when our lives are getting good." His transformation from freak to person is convincing and highlights still further Nadine's extreme difficulty in coping with life.

Techniques

Attachments begins with a chatty tone that some critics have found annoyingly close. The language in the opening pages is clever and witty, as when Nadine calls the East, "The Yeast . . . thus conveying, quite unconsciously, both my awe of it as a mysterious place of feverishly fermenting intellects and my fear that I would not readily find a place in this mass." Soon, however, Rossner's persona runs out of verbal energy, and the narrative settles into a calmer but far less interesting flow of words. Critics have faulted the book for too much heavy underlining and an unattractive self-consciousness, which are probably valid complaints. As in *Looking for Mr. Goodbar,* Rossner uses dreams to convey inner feelings and desires, though the device is less necessary here since, as the narrator, Nadine can tell the reader directly what she is thinking.

Literary Precedents

No one has written fiction about this particular subject matter before, though there is some basis in fact for the marriage of Siamese twins. Judith Rossner became fascinated by a picture of real Siamese twins who married sisters and had 21 children between them. When the sisters couldn't get along, they moved to two houses, and the twins divided their time between them. They were never separated, dying in 1914, before successful operations were possible.

Though the subject matter is unique, *Attachments* has been called by Jerome Charyn "a kind of *Lolita* in reverse: the female's terrifying quest for identity through sexual power and lust. We purr at the exotic. We fondle it, we move up close to it, smother it, until it becomes more and more like ourselves . . . . Funny, sexy, and sad, *Attachments* is a crazy treatise on 'love' as the ultimate executioner."

Related Titles

Judith Rossner takes the fear of loneliness another step forward in this book. She states more explicitly a theme that was begun in *Looking for Mr. Goodbar,* that a woman needs to have a meaningful life of her own. The friendship between Nadine and Dianne in *Attachments* sets the stage for the full development of the bonds of female friendship to be explored in *August.*

AUGUST

August, 1983, novel.

Social Concerns

In *August,* Rossner again argues the need for a woman to have a meaningful life of her own through Dr. Lulu Shinefield, a Manhattan psychiatrist, whose professional life works smoothly but whose private life is filled with "attachment" problems. She is not, despite her career, the "New Woman," the terrific career type she both admires and fears. Lulu, by carrying her training to her own home, manages to make serious mistakes in dealing with her daughter, her husbands, and her lover.

The book also focuses on psychiatry itself through the developing relationship between Lulu and her analytic daughter Dawn Henley. The title *August* highlights the tremendous dependence that develops between a patient and her analyst. In August, when New York analysts all take their vacations, patients must survive on their own, and insecurity mounts. Each successive August in Dawn's five-year analysis is less traumatic, though, as she grows more and more healthy mentally. Dawn's problems are the ones Rossner has developed in other books—a loneliness and fear of loss caused by abandonment by her parents in her infancy, and the recent "divorce" of the two women who raised her—but here a solution is offered through psychiatry. The doctor's office is reality to Dawn and becomes her "home." She tells Lulu, "You're the person who turned my life into a life." Dawn's recovery and the closeness that develops between her and Dr. Lulu Shinefield come to rehabilitate the doctor as well, bringing satisfaction and love to her troubled life.

Another social concern developed at some length in *August* is sexuality, including homosexuality and lesbianism. Dawn's adoptive "parents" are a lesbian couple and her father, Dawn discovers, was a homosexual. The relationships are explored frankly and non-judgmentally. The book also deals with the attitude differences between men and women. Dawn tends to equate being a woman with "being sick and messed up" and sees it as a sign of weakness, but through analysis she comes to accept that women aren't really sicker, only more likely to seek help when they need it. Dawn generalizes that "men are always looking on the outside to solve problems and women are always looking into our own . . . our own heads." Rossner's conviction that friendships between two women are deeper than between men and women because women put things into words is demonstrated by the relationships in this book. None of the male-female relationships really satisfies here, while close female bonds are the main source of strength.

Themes

The need for love is once again a major theme. Dawn, abandoned by her mother, who committed suicide when Dawn was six months old, and her father, who went sailing with a friend a year later and drowned, is constantly searching for parents. Her loss is all the more traumatic since her father left her totally alone the day he died, so that she cried in terror in her crib for hours before a neighbor found and rescued her. Now her lesbian aunt Vera, who raised her and whom she called "daddy," has separated from her "mother," Tony, and she feels once again abandoned. To intensify the loss further, Tony is now married and has two step-daughters, of whom Dawn is jealous, and has had a mastectomy. Dawn so fears losing Tony that she won't even visit. Feeling both sets of parents unavailable, Dawn attaches to a series of men, including one old enough to be her father, and to her doctors, first Dr. Seaver, a male psychiatrist who saw her through her adolescence and recently declared her analysis completed, and now Lulu, to whom she feels she is a daughter. Her fear of loss is so great that she snaps pictures of Lulu on the street to have something to keep, leaves paintings behind in her office so Lulu will have something to remind her of Dawn, and is intensely jealous that Lulu has a daughter of her own.

Gradually, through analysis, Dawn rediscovers her birth parents and brings them to life. Through old letters and belongings in her aunt's attic, she finds her mother was a talented artist and that she wanted an abortion when she found she was pregnant with Dawn. Dawn feels terribly guilty about her death at first but comes to terms with that and other elements of the past through her analytic sessions. By the end, she is strong enough to re-establish relationships with both Vera and Tony and to voluntarily terminate her analysis, moving to Washington to start a new life. She wants something of Lulu to keep as proof that she exists but then realizes she herself is the proof, for Lulu *has* given birth to her. Instead of taking something, Dawn gives Lulu something to keep, a painting of herself with a smaller Lulu inside of her, with Lulu's head "reach[ing] the place where the large one's heart might have been."

Characters

In *August* the two heroines must be viewed as a unit, for together they illustrate Rossner's major theme, the power of friendship and understanding in combating loneliness. Both Dawn and Lulu have a tremendous need for love. At first, the relationship is one-sided and professional only, but as Dawn matures and recovers, Lulu becomes an equal recipient in the exchange. Together, the two of them demonstrate the power of friendship, and both benefit from it. For both, reality seems to exist only in Lulu's office. When Rossner depicts Lulu with her friends and family, her private life seems drab and unreal and the reader, too, wants to hurry back to the couch.

Lulu's own life shows many parallels to Dawn's. Her mother was an unfulfilled artist-type, her father an alcoholic. She too has suffered loss, with her mother committing suicide, her first husband finding another woman even before their daughter Sascha's birth, and her daughter running from home in search of her birth father during her teen years, breaking her stepfather's heart and breaking up Lulu's second marriage. Sascha is still estranged from Lulu as the story opens, though at the end she has returned and the reader can see hopeful signs that she will help replace Dawn in Lulu's life. Lulu's two "daughters" pass each other in Lulu's waiting room, in fact, on Dawn's last day of analysis, making the transfer of roles complete. Sascha is jealous of Dawn's beauty and her apparent closeness with Lulu, and when she confesses her feelings to her mother, Lulu and Sascha cry together. Lulu tells Sascha how beautiful she is and together they go out to lunch, and, by implication, on through life.

Techniques

August is told in a subdued manner, almost entirely dialogue. All of the action of Dawn's life is reported secondhand, from the couch in Lulu's office. The alternate chapters, in which Lulu emerges from the office into her private life, are not nearly so interesting, heightening the impression that reality in this book lies in the talking. The pace is extremely slow, with all the hesitations and even redundancies of analysis sessions written in. Occasionally the dialogue bogs down as it belabors a point, and the reader might wish for a change in setting or tone, but the illusion that he is overhearing real psychoanalysis is well maintained and accomplishes Rossner's purposes.

At first Dawn's and Lulu's lives are kept very separate, in self-contained chapters, but then overlaps begin to occur. By the middle of the book, Sascha and Dawn are in direct competition for Lulu. Leaving her August vacation to meet Dawn in the city, Lulu must answer to Sascha. "Was that your precious patient?" she asks. "I hope It's going to get what It wants, even if I'm not. Actually, I know it's a She." The alternation and intrusion of one life into the other become more and more frequent. There are parallel actions, too, as when Lulu goes in search of her own childhood and home as she realizes the end of her relationship with Charles is imminent. Lulu is the analyst but she too is constantly in need of analysis herself, as proven by her long treatment in her youth, her choice of analysts as husbands and lovers throughout her life, and her own rehabilitation from the other side of the couch in her treatment of Dawn. The meshing of the two stories is skillfully handled.

Literary Precedents

August's heavy use of psychoanalysis is in keeping with a recent interest in the subject by both novelists and journalists. According to Walter Kendrick in the *New York Times Book Review,* "*August* is testimony to this new interest and a valuable contribution to it. I know of no other account, imagined or factual," he writes, "that gives such a vivid picture of the analytic experience, on both sides of its intense, troubled, ambiguous relationship."

Related Titles

In *August,* Judith Rossner deals once again with the need for love and fear of loss, but here the remedy is different from that in earlier books. Where Terry leaped into bed with whomever seemed willing and Nadine seduced and married a pair of Siamese twins to combat loneliness, Dawn talks it out and is able to overcome it. Both she and Lulu use sex to some extent, but in the end they find that the only permanent fix is in non-sexual attachments, in talking with and truly understanding another person. Here the talking is formalized in psychoanalysis, but the same potential benefit could be offered by Dianne and Nadine's friendship in *Attachments,* or by Lulu and Sascha's bond or Dawn and Tony's bond in *August,* provided they take advantage of it. *August* is clearly the most hopeful of Rossner's books thus far, for it shows a way out of the fearful, lonely trap into which her main characters always seem to fall.

Additional Sources

Rossner, Judith and Liz Driven, "An Interview with Judith Rossner," *Vital History Cassettes,* Encyclopedia Americana, CBS News Audio Resource Library, No. 3 (September 1977).

"Rossner, Judith," *Book Review Digest,* 1967, 1969, 1972, 1975, 1977, 1980, 1983.

"Rossner, Judith (Perelman)," *Contemporary Authors,* ed. James M. Ethridge, Barbara Kopala, Carolyn Riley. Detroit, Michigan: Gale Research Company, 1968.

"Rossner, Judith," *Contemporary Literary Criticism,* 6, ed. Carolyn Riley and Phyllis Carmel Mendelson. Detroit, Michigan: Gale Research Company, 1976.

"Rossner, Judith," *Contemporary Literary Criticism,* 9, ed. Dedria Bryfonski. Detroit, Michigan: Gale Research Company, 1978.

"Rossner, Judith," *Contemporary Literary Criticism,* 29, ed. Jean C. Stine and Daniel G. Marowski. Detroit, Michigan: Gale Research Company, 1984.

"Rossner Says Hollywood Cheapens Books," *New York Times,* III, 21 (November 10, 1983): 1.

Mary G. Bernath
Bloomsburg University

PHILIP ROTH
1933

Publishing History

Philip Roth began his writing career as a student and published his first stories in *Et Cetera* (Bucknell University) in 1952. "The Day It Snowed" was published in 1954 in the *Chicago Review*. "The Contest for Aaron Gold" appeared in *Epoch* and was also included in *The Best American Short Stories of 1956* which served as his springboard to a very successful career. In 1960, Roth's collection of five short stories and a novella *Goodbye, Columbus* (1959), depicting conflicts of Jewish middle class life in America, won the National Book Award and was later released by Paramount in an enormously successful movie version. "Defender of the Faith" was included in *The O. Henry Prize Stories, 1960*.

In 1969 his *Portnoy's Complaint*, a controversial novel concentrating on sexual exploits and psychic fears of a Jewish male, became the number one best seller and the film version was later released by Columbia-Warner. *The Breast* (1972) deals with the metamorphosis of a man who turns into a huge breast. It was followed within a year by *The Great American Novel*, a hilarious account of a baseball band during the summer of 1943-44. His next novel *The Professor of Desire*, published in 1977, is a portrait of a young Jewish intellectual caught between temptation and restraint. His trilogy *The Ghost Writer* (1979) was awarded the "Present Tense" award for fiction, and was also made into a film and broadcast on Public Television in 1983. *Zuckerman Unbound* (1981) and *The Anatomy Lesson* (1983) were completed in *Zuckerman Bound* with a novella length epilogue called *The Prague Orgy* (1985), which deals with the problem of a Jewish writer of the post-World War II Holocaust generation and his compulsion to his literary vocation.

Critical Reception, Honors, and Popularity

Even though Roth is one of the most prolific and popular of novelists, he has received mixed critical attention. He is famous for being controversial, for being associated with bad taste and offensive language, and is even considered the most renegade of renegades, an anti-Semitic Jew. He was labeled by some as the "enfant terrible" of American Jewish fiction while other critics praised him for taking aim at the idiosyncrasies of Jewish middle class life. Many consider Roth to be a highly respected American writer, with an acute ear for dialogue, who deals frankly with sexual, political, and intellectual themes.

In 1959 he received the Houghton Mifflin Literary Fellowship, a National Institute of Arts and Letters grant, a Guggenheim Fellowship, the Daroff award, the *Paris Review* Aga Khan award, and in 1965 a Ford Foundation grant. In 1954 Roth was elected to Phi Beta Kappa at Bucknell University and in 1970 to the National Institute of Arts and Letters.

At present, Roth's reputation is solid and his success is a fact of certainty, regardless of the controversy associated with his name. He is considered to be one of the most talented and popular American novelists.

Analysis of Selected Titles

PORTNOY'S COMPLAINT
Portnoy's Complaint, 1969, novel.

Social Concerns

Portnoy's Complaint is a tour de force novel of the 1960s containing flashbacks to the 1930s. Portnoy, the main protagonist, is plagued by masturbation problems and by a possessive Jewish mother. He rejects conventional morality but is overwhelmed with a guilt complex, from which he cannot free himself. He is guided by social and psychological forces beyond his control; he tries to assert himself boldly but at the same time is held back by his own defense mechanism. He is tormented because he cannot justify his role in society. Portnoy's actions expose the stratum of the stereotyped American-Jewish middle class suburbia where obscenity represents a violation of what his Jewish past stands for: strict social laws and a high respect for moral behavior.

Themes

The novel frankly exposes the unsatisfactory sexual life of a constantly masturbating immature adolescence and the neurotic experience of a *ménage à trois* by a guilt-ridden young man for whom sex is not a pleasure but a self-torturing necessity. This desperate young protagonist rebels in a rage against his Jewish heritage. The novel is hilarious saga exposing a mother-son confrontation as well as the tension between public and private life. Portnoy's persistent self-examination of consciousness and unconsciousness lead nowhere. His story is an endless confession to Dr. Spielvogel, a New York psychiatrist, who is able only at the end of the novel to give a glimmer of hope to Portnoy.

Characters

Alexander Portnoy, the main character, is a self-tortured young man full of complaints and obsessed with sex. He tries to be mother's good boy and a successful student; he attains a job of prestige as the Assistant Commissioner of Human Opportunity for the City of New York. Because of his hilarious confessions and his fear of exposure, he is depicted as an "unloved and unloving" person. After numerous sexual encounters with non-Jewish girls (with names such as The Pumpkin and The Pilgrim), he finds satisfying sex and love only with an intellectually unsophisticated, almost illiterate mistress, named The Monkey, a girl from the coal fields of West Virginia. However, Portnoy realizes that because of her limitations even she is not a solution to his problem. In the end, this almost idyllic love encounter leaves him unsatisfied. A visit to Israel does not bring satisfaction to his expectation and he realizes that simplicity is not the solution to his tormented life.

Alexander's life is ruled by Sophie, his Oedipal mother. Her compulsive neatness and cleanliness control her son, the kitchen, food, the bathroom, and sex. Jack, his father, is an insurance salesman and a lifelong liberal who lives in constant fear of his WASP employer.

Techniques

Portnoy's Complaint combines fact and fiction to expose occurrences of everyday life in great detail. A brilliant exploitation of the new freedom in language as the voice of the 1960s, the novel is lively, articulate, often hilariously funny American *Bildungsroman*; a confessional and self-explanatory monologue; an obscene book but not pornographic; a satirical farce but not ironic; an intelligent mixture of black comedy and pathos; a harsh view of middle class experience combined with a rebellion toward freedom expressed sexually by a young man.

Literary Precedents

The main character of *Portnoy's Complaint* follows the footsteps of Joyce's Dedalus. In this novel of consciousness and subconsciousness, however, the Rothian hero does not grow up as an artist. Portnoy tries to mature but basically remains a complaining Jewish hero. Roth follows the path of Bellow, Malamud and others who write of American-Jewish moralists and traditionalists. However, Roth dares to demythologize the belief in tradition and faith. Portnoy is alienated by the pressures of pleasing his family and maintaining sexual relationships. The ineffectuality of liberalism disillusions and further alienates him.

Related Titles

The Rothian characters are basically of the same ethnic background so they relate to each other easily. For instance Neil Klugman of *Goodbye, Columbus,* is caught between conflicting life styles as is Alexander Portnoy. Klugman demonstrates psychological insight as well as comic revelation, as does his girlfriend Brenda Patimkin. As the archetypical Jewish-American-Princess, Brenda characterizes the nouveau riche of the American suburbs. Like Roth's other characters, these two are strongly attached to their Jewish roots and have to learn how to cope with their past.

Adaptations

Portnoy's Complaint was made into a motion picture in 1972. The film was produced by Ernest Lehman, directed by Philip Lathrop, released in Technicolor and Panavision by Warner Brothers. It starred Richard Benjamin, Karen Black, Lee Black, Jack Somack, Jill Clayburgh, and Jeannie Berlin. It was a disappointing adaptation of the novel.

THE BREAST

The Breast, 1972, novel.

Social Concerns/Themes

Like *Portnoy's Complaint*, *The Breast* is an arresting tour de force. David Kepesh, a thirty-eight-year-old professor of comparative literature, awakens on the morning of February 18, 1971, and finds himself changed into a six-foot female breast. He feels victimized by his glands and calls the metamorphosis "a massive hormonal influx," as well as "an endocrinopathic catastrophe," and "a hermaphroditic explosion of chromosomes." The exploration of the frustrations suffered by the protagonist as a victimized individual is camouflaged as a search for a scientific explanation of his metamorphosis. Kepesh has to face up to the fact that his middle-class Jewish American upbringing did not prepare him to accept his embarrassing predicament. His hopelessness and alienation are realities of modern existence.

Characters

The main protagonist, David Kepesh, investigates all possibilities of the cause of his bizarre metamorphosis. He intellectually agonizes over his grotesque situation and feels imprisoned by it. He consults with Dr. Gordon, his physician, whose scientific explanations depict it as irregular occurrence of nature. Kepesh turns to Dr. Klinger, a psychiatrist, just as Portnoy did. However, Dr. Klinger is an anti-apocalyptic listener, a rational realist who objectively clings to the facts of reality and sees the possibility of salvation for Kepesh in the acceptance of his grotesque self. Similarly, Claire Ovington, his mistress, accepts him as he is and offers him a relatively stable life after his ordeal of a broken marriage and five years of painful psychoanalysis. Arthur Schonbrunn, a stodgy and pedantic colleague of Kepesh, also insists on exact adherence to rules of reality.

Techniques

The Breast is a most innovative brilliant novel. The narrative fiction focuses on a human character's acceptance of a bizarre surprise; the result is a keen character study of modern man caught in an existential anguish enhanced by metaphysical images. The events, based on an erotic fantasy, are farcical rather than tragic. According to Roth the novel is a description of a nightmarish dream envisioned in a Dali painting.

Literary Precedents
The novel is indebted to Kafka's *Metamorphosis* and Gogol's *The Nose* and shows the frustrations suffered by the protagonist. In addition Rilke's literary influence can be detected as well as a reminiscence to Swift's style.

Related Titles
The hilarious fantasies of *Portnoy's Complaint* are more realistically and painfully examined in *The Breast*. The imbued characteristics of a traditional Jewish home life are exposed more frankly; Kepesh de-mystifies his past with the help of Dr. Klinger, a rational realist. Through the ordeal of this almost surrealistic metamorphosis the seeds of the immature Rothian adolescence ripen to a sexually mature professor who daringly exposes his encounters in *The Professor of Desire*.

THE PROFESSOR OF DESIRE
The Professor of Desire, 1977, novel.

Social Concerns/Themes
In this challenging and engaging novel, the principal character, David Kepesh (called by the same name in *The Breast*), is an adventurous but also intelligent man who sees sex as exemplifying his right to the pursuit of happiness. Nevertheless, he is torn between reckless erotic ambitions and conscientious intellectual devotion. Here too, the social mimicry is exposed as embarrassing the Jewish stereotype but is combined with a realistic rendering of the exposure of a professional academic teacher. The novel is observant; it is an honest explication of human feelings; it is erotic but also serious in intent.

Again, Kepesh confronts the embarrassment of love. The protagonist makes an honest attempt to cope with life by letting his sexual desires mature to human feelings. The result is a modern tale of the age old struggle between body and spirit, depicted in striking mental images that expose the hero who tries to put order to his life. The maturing of Kepesh is recounted with feeling and with an awareness that somebody else's feelings can be respected, too.

The title of the novel indicates the hero's occupation as well as the main theme of the saga.

Characters
Professor of Humanities, David Kepesh, is basically an egotist who is indifferent to the needs and feelings of others. In his vivid sexual encounters with Elizabeth, Birgitta, Helen, and others, the paradox of male desire becomes apparent. This is intellectually reenforced via the erotic literature course he teaches called "Desire 341." Only towards the end of the novel does Kepesh show sincere feelings toward Claire Ovington, a likeable and orderly woman with whom he is able to enjoy domestic pleasures. The novel ends with a deeply moving idyllic scene describing a reunion with his parents and tenderly portraying Mr. Barbatnik, a dying older Jew. The characters are human beings, not caricatures. Only Herbert Bratsky is depicted as a vulgar comedian.

Techniques
Roth confronts the embarrassment of love more maturely here. The novel, an impressionistic description of facts and fiction, is a clear explication of human feelings. Roth has an acute ear for dialogue here as well. Written in a relatively narrow scope but with a broad vision, the confessional prose is funny, entertaining, and often piquantly witty. A buoyant handling of self scrutinizing monologue gives detailed information of a Jewish intellectual's sex life.

Literary Precedents
Kepesh teaches Chekhov and makes references to Flaubert but most often alludes to Kafka. *The Professor of Desire* follows the ethical traditionalism of Saul Bellow; it is also similar to the novels of Norman Mailer and James Baldwin.

Adaptations
"Eli, the Fanatic," by Irv Bauer for Broadway, 1964; "Unlikely Heroes," by Larry Arrick for Broadway, 1971; "The Watergate Follies," for Yale Repertory Theater, 1973.

Other Titles
Novels: *Goodbye, Columbus*, 1959; *Letting Go*, 1962; *When She Was Good*, 1967; *Our Gang*, 1971; *The Great American Novel*, 1973; *My Life as a Man*, 1974; *The Ghost Writer*, 1979; *Zuckerman Unbound*, 1981; *The Anatomy Lesson*, 1983; *Zuckerman Bound*, 1985; *The Counterlife*, 1987.
Selected Stories: "Philosophy, Or Something Like That," *Et Cetera* (May 1952): 5, 16; "The Box of Truth," *Et Cetera* (October 1952): 10-12; "The Fence," *Et Cetera* (May 1953): 18-23; "Armando and the Frauds," *Et Cetera* (October 1953): 21-32; "The Final Delivery of Mr. Thorn," *Et Cetera* (May 1954): 20-28; "The

Day it Snowed," *Chicago Review* 8 (Fall 1954): 34-45; "The Contest for Aaron Gold," *Epoch* 5-6 (Fall 1955): 37-51; "You Can't Tell a Man by the Song he Sings," *Commentary* 24 (November 1957): 445-450; "The Conversion of the Jews," *Paris Review* 18 (Spring 1958): 24-40; "Epstein," *Paris Review* 19 (Summer 1958): 13-36; "Heard Melodies Are Sweeter," *Esquire* 50 (August 1958): 58; "Expect the Vandals," *Esquire* 50 (December 1958): 208-228; "Defender of the Faith," *New Yorker* 35 (14 March 1959): 44-50; "Eli, the Fanatic," *Commentary* 27 (April 1959): 292-309; "The Love Vessel," *Dial* 1 (Fall 1959): 41-68; "Good Girl," *Cosmopolitan* 148 (May 1960): 98-103; "The Mistaken," *American Judaism* 10 (Fall 1960): 10; "Novotny's Pain," *New Yorker* 38 (27 October 1962): 45-56; "Psychoanalytic Special," *Esquire* 60 (November 1963): 106; "On the Air," *New American Review* 10 (August 1970): 7-49; "Salad Days," *Modern Occasions* 1 (Fall 1970): 26-46; "Courting Disaster (or Serious in the Fifties)," *Esquire* 75 (May 1971): 93-101; " 'I Always Wanted You to Admire My Fasting'; or Looking at Kafka," *American Review* 17 (May 1973): 103-126; "Marriage à la Mode," *American Review* 18 (September 1973): 211-244.

Collections: *Reading Myself and Others*, 1975; *A Philip Roth Reader*, 1980.

Nonfiction: "Mrs. Lindbergh, Mr. Ciardi, and the Teeth and Claws of the Civilized World," *Chicago Review* 11 (Summer 1957): 72-76; "The Kind of Person I Am," *New Yorker* 34 (29 November 1958): 173-178; "Writing American Fiction," *Commentary* 31 (March 1961): 223-233; "Writing About Jews," *Commentary* 36 (December 1963): 446-452; "Pictures of Malamud," *The New York Times Book Review* (20 April 1986): 1, 40-41. Roth has also published numerous reviews, letters, essays, etc.

Additional Sources

Jones, J.P., and Nance, G.A., *Philip Roth*. New York: Frederick Ungar, 1981. On his writings with biographical references up to 1980.

Lee, Hermione, *Philip Roth*. London: Methuen, 1982. An analysis of Roth's stylistic and emotional range over the last three decades.

McDaniel, John N., *The Fiction of Philip Roth*. Haddonfield: Haddonfield, 1974. A detailed study of his works up to 1973.

Pinsker, Sanford, ed., *Critical Essays on Philip Roth*. Boston: G.K. Hall, 1982. A collection of essays.

Rodgers, Bernard F., *Philip Roth: A Bibliography*. Metuchen: Scarecrow, 1974; second edition 1984. See particularly for a full list of reviews and essays by and about Roth.

_____, *Philip Roth*. Boston: Twayne, G.K. Hall, 1978. A comprehensive study of his life and opus until 1977.

Elizabeth M. Rajec
City College of the City University of New York

JOANNA RUSS
1937

Publishing History

Joanna Russ published her first short story, "Nor Custom Stale," in *The Magazine of Fantasy and Science Fiction* (1959). She has published numerous short stories since, and six novels, including *Picnic on Paradise* (1968), *And Chaos Died* (1970), *We Who Are About To* (1977), and *On Strike Against God* (1985). Her story for children, *Kittatinny,* was published in 1978, and her short fiction has been collected in three volumes, *The Adventures of Alyx* (1983), *The Zanzibar Cat* (1984), and *Extra (Ordinary) People* (1984).

An apparently pivotal event in Russ's career occurred with the publication of her short story "When It Changed" in Harlan Ellison's collection, *Again, Dangerous Visions* (1972). The impact of this Nebula-winning story is clear from its subsequent history: it has been reprinted in Russ's own collection, *The Zanzibar Cat,* but also in Pamela Sargent's feminist collection, *The New Women of Wonder,* and most recently in Gilbert and Gubar's widely praised *Norton Anthology of Literature By Women.* Although Russ had published two novels and many short stories before this, "When It Changed" generated enough controversy and praise to establish Russ in the ranks of the foremost contemporary writers of speculative fiction, including Ursula Le Guin, Thomas Disch, Sonya Dorman, and Samuel R. Delaney. Russ's distinctive feminist stance leads her to explore the fictional possibilities of portraying the lives of women freed of the psychological constraints and stereotypes of patriarchal or male-dominated social structures. Her most complex work, *The Female Man,* further develops the themes associated with the planet Whileaway of "When It Changed," juxtaposing that all-female society with several parallel universes.

Critical Reception, Honors, and Popularity

Reviewers have reacted gingerly to Russ's novels, almost certainly because of the vigorous feminist challenges to conventional expectations that characterize her work. One reviewer, who calls *The Female Man* "a scream of anger," claims that "Russ has excluded men from participation in her novel, either as readers or characters." This is a predictable male response, just as are more positive responses from feminist readers such as Marge Piercy, who acknowledges the anger and occasional crudity of Russ's storytelling, but who affirms the balancing "quality of outraged, clear-sighted, pained intelligence, at once incandescent and exacerbated." Male critics, such as Gerald Jonas, Samuel R. Delany, and Harlan Ellison, have found ways to "enter" her work, in spite of the distancing tactics she uses. Frederick Pohl, referring to the special pleasure he has gained from publishing "daring" works in the series he has edited, speaks of *The Female Man* as "a searing radical-feminist dystopia-Utopia, filled with love and rage." It is arguable that Russ's anger is not exclusive if it is shared by the reader, male or female. Piercy says of Russ's fictions, "They ask nasty and necessary questions." This is true of most significant speculative fictions, all of which define their audiences by the expectation that they will be willing to experience discomfort in their search for illumination.

In spite of the controversy some of Russ's fictions have aroused, she has been acknowledged an important writer both by her peers in the SFWA and by readers and fans. Her first novel, *Picnic on Paradise,* was nominated for a Nebula Award. "When It Changed" won the Nebula in 1972. The novella, "Souls," first published in the *Magazine of Fantasy and Science Fiction* and reprinted in *Extra (Ordinary) People,* won the Hugo Award and two other awards as the best novella of 1983.

Analysis of Selected Titles

WHEN IT CHANGED
"When It Changed," in *Again, Dangerous Visions,* 1972, short story (rpt., *The New Women of Wonder,* 1978; rpt., *The Zanzibar Cat,* 1984; rpt., *Norton Anthology of Literature by Women,* 1985.

Social Concerns/Themes
The central event of "When It Changed" is the arrival on the planet Whileaway of a space vehicle full of men. Whileaway had been colonized by men and women from earth, but all the men had died of a mysterious plague some 600 years before the the story begins. The women have devised technologies of survival—both for reproduction by the merging of ova, and for conducting the heavy labor needed to sustain civilization—and have evolved a society that is not presented as perfect, but that is richly satisfying to most of the women so long as they are willing to accept both its limitations and its communal character. The narrator, Janet, is caught between her wife Katy's violent reaction to the men's arrival (Katy feels they "should have burned them down where they stood") and their daughter Yuki's derisive dismissal of the men as "ten-foot toads." Janet senses that neither violence nor humor will suffice to head off the inevitable changes in their world when the men return. She explores a number of consolatory rationalizations, but realizes the most devastating change the men will bring to Whileaway will be their ability to drain away the meaning, so painfully created over several hundred years, of the women's lives. Her final protest, "Take my life but don't take away the meaning of my life," is both defiant and despairing. The implication that men are incapable of respecting women's accomplishments, and that they will always cast women in subordinate roles, seems to spell the doom of Whileaway. It would be mistaken, however, to take this as a defeatist story; Janet certainly has not given up hope, in

spite of her evocation of the original name for the planet—"For-A-While." She has simply reached a stage of awareness from which she can begin to mobilize the necessary moral and imaginative forces needed to protect the planet from reabsorption into the male-dominated universe.

Characters

Janet, the first person-narrator of "When It Changed," is adept with languages ("I can talk the old tongues in my sleep"), which is one reason she is called to meet the arriving men. She is thoughtful, perceptive, and inclined to worry about her wife and children, even though she has fought "three duels" and has the scars to prove it. Janet's wife, Katy, drives wildly, but refuses (until the crisis of the story) to handle guns. Their daughter, Yuriko (Yuki), is an ebullient 12-year-old whose future is the focus of Janet's anxiety. Several other women are named, and their descriptions help fill in other characteristics of the society of Whileaway.

Of the four unnamed men who arrive from the space ship, only two actually speak. The first reveals his obtuseness by asking twice "Where are all the people?," even though Janet has explained the history of the plague to him. After his second question, she tells us "I realized then that he did not mean people, he meant *men,* and he was giving the word the meaning it had on Whileaway for six centuries." The second man acknowledges the stupidity of his colleague and reveals the purpose of his visit: "There's been too much genetic damage in the last few centuries. Radiation. Drugs. We can use Whileaway's genes, Janet." His revelation drives the normally gun-shy Katy to threaten him with Janet's rifle. Given the attitudes of the men, Katy and Janet both fear their children will be "cheated of their full humanity and turned into strangers."

In an important sense, it is the six hundred year history of the women's planet, Whileaway, that is the true central character of "When It Changed." Each of the individual women described, and especially the sharp contrasts between their personalities and those of the men, help the reader to construct a composite picture of a world as it would be if no one felt the need to "play the role of the man."

Techniques

By their very nature, short stories require the reader either to infer a great deal of unwritten contextual material, or to take a great deal on faith. "When It Changed" requires both; it also provides an excellent example of the economy and efficiency of an accomplished storyteller. The exposition is both revelatory and tricky. An unsuspecting reader may fail to notice that the narrator is female until halfway through the story. The narrator refers to "my wife" and alludes to "three children between us, one of hers and two of mine." When she first describes the plague to the visiting man, she states "We lost half our population," but only after further description of post-plague history does she explain that the lost half was all the men. The reader, at this point, must accept the premise that "the merging of ova" is biologically possible, but that is one of the few science fictional elements of the story other than that it is set on another planet sometime in the future.

Janet's explanations to the men of the history of her society, and her brooding about the implications of the arrival of the men, serve to inform the reader of the special character of the planet and to convey the complex interactions that make up the society. Russ employs some familiar types (the *miles gloriosus* who is the first man to speak, the "benevolent colonizer" who is the second), but in the very use of these conventions she discredits them by showing the degree to which they can function only in mutually agreed interactions with other stereotypes. If the women of Whileaway refuse to acknowledge the roles the men cast them in, then the men's roles must also be deconstructed. This is the hope for the future.

Literary Precedents

In her afterword to "When It Changed," published in *Again, Dangerous Visions,* Russ states that the story is, at least in part, a response to some questions and problems suggested by Ursula Le Guin's *Left Hand of Darkness,* in which an androgynous civilization is depicted. The story is thus associated with a considerable body of utopian and dystopian fiction that depicts the impact of encounters between representatives of disparate or mutually exclusive cultures. An early example might be the fourth book of *Gulliver's Travels,* but in more contemporary terms one of the earliest and best examples is Stapledon's *Starmaker.* A number of women have written works that transpose familiar male-oriented story types into feminist forms, Suzy McKee Charnas's revision of the post-nuclear holocaust type—*Walk To the End of the World*—and Marion Zimmer Bradley's revision of the Arthurian corpus—*The Mists of Avalon*—come to mind. Russ has adapted the persona of the hardboiled enforcer-detective in "When It Changed," as elsewhere: tough but thoughtful, sensitive but guarded, ruthless when necessary.

Related Titles

Although Joanna Russ has stated "My feminist novel, *The Female Man,* was a later and very different project" (*Zanzibar Cat* 9), the connection between the two works is difficult to ignore, since the first narrator in the novel is Janet Evason, who announces "I was born on a farm on Whileaway." Certainly the novel—which traces the lives of three other women from parallel universes, and which gives a great deal more background about Janet—is a more complex and demanding work, but it is hard to see how it can be a very different project. The adventurous, even swashbuckling characters of Russ's other fictions (e.g., Alyx, of *Picnic on Paradise* and other stories) also constitute links among her various works.

PICNIC ON PARADISE

Picnic on Paradise, 1968, novel. Collected with other stories about Alyx in *Alyx*, 1976, and *The Adventures of Alyx*, 1983.

Social Concerns/Themes

As is the case with most of Russ's titles, *Picnic on Paradise* is both ironic and paradoxical in relation to the narrative it stands for. The planet Paradise has the same tourist appeal (and beguiling danger) as would the South Pole if it were fitted up with heat-controlled domes complete with Hyatt Regency interiors. The "picnic" is to be a desperate trek across the frozen landscape of the planet, and peopled by an assortment of variously unqualified, unfit, and obnoxious pilgrims. (The title may well allude to Manet's well known painting, "Dejeuner Sur l'Herbe," which depicts passive nude women in a vernal landscape, surrounded by more or less well-dressed and competent looking males. If so, it would participate in a complex system of imagery having to do with the roles of women in various gardens, paradises, or *loci amoeni*. Russ inverts the value systems implicit in the tradition, making the images ironic in the process.) The people dependent on Alyx's skills are not quite so debilitated as are the Eloi in Wells's *The Time Machine*, but they are far less appealing. Their various psychological and physical dependencies represent aspects of Russ's critique of contemporary bourgeois consumerism and patriarchy. (It is mistaken to view Russ's satire as directed solely at male chauvinism, though that is certainly a prime target.) While she is less overt in her attack on state capitalism than have been, for example, Philip K. Dick or Pohl and Kornbluth in *Space Merchants*, her satire is no less comprehensive.

Characters

Alyx is the only real "character" in *Picnic on Paradise*. The reader's first reaction to her may be that she is a feminine version (transvestite or transsexual?) of the tough narrators of male detective fiction (Mike Hammer, Travis McGee) or of chauvinist science fiction (Heinlein's *Starship Trooper*, Dickson's *Soldier, Ask Not*). Alyx talks tough, disdains the weaknesses of her companions—at least initially—and performs forcefully in a number of confrontations of the type now associated with "heroes" played by Stallone, Schwarzenegger, and Norris. But the association does Alyx a disservice. She is, after all, a representative of TransTemp, and has the breadth of understanding available to a being who has lived in many civilizations, many centuries, many cultures.

The other persons named in *Picnic on Paradise* are little more than types, each representing a negative aspect of the future development of a chauvinist/ consumerist culture. Physical weakness, vanity, drug dependency, and general lack of survival skills sum up the group. That Alyx must bring the accumulated skills of thousands of years of experience to the effort to save these feckless individuals becomes not so much a drama concerned with their survival as yet another test of Alyx's strength and ingenuity. She is the sum—but not the total—of women's efforts to sustain life and strength against the forces of greed, self-indulgence, and death associated with the worst of patriarchal institutions. Her interest in Machine, the young man in an iron mask who cannot endure emotion, suggests the possibility of some future positive relationship with the masculine element if it can open itself to its feminine component.

Techniques/Literary Precedents/Related Titles

Picnic on Paradise, and the other Alyx stories, fit into a small tradition of narratives that carry their central figures through many ages of human history. It is not, strictly speaking, a time-travel narrative, nor is it a story of the "undead" (as are most vampire stories); rather, it is a story of the persistence of a character, or a type of character, through many ages, divorced either from the technology of time-travel or the supernaturalism of the vampire narratives. True, the TransTemp super-structure suggests the former, but that does not form the center of interest, nor does it seem more than instrumental in placing Alyx in different contexts. This work in progress is more like Virginia Woolf's *Orlando,* or Djuna Barnes's *Ryder,* stories of the persistence of a principle consciousness through many centuries, including the occasional change of gender of the central character. That Alyx is always female does not except her from this, since her actions are not always gender-determined.

AND CHAOS DIED

And Chaos Died, 1970, novel.

Social Concerns/Themes

And Chaos Died is about the ways in which societal boundaries around behavior and consciousness constrain one from full realization of one's potential existence. The title, characteristically ironic, alludes to a passage from the Chinese sage, Chuang Tzu, describing the well-intentioned efforts of demigods to give organs of perception to the god Chaos. In its original form, this fable suggests that the sensory organs are necessary to help Chaos organize experience, but that their creation necessarily implies the destruction of "chaos," or the lack of such organi-zation. (The village is destroyed to save it.) In Russ's version, the existence of the usual human organizations of perception constitutes a limitation of human poten-tial; the development of a new sensory aperture (the ability to communicate di-rectly with other minds) necessarily leads to the "death" of the old consciousness and access to a new level of existence and consciousness. Some humans are able to sustain the shock of the new consciousness, others are not. In this story, the devel-opment of "psi-powers" assumes total and unconcealed communication among all minds that have developed such powers; this represents a devastating challenge to the conventional bourgeois notions of individuality and privacy. *And Chaos Died* dramatizes the implications of the potential evolution of isolated human consciousnesses toward a condition of universal consciousness.

Characters

Jai Vedh, a homosexual environmental designer, is the central character of *And Chaos Died*. The starship in which he is travelling explodes and he, and the Captain, are the only survivors together on a planet inhabited by a race of beings who have developed full telepathic powers. The Captain, a tough macho military type who has unquestioning faith in "science," initially reacts with contempt to the inhabitants of the planet, who live in an edenic climate: "Sit a man on his ass with nothing to do but eat and the first thing that goes is his mind." He is similarly hostile to Jai Vedh, as much because he is a civilian as because he is homosexual. It is the captain's mind, however, that "goes" in the face of this, to him, incomprehensible civilization. He frantically tries to reconstruct a communication device to summon help, but as Jai Vedh observes, "that thing you're making is going to broadcast about as well as a Christmas tree." The last the reader sees of the Captain, he is obsessively tinkering with his contraption and, as Jai Vedh observes, reduced to the same "primitive" condition he has accused the planet's inhabitants of living in: "He's worshipping it, thought Jai."

Jai Vedh learns to communicate with the inhabitants of the planet in their own manner, starting with Evne, a multi-faceted female who both does and does not have a "body" and an "identity." He encounters other "individuals," but it is the nearly universal metamorphic power associated with the collective consciousness of the beings on the planet that he is truly "in touch" with. The more he learns about this new consciousness, the more he realizes the irrelevance of the sense of boundaries that conventionally protect humans from experiencing the full power of their own consciousnesses. As Evne says, "What you call psionics . . . is the result of perception and education, nothing more, although you don't believe that." In this sense, the "powers" of these beings are not altogether unlike those of the imagination in William Blake's worldview—the cleansed doors of perception give access to infinity, but *not* by obliterating physical reality.

Techniques

Russ employs sharp shifts from "reality" to "dream" or unreality, and sudden implosions of imagery akin to surrealism in order to convey the experience of telepathic consciousness. At first, the Captain and Jai Vedh are catechized by the inhabitants like small children, but even with their gradual initiation, there is disorientation and fear, especially for the Captain. Jai Vedh, professionally trained to perceive patterns, techniques, strategies in ways that the Captain is unable to do, begins quickly to organize elements of the pattern—starting significantly with his discovery of a very large (numerically) prime number that can be pronounced, in the inhabitants' language, in one syllable. This helps him to understand the complexity and simplicity—the sophistication—of the civilization they have encountered.

Literary Precedents/Related Titles

Fictions about races with telepathic or psionic powers frequently portray them as threats to the human race, or to civilization. John Wyndham's *The Midwich Cuckoos* is an especially scary example; the total annihilation of the beautiful but ruthlessly destructive "children" who can communicate directly with each other's minds across great distances, and read the minds of their human hosts with ease, is justified in the name of protecting humanity from domination by a race with such unfair advantages. Other writers, notably Ursula Le Guin in *The Word for World is Forest* and Russ in *And Chaos Died,* portray such powers as an evolutionary advance or as a parallel evolutionary development that would lead to a more peaceable and creative civilization. In Le Guin's story, the "natives" are as much in tune with their environment as they are with each other; the earthmen's intended despoliation of the planet is as much a product of their inability to perceive the life of the environment as it is of their greed. Similarly, in Russ's novel, the Captain's dismissal of the inhabitants' powers ensures his mental and subsequent physical dissolution. The spiritual union (lovemaking) of Milton's angels, in *Paradise Lost,* and the "fourfold vision" of William Blake's cosmology may not be exact parallels or precedents, but both Le Guin and Russ are thinking on analogous lines.

THE FEMALE MAN

The Female Man, 1975, novel; rpt. Gregg Press, 1977.

Social Concerns/Themes

The many modes of domination of women by men, and the potential for the termination of that dominance in a new sociopolitical order, are the primary themes of *The Female Man.* Each of the four main characters embodies a different response to male oppression, depending in part on her social context. Russ creates several parallel universes in which the roles of men and women differ. In Whileaway, men have no roles, all of them having died centuries ago in a plague; women have evolved a society in which they fulfill all necessary roles. The very different world of Alice-Jael is in a constant state of war—the Men against the Women—and Alice-Jael is just as cunning and ruthless as the biblical heroine after whom she is named, though her weapons are technologically more sophisticated than a tent stake. Jeannine is a passive victim of a society rather like today's would be if it had stopped developing in the 1930s or 1940s. Joanna is a woman in the early stages of feminist consciousness, not yet ready to break completely with the patriarchal system. Behind them all is the shadowy figure—the author—who is all of them and more. Their responses to each other, and to the different social and political contexts in which they live, provide the satiric and analytical moments in this complex novel. One crucial underlying concept—most fully developed in the person of Janet and in the society of Whileaway—is that "gender" is not biologically or psychologically determined, but rather is an ideological product of the dominant forces of society.

Characters/Techniques

At the end of *The Female Man* the reader realizes that there is really only one "character" in the novel—the speculative imagination of the author who has subdivided herself into four women, each an aspect of (perhaps) her own personality, each responding in different possible ways to situations encountered or imagined by the author. It is rather a highly elaborated version of the after-the-fact musings of a person who wonders "what if I had—?". Such a format is more or less typical of parallel universe narratives. As Alice-Jael explains in some detail, all four of the "characters" are the same person: "we started the same . . . We ought to think alike and feel alike and act alike, but of course we don't. So plastic is humankind. . . . Between our dress, and our opinions, and our habits, and our beliefs, and our values, and our mannerisms, and our manners, and our expressions, and our ages, and our experience, even I can hardly believe that I am looking at three other myselves." By shifting from one character's perspective to another's, juxtaposing the attitudes and reaction of each of the four women to the others' behavior, Russ emphasizes both the sameness and the important differences among them. These differences include differing attitudes about the use of violence, varieties of sexuality, and conflicting views of the relative usefulness or uselessness of men. Two highly erotic scenes emphasize these differences. Janet Evason, splitting from the ambivalent voice of the narrator, succumbs to the seduction of Laura Rose and, in the succeeding narrative, destroys all the cliches about "lesbian" love. Later, Alice-Jael takes the "J's," as she calls them, to her Vermont mountain retreat where she keeps Davy, "the most beautiful man in the world," a blue-eyed blond house-pet and sexual toy who is controlled by the house computer by means of implants in his brain. While some might argue that these two scenes suggest that mature sexuality is possible only between women, and that men's sexual functions are nonessential or recreational in a potential world, these are only two possibilities explored among many potential "universes."

The sexually explicit nature of many passages in *The Female Man* is another evidence of Russ's position in relation to what has been called the "new wave" in science fiction. Before the 1960s, sexuality was virtually invisible in science fiction, but the writers of Russ's generation broke with that tradition and began to explore not only the uses of sexuality in conventional terms, but the many varieties available once the physical and psychological limits of conventional human behavior are dismissed.

While the parallel-universe narrative is familiar to science fiction readers, there is little else about *The Female Man* that can be called conventional. Not only do the unusual personalities of the several characters force the reader into unfamiliar modes of thought, but the frequent shifts of point of view and the sudden appearance of satirical lists or hypothetical dialogues between nameless character types tend to keep the reader off balance. Russ might not appreciate comparisons with earlier male satirists, but the portrayal of the Manlanders, for example, has both a Rabelaisian grotesquerie and a Swiftian bite. The games (such as "The Great Happiness Contest," or "Ain't It Awful") are like scenes from Restoration Comedy, as the names of the participants—Saccharissa, Wailissa, Lamentissa—suggest. Russ uses a remarkable range of comic and satiric techniques to break down conventional expectations and attitudes and to expose the absurdity of the false consciousness generated by patriarchal society.

Other Titles

Alyx, 1976 (novella and short stories); *We Who Are About To . . .*, 1977 (novel); *The Two of Them*, 1978 (novel); *Kittatinny: A Tale of Magic*, 1978 (novel); *The Adventures of Alyx*, 1983 (novella and short stories); *How To Suppress Women's Writing*, 1983 (critical essay); *The Zanzibar Cat*, 1984 (short stories); *Extra (Ordinary) People*, 1984 (novella and short stories); *On Strike Against God*, 1985 (novel); *Magic Mommas Trembling Sisters Puritans and Perverts: Feminist Essays*, 1985 (essays).

Additional Sources

Contemporary Literary Criticism, Vol. 15. Detroit: Gale Research, Reviews by Marge Piercy, Gerald Jonas.

Delany, Samuel R., Introduction to *Alyx*. Boston: Gregg Press, 1976, pp. v-xxiv.

Dictionary of Literary Biography, Vol. 8, Part 2, Detroit: Gale Research, pp. 88-93.

Hacker, Marilyn, "Science Fiction and Feminism: The Work of Joanna Russ," *Chrysalis* 4 (1977): 67-79.

Rosinsky, Natalie M., "A Female Man? The Medusan Humor of Joanna Russ," *Extrapolation* 23.1 (1982): 31-36.

Thomas F. Dillingham
Stephens College

J. D. SALINGER
1919

Publishing History

It is said that J.D. Salinger first offered *The Catcher in the Rye* to a famous publishing house, but his editor there thought Holden Caulfield was "crazy." If so, that editor made one of the biggest mistakes in publishing history. Angered, Salinger next offered the book to Little, Brown, which set publication for the spring of 1951. But when the Book-of-the Month Club made *The Catcher in the Rye* its midsummer selection, the publication date was pushed back to July 16, 1951, and the rest is history. By the end of July, it had been reprinted five times and entered the best seller list of *The New York Times* in fourteenth place. It reached as high as fourth place and remained on the list twenty-nine weeks.

But this was only the beginning. Instead of dropping off sharply in popularity, as most best sellers do after their initial run, *The Catcher in the Rye* maintained its momentum. It became especially popular in high schools, colleges, and universities. When asked in 1962 which American books published in the last thirty years deserve "to be included in a college course in American literature" and "have already begun to attain the stature of modern classics," professors in California put *The Catcher in the Rye* at the top of both lists. Ten years later, in response to the same questions, professors in Illinois placed it second only to *Invisible Man*. Similarly, in 1981, *The Catcher in the Rye* was second only to *Of Mice and Men* as the most frequently taught novel in public schools. And all this occurred despite the militant opposition of conservative groups to the novel's "profanity." By 1961, the book had sold 1,500,000 copies; by 1965, about 5,000,000; and by 1975, over 9,000,000, placing it third or fourth among all novels in American sales. In 1981, *Esquire* reported that the Bantam paperback continued to sell twenty to thirty thousand copies a month, so the grand total of sales today is approximately 12,000,000. In addition, *The Catcher in the Rye* has been translated into at least 27 languages and now includes readers in such diverse places as Iceland and Vietnam.

Salinger has also published 35 short stories. In 1939, he studied short-story writing at Columbia University with Whit Burnett, who published "The Young Folks," Salinger's first story, in his *Story* magazine in 1940. Salinger was soon publishing in the mass circulation magazines—*Collier's, Esquire, The Saturday Evening Post, Cosmopolitan,* and *Harper's*. As early as 1941, he sold a Holden Caulfield story, "Slight Rebellion Off Madison," to *The New Yorker,* but the magazine held off publication until 1946. By 1953, he was publishing exclusively in *The New Yorker,* considered at that time to be the finest short-story magazine in the country.

The turning point in Salinger's career was, of course, *The Catcher in the Rye.* After that triumph, demand increased for Salinger books. In 1953, he collected his most mature work and published *Nine Stories*. It made ninth place on *The New York*

Times best seller list and remained on the list for over three months, a unique achievement then for a book of short stories. It has been translated into at least 17 languages. The first of the *Nine Stories,* "A Perfect Day for Bananafish," begins the saga of the Glass family that was to occupy Salinger for the rest of his publishing career. In 1955, he published "Franny," and in 1957, "Zooey." The book, *Franny and Zooey* (1961), proved even more immediately successful than *The Catcher in the Rye.* It quickly rose to first place on *The New York Times* best seller list and remained there for six months. It sold more than 125,000 copies within the first two weeks of publication. It has been translated into at least 15 foreign languages. *"Raise High the Roof Beam, Carpenters"* and *"Seymour: An Introduction"* (1963), whose stories had originally appeared in 1955 and 1959 respectively, represented a falling off in Salinger's popularity, although by almost any other standard the book must be considered a commercial success. It, too, was translated into at least 15 foreign languages. Salinger's last story, "Hapworth 16, 1924" (published on June 19, 1965), has never appeared in book form. Salinger has published no fiction in the last 21 years, and it now appears that the Glass family saga will never be completed.

Critical Reception, Honors, and Popularity

Despite its enormous popularity among the general reading public, and especially students, *The Catcher in the Rye* has been attacked by two diverse but influential groups. First, non-literary guardians of public taste have condemned the novel because of its "profanity." At times, their criticism has extended to the life style and attitudes of the teen-age protagonist, hardly a worthy model for impressionable adolescents. This group wields considerable power in local schools and libraries and has enjoyed considerable success. *The Catcher in the Rye* is one of the most banned books of the late twentieth century.

Second, highly literate academic critics have reacted against the very success of the novel. The early reviews were generally favorable. But when *The Catcher in the Rye* became a popular sensation, the critics became excessive in their praise, comparing this short first novel with some of the world's greatest fiction. The inevitable reaction followed. In a famous criticism, George Steiner castigated "the Salinger industry" for its failure "to distinguish what is great from what is competent." Recent criticism has moderated its claims and tried to assess the novel's true position. The consensus today seems to be that *The Catcher in the Rye* is a minor masterpiece.

Time has been less kind to Salinger's other works. The three volumes of short stories apparently owed their initial popularity largely to considerations other than their intrinsic merits as literature. They were written by the author of *The Catcher in the Rye;* they presented the evolving story of the Glass family; and they anticipated the emerging interest in Eastern modes of thought, most notably Zen. But America in the 1980s seems less interested in the life of contemplation, and

Salinger, having published no fiction for 21 years, seems determined to leave the Glass saga unfinished. Contemporary criticism believes that Salinger will be best remembered as the author of *The Catcher in the Rye*.

Salinger's work has received some formal recognition. "A Girl I Know" won a place in Martha Foley's *Best American Short Stories of 1949*. "For Esmé—with Love and Squalor" appeared in *Prize Stories of 1950*. "Uncle Wiggily in Connecticut" was transmogrified by Hollywood into "My Foolish Heart," a romance starring Susan Hayward and Dana Andrews. Salinger has since refused to sell movie or television rights to any of his works. In a similar vein, *The Catcher in the Rye* was a midsummer selection of the Book-of-the-Month Club, but Salinger then rejected several lucrative book-club offers for *Franny and Zooey*. Finally, Valley Forge Military Academy chose him as one of its distinguished alumni for 1952, but his sister replied that he was in Mexico and could not attend. For an author of Salinger's ability and notoriety, he has received remarkably few honors; no one continues to offer awards to a recluse.

Analysis of Selected Titles

THE CATCHER IN THE RYE
The Catcher in the Rye, 1951, novel.

Social Concerns

The Catcher in the Rye heralds the America of the 1950s: the Eisenhower-Nixon administrations, the McCarthy investigations, the men in the grey flannel suits. It was a world of economic expansion and social complacency. The young, blacks, and women had little power, yet the voice of protest was muted. It seemed that things would go on in the same way for a long time.

This is the society in which Holden Caulfield lives. Speaking for many of his generation, he rails at the phoniness of his world but feels incapable of effecting any meaningful change. He cannot even connect with another individual. His instinct is to cut and run. In vivid and concrete detail, *The Catcher in the Rye* thus anticipates the major catchwords of the 1950s: alienation, the silent generation, the lonely crowd. Although the novel has been criticized for not dealing with specific social issues, time has shown that it caught the peculiar social malaise of the 1950s with remarkable accuracy.

Themes

The most obvious theme of *The Catcher in the Rye* is the conflict between the individual and society. Holden abhors the phoniness of his world. An idealist, he wants people to meet on a purely human basis, an I-thou relationship; but this son of a wealthy corporation lawyer is sensitive to the barriers erected between individuals and classes by the bourgeois materialism of mid-century America. Genuine communication remains problematical. The novel suggests the rich ambiguities latent in this theme. Is something wrong with the individual because of his inability to adjust to his society? Or is something wrong with a society that alienates such an individual? Must Holden choose between the extremes of conformity and dropping out, or is there a possibility of improving the society?

The novel also has a more "philosophical" theme. Holden struggles not only with society but also against Time, the bringer of old age, decay, and death. During puberty, Holden learns that Time is the great destroyer when his beloved younger brother, Allie, dies of leukemia. Consequently, Holden wants to stop time. He loves the Museum of Natural History because "everything stayed right where it was. Nobody'd move." Holden wants to be "the catcher in the rye," to catch the kids before they fall over the cliff into the phony adult world of time and death. But his young sister, Phoebe, teaches him a better way. First, she reminds him that the line is "If a body *meet* a body coming through the rye," that one must encounter "the other" as an autonomous equal, not as a dependent to be protected in accordance with one's own fears. Then, at the climax, as Holden watches Phoebe ride the carrousel and grab for the gold ring, he says, "I was sort of afraid she'd fall off the goddam horse, but I didn't say anything or do anything. The thing with kids is, if they want to grab for the gold ring, you have to let them do it, and not say anything. If they fall off, they fall off, but it's bad if you say anything to them." Holden begins to accept time and process and change, to accept life.

Characters

Think of *The Catcher in the Rye*, and one immediately thinks of Holden Caulfield. He is one of the great characters of fiction, the model of the sensitive, idealistic, and confused young man. His struggles with society and against Time, told from his own point of view, make the book intensely real for most readers who empathize with Holden. But something bigger and stranger happens. Like Huck Finn, Jay Gatsby, and other memorable characters, Holden breaks the bounds of his own fictional world and achieves an independent existence. Readers imagine him as a real person in real-life situations.

Holden is the only fully drawn character in the novel; the others are character sketches. Phoebe and Allie are rare creations: intelligent and lovable children, yet believable and unsentimentalized. Like Dickens, Salinger has the uncanny ability to make even his most minor characters into memorable individuals—Harris Macklin, for instance, who was such a terrific whistler. The only stereotypes are several of the adult figures: Holden's father, the corporation lawyer; Holden's mother, the worrier; Haas and Ossenburger, the phony businessmen. But even these stereotypes serve to characterize Holden. Since all of the characters are presented from his point of view, his vision of vital, loving kids and cold, phony adults tells the reader a great deal about Holden.

Techniques

The popularity of *The Catcher in the Rye* largely depends upon its plot and its language. It employs that most archetypal of all plots: the quest. From *The Odyssey* on, Western literature has dramatized the adventures of a quester. Escaping from Pencey Prep to New York City, Holden Caulfield encounters various figures in his search for human connection and meaning. The fabulous creatures and adventures of early quest narrative have become realistic here, but Holden's story is no less terrifying than that of Odysseus. Like Odysseus, he finally reaches, thanks to Phoebe, home. Has he learned anything? Has the quest been meaningful? He has certainly learned that he cannot be "the catcher in the rye." In addition, the fact that he is recounting his odyssey to a psychiatrist suggests that he is shaping and gaining control of his experience. Perhaps understanding even leads to love; after all, he misses everybody he tells about, even old Maurice.

When *The Catcher in the Rye* was published in 1951, much attention was focused on its "obscene" language. Now, in a more permissive age, more attention can be paid to the brilliance of its language. Holden's speech sounds authentic to almost all readers of the book. He uses the diction, slang, rhythms, and repetitiousness of the 1950s American teenager, shaped by Salinger to give it point, humor, and meaning. The question is, how can such a realistic example of teenage speech serve as such an effective medium of communication? While creating the illusion of realistic speech, Salinger contrasts Holden's sensitivity to an era of comformity.

Literary Precedents

Because *The Catcher in the Rye* deals with those perennial themes of American fiction, the struggle of the individual with society and the struggle against Time, it has been compared with almost all of its major predecessors. Holden has been related to such diverse figures as Jay Gatsby, sensitive to the rich possibilities of life but trapped in an acquisitive and phony society; Henry David Thoreau, drawn to a purer life in the woods; and even Captain Ahab, on a quest for the Absolute. If nothing else, these genealogical charts show that *The Catcher in the Rye* lies in the mainstream of American literature.

One literary precedent stands out strikingly: *The Catcher in the Rye* is a kind of updating of *The Adventures of Huckleberry Finn*. Both stories are told by their adolescent heroes in vivid, colloquial English. Both young men are loving, sensitive, perceptive, and troubled. Both escape from their conventional circumstances, which they feel to be constraining and phony, to seek a more authentic existence. During their flights, both encounter a series of strangers, many of whom are threatening. Each boy becomes the vehicle for a devastating criticism of his loveless society. Finally, each returns home. But the differences between the two books are at least as important as the similarities and measure the road that America traveled in the intervening 67 years. Huck is more accepting of reality; Holden is more alienated. Huck is freer and cheerier floating down the Mississippi; Holden is trapped in the modern wasteland. Huck can light out for the still existing Territory; Holden is recounting his story to a psychiatrist in California. Written after two world wars and the depression, *The Catcher in the Rye* presents a darker vision of the world.

Related Titles

The Catcher in the Rye develops from six short stories that include the two Caulfield brothers, Vincent and Holden, and a lovely sibling relationship between Babe and Mattie Gladwaller. In "Last Day of the Last Furlough" *(Saturday Evening Post*, 15 July 1944), Babe Gladwaller speaks with his ten-year-old sister, Mattie, whose understanding of him anticipates Phoebe's relationship with Holden. Babe is concerned over his friendship with Vincent Caulfield, whose brother Holden has run away from school again. In "A Boy in France" *(Saturday Evening Post*, 31 March 1945), the troubled Babe lulls himself to sleep by rereading a letter from Mattie. In "The Stranger" *(Collier's*, 1 December 1945), Babe takes Mattie to New York to tell Vincent Caulfield's ex-girl friend about his death in the war. The woman reveals that Vincent had become very cynical after his young brother, Kenneth Caulfield, died.

The other three stories feature the Caulfields directly. In "This Sandwich Has No Mayonnaise" *(Esquire*, October 1945), Vincent becomes depressed over the news that his nineteen-year-old brother, Holden, is missing in action in the Pacific. In "I'm Crazy" *(Collier's*, 22 December 1945), the "real" Holden Caulfield appears at last. The story is an early version of the scenes with his history teacher at Pencey Prep and with Phoebe in the bedroom at home. This Holden is a less complex and less lovable character than the protagonist of the novel, and he ends up with an office job. The profane language is absent from *Collier's*. In his first *New Yorker* story, "Slight Rebellion Off Madison" (21 December 1946), Salinger presents (from the third-person point of view) the relationship between Holden and Sally, combining the ice-skating episode and the later phone call. Again, Holden is not allowed to say to Sally, "You give me a royal pain in the ass," in the magazine. Finally, it is important to note that Salinger sold an earlier version of "Slight Rebellion Off Madison" to *The New Yorker* in 1941. It was not published but reveals that he was working on the material that was to become *The Catcher in the Rye* in another ten years.

Adaptations

Two scenes from *The Catcher in the Rye* were dramatized by Barbara Wells and presented at the Repertory Theatre Circle in New York on June 7 to 9, 1962.

Otherwise, Salinger has remained adamantly opposed to adaptations of his masterpiece. Although he has been offered immense sums to allow *The Catcher in the Rye* to be made into a movie, he has steadfastly refused them. Like Holden, he undoubtedly fears that Hollywood would turn the book into something phony. "My Foolish Heart," the 1950 Hollywood transmogrification of "Uncle Wiggily in Connecticut," taught him a lasting lesson.

Other Titles

Nine Stories, 1953 (short stories); *Franny and Zooey,* 1961 (short stories); *"Raise High the Roof Beam, Carpenters"* and *"Seymour: An Introduction,"* 1963 (short stories).

Additional Sources

French, Warren, *J.D. Salinger.* Boston: Twayne, 1976. A reprint, with revised and updated bibliography, of the original 1963 book that examines all of Salinger's major work.

Grunwald, Henry Anatole, ed., *Salinger: A Critical and Personal Portrait.* New York: Harper, 1962. A collection of landmark essays on Salinger, including those by Arthur Mizener, Alfred Kazin, George Steiner, Dan Wakefield, Edgar Branch, and Donald P. Costello.

Miller, James E., Jr., *J.D. Salinger.* Minneapolis: University of Minnesota Press, 1965. A short but authoritative account of the alienation theme in Salinger.

_____, *"Catcher* in and out of History," *Critical Inquiry,* 3(1977): 599-603.

Ohmann, Carol and Richard, "Reviewers, Critics, and *The Catcher in the Rye,*" *Critical Inquiry,* 3(1976): 15-37.

_____, "Universals and the Historically Particular," *Critical Inquiry,* 3(1977): 773-777. A fascinating interchange over a question that has implications far beyond *The Catcher in the Rye:* is the novel entirely conditioned by its social and economic context, or is it a universal work?

Sublette, Jack R., ed., *J.D. Salinger: An Annotated Bibliography, 1938-1981.* New York: Garland, 1984. An indispensable guide to works by and about Salinger.

Mark A. Weinstein
University of Nevada, Las Vegas

JACK SCHAEFER
1907

Publishing History

Jack Schaefer's development as a writer is atypical, in that he did not publish his first novel *(Shane,* 1949) until he was in his forties; further, that book's success has overshadowed much of his subsequent production. Schaefer's earlier careers gave little indication that he would one day become an eminent chronicler of the American western frontier. Before turning to free-lance writing, Schaefer labored variously as an Eastern journalist, an educator in a Connecticut prison, and as an associate in a New Haven advertising firm. Indeed, Schaefer had never been west of his native Ohio at the time he wrote *Shane,* the bulk of which was written in Norfolk, Virginia.

In submitting an early version of the novel to *Argosy* magazine, Schaefer neglected to include return postage, but his manuscript miraculously was not ignored and was published (although the author's name was misspelled) in the fall of 1946 under the title *Rider from Nowhere,* serialized into three parts. Houghton Mifflin picked up the revised novel in 1949, and *Shane* has enjoyed solid sales ever since. By 1951 the book was selling 8,000 hardbound copies a year; a Bantam paperback edition has averaged yearly sales of 12,000 since 1950. The novel has passed through some seventy editions in thirty languages and was adapted into an epochal 1953 film. Recently honored by the Western Writers of America as the best Western novel ever written, *Shane* has clearly found a durable niche within the halls of popular fiction.

Critical Reception, Honors, and Popularity

Although *Shane* was by no means an immediate best seller, its critical reception was warm from the start. Early reviewers were quick to appreciate the novel's spare prose style and its sharp delineation of character.

Nonetheless, Western literature as an identifiable genre enjoys little respect among academic critics, who often dismiss Schaefer as a writer of escapist melodrama. Schaefer's admirers, conversely, maintain that his stubborn regionalism should obscure neither the excellence of his prose nor the universality of his themes; such critics applaud the historical accuracy of his tales, a quality which, for them, removes Schaefer's work from the body of "blood and bullets" Westerns with which it is sometimes linked. In the long run, however, it seems likely that only *Shane* and perhaps a handful of Schaefer's short stories will continue to attract a large reading audience.

In addition to the honors garnered for *Shane,* Schaefer received an Ohioana Book Award (1961) and an American Library Notable Book prize for *Old Ramon.* He was also honored in 1975 with a distinguished achievement award from the Western Literature Association.

Analysis of Selected Titles

SHANE

Shane, 1949, novel.

Social Concerns

Much of *Shane*'s early popularity may be traced to the fact that it addresses societal changes on a vast scale, a theme which speaks tellingly to the concerns of post-war generations. In the tradition of Stephen Crane's "The Bride Comes to Yellow Sky," *Shane* treats the *fin de siècle* American West in which an era of lawless individualism is being supplanted by the rooted, domesticated values of an intrusive and inexorable civilization. Ironically, both the gunfighter Shane and his antagonist Luke Fletcher, a pioneering and land-hungry cattleman, are among those who are being shunted aside by the urgent drift of historical progress; both men are fated to be subsumed by the legions of civilized farmers represented in the story by the Starrett family. Throughout the novel, Shane struggles desperately to associate himself with the values and visions of these homesteaders, and he becomes their staunchest champion in their final stand against Fletcher. But Shane is ultimately unable to deny his own heroic role within the fading age that molded him; appropriately enough, his desertion of the Starretts has him riding alone into a Western sky from which the sun has already departed.

Themes

Shane is told from the point of view of young Bob Starrett; the novel involves the adolescent narrator's initiation into the positive moral values of both Shane, whom he idolizes, and of his own stalwart father, Joe. These two men reflect opposing approaches to life: Joe Starrett represents the civilizing ethos of domesticity, while Shane is the archetypal loner, irretrievably cut off from the burgeoning society that he momentarily serves. Nonetheless, Bob's two "fathers" share a common conviction that life is a persistent struggle in which the mettle of a man is tested and shaped by the overcoming of contentious obstacles. As Bob witnesses Joe and Shane's epic battle with a monstrous tree stump, Shane's inner struggle to conform to the life of the farmer, and the gunfighter's expert dispatching of Fletcher and Wilson, he learns to appreciate and adopt the best values of both the "Old" and "New" West.

Characters

Shane is peopled by so-called "stock" characters: the stolid-but-honest farmer, the "house-proud" farmwife, the enigmatic and black-clad gunfighter, the rapacious land baron. In the case of *Shane,* however, the familiarity of these characters serves to lend mythic dimensions and a certain timelessness to Schaefer's overtly simple plot. Still, the archetypal patterns of ancient myth are reversed here: Shane's quest is not so much to enter a dark wood of violent adventure as it is to divest himself of his heroic past and to take on the trappings of the new order. In this sense, therefore, Shane is the one dynamic character in the novel. He struggles valiantly to deny his true calling and to assume the factitious role of homesteader, even to the point of dressing the part, putting away his ebony Colt, and falling half in love with Marian, Joe's wife. But that domestic role is artificial at its heart for Shane, a fact which he ultimately acknowledges when he answers the siren call of Wilson, Fletcher's hired gun. Shane again straps on his revolver, thereby becoming "complete" and at one with his heroic stature, a lone rider into the dark depths of the soul's hidden violence. As in classical myth, Shane-as-hero vanquishes the evil forces threatening the larger community, revivifying the agricultural village from which he himself is permanently (and ironically) barred.

Techniques

Schaefer was a newspaper editor for many years, and the journalist's penchant for clear, simple and emphatic language is apparent throughout *Shane.* This simplicity of style, however, harbors a variety of complex literary devices—including foreshadowing, symbolism, and counterpoint—all of which add immeasurably to the work's appeal. The central conflict in the novel is not so much the literal one of cattleman vs. homesteader as it is the struggle that rages within Shane himself; the reader of *Shane* is absorbed from the outset by the question of whether the loner, provoked by Fletcher's outrages against the Starretts, will take up his gun and revert to his former ways. The first time Shane appears in the novel, he is seen hesitating at a symbolic fork in the road; finally he chooses to ride on toward the Starrett's farm and its life of happy domesticity. But Shane's brief career as a farmer is punctuated by recurring episodes that reveal the insistent pull of the life he has tried to renounce. For example, Shane at one point gazes longingly at the wild mountain ranges that border the farm; he coaches Bob lovingly in the use of a gun; he bridles as Fletcher's assaults begin to focus on Joe. By the time Shane reassumes his former identity, therefore, the reader has been well prepared for his critical decision; nonetheless, Schaefer's craftsmanship as a storyteller is such that this foreshadowing does not diminish the plot's informing texture of suspense.

Literary Precedents

Early reviewers of *Shane* likened Schaefer's novel to the works of Owen Wister (especially *The Virginian* (1902)), Mary Hallock Foote and Helen Hunt Jackson. To a certain extent, *Shane* is an apotheosis of the Western story as it has become known to generations of movie goers, pulp novel readers, and television viewers: the conflict between society and outlaw, culminating inevitably in a fiery show-down, has become so familiar as to have permanently entered the American mythic consciousness. As mentioned above, however, Schaefer's themes are more closely linked with Stephen Crane's; Schaefer deals repeatedly with that twilight era of the Old West in which frontier individualism and values are being usurped by Eastern notions of order and degree. In his substantial canon of novels and stories, Schaefer increasingly strikes an elegaic chord, lamenting the passage of those giants who once walked the American West and finding fault with the so-called "civilized" life that effectively eradicated them.

Adaptations

Shane was made into a justly famous motion picture in 1953 (produced and directed by George Stevens for Paramount; screenplay by A. B. Guthrie, Jr.). The film starred Alan Ladd in the title role and featured such well-known actors as Van Heflin, Jean Arthur, Brandon De Wilde, and Jack Palance (who brilliantly por-trayed the malevolent Wilson).

The production received general praise from critics. Although the film lacks the novel's complexity of characterization, internalized descriptions, and mythic di-mensions, it nonetheless follows Schaefer's plot faithfully as it graphically depicts Shane's essential separation from the farmers whom he champions. In one scene, for example, Shane stands outside in the rain while talking to Marian, who remains inside the snug Starrett house; the soundtrack plays "Beautiful Dreamer" at this point, accentuating the unreality of Shane's desire to fit in with the homesteaders.

OLD RAMON

Old Ramon, 1960, novel.

Social Concerns/Themes

Old Ramon is Schaefer's award-winning short novel for juvenile readers. Its plot is straightforward: Old Ramon, an ancient shepherd, "wise in the ways of sheep," takes his employer's young son with him as he drives his sheep across the Western desert toward their seasonal grazing lands. In the past, Ramon has similarly been a mentor for the boy's father and grandfather, initiating them into the mysteries of the flock and the outdoor world. Like his forebears, the youngster learns much practi-cal knowledge from Ramon, as man and animal confront the challenges of snakes, swollen rivers, wind storms and wolves. More importantly, the boy is exposed to the old man's simple philosophy of fidelity, courage, persistence, and respect for the wilderness. By the story's end, the boy is more nearly ready, in his turn, to become Ramon's respectful *patrón.*

Characters

Old Ramon is intended for young people, and adult readers may find the short novel heavy-handed and sententious. Nonetheless, Schaefer has created in Ramon one of his most sympathetic and clearly-etched characters, one who shares common traits with the heroes of Schaefer's adult fiction. Like Shane, for example, Ramon represents the dying breed of men who are adept at skills and approaches to life that are quickly fading from the Western scene. The boy's father turns the youngster over to Ramon for a period of instruction in the central virtues that cannot be learned from books. In his own classroom of the shrinking American wilderness, Old Ramon imparts those values which Schaefer clearly sees as headed toward a premature and lamentable extinction.

MONTE WALSH
Monte Walsh, 1963, novel.

Social Concerns/Themes

Perhaps Schaefer's most ambitious work, *Monte Walsh* encompasses, through a review of the title character's troubled life, the entire historical era of its author's interest. Monte, born in 1856, runs away from an unhappy home at sixteen and gradually learns the impressive skills of an expert cowboy. In 1879, Monte forms the chief friendship of his life with Chet Rollins, a fellow cowpuncher who proves to be distinctly more adaptable than Monte to the West's changing ways. As the cattle business evolves into a corporate, structured enterprise, Monte is in danger of becoming a living anachronism, a man whose fierce independence and reliance on old ways ill suit him to the industry's modernity. The death of a veteran gunfighter, William (Powder) Kent, and the cattle corporation's insistence on breaking and then destroying a wild horse named Hellfire serve as presagers of Monte's own fate. Nonetheless, Monte demonstrates through a final act of heroic horsemanship that the arts and hardiness of the Old West are being forfeited only at a considerable cost. His death in 1913 (his epitaph lauds him as "A Good Man With A Horse") marks as well the end of an era, one to which Schaefer consistently refers with longing, nostalgia, and reverence.

Characters/Techniques

Schaefer's familiar thematic concern with civilization's encroachment on the wilderness receives its fullest treatment in *Monte Walsh,* finding expression in a wealth of specific detail. Monte pays three visits to Dodge City, for example, and discovers on each succeeding trip that the community is becoming ever more civilized, more staid. This development has its merits: at one point, communal efforts are successful in controlling a wild range fire that would have been even more devastating but for the cooperation of settled townspeople. But Monte resolutely refuses to conform himself to the society of the "autymobile" and the corporate manager.

Schaefer contrasts Monte's intractability with Chet Rollins' willingness to adapt to the changing times. Rollins, who becomes a successful businessman and statesman, is himself an admirable character, comparable to the similarly adaptable Joe Starrett and the patrons of Old Ramon. Nonetheless, Monte remains in Chet's eyes a shining symbol of the good days when the West, like the cowhands Chet and Monte, had been young and stirringly vibrant. As in all of Schaefer's works, here the passing away of the Old West is couched in terms of regret and elegaic ruefulness.

Other Titles

First Blood, 1953 (short novel); *The Big Range,* 1953 (short stories); *The Canyon,* 1953 (short novel); *The Pioneers,* 1954 (short stories); *Out West: An Anthology of Stories,* 1955; *Company of Cowards,* 1957 (novel); *The Kean Land,* 1959 (short stories); *The Great Endurance Horse Race,* 1963; *The Plainsmen,* 1963 (novel); *Stubby Pringle's Christmas,* 1964 (short stories); *Heroes Without Glory: Some Goodmen of the Old West,* 1965 (nonfiction); *Adolphe Francis Alphonse Bandelier,* 1966 (nonfiction); *Collected Stories,* 1966; *Mavericks,* 1967 (novel); *New Mexico,* 1967 (nonfiction); *The Short Novels of Jack Schaefer,* 1967; *Hal West: Western Gallery,* 1971; *An American Bestiary,* 1975; *Conversations with a Pocket Gopher,* 1978.

Additional Sources

Haslam, Gerald, *Jack Schaefer.* Boise State University Western Writers Series, No. 20. Boise: Boise State University, 1975. A brief, sympathetic discussion of Schaefer and his works, with special attention paid to *Shane, The Canyon, Monte Walsh,* and *Mavericks.*

Work, James C., ed., *Shane: The Critical Edition.* Lincoln: University of Nebraska Press, 1984. In addition to the 1949 *Shane* (retaining the profanity that had been largely excised in the 1954 edition), this text contains reprints of most of the important secondary material on Schaefer, including Fred Erisman's "Growing Up With the American West: Fiction of Jack Schaefer;" James K. Folsom's *"Shane* and *Hud:* Two Stories in Search of a Medium;" Pauline Kael's ideologically acerbic 1968 review of the film version of *Shane;* Robert Mikkelsen's "The Western Writer: Jack Schaefer's Use of the Western Frontier;" and Henry Nuwer's "An Interview with Jack Schaefer."

William Ryland Drennan
University of Wisconsin Center—
Baraboo/Sauk County

JAMES H. SCHMITZ
1911

Publishing History

James H. Schmitz had his first short story accepted for publication in 1941, shortly before the attack on Pearl Harbor. Service in the Army Air Corps during World War II and a short period as a self-employed manufacturer interrupted his writing career, which resumed in the early 1950s with sales to *Astounding* and *Galaxy* Science Fiction magazines. These stories were later anthologized as the popular *Agent of Vega*. His first novel, *Legacy* published in 1962, established a favorite locale, a fictional galactic civilization called the Federation of the Hub, in which most of his later work would be based.

His best-known work is a fantasy-science fiction novel, *The Witches of Karres* (1966). His total works comprise five novels, three collections of novelettes, and numerous short stories.

Critical Reception, Honors, and Popularity

Schmitz's critical reception has been generally positive. Many critics appreciate his fresh, unstereotyped treatment of character, human and alien alike, and his rich imagination. Particularly noted also is the implicit treatment of male and female as equally competent and adventurous in a genre and era where females were regarded as deficient in both brain and nerve. This may help explain Schmitz's continuing popularity. His unprejudiced tone, neither condescending nor militant, keeps his work from being too readily dated. In addition, most critics compliment him on his ability to flesh out his galactic civilizations with non-human species, some humanity's equal, some its superior, all in lively competition for a piece of the galactic action.

Schmitz has been honored by his colleagues in the Science Fiction Writers of America with the inclusion of the 1949 novella "The Witches of Karres" in their *Science Fiction Hall of Fame* (1973), a multi-volume collection of the most highly-regarded science fiction ever written. In a more puckish vein, he received in 1973 the Invisible Little Man Award from the Elves', Gnomes' and Little Men's Science Fiction, Chowder, and Marching Society.

Analysis of Selected Titles

THE WITCHES OF KARRES

The Witches of Karres, 1966, novel (expanded from the 1949 novella of the same title).

Social Concerns/Themes

Of special interest to adolescent readers, *The Witches of Karres* combines an unconventional young man's search for his niche in life with an elaborate narrative of political and commercial intrigue on a grand scale. In this book, set in the distant future, humanity has colonized much of the galaxy, and has diversified into a variety of types, some with very special powers. It is a chance encounter with three young citizens of the planet Karres, whose metaphysical powers have earned them and their community the title of witches, that propel the young man into strange adventures.

Among its most timely themes, common to Schmitz's work, is the idea that each individual needs to be capable of taking care of himself. Female and male characters, human or otherwise, are equally represented in every profession, from shipwright to secret agent. In Schmitz's universe, no one wastes time being ornamental, or can afford to do so.

Characters

In *The Witches of Karres,* the plot focuses on Captain Pausert of Nikkeldepain, a young shiphandler who takes an old exploration ship out into the wide galaxy to redeem his dwindling fortunes and win the esteem of his fiancee's family so that he can return to that stuffy commercial planet, marry, and settle down to be the most ordinary of citizens. In the course of his journey he does a good deed, and because no good deed ever goes unpunished, the Captain is forced into a new path of self-discovery.

By making his protagonist a galactic ship's captain, Schmitz is able to demonstrate the complexities of navigating among the stars, running a small commercial venture, getting to know one's allies from one's opponents, and surviving local politics long enough to make a profit. The young man must also decide over the course of the novel to which community he belongs: his comfortable, dull native world of Nikkeldepain with its self-absorption, or Karres, a world peopled by galactic-minded odd birds with a gift for finding dangerous tasks and staying with them.

Karres is represented in the novel by Goth, a wily child who, like Pausert, is on a journey of self-discovery that draws on her extrasensory powers to stay just one step ahead of the situation—one that grows rapidly from the problems aboard one ship, to those of a world, to that of a galaxy on the brink of being overrun by a sinister force. Together, she and Pausert take on ever-larger challenges, hoping their growing capabilities will enable them to keep pace.

Techniques

The Witches of Karres is a fantasy-science fiction novel of intrigue and magic. In order for tension to be maintained throughout the novel to a satisfying conclusion, the magic must have limitations, to avoid making life too easy and success too predictable, and to enable its characters to experience the fascinating, frustrating process of growth, thus developing the admirable qualities of bravery and competence—this last important especially for the adolescent reader.

So, for the aforementioned reasons, it makes sense that the two principal characters be young people in the process of developing, in unpredictable order, their respective talents, as well as learning to get along with each other. It is also appropriate that they travel widely, encountering many types of people and new cultures, as well as strange and new dangers. Schmitz peoples his fantasy world with many kinds of eccentric but believable characters, from the stuffy high society of Nikkeldepain, to the friendly, far-traveling and mysterious inhabitants of Karres, to the cagey business-people of the "reformed" pirate-planet of Uldune, to the wide assortment of strange folk who inhabit and occasionally menace the spaceways.

Finally, by setting his adventure on a galactic scale in the far future, Schmitz has plenty of room to let his imagination run fruitfully wild. Not many writers, even the best, can successfully write an imaginative adventure on such a grand scale as a galactic one, with a civilization steeped in its own ancient history, with a multitude of competing cultures either drawn out or implied. Schmitz manages to weave together all these elements: the protagonist's growth, an interesting cast of supporting characters, a vast and complex environment as a stage for those characters to move about, and a problem of the highest importance to solve—the very survival of civilization. His style of writing is not self-consciously literary; like that of a good journalist, his writing style is direct and uncomplicated. With a gift for good, straightforward description and pithy dialogue, Schmitz knows how to invent a good action tale and how to tell it well.

Literary Precedents

Stories of picaresque adventure have been popular since the ancient days when the *Odyssey* of Homer was sung. Recent favorites include Rudyard Kipling's *Kim,* set in India in the days of the British Raj, and Mark Twain's *Huckleberry Finn,* set in the antebellum South. The modern-day versions of these tall-tale epic journeys are often found in the realm of science fiction. Like the Great Trunk Road of British India, or the Mississippi River, the imagined future traffic arteries and trade routes of a yet unborn civilization offer great opportunity to portray the people who make a living servicing, regulating, or robbing the traveler. Like Kim Rishti or Huck Finn, Pausert and Goth operate on the side of right rather than the side of bureaucracy, which gains them the emnity of certain authorities but guarantees them the sympathy of the reader.

THE UNIVERSE AGAINST HER

The Universe Against Her, 1964, novelettes. Sequels: *The Telzey Toy*, 1973, novelettes; *The Lion Game*, 1973, novel.

Social Concerns

In *The Universe Against Her*, the adventures of a brilliant young telepath are set in a future civilization clustered about the galactic core, called the Federation of the Hub. Telzey Amberdon's discovery, exploration, and, finally, application of her telepathic gifts make for entertaining reading but also a well-thought-out presentation of how an intelligent young person makes use of a highly unusual and potentially dangerous new ability. In this modern age of rapidly advancing and sometimes frighteningly powerful technology, many readers, particularly adolescents with a creative bent, can identify with both Telzey's ambition and caution. She learns that her high intelligence and will to use it have earned her the jealousy of others not so gifted; her emerging extrasensory talents threaten to get her looked upon as a freak even by those in her life who accept her intellect.

She is reluctant to take the path of least resistance: to squelch her talents in order to fit in, and to avoid the responsibilities that come with power. Neither is she eager to put herself in the harness of any public agency, which would decide for her where, when, and how much of her talent she would use and develop. A strong-willed girl, Telzey trusts herself to explore wisely, to apply her powers humanely, to oppose evil with no less power than is necessary to defeat it.

Themes

The Universe Against Her and its sequels explore the theme of the individual being at her best when thrown on her own resources. It emphasizes not only the potential strength of rugged individualism but also its sureness—that the best guide to the development of talent, provided that one has a solid foundation of good character to lay it on, is the intelligent person's own sensibility. Many times in the novel, this independence flies in the face of a large, complex society's tendency to over-control its members, even those who are already quite conscientious. It can hobble its most productive members and blunt its own natural defense systems against criminals by its own distrust of the very individuals that make up its body.

Telzey not only learns about these tendencies of civilization in order to overcome them; she also learns to make some of them work for her. She discovers that it can be to her advantage to outwardly appear, to everyone but her compatriots, to be a bright, pretty but otherwise quite ordinary teen-age girl, especially to her criminal prey. Schmitz has an awareness of what might be called the psychological ecology of human society—the emergence of mental defenses similar to those physical ones seen in animal species in nature, such as camouflage, armoring, aggressiveness, or swift automatic responses.

James H. Schmitz 1231

Characters

Telzey first uncovers her telepathic (or "psionic") powers through a relationship with her pet, Tick-Tock, a kitten-like creature she had found as a stray and taken in. As the years pass she has discovered that she can pick up mental images and feelings from her pet, now grown much larger and mentally more mature—less a pet and more a companion. It is the question of Tick-Tock's fate as a possibly intelligent creature and a friend in trouble that motivates Telzey to push onward through strange, new and even frightening experiences to expand what had simply been a telepathic form of child's play into the means to save her cat-like friend.

As the novel progresses, so does Telzey's scope. She ventures far beyond the resolution of Tick-Tock's problem and into the arena of government agencies like the Psychology Service and private investigative firms like the Kyth Interstellar Agency who are trying to defend a young friend of Telzey's who is caught up in a private war. Telzey must struggle to avoid becoming an easily dispatched pawn in a chess game with many other pieces: some sympathetic, others distantly manipulative, and the last group coldly, criminally ruthless. It becomes obvious in the course of the "game" what the basic character of each group is, and what Telzey must do, despite fear or distaste, to win for decency's sake.

Techniques

Schmitz establishes and maintains interest in his stories with two devices: intricate, cloak-and-dagger plots and an emphasis on the humanity of the telepathic protagonist. Schmitz's plots are elaborate puzzles where the use of telepathy is essential to investigate the criminal activities of people who have covered their tracks too well for conventional methods of detection to find them in time. But since telepathy is a mechanism used on sentient beings who have to be convicted on the basis of physical evidence, it is a device that needs an expert touch. Therefore, Schmitz has created a character, Telzey, who is both a law student and a powerful telepath, to bring such criminals to justice. In her, he has also created a human being whom the reader can find interesting because of the moral and practical decisions she must make on the job. These decisions include ones about if and when to intervene, and if so, what methods to use. These decisions promote her growth of character and nurture her telepathic talents, and make her a strong figure with whom the reader will want to identify.

Literary Precedents

While Schmitz is not an obvious imitator of other writers, his tendency to write "series" stories, later novelized into *The Universe Against Her* and its sequels, follows a pattern set by another prominent science fiction writer, Robert Heinlein. Much of Heinlein's work, which like Schmitz's includes short stories, novelettes, juvenile fiction, and short adventure novels, can be organized into what has been called a "future history." That is to say, his stories all take place in different historical eras in the same future galaxy of Heinlein's invention and are historically consistent with each other. Much of Schmitz's work deals with the Federation of the Hub, a vast alliance of largely human-inhabited worlds whose political and defense affairs are coordinated but not strictly controlled by an "Overgovernment," a power which Hub citizens almost forget is there because it does its job quietly and with a light touch. The Telzey Amberdon novels are only part of Schmitz's works that can be classified under "history of the Hub," although Telzey can easily be said to be the most popular continuing character that Schmitz ever created.

The major difference between Schmitz, Heinlein and many other writers of the post-World War II era is that Schmitz's work was not primarily Earth-centered, or even set in the Earth's solar system. In the Hub civilization, as with most of his other fiction, Earth is but a distant memory, even more remote than ancient Greece is today. This difference has made for a bigger physical scale, more depth of history, more complex political maneuvering. Other galactic-scale series, such as Issac Asimov's *Foundation* trilogy and Frank Herbert's *Dune* books, are based on past Earth empires; in Asimov's case the Roman Empire and in Herbert's, the Arabian Empire of Mohammed's followers (the Nation of Islam). Schmitz's Federation of the Hub has a much more modern feel to it, as if it were based on the present-day system of cold-war alliances, although aggression must be deterred more subtly than in previous eras. In Schmitz's universe, powers of the mind, such as intelligence, telepathy and creativity are preferred to prevent physical warfare from breaking out.

Related Titles

With the success of the first Telzey Amberdon stories, Schmitz wrote more novelettes, first published in *Analog* magazine, then gathered into novel form under the title *The Telzey Toy.* This book draws Telzey deeper into investigative and intelligence work. The Telzey Toy is an android made in physical and mental imitation of Telzey as a part of an egotistical inventor's plan to perfect his product line of androids, with her unwilling cooperation. *The Telzey Toy* plays with the question of what constitutes a human identity; whether it consists of a body, a set of memories, or a unique location in physical space.

The Lion Game, a sequel to *The Telzey Toy* that was first published in serial form, again in *Analog,* is a densely-plotted novel about a mysterious race of telepathic giants pursuing a ruthless game of power politics and assassination within the Federation of the Hub. Telzey nearly becomes a victim of their deadly tactics. When she survives an assassination attempt she knows that she must track down her attackers or succumb to inevitable future attempts on her life. In this book Schmitz explores the theme of the weakness inherent in selfishness. The villains are very strong; they are giants, physically and telepathically. They have conquered races to do their inventive work for them while they concentrate on competing with each other for power. But they have become lazy in their success; they use the same brutal strategy over and over again until they have forgotten how to adapt to new circumstances. Thus Telzey, who has cultivated a sense of responsibility and compassion along with her strong talents has retained the ability to adapt, invent, and cooperate, can fight back successfully and defeat them.

THE DEMON BREED

The Demon Breed, 1968, novel. First published in *Analog* under the title *The Tuvela* (1968).

Social Concerns/Themes

The Demon Breed, a novel of adventure and battle set on one of the Federation's water planets, is thematically the most complex of Schmitz's novels. It explores the issue of survival in an unpredictable universe and what strategies work best for a sentient species over the long haul. *The Demon Breed* is an ecological novel which includes sentient species like humanity as intimate parts of ecological systems, subject to the same laws that govern the competition among lower forms of life. The crucial difference between intelligent and unintelligent life-forms in matters of competition is that intelligent forms must make choices, such as long-term implications of their strategies. In this novel Schmitz presents a confrontation between two intelligent species who have made this choice very differently.

The two societies meet on the planet of Nandy-Cline. The way they interact is the result of choices made by the invaders, the Parahuans. The Parahuans are a warrior society; they choose to interact with other species as enemies or as allies in war. They are very successful professional predators; they have succeeded before in destroying entire competing species and taking over their territory. Now against the Federation of the Hub, composed of Humans and their (non-human) allies, the Parahuans plan to expand their range again.

The Federation of the Hub is a society of trade and industry, one at peace after centuries of wars among the star systems that now compose it. It has taken on the difficult task of civilizing its inborn aggressiveness, neither eliminating it, nor allowing it to run wild. The drives for power, wealth, longevity, predictability, and perfectability are common among intelligent species. The reward for supremacy in Parahuan society is that they may indulge these drives without limit, at the expense of any creatures they happen upon. It is a formidable society of indescriminate ruthlessness.

How, then, is such a highly specialized military machine to be resisted? Schmitz's answer may be unsettling, for he puts forth in this novel what could be called a policy of defensive discriminate ruthlessness. Schmitz calls the Federation a "balanced anarchy" where complacency gets no encouragement. The Overgovernment deliberately maintains a "hands-off" policy in areas where it could be more efficient, in order to foster initiative to solve problems on the planetary level by the local citizenry. Developing initiative is not a painless process, but it does not produce the dreary regimentation of a society constantly at war, nor a stifling bureaucracy where the citizen is in danger of being either degraded or infantalized by his government.

Primarily a work of entertainment, and not a serious treatise on the arts of warfare and defense, *The Demon Breed* is nevertheless carefully and imaginatively thought out. The modern appreciation for the ecology of natural systems is displayed here in the detailed descriptions of Nandy-Clines floatwood island environment. A modern appreciation for one's adversary is also notable; the Parahuans are portrayed, not sympathetically, but with an understanding of their integrity as villains. Once they have decided on a course of action in the context of their culture, they are not diverted by anything but a strength that exceeds their own.

Characters

The main character of the novel is Dr. Nile Etland, a young woman of no extraordinary powers (like "psi") but a remarkable combination of intelligence, knowledge, and nerve. A biochemist and native of the planet, Nandy-Cline, on which the novel takes place, Dr. Etland has arranged to keep tabs on Dr. Ticos Cay, an elderly but very hale researcher into the life-forms of a "floatwood" island, searching for biochemical methods of lengthening the human life-span. It is between her monthly visits to the island a sort of huge jungle adrift on the ocean currents of Nandy-Cline, that the Parahuans, a race of sentient amphibians from an empire adjacent to the Hub, capture Dr. Cay to question him.

Dr. Etland reaches the island with Sweeting, a mutant hunting-otter who speaks, discovers the desperate scam that Dr. Ticos Cay is trying to pull on the Parahuans, and decides that she must go along with it, at her peril. She must rely on her deep knowledge from childhood, of how to hunt on the Floatwood, in order to appear to be an invincible "Tuvela" until she can smuggle out a message to warn the rest of the planet. She and Ticos are often frightened during their ordeal, but they conceal their fear from the Parahuans and press on.

The Parahuans are based on the Axis powers of World War II. Like the Fascist empires of the mid-twentieth century, the Parahuans are organised into rigid hierarchies, with a few very powerful individuals at the top and the vast majority of the population at the bottom. The "Palachs" command enormous power, wealth, and longevity, although they are not born into their social position but have risen through the ranks. The "Oganoon" are conditioned to unquestioning obedience through fear: a Palach can kill one in a fit of pique with impunity.

The humans and their non-human allies of the Federation are organized along more self-reliant lines. The principal characters among them have sufficient audacity, imagination, and initiative to begin immediate resistance based on their own strategy. They are not the first humans to encounter the Parahuans on Nandy-Cline, but they are the best-equipped to deal with them. Schmitz calls these types of characters "anti-predators." They are the mirror-image of the predator: they have similar aggressiveness but lack its greed and callousness. When not needed, they return to harmless pursuits. The Federation preserves this policy by turning its population's attention toward non-bellicose events as soon as possible after the news of the Parahuan defeat on Nandy-Cline gets out.

Techniques

The story develops by setting representatives of the sentient species at war with each other in a microcosm: a strange floating island in an isolated sea. A quick acid test will determine the quality of each culture by seeing who will survive the next few days in the most desperate of circumstances. At stake are not only the lives of the people immediately involved, but the survival of a planetary culture, and other similar worlds beyond.

The Parahuans, old enemies of the Federation and losers in a previous clash almost a century before, have returned secretly to certain water planets of the Hub. They plan to conquer those planets, expanding their empire and redeeming themselves for their earlier defeat. Only one factor prevents them from launching a new war of conquest: the leaders are split into two factions at odds with each other over whether a new war can be won. The two factions, called the Voice of Action and the Voice of Caution, need an important piece of information from Dr. Cay before they can resolve their differences.

The parahuans cannot believe that such a loosely-governed, egalitarian society like the Federation has succeeded in repulsing them and similar invaders. They believe that theirs is such a perfect society that only one similar in organization could successfully oppose them. Therefore, they have hypothesized that a secret class of immortal super-intelligent rulers, "Tuvelas," is actually running the Federation. Dr. Cay plays along with this theory, hoping to frighten the Parahuans into retreat before a planetary war begins.

Not surprisingly, the Parahuans' style of warfare, like that of the Axis high commands, shares the strengths and weaknesses of a hierarchy where most of the initiative is concentrated at the top ranks. Their strong suit is detailed, intelligent planning and preparation in advance, carried out in secrecy and with precision. Their weaknesses are their vulnerability to sabotage of the top levels and their lack of imagination outside military matters. They have over-specialized.

Schmitz demonstrates his theme dramatically by creating an adversary for the Parahuans who hits them directly in their vanity. Young, female, and alone, Nile Etland should be no match for the well-armed and numerous amphibians. Yet she not only evades capture, but begins the work of "decapitating" the Parahuan organization with a combination of skill and quick thinking to capitalize on her luck.

Other Titles

An Agent of Vega, 1960 (novelettes); *Legacy,* 1962 (also published as *A Tale of Two Clocks*) (novel); *A Nice Day for Screaming and Other Tales of the Hub,* 1965 (short stories); *A Pride of Monsters,* 1970 (short stories); *The Eternal Frontiers,* 1973 (novel).

Additional Sources

Barbour, Douglas, *"The Witches of Karres," Survey of Science Fiction Literature,* vol. 4, Frank N. Magill, ed. Englewood Cliffs, NJ: Salem Press, 1979, pp. 2482-2487. An extensive critical commentary on Schmitz's most popular novel.

Meyers, Walter E., "Schmitz, James H(enry)," *Twentieth Century Science-Fiction Writers,* Curtis C. Smith, ed. London: Macmillan, 1981, pp. 472-473. A brief discussion of Schmitz's career, focussing on his major themes.

Reginald, R., "James H. Schmitz," *Science Fiction and Fantasy Literature: A Checklist, 1700-1974.* Detroit, MI: Gale Research, 1979, pp. 1065-1066. A short biography and a commentary by Schmitz himself, in which he discusses how his major works came to be.

Rutledge, Amelia A., "James H. Schmitz," *Twentieth Century American Science Fiction Writers,* David Cowart an Thomas Wymer, eds. Detroit, MI: Gale Research, 1981, pp. 100-101. A short critical discussion of Schmitz's characters and techniques.

Suzanne M. Munich
University of California, Davis

ERICH SEGAL
1937

Publishing History

Erich Segal, Professor of Classics at Yale University, has been a master of many trades since his youth. At present he is an educator, editor, translator, critic, marathoner, playwright with specialization in screenplays, and classicist. Segal also served as TV commentator several times for three Olympic Games.

There are two versions of how Segal came to write the phenomenally successful *Love Story*: one version tells of how he became involved in writing popular literature when he was informed, one Christmas vacation, of the tragic death of the brilliant and charming wife of one of his former students. He was so moved with compassion that he wrote *Love Story*, not so much as an elegy, but as a celebration and commemoration of genuine, innocent love, and to recreate the ideal life and love to which the couple had aspired. Their romantic and perfect love is aptly summed up in the dedication of *Man, Woman and Child*. "A wife of valor who can find? She is far more precious than jewels." (Proverbs 31:10). The second version refers to a student conversation Segal overheard about two people, and that he changed all the details of the story except for the death of the girl and the fact that she worked to put her husband through law school.

The NAL Signet paperback edition of *Love Story*, at five million copies, was the largest first printing of any paperback edition in the history of the publishing industry. Rollene W. Saal, in *Saturday Review* (December 26, 1970), discussing statistics pertaining to *Love Story* elaborates, "The publishers have put forth all kinds of extravagant statistics on it, such as that enough paper was used to fill twenty railroad freight cars, or that, laid end to end, their first printing would reach from here to Outer Mongolia," further attesting to its popularity. One of Segal's academic colleagues teasingly referred to *Love Story* as "ancient history," and to the idea that it came straight out of the 1740s. Segal's reply was that love is a time-honored theme and that his novel, like *Romeo and Juliet*, has caught the imagination of contemporary youth. As he himself explains, "Sure, it is old-fashioned. It even has a bit of *Our Gal Sunday* in it. But the kids today are sentimental. Just listen to the Beatles, all that tenderness." First written as a screenplay, *Love Story* (1970) has been followed by a sequel, *Oliver's Story* (1977), by *Man, Woman and Child* (1980), and by *The Class* (1980). Each of these novels became an instant best seller and the first three have been made into successful movies.

Critical Reception, Honors, and Popularity

Generally, *Love Story* generated positive critical reaction. It was acclaimed outside of academic circles (where the novel was regarded as pulp fiction). It became an instant best seller and remained on the nation-wide best seller list for over one year. The novel's appeal extended over a wide spectrum, ranging from college students to housewives. The Avon paperback edition attests to the novel's popularity by citing an American couple's letter to the publisher, where they confess spending their wedding night reading *Love Story* to each other. Students of one of Wellesley College's dormitories tearfully telephoned the author for an explanation of why Segal had to kill off Jenny at *Love Story*'s end. At Monmouth College, each entering student received a copy of *Love Story* from the college's administration, partly for the moral lesson imparted by the work, and partly for the sheer enjoyment of reading. In the U.S. alone, 9.5 million copies were sold, with additional sales in overseas English-speaking countries. *Love Story* has been translated into thirty-three languages, and as a movie in the USA, it attracted over thirty million viewers. Three major book clubs adopted the novel as a first-choice offering.

Younger readers, mostly college students, have formed "devotional cults" and discussion groups to analyze the novel. "*Love Story* evokes such beautiful gestures from people. One girl at Berkeley gave me a floral arrangement she had made in memory of Jenny" (the heroine).

In regard to the popular reception of *Love Story*, which has been read by one out of every five Americans, Segal admits that the novel appeared at "the right time. My book is an expression of today's youth, their values and their truths." The critic Mark Spilka attributes its popularity to the fact that readers see in the novel a realization of their own, as well as the author's fantasies in terms of sexual dreams and longings, the solutions to problems raised by sexual roles and by parent-child and family connections. Of course, these difficulties are not confined to the poor.

On the other hand, some academic critics and literati condemned the novel as "maudlin and bathetic," for the most part after the popular success of the film. One of the most acidic attacks came from *Newsweek*'s S. K. Oberbeck: "The banality of *Love Story* makes *Peyton Place* look like *Swann's Way* as it skips from cliché to cliché with an abandon that would chill the blood of a *True Romance* editor."

Erich Segal's reputation is well-established world-wide, both as a scholar and as an artist. In 1968 Segal won a Guggenheim Fellowship, and in 1970, the film version of *Love Story* won the Golden Globe Award for Best Screenplay; it was nominated for an Academy Award in the same year. In 1971 it was nominated for the National Book Award, but was dropped from consideration at the complaint of William Styron. Segal received the Presidential Commemoration for Service to the Peace Corps in 1971.

Analysis of Selected Titles

LOVE STORY

Love Story, 1970, novel; Sequel: *Oliver's Story*, 1977, novel.

Social Concerns/Themes

One of the crucial social concerns and themes raised by the novel is the question of an ideal marriage. Does such a marriage exist? When a match takes place between a brilliant but poor young woman, with "zero social status" and an equally brilliant, athletic, rich Ivy-leaguer, what are the common denominators to insure an ideal and successful marriage? The parents of the wealthy young man object to the match because the young lady is a commoner; will love alone be strong enough to sustain the marriage, without the parents' blessing? In spite of initial disapproval, Jenny's self-sacrifice and hard work bring about a greatly successful marriage, almost idealistic in nature. The question of whether to attend the anniversary of Oliver's parents brings a misunderstanding between the couple but reconciliation follows swiftly.

This question of ideal marriage leads Segal to an examination of the important theme of love and of growing up. In that sense, *Love Story* can be seen as a variation on the *bildüngsroman* with both central characters coming from extremely different backgrounds. These polarities represent wealth and poverty. Even after marriage the process of growing up continues since the couple must support themselves financially. (Though the Barretts are very wealthy, Oliver's father cuts him off after his marriage.) Oliver, too, has learned the meaning of responsibility, the pains and tribulation of poverty, and the triumphs of success.

Love, in its many variations, is a quintessential theme in the novel. Reciprocal love between father and daughter is clearly outlined in Jenny's entire upbringing and personality. However, in the case of the Barrett family, the relationship between father and son revolves around hatred and suspicion. Oliver III's assumed hatred of his son stems from the fact that the father tries to push the reluctant Oliver into fulfilling his expected role in the Barrett family tradition. Oliver's mother invariably sides with her husband. This hatred constantly manifests itself in sarcastic verbal fencing. Oliver holds a very negative image of his father.

The notion of self-sacrificing love, with its now famous dictum "love means not ever having to say you're sorry," has taught Oliver a grand lesson. The overall moral lesson, as far as *Love Story* and even *Oliver's Story* is concerned, is that Jenny has taught Oliver the true meaning of love, love for a spouse and love for a parent. Her death acts as the magnet for reconciliation between father and son.

Another implicit social concern in the novel is the question of incest. The closeness of Jenny to her father, Phil, would perhaps create the impression of an incestuous relationship, but some critics, notably Mark Spilka, have pointed to Oliver's fear of homo-erotic love with his father.

Coping with hospitalization, dying and death in its psychological and financial aspects forms another important theme and social concern in the novel. Oliver is forced to borrow money from his father to pay for Jenny's hospital expenses. David Hendin in his book, *Death As a Fact of Life*, states that "Death is simply un-American. Its inevitability is an affront to our unalienable right to 'life, liberty, and the pursuit of happiness,' " and thus explains readers' reluctance to accept Jenny's death in *Love Story*. In effect, *Love Story* not only deals with the agony of death, but with the psychology of dying and the actuality of the loss. Death as a theme is prevalent in American letters, in Hemingway, in Agee's *A Death in the Family* and in Plath's enactment of the suicide scene in *The Bell Jar*. The book version of *Love Story* poignantly captures Jenny's passing, as opposed to the movie where Ali MacGraw just fades into the hospital to die. In both cases, the emotional impact on the reader or viewer is profound. Oliver's emotional confusion at Jenny's impending death is strongly drawn in the movie version.

Other specific issues are the Peace Corps (an idea that originated in the 1960s), sterility vs. virility, insufficiency vs. fertility, of spontaneous vs. programmed sex.

Anti-Semitism is a significant social issue present throughout Segal's fiction, although it is handled with subtlety and restraint. In *Love Story*, even though Oliver has graduated third in his class, he lands the most desirable position in the legal firm: The two candidates who finished first and second place are Jewish, and are thus rendered ineligible.

Characters

Apart from time-honored quotations in the novel, Segal has created memorable characters. The major characters are obviously the hero and heroine, Oliver Barrett IV and Jennifer Cavilleri Barrett. Minor characters, such as Oliver Barrett III and his wife, and Phil Cavilleri, Ray Stratton, and Alf Johnston enable readers to view the protagonist from different perspectives.

In some ways, Oliver Barrett IV is a chip off the Oliver Barrett III block. They are both brilliant and wealthy, and both are supremely egotistical. They obviously make a good family and Oliver Barrett III represents an authoritarian, disciplined father-figure. As far as success and the Barrett tradition are concerned, the father always strives after perfection. While the son is egomaniacal, all his statements and actions relate to his wealth, family, academic achievements and his aspirations. Both Barrett men display the traditional Barrett athletic prowess; both have won many athletic awards. The father was a member of the 1926 Olympic team. Their common goal, excellence in all, is to uphold family tradition, pride and heritage. For a Barrett, being Number One is of paramount importance. Oliver Barrett IV could not become reconciled to the idea that Mozart, Bach and the Beatles supersede him in Jenny's estimation. The Barrett name lands Oliver a very lucrative job, even though he is third on the list of graduates.

The differences between father and son are equally striking. Oliver is very conceited (witness his desire to have the number seven jersey retired). He hates his father and wants independence from the Barrett success formula. There seems to be some undeclared conflict between father and son, who can never discuss an issue without sarcasm and hostility, such as the scenes where they discuss the Harvard/Cornell hockey game, the discussion of Oliver's attendance at law school, and the marriage to Jenny, who comes from a lower social class. In fact, the son seems to fear the father, always referring to him as "Sir." He seems to have no respect for the father until the sequel, *Oliver's Story*, where he discovers that his father has sacrificed a great deal to maintain the Barrett tradition. Oliver refers to his father as a "son of a bitch; a walking, talking Mount Rushmore; a stony face." True, Oliver's father is a snob, but he does seek only his son's best interests.

Some critics maintain that Oliver is too shallow a character. Others charge that he lacks credibility because he is too genuine to be believable.

Jenny is of Italian descent and her name alone—Jennifer Cavilleri—indicates her scoffing, jeering, satiric nature, since it is drawn from the Latin verb *cavilor*, to scoff. Oliver's mother dubs Jenny "Cavilleri Rustica," conjuring up a derogatory, rustic image of Oliver's chosen. Jenny's adoration of her father stands in direct contrast to Oliver's hatred of his father. She is a brilliant, serious musician and plays piano with the Bach Society. Jenny loves the simple things in life, and has had to sacrifice her comfort and Paris scholarship to be together with Oliver. Her main role in the novel is to reconcile Oliver with his father. Her death accomplishes this. The marriage vows exchanged by the couple show the modern nature of these characters who have gone against their *status quo*. Jenny reads a sonnet by Elizabeth Barrett Browning, with all its erotic implications and predictions of early death. Oliver reads a Walt Whitman poem which connotes faithful companionship. Thus the contemporary 1960s couple is portrayed.

As Spilka points out, "Jenny's role is to bring the Barretts together, to make them realize their true affection. All her schooling of Oliver—her systematic deflation of his self-importance, her correction of his views on sexual love—is designed to make him less adamant in his pride, less resentful in his rivalry, and less afraid of his own tender feelings."

The general absence of mothers in the novel (Oliver's mother is but a cypher and Jenny's mother died much earlier on) is an interesting omission. The most compelling mother-figure in Segal's work is Sheila Beck in *Man, Woman and Child*; in *The Class* there is the strong presence of a mother who visits her student son after his attempted suicide. Nicole Guerin, in *Man, Woman and Child*, figures as the dynamic single parent. Jenny in *Love Story* never becomes a mother.

Phil Cavilleri as father is the exact opposite of Oliver Barrett III. He is warm, affectionate, dedicated and demonstrative. Even the death of Jenny does not totally shatter his world. Like Jenny, Phil tries to reconcile the Barretts.

Techniques

One outstanding technical accomplishment of the novel is its simplicity, remarked upon by many critics. In fact, simplicity in terms of plot, construction and subject is the hallmark of this novel. The *denouement* is revealed at the start when the author asks the reader, "what can you say about a twenty-five year old girl who died." This opening sentence sets the tragic tone for the novel. Coupled with the opening scene, the marriage vows and the leukemia all point to a sad end for a brilliant and likeable character. The very start of the novel evokes the essence of love, tenderness, family tradition, conflict and brilliance.

As far as style is concerned, the diction is contemporary and collegiate. Segal has been praised for his sensitive, flashy, endearing ear for dialogue. Indeed, the entire novel is built upon dialogue. One critic believes that Segal uses dialogue as a device to animate "a spineless, mediocre, spiritless novel." The writing style is economical, tight and well-constructed, leaving much to the reader's imagination. Segal's originality is superb, with excellent characterization. Almost all protagonists are smart, or rich, or brilliant, or beautiful, or cultured ladies and gentlemen.

Literary Precedents

Love Story's premise harks back to the medieval conception of the connection between love, hatred and death. In the medieval romance tradition, such tales as *Tristan and Iseult*, and in the Shakespearean *Romeo and Juliet*, star-crossed lovers abound. In all such cases, the lovers are unable to sustain the relationship on a permanent basis due to death's intervention. The successful utilization of this genre by Segal is evident when *Love Story* is compared with countless other works written in the same tradition.

Related Titles

In a certain sense, *Love Story* would be incomplete without its continuation, *Oliver's Story*, set in New York City, Rhode Island, Boston, and Hong Kong. The lessons that Oliver Barrett has learned from Jenny and from Jenny's death in *Love Story* have helped him to better cope with life, although he is still very much confused and psychologically off-base. The inability to forget Jenny destroys the possibility for other relationships, especially the potential with Marcie Nash, the modern, dynamic, successful independent tycoon, of the same social class as the Barretts. *Oliver's Story*, therefore, deals with the following themes and social concerns: the fear of commitment and intimacy, vulnerability in personal relationships; the modern idea of seeking psychiatric and therapeutic help; and the Vietnam protests. Other more contemporary issues concern the ideas of open relationships, adultery, cohabitation, and free sex; women's roles, the liberated woman who has her own career and independent life; divorce and alimony; celebrity worship; exploitation of workers, child labor, the plight of the poor with particular reference to "sweat equity"; how the fabulously rich acquired their wealth, and the laundering of dirty money.

One interesting conclusion of the *Love Story/Oliver's Story* connection that began at *Love Story*'s end has been completed at the end of *Oliver's Story*. Not only has Oliver learned to love his father but he has come to appreciate his father's hard work, integrity and respect for family tradition. Oliver has agreed to return home to perpetuate the Barrett dynasty. The characters carried over from *Love Story* have fully matured. Oliver Barrett III is no longer the dictatorial father of *Love Story*: Retired now, he is understanding and sympathetic, treating his son as an independent and matured individual. Oliver's mother is still as steadfastly behind her husband as ever. Phil Cavilleri is fine in Florida, in the pastry business. Although Oliver never remarries, he maintains an amicable relationship with a young Boston woman. Marcie Nash marries a Washington attorney; Joanna Stein marries a doctor and settles in California. The phase of tragedy has ended.

MAN, WOMAN AND CHILD

Social Concerns/Themes

Man, Woman and Child, Segal's novel following the Barrett family saga, addresses the conception of the so-called perfect family. Again, adultery, free love and its consequences are examined. Emotional turmoil, caused by casual sex, is closely delineated. In the movie version, *Man, Woman and Child* deals with the de-emphasizing of the humanities in American education, as opposed to the novel, which glorifies the sciences. Natural childbirth, with both parents participating, is another social concern raised in *Man, Woman and Child*.

Characters

In typical Segal fashion, the protagonists are a brilliant, happily married couple. Priscilla Johnson refers to *Man, Woman and Child* as "pure soap, with no characterization to break it up. The style is flat, spare, but not tight. In spite of all these weaknesses, this will be a successful novel because of the following built up from *Love Story*." Robert Beckwith, Professor of Statistics at M.I.T., is married to Sheila, a first-rate editor at the University of Harvard Press. As in *Love Story*, their relationship began in college, when both were undergraduates, Sheila at Vassar and Robert at Yale. Later they married, and established the ideal family. Fate intervenes when Robert's brief affair with Dr. Nicole Guerin results in the birth of Jean-Claude Guerin. His son's existence is only disclosed to Robert ten years later, when Nicole is tragically killed. The idyllic family life is shattered when Robert's daughter discovers the truth. Through much pain, remorse and pity, Sheila and the family come to love Jean-Claude. However, he returns to France after one summer to his guardian, much to the family's sorrow.

Again, Segal is charged with creating a cast of characters too angelic to be real. Even Sheila, who is tempted to engage in an affair with Dr. Garvin Wilson in order to get even with Robert, cannot carry out her plans. The children in general are adoring and adorable, although sibling rivalry is commonplace. The only semblance of a villain in the entire novel is the young son of their family friend and lawyer, who reveals Jean-Claude's true identity.

Adaptations

All three novels, *Love Story* (Paramount, 1970; nominated for seven Oscars); *Oliver's Story* (Cinema International Corporation, 1979), and *Man, Woman and Child* (Columbia, EMI, Warner Brothers, 1983) have been adapted for film and all appear on pre-recorded videocassette.

The screenplay of *Love Story* (with Ali MacGraw and Ryan O'Neal in the title roles) actually prefigured the novel, and though very popular, only readers of the novel and viewers of the movie would have noticed minor variations, whereas the novel stresses the readers' reliance upon parental guidance and leadership which was either given in overabundance (as in Jenny's case) or withheld (as in Oliver's).

The remorse and tenderness stressed in the novel give way in the movie version to a much more aggressive, macho Oliver. Even the concluding reconciliation scene lays the burden of guilt more upon the father than the son.

In *Man, Woman and Child* substantial changes are evident in the film version. The novel is set in the Boston area at M.I.T.; the movie is set in California. Again in the novel, Professor Beckwith is a teacher of and authority in statistics and attends a scholarly conference in France where he meets Dr. Nicole Guerin. In the movie, Martin Sheen, who plays Beckwith, is a Professor of Literature, who gives a scholarly talk on Baudelaire, also in France. The accident that led to their opportune meeting also differs in novel and movie. In the book, the police harass Dr. Nicole Guerin and friends; in a rescue attempt, Beckwith is badly beaten up. In the hospital the two meet. However, in the movie, Beckwith is hospitalized from an auto accident and meets Dr. Guerin who is on call that night.

The reconciliation scene at the end of the film version has been given a very pathetic, graphic treatment with genuine love for the young boy stressed. An incident that nearly destroyed the family turned out to be their salvation.

The movie, *Oliver's Story*, is a more faithful reproduction of the novel, again with only minor variations: In terms of the characters, Joanna Stein was a medical intern, but in the movie she is a furniture designer. It seems as if the musical scene of the Stein family was omitted from the film version. The movie lays more emphasis on Oliver's psychological problems as well as his philanthropic activities, ending in reconciliation between Oliver and his father, when Oliver decides to return to his hometown to run the family business.

What both versions stress are the basic problems of a seemingly perfect and ideal family couple.

Other Titles

Aside from several academically acclaimed scholarly texts and various screenplays, Segal has written the following:

Fairy Tale, 1973 (a children's book); *Odyssey*, 1975 (play); *The Class*, 1985 (novel).

Additional Sources

Anderson, H.T., *"Love Story*: A Review," *Bestsellers* (June 1977). A positive review of the novel.

Galloway, David D., "The Love Ethic," *The Absurd Hero in American Fiction.* Austin, TX: University of Texas Press, 1970, pp.140-169. An indictment against modern American life and culture seen from the perspectives of Salinger's characters, who are desperately looking for love.

Inge, Thomas M., ed., *Handbook of American Popular Culture.* Westport, CT: Greenwood Press, 1980. A collection of critical bibliographic essays in three volumes by various scholars on the history of over forty-eight topics in American culture. Volumes 1 & 2 include essays on the detective, mystery and science fiction novels, films, best sellers and the pulps.

Lingeman, Richard R., "The Son of *Love Story*," *The New York Times Book Review* (March 1977): 6-7. A comparative analysis of *Oliver's Story* in relation to *Love Story* with emphasis on the polarity of opposites between the heroines in the two novels.

Spilka, Mark, "Erich Segal as Little Nell or The Real Meaning of *Love Story*," *Journal of Popular Culture* (Spring 1972): 782-798. A scholarly treatment of the themes, style and characterization in *Love Story*. Compares Segal's Jennifer and Dicken's Little Nell.

C. Lasker
K. Amoabeng
State University of New York
at Stony Brook

MARY LEE SETTLE
1918

Publishing History

As a young woman, Mary Lee Settle started out to be an actress, and her first ten literary efforts were in dramatic form: six plays and four film scripts, all unproduced and unpublished. Her first published novel, *The Love Eaters* (1954), is about a small-town play production. Her second published novel, *The Kiss of Kin* (1955), is a reworking of one of her plays, and was actually written before her first published novel.

During her early career, Settle sometimes earned living expenses by working as a free-lance journalist. Under the pseudonym Mrs. Charles Palmer, she wrote an etiquette column for *Woman's Day;* she was British correspondent for *Flair* magazine, which folded; and she rewrote articles for *American Heritage.* She resigned her only full-time position in journalism, as assistant editor at *Harper's Bazaar,* in order to pursue her own writing. She vowed not to tie herself down to a similar position again.

Through ten novels and one autobiographical work, Settle has experienced notable transatlantic success by getting her books published almost simultaneously in the United States and Great Britain. She has not, however, always been happy with her American publishers. Viking Press published the first three Beulah novels separately but not as a trilogy (in 1965 Ballantine Books published the "Beulah Land Trilogy" in paperback; later, with the addition of two other novels, the trilogy was expanded into the Beulah Quintet). Settle also maintained that Viking's editorial cutting of *Fight Night on a Sweet Saturday* (1964) rendered it unsuitable as the concluding volume of the Beulah series; she later reworked *Fight Night on a Sweet Saturday* and publishing it as *The Killing Ground* (1982).

Critical Reception, Honors, and Popularity

Throughout much of her career, Settle had to struggle against a tendency of the American public and critics to forget about her work. For example, between 1964 and 1977, no New York publication reviewed any of her books. Her early novels were well received as the work of a promising new writer, but periodically she had to be rediscovered. One such rediscovery was the Granville Hicks preface to the "Beulah Land Trilogy" published in 1965; no less a critic than Malcolm Cowley recommended Settle to Hicks. Another rediscovery was the prestigious 1978 National Book Award in fiction for *Blood Tie* (1977), but a number of journalists and critics, taken by surprise, cried foul at the award given to an "unknown."

Still, the controversial award seemed to be what was necessary for American recognition of Settle to stick. Since then, she has been given serious attention. *The Scapegoat* (1980), for example, was carefully reviewed by such writers as Robert

Houston and fellow novelists Anne Tyler and E. L. Doctorow. Critical articles on her work have also begun to appear, especially by critics who want to claim her as one of their own, such as women and/or Southerners. A native of the West Virginia coalfields, Settle has in particular been claimed as a leading author of the contemporary Appalachian Awakening. Her reputation, however, is transatlantic and has indeed remained steadier in Britain than in the United States: *The Times Literary Supplement* has faithfully reviewed her books, generally with more perceptive comments than American reviewers.

The main complaint against Settle, through her first five books, was that her work did not cohere. Her stereotyped characters and subject matter, so the critics stated, did not merit the shifting points of view, complicated time schemes, lushly overwritten style, and other efforts at sophisticated technique. They also argued that her historical novels did not offer enough sense of history, even though she did her research in the British Museum. Settle was ambitious, but her ambition seemed to outstrip her skill.

Throughout this period, Settle was apparently developing her skill and absorbing various influences, particularly William Faulkner's. A landmark in her development was her autobiographical work, *All the Brave Promises* (1966). Autobiography not only allowed her to sort out her ideas, especially her political beliefs, but also seemed to teach her the importance of knowing her material through personal experience. Her complicated techniques and personally experienced material all came together finally in *Blood Tie* and *The Scapegoat*.

Analysis of Selected Titles

BLOOD TIE

Blood Tie, 1977, novel.

Social Concerns

Reviewers admired the convincing way Settle portrayed Turkish characters and society in *Blood Tie,* which is set mostly in and around Ceramos, a fictional small town on the southwest coast of Turkey. Settle lived in the area for a couple of years, but in addition she found plenty of parallels in Turkish society to Appalachian coal towns and even to the seventeenth-century British society in *Prisons,* which she had just finished writing before *Blood Tie.* The main social concern in *Blood Tie,* as elsewhere in Settle's work, is the domination of society by bosses, whether they are called landowners, mine operators, padrones, or aghas (as in Turkey), and the consequent stifling of democracy.

Ceramos is dominated by Dürüst Osman, the old agha, and his corrupt son Huseyin. They are the local land-owning aristocracy, but here, as in Settle's other books, the aristocrats have grimy and disreputable origins. The high and mighty agha began his career as an *ibne*, the kept boy of a homosexual German military attaché. Trying to forget his days as a powerless orphan, the agha now exercises power ruthlessly. Nor is the agha's power merely local. He can also reach into the national government and influence its decisions, suggesting that the real national government is a network of good old aghas, despite the democracy supposedly installed by Ataturk. The entrenched agha system seems an unhappy legacy of a country where, as one character jokes, two of the national heroes are Attila the Hun and Genghis Khan (the Turks are descendants of historic marauders from the central Asian steppes).

In *Blood Tie,* the boss system has an international dimension, naturally involving Americans, who have replaced the one-time Germans. The CIA works hand in iron glove with the aghas and the nominal authorities to control development and dissidents, and to keep the coast safe for NATO. A circle of expatriate Americans also associates socially with the local power elite; in fact, one rich American girl is sleeping with the agha's son. *Blood Tie* seems to warn that, with their wealth and power, Americans are in danger of becoming the biggest bosses of the world.

Themes

The title *Blood Tie* suggests something high-minded like brotherhood, the recognition of common humanity among diverse peoples, the forming of close relationships. There are examples of all these in *Blood Tie,* but the title also evokes a more sinister theme—the complicity of bloodshed. In the three instances of death in the novel, numerous people are implicated as partially responsible, some unwittingly or ignorantly. The first instance involves only Turks: one of Huseyin's overloaded passenger boats, habitually ignored by the authorities, swamps and sends several young people to their doom, including Huseyin's fiancée, daughter of a rich Istanbul agha. In the second instance, an American woman who sleeps around with the young Turkish men is caught in the act by her husband, who commits suicide by scuba diving deep into the ocean and then shooting to the surface like a human missile. In the third instance, many people are involved—the same sluttish woman, the CIA, Huseyin, and the local police—in tracking down a young dissident (guilty only of taking part in Istanbul demonstrations), who is beaten to a pulp with a rifle butt. The three instances show how easy it is to become implicated in bloodshed, and the widening circles of implication ultimately take in even the reader.

Characters

Settle's greatest achievement in *Blood Tie* is her characters. They are authentic and memorable, including the minor characters such as old Attila the donkey driver, who wears a faded Harvard sweatshirt and whose right hand was cut off for smuggling. Settle is as good with the Turkish characters as with the Americans, perhaps better. With the Turkish characters, the reader gets the sense of going inside a foreign culture. With the American and European characters, the reader gets a similar feel for the close-knit expatriate circle.

Even the characters who seem stereotypical have unique features. The old agha resembles a movie Mafia godfather, but he has a definite Turkish accent, worrying about his lemons instead of his tomatoes. Frank Proctor, the local CIA man, obviously works for the company: he is a "team player" who does not question his superior or policy even when they are wrong. But his motives are carefully probed, showing the roots of "bossism" in his paternalistic belief that he is doing good for the Turks (besides, of course, for America).

There is no single protagonist in the novel. The characters who come closest are Ariadne, a divorced middle-aged American who mothers the young people, and one of her charges, the mute Turkish boy Kemal. The good-hearted Ariadne, at home in the Turkish setting and accepted by the Turks, is forced to leave the country for being too friendly with suspected dissidents. Kemal, younger brother of the slain dissident, has risked his life repeatedly to hide and feed his brother. When he loses both his brother and Ariadne, he is so grief-stricken that he breaks out of his muteness. On the book's last page, he stands on the mountainside above the town and screams out "HELE HELE!," meaning "Tell me the truth!"

Techniques

The fine characterization in *Blood Tie* is related to Settle's main narrative technique, a shifting third-person point of view. The point of view allows for detailed exploration of each character, including the character's past. Then the point of view shifts every few pages, resulting in the same treatment of a whole range of characters. How many times Settle returns to the same character depends on how important the character is to the action. The action itself is slow-moving and fragmented, deepening and coming together only through the different points of view.

For readers wanting fast action and immediate explanations, the technique is frustrating, though it does offer some suspense, like the old Victorian novels with several lines of action. The technique is superb, however, for showing multicultural perspectives and the normal little misunderstandings of life—such as Huseyin's notion that the rich American girl is admiring him from a distance, when she is practically blind without her contact lenses. Most of all, the technique places the action in context, mirroring the complex nature of reality. The hidden aspects of reality, its historical and cultural contexts, are symbolized by the undersea landscape containing ruins and by the mountain overlooking Ceramos. The mountain is honeycombed with secret passageways and tombs (maybe the tomb of the mythical Endymion) which only Kemal and his brother know about and to which the rest of Ceramos, except for a young German archaeologist who suspects their existence, is oblivious.

Literary Precedents

Perhaps the oldest literary ancestor of *Blood Tie* is Mark Twain's *Innocents Abroad,* but over the decades the tone of novels describing American innocents abroad has changed from comic to somber, as American power has grown in the world. Henry James started the trend with his tales of American women who got themselves into trouble in Europe, a kind of story which bred many imitators. In *Blood Tie,* American women are still getting themselves into trouble in Turkey, and for the most part they are still walking away and letting others pay. Their pattern of individual behavior is atrocious, but when the pattern of behavior is adopted by the CIA, it has the makings of foreign policy disaster, as described in Graham Greene's *The Quiet American* and similar works. *Blood Tie* has something in common with *The Quiet American,* except that Ariadne shows that not all Americans abroad are walking disasters.

Blood Tie also has some close Turkish relatives, particularly the early novels of Yashar Kemal describing the behavior of aghas. The best known of these is *Memed, My Hawk,* now a Turkish classic. Unhappily, the behavior of aghas has not changed at all over the decades.

THE SCAPEGOAT

The Scapegoat, 1980, novel. Predecessors: *Prisons,* 1973 (published in Britain as *The Long Road to Paradise,* 1974); *O Beulah Land,* 1956; *Know Nothing,* 1960. Sequel: *The Killing Ground,* 1982.

Social Concerns/Themes

Some reviewers considered *The Scapegoat* Settle's best novel. She wrote it next after *Blood Tie,* to which it bears many resemblances, even though *The Scapegoat* is set in the 1912 West Virginia coalfields. In *The Scapegoat,* the main issue is still the domination of society by bosses and the consequent denial of democracy. Here the bosses are mine operators instead of aghas, and the coal miners are hillbillies and immigrants, many from Italy. It is a time of transition in the coalfields, with local paternalistic mine owners being bought out by absentee owners, big capitalists and corporations, who are in some ways worse than the aghas.

The main thematic difference between *Blood Tie* and *The Scapegoat* is that here the issue is more out in the open, violently so, with a strike on and a confrontation between union and owners. While the local owners want to settle with the union, the absentee owners, with lots of resources and an ideological stance (rather like the CIA), want to break the union. The absentee owners prevail over the local owners, bringing in thugs and scabs to fight their battle; ironically, many of the scabs are new immigrants who came to America expecting democracy. With the miners likewise armed, there is potential for mass violence; but within the novel's main action, which covers just one day of the strike, only one person dies. He is an innocent scapegoat, an Italian who arrived the day before and cannot even speak English, but the thugs vent their fury on him much as the police do on the poor dissident in *Blood Tie*. The novel does not resolve the union-owners confrontation; though, historically, the union prevailed after a few "mine wars."

Characters

Settle covers a wide spectrum of characters here as she does in *Blood Tie*, showing the social distinctions between blacks, immigrants, hillbillies, thugs, managers, local owners, and big capitalists. Even better than the union-owners confrontation, the class system already in place drives home the theme of democracy denied, though limited socializing does occur across class lines, particularly between the hillbillies and local owners, some of whom are related. With one exception, the fine ladies at the top, concerned with clothes and relationships, behave as if they are in a novel of manners rather than a class war.

The one exception is Lily Lacey, daughter of a local mine owner. Always a political rebel, she has been east to Vassar and contracted a case of liberal guilt. She sympathizes with the miners and drives her parents frantic by taking long hikes in the woods with Eddie Pagano, handsome son of immigrants. Lily's parents need not worry, since all she does is read books to Eddie in an attempt to educate him. But her indiscretions fan the volatile situation and indirectly lead to the death of the innocent scapegoat, who makes a good substitute when the aroused thugs cannot find Eddie Pagano. In the end, Lily decides to leave town, with new worlds to conquer in New York City, thereby fulfilling the pattern of the indiscreet women in *Blood Tie*.

Part of the reason Lily leaves town is her public putdown by Mother Jones, famous labor leader whom Lily idolizes and considers a political ally. Cussing, crusty Mother Jones sees it differently. At a labor rally, she calls Lily to the front and presents her as an exhibit of what the miners are fighting. She tells Lily that Lily cannot be rich and right at the same time, going home to the big house after hitting the barricades all day. After this humiliation, Lily gives up on coal miners and adopts women's suffrage as her next cause.

Women play the major roles in this novel, which has no one protagonist. Besides Lily and Mother Jones (an actual historical figure), other major characters are Annunziato Pagano, Eddie's tough mother, and Lily's mother and two sisters. The men in the novel are not as memorable as the women, but Settle still does a better than adequate job of presenting them. Again, some of the minor characters stand out, such as a couple of orthodox Jews and a young French chef who, fresh off the boat, arrive by mistake in the West Virginia coal town.

Techniques

Settle utilizes much the same techniques in *The Scapegoat* as she does in *Blood*

Tie, shifting points of view from character to character and providing extensive character analysis. The only difference here is that Settle uses first person and omniscient points of view in addition to third person. The first person point of view gives the flavor of West Virginia talk and class attitudes, especially in the gossipy opening section narrated by Mary Rose, the youngest Lacey daughter. Settle does not go into the mind of Mother Jones, except briefly in the omniscient sections. Again, the shifting points of view make the action slow-moving and disconnected, but it comes together swiftly at the end, as it does in *Blood Tie.*

One departure from the techniques of *Blood Tie* is a flash-forward, shortly before Lily's political humiliation, showing her as a volunteer nurse in World War I. She finally vindicates herself by volunteering as an ambulance driver and getting blown up; thus, in a sense, she is also the scapegoat of the novel.

Literary Precedents

Although *The Scapegoat* contains elements of various traditions, it has no clear literary precedent. Its lack of precedent is suggested by two literary extremes which it recalls: on the one hand, such coal-mining novels as Émile Zola's *Germinal* and D. H. Lawrence's *Sons and Lovers;* and on the other hand, the novel of manners such as Jane Austen's. Perhaps the unifying concern here is a preoccupation with social class, in the fashion of nineteenth-century French novels. But *The Scapegoat* also recalls nineteenth-century English novels seeking to reform the workplace and such naturalistic American novels as Frank Norris's *The Octopus.* Settle's portrayal of an early twentieth-century woman radical, Mother Jones, is reminiscent of E. L. Doctorow's treatment of Emma Goldman in *Ragtime.*

Related Titles

The Scapegoat is book four of the Beulah Quintet, a series of related novels covering over three hundred years of history. In chronological order the five novels are *Prisons* (1973), *O Beulah Land* (1956), *Know Nothing* (1960), *The Scapegoat* (1980), and *The Killing Ground* (1982). Each novel can stand alone, read separately, but together they unwind an intricate and interesting story.

The novels are related in part through their characters. All of the major characters belong to a few families who mingle and intermarry through the centuries and who move up and down in the social order: mainly the Laceys, McKarkles, Catletts, Kreggs, Neills, Brandons, Crawfords, Cutrights, and Paganos. Together their stories constitute a fascinating socio-economic history, representative of America, and symbolically their kinships (sometimes unknown to them) suggest the blood relationships binding together the American population as a whole.

Prisons, set during the English Revolution, tells the story of young Johnny Church, one of Cromwell's soldiers executed for his Leveller sympathies. *O Beulah Land,* set in prerevolutionary America, introduces the wilderness Catletts and shows Church's descendant, Johnny Lacey, establishing the Beulah plantation in West Virginia (then part of Virginia). *Know Nothing* depicts their descendants preparing for the Civil War, and *The Scapegoat* treats the various families involved in economic struggles prior to World War I. *The Killing Ground,* with a contemporary setting, shows Hannah McKarkle trying to understand her drunken brother's death by reconstructing family history (and in effect, writing the Beulah Quintet).

The first four novels are associated with wars supposedly fought for freedom, and the theme running through the Beulah Quintet is the search for freedom, primarily in America. America is the promised land of the old gospel hymn (based on Isaiah 62):

O Beulah Land, sweet Beulah Land,
As on thy highest mount I stand,
I look away across the sea
Where mansions are prepared for me,
And view the shining Glory Shore,
My Heaven, my Home, forevermore.

In the Beulah Quintet, these words ring forth with both idealism and irony.

Other Titles

The Love Eaters, 1954 (novel); *The Kiss of Kin,* 1955 (novel); *Fight Night on a Sweet Saturday,* 1965 (novel, first version of *The Killing Ground); The Story of Flight,* 1967 (juvenile nonfiction); *The Clam Shell,* 1971 (novel); *The Scopes Trial: The State of Tennessee vs. John Thomas Scopes,* 1972 (juvenile nonfiction); *Water World,* 1984 (juvenile nonfiction).

Additional Sources

Doctorow, E. L., "Mother Jones Had Some Advice," *The New York Times Book Review* (October 26, 1980): 1, 40-42. Excellent review of *The Scapegoat* by a novelist who shares many of Settle's narrative techniques.

Dyer, Joyce Coyne, "Embracing the Common: Mary Lee Settle in World War II," *Appalachian Journal* 12, 2 (Winter 1985): 127-134. Finds Settle's wartime WAAF service described in *All the Brave Promises* pivotal to her political attitudes.

Garrett, George, "Mary Lee Settle," in *Dictionary of Literary Biography,* Vol. 6: *American Novelists Since World War II,* Second Series, ed. James E. Kibler, Jr. Detroit: Gale Research, 1980, pp. 281-288. Good introduction to Settle's life and work by a friendly fellow novelist.

Schafer, William J., "Mary Lee Settle's Beulah Quintet: History Darkly, Through a Single-Lens Reflex," *Appalachian Journal* 10, 1 (Autumn 1982): 77-86. Highly critical analysis of Settle's techniques of depicting history.

Settle, Mary Lee, "Recapturing the Past in Fiction," *The New York Times Book Review* (February 12, 1984): 37. Settle discusses her writing of the Beulah Quintet.

Shattuck, Roger, "Introduction," *The Scapegoat.* New York: Ballantine Books, 1980, pp. V-XV. Introduction to the Beulah Quintet, also appearing in the other volumes.

Vance, Jane Gentry, "Mary Lee Settle's *The Beulah Quintet:* History Inherited, History Created," *Southern Literary Journal* 17, 1 (Fall 1984): 40-53. Explains how the Beulah Quintet holds together, especially thematically.

Harold Branam
University of Pennsylvania

BETTY SMITH
1904-1972

Publishing History

Betty Smith wrote her popular novel, *A Tree Grows in Brooklyn*, over a period of three years (1935-1938) at the University of North Carolina at Chapel Hill where she held, in succession, a Rockefeller fellowship in play writing and a Rockefeller Dramatists Guild fellowship. During the same time she wrote and published seventy-five one-act and five full-length plays. *A Tree Grows in Brooklyn* (1943) was a best-selling phenomenon that by 1955 had sold over three million copies and had been translated into sixteen languages.

A Tree Grows in Brooklyn was followed by *Tomorrow Will Be Better* (1948), *Maggie-Now* (1958), and *Joy in the Morning* (1963). All have been recently re-issued in paperback in Harper's Perennial Library series. All except *Joy in the Morning* take place in the squalor of Williamsburg, Brooklyn, in the second and third decades of the twentieth century. All have as the central character a young girl struggling against that squalor, reaching for a better life. In *Joy in the Morning* the girl from Brooklyn follows her husband to a college in the midwest where she discovers her vocation as a writer.

Critical Reception, Honors, and Popularity

A Tree Grows in Brooklyn was an astounding success, well-reviewed even by *The New Yorker* which said, "A remarkably good first novel. The author sees the misery, squalor and cruelty of slum life but sees them with understanding, pity and sometimes with hilarious humor." Smith was bemused by the novel's popularity. At a *New York Times* meeting of authors on February 24, 1944, she said, "I, Betty Smith, wrote a novel. I had no axe to grind. I just wanted to write, but it seems I didn't know my own strength." She insisted she had no intention of writing a novel of "social significance," and said she wrote about the people of her book because they were "the kind of people I know and the kind of people I like." On May 5, 1946, the *New York Times* reported that in a survey of the taste of the reading public in the first six months of 1945 " . . .the Bible [has been] pressed in popularity by *Forever Amber* and *A Tree Grows in Brooklyn.*"

None of Smith's later books enjoyed the success of *A Tree Grows in Brooklyn*, which apparently had the power to touch the lives of the reading public with immediacy. In the author's note dated Chapel Hill, June, 1947, and included in the first Harper Perennial edition (1968) and in the current reprint, Smith discusses the constant influx of letters from people all over the country who say things like, "I was a girl like Francie Nolan"; "My family had the same kind of struggle. My mother was like Katie [Francie's mother]"; "I've never lived in Brooklyn but someone must have told you the story of my life because that's what you wrote."

Analysis of Selected Titles

A TREE GROWS IN BROOKLYN
A Tree Grows in Brooklyn, 1943, novel.

Social Concerns

Although Smith denied that she wrote a novel of social significance, there are societal themes in *A Tree Grows in Brooklyn*. The grinding desolation of urban poverty is closest to the surface and it is this, in all its naturalistic detail, that Smith concentrates on. However, she washes over the images of squalor with sentimentality, as in the figure of the tree: "It grew in boarded up lots and out of neglected rubbish heaps and it was the only tree that grew out of cement. It grew lushly but only in the tenement districts." Though mean and poor, Smith's Brooklyn teems with life, overflows with the irrepressible good nature of its main characters who refuse to be daunted by the squalor that always threatens to destroy them. Francie Nolan, the protagonist, resists the inadequacy of her life, insists on reading every book in the local library despite that fact that the librarian never once, over a period of six years, looks at her when Francie checks out a book. The Nolans fight against poverty by stuffing every grubby cent they can spare into a tin can nailed into the floor in a dark corner of their bedroom closet to insure future solvency. They also fight against their own hard circumstances, mainly that the father, Johnny Nolan, is a hopeless drunk who dies of alcoholism halfway through the novel, leaving his pregnant wife, Katie, Francie and her younger brother, Neely, to carry on the battle from which he had withdrawn into alcohol. All around them are the tenement people, crude, careful, getting by on nickels and dimes, brawling, singing, pawning their overcoats until they can collect their next pay envelopes.

Another social concern is the integrity of the family unit, which closes ranks against outsiders, protecting and supporting its members without judging them. Even though Johnny Nolan is a drunk who must weave through his taunting neighbors to get home to his tenement flat, when he arrives there he is treated as the head of a family must be treated, with love, kindness and respect. Johnny is Francie's adored father who, with his physical beauty and innate Irish charm, has a special place, a haven, to come to every day. Katie, who must clean three other tenements to keep the family in rent and food money, is still jealous of the woman Johnny rejected for her when that woman shows up at his funeral. Johnny's alcoholism is viewed as a result of unfortunate circumstances, not something to censure him for.

What firmly anchors *A Tree Grows in Brooklyn* in popular fiction, however, is that its social significance is merely the background against which Francie's life unfolds. Smith was a playwright first and there is a real sense that the details of the poverty of tenement life in Brooklyn are placed carefully, like a set of props around a stage on which a girl cheerfully recites her part in an essentially comic play. Everything comes up, if not roses, at least ailanthus trees.

Themes

The central theme of *A Tree Grows in Brooklyn* is the great story of life triumphant against adversity, which probably accounts for its spectacular popularity. Francie Nolan is the protagonist in a *Bildungsroman*. Francie's life grows as the symbolic tree grows, pushing through the cracks and rubble that oppress tenement life. She is eleven when the novel opens and seventeen at its close and she spends the intervening six years discovering who she is, that she is different from the other slum children and destined for a better life than they are. Since this is the coming-of-age of a girl rather than a boy in a novel about "serenity" nothing really bad is allowed to happen. For example, as Francie passes through puberty the shadow of sexual threat appears but is dispatched cleanly: Katie Nolan shoots the child-molester who corners Francie in the dark, narrow tenement hallway, a deliriously satisfactory fictional device.

Using the conventional method of having Francie keep a diary, Smith shows the child inventing a role for herself in the world as a writer. On her voyage to self-discovery, Francie passes through occasional rough seas, but her exuberance never flags and the good ship Life carries her safely into port.

As a subsidiary theme, there is a somewhat hesitant representation of a Freudian family romance threaded through the story of the Nolans. Francie knows well that Katie loves Neely better than she loves Francie; and Francie adores her father who reciprocates in a hazy alcoholic way. To compound Francie's confusion, Neely inherits his father's handsome face and light-footed Irish grace (but not his tendency to drink) while Francie remains plain—not unattractive, but plain. This is not quite a version of Cinderella, nor do the Freudian/sexuality themes predominate. *A Tree Grows in Brooklyn* celebrates, in a sentimental way, the possibility of a good life developing in a mean environment, but the environment itself, Smith's Brooklyn, is, as Francie says, " . . .a magic city and it isn't real."

Characters

Francie Nolan is the protagonist of *A Tree Grows in Brooklyn*. Her parents endow her with two traits that enable her to conquer adversity; from her second-generation German mother, Katie, Francie inherits the strength, determination and indominitable sense of respectability that guide her into a future that holds promise; from her weak Irish father, Johnny, she inherits the ability to see and hear beauty in an ugly world. The foreground of the novel is full of strong female characters: Katie; Katie's solid, immigrant German mother; Katie's sisters; and Francie herself, whose strength increases as she learns to solve the problems of her young existence. It is she who convinces her father to connive to have her transferred to another, better neighborhood school. Although Francie is a good, obedient girl, her apparent passivity masks a will that eventually prevails over her domineering mother's. There is no real conflict, however, between mother and daughter. The values of hard work, education, cleanliness and decency are established as normative and Francie embraces them. Most of the male characters are weak and tend to inhabit the novel's background as biological, social and economic entities, but with no real importance. The women do not despise the men; rather, they accept their flawed husbands, brothers and fathers as necessities and move on with their lives. *A Tree Grows in Brooklyn* is Francie Nolan's quest for identity, an enactment of the central theme of the irrepressibility of life.

Techniques

A Tree Grows in Brooklyn is loosely constructed, anecdotal, digressive and episodic rather than carefully plotted. There is occasional foreshadowing, as in the saga of Francie's promiscuous Aunt Sissy's attempts to have a baby. Sissy finally succeeds after bearing nine still-born infants and adopting one who turns out, it is hinted, to be her third husband's illegitimate child. But Smith is not interested in subtlety and most of her attempts at plotting are heavy-handed and obvious. Francie's development provides the book with its central structure and around this are stacked other related stories about the Nolan family and their neighbors. Almost all of this is told with energy and good humor. Smith writes in the plain style of the vernacular of Brooklyn with its slang and ungrammatical constructions. Even the omniscient narrator speaks in a simple, slangy way, injecting exclamatory statements to emphasize dramatic events and emotional responses. Much of the book is dialogue and although there is a sameness about the characters' speeches, there are enough action and signalling devices to keep the characters distinct. *A Tree Grows in Brooklyn* is the work of an amateur, in both senses of the word, and its lack of literary refinement, its simplicity and forward-marching, predictable story line make it both charming and ephemeral.

Literary Precedents

Because of its conventional coming-of-age theme, *A Tree Grows in Brooklyn* fits the *Bildungsroman* genre, but it is a sentimental, simplistic example of the type. Its lack of serious literary achievement precludes it from formal critical commentary. Smith uses both realistic and naturalistic techniques, concentrating on sometimes exhaustive physical description of the economic poverty of her characters' lives, but she undercuts the effects of poverty by denying its importance and its repressive potential. Therefore, while it is tempting to cite Crane, Dreiser or Howells as Smith's literary influences, and to suggest that Francie's mean environment has a deadening effect on her development, the novel's basically optimistic drive raises it from the lower depths and propels Francie merrily through the streets of Williamsburg.

A Tree Grows in Brooklyn is a woman's novel, and therefore it might be compared to the comic novels of Barbara Pym, whose *Excellent Women*, for instance, also relies on the realistic description of reduced circumstances to depict the life of its heroine, Mildred Lathbury. But in *Excellent Women* the bleak, paralyzing details of middle class life in postwar London function as a metaphor of the heroine's class status. The reader can feel the teacups and jumble sales constricting Mildred while simultaneously and properly confining her to her gentlewoman's place in a rigorously ordered social structure. Smith never develops the layered density of metaphor with her intentionally pathetic details. The reader knows, from the first paragraph, that Francie is destined for a happy future regardless of the pathos of her present circumstances.

Related Titles

Smith continued her story of the girl who grew up in Brooklyn in her succeeding three novels, *Tomorrow Will Be Better*, *Maggie-Now*, and *Joy in the Morning*. In each, the central character is a young woman who, recognizing that she is different from the other tenement girls, knows she must control her life so that she succeeds in fulfilling the promise of that difference.

Tomorrow Will Be Better (1948), though not a spectacular best seller like *A Tree Grows in Brooklyn*, nevertheless received fairly good reviews but dropped out of sight, perhaps because its heroine, Margy Shannon, temporarily fails in her quest for happiness. Margy chooses marriage as the only way to improve her life, but the marriage comes apart after she gives birth to a stillborn child and then realizes that her husband, while not quite homosexual, is at least sexually repressed. The homosexual theme had, as yet, not found a place in popular fiction that was designed to appeal to women at a time when they were occupied in building lives around the men who had just returned from fighting World War II.

Maggie-Now, the eponymous novel Smith published in 1958, constructs a heroine who attains a place for herself through marriage with the mysterious Mr. Bassett. Maggie-Now's struggle is not only against lower middle class poverty, but against the men who impinge on her life: her cantankerous, possessive father; her irresponsible brother and, finally, Claude Bassett who disappears from March to November during every year of their marriage until he dies. Maggie's strength, kindness and fundamentally Christian ability to forgive allow her to maintain her sense of individuality and to build a rewarding life despite her problems.

Joy in the Morning (1963), apparently the most autobiographical of Smith's four novels, takes the girl who grew up in Brooklyn to a college in the midwest where she marries the Brooklyn boy who is enrolled there in law school. The novel describes the traditional difficulties of adjustment, money, pregnancy and childbirth that occur in the first year of their marriage. The girl, Annie, is the center of the book which is a continuation of *A Tree Grows in Brooklyn*. Annie is a thinly disguised Francie Nolan, transported to a world very different from Williamsburg, who nevertheless takes with her Francie's good-spirited ability to control and build a life. *Joy in the Morning* resembles the earlier book also in that it is an example of a similar genre, the *Künstleroman*; it traces Annie's development as a serious writer, from her first scribblings of dramatic dialogue to her recognition by the members of the English Department of the college, who criticize and praise her work.

Adaptations

Betty Smith and George Abbot wrote a musical comedy version of *A Tree Grows in Brooklyn* which played on Broadway in 1944. It was produced by Elia Kazan who then directed the movie version, Kazan's first feature film, released in 1945. The movie starred James Dunn as Johnny Nolan and Peggy Ann Garner as Francie. Reviewing it in *The Nation*, James Agee (with the *caveat* that he hadn't read the book) praised the movie for its attention to the details of poverty in the big city while damning it for not taking poverty seriously enough and for playing safe with the Freudian mother-son/father-daughter theme. However, Agee recommended that the movie not be dismissed by intelligent people who automatically dismiss best sellers. *Joy in the Morning* was made into a feature film starring Richard Chamberlain and Yvette Mimieux.

TOMORROW WILL BE BETTER

Tomorrow Will Be Better, 1948, novel (published in England as *Streets of Little Promise*).

Social Concerns/Themes

Margy Shannon, who is seventeen at the beginning of *Tomorrow Will Be Better* strains against the restrictions of her drab, domineering mother, Flo and, hoping for a better life than her parents', resolves to marry Frankie Malone, whose full name, Francis Xavier Malone sounds "important—like a mystery revealed" when she first hears it. It is this hope that expresses the primary social significance of the book: a bright and promising life is possible only if one breaks free from the awful bonds of lower middle class drudgery. Smith also touches, in passing, the stifled, hopeless sterility of workingmen's lives by showing Henny, Margy's father, who has been "pushed around" all his life by bosses, making feeble connections with other workingmen—with the trolley driver who passes Henny's street, forcing him to walk back a couple of extra blocks after a long day at work; with Margy's future father-in-law, who is taking a correspondence course in undertaking to upgrade his life—to form a union of sympathy in a society that has yet to allow labor unions.

Through their own union, Margy and Frankie climb at least one rung on the ladder of respectability, but Frankie proves inadequate to the sexual demands of marriage and the novel ends with the potential separation of the couple. However, tomorrow will be better because the novel ends with Margy rekindling a romance with her ex-boss who has had to work his way free from his own mother's grasp.

Tomorrow Will Be Better is not a *Bildungsroman*. Margy lacks both Francie's optimistic assertion of individuality and her talent; rather than searching for identity, Margy wants just to be free to be the self she knows.

Characters

Margy Shannon is another Brooklyn girl who finds ways to make a good life for herself despite the massive constraints of family and environment. Unlike Francie Nolan, however, Margy is not particularly intelligent, has no interest in education beyond two years of high school and is perfectly happy with her job as a reader in a mail-order house. She has no aspirations beyond marrying Frankie Malone and fixing their flat so it looks "nice." Smith expends a good deal of realistic detail on the scenes of the girl furnishing the apartment, showing how Margy takes great pleasure in adding "artistic touches" like a fringed artificial medieval tapestry. Margy's limitations are the result of her cruel, ignorant mother, Flo, the book's second most memorable character. Given Flo's brutalizing smallness of spirit, it is to Margy's credit that she has the energy to pursue Frankie let alone leave home and marry him. Henny and Frankie are two more of Smith's weak male characters, Henny unable even to ask for a better meal than the two eggs fried in lard that Flo grudgingly provides every night and Frankie, a momma's boy, who lies rigidly in bed with his back toward Margy, recoiling when she touches him. *Tomorrow Will Be Better* is devoid of humor and it lacks the rich density of characterization that distinguishes *A Tree Grows in Brooklyn*.

Techniques

Tomorrow Will Be Better is thinner, more tightly structured than *A Tree Grows in Brooklyn*, without the latter's disgressions and fully developed episodes. This makes it drab in comparison and its lack of humor reinforces the drabness. The book is Margy's story, told in straight chronological order except for one long flashback at the beginning, the horrifying narrative of Margy as a very young child getting lost on a walk with her mother through the streets of Brooklyn. This episode establishes Flo's cruelty and contributes to the desolation of Margy's spirit.

Again, Smith uses dialogue to develop character and action and concentrates heavily on specific, realistic detail to create the atmosphere of the slums and their downtrodden inhabitants. Yet even with its lack of cheer, *Tomorrow Will Be Better* fails to suggest that its heroine would have been much different from the way she is if her circumstances had been better. The plotting is thin and transparent; for example, the scenes of Frankie's father studying the mortuary business foreshadow the death of Margy's baby.

Additional Sources

Agee, James, *Agee on Film*, vol. 1. New York: Grosset and Dunlap, 1967, pp. 141-143. A two volume collection of Agee's movie reviews.

New York *Times* (February 24, 1944):20. Source of the quotation that begins "I Betty Smith wrote a novel . . ." News article reporting a meeting of authors sponsored by the New York *Times*.

New York *Times* (May 5, 1946):14. News article reporting popularity of *A Tree Grows in Brooklyn* and *Forever Amber*.

New York *Times* (January 18, 1972). Betty Smith's obituary.

Janet Alwang
Penn State University

MARTIN CRUZ SMITH
1942

Publishing History

Born "Martin William Smith" ("William" having been changed to "Cruz" in 1977), this still relatively young and extremely successful author learned his trade by working as a newspaperman and magazine writer from 1965 to 1969. His first novel, *The Indians Won,* was published in 1970, and for the next several years he turned out mysteries, westerns and movie novelizations under a variety of different pseudonyms as well as "Martin William Smith." In 1977 his novel *Nightwing* was a surprise best seller, and with his approximately $500,000 earnings from the book Smith was able to begin working full time on what would eventually become *Gorky Park.*

In 1972 Smith had begun talking with G.P. Putnam's Sons about his ideas for *Gorky Park.* Although the firm was interested, they were not happy about Smith's plan to feature a Soviet detective—rather than an American one—as his protagonist, and in 1977 Smith bought back the rights to the novel from them. Random House showed no such hesitation about *Gorky Park,* and in 1981 it was published to almost unanimous acclaim. Smith's most recent novel, *Stallion Gate,* appeared in 1986 just as this volume was going to press, and seems to be headed for a similar kind of success.

Critical Reception, Honors, and Popularity

Smith's career divides into two very distinct phases, with *Nightwing* being the pivotal event that separates them. Prior to its publication in 1977, he had received little in the way of critical recognition or mass popularity, since much of his writing was pseudonymous and the remainder largely consisted of undistinguished genre work. *Nightwing* received generally positive notices, sold over a million copies and was made into a popular film, and the cumulative effect of these successes was to make him an instant member of the fraternity of best-selling writers.

This status was confirmed by the reception accorded *Gorky Park,* which found many reviewers commenting upon the reasons why it merited special attention in a publishing milieu by no means supplied with competent thrillers. It was lauded as a new and improved variety of the adventure novel, praised to the skies for the authenticity of its Russian characters and settings, and often cited as the American equivalent of the work of le Carré and Deighton. Although it is still too soon to tell whether or not Smith will continue to produce books of this quality, as of this moment he must be considered one of the major American entertainment writers of his generation.

Analysis of Selected Titles

GORKY PARK

Gorky Park, 1981, novel.

Social Concerns/Themes

Gorky Park is such an exciting and entertaining story that on a first reading one is seldom conscious of anything other than the events of its fast-paced narrative. But a more reflective consideration of the book reveals that it does possess a few abstract aspects which, although generally muted by the color and energy of their surrounding context, periodically indicate some of the author's broader concerns.

The primary social question in *Gorky Park* is the quality of life in the Soviet Union. Smith has structured the novel in a way that reveals ever-widening circles of corruption within the Russian social and political systems, and the plot turns upon the efforts made by members of the elite to frustrate, block and finally kill Arkady Renko, the police investigator charged with solving a bizarre triple murder. This emphasis upon the widespread rottenness of Soviet society as a whole is reinforced by frequent criticisms of the material quality of Russian life, as everything from cigarettes to clothing to large appliances is denigrated as the inferior product of a barely functioning economy. Although the final section of *Gorky Park* (about one-fifth of the book) takes place in New York City, where Smith exhibits an equally keen eye for the shabbier aspects of American life, it is the novel's vivid portrayal of the Soviet Union's general social decay that makes the greater impression upon the reader.

Thematically, *Gorky Park* bears some similarity to the "down these mean streets a man must go" tradition exemplified by Raymond Chandler's Philip Marlowe. Smith's Arkady Renko is also a lone wolf in a dog-eat-dog world, and like Marlowe it is only his exceptional personal integrity that keeps him going when most people either ignore him or attempt to kill him. For Renko, however, there is an ironic twist to this situation. His society is supposedly dedicated to the abolition of the individual selfishness that causes crime and the creation of an internalized concern for the general social welfare; thus Renko's attempts to pursue truth are to this extent subversive, since they challenge the established order, rather than merely ill-judged, as in Marlowe's case. The contrast between the not very powerful, but nonetheless brave individual, and the omnipotent but ethically barren state is a source of moral as well as dramatic tension for *Gorky Park;* and if this is an essentially romantic and probably quite unrealistic myth, it is also one of the most appealing conceits remaining to contemporary sensibilities.

Characters

Arkady Renko, *Gorky Park*'s protagonist, is the alienated citizen of a culture that prides itself upon its elimination of capitalism's exploitative alienation of workers from the fruits of their labor. In a sense, Renko is a model of proletarian consciousness: he performs his police duties conscientiously and well, even though he is poorly paid and has been passed over for promotion despite an excellent record of solving cases. It is precisely his high professional competence, however, which has kept him from being better rewarded by his society, since he has failed to conform to the covert ethos of materialistic selfishness that really governs life in the U.S.S.R. Renko is certainly aware of the kind of conformist behavior which would earn him a larger slice of the communal pie, but he is also cognizant of the spiritual impoverishment which would result from surrendering to social pressures.

If this makes Arkady Renko seem like some sort of intolerably self-righteous saint, it should be emphasized that Smith offers a much more complex portrait of his protagonist. Renko smokes and drinks, as well as thinks, far too much, and his desire to remain independent leads him to reject genuinely helpful suggestions as well as advice that contains ulterior motives. His integrity regarding larger matters often leads him into priggishness in small ones, and his ability to grasp the meaning of tiny physical clues is matched by an inability to correctly interpret major psychological outbursts. Although Renko is a basically good man in a deeply flawed society, Smith takes care to endow him with the kinds of quirkily idiosyncratic traits that make for a compelling "warts and all" characterization.

Renko is the center of attention for almost all of *Gorky Park,* and as a consequence the other *dramatis personae* are much less fully sketched. The man responsible for the triple murder, John Osborne, is a shadowy figure whose motives are not well articulated, and the characters of Renko's wife, mistress and colleagues are made up of predictable and at times even stereotyped elements. It is a tribute to Smith's narrative skills that the impetus of his plot is more than sufficient to maintain interest in *Gorky Park,* a book in which one well-developed character holds the stage while a host of lesser entities make their alarums and excursions at an ever-accelerating, and almost always exhilarating, pace.

Techniques/Literary Precedents

Although critics have often assumed that *Gorky Park* is simply a thriller or adventure novel, a good case can also be made for including it in the police-procedural tradition. This increasingly popular genre, whose major exponents have been the American writers Ed McBain and Hilary Waugh and their English counterpart J.J. Marric, typically provides a nuts-and-bolts account of a police force's standard operating procedures along with the usual components of a mystery story. The sociological material that results can, if effectively utilized, add a firmly realistic foundation to what might otherwise be just another cops-and-robbers story; and while *Gorky Park* is certainly not one of the latter, its descriptions of Arkady Renko's methods of work are both intrinsically fascinating and exotically unfamiliar to Western readers. The second half of the book introduces a New York City detective into the middle of Renko's investigation, which gives Smith additional opportunities to contrast American and Russian versions of proper police procedure. *Gorky Park* does contain elements not commonly found in the police-procedural—the extensive criticisms of Soviet society and the action-packed plot are both atypical—but it is, in essence, the story of a dedicated policeman's methodical pursuit of a criminal, and should thus be considered in the context of a genre that has appealed to a number of contemporary writers.

Adaptations

The film version of *Gorky Park* was released in 1983. Directed by Michael Apted, produced by Gene Kirkwood and Howard W. Koch, Jr. and with a screenplay written by Dennis Potter, it featured William Hurt in the role of Arkady Renko and Lee Marvin as the villainous John Osborne. Among the supporting cast were Joanna Pakula, Brian Dennehy and Ian Bannen. Most reviewers found it an entertaining and enjoyably fast-paced movie, although several also commented upon its failure to fill in the flavorful Russian social context that constituted one of the book's major strengths. Despite a strong performance by star attraction Hurt—who was widely praised for the subtlety of his characterization of Arkady Renko—the film enjoyed only moderate success at the box office.

NIGHTWING

Nightwing, 1977, novel.

Social Concerns/Themes

The protagonist of *Nightwing* is Youngman Duran, a Hopi Indian deputy sheriff on a Southwestern reservation who is torn between the White and native worlds. With one foot in each camp and his fundamental allegiances in neither, Duran's cultural ambivalence makes him a uniquely sensitive instrument for recording the conflicts between traditional and technological forces that recur throughout *Nightwing*'s account of an invasion by bloodthirsty vampire bats. Although Smith is careful to provide a plausible natural explanation for the bats' terrifying depredations, they also function as a symbol of the different kinds of control over nature exercised by Whites and Indians: if White technology is ultimately powerful enough to destroy the bats, it is traditional Indian magical practices that invoke the bats' appearance and—to an extent left ambiguous by Smith—are in some sense responsible for their attacks upon humans.

Nightwing's portrait of Hopi society and its reactions to alien encroachment is one of the most attractive aspects of the book, not least because it is far more sophisticated than the revisionist good-Indians bad-Whites attitude that has largely supplanted its vicious savages-virtuous settlers predecessor among the American intelligentsia. Smith depicts a broad variety of individual responses ranging from the assimilationist to the isolationist, and he implies that it is the former which will prevail in the long run. At the same time, however, he presents a cultural defense of Hopi life that manages to be compelling without lapsing into sentimentality: their rich heritage of myth, ritual and folktale is described at some length, and the reader certainly comes to understand how and why they have resisted taking on the values of White society.

Although their way of life is under attack, the Hopi are seen as much better adapted to their natural environment than are the alien newcomers. The Hopi comprehension of nature, which strikes the Whites in *Nightwing* as an almost occult phenomenon, is perceived as a profound sympathy that leads to an equally profound understanding. The scientific technology of the invaders is in some respects far more powerful, but its inability to transcend its basic intellectual premises is viewed as a definite limiting factor: although technology can be used to wipe out the bats once they have been identified as the cause of the attacks, it is the Hopis who have from the beginning understood what is going on and the reasons for it. *Nightwing* offers a sustained meditation upon the question of the proper relationships between men, their societies and the natural world, and it does so in a thoughtful, open-ended manner that provides no final answers but instead encourages readers to come to their own conclusions on such vital matters.

Characters

Youngman Duran's uncertainty about his cultural identity makes him the ideal protagonist for *Nightwing*'s story of conflict between divergent societies. The clashes between Hopi and White values are played out in his own consciousness as well as in the events of the plot, which gives his character dramatic depths seldom found in contemporary popular fiction. The special qualities of his Indian heritage are conveyed through Duran's encounters with Abner Tusapi, an elderly medicine man who has decided to destroy the White intruders by calling down a plague upon their cities. Tusapi has recognized a true Hopi spirit underneath Duran's White-oriented exterior, and as he explains his rituals and spells to the deputy, the reader comes to understand the religious beliefs upon which Hopi society rests.

Duran's mistress and the other White characters of *Nightwing* are much less fully sketched than his Indian acquaintances. Most of Smith's readers will be familiar with the cultural context that he opposes to the Hopi worldview, but the book might have been even more affecting if the primary representative of technology—a mad scientist obsessed with killing vampire bats—had been made as articulate a spokesman for his credo as is Abner Tusapi. The failure to make the behavior and values of the White characters completely intelligible tends to romanticize their Indian counterparts, and to add a slight air of unreality to a book that otherwise seems totally authentic.

Techniques/Literary Precedents
The combination of a detective story plot and an anthropological account of an unfamiliar culture has produced some interesting literary hybrids. Arthur Upfield's mysteries featuring the Australian aboriginal detective "Bony" and James Mc-Clure's South African police-procedurals rely heavily upon the unusual details of their cultural settings; and there is an interesting parallel to *Nightwing* to be found in the novels of Tony Hillerman, whose *The Blessing Way* (1970) began a series featuring Navajo policemen Joe Leaphorn and Jim Chee. Hillerman works extensive descriptions of both Navajo and Hopi ways of thinking and feeling into his narratives, and like *Nightwing*'s Youngman Duran his protagonists must function in both the White and Indian worlds without being full citizens of either. Although *Nightwing* is more of a suspense novel than a police-procedural, its contexts and themes are so similar to those of Hillerman that it may well have been influenced by them.

Adaptations
The film version of *Nightwing* was released in 1979. Directed by Arthur Hiller, produced by Martin Ransohoff and with a screenplay by Smith, Steve Shagan and Bud Shrake, it starred Nick Mancuso and David Warner, with supporting roles played by Kathryn Harrold, Stephen Macht and Strother Martin. The movie was well received by the critics, with the special effects work's depiction of the rampaging bats often lauded, but the film's relatively high intellectual content and the absence of a major star resulted in only mediocre returns at the box office.

Other Titles
As Martin William Smith: *The Indians Won*, 1970 (novel); *Gypsy in Amber*, 1971 (novel); *Canto for a Gypsy*, 1972 (novel); *The Human Factor*, 1975 (novel).
As Simon Quinn: *The Analog Bullet*, 1972 (novel); *His Eminence, Death*, 1974 (novel); *Nuplex Red*, 1974 (novel); *The Midas Coffin*, 1975 (novel); *Last Rites for the Vulture*, 1975 (novel).
As Jake Logan: *North to Dakota*, 1976 (novel); *Ride for Revenge*, 1977 (novel).
As Martin Quinn: *Adventures of the Wilderness Family*, 1976 (movie novelization).
As Martin Cruz Smith: *Stallion Gate*, 1986 (novel).

Additional Sources
Hubin, Allen J., *Bibliography of Crime Fiction 1749-1975*. San Diego: University of California, 1979, pp. 381-382. Useful for the identification of Smith's pseudonymous work.

Stine, Jean C., ed., "Martin Cruz Smith," *Contemporary Literary Criticism,* Vol. 25. Detroit: Gale, 1983, pp. 412-415. Offers a good overview of critical reaction to Smith's novels.

Straub, Deborah A., "Martin Cruz Smith," *Contemporary Authors,* New Revision Series, Vol. 6. Detroit: Gale, 1982, pp. 478-480. The best source of biographical information, as well as a comprehensive bibliography.

Paul Stuewe

TERRY SOUTHERN
1924

Publishing History

Terry Southern began writing abroad in the early 1950s, some of his pieces being published in the *Paris Review.* He struggled as a writer subsequently, working at odd jobs in upstate New York. His novel *Candy* (1958) was censored and condemned when first published by Olympia Press in Paris. However, his fortune was soon completely altered. His novel, *The Magic Christian* (1959-1960) caught the eye of Stanley Kubrick, who recruited Southern to help write the film script of "Dr. Strangelove," a violent satire and highly-touted cinematic success. When *Candy* was finally published in the U.S. in 1964, it vaulted to the best seller lists, remaining there for a lengthy period of time. Where *Candy* had originally earned its author only $350 in Paris, he was now awarded an advance by Random House of $35,000 for his next novel. Although controversial, Southern has been much interviewed and widely admired; he began writing a series of Hollywood film scripts in the 1960s, in addition to publishing other novel-length work and short fiction.

Critical Reception, Honors, and Popularity

Although Southern has written successful novels and a long string of impressive film scripts, he is essentially greeted with mixed reviews. Because his satire regularly goes too far, what he himself calls the "testing of limits," and because he seeks, in his own words, to "astonish," his work is often received as "sick," excessive, immoral. Furthermore, most of his fiction satirizes, flirts with, and otherwise openly employs pornography. Hence, many a critic has treated him as unacceptable, in bad taste, and beyond the pale. Admittedly, too, Southern, while sparkling and inventive, does have difficulty in sustaining a plot, or in deepening a character, or in managing extensive structuring of his longer fiction. On the other hand, much of his writing is deliberately picaresque, episodic, lightly and quickly sketched of necessity, yet many a critic cannot forgive him for any of his foibles or seeming flaws.

Nevertheless, a number of important writers, like William Styron, have at one time or another praised his fictions. He is expert in capturing the current argot of various crackpot professions—young nymphs, doctors and psychiatrists, religious zealots, complacent middle-class hypocrites, and the entire cast of Hollywood filmmaking. There is no doubt of his major talent as a scriptwriter. He received the British Screen Writers Award in 1963 for *Dr. Strangelove,* and several of his films have been nominated for Academy Awards (*Dr. Strangelove* in 1963; *Easy Rider* in 1968). In fact, *Easy Rider* has been broadly acclaimed as a unique and masterful script. Clearly, Southern has been a challenging and successful writer, a "black humorist" who has invented wildly and startled mightily, along with the best of his post-World War Two literary generation.

Analysis of Selected Titles

CANDY

Candy (with Mason Hoffenberg, under the joint pseudonym of Maxwell Kenton), Paris, 1958 novel; banned by the French government and reissued there under the title, *Lollipop,* 1962; published in the U.S. as *Candy* under the authors' actual names, 1964.

Social Concerns

Candy literally satirizes everything in sight. It particularly provides a send-up for a number of relevant issues in the 1950s and 1960s—the pornographic novel itself, and clusters of wildly liberal, nay, leftish fads of the era, such as Zen Buddhism, Taoist mysticism, tourism, Bohemian life in Greenwich Village, pop psychiatry with its experiments and fixation upon sex, group therapy, commune-living and commune jargon, Chinese acupuncture, dabblings in kinky sex, lascivious filmscripts, bathroom comedy of manners, and a quaint fondness for incest and freaks. The era was witnessing the "opening up" of Liberalism—even to the end of its tether—and was bending over backwards to embrace new extremes in theorizing, the sexual revolution, and acceptance of pornography as admissably possessing "redeeming social values." *Candy* pillories the entire stock of these fads with flare and tipsy bad taste. It must also be admitted that *Candy* is nevertheless ambivalent. Like numerous film Westerns of the period, this novel simultaneously spoofs its subject while nonetheless serving loyally as a serious and juicy example of the very genre it portends to roast.

Themes

Just as Voltaire's *Candide* had mocked naive eighteenth-century philosophy that "all is for the best in this best of all possible worlds," so does *Candy* mock modern permissive ideas that free love, frantic travel, and rabid experimentation in religions, mores, and life-styles are eagerly-to-be-fostered and endured. Beneath the masks of most "mod" performers is merely the rampant libido of another me-first generation of individuals who will exploit any and all ideas and men (and especially women) for purposes of self-aggrandizement. Yet, disquietingly, as in Voltaire, Nature herself—with accidents, reversals, small floods, and large earthquakes—contributes both to unsettle all things but at times even to advance the sexual promiscuity and carnage. Almost every single piety, faction, movement, and group protestation is reduced to shambles, for behind every civic movement stands a selfish (and sometimes lunatic) manipulator and solipsist. For all of its humor, *Candy* partly wishes to leave with the reader the least modicum of a bitter taste.

Characters

Candy Christian is the central protagonist. Like Candide, she is a young *naif,* a willing victim of all the "-isms" and fads abroad (and well touted) in an age of rapid transit and instant communications. Her favorite expressions are backwoods middle-class provincial exclamations: "Darn" and "Gosh" and "Good Grief." She is repeatedly the victim of every con-man in her vicinity, all of whom preach some supposedly pious and self-serving species of so-called "contemporary ethics." In such a novel, there are only two classes of character: the foolish Candy and a herd of knaves. For the rest, incident clearly plays a more dominant role than does character, as is frequently the case in fast-paced satiric novels.

Techniques

Following in the steps of Voltaire, the authors create a satiric adventure tale with many of the earmarks of the original *Candide*. It is deliberately episodic, each chapter detailing a complete new adventure. Furthermore, it is ludicrously fast-paced, events unrolling at incredible speeds. The effect of such rapidity is to reduce actions and events to the level of absurdity and farce. In every single episode Candy is either duped into a sexual imbroglio or naively volunteers her services (without realizing her partners' motives). A recurrent feature of such a fiction is the comic "cognitio." Characters like Daddy, Uncle Jack, Aunt Livia, a guru disappear only to turn up and be suddenly recognized under very astounding circumstances. In addition, a dynamic satiric ploy recurrently utilized is anti-climax; Candy is again and again manipulated into a sexual encounter of great violence, yet most often the event is not consummated; instead, some third character arrives, some catastrophe ensues, and the result invariably is *coitus interruptus*—and some species of mayhem and letdown. In short, sexual fulfillment is usually nipped or curtailed, and the disruptions can only be conducive to laughter. By such means, of course, the characters, prevalent ideas, and even the pornographic novel itself are tilted, debilitated, and derided.

Literary Precedents

A major strand of the modern novel has been the picaresque tradition, which uses small, illicit characters as anti-heroes or anti-heroines, conducting them through a vapid sequence of satiric misadventures. Such is the *mythos* in Petronius' *Satyricon,* in the anonymous Spanish *Lazarillo de Tormes* (1554), in Voltaire's *Candide*. Dickens' Mr. Pickwick belongs in this genre, and a number of important twentieth-century authors have experimented with it, notably Evelyn Waugh, Nathanael West, Saul Bellow, John Barth, and Günter Grass. Moreover, by entitling their main character Candy *Christian,* Southern and Hoffenberg invoke one further precedent, suggesting the pious journeys through this world (toward the next) of John Bunyan's Christian in *Pilgrim's Progress* (1678). By no stretch of the pious (or gullible) imagination can it be presumed for an instant that Candy is somehow stumbling toward sexual or ethical salvation of any sort whatsoever, despite the claims and protestations of "mod" idea salesmen, con-men, and ravishers. Needless to say, even the merest suggestion of any similarity between Candy and Christian (or his wife Christiana) is likely to conjure visions of sacrilege for a considerable gaggle of critics, and provoke chagrin.

Adaptations

The film of *Candy* was released in technicolor in the U.S. in 1968 by Selmur. Terry Southern developed the script, and the motion picture featured, among others, Richard Burton, Marlon Brando, John Huston, and Ewa Aulin. It was a mild success as a picture, by no means so well received as the novel had been when published in the United States in 1964.

THE MAGIC CHRISTIAN
The Magic Christian, 1960, novel.

Social Concerns/Themes

As a billionaire dupes much of society in this novel, the populace is exposed as "having its price," as being purchasable—if the price be high enough. In the pranks that prevail throughout the novel, businessmen, whole industries, the police—all are acquired and manipulated with money. This is especially true of the so-called "middle Americans," the men in the street. Everyone is made into a dupe, and the wealthy perpetrator of all the shenanigans is repeatedly able to buy his way out of any shady entanglement. The implication throughout is that normative Americans are too staid, serious, lackluster, materialistic, and gullible; therefore they deserve to have their quietus and peace of mind violated and broken.

Characters

Clearly Guy Grand, the billionaire investor in steel, rubber, and oil, occupies stage-center in this episodic satire. Outside the normal decorum of his Wall Street offices, Guy Grand is a lunatic chortling eccentric, intent upon devoting his life to *"making it hot for"* mankind. He dons a pig mask, tampers with classic cinema films, opens virtual give-away grocery stores, and generally disrupts normalcy. He will introduce a panther in disguise at a dog show, create an elaborately monstrous series of Vanity Products, or even pay millions to hire an ocean liner for the elegant (named the *S.S. Magic Christian*)—only to be able to exercise hundreds of noisy, disquieting, and senseless pranks upon a captive audience. At his worst, Grand will introduce in crowded downtown Chicago a vat filled with hot wet cement, urine, manure, and offal, into which 10,000 hundred-dollar bills have been stirred, beside a candid sign: "Free $$ Here." All of his machinations have been exercised solely for the opportunity of watching the pitiful multitude of men succumb to the temptation of the cash nexus and take a noxious plunge into the vat. But, because his ploys are interchangeably vast and petty, and because he childishly enjoys them all, the novel seems too randomly organized, and Guy Grand appears easily implicated as something of a victim himself.

Techniques

Southern is most comfortable with episodic structures, where each action is self-contained, complete-in-itself. Yet even these units are not often well integrated, and, seldom does his work coherently build toward climax. As usual, however, Terry Southern's strong point is his use of concrete details—hosts of characters from all walks of life, dozens of speaking styles, and cart-loads of physical products and data, lovingly described and manipulated in his fiction. Even Guy Grand may be perceived, in a way, as a specific detail, an emblem of Terry Southern himself; both like to travel up and down in the land, shocking the bourgeoisie and rather devotedly, in an excessive and puerile way, making it "hot" for just about everybody around.

Adaptations

The Magic Christian was made into a motion picture in Great Britain in 1970 by Commonwealth International. It featured a number of major artists, including Peter Sellers, Laurence Harvey, Raquel Welch, Yul Brynner, Roman Polanski, Ringo Starr, and Terry Southern himself. The picture was a modest box office success.

BLUE MOVIE

Blue Movie, 1970, novel.

Social Concerns/Themes

The novel *Blue Movie* is Southern's satiric examination of Hollywood, its mores, its goals, its conduct, and its values. The film industry is its essential target, and its ideals are presented as consisting of little other than Money and Sex, the chief concerns on the company lots and at Malibu beach parties. In the novel, Hollywood censorship of blatant sexuality is still strong, outside the realm of stag films. But one of the so-called great directors, "King" B. (Boris Adrian), almost dreamily plans a pornographic film to end all pornographic films, one "noncontrived," "relevant," "beautiful and pure," and dedicated to "art" and "aesthetics." The film, *The Faces of Love,* is shot on location exclusively in Liechtenstein, without the knowledge of Metropolitan Pictures' top executives. The film is almost exclusively a raunchy series of mad orgies, entailing massive ensembles of copulation in a Casbah setting, and other heated episodes of sodomy, incest, and lesbian encounters. Only at the last minute is a Papal vigilante team able to assault the offices of the cinemakers, confiscate, and destroy all of the steamy footage. Hollywood filmland, and its frequent pretentions of devotion to Art and Aesthetics, is the satire's victim here. But sexual mores generally and society's increasing liberalization of torrid sex on the silver screen also come in for some sound pommeling. Unfortunately, blatant sex and pornography surface almost incessantly, and the satire is finally submerged and nearly lost in the licentious melee. The attempts at comedy in this novel are less successful than in *Candy,* and the reader is too often left with some lackluster prose and heavy-handed obscene language and violent eroticism. And yet, on the outskirts of the set, the world in this fiction is also portrayed as benighted by chaotic civic actions: processions of anarchists, parades of political factions hailing and condemning acid, war, and the Viet Cong. The landscape outside filmland, it is implied, is equally chaotic, diseased, and obsessed.

Characters
The focus of the novel is Boris Adrian, the star director, and his low-grade assistant, the B-filmmaker and crass materialist Sid H. Krassman. Various international stars are solicited for the gala sexual activities—Angela Sterling, Debbie Roberts, Arabella, and Pamela Dickenson. As frequently is the case in satire, these characters are little more than absurd puppets, cogs, so to speak, in an enormous and ever-turning sexual grindstone. Nonetheless, Boris Adrian, as a virtual Ingmar Bergman or Federico Fellini of the triple-X-rated movie, is far more tepid and nondescript than is necessary.

Techniques
Blue Movie too is episodic, but not so much so, nor so carefully constructed as *Candy.* It attempts to unfold a single, continuing story, but technical control of the plot is not evident. Like a circus, much of the work's success lies in cluttering its scenes with dozens and dozens of Hollywood types: actors and cameramen and technicians, and loads of extras: black Morrocans, Hamburg whores, and a bevy of translators and miscellaneous hangers-on. Indeed, overcrowding and exaggerated delineations of sexual encounters—both on and off the set—constitute the novel's primal strategies for generating mayhem and laughter. Too frequently, such maneuvers do not wholly succeed.

Other Titles
Flash and Filigree, 1958 (novel); *The Journal of "The Loved One": The Produc-*

tion Log of a Motion Picture, 1963 (narrative); *Red-Dirt Marijuana and Other Tastes,* 1967 (short stories); *The Rolling Stones on Tour,* 1978 (narrative).

Filmscripts: *Candy Kisses,* with David Burnett, 1955; *Dr. Strangelove,* with Stanley Kubrick and Peter George, 1963; *The Loved One,* with Christopher Isherwood, 1964; *The Cincinnati Kid,* with Ring Lardner, Jr., 1965; *Barbarella,* with Roger Vadim, *et al.,* 1967; *Candy,* 1968; *Easy Rider,* with Peter Fonda and Dennis Hopper, 1968; *The End of the Road,* with Aram Avakian, 1968; *The Magic Christian,* 1970; *Meetings with Remarkable Men,* 1979.

Additional Sources

Howard, Jane, "A Creative Capacity to Astonish," *Life* 57 (August 21, 1964): 39, 40, 42. An interview, which also reviews Southern's controversial career and his works' mixed reception.

Murray, D. M., "Candy Christian as a Pop-Art Daisy Miller," *Journal of Popular Culture* 5 (Fall 1971): 340-348. Places *Candy* in Voltaire's tradition as picaresque parody and satire.

"No Limits," *Newsweek* 63 (June 22, 1964): 86, 86B. Interview, stressing Southern's interest in attacking smugness and in testing the limits in a society that is fast abandoning limits of every kind.

Silva, Edward T., "From *Candide* to *Candy:* Love's Labor Lost," *Journal of Popular Culture* 8 (Spring 1975): 783-791. Discusses *Candy*'s traditions and its uses of parody, especially of pop psychology.

"Southern, Terry," *Contemporary Literary Criticism,* vol. 7, Mendelson, Phyllis Carmel, and Bryfonski, Dedria, eds. Detroit: Gale, 1977, pp. 452-454. Presents excerpts from major reviews of Southern's novels.

"Southern, Terry," *World Authors 1950-1970,* Wakeman, John, ed. New York: H. W. Wilson, 1975, pp. 1354-1356. Outlines Southern's career and achievements.

Styron, William, "Tootsie Rolls," *New York Review of Books* (May 14, 1964): 8-9. A review of *Candy,* treating it as healthy and exuberant satire.

"Terry Southern," *Dictionary of Literary Biography,* Vol. II: *American Novelists Since World War II,* Helterman, Jeffrey, and Layman, Richard, eds. Detroit: Gale, 1978, pp. 452-455. Surveys Southern's career.

John R. Clark
University of South Florida, Tampa

SCOTT SPENCER
1945

Publishing History

When he was eight years old, Scott Spencer wrote his first novel, the story of a horse captured by Nazis and rescued by an American film maker. He continued to write throughout his childhood. Spencer's first two published novels, *Last Night at the Brain Thieves Ball* (Houghton, 1973) and *Preservation Hall* (Knopf, 1976) received little recognition although Spencer was praised by critics as a writer to watch. His third novel, *Endless Love* (Knopf, 1979) was reviewed widely, became a popular as well as a critical success and established Spencer's reputation as a writer of exceptional depth and power. In May 1986, Knopf published Spencer's fourth novel, *Waking the Dead,* with a first printing of 35,000, conferring upon the book best seller status before it was even reviewed. Between the publication of *Endless Love* and *Waking the Dead,* Spencer wrote the screenplays of *Split Images* and *Act of Vengeance,* the latter directed by Brian DePalma for HBO. Spencer has also contributed stories and articles to *Harper's, The New York Times Book Review, Vanity Fair, Redbook* and *Ladies' Home Journal.*

Endless Love inspired praise for Spencer's descriptive powers, for his creation of a fictional Chicago that, as one reviewer said, Saul Bellow would recognize. Critics commended Spencer for having mastered his craft in a book that was cited as compellingly readable. Because of its dramatic rendering of adolescent passion, *Endless Love* appealed particularly to young people among whom it developed almost cult status.

Critical Reception, Honors, and Popularity

Beginning with *Last Night at the Brain Thieves Ball,* Spencer has enjoyed favorable treatment by critics. In its one published review, *Last Night at the Brain Thieves Ball* was compared to the work of Kurt Vonnegut because of its mix of comedy, social comment and science fiction. With *Preservation Hall,* Spencer was praised for his powers of description and for confronting, albeit obscurely, the universal paradox of the improbable debt that happiness owes to misery. But it was *Endless Love* that propelled Spencer into public recognition. With its explicit passages of teen-age eroticism, its claustrophobic rendering of the narrator's psychotic infatuation with his girlfriend and her family, *Endless Love* had an almost stunning effect on critics. Many reviewers seemed to identify with the narrator, David, and his depiction of the overmastering passion of adolescent love, calling it both a romantic and harrowing portrayal and praising the author for the convincing details of his characters and situations. However, at least one critic objected to the portrait of Jade Butterfield, the girlfriend, on the grounds that Jade is hardly there as a person; she merely represents "affection's symbolic locus."

Endless Love sold very well, was named a notable book of 1979 by the American Library Association and in 1981 was nominated for an American Book Award. Spencer's latest novel, *Waking the Dead,* so far has received fairly good reviews. Critics praised Spencer for moving away from the claustrophobic, self-referential adolescent world of *Endless Love* into the more mature, other-directed realm of politics he creates in *Waking the Dead.* As before, the reviewers commend Spencer for his writing style, for his verbal intensity, for his talent, and for his ability to create memorable characters.

On the negative side, *Waking the Dead* is perceived as slick in that it appears to some critics to have been written with a future Hollywood movie deal in mind. The protagonist, Fielding Pierce, a man with political ambitions, has already been compared to the James Stewart character, Mr. Smith, in *Mr. Smith Goes to Washington.* The eerie subplot, in which Pierce is haunted by the ghost of his former girlfriend can be, it is said, worked into film even more convincingly than it can be worked into a novel. The book also suffers from the limitations of the first-person narrative device: as one critic says, what is gained in intensity is lost in breadth of vision.

However, *Waking the Dead* confronts issues of political corruption, of the dilemma of the moral struggle that a good man must engage in if he wants to do good deeds in a fallen world. For speculating about answers to the questions these issues raise, *Waking the Dead* has earned the respect of critics.

Analysis of Selected Titles

ENDLESS LOVE

Endless Love, 1979, novel.

Social Concerns

Focused on adolescent passion, a traditionally powerful, emotional topic, *Endless Love* opens up the tortured mind of its narrator, sixteen-year-old David Axelrod, and exposes the wreckage left there by the conflict between sexual indulgence and sexual deprivation. David might have been, like Romeo, a symbol of that tender part of the human spirit that ordinarily dies when first love ends. But first love's searing sensation never ends for David and he becomes a misfit, for a time a sociopath, who learns to outwit authority in order to feed the flames of his destructive love for Jade Butterfield.

Most of the action takes place in the late 1960s against a background filled with that era's social concerns juxtaposed against the social concerns of David's parents, leftist Jews who had been active in the labor movement. David's predicament, however, depends less on social issues than on psychological disintegration. Although he appears to be caught between the hedonistic social awareness of the

Butterfields and his parents' legacy of leftist labor union activism, David is essentially isolated, caught in the centripetal vision of the disordered personality.

Themes

Endless Love is about the destructive power of unbridled passion. The book opens with David's setting fire to the Butterfields' house, a desperate publication of David's love for Jade, the seventeen-year-old daughter of Hugh and Ann Butterfield. In Freudian terms, David is the victim of his id, a boy who, in rejecting his conservative parents for Jade's permissive ones, denies his superego; when Jade's father asserts his authority and throws David out of the Butterfield house, (where David had lived for six months, during which time he and Jade had made love almost endlessly) David burns the house down, not in revenge, he says, but to drive Jade out of the house simply so he can see her again. Of course his plan fails and David is committed to three years in a private mental institution. After his release he tries to reunite the now-dispersed Butterfield family and to become part of it again, but the book ends with David alone, ten years older than he was at the book's beginning, but just as pathologically obsessed with Jade as he was then.

David's love for Jade is his only motivating force. It is the *sine qua non* of his life. *Endless Love* reveals the pathetic interior of David's mind, virtually empty except for the furniture of his passion. Because he has failed to develop other aspects of himself, David becomes a symbol of all-consuming lust, a passion that destroys him just as the fire he set destroys the Butterfield house.

Characters

David Axelrod is the narrator and protagonist of *Endless Love.* The reader sees most events through the distorting lens of David's eye, yet the account seems fair. David, not Jade, is the center of the novel and David's feelings for Jade constitute the novel's purpose. Like many neurotic characters, David is hypersensitive, can read others' feelings and motives with uncanny accuracy, and, because his is a single-purpose existence—to get back into bed with Jade—he succeeds to a far greater extent than he has a right to expect.

Unfortunately for him, David's obsession detaches him from the rest of society, which is formed to protect those who cooperate, not those who defy the rules to satisfy their needs. David is doomed to isolation, partly because his neurotic/psychotic attachment to Jade is self-isolating but partly, too, because he refuses to cooperate or to compromise. Like many neurotic people, David manipulates others in his need to fulfill the terms of his own desire. Thus David is the heart of *Endless Love;* the other characters, even Jade, are there only to show how much need one out-of-control heart harbors.

Techniques

Spencer effectively uses the device of the first person narrator to show David in isolation and to emphasize his megalomania. Through flashbacks and other methods of distorting time, David tells his story in great detail, total recall adding to the burden of his neurotic preoccupation with everything that has ever happened to him. At one point, David receives a letter from Ann, Jade's mother. This device expands David's portrait. The letter shows that, though fairly reliable as a narrator, David has not been entirely successful in penetrating the secrets of the Butterfield family; Ann tells him that it was Jade who orchestrated David's banishment from the Butterfield household, not just Hugh, Jade's father.

Thus, though almost all events are filtered through the screen of David's perception, Spencer allows other points of view to seep into David's story, through dialogue and through David's direct encounter with other characters: his parents, his therapists, the Butterfields. All these people directly affect David's well-being, yet all are peripheral to his central concern with his feelings about Jade. Although during most of the book David speaks of Jade in the third person, at very dramatic moments he speaks directly to her. This shift, whether calculated or accidental, underscores David's precarious hold on reality. When at the very end of the novel he addresses Jade and commends the entire account to her as an *apologia,* it is clear that David's condition is hopeless and that rather than defending or vindicating him, the book has revealed that hopelessness.

Literary Precedents

Because it is about an obsession, *Endless Love* may bear some resemblance to *Lolita,* Vladimir Nabokov's exploration of the same territory. In both, the central character lives only for the object of his love and love for the object drives out every other consideration from his mind. Like Humbert Humbert with Lolita, David Axelrod is completely absorbed in Jade, fantasizing about her in her absence, transformed into a helpless supplicant in her presence. Both books present narrators who reveal all the dark secrets of their lives, wrapping their beloved ones in the thick, palpable mist of their desire. And in both, the destructive potential of wholly physical passion is part of the theme.

However, *Endless Love* lacks the dense, textured complexity of *Lolita,* its playfulness and self-deprecating good humor. Spencer creates a fully-detailed, realistic world where the suffering of the narrator, the real focus of the book, is meant to be taken seriously. When David describes the intensity of his passion for Jade, he appears to mean exactly what he says and intends to engage the reader's sympathy if not empathy for his travail. Unlike Nabokov, Spencer uses few, if any distancing devices like humor or irony; he wants the reader to experience what David experiences, relying on the seriousness of David's purpose to convey the admonitory theme.

Adaptations
Endless Love was made into a movie produced by Universal Pictures in 1981. The script was written by Judith Rascoe; the movie starred Brooke Shields and was directed by Franco Zefferelli.

WAKING THE DEAD
Waking the Dead, 1986, novel.

Social Concerns/Themes
While *Waking the Dead* does not repeat the adolescent, destructive-passion theme of *Endless Love,* there is a thread of obsessional memory running through it. Fielding Pierce cannot forget his dead lover, Sarah Williams, a 1960s social activist blown up by a car bomb while transporting Chilean refugees five years before the main action of the book begins. Fielding is not David Axelrod grown up, yet he has the same intense focus on feeling that characterizes David. And since *Waking the Dead* is also a first-person narrative, the protagonist's deepest emotions are exposed as a matter of course and form a substantial part of the novel.

But *Waking the Dead* operates in a wider, more public arena than *Endless Love* does. Pierce is an assistant district attorney from Cook County, Illinois, engaged in running for congress to fulfill a lifetime's ambition. He finds himself contending with big-city political corruption while carrying the banner of the honest man. That Pierce persists despite personal misgivings and growing cynicism about politics attests to his fundamental worth and it is this worthiness that forms the major theme of the novel. In a way Fielding Pierce represents modern, ambitious, selfish yet moral America, rising out of the decay of the past to attend to the business of the present and future.

Characters/Techniques
Like David Axelrod in *Endless Love,* Fielding Pierce is the narrator and protagonist of *Waking the Dead,* a circumstance that accounts for the limited vision of the novel. Pierce tells all about himself and reveals a certain amount of self-righteous, self-pitying attitudinizing in the telling. The success of the book depends entirely on the degree to which the reader sympathizes with the narrator; the danger in this structure is that the narrator, to be a truly round character, must reveal his hidden motives, his pettiness, his smallness of spirit as well as his strengths. As in autobiography, the constant progression of the first person pronoun, I, me, my, mine, can alienate as easily as it can captivate. Then, in telling the story of a politician whose ego necessarily contributes to his success, the novelist runs the risk of creating a monster. But Spencer avoids all these pitfalls, creating in Fielding Pierce a likeable, flawed modern man who will probably contribute as much as any other good

man can to the welfare of the body politic.

The mystery of Sarah Williams forms the subplot to *Waking the Dead* and of course the occasion of the title. Whether Sarah really haunts Fielding or whether she is merely a metaphor of his subconscious, or of his dead past or of the death of American political ideals must be decided by the individual reader.

Additional Sources

Batchelor, John Calvin, "Fashioning a Life for Politics," *The Philadelphia Inquirer* (25 May 1986): T8-9. Review of *Waking the Dead*.

Broyard, Anatole, "The High Cost of Loving," *New York Times* (19 October 1976): 43. Review of *Preservation Hall*.

Contemporary Authors, vol. 113. Detroit: Gale Research, pp. 461-462.

Gray, Paul, "Ambitions," *Time* (19 May 1986): 102. Review of *Waking the Dead* by Scott Spencer.

Kolson, Ann, "Is it Obsession?" *The Philadelphia Inquirer* (7 June 1986): C1, 8. Discusses *Waking the Dead*.

Psychology Today (November 1973): 140. *Review of Last Night at the Brain Thieves Ball.*

Weldon, Fay, "The Moral Struggle of a Cad," *New York Times Book Review* (18 May 1986): 11. Review of *Waking the Dead*.

Janet Alwang
Penn State University

MICKEY SPILLANE
1918

Publishing History

Among modern day detective writers, Mickey Spillane has positioned himself as the most "commercial." By his own account, he writes for money, not pleasure, and his publishing career indicates that he has achieved his purpose. Since the publication of his first novel, *I, the Jury*, in 1947, he has produced over 20 best-selling suspense novels, several of which have been made into movies.

Spillane's ego and bombastic speeches are, in part, accountable for his public image. He has appeared both as the model for the cover of one of his books and as the lead role in *The Girl Hunters*. He fancies himself to look like Mike Hammer, he married a model who posed for the same book jacket as the one he appeared on, he ridicules his critics, and seems indifferent to his readers. He claims to have written one novel in three days, and that most are written in two weeks. Television has also contributed to his success, both as a forum for his Mike Hammer stories and as a place for him to appear in commercials. Spillane's self-assurance, resourcefulness, and endurance have characterized his career. He began selling stories at 17, supported himself through college by writing comic books, served as a fighter pilot and flight instructor in the Air Force during World War II, and worked as a trampoline artist for Ringling Bros. circus before declaring himself a full time writer. His personality has helped to shape both his characters and the direction of his publishing success.

Critical Reception, Honors, and Popularity

Nearly all critics and readers alike agree that Spillane's brand of detective-suspense fiction is derivative of Dashiell Hammett, Raymond Chandler, and Ross Macdonald, and Spillane is frequently criticized for his gratuitous sex and violence. Nonetheless, he has developed a devoted readership who are attracted to his Mike Hammer figure and his proclivity for telling a fast paced story. As many as fifty million of his books may have been sold, six million sales attributed to *I, the Jury*, alone. That Spillane himself is an adventurous, tough, romanticized personality contributes to his popularity and, in readers' minds, establishes his credibility as a writer of detective fiction.

Analysis of Selected Titles

I, THE JURY

I, the Jury, 1947, novel.

Social Concerns/Themes

Spillane is a product of a generation which was toughened by hardships of World War II, romanticized by the hope of a better world, shaken in its belief of the goodness of mankind, and fiercely self-reliant and proud of its performance in the war. Perhaps more than any other fictional character of his time, Mike Hammer reflects the mood of the country which spawned him. If Norman Mailer's *The Naked and the Dead* profiles the horrors and difficulties of heroism during World War II, Mike Hammer in *I, the Jury* is the earliest prototype of the modern "anti-hero"; a type of literary character which shaped much post World War II fiction. Readers shouldn't lose touch with the significance of *I, the Jury* as a war novel, published shortly after the armistice and three years before *The Naked and the Dead*.

As the anti-hero came to be defined, his characteristics were: (1) mistrust and irreverence for all establishments, (2) joy in using the establishment to attain ends which were contrary to the establishment's purposes, (3) cleverness in turning the establishment against itself, and (4) atypical moral values which permitted the anti-hero to break the rules with a clear conscience. Hammer's brand of anti-heroism included revenge and murder, and it is a fine line between Hammer as anti-hero and Hammer as criminal. For Hammer, the end justifies the means, and in *I, the Jury*, the revenge of his friend's murder isn't particularly noble. In Hammer's world, the "establishment" includes drug rings, the Mafia, and gangs, as well as society's establishments of the police force and court system. Hammer regards all organizations/establishments as havens for criminals, and so he appoints himself a one-man vigilante—a kind of Lone Ranger, Batman, or Superman who is justified in dealing out punishment.

The most shocking social concern in *I, the Jury*, and in succeeding Mike Hammer novels, is Hammer's willingness to embrace being judge, jury, and executioner. As a resourceful, self appointed keeper of anti-heroic principles, he feels completely justified in dealing with hoodlums any way he pleases. Hoodlums are as much an enemy as the Germans during the war, and so he approaches his mission as if it were combat. Charlotte, his lover and the killer of his friend, is as cunning and seductive as a war spy. His cold blooded murder of her defiantly establishes that he is above the law.

Readers should not make too much of social concerns in most detective fiction. It isn't a genre for conveying ideas, and Spillane is the first to say that there's nothing more to his stories than a good story. But the popularity of his Mike Hammer books, published between 1947–1952, and readers' admiration for Hammer's style indicate a shift in values after World War II. That he is willing to shoot his lover while she is performing a strip tease to distract him from his deadly intention reflects a modern American propensity to conclude that people get what they deserve. Charlotte gets hers, and Hammer walks away satisfied that he's performed his duty. His coolness in such a personal killing, his loyalty to his dead friend, and his resoluteness to his goals cause the character to rise above his society, reaffirming the value of the individual above all else.

Characters/Techniques

Hammer is so egocentric that he considers only certain types of white men worthy of his loyalty. He is a bigot, a racist, and a sexist, unlike, say Perry Mason, who is at all times considerate. Hammer's attitudes toward the people he considers less worthy, combined with his anti-heroic persona, make him into a destructive role model for unaware readers. Although James Bond is as headstrong and independent of the law as Hammer, he stands for certain admirable social values, while Hammer is admired for his flippancy, irreverence, intolerance, and lack of emotion.

It is critically unfair to attack Hammer's character because he doesn't personify noble human traits. Hammer's world is not the reader's world. It isn't even the real criminal world but a romanticized, closed world where one exceptional man can conquer. While James Bond has the technical devices of Her Majesty's Secret Service to help him, and Perry Mason is supported by the courts, Hammer is alone. Neither especially brilliant nor physically strong, he is able to follow a trail of clues, discover the killer, and take revenge.

In comparing Hammer's world to Bond's or Mason's, it becomes clear that Spillane is creating characters who represent extremities rather than real people. It is useful to know that Spillane supported his way through college writing comic books and considers himself one of the creators of the Captain Marvel, Captain America generation. Spillane populates his novels with very odd, different-than-life characters. In *I, the Jury*, the suspects include identical twins, one of whom is a nymphomaniac, a reformed gangster, and a moron beekeeper. By using psychologically and physically deformed people, Spillane drops a curtain between reality and entertainment so that whatever fate befalls any character except Hammer isn't a disturbing loss.

Hammer also tends to render scenes in frames similar to the panels of a comic book. If each panel is whole and logical, Spillane doesn't worry that the logical continuity from panel to panel works. The clues which Hammer uncovers in one panel lead him to the next, but the logical framework of the previous panel doesn't matter as the novel unfolds. The breaks in logic don't bother Spillane as much as they have some readers, perhaps because he thinks the entertainment value of his books is more in the picture he draws than in the reader's involvement in solving the mystery.

Literary Precedents

Mike Hammer is both derivative of his predecessors and frequently imitated by his successors. He is much like Dashiell Hammett's Sam Spade, and equally unlike Perry Mason and James Bond. Both Erle Stanley Gardner and Ian Fleming are competitors for Spillane's readership, and he is frequently compared to them, as well as to Ross Macdonald. The difference between Hammer and Mason/Bond are important. Perry Mason, in the tradition of Agatha Christie's detectives, uses a public forum (usually the courtroom) to untangle the mystery and expose the killer. Hammer solves the mystery himself, confronts the killer, reiterates the killer's crimes to his face, elicits a silent consent of guilt, then kills him/her. For instance, as Charlotte Manning fights for her life by stripping while Hammer holds a gun on her, he outlines the methodical evil of her brutal spider web. Mason works within the law, believing in its ultimate ability to control society, while Hammer uses the law only as a tool to reach his own ends. Mason depends on intellect to construct the logic of his clues; Hammer depends on his powers to force clues out of hiding.

James Bond is more of Mike Hammer's ilk than Perry Mason. Bond is willing to kill, although he seldom uses his 007 license. Bond's adversaries are often physically and emotionally deformed. The solution to Bond's dilemmas are often a result of chance rather than logical deduction. The differences between Hammer and Bond, however, are more significant than appearances of the stylish, refined Bond and the natural, rough Hammer. Bond believes that order can be restored to a world structure that governs society. Bond will not use his superior prowess to take advantage of other people (even his women are willing, equal partners in bed), and while Bond is totally self-sufficient and alone in life, he isn't fighting to prove that his will is greater than society's. Hammer is a struggling hero, Bond is a completed one.

More interesting comparisons to Spillane than his contemporary mystery writers are the books which develop the anti-heroes of post-World War II literature. While these books had no influence on Spillane's development as a writer, they can offer the reader pleasure in understanding why Mike Hammer is appealing as a tough guy hero. Two useful examples are Ken Kesey's *One Flew Over the Cuckoo's Nest* and Joseph Heller's *Catch-22*. Both novels, published in 1962, use larger-than-life, comic book like characters. McMurphy, in *One Flew Over the Cuckoo's Nest*, is a Captain Marvel type hero while Big Nurse is a Spider Lady type villain. Yossarian, the quintessential anti-hero of *Catch-22*, passes through the establishment almost untouched by its ludicrousness, while Milo Minderbender completely manipulates the establishment for his selfish gain. All four characters can exist only in a world in which reality is measured in severely different terms. One recurring theme in these two novels, as well as Kurt Vonnegut's *Slaughterhouse-Five*, is depicting the only means of survival in an absurd world in which the old order establishment is not only useless but evil in the chains it uses to shackle the modern hero. Mike Hammer's world is equally absurd and Hammer cuts the same kind of self-reliant, defiant figure as McMurphy and Milo. Readers who are willing to accept Spillane as a product of World War II who reflects a radically different, naive American society, may see interesting parallels between *I, the Jury*, *Catch-22*, *One Flew Over the Cuckoo's Nest* and *Slaughterhouse-Five*.

Adaptations

Spillane's novels have been adapted into six full-length Hollywood movies, one made for television movie, and two television series. United Artists produced four of the six Hollywood versions: *I, the Jury* (1953, with Biff Elliott), *The Long Wait* (1954), *Kiss Me, Deadly* (1955, with Robert Gray), and *My Gun Is Quick* (1957, with Ralph Meeker). Spillane, himself, plays Mike Hammer in *The Girl Hunters* (1963, produced by Colorama). *The Delta Factor* was released in 1970 by Continental. *Murder Me, Murder You* starring Stacy Keach was the title of CBS' 1983 movie. NBC produced the first series in 1958 (*Mike Hammer, Detective*), and CBS produced *Mickey Spillane's Mike Hammer* in 1984, which continues to air.

Other Titles

Vengeance Is Mine! 1950, (novel); *My Gun Is Quick*, 1950 (novel); *The Big Kill*, 1951 (novel); *One Lonely Night*, 1951 (novel); *The Long Wait*, 1951 (novel); *Kiss Me, Deadly*, 1952 (novel); *The Deep*, 1961 (novel); *The Girl Hunters*, 1962 (novel); *Me, Hood!*, 1963 (stories); *Day of the Guns*, 1964 (novel); *The Snake*, 1964 (novel); *The Flier*, 1964 (stories); *The Death Dealers*, 1965 (novel); *Bloody Sunrise*, 1965 (novel); *The Twisted Thing*, 1966 (novel, published in 1971 with the title *For Whom the Gods Would Destroy*); *The By-Pass Control*, 1967 (novel); *The Body Lovers*, 1967 (novel); *The Delta Factor*, 1967 (novel); *Killer Mine*, 1968 (stories); *The Tough Guys*, 1970 (stories); *Survival*, 1970 (novel); *The Erection Set*, 1972 (novel); *The Last Cop Out*, 1973 (novel); *Tomorrow I Die*, 1984 (novel).

Additional Sources

Collins, Max Allan, and Traylor, James L., *One Lonely Night: Mickey Spillane's Mike Hammer*. Bowling Green, OH: Bowling Green State University Press, 1984. Analyzes Mike Hammer's character and function through all of the novels in which Hammer appears as the hero. This is an exhaustive, excellent source for readers who want to understand what makes Hammer such a receptive hero.

Van Dover, J. Kenneth, *Murder in the Millions: Erle Stanley Gardner, Mickey Spillane, Ian Fleming*. New York: Frederick Ungar, 1984. Although at times too lengthy on plot summary, Van Dover offers some astute critical insights into the social significance of these three writers, and suggests provocative comparisons between them.

Walton Beacham

DANIELLE STEEL
1947

Publishing History

Over 60 million copies of books written by Danielle Steel are currently in print, and the American Booksellers Association reported in September 1982 that the top seven titles in the mass market romance paperback category were written by Steel. Another survey showed that Danielle Steel is the only woman among the five most popular writers in America today. Her publisher reports that, since 1981, there has not been a week when one of her books was not on the *New York Times* Best Seller List.

One of the reasons for this phenomenon is the frequency with which new Danielle Steel books appear on the shelves. *Passions' Promise* appeared in 1976, three years after her first novel *Going Home*. In that gap Danielle Steel had turned out four novels that no publisher wanted. But then she hit it big producing paperback romances for Dell, and the books arrived annually, *Passions' Promise* in 1976, *Now and Forever* and *The Promise* in 1977, *Season of Passion* in 1978, *Summer's End* and *To Love Again* in 1979, *The Ring* and *Loving* in 1980, *Palamino* and *Remembrance* in 1981, *A Perfect Stranger* and *Crossings* in 1982, *Changes* and *Thurston House* in 1983, *Full Circle, Love* and *Family Album* in 1984, *Secrets* in 1985 and *Wanderlust* in 1986.

The story behind this prolific writer is in many ways similar to the plots of her novels. Born of a German father, a member of Munich's Lowenbrau beer dynasty, and the daughter of a Portuguese diplomat, who divorced when Danielle was eight, she lived with her playboy father, attended schools in New York, married first a wealthy French banker, then a supportive social worker, and finally a shipping executive. She also produced six children, so that the adventures, the choices, the search for a workable marriage relationship which her heroines experience is based to some degree on her own experiences. So too are the trials and joys of raising a family, which feature so largely in her later novels.

Critical Reception, Honors, and Popularity

The popularity of Danielle Steel can be assumed from the eagerness with which readers await the arrival of her latest book. Critics at first ignored her writing, placing it in the category of formula pulp romance, considered beneath their notice, until her popularity and longevity were confirmed. Once sampled, critics were surprised at the credibility of the conflicts facing Steel's protagonists and the primacy of personal choices and concerns over glamorous adventures among the rich and ruthless. Critics agreed that the cliches were still present in large numbers, and plots suffered from some contrivance, but they agreed also that these novels were "a good read."

Each subsequent Steel novel has received full and serious criticism in major review journals, in which praise has been extended to her well-crafted plots and attention to private personal reality. Criticism has been levelled at the rapid developments and narrow focus on love relationships which are inherent to the genre of romance.

Analysis of Selected Titles

LOVING

Loving, 1980, novel.

Social Concerns/Themes/Characters

This, as with many of Steel's books, is an examination of a young woman's journey from youth to maturity, from ignorance in the art of loving, through a series of relationships with men, to self knowledge and a mature, balanced relationship. As all of Steel's novels deal with the nature of love between men and women, this book provides a compendium of possible relationships.

The first significant man in Bettina's life is her father, a celebrated and egotistical author. Although Bettina's life appears to be all that is glamorous and desirable, it is in fact hollow and destructive, a perfect example of the seductive quality of fame and wealth. Bettina lives in a jeweled cage, pampered and protected, but also used, as her entire life is geared towards pleasing her father at the expense of her own personality.

Bettina's father dies, and she is comforted by her father's friend Ivo Stewart, and then unfolds another fantasy story in the Cinderella mode. This cultured and much older man offers Bettina a more generous love than her father did, but it is still paternalism. Ivo allows her to explore her love of theatre while maintaining the gilded cage of wealth and nurturing. For example, Bettina gets a job in an experimental theatre but is picked up every night after the show by her husband's limousine.

The best thing Ivo does for Bettina is force her to leave him, again like a father who observes that the beloved young woman has grown up and is ready to fly the cage. Bettina precipitates this by falling into an affair with a very attractive actor, Anthony Pierce, but even before Bettina realizes it, Steel signals to the reader that this young man spouts the dangerous and egotistical charm of Bettina's father. So Bettina falls into the pattern of subjugating herself to the needs of others, as with Anthony, who dumps Bettina as fast as possible when she finds herself pregnant.

This appears to be the lowest point this still young heroine can experience. She loses the child and attempts suicide, but in the hospital another romantic fantasy appears to be unfolding. The handsome young doctor attending her reveals that he, too, is lonely and eager for someone to love, and Bettina finds herself ensconced in an urban gilded cage. John Fields is supportive of her emotional and physical needs, but tries to squeeze Bettina into the mold of wife and mother to which he ascribes. Bettina is forced to hide her play writing attempts, a clear sign of the destructive qualities of this superficially attractive relationship. But it is at the birth of her first child that the husband's true nature is revealed. All of the needs of the woman are ignored in pursuit of the perfect delivery from the obstetrician's point of view, and John, a doctor, sides with his medical colleague instead of his wife.

Bettina's growth as an individual is signaled by her ability to think through the faults of the situation and leave it of her own accord, as opposed to all of the previous relationships, which were ended by the man. She finds herself in New York, having received a rather implausible "lucky break" in finding a producer for her first play. She also meets one of the breed of new men, gentle, loving, and as giving to Bettina's needs as she had always been to men around her. In fact, he is willing to put his career as a successful theatre critic in second place behind Bettina's growing success as a playwright.

This appears to be the perfect relationship, but Steel suggests otherwise. There is no spark, no fire, no tension between two equally vivid and dynamic individuals. Bettina needs a man as powerful and successful and special as she is, a man like her father as she is now a woman like her father, and Steel contrives that she be free and ready to fall in love when this ideal mate appears in the final chapter of the book.

Loving is a compendium of traditional female fantasy relations, celebrated so often in romance, and Steel takes each one and shows how it is potentially a trap for a woman, particularly one who has not learned much about her own needs, her own personality. Yet the book is not anti-male. There is never any suggestion that the entire system is geared by men to exploit women. Rather, women are responsible to learn about themselves, to grow up, and if need be, to experiment with relationships until they are capable of loving as fully and maturely as possible.

In this book, as in several others, Steel explores relationships which, traditionally, have been frowned upon. In this case, Bettina is a much divorced woman, yet her experiences are shown in a sympathetic light, so that the reader understands how such things might come about, without either judging harshly or glorifying unduly.

Literary Precedents

All of Danielle Steel's novels are shelved with mass market romance paperback fiction; yet, in many ways she transcends the genre. The central concern of her novels is the search for a lasting love relationship. While the characters are uniformly wealthy, beautiful and involved in exciting occupations, events or experiences, beneath the surface level of plot and character description is the real key to Steel's phenomenal popularity. She uses all of the traditions of the formula, but they are secondary to the real focus, which is the uncertainties, conflicts, choices and mistakes that anyone could and most people do experience. Readers are treated to extraordinary, exciting and exotic events which provide escape from the daily grind of ordinary existence, and also ordinary, familiar and recognizable problems, which are not easily solved but which fail to destroy or defeat the love at the center of the story. Readers can make direct application of the choices and triumphs of the fictional characters to their own lives.

FULL CIRCLE

Full Circle, 1984, novel.

Social Concerns/Themes/Characters

In this novel Steel presents another young woman living and growing and learning about herself and the nature of love between men and women. Tana observes and judges harshly her mother, caught in a long term affair with her boss who fails to offer marriage even after his wife has died. Tana's first encounter with sex is also negative: she is raped by this same boss's son, and her mother refuses to believe her. Tana slowly overcomes the scars of these early experiences, but in the course of her life makes her own mistakes. She maintains a close platonic relationship with one man, has a brief, passionate and ultimately untimely affair with that friend's father, and then finds herself in a situation which mirrors her mother's. She meets an attractive, compatible man with just one problem: he has just separated from his wife. Tana's mother warns her that he might not be emotionally separated, and sure enough, Tana becomes the other woman, left alone at Christmas, always waiting for the phone to ring. Tana, and the reader, must reevaluate the harsh judgement placed on the first mistress, and to understand how such things come about. Tana is able to summon the courage to end the relationship, and begin another based entirely on compatibility. This, too, is finally revealed to be a dead end, and in the final chapters of the book Tana has the good fortune of meeting and marrying a suitable man.

Tana's life raises another social issue, for she is a very successful lawyer, and a great deal of her conflict with her mother and with the men in her life centers on her enjoyment in her work and the traditional view of the role of women. Tana's mother wants her to marry for wealth, security and a place in society. Tana argues that she has achieved all these on her own. Her compatible lover is offended when Tana's career is more successful than his own, and subtly and overtly presents blocks to her advancement. It is only in her final relationship, and only marriage, that Tana makes the important discovery, with her husband's help, that she can have it all, a happy marriage, an exciting career, and a family too.

Techniques

Steel spans two full generations in this novel, showing the early years for Tana's mother during and after World War II, in an attempt to explain the older woman's options and choices. This provides a contrast with Tana's life, and heightens the irony of Tana ending up in the same compromise relationship that her mother chose. Steel also touches on contemporary political issues by having Tana attend a southern girls' college and be roomed with its first black student. Tana finds herself drawn into the civil rights movement, and tragedy occurs when both her roomate's brother and the young girl herself are killed. But this is just a brief interlude in Tana's life, and she does not remain involved in the civil rights movement.

Similarily, the war in Vietnam makes itself felt, as Tana's platonic friend allows himself to be drafted, to Tana's horror, and returns paralyzed from war wounds. But this too is a personal rather than political issue for Tana, and she marshalls her considerable energies getting her friend interested in life again rather than fighting against the war. She has a brief sexual relationship with a student radical, but refuses to become involved in his activities, which is just as well because he is caught trying to blow up the governor's house.

These political and historical events ground the novel in American history, and thus lend the story credibility, but remain secondary to the main concern, which is Tana's growing understanding of the complexities of love.

CROSSINGS

Crossings, 1982, novel.

Social Concerns/Themes/Characters

This novel is set during World War II, and although relationships between men and women remain Steel's dominant concern, the social and political realities of the period are also explored. Liane is happily married to her French husband Armand de Villers at the beginning of the novel, so that when she first meets Nick Burnham, unhappily married to the spoiled Hilary, she offers him sensitive sympathy only. Nick realizes that this is the sort of woman he considers ideal: a good mother, a loyal wife, and gently, purely beautiful as opposed to his own wife's flaunted sexuality. Nick's marriage is held together only by his concern for his son, but Liane's much stronger relationship is torn apart by external pressures. Armand is returned to France at the beginning of the war and then, at the fall of France, is forced to choose between his love of his wife and children and his love for his country. He chooses to send his family back to America and remain in Nazi-occupied France, apparently cooperating with the Germans but secretly assisting the underground.

Liane, in turn, remains loyal to her husband despite the public knowledge of his collaboration and the cruel prejudice of her old friends. Even her family attempts to force her into a divorce, but she remains married to Armand. Besides the external pressure, there is a private conflict; Liane and Nick have met again, fallen in love, and now struggle to suppress their passion in loyalty to her husband and in hopes of saving his son from a messy divorce.

Steel presents a tortured love affair, where neither of the lovers is wicked, where both try to do the best they can, and yet where people are still hurt, where tragedy cannot be avoided. The novel suggests that actions should not be judged unless one knows all the facts; an apparent traitor may be a loyal citizen sacrificing all, and an errant wife may be caught between loyalty and passion and be simply trying to hurt the fewest number of people.

Adaptations

Crossings was made into a mini-series on ABC-TV. Cheryl Ladd played Liane, Christopher Plummer was Armand, Lee Horsley was Nick and Jane Seymour was the bitchy Hilary.

CHANGES

Changes, 1983, novel.

Social Concerns/Themes

This novel explores the problems of a working woman juggling children and a challenging career. Melanie Adams seems to have it all: a high-profile and high-paying job as anchor of a national news broadcast, and attractive and well-adjusted teenage twin daughters. But at what price? She has not allowed herself to risk deep involvement with a man since the father of the twins walked out on her years before the story begins. When she does meet a special man, all sorts of questions are raised which she and her lover must answer.

Peter Hallman has an equally successful and glamorous career; he is a heart surgeon, and he, too, is leery of falling in love as he is still recovering from the death of his wife. But despite their uncertainty and a lengthy courtship, they finally must admit that they are in love. And now the trouble begins.

Melanie and Peter explore the sorts of compromises which make a mature relationship survive. This story doesn't end with the marriage ceremony, for Steel is very interested in just how one lives happily ever after. She shows the tensions which exist between husband and wife, no matter how loving they might be. The situation for Melanie and Peter is complicated by the new extended family; Melanie's two girls must share their mother with Peter and his three children.

Steel explores some of the problems parents must face. The youngest boy is lost in the mountains over night. Then Peter's son and Melanie's daughter begin a relationship, and a pregnancy results. Neither Melanie nor Peter deal with these problems perfectly, which endears them to the reader. In fact, there is no perfect solution, because the daily tensions, large and small, cannot be eliminated except in fantasy.

Underlying all the tensions, though, is a single problem which is finally addressed and solved, giving hope for a smoother life ahead. Both Peter and Melanie are afraid of change, but Melanie conquers her fears and commits herself to a new life. Peter, however, is less willing to change, to compromise, to adjust his life to accommodate his new partner. Finally Melanie leaves him for a time, and he realizes not only what she means to him but also how limited he has been in his growth. Life demands constant change, and rigidity can only destroy the positive aspects of living and loving.

Characters

Melanie and Peter are both, on the surface, stereotypes of contemporary fantasy characters. Melanie is the new superwoman, a success as mother, in her career, respected, financially secure as a result of her own hard work, and also beautiful, warm, loving and loved. Yet readers see the flaws in her otherwise perfect life, the emptiness at the center. And when she chooses change and chance over secure success, they applaud her growth.

Peter first appears as the attractive doctor of romance, dedicated to work, but also lonely and longing for love. Beneath this surface lies the truth that the very things that make him a good doctor make him a poor husband; he is rigid, unwilling to change, and he cares so much for his patients that his family suffers. As his character unfolds, the reader likes him more, for his fears and weaknesses make him more believable and approachable a character.

This then is the key to Steel's success in creating appealing characters. They are uniformly attractive and usually wealthy and successful, but on closer examination she reveals flaws which mark them as little different from the ordinary reader. All the wealth and beauty is little help in dealing with the most important aspects of life: the relationships between men, women, and their children.

FAMILY ALBUM

Family Album, 1984, novel.

Social Concerns/Themes/Characters

At first glance this novel appears to be set in the familiar mode of Hollywood saga of stardom, scandal and secrets. But Hollywood is merely the background for the relationships of family members. In this case, the tension between parents and children is even more central than the working out of the love between husband and wife.

Faye and Ward Thayer have their ups and down as a couple, but their children experience some of the problems which worry parents from California to New Jersey and beyond. Lionel, their oldest son, is a homosexual, and Steel presents his search for identity and love sympathetically. Faye and Ward, particularly Ward, are horrified by the discovery, but Steel asks her readers not to judge but to understand. She also presents tasteful sexual scenes and a homosexual marriage situation, a first in her writing and perhaps a surprise to many of her readers. Steel avoids stereotypes in Lionel, and places no blame for his sexual preference. Rather, it is presented as simply an aspect of his character, and he, like everyone else in the novel, is searching only for love and security.

Greg, the second son, is an all-American hero but, for all his success with women and on the football field, is a less appealing young man than his brother. With his character Steel explores another shared family experience, the loss of a son and brother in Vietnam. Both Lionel and Greg serve in Vietnam; Lionel volunteers after a lover is tragically killed and Greg is drafted when he flunks out of college. He dies when he steps on a land mine two weeks after being sent overseas. The cruelty of the loss, in the irony of the statistics is brought home in this sudden and unexpected death.

Ward and Faye have twin daughters, Valerie and Vanessa, and with these two girls Steel explores various options in relationships and life choices for young women. Vanessa is the wild one, battling with her mother, sexually promiscuous, but finally fulfilling her promise and emerging as an outstanding actress. Valerie opts for college, where she finds a compatible, if not perfect, lover. In contrasting the two girls, Steel avoids judgements, but suggests that, despite their different avenues, both were seeking the same thing: fulfillment of their talents and energies as individuals, and only then a lasting, loving relationship.

The youngest child, Anne, presents the most problems for her parents, but Steel lays the blame firmly at Faye's door. When the other children were little, the Thayers had lots of money and Faye was able to devote herself to nurturing her family. But just after Anne's birth, it becomes apparent that Ward has squandered the family fortune, and Faye becomes the sole supporter of the family. Suddenly, she is just too busy to pay any attention to her youngest child. Anne grows up in the shadows, and makes the most spectacular and sensational mistakes of the children. She runs off to Haight Ashbury and joins a cult which indulges in multiple drug and sex orgies. Her family rescues her, but she is pregnant, and Faye forces her to give the child up for adoption. Only near the end of the novel is Faye able to admit that she was wrong in this, though she did it for the best, and Anne is able to agree. By this time Anne has followed a completely different route in her search for love and security. She has formed a relationship with the father of one of her friends, and this unconventional marriage turns out to be a suitable one for her.

At the center of the novel is Faye, a strong woman who makes choices and then lives with the results of her choices, admirable in her determination and endurance, and frightening in the force of her personality. She fights to keep the family together, observes the mistakes she makes. She demands a great deal from others as well as from herself, and loves as best she can. In this character Steel has created a complex, flawed and yet heroic woman. One understands why her children fight her influence and seek her approval. Externally, she is a figure from fantasy: beautiful, intelligent, the first major female director in Hollywood. But at home, she is just a mother, doing the best she can in the complex and imperfect relationships which are part of ordinary and real life.

Other Titles

Novels: *Passions' Promise*, 1976; *Now and Forever*, 1977; *The Promise*, 1977; *Season of Passion*, 1978; *Summer's End*, 1979; *To Love Again*, 1979; *The Ring*, 1980; *Palamino*, 1981; *Remembrance*, 1981; *A Perfect Stranger*, 1982; *Thurston House*, 1983; *Love*, 1984; *Secrets*, 1985; *Wanderlust*, 1986.

Additional Sources

Cosmopolitan (February 1985). Biographical sketch of Steel.

New York Times Book Review (October 3, 1982). First major review of Steel's work. The reviewer asserts that due to the author's phenomenal popularity, *Crossings* is "worth at least a cursory examination." Though skeptical of Steel's brand of fiction, the reviewer concludes that the novel is entertaining, with a well-structured plot and endearing characters.

New York Times Book Review (September 11, 1983). Review of *Changes*. Steel is credited with creating poignant scenes without descending into melodrama, and particularly praised for her credible telling of familiar painful family crises.

People Weekly (February 5, 1979). Brief biographical article.

Ramsey, Nancy, *New York Times Book Review* (August 19, 1984). Brief, mixed review of *Full Circle*. Ramsey concludes that: "Cliches abound, characters come and then go just as quickly, but the lively plot and fast romp over the past three decades make the book a good read."

Time (February 24, 1986). Biographical sketch.

Leslie O'Dell
Wilfrid Laurier University

MARY STEWART
1916

Publishing History

Mary Stewart grounded herself thoroughly in English literature before she decided to become a writer. In 1938 she received her B.A. with first-class honors in English language and literature at Durham University. Three years later she earned her master's degree and subsequently taught English as a lecturer at her alma mater. She began writing in 1949 when she found "this I could do, this I must do. Storytelling came as naturally as leaves to a tree, and it was a pity (I told myself) that I had wasted so much time." She had published literary articles and poems before, but now she began work on a story called "Murder for Charity" which later became her first novel *Madam, Will You Talk?*

Although she had no intention of publishing *Madam, Will You Talk?*, her husband persuaded her to send it away. After its success, she published ten more romantic suspense novels—all of which have been best sellers—and by 1967 had a following of four million readers. She then switched to historical romance with her Merlin trilogy and achieved her greatest popular and critical success. *The Hollow Hills,* the middle book of the trilogy, for example, was on the New York Times Best Seller List for thirty-five weeks.

Since writing the trilogy, she has published another suspense novel and one more Arthurian novel, as well as three books for children. Her stories have been serialized in magazines and on the radio; *The Moonspinners* became a popular Walt Disney movie; and her books have been translated into sixteen languages, including Hebrew, Icelandic, and Slovak.

Critical Reception, Honors, and Popularity

Mary Stewart's suspense and historical novels have both received praise and honors. She was elected Fellow of the Royal Society of the Arts in 1968. *The Crystal Cave* appeared on the ALA Best Young Adult Book List and received the Frederick Niven prize from the Scottish Chapter of the International PEN Association in 1971. She has also been honored by the Scottish Arts Council.

Stewart's credible, sensible heroines and careful evocation of place have helped her romantic suspense stories rise above the formulas of her two most popular contemporaries, Victoria Holt and Phyllis Whitney. Of her romances, the earliest are considered to be her best. These stories have been called "genuine triumphs of a minor art." In her Merlin trilogy, however, Stewart displayed her greatest talents in storytelling and created what is regarded as her most enduring literary contribution. Although Stewart will never be categorized on the same level as such major contemporaries as Graham Greene, her works will continue to be appreciated for their richly imaginative prose, complex characterization, and suspenseful plotting.

Analysis of Selected Titles

THE HOLLOW HILLS

The Hollow Hills, 1973, novel, second in the Merlin trilogy, which includes: (1) *The Crystal Cave,* 1970; (3) *The Last Enchantment,* 1979. Continuation of Arthur story in *The Wicked Day,* 1983.

Social Concerns

The Hollow Hills shows a nation in the midst of political and religious turmoil, half-faithful to the old gods and to a kingdom united under a Roman-type of government and half-accepting of Christianity and of individual scheming for glory. As such, the novel's concerns are not far from those of American society in the early 1970s, a society confused by the upheaval of values brought on by the Vietnam War and Watergate and undergoing a revival of "born-again" Christianity. As the Britons of the sixth century sought in Arthur a hero-king to unite the kingdom and clear the confusion, so Americans of the 1970s looked back with nostalgia to the "Camelot" days of the young and vigorous President John F. Kennedy and longed for a new white knight to cleanse the nation of moral decay and to infuse hope.

Another social preoccupation of the 1960s and 1970s which *The Hollow Hills* mirrors is the interest in psychic powers, into predicting the future and into the consequences of knowing the future. In *The Hollow Hills* Merlin often muses about his powers and the difference they have made in his life, a difference which has not always been comfortable. In many ways this interest in foretelling the future and extra-sensory powers grows out of the before-mentioned political despair and the turning to religion for solace and answers.

Themes

Closely related to the social concerns of *The Hollow Hills* is its main theme and indeed the main theme of the entire Merlin-Arthur story: man's free choice and reconciliation to his destiny. Merlin in *The Crystal Cave* has the choice between manhood and power, chooses power, and spends the rest of his life helping his second self—Arthur—achieve power over the nation. Arthur in *The Hollow Hills* follows his destiny to become the warrior king but sows the seed of his own death when he sleeps with his half-sister Morgause, impregnating her with Mordred. Mordred in *The Wicked Day* knows of the prophecy that he will bring about his father's death, loves and serves his father, yet becomes enraptured by power and trapped by circumstance into living out the prophecy. Stewart thus seems to believe that man has some measure of free will but that this free will carries awesome responsibility and always works in keeping with the greater will of God, destiny or fate.

Characters

Stewart's impetus in writing the Merlin trilogy was to invent a life for Merlin, who most often appears in the King Arthur stories as an old man. In *The Crystal Cave* Merlin appears as a boy and comes to terms with his prophetic powers. In *The Hollow Hills* Merlin, now a young man in his twenties, becomes a conduit between this world and the otherworld as he seeks to bring about the will of the gods. In addition to facilitating the plot, he narrates the story; and, because the reader often sees into his mind, to Merlin also falls the majority of the thematic statements of the book.

Stewart works hard to make Merlin more than a character of legend. Besides having him comment on the physical painfulness and yet the joy of the gift of prophecy, she has him be very much aware of what he has sacrificed in service to the gods: having his own family and claiming his own rights to the kingdom. Yet he is not the typical hermit or holy man—several characters comment on the command in his bearing and his walk. Despite Stewart's efforts, though, Merlin's main function remains as mouthpiece and plot facilitator, and he still seems an old man. The real focus and interest of the story continues to be Arthur, as perhaps the events of the legend make inevitable.

Techniques

Stewart's background as a writer of eleven novels and as a writer of suspense stands her well in the writing of the Merlin trilogy. Her challenge was to invest a legend retold hundreds of times in verse, prose, drama and film with enough imagination and tight-plotting to make it interesting to readers on all levels of familiarity with the story. The imagination appears most clearly in her use of striking metaphors, similes and imagery to embody themes and convey character— Merlin's visions "real as pain in the blood, and piercing the brain like ice" or Ygraine, once a "wild bird beating her wings against the wires of the cage" now brooding "wings clipped, gravid, a creature of the ground."

Stewart also knows how to build suspense, particularly by the sense of foreboding which Merlin often feels. Yet she also can quickly dissolve the fear, as she does best in *The Hollow Hills* when Cador, a possible threat to Arthur's future, draws his dagger, but only to "draw patterns in the wild thyme."

Because of Stewart's skill with language and plot, the most ardent readers of Arthur enjoy her versions (she explains the choices she has made among the legends in her notes at the back of each volume).

Literary Precedents

With the possible exception of *The Canterbury Tales,* no group of medieval stories has so caught the modern imagination as the Arthur stories. The "father" of Arthurian romance, Geoffrey of Monmouth, wrote his *History of the Kings of*

Britain in the twelfth century, and Stewart relies on Geoffrey as an important source. Tales of Arthur continued to be told, most notably by the French troubadours, by Sir Thomas Malory, by Edmund Spenser, and by Tennyson. In the twentieth century T. H. White is perhaps the best known writer of the Arthurian legend, having published his *The Once and Future King* tetralogy in 1958. From White's book came the Broadway musical *Camelot* and even a Walt Disney cartoon, *The Sword in the Stone.*

Though Stewart's and White's antecedents are similar, their aims and methods differ. White emphasizes Merlin's magical powers, particularly his ability to transform himself and Arthur into animals in order to learn valuable lessons, and characterizes Merlin as powerful but somewhat muddled. A pacifist struggling with his conscience during World War II, White uses Merlin as a mouthpiece to harangue man for his glorification of war. The theme of his work is the immorality of war and the need for an antidote to it.

Stewart, on the other hand, tries as much as possible to portray Merlin as a real man. Her Merlin gives Arthur lessons in history and does not transform him into animals. Never a bumbler, Merlin works to give Arthur a sense of his family, of the responsibility of power, and to prepare him for his destiny. Merlin, to Stewart, epitomizes the confusion and seeking of the Dark Ages, a real man trying to make sense of the world of men after the collapse of the Roman empire and during the building of the new world dominated by the Christian god.

Related Titles

Stewart's original intent in writing her trilogy was to focus on Merlin; and in *The Crystal Cave* (1970), *The Hollow Hills* (1973) and *The Last Enchantment* (1979), she has him narrate his own story—his learning of his prophetic powers, his preparation of Arthur, and his role of adviser to King Arthur. The main themes of the novels are the same—power and its proper aims, and destiny and man's acceptance of it. The quality of writing in each of the trilogy remains high, and each novel can be read as a complete story.

In Stewart's more recent work, *The Wicked Day* (1983), however, Nimue has taken over for Merlin as adviser to Arthur, and Merlin never appears (though his presence is felt, particularly in a scene where Mordred struggles to come to terms with the prophecy that he will kill his father). The story of *The Wicked Day* can be seen as embodying the consequences of Merlin's life and work, but the focus is much more on Arthur and Mordred. A new theme appears: the need of the new generation to supplant the old (though this was a minor theme in *The Hollow Hills* with Arthur supplanting Uther). The quality of Stewart's writing is still good but not as evocative and imaginative as in the trilogy.

MY BROTHER MICHAEL
My Brother Michael, 1959, novel.

Social Concerns
My Brother Michael, written thirteen years after the end of World War II, shows a Europe still unsettled and people still trying to come to terms with what happened to them on a personal level during the war. Simon Lester has come to Greece to find out the truth about his brother who died near Delphi during the war. On a related level, the novel is about personal identity and discovery, another important concern of the post-World War II world. Camilla Haven, the heroine, has come to Greece after breaking off her relationship with dashing but overwhelming Philip. Having been linked for a long time with an overpowering figure, she has little knowledge of herself apart from him. Thus, *My Brother Michael* reflects a need for personal stability on an individual and international level.

Themes
Stewart combines the ideas of Shakespeare and Donne to create the major theme of *My Brother Michael:* being true to oneself while being involved in mankind. According to the hero Simon who quotes both Shakespeare and Donne, the really great man sees the pattern of life and his own place in it. He stands for the ideals which ancient Greece gave to the Western world—"truth, straight thinking, freedom, beauty." While committed to personal growth, Stewart's characters also care for each other, and not only on a romantic basis. Stewart thus wants her books to convey positive, humane values to her readers. In interviews she has clarified her position: ". . . I don't want any one made troubled or unhappy by anything I've written; perhaps 'depressed' and 'hurt' are better words." She expressed her disgust with the "anti" trend of the 1950s, "all the 'anti' brigade, the dirt brigade, the sicks and the beats." Instead, readers need to be shown "some living pattern of rightness that fits our times."

Characters
Camilla Haven, the heroine and narrator of *My Brother Michael,* is not the typical romantic heroine. At times impulsive, she is nevertheless intelligent in her investigation of Delphi and its secrets. Unlike the other mindless tourists, she has read a great deal about Greece and seeks more than a superficial understanding of its culture and impact. In contrast to Danielle, the femme fatale of the novel, Camilla is sensible and very aware of the importance of manners in sparing the feelings of others and upholding civilized society. Her warm heart and sense of responsibility for others keeps her involved with Simon in Delphi, even though she would be financially better off and physically safer if she left. Perhaps the literary

character Camilla is most reminiscent of is Jane Eyre, though Camilla is not mousy and is much more sure of her own self-worth. Though not quite a "liberated" woman, Camilla is one of the good, solid girls who populated women's popular fiction from the 1930s through the 1950s.

Techniques

"Nothing ever happens to me," *My Brother Michael* begins, and the rest of the novel disproves the heroine's opening statement. Stewart creates suspense in this novel through her characterization. The heroine provides a stable, unmysterious center to the activities. Each character Camilla encounters has some tension within him or between others and him which Camilla detects but cannot explain, and the subsequent workings out of the plot reveal the characters' motivations. When Camilla first meets Simon, for example, the villagers react with suspicion towards him yet he seems cool and unruffled. She later learns that Simon is very much a caring person and that the villagers' hostility is caused by old Communist vs. Allied war wounds. The novel is, then, an interweaving of characters and their true motivations which only becomes a whole cloth of explanations at the end.

Literary Precedents

Stewart's non-Merlin novels are difficult to classify because they really are not romances, mysteries or whodunits. Although they have a romantic background, the romance is very understated, especially by more modern standards. They certainly have a strong element of mystery, but it is not as important as other aspects such as the values expounded and the human relationships explored. And the thrust of *My Brother Michael* is not towards who killed Michael since the murderer has been known for years. Stewart, when asked about the problem of classification, has said, "I'd rather just say that I write novels, fast-moving novels that entertain." Other categories under which critics have tried to place her works include gothic novels, thrillers, and romantic suspense novels.

Related Titles

Though none of Stewart's pre-trilogy novels have sequels, they do share similar plot ingredients, heroines, values, and sense of place. Each plot contains adventure, danger and innocent romance. The heroines are spirited, resolute and selfless. It is their maturity and commitment that make them attractive to the heroes. The biggest variation in the novels occurs in the setting, from the Isle of Skye for *Wildfire at Midnight,* Corfu for *This Rough Magic,* Austria for *Airs Above the Ground,* to France for *Nine Coaches Waiting.* Though the number of varied settings might tend to make Stewart's novels travelogues, she rises above this temptation to make her settings not only authentic but integral parts of the story.

Other Titles

Madam, Will You Talk?, 1955 (novel); *Wildfire at Midnight*, 1956 (novel); *Thunder on the Right*, 1957 (novel); *Nine Coaches Waiting*, 1958 (novel); *The Ivy Tree*, 1961 (novel); *The Moonspinners*, 1962 (novel); *This Rough Magic*, 1964 (novel); *Airs Above the Ground*, 1965 (novel); *The Gabriel Hounds*, 1967 (novel); *The Wind off the Small Isles*, 1968 (novel); *The Little Broomstick*, 1971 (children's fiction); *Ludo and the Star Horse*, 1974 (children's fiction); *Touch Not the Cat*, 1976 (novel); *A Walk in Wolf Wood*, 1980 (children's fiction/fantasy).

Additional Sources

Commire, Anne, *Something about the Author*, Vol. 12. Detroit: Gale Research, 1977, pp. 217-219. Brief biography and history of Stewart's beginning as a writer.

Herman, Harold J., "The Women in Mary Stewart's Merlin Trilogy," *Interpretations*, 15(2) (Spring 1984): 101-114. Examination of the role of women in Arthurian legend.

Newquist, Roy, *Counterpoint*. Chicago: Rand McNally, 1964, pp. 561-571. Interview with Stewart on her life, philosophy and work.

Ann W. Engar
University of Utah

IRVING STONE
1903

Publishing History

Irving Stone's first published work was in drama, not historical fiction, for which he became famous. *The Dark Mirror* ran for six weeks in 1928 in an off-Broadway production. Although his play was modestly successful, Stone turned to fiction, publishing his first novel, *Pageant of Youth* in 1933. While working on this non-historical novel, Stone researched the facts of Vincent Van Gogh's life and produced the manuscript for the biographical novel *Lust for Life*. Seventeen publishers and three years later, *Lust for Life* (1934) appeared and immediately became a best seller.

His research on Van Gogh demonstrated to Stone that his interests lay in biography, and although he wrote a second play (which opened and closed the same night), as well as edited a collection of letters between Vincent Van Gogh and his brother Theo, his next major effort was to write a biographical novel on Jack London. Having established a solid reputation with *Lust for Life*, Stone was able to secure the trust of London's relatives. With their assistance and with access to family papers and London's original manuscripts, Stone completed *Jack London: Sailor on Horseback*, which was serialized by the *Saturday Evening Post*, then published in book form in 1938. London's immense popularity, his exotic and adventurous lifestyle, and the mysterious circumstances of his untimely death, gave *Sailor on Horseback* the ingredients for the popular success which it achieved.

The reasons why these two novels were exceptionally successful also were in part the same reasons why Stone began to receive unfavorable criticism. Both Van Gogh and London were creative geniuses whose lives were turbulent and full of emotional stress. Both were driven by madness and obsession. In the course of their lives, both men went to extremes, and Stone's "fictionalized" interpretation of their extremities caused academic historians to denounce the value of Stone's books. It is preferable to have no biographies at all than to have misleading ones, the critics argued, no matter how entertaining they may be. Certainly, Van Gogh became known to Americans far beyond his popularity as an artist, and Stone has always believed that he provides a valuable service to both his readers and the subject of the biography.

Emerging from these two novels came a pattern which Stone has followed throughout his career, and which has led to further criticism of him as a "formula" writer. He selects historical personalities who are sensational, researches them thoroughly, and selects the facts of their lives which can be shaped into good fiction. Stone's counterpart in making biographical/historical fiction so popular during this century is James Michener, who is also criticized for being a formulist who tends to play up the sensational elements, and together Stone and Michener have defined the genre.

Stone's third biographical novel, *Clarence Darrow for the Defense* (1941), came from materials provided to him by the Darrow literary estate, which included briefs, manuscripts, and private papers. Darrow, famous for his defense of the theory of evolution in what became the sensational "Scopes monkey trial," was one of the most controversial figures of his decade. In Stone's hands, and with the novel being a Literary Guild selection, *Clarence Darrow for the Defense* was an immediate success and has been a continuing best seller ever since.

Stone's next book, *They Also Ran* (1943), was the story of all the men who had been defeated for the presidency, from Henry Clay through Thomas E. Dewey. Receiving critical acclaim, this book became a standard desk reference for people who deal with the presidency.

Stone's next three biographical novels took women as their subjects. *Immortal Wife* (1944) is the story of Jessie Benton Frémont; *The President's Lady* (1951) is about Rachael Jackson, Andrew Jackson's wife; and *Love Is Eternal* (1954) is about Mary Todd Lincoln. This trilogy, of women less famous than their husbands, touched a post World War II readership who was ready to appreciate the strength and contributions of women to the direction of history. All three books were best sellers, with *Immortal Wife* becoming one of the biggest best sellers and assuring Stone's dominance as an important genre writer.

Stone's next two biographical novels were equally well received by a reading public which now had high expectations and demands of Stone's work. *The Agony and the Ecstasy* (1961) and *The Passions of the Mind* (1971) treated Michelangelo and Sigmund Freud respectively, figures who changed the course of the world through ideas and politics. Unlike either Van Gogh, Darrow, or the "vilified" ladies, Michelangelo and Freud represented the "super intellect," and Stone was confronted with the challenge of handling complex ideas in a way which his readership could understand and which would not detract from the entertainment quality of the fiction. He spent four years researching materials on Michelangelo, even living near the places where Michelangelo lived and worked, and although art historians were quick to point out the factual mistakes, such as Chianti wine not being named until long after Michelangelo's time, most critics agreed that Stone had skillfully handled difficult material. Most recently, Stone has returned to his *Lust for Life* type novel with the life of Camille Pisarro (*The Depths of Glory*, 1985), but it is clear that over his long career Stone has improved his formula and been willing to undertake more difficult subjects.

Critical Reception, Honors, and Popularity

Because Stone was a pioneer in the bio-historical novel genre, he has been given a wide range of critical attention. *Lust for Life* was received with great enthusiasm and good press, and it remains one of his best known works. Yet his handling of Van Gogh in a fictionalized manner angered some critics. They complained that phrases shaped in the mouth of the artist, as well as invented thoughts, actions, and reactions, all seemed somehow unreal. They called his narrative a "pseudo-biography" which, they felt, embroidered too fancifully and sentimentally on his subjects' lives. More recent commentators, perhaps because of the immense popularity of his novels, now view and accept Stone as a "bio-historical novelist." That is, they place him at the head of a group of writers for whom historical figures and plots are of greater importance than straightforward historical facts. Although they are surprised at his apparent disregard for extensive research and painstaking accuracy in historical matters, they seem to accept this oddity as necessary for Stone's technique. He did develop his narrative into a form which he has made uniquely his own and which has been universally accepted by the public.

At present Stone's reputation is secure. The majority of critics believe that his novels stand as solid efforts. Regardless of some critics' discontent, they recognize the author's success and world-wide popularity in the realm of bio-historical novels. They realize that the public has greater knowledge and perhaps even greater compassion for outstanding historical figures than it could have had otherwise. They praise Stone for bringing to the public certain facts that have been hidden and revealing prejudices and half-truths that present more complete portraits of his subjects than the public had seen before. One example in this regard is Van Gogh's unusual personality. It is more believable and understandable through Stone's ability to create a violent, clumsy fellow driven to the extremity of exhaustion by his gnawing passion to get the essence of life on his canvas. Other examples include two of his "women trilogy" novels, *Love is Eternal* and *The President's Lady,* which bring an understanding of two first ladies who, prior to these novels, had been misunderstood and misrepresented.

Stone belongs to many organizations and has attained recognition throughout literary and other professional circles. Two of his outstanding decorations came from his translation of *The Agony and The Ecstasy.* They are the *Florentine Giglia d'Oro* (Golden Lily) "for distinguished service" in 1964 and the Republic of Italy's Knight Commander award in 1965.

Analysis of Selected Titles

LUST FOR LIFE

Lust for Life, 1934, bio-historical novel. Reprinted, Grosset, 1961, published with reader's supplement, Washington Square Press, 1967.

Social Concerns/Themes

Besides receiving the best press and remaining one of his best known works, *Lust for Life,* Stone's first successful fictionalized biography, gave direction to his career. In this novel, the biographer sets forth well-researched factual material about Van Gogh's life based chiefly on the three volumes of the artist's letters to his brother, Theo, and on material unearthed in research, while dramatizing, often very romantically, the artist's thoughts and conversations. The novel presents a lonely, intense man, suffering from epilepsy, driven by an obsession to create life from his paints. It is a thoughtful examination of his passions, his search for love and his battle against loneliness and physical collapse.

Stone's belief that Van Gogh was misunderstood in his lifetime and subsequently treated unfairly in biographies provided a good deal of the inspiration for *Lust for Life*. Prior gossip and publicity presented Van Gogh as having driven himself insane through his obsession with art. Stone's desire to set the records straight resulted in a benefit to both Van Gogh's personal reputation and to the public. Whoever reads this novel will gain most, if not all, the important facts concerning the life of the painter in a poetic and touching portrayal.

Characters

As in any fiction, the quality of a novel depends largely upon its characters seen in the round and presented in the process of growth, development, and change under stress. Van Gogh is one of these characters. Stone skillfully reveals Van Gogh's frustrations, desires and ill health, as well as the limited successes in his own life time. The artist's character is elaborately worked out on one level where the reader understands his problems and realizes that in addition to epilepsy, Van Gogh suffered torment, frustration, and subsequent nervous breakdowns which included his cutting off an ear and shooting himself. The reader further discerns the artist's relationship to his work as Van Gogh visits and paints universal man in his own surroundings, including the coal mines, the fields, and towns. Because Stone brings reality to his pages, the reader envisions Van Gogh's genius, his ability to bring reality to his canvas and to the world of art. As *Lust for Life* progresses from one scene to the next, Van Gogh's loneliness, coupled with his obsession to create objects on canvas as they appear in real life, becomes the central concern and leads to his physical destruction and early death. When the artist loses himself to nervous collapses at a relatively early age and must fight his way back to health, this struggle becomes one of the themes in which there is the classic confrontation of a character facing his own mortality. The stress of confronting death is often used to reveal the essence of a character. Van Gogh, for example allegorizes it in one of his later paintings as a reaper working in a field of gold.

Techniques

Lust for Life is an excellent example of how an author may resolve the potential conflict between a novel that contains entertaining narrative and an historical novel. Stone turns a biography of Van Gogh, who is a far-from-perfect hero because he is driven by passion and lacks certain endearing qualities, from a textbook rendition, which it could have easily become, into a context which entertained while including the many facts of Van Gogh's life that Stone had uncovered. To accomplish this, he develops Van Gogh's rejection of love on a parallel with his devotion to art. By taking Van Gogh's rejection and allowing his character to turn it into energy that creates masterpieces, Stone combines an entertaining story with the facts of Van Gogh's life and the rise of Impressionism.

Literary Precedents

Many critics believe *Lust for Life* was the first of a new genre, the bio-history novel. This is, perhaps, the reason why several reviewers reacted so severely to it. The offspring of such literary works as Boswell's biography of Samuel Johnson and Claudius' history writings of Rome before the fall, it is also related to such narratives that began with Daniel DeFoe and Laurence Stern in the eighteenth century. Like James Michener, a contemporary historical novelist, Stone compiles and translates years of data and research into novels, but he is a biographer first; he concentrates on the person. Michener is a historian first and concentrates on historical data. They both, however, incorporate fiction with history, and as Michener's predecessor, Stone has accomplished much to pave the way for this artistic/historical form.

Adaptations

Lust for Life was filmed, and was released by Metro-Goldwyn-Mayer in September, 1956. Produced by John Houseman and directed by Vincente Minnelli, it was designed and promoted primarily as an extravaganza. The stars, Kirk Douglas as Van Gogh and Anthony Quinn as his contemporary and friend, Gauguin, helped the film gain a rather successful box office return. The film's critical reception was mixed, as was Stone's novel, with some critics admiring its visual effects and others complaining that, since lives of artists or great men can't be told honorably within the limits of popular entertainment, Van Gogh was presented as less than heroic. Basically, the complaining critics' accusation was that the public is made to look at Van Gogh, a great artist, with shallow eyes. Perhaps this criticism is more of popular biography's art form than of this particular picture. The critics agreed, however, that *Lust for Life* came to the screen with impressive fidelity.

THE AGONY AND THE ECSTASY

The Agony and The Ecstasy, 1961, abridged juvenile edition published as *The Great Adventure of Michelangelo,* 1965; (author of introduction) *The Drawings of Michelangelo,* Borden Publishing, 1962 (editor with wife, Jean Stone).

Social Concerns/Themes

The combination of Michelangelo's varied background as sculptor, painter, poet, architect and engineer, his own personal weaknesses and vanity, and his unremitting drive which enabled him to conquer overwhelming disappointments and find satisfaction in difficult and backbreaking work has made *The Agony and the Ecstasy* one of Stone's most well-read books. Michelangelo is the artist's everyman as his biographer combines the focus on art and will with insights into human behavior, and provides an excellent account of his struggles and achievements, desires and despairs. The events of the novel, historical in fact and theme, cover the periods of Lorenzo the Magnificent, who first befriended the young artist, through the harshness of Pope Julius II, who literally forced Michelangelo to paint the ceiling of the Sistine Chapel in Rome, to Pope Pius IV, who finally gave him full authority to plan and complete St. Peters. Yet, Stone's important contribution has not been solely to the realm of history. Rather, Michelangelo's struggles to become an artist and maintain his craft is of major importance. It is generally agreed among the critics that Stone communicates to the reader a feeling for the physical effort which goes into the great art of bringing forth an inspiring image from marble. His descriptions of the "scalpellini," the stonemen, and the "pietra serena," the serene stone of Florence, help to explain his success in depicting the human figure in motion. Another aspect of the artist at work is Stone's presentation of Michelangelo's "do-it-yourself" anatomy experiments on corpses secretly put at his disposal against the laws of his time. In an effort to illuminate his reader further, Stone has included additional biographical notes, bibliography and indications of where the extant works of Michelangelo may be viewed today.

Characters

In *The Agony and the Ecstasy,* the essential plot involving what many critics believe to be the ultimate of Michelangelo's painting focuses on the close but abrasive relationship between Pope Julius II and Michelangelo. Since this personal conflict resulted in the artist reluctantly painting the Sistine Chapel ceiling, by concentrating on this struggle, Stone is able to explore in detail the affect of a genius at work. Further, because the biographer apprenticed himself to a sculptor in order to achieve a greater understanding of Michelangelo's unique art, he could more accurately probe the imaginary mental processes by which Michelangelo finally carried his ideas from marble blocks to his paint and spent hour after hour forty feet from the floor, on his back, painting the ceiling of the Sistine Chapel. Thus, the reader is able to visualize more clearly how Michelangelo probably received his inspirations, how he analyzed and broadened his ideas, how he looked for models, reached for inspiration and, putting these ideas aside, evolved his own interpretations of biblical figures, including those of the Blessed Virgin and Jesus.

Critics believe that most characters in the book are well-drawn, although those who are of the Medici family are perhaps drawn with the most understanding and vividness. There is a variety of characters who act and interact with Michelangelo from the women in his life to his assistants on the Sistine scaffolds. The result is a pageant, an opera, and in every sense a much broader canvas on which to explore the artist's complexity than Stone's memorable biographical novel of Van Gogh, *Lust for Life*. Some critics argue that in individual sequences, Stone does not make the master come alive as a human being and that some dialogue clutters the High Renaissance tapestry effect of the piece. While they say, as fiction, the book is not a substitute for the biographical studies of DeTolnahy or John Addington Symonds, as fiction, it is an outstanding and readable performance.

Techniques

Some critics have been particularly harsh in their estimation of Stone's techniques in *The Agony and the Ecstasy*. They contend that while he researches the facts of his subject completely, he changes, adds and rejects at will. The scholars who admit this best seller is a successful novel recognize the question of the dilemma of truth versus entertainment. They say that to fictionalize an artist's life is to compromise the truth no matter how carefully the story is documented. Yet, it is the job of a biographical novelist to know all and tell all as he ties together loose threads with excellent crochet-work. Stone apparently came to Michelangelo knowing him first as the standard genius of popular folklore. He entered into research with this icon and, deciding not to change it, suppressed any truths that interfere with a wholesome interpretation. Thus he neglects to include many of Michelangelo's alleged faults, particularly his extreme arrogance, cynicism, and vicious temper. He also excludes any mention of the strong possibility that the artist was bisexual. In the twentieth century world of realism, some would have Stone less idealistic and more realistic. In addition to what they term alterations, they dislike what they call shattering, puerile dialogue; yet, they believe that Stone stays with the ascertainable facts and has not hesitated to set down innumerable details. They admire Stone's dedication, and they agree that his experience as apprentice to a sculptor has resulted in some of the best passages in the novel. While those critics who dislike biographies and/or histories, dislike this novel, the majority of the reviewers believe that, using his novelist's license as he has every right to do and coloring his narrative with bold, free strokes, Stone has written an important and thoroughly enjoyable novel.

Adaptations

It seems apparent that in adapting *The Agony and the Ecstasy* to film, Scriptwriter Philip Dunne had artistic license in mind. He and the creative forces at Twentieth Century Fox Studios chose to concentrate only on the four years through which Michelangelo suffered pangs of creation as he painted the first book of the Bible on the ceiling of the Sistine Chapel. Reviewers credit Dunne as having succeeded in conveying the tormenting struggles of a genius, as well as portraying two strong men whose opposition to each other often erupted in rage, but whose high regard for each other softened this anger. Tall, rugged Charlton Heston portrays Michelangelo as a willful man who argues with his pope, Pope Julius II, and insists his work should be in sculpture, not paint. Rex Harrison as Pope Julius II is also a willful man, more cunning than the artist, and more skillful at getting what he wants. Neither Heston nor Harrison are type cast for this movie. Michelangelo was far from the tall, muscular character whom Heston creates, and Harrison is much younger and less power conscious than Pope Julius II. Nevertheless, their portrayals of these great men are significant, if not impressive. There is a large supporting cast which illuminates the majority of Stone's novel and helps to create the reality of Michelangelo's Renaissance Italy. The introduction, a short documentary about Michelangelo's art filmed in Todd A and color, pleased the moviegoers. The first scene is of a rising helicopter shot of St. Peters in the early morning light and takes the observer into an aerial view of buildings that house the Michelangelo sculptures, then scans the tombs and statutes themselves and sets the mood for the movie.

Other adaptations of Stone's work include *False Witness,* filmed by Republic Studios and released in 1941, and *The President's Lady,* filmed by Twentieth-Century Fox and released in 1953.

THE ORIGIN
The Origin, 1980, novel.

Social Concerns/Themes

The Origin, the principal character of which is Charles Darwin, is bio-history writing on a grand scale. Darwin, by proving that the only constant force in nature is change, caused theorists to question if the world was created by a single, instantaneous act of God, or by a series of acts each time the creator changed his mind. The drama of *The Origin* is that Darwin, for years after his world circling voyage on the *Beagle,* developed a theory about the origin of species, their development and differentiation through processes of natural selection and survival of the fittest. In time he came to believe that man was included in the ascent through the same kinds of evolutionary processes. The release of this information in "The Evolution of the Species" caused an uproar around the world.

Darwin's overpowering research was made over a period of years and, in *The Origin,* Stone develops a manner through which he made much of this information available to the public. Utilizing the great minds of the naturalist's time and exploring their effect upon Darwin's ultimate theories, Stone sets out to paint a picture that is more than a portrait of a scientific genius. It is also a panorama of the intellectual landscape of his time.

Characters

Stone helps to demythologize the great naturalist and thus make him more accessible to the reader by presenting him within the circle of brilliant scientists of nineteenth century England such as Charles Lyell, Joseph Hooker, Thomas Huxley, and Alfred Wallace. While presenting these learned men in terms a twentieth century reader can understand, Stone evokes Darwin's character, making him warmly, humanly appealing as well as possessing characteristics of a genius. Stone captures Darwin's exterior defenses, the socially retiring modesty which his visitors often took as genuine simplicity; his private life is also illuminated as the biographer presents a man devotedly loved and nursed by a loving wife who feels the strain of her husband's work.

As various critics point out, Darwin, a man full of contradictions, was not an easy fellow to capture. He was a gregarious recluse; an energetic invalid; modest yet eager for scientific immortality; meticulous over observation and fact, yet hesitant to publish or to acknowledge his mentors and predecessors. Perhaps the key to capturing this paradox lay in Stone's sensibilities about him. The biographer rejected prior diagnosis of eye strain, of an "inherited peculiarity of the nervous system," of an unconscious desire to kill his father (transferred to an attempt on "the Heavenly Father") and of an infection of the protozoan *Trypanosonia cruzi* which causes Chaga's disease. He decided, instead, in favor of chronic overwork and severe anxiety, induced by an understandable apprehension of the probable effects of altering mankind's perception of itself. Because the reader can identify more readily with this latter choice, Stone is successful in placing Darwin within the reader's grasp and allowing the causes of these contradictions to be at once clear and, although not always understandable, at least acceptable.

Techniques

According to some critics, Stone has been remarkably restrained both in his choice of title for this massive novel, and in the selection and presentation of its contents. They believe that he successfully joined together the three genres of biography, history and fiction and solved the problem of crossbreeding through his lucid narrator, the structure of the novel, and the handling of details.

The structure of the novel is built to introduce the reader first to Darwin, the fact-finder and scientist, then later to Darwin, the family man. In the first section of the novel, Stone describes Darwin's off-shore and onshore experiences on a surveying trip to South America. Describing the journey in lavish detail, he gives proper emphasis to the visits that young Darwin took to the Galapagos Islands and the data he found there which ultimately sowed the seed for "The Origin of Species." (Stone even furnishes a clear map of the voyage for the reader's benefit.) The reader is able to understand how the trip trained the potential scientist's mind, building onto his love of science habits of concentrated attention, observation, fidelity to nature, and patient induction through long, hard, and solitary work.

When he returns from the *Beagle* voyage, he is armed with bits and pieces of natural history and the desire to resolve their puzzle.

The second section involves Darwin's family, scientific associates, study, writing, and his long struggle with delicate health. Stone explores Darwin's thinking as it developed from doubts about fixity of species to convictions of some theory of organic descent, to the development of a coherent theory of selection (with the help of Molnius' work). Each step is logical and consistent. Then, five years after the voyage, Stone settles Darwin into the life of a happy husband and successful author-naturalist, before precipitating (and finally weathering) a storm of controversy with his outrageous theory of evolution.

A few critics say that Stone's objective to characterize Darwin gets lost as he concentrates on detail in the "multitudinously different minutiae of the external world." They point to a few errors: There are no lions in South Africa and the "stinkhorn mushroom" is not a mushroom at all but a toadstool. Some critics object to the "lists" Stone uses to categorize various sections of his information in the novel. Others say he has a fussy gathering of historical detail and instead of breathing life into his characters, he stores them away in a museum. Nevertheless, *The Origin* has much to offer a twentieth-century reader who wishes to learn about the man who changed the theory of "the origin of man," perhaps forever.

Other Titles

"The Dark Mirror," 1928 (drama); "The White Life," 1929 (drama on Spinoza); *Pageant of Youth*, 1933 (novel); "Truly Valiant," 1936 (drama); *Dear Theo*, (autobiography of Van Gogh); *Sailor on Horseback*, 1938 (fictional biography of Jack London); *False Witness*, 1940 (novel); *Clarence Darrow for the Defense*, 1941 (fictional biography); *They Also Ran: The Story of the Men Who were Defeated for the Presidency*, 1943 (non-fiction); *Immortal Wife*, 1944 (fictional biography of Jessie B. Frémont); *Adversary in the House*, 1947 (fictional biography of Eugene V. Debs and his wife); *Earl Warren*, 1948 (biography); *The Passionate Journey*, 1949 (fictional biography of John Noble, artist); *The President's Lady*, 1951 (fictional biography of Rachael Jackson); *Love is Eternal*, 1954 (fictional biography of Mary Todd Lincoln); *The Drawings of Michelangelo*, 1962 (edited with Jean Stone); *Lincoln: A Contemporary Portrait*, 1962 (non-fiction); *The Irving Stone Reader*, 1963 (selected writings); *The Story of Michaelangelo's Pieta*, 1964 (non-fiction); *Those Who Love*, 1965 (fictional biography of Abigail Adams); *The Passions of the Mind*, 1971 (fictional biography of Sigmund Freud); *The Greek Treasure*, 1975 (fictional biography of Henry and Sophia Schliemann); *The Depths of Glory*, 1985 (biography of Camille Pisarro).

Additional Sources

Contemporary Authors, New Revision series, vol. 1. Detroit: Gale, 1981. Biographical and some critical information.

Contemporary Literary Criticism, vol. 7. Detroit: Gale, 1977. Excerpts reviews of Stone's work.

Current Biography Yearbook. New York: H. W. Wilson, 1967. Biographical information concentrating on Stone's childhood and early career.

Newquist, Roy, *Counterpoint*. Skokie, IL: Rand McNally, 1964. Includes a rather extensive interview with Stone.

Stone, Irving, *The Irving Stone Reader*. New York: Doubleday, 1963. This collection includes excerpts from the major novels, short stories previously collected in periodicals, a prologue in which Stone discusses the craft of writing biographical novels, and introductions by Joseph Henry Jackson and Allan Nevins.

Wanda La Faye Seay
Oklahoma State University

ROBERT STONE
1937?

Publishing History

Dropping out of school at seventeen, Robert Stone joined the Navy presumably to "see the world," and judging from his fiction, he learned a great deal about people, places, and the times in which he lived. Returning to New York City, Stone briefly attended New York University, worked periodically as a journalist as a means to earn his livelihood, and began to write poetry in association with the Beat movement of the late 1950s. Eventually, Stone gravitated to New Orleans and to California as the recipient of a Stegner Fellowship based on the first chapter of a novel-in-progress. Once there, Stone was assimilated into the San Francisco Bay Area where he lived out a psychedelic fantasy as part of the blossoming counterculture of the 1960s. Afterwards, as a participant in a Stanford University writing workshop, Stone was awarded a Houghton Mifflin Literary Fellowship in order to complete his novel entitled *A Hall of Mirrors*. Published in 1967, the novel jettisoned the thirty-year-old Stone into the forefront of new American writers.

Stone's fiction appeared in *New American Review, Fiction,* and *The Best American Short Stories 1970* prior to a journalistic assignment to Vietnam in 1971. Characteristic of his generation, Stone would be permanently transformed by the Vietnam experience, which would serve as the backdrop for his next two novels, *Dog Soldiers* (1974) and *A Flag for Sunrise* (1981). Today, Stone is considered one of the most original and talented writers in the United States. Most recently, Stone published the critically acclaimed *Children of Light* (1986), and is presently at work on a forthcoming novel.

Critical Reception, Honors, and Popularity

The publication of *A Hall of Mirrors* was greeted with refreshing enthusiasm and critical praise. Stone's debut as a novelist was considered a significant literary event, signaling the arrival of a gifted, provocative author. In the novel, Stone intertwines the lives of three characters "on the edge" of both society and sanity: unpredictable, complex, and misguided. Stone presents a profoundly dark image of contemporary America festering with infection. Plagued by immorality, malevolence, and greed, *A Hall of Mirrors* has been compared to Nathanael West's *The Day of the Locust* for confronting the terrifying consequences of madness and chaotic violence, Malcolm Lowry's *Under the Volcano* for probing the tormented world of alcoholism, and John Dos Passos' *U.S.A.* for entering the smoke-filled arena of political intrigue and dementia.

The film version of the novel was written by Stone and released in 1970 under the title of *WUSA* (produced by John Foreman for Paramount Pictures and directed by Stuart Rosenberg). Conceived as a vehicle for Paul Newman, the actor considered the film a political project and one of his most significant achievements. Starring Newman along with his wife Joanne Woodward, Anthony Perkins, Laurence Harvey, and Pat Hingle, the film was disastrously reviewed by critics and considered a disappointing box office failure.

Stone's early and relatively sudden recognition as a writer, considered premature by some critics, was reinforced by the appearance of his second novel, *Dog Soldiers.* Similar in shape and style to *A Hall of Mirrors,* the novel continued Stone's exploration into the existential essence of America. Extremely well received, *Dog Soldiers* established Stone as a major spokesperson for the underside of life caught between expectation and truth. His is the voice of pessimism; of note, however, is that Stone presents a message recognized and understood all too well by the reading public.

Sharpening his ability to produce fiction of contemporary relevance and impact, Stone created in *A Flag for Sunrise* an imaginary Central American country from which to witness the birth of revolution within the grim landscape of brutality, corruption, and moral decay. Clearly demonstrating a distinct pattern of development, Stone's third novel received a generally mixed critical reception. Most critics were impressed with the work as an adventure story but considered Stone's message obscured by complicated plot development and abstraction.

It seems apparent that Stone has regained his momentum with the recent publication of *Children of Light.* Utilizing narrative and characterization to weave an intricate tapestry of lives dominated by detachment and despair, Stone evokes the "new" Hollywood as the metaphysical presence of evil. Critical reaction was generally favorable to the novel, yet the question remains whether or not Stone has the capability of becoming a best-selling author. Based solely on his literary output, Stone has failed to achieve widespread popularity. However, his fiction has the potential to translate well to the screen and the consensus is that both *A Flag for Sunrise* and *Children of Light* will be adapted for film. Consequently, depending on the quality of production, the film versions of Stone's novels could produce increased accessibility and dimension to his creativity.

Consistently mentioned among America's leading writers, Stone received the William Faulkner Foundation Award for "notable first novel" in 1968 for *A Hall of Mirrors* and the National Book Award for fiction in 1974 for *Dog Soldiers.*

Analysis of Selected Titles

DOG SOLDIERS
Dog Soldiers, 1974, novel.

Social Concerns
Dog Soldiers is a vastly disturbing if not horrific vision of contemporary Amer-

ica. Scanning the emotional well-being of the nation, Stone envisions a decidedly bleak landscape inhabited by a sordid collection of life's "soldiers" unceremoniously waging a losing battle against their own undoing. Passing judgment as if pronouncing death, Stone forces the reader to look at the world around him while simultaneously forcing him to look closely at himself. Unfortunately, the result is a sad commentary on history and the lack of promise in the generation of the 1970s.

The novel tells the story of an American journalist in Vietnam who schemes to smuggle heroin into the United States aided by his wife in California and an ex-Marine accomplice. As the plan goes askew, Stone creates a harrowing struggle for possession of the drug while investigating the psychological motivation and interrelationships of the major characters.

Having experienced the American involvement in Vietnam first-hand, Stone is seemingly more concerned with analyzing the aftermath of the conflict rather than raising a moral objection to war itself. However, Stone is certainly communicating that there exists an inherent attraction or propensity in the American psyche toward violence and that the horrors of the war unfold as a logical extension of illogical fascination.

Ironically, the heroin takes possession of the novel in much the same way as it does the lives of those who either possess or desire it. Heroin is used by Stone as a vehicle to explore the depth of man's indifference or baseness toward the destruction of self or others. However, the novel is also concerned with the prevailing environment capable of producing such disregard for human dignity and continuance.

Themes

"Part melodrama, part morality play," *Dog Soldiers* brings the Vietnam conflict home to America. Demoralized and victimized by the reality of war, the protagonist of the novel, John Converse, escapes into delusion and sophistry to negate the consequences of smuggling heroin. By illustrating the impact of the drug on the lives of his characters, Stone is acknowledging the terrifying connection between the war and the American counterculture. As the scheme is discovered by a corrupt federal agent seeking the heroin for his own personal gain, the action of the novel flows from Saigon to Los Angeles to the California desert near the Mexican border as Converse's wife and his accomplice take flight to avoid pursuit and self-actualization.

Stone depicts a world void of decency and morality, a world marked by violence where fear has become a permanent condition of daily living. Accordingly, the only means of survival is either absolute despondency or total escape into a netherworld of drugs, mania, or perversion.

Characters

Although Converse surfaces in the novel as the primary focus of attention, the spotlight is shared by Marge, Converse's wife, and Ray Hicks, his partner in crime. All are deracinated, complex characters: troubled, detached, and morally bankrupt. Similar to the character of Rheinhardt, the protagonist in *A Hall of Mirrors,* Converse is self-indulgent and manipulative, hoping to survive in the modern world by the willful exploitation of others. His scheme to smuggle heroin is motivated by profit but also a perverse attraction to the exploit itself.

Seemingly destined for self-destruction, Marge represents a pathetic victim rather than an active participant in the scheme. As a drug-user, Marge is drawn to the heroin by association, but interestingly she develops a romantic attachment to the irrational and violent Hicks. A mixture of raw physical prowess and superimposed pathology, Hicks is a terrifying enigma, enticed into the crime by excitement and danger. Referred to by one critic as "a kind of latter-day samurai," Hicks ironically possesses the necessary qualities for survival in Stone's frigid landscape except for his loyalty to Marge which ultimately proves to be a fatal weakness.

Aimlessly drifting toward apocalypse, Stone's characters are distinctly "unlikeable," and consequently questionable in relation to public acceptance. Pitted against a world offering neither hope nor redemption, it is little wonder his fictional characters tend to confront the reality of their existence by allowing themselves "to speed up the trip towards death."

Techniques

Utilizing plot as a primary means to articulate his thematic concerns, Stone is unquestionably a masterful storyteller. *Dog Soldiers* is methodically developed by sustained and riveting suspense. The reader becomes engrossed in the intricacies of the narrative and personalities of the major and minor characters. Noted for his descriptive and compulsive sense of detail, Stone creates a vivid picture of a place in time realized by few. Employing convincing and powerful dialogue, Stone produces a tightly written, cynical, and relentless novel worthy of admiration and respect.

Literary Precedents

Stone admits to being a voracious reader and acknowledges the influence of diversified and numerous authors. Most implicitly, Stone derives from the narrative tradition of writers such as Joseph Conrad, Ernest Hemingway, and F. Scott Fitzgerald. Extremely engaging and intensely paced, *Dog Soldiers* is considered the literary descendent of Conrad's *Heart of Darkness.* Of interest, however, is that Stone incorporates cinematic techniques into his fiction prevalent among screenwriters such as Dashiell Hammett, Raymond Chandler, and especially B. Traven, as illustrated in *The Treasure of Sierra Madre.*

In addition, Stone has publicly commented on his indebtedness to the French novelist Louis Ferdinand Céline. Stone's ability to populate his fiction with dark, disturbing personalities drawn from the counterculture of contemporary society is clearly reminiscent of Céline, most notably in his perverse artistic triumph entitled *Journey to the End of Night.* Likewise, the religious quality of Stone's fiction, first introduced in *A Hall of Mirrors,* present in *Dog Soldiers,* and later realized to a far greater extent in *A Flag for Sunrise,* is comparable to the novels of Graham Greene and the short stories of Flannery O'Connor. Of most importance is that Stone is mentioned in connection to writers of serious literature which is indicative of his growing recognition as an author.

Adaptations

Following his initial, unsuccessful venture into film, Stone was considerably more cautious with the film version of *Dog Soldiers,* grievously retitled as *Who'll Stop the Rain* (produced by United Artists, directed by Karel Reisz, adapted by Stone and Judith Rascoe, and released in 1978). The film, starring Michael Moriarty, Nick Nolte, and Tuesday Weld, received critical acclaim but was only mildly successful at the box office. Most critics commented that despite an action-packed sequence of events and moving performances, especially by Weld, the film was flawed in relation to continuity and character development. Creating unsympathetic and overtly unappealing characters seemed to present insurmountable consequences for the film.

A FLAG FOR SUNRISE

A Flag for Sunrise, 1981, novel.

Social Concerns/Themes

Recognizing striking and disturbing similarities between the Vietnam experience and the current political situation in Central America, Stone sounds a timely and volatile note in his third novel, *A Flag for Sunrise.* Set in the republic of Tecan, modeled in part after present-day Nicaragua, the novel is at once a political thriller and metaphysical journey into an unequivocal hell on earth. Representative of other Third World countries embroiled by American presence and dictated by corruption, abuse, and brutality, Tecan will become the stage for a drama of events and ideas bound together by the spiritual death of innocence.

Having previously worked in an unexplained capacity for the CIA in Vietnam, Frank Holliwell is approached by a former associate to investigate the political rumblings in Tecan while on a university lecture tour in a neighboring country. Initially refusing his services, Holliwell later consents not by any sense of duty but rather by impulse and curiosity. The focus of the investigation is a Roman Catholic mission run by an aging priest and young, idealistic nun who are suspected of having revolutionary leanings. Awaiting his arrival, however, is a nightmarish amalgram of contemporary horror, and Holliwell is immediately swept into the turbulence of the country.

In the novel, Stone utilizes the aftermath of the Vietnam conflict as a thematic element, analyzing as he did in *Dog Soldiers* the impact of the war on American sensitivity. Convinced that Vietnam evoked a contemporary "fascination" with the concept of violence, Stone is issuing a warning that Vietnam could well repeat itself in Central America. His characters serve to illustrate the price of American intervention: fear, alienation, paranoia, and despair.

Characters

Caught up "among spies, gun runners, murderers, maniacs, and revolutionaries," the protagonist of *A Flag for Sunrise* is clearly Frank Holliwell; his character, however, is delicately interwoven with those of Father Egan, the rector of the mission Holliwell is sent to investigate, his assistant, the morally earnest Sister Justine, and the erratic nomad Pablo Tabor, a Coast Guard deserter who drifts into the turmoil in Tecan by hypothetical accident. Similar to the protagonists in Stone's earlier fiction, Holliwell is alcoholic, self-destructive, and amoral. Anthropologist by profession and former freelance CIA agent by design, Holliwell apparently enjoys flirtation with danger. Characteristic of the fictional hero-adventurer, Holliwell is drawn to Tecan by the scent of excitement and intrigue. Obsessed with the spiritual need to discover self, Holliwell ends his journey with a ritualistic confrontation with his own mortality.

Bristling with religious overtones, the novel serves as a platform for the characters of Father Egan and Sister Justine to test the parameters of faith in the modern world. Weathered by the storm of contemporary absurdity, the philosopher-priest is observed sinking into a form of mystical gnosticism while Sister Justine attempts to reaffirm her distorted sense of devotion by sacrifice in the name of liberating revolution. Striving for perfection in an imperfect world, Sister Justine is characteristic of other Stone heroine-victims, including Gertrude in *A Hall of Mirrors* and Marge in *Dog Soldiers,* primarily existing for man's solace or salvation. Seeking a far more disturbing liberation is Pablo. Burnt-out, homicidal, and intrinsically doomed, Pablo replaced God with pills and the price of exaltation is physical release by death.

Attesting to Stone's artistic development as a writer, *A Flag for Sunrise* incorporates a vast assortment of supporting characters to accenuate the action of the novel. Whether participants, observers, profiteers, or casualties in the human drama unfolding in Tecan, Stone's characters either electrify or mesmerize the reader. In addition, Stone achieves a stunning success in paralleling the lives of the major characters, especially Holliwell and Pablo, to eventually collide by the novel's end in a perverse configuration of unity.

Techniques

In *A Flag for Sunrise,* Stone creates a realistic and suspenseful novel seemingly possessed by a menacing sense of impending doom. Drawing heavily on plot development and enhancing the action with a continuous stream of complex, engaging characters to attract attention, Stone is attempting to both entertain and instruct his readers. Criticized for being episodic and disjointed in structure, the novel represents an artistic challenge for Stone. Consequently, the novel's most successful quality is Stone's ability to re-create real experience into the fictional lives of his characters. In the process, Stone provides vivid and often transcendent description to supplement his thematic concerns. Likewise, his dialogue is at once capable of vibrant intensity and lyrical brilliance. Although flawed as a serious work of art, the novel represents a significant step in Stone's progression as an artist.

CHILDREN OF LIGHT

Children of Light, 1986, novel.

Social Concerns/Themes

Moving his fiction from New Orleans, Vietnam, Los Angeles, and Central America, Stone relocates to the coast of Mexico to continue his exploration of contemporary society in his most recent novel, *Children of Light.* Considered an artistic departure for Stone, the novel replaces the eccentric, menacing characters of his earlier work with the inhabitants of present-day Hollywood. The "children of light" are the self-illuminating, talented individuals so often consumed by the fantasy world of illusion.

The novel focuses on the protagonist Gordon Walker. Recently deserted by his second wife, Walker decides to visit the location shooting of a film based on his screenplay and starring his ex-lover Lee Verger, the stage name for Lu Anne Bourgeois. Once again, Stone produces fragile and nearly broken characters precariously dangling before an emotional abyss, desperately seeking reconciliation with the modern world and a renewed sense of purpose in life. Unfortunately, the destructive lives of his characters are beyond repair, and salvation if at all possible is momentary and fleeting.

At first glance, *Children of Light* does not reflect the harsh reality and violence so commonplace in Stone's fiction. Seemingly quieted by the serene locale, his characters appear less terrifying than previous prototypes; however, as the novel unfolds, an unnatural and unconscionable evil surfaces to take hold of the action and characters in the form of manipulation, degradation, and insanity.

Characters

An alcoholic screenwriter and sometime actor, Walker is a familiar figure in

Stone's fictional terrain. Inherently intelligent and not without promise, Walker is presently spent on cocaine and depression. Alone, adrift, and tormented by his existence, Walker is rushing headfirst into self-annihilation. Blinded by the glare of truth, Walker attempts to retreat into a dreamscape of drug-induced euphoria. However, the spell is short-lived and reality will undoubtedly reappear to claim its inheritance.

Akin to Walker, Lu Anne is another unsusceptible victim within the novel. Vulnerable to the unnatural forces that take possession of the mind and body, Lu Anne is schizophrenic, dependent on a daily dosage of medication to control her interior state of madness. Demoralized and desensitized, Lu Anne attempts to break free of her bondage by artistic and ultimately spiritual triumph. Walker is compelled to intercede in her behalf, more for his benefit than for hers, yet he is unable to overcome his own limitations. Similar to Rheinhardt, Converse, and Holliwell, Walker survives to face another day regardless of the bleak uncertainty of the future. Lu Anne, on the other hand, will join Gertrude, Marge, and Sister Justine in a brief moment of transcendence.

Increasingly aware of the possibilities and intrinsic value of his secondary characters, Stone dispenses an entire colony of film personnel to supplement the authenticity and rhythm of the novel. Among his realistic, insightful, and often comic creations are the film-directing Drogues, junior and senior, the viciously omnipotent journalist, the rising young starlet, and a colorful array of the various and sundry "extras" of the business. All are under the watchful and sarcastic eye of Stone, observing the scene from a safe distance and shaking his head in saddened disbelief.

Techniques/Literary Precedents

Considered Stone's most realistic achievement, *Children of Light* is polished narrative strikingly similar in development to Ernest Hemingway's *The Sun Also Rises*. Immensely dependent on dialogue, the novel exposes the innermost depth of human suffering as well as the day-to-day routine of the film industry. Stone creates diversified voices within the novel but exercises complete control over the diction and intonation of his characters.

Stone is particularly successful, as he was in *A Flag for Sunrise*, in producing intricate plot development while orchestrating the actions of his major characters to intersect at the climax of the novel. Likewise, Stone creates an interesting parallel, similar to the relationship between Holliwell and Pablo, with Lu Anne and the character she is playing in the film. As fantasy and reality become interchangeable for Lu Anne, she realizes her destiny is to follow the precedent set by her fictional counterpart. Striving for a final display of epiphany, Lu Anne disappears into the beckoning and comforting sea. Stone leaves, as he has before, a surviving protagonist, no wiser for having made the novel's journey, and a heroine as victim on the altar of the modern world.

Additional Sources

Contemporary Authors, Volumes 85-88. Detroit: Gale Research, 1980. Limited biographical information and discussion of *A Hall of Mirrors* and *Dog Soldiers.*

Contemporary Literary Criticism, Volume 5. Detroit: Gale Research, 1976; Volume 23, 1983. Quotations form selected reviews of Stone's novels through *A Flag for Sunrise.*

Epstein, Joseph, "American Nightmares," *Commentary* 73 (March 1982): 42-45. Critical analysis of Stone's work through *A Flag for Sunrise* offering insight and evaluation of stone's literary reputation.

"Robert Stone," *The Paris Review* 98: 24-57. Candid and informative interview with Stone providing biographical information and commentary concerning Stone's novels through *Children of Light.*

Ruas, Charles, "Talk with Robert Stone," *New York Times Book Review* (October 18, 1981): 34-36. Supplementing the review of *A Flag for Sunrise* by Michael Wood, Ruas' interview with Stone offers brief biographical and critical information.

Steve Serafin
Hunter College
City University of New York

REX STOUT
1886-1975

Publishing History

Like many writers who have specialized in narratives of crime and detection, Rex Stout became a novelist after succeeding in another career. His first Nero Wolfe novel appeared in 1934, when Stout was forty-seven years old. Because it was an immediate success, Stout continued to write about Wolfe, Archie Goodwin, and the brownstone mansion on West Thirty-Fifth Street during the next forty years. Stout contributed thirty-three novels and more than forty novellas to the literature of crime and detection.

Striking parallels exist between the evolution of Stout and two writers of detective fiction who figured prominently as literary influences on him. Sir A. Conan Doyle, the creator of Sherlock Holmes, had been a successful physician and adventurer before he began to chronicle the adventures of his great detective. Raymond Chandler, who created Philip Marlowe, had an eventful career as an executive in several oil companies before he wrote his studies of the California waste land. Stout, too, was a businessman who later took up the pen.

Born in Indiana, Stout first achieved recognition as a child prodigy. Biographer John McAleer holds that Stout's measured I.Q. was an astonishing 185. He left the University of Kansas without completing his degree to join the navy and served a tour of duty aboard President Theodore Roosevelt's yacht. Later he entered the financial world and, in 1916, designed the Educational Thrift Service, a system encouraging savings by children that was eventually installed in more than four hundred school districts throughout the country. Until the depression, this invention made the Stout family financially independent, and Rex retired from business in 1927. He moved to Paris to take up a career as a writer. His first novels received favorable reviews, but did not meet with popular success. With the publication of the first Wolfe novel in 1934, his career as a popular writer with serious concerns was launched.

Stout's methods of composition are almost unique. Although they are not a model for other writers, they indicate the exceptional quality of Stout's mind. Stout almost never revised a line. He planned each story or novel so thoroughly that he knew what situations, clues, and characters he would need to include before he began to write. The first draft was always final. He worked at a typewriter and explored all the possible variations for each sentence in his mind. When he had the right version, he typed it out. Working with this precision, he usually wrote four to six finished pages each day.

The result of this method is a style that compares with Chandler's in intriguing ways. Stout's style never reaches the brilliance of some of Chandler's inspired descriptions or philosophical meditations. At the same time, it is never crude or trite or artificial as Chandler (like most writers of detective fiction) is at his worst.

Perhaps the best word to describe Stout's style would be "stable." It is always carefully controlled and pleasingly varied. Stout seldom becomes monotonous because he adeptly varies sentence length and rhythm and because he uses wit and humor more effectively than most mystery writers.

Critical Reception, Honors, and Popularity

Detective fiction has always appealed to a special audience. Statesmen, philosophers, poets, and executives frequently confess that their favorite casual reading includes detective novels. Among leaders of government, business, and the intellectual world, Stout has had a following comparable with that of Doyle or Dame Agatha Christie. When Stout died in 1975, Harry Reasoner, one of the more erudite television journalists, ended his commentary with the sentence, "A lot of more pretentious writers have less claim on our culture and our allegiance."

A very selective listing of those who have expressed admiration for Stout's achievement will give some sense of his appeal to leaders and intellectuals. Political figures include Chief Justice Oliver Wendell Holmes, who felt that Wolfe "is the best of them all"; Senator and Vice President Hubert Humphrey; President Dwight Eisenhower, who read *Prisoner's Base* while recovering from a heart attack; and British Prime Minister Anthony Eden. Philosophers like Bertrand Russell, theatrical people diverse as John Wayne or Lynne Fontiane, and literary critics like Joseph Wood Krutch, Mark Van Doren, or Jacques Barzun have all indicated appreciation for Stout's achievement. Praise also came from "serious" writers like Graham Greene, Robert Penn Warren, John Steinbeck (whose *Travels With Charley* Wolfe reads in *The Mother Hunt)*, and William Faulkner. The greatest praise came from Ross Macdonald, himself one of the giants in the development of a serious American detective literature, when he said, "Rex Stout is one of the half-dozen major figures in the development of the American detective novel."

Praise from these leaders in the world of the intellect and practical affairs meant much to Stout, but equally treasured were communications from students, doctors, housewives, professors, and cab drivers—in short, the whole range of contemporary life. Readers from all segments of society found something to value in the Nero Wolfe stories. Even readers behind the Iron Curtain, where Stout's books are censored, rate Stout as one of the most popular authors.

A statistical measure of Stout's wide appeal is that more than forty-five million copies of his works have been sold. Translations include more than twenty-two languages. In 1985, Bantam Books announced its intention to bring back into print one Wolfe book each month until the entire corpus is available to readers.

A final indication of the importance of Stout's creation is the publication in 1986 of Robert Goldsborough's *Murder in E Minor*. This novel uses the characters, literary techniques, and conventions of Stout's Nero Wolfe books. As Ian Fleming's James Bond (Fleming unsuccessfully proposed collaborating with Stout on a novel) was taken up by subsequent authors including Kingsley Amis and John Gardner,

Stout's major achievement struck so important a chord that even the author's death could not eliminate the public's wish to hear more about Wolfe and the other inhabitants of the brownstone mansion.

OVERVIEW

Characters/Literary Precedents

Because all the books depend on Wolfe and Goodwin—*Too Many Women* is unique in that Goodwin is the central character and Wolfe has a secondary role— the major characters are best examined in a unified way. A consideration of literary traditions behind each of the principals is necessary in order to understand the thematic significance of the characters.

At the heart of Stout's achievement is his unique synthesis of literary traditions. Detective novels have historically fallen into two categories, which may be called the British "master sleuth" and the American "tough guy." Stout's work is exceptional in that it combines the strong points of each genre.

The British "master sleuth" originates with Edgar Allen Poe, but reaches its finest expression in Sherlock Holmes, on whom Wolfe was modeled. This model of writing, which has not, except for Stout, been critically successful in America, offers the pleasures of exotic and imaginative crimes and the delights of an exercise in problem-solving. The doctrine of fair play demands that the author share all relevant information with the reader, but the detective, blessed with a superior intellect, is able to systematize the information and assign each detail the correct priority. Readers therefore engage in a contest with the sleuth, trying to solve the mystery before the detective reveals the solution. Because of the influence of Holmes and Dorothy Sayers' Lord Peter Wimsey, it has become customary for the detective to be personally eccentric as well as cerebral and sometimes contemptuous of his intellectual inferiors.

Nero Wolfe falls clearly in this tradition. He is thoroughly eccentric. He weighs 286 pounds and has a specially designed chair to accommodate his bulk. He dresses flashily, usually with yellow shirts, and his bright yellow pajamas must resemble a sail on a medium-sized yacht. He is a misogynist, so his staff is all male, but he is elegantly polite to most of the women who visit the office. He is an avid reader and a devoted lover of language. He regrets in *Please Pass the Guilt* that he speaks only six languages because "I would like to be able to communicate with every man alive." His reading, even while engaged in a case, indicates an ecletic interest in the life of the mind, but in *Gambit* he systematically burns, despite philosophical objections to book-burning, a book he finds "subversive and intolerably offensive." The book is Webster's New International Dictionary, the third edition, which many traditional grammarians found offensive because of the editorial choice to describe the current uses of the language rather than to seek to regulate its use. Wolfe's most obscure demonstration of literary knowledge occurs in *The League of Frightened Men* when he recognizes a line as plagarized from Edmund Spenser's "The Shepherd's Calendar," but in *A Family Affair,* the final Wolfe novel, he compares the Robert Fitzgerald translation of *The Iliad* with several others on his shelves.

More familiar eccentricities include Wolfe's appetites for gourmet food and beer. He employs Fritz Brenner, who has a reputation as one of the finest chefs in New York City, and on occasions prepares feasts himself when he is absent from his home. He drinks great quantities of beer while consulting with clients or suspects and keeps track of his consumption by placing the cap from each bottle in his desk drawer. He cultivates exotic orchids in a hothouse on the roof of his mansion, and employs gardener Theodore Horstmann to help with this avocation. Gourmet cooking and exhibiting his orchids cause most of his rare departures from the house. Tending the orchids leads Wolfe to keep a rigid personal schedule much like the legendary walks of the philosopher Immanuel Kant. From nine until eleven o'clock in the morning, and from four until six in the afternoon, he is not available for consultation because he is in the orchid rooms. Any intrusion on this time, whether by a client, a police officer, or even Goodwin, is an invasion of privacy and is greeted with a bellow or a sulk.

The most familiar convention of the series is the detective's refusal to leave his mansion. This may be Wolfe's crucial thematic eccentricity, and it certainly involves Goodwin and Stout in logistical problems of getting suspects and witnesses to come to the mansion during the hours Wolfe is available for consultation. Stout's genius is clearly illustrated in that this important convention is frequently violated. Several of the best novels, including *Some Buried Caesar* and *In the Best Families,* require extended stays away from the mansion, and Wolfe voluntarily travels to Montana, overcoming phobias about automobiles and airplanes, to help Goodwin with a case he cannot solve in *Death of a Dude.* Despite the uncomfortable chairs, poor beds, lack of orchids, and canned soup, Wolfe never discusses a fee and behaves as an ideal guest. He also travels to West Virginia for a gourmet convention in *Too Many Cooks.*

Wolfe's origins remain mysterious throughout the series of books. He is fifty-eight years old in all stories, for Stout decided to incorporate contemporary developments of the time of each book's composition, but to keep his principals at the same age. Readers learn fragments about the detective's past. He owns a home in Egypt, but never expresses a desire to go there. He grew up in Montenegro, Yugoslavia, with one of the few men who call him Nero, restauranteur Marco Vukcic. His occasional anecdotes about escaping from prisons in Algiers and Budapest suggest a past life of political intrigue—if they are true—and this sense of the past might account for his reluctance to journey away from home. He tells a suspect in *The League of Frightened Men* a story of a wife who tried to poison him in Hungary, but this too may be fabricated because the woman he is talking to is capable of murder. He mentions many political intrigues in his past in *Over My*

Dead Body and reveals that he once adopted a daughter in Montenegro.

His past in question, Wolfe has little concern for the future. He is a hedonist, concerned with the pleasures of the present. His profession as a detective is a way to generate an income sufficient to maintain those pleasures. His method involves a more intricate analysis of the facts than is possible for either Goodwin or the police. He refuses to go over the ground covered by the police because, unlike many fictional detectives, he respects the integrity and ability, within limits, of most officers of the law. He gets his results by asking different questions and proceeding on different hypotheses from those of the police force.

Archie Goodwin is in many ways Nero Wolfe's alter ego. His origins are not at all exotic. He grew up in Ohio with a normal set of childhood experiences. Thirty-four years old in all the books, he is fairly handsome, reasonably athletic, certainly no misogynist, and generally competent in the business of detection. His exceptional qualities include an outstanding memory, presumably cultivated by long association with Wolfe, which enables him to report verbatim conversations with others. He is justifiably proud of his typing skills, both faster and more accurate than those of professional secretaries.

Archie is Wolfe's eyes and ears, but he is a capable investigator on his own. Wolfe often tells him to act on his "experience guided by intellect" and to exercise independent judgment. He often prods Wolfe to get involved in a case, and in *Please Pass the Guilt* actually solicits business for his employer. Wolfe appears to some readers as materialistic (he does work for an exclusive clientele and charge outrageous fees), but it is in fact Goodwin who frets over the bank balance and the expense accounts and complains of Wolfe's habitual laziness.

Goodwin completes Stout's design because he derives from a native American tradition in detective fiction. Like Chandler's Marlowe, Archie is a "tough guy" who depends on perseverance and commitment rather than pure intellect. His sense of humor, occasionally self-deprecating, rivals Marlowe's. Archie is knowledge-able and effective in what Chandler calls "the mean streets," where criminals operate. He is ready, if necessary, to fight or even kill to discharge his obligation or protect his pride.

He also resembles Marlowe in his conflicts with the police. He often spends time in jail as either suspect or material witness because he refuses to cooperate with the officials. Like Marlowe, he uses the technique of the wise-crack as an offensive weapon against the stubbornness or stupidity of the officers, especially Lieutenant Rowland, who was probably based on a Naval officer under whom Stout once served, and who gets his comeuppance in *Please Pass the Guilt* because he un-knowingly divulges privileged information to a suspect.

Unlike Wolfe, Archie is well-adjusted sexually. Although his attitudes are tainted by male chauvinism when he stereotypes women in terms of sexual appeal, he enters into healthy relationships with women he encounters in several novels. Wolfe once suggests—half jokingly—that Archie seduce a client's daughter. Goodwin has a lasting emotional relationship with Lily Rowan, whom he first meets in *Some*

Buried Caesar, and the progress of this relationship from physical attraction to genuine love (although a tough guy like Goodwin would not use that word) provides yet another unity in the series.

By combining the sleuth with the tough guy, Stout created something rare and fine in detective literature. The achievement was more than a technical triumph, but technically it does combine the fantasy element of the "sleuth" story with the realism of the "tough guy" chronicle. Stout was able to preserve with minimal compromise the characteristics appropriate to each type of detective novel. With the constant tensions that exist between two men who work closely together and depend on one another more than either would like to admit, Stout's combination strikes a subtle balance between personality types. Wolfe represents the Renaissance man, committed to idealism, aesthetics, and the life of the mind, whereas Goodwin is a synecdoche for contemporary man, devoted to pragmatism, results, and the world of action. Neither is complete without the other.

Themes

Crime literature usually treats the theme of the fallen world, and Stout's fiction approaches this idea in a unique way. The very existence of serious crimes like theft, kidnapping, or murder suggests a breakdown in the social contract. By violating another person's right to property, freedom, or even life, the criminal presumes to set himself above the laws that enable human beings to live in a civilized, rather than barbaric, state. In an important essay on detective fiction, poet W. H. Auden argues that murder is "negative creation," and that murderers in effect approximate ironically the role of god. The detective is civilization's last outpost. By discovering the criminal, he assures that some form of retribution will be exacted on those who would set aside the very principles of civilization for their own interests.

Nero Wolfe would not consider himself the champion of a principle of civilization. He is generally reluctant to take a case at all and seldom does so until a substantial retainer has been paid him. He often cautions Goodwin to stay out of cases in which they have no "legitimate interest"—no client or prospect of a fee—and prefers to allow the police to find the solution in their own slow ways. A discrepancy exists, however, between the role Wolfe accepts for himself and that designed by his creator. Stout treats Wolfe as representative hero in the romance that exists behind all worthwhile detective fiction: after the official constabulary has failed, there is someone who has the resources and intellect to expose the criminal and return society toward a rational course.

These themes are characteristic of the detective romance, but a unique element in Stout's creation depends on his hero's eccentricities. Wolfe's rigid schedule and reluctance to leave the mansion suggest the additional theme of an artificially created world. In this context, two objects in Wolfe's house become revealing symbols. The hothouse, in which Wolfe spends four hours each day, is an artificial environment, carefully engineered to nurture the delicate orchids of which Wolfe is so proud. Its temperature and climate are regulated alternatives to the natural conditions under which the orchids could not live. This symbol represents the entire created world of Nero Wolfe. It is artificial and vulnerable. The hothouse is destroyed by one of Wolfe's enemies in *The Second Confession,* and he regards any intrusion into it as an invasion of privacy. It, like the mansion and lifestyle of its owner, represents the ability of human intellect to create an environment in which human aspirations toward beauty, civility, and order can thrive.

The second important symbol is Wolfe's chair. It was custom made to accommodate his unusual bulk, and when he must leave the brownstone a chief inconvenience with which he must contend is chairs made for ordinary men. This symbol suggests the unique needs of individuals in a world where things are standardized. Wolfe will not let himself be governed by this standardization. His chair, indeed the mansion itself, are attempts to create a world that meets with his dreams and aspirations. Like his fondness for fine foods, good books, and a household free of what he perceives as the irrationality of women, his chair represents a desire for a rationally ordered world that serves human needs.

Three times in *Fer-de-Lance* Wolfe admits that he has a "romantic disposition" and in *Too Many Cooks* he calls himself "an incurable romantic." By contrast with more pragmatic minds, he longs for a world ordered to meet human needs and within his own closed system is able to design an artificial version of such a world. This is not to say that he ignores the imperfections of the real world. He is keenly aware that the world, with its corporations ruled by ruthless ambition as in *Too Many Women* or its families governed by hostility and unresolved tensions rather than love as in *The Final Deduction,* exists and presents a constant threat to his own environment. Each time the door of the brownstone mansion opens for a client, a police officer, or a suspect, the order of Wolfe's world is in jeopardy. Many of the best stories contain an episode in which that threat is made explicit when an object that threatens the lives of the inhabitants is brought inside the mansion, including a poisonous snake, a tear-gas bomb, and a bomb.

Wolfe recognizes the artificiality of his creation and the necessity of dealing with the imperfect world of human society but chooses to deal as much as possible with that world through emissaries. His principal ambassador is Archie Goodwin, to whom he delegates the task of working directly with the imperfect world. Goodwin's principal job is to gather information and report to Wolfe. Although Goodwin's charge is gathering information, the special character of his association with Wolfe suggests that the implication of his duty is the protection, as far as possible, of the created world of his employer. Archie is not alone in this commitment. The several independent operatives who help him gather information—Saul Panzer; Fred Durkin; Johnny Keems, who is murdered while following leads in *Might As Well Be Dead;* and Orrie Cather, who causes special problems in *Death of a Doxy* and *A Family Affair*—variously emerge as champions of the order Wolfe establishes around himself.

Techniques

The success of any detective fiction depends on careful plotting and surprise. Stout is very adept in plotting his narratives. The reader's expectations are almost always foiled by an unexpected twist in the motivation behind the crime. The formula of Stout's fiction is that the crime is usually very complex, but the motive is generally simple after Wolfe has been able to deduce it. Usually the criminals are motivated by greed, ambition, the need to cover up a different misdeed, sexual jealousy, or a familial grievance. One remarkable instance of Stout's plotting is *The League of Frightened Men,* in which the deaths Wolfe investigates prove to have been an accident and a suicide, but the suspect has used these to launch a psychological campaign of terror against those who injured him years before in a fraternity hazing.

The challenge that confronts writers of the "sleuth" variety of detective fiction is providing the reader with all the pertinent information but maintaining suspense by not sharing the relative importance of each detail. To meet this challenge, Stout adapted the literary convention of peripheral first-person narrative more effectively than any of his predecessors. Years before, Doyle had successfully used Dr. Watson as his narrator. Watson knows all that Holmes does but cannot discern the relative significance of crucial details. Watson thus serves as an intermediary between the reader and the genius of Holmes. Often, however, he seems merely befuddled and his expressions of admiration for Holmes' genius often sound like Victorian pomposities.

Stout improved upon the method used by Doyle by casting his first-person narrator as himself a competent investigator. Goodwin therefore evaluates data with a professional mind, and this adds significance to the prodigious mental feats by which Wolfe sorts out detail. Unlike Watson, Goodwin does not express unqualified admiration for Wolfe. He is often exasperated by his employer's habits and secrecy, so much so that he often threatens to resign—or Wolfe to fire him, as he pretends to do in *Gambit* to deceive a suspect. A charming moment in one of the few extensively revised novellas, "Assault on a Brownstone," occurs when Goodwin returns from a second failure to bring in a person for questioning and sees Wolfe staring at his cherished globe. Goodwin suspects that his employer is "probably picking out a spot for me to be exiled to."

It is finally the complex interpersonal relationship between Wolfe and Goodwin that marks Stout's adaptation of the convention of the detective novel as unique. The contest has ultimately three components. Readers challenge both detectives in solving the crime, and Goodwin wishes passionately, just once, to prove his solution before Wolfe does. This complex challenge among characters and readers may be the most satisfactory method of writing a detective story. The relative lack of success of Stout's other detective stories, *Double for Death* and *Bad for Business* (later rewritten as the Wolfe novella "The Bitter End"), which use an omniscient narrator, indicate how much the success of the Wolfe canon depends on the adaptation of literary technique and the brilliance of Stout's characterization.

Analysis of Selected Titles

FER-DE-LANCE

Fer-de-Lance, 1934, novel.

Social Concerns

The first of the Nero Wolfe books and among the most successful, *Fer-de-Lance* introduces the principal characters and conventions of the Wolfe canon. Because of this, it is the best possible introduction to Stout's work. The crime is exotic and completely unmotivated. A college president who has no known enemies suffers a heart attack after hitting a drive on the golf course. Brought into the case by indirect methods, Wolfe concludes that Dr. Barstow was poisoned by a projectile fired from a golf driver adapted so that the impact on the ball would serve as a trigger. After a complicated wager with the District Attorney to have the body exhumed, an autopsy proves Wolfe correct. This creates more problems than it solves, for no one hated the victim. Wolfe's patient questioning of the caddies discloses that Barstow used a borrowed driver, so a different victim was intended.

One social concern of this story regards the self-interest of Westchester County District Attorney Fletcher Anderson. In 1928, Wolfe had provided Anderson with crucial evidence on a case but Anderson took full credit for solving it. This in itself gives Wolfe a motive to get revenge by exposing Anderson's incompetence. Moreover, Anderson is politically ambitious and personally a snob. Wolfe must coerce him to admit that there was a crime and he must contend with the intransigence of Anderson and the police force, especially "oafs" like Officer O'Grady and bullies like Corbett, to seek justice. Part of his satisfaction is that he wins a large wager from Anderson and is able to put him in his place. The larger implication is that without Wolfe's prodding, the district attorney would have allowed a murder to go undetected and a killer to remain free.

The killer is totally amoral. He inadvertently kills an innocent, respected member of the community and murders a poor mechanic to cover up this crime. As Wolfe moves toward exposing him, the killer makes an ingenious attempt on the detective's life by concealing a poisonous snake in his desk drawer (the first of many threats to the created world). Despite this occasion for hostility toward the killer, Wolfe allows him to complete his design by killing the man he originally set out to murder.

Why he allows the killer to complete his design indicates a second major social issue, one with which Stout was consistently concerned. The failure of the family to provide a stable basis for ethical conduct remained a paramount concern for Stout as it did for his contemporary Ross Macdonald. In the course of his investigation, Wolfe learns that the victim's widow, suffering from psychological problems, had once tried to kill her husband. The killer was abandoned as a child and witnessed the killing of his mother by his enraged father. His obsession is to avenge his mother's death and his own neglect. After establishing his guilt, Wolfe telephones the murderer and explains the evidence the detective must turn over to the authorities. This allows the killer time to kill his father and himself, and Wolfe feels no guilt about serving poetic rather than legal justice.

SOME BURIED CAESAR
Some Buried Caesar, 1939, novel.

Social Concerns

Stout's own favorite among his novels is unusual because, like *Too Many Cooks* and *Death of a Dude,* it is set entirely outside the artificial world of the brownstone mansion. Wolfe and Goodwin become involved in the case because of accidental circumstances. On the way to an orchid exhibition in Crowfield, Archie confirms Wolfe's suspicions about automobiles by having an accident. This strands the two temporarily at the estate of Thomas Pratt, owner of a chain of convenience restaurants in New York. Pratt has enraged local cattlemen by planning to butcher a prize bull as a publicity stunt for his restaurants. The book opens with a very funny scene involving Wolfe standing on a very large rock threatened by an angry bull.

While accepting Pratt's hospitality, Wolfe nearly witnesses the apparent mauling of the son of the patrician landowner Osgood by Caesar, the bull that had recently kept the fat detective on a rock. Wolfe immediately knows the young man was murdered and placed in the vicinity of the bull to create the impression of an accidental goring. Hired by the victim's father, he quickly discerns the identity of the killer, but the evidence keeps disappearing from his grasp. The bull contracts anthrax and its remains are incinerated before Goodwin can examine them. A suspicious character, Howard Bronson from New York, is found impaled by a pitchfork in a pile of straw. Goodwin, arrested as a material witness in Bronson's death, passes his time in jail in a delightful pursuit, but the incompetence of the Crowfield police is so great that Wolfe speaks kindly of his nemesis on the New York Police and even calls him "Inspector" rather than "Mister" Cramer.

Although Goodwin has no idea who committed the crimes, Wolfe has known all along. He cannot prove it because incriminating evidence keeps escaping, so he decides to invent some. This requires instant comprehension of the subtleties of the art of cattle judging, but Wolfe is up to the challenge. The killer he exposes is allowed time to take his own life. Again, Wolfe has opted for poetic rather than legal justice. The killer he exposes is a fundamentally decent man who was driven by misfortune and economic disaster to recover some of his fortune and his status as a cattleman. The murders, really attempts to cover up a fraud, were irrational acts of a desperate man.

Admirers of Goodwin will find this story interesting because it initiates a long romantic involvement with Lily Rowan, who pursues Archie in this book. Rowan will become so trusted a love interest that, in *In The Best Families*, Archie will trust her with his own and Wolfe's lives. After significant interludes in *Too Many Women* and especially *The Second Confession*, Archie's romantic interests in the cases will be less important than they were before because of his growing commitment to Lily.

IN THE BEST FAMILIES

In The Best Families, 1950, novel.

Techniques

Many readers feel that this is the best of Stout's narratives. It is also his most unique in that the case upon which Wolfe is working is less important than a personal crusade Wolfe undertakes to rid New York of its most dangerous master criminal. This quest requires that Wolfe retire from the detective business, find alternative employment for his chef and his gardener, put the mansion up for sale at a ridiculous price, and undertake a disguise that involves growing a beard and losing more than one hundred pounds. With Wolfe gone, and no one except his boyhood friend Marko Vukcic has a remote idea where he is—Archie speculates that he has taken up residence in his house in Cairo—Goodwin goes into business for himself and proves that he can function independently as a detective.

Rex Stout had labored for sixteen years to establish the character of Wolfe and the conventions of his created world. With a daring stroke at the height of his career he challenged every single convention he had developed. This was a great risk, for readers of detective novels resist changes in the assumptions they have learned to accept. Taking this risk, Stout wrote his finest novel.

Social Concerns

Wolfe reluctantly takes the case of a wealthy wife who wants to learn the source of her gigolo husband's income, and the client is murdered before the investigation is well under way. What he sees at the Rusterman estate convinces Goodwin that the promise of equal justice for all does not pertain among the very rich, but a greater threat prompts Wolfe to disappear leaving no trace before Goodwin returns to report on his client's death.

Before Mrs. Rusterman dies, master criminal Arnold Zeck sends a tear gas bomb to warn Wolfe to stay out of this case. This same Zeck warned Wolfe to stay out of a case in *And Be A Villain*, then sent a hit man to blast the hothouse in *The Second Confession*. In that book, Wolfe outlined to his clients the criminal operations and political influence of Zeck. He mentioned a contingency plan to go underground if necessary to destroy Zeck, but the man he was investigating to learn whether he was a communist (Zeck's interest in the matter ruled this out) was murdered—the weapon was Wolfe's sedan—so Zeck's and Wolfe's interests were temporarily the same.

The crisis cannot be avoided in this novel. When Zeck interferes, Wolfe knows that Rusterman's secret income is the result of a connection with organized crime and he determines that he must destroy Zeck in order to preserve the personal freedom he has created. As he tells Archie, "that confounded voice will presume to dictate to us." When Goodwin returns from the Rusterman estate, he finds the door of the mansion open—an invitation for the corrupt world of the streets to enter Wolfe's created environment.

By disguising himself as a criminal, Wolfe penetrates Zeck's operation. What he learns is of no legal use, however, because it is impossible to determine how far Zeck's influence extends. His chief weapon is blackmail, and many police officers and judges have been compromised in the past. Wolfe cannot trust even Inspector Cramer, whose integrity he has never before doubted even if he has had reservations about Cramer's intellect. Cramer himself warns Archie that Zeck is "out of anybody's reach" and Goodwin's suspicion that he is acting as a messenger for Zeck leads to a fistfight.

There is no recourse to justice, so Wolfe must cause Zeck's destruction. It is beneath his principles, and physically impossible, to assassinate him, so he and Goodwin execute a complicated scheme to force Rusterman to murder Zeck and be in turn killed by his bodyguards. After completing this task, Wolfe solves the murder of Mrs. Rusterman and begins to put on the weight he has lost.

In delineating this confrontation with Zeck, Stout addresses the theme of a system of crime so insidious that institutional justice is impossible and no one is above suspicion. The only recourse available to Wolfe reminds readers of the work of Chandler or Macdonald. The man of integrity must stake everything to combat the influence of evil. Stout would write many splendid books after *In the Best Families,* but he would never again aim at so daring a theme or achieve so much.

A FAMILY AFFAIR

A Family Affair, novel, 1975.

Social Concerns

Written in Stout's eighty-eighth year, this novel shows absolutely no indication of diminishing ability. It abounds in topical references to women's liberation and the first American energy crisis. Watergate is mentioned several times, and Wolfe confides to his associates that one reason he is interested in this case is that it may help to expose the malfeasance of President Nixon, whom all the characters despise for betraying the national trust.

Wolfe is not candid in his intention to reveal new information about Watergate. He knows the killer is one of his free-lance operatives, to whose defense he had come in *Death of a Doxy,* but he cannot prove it. Worse yet, one of the victims was killed in Wolfe's house, where he had come for safety. The detective's created world has been doubly violated. His hospitality has been rocked by a bomb blast and his professional family harbors a killer. When Inspector Cramer urges, as a friend, that he share his information with the police, Wolfe spends a weekend in jail as a material witness.

After Wolfe tells Saul Panzer and Archie figures out independently the identity of the killer, the two men labor to find the incriminating evidence. When they succeed, Wolfe leaves the disposition of the matter to the men he trusts. They coerce the killer to commit suicide.

In this final novel, Stout suggests the fallibility of Wolfe's created world. But he also indicates that ethical responsibility cannot be designated to the authorities, a theme implicit in all his fiction.

Adaptations

During the early 1980s, a commercial television network attempted a series based on Stout's characters and situations. The series was unsuccessful both commercially and critically. Some of this failure must be attributed to the inability of both script and cast to capture the subtlety of Stout's characters and themes.

The failure of the series points to an important merit of the Nero Wolfe books. They depend upon a subtle, coherent vision of reality. The medium of television, with its tendency toward simplification of issues and the mechanics of plot, did not effectively capture those premises upon which the fabric of Stout's book rests. All the viewer had was the plot. For Stout, the plot is an instrument closely allied with theme and character. An almost poetic justice occurs here, for Wolfe tells an audience in *Please Pass the Guilt,* in which many characters are involved in the television industry, that he watches television only occasionally to remind himself of the mediocrity of the medium. Goodwin, while less hostile to television than his employer, watches primarily baseball games involving the New York Mets.

Other Titles

Selected Novels: *The League of Frightened Men,* 1935; *The Red Box,* 1937; *Too Many Cooks,* 1938; *Over My Dead Body,* 1940; *The Silent Speaker,* 1946; *Too Many Women,* 1947; *And Be a Villain,* 1948; *The Second Confession,* 1949; *Prisoner's Base,* 1952; *Might As Well Be Dead,* 1956; *Champagne for One,* 1958; *The Final Deduction,* 1961; *Gambit,* 1962; *The Mother Hunt,* 1963; *A Right to Die,* 1964; *The Doorbell Rang,* 1965; *Death of a Doxy,* 1966; *Death of a Dude,* 1969; *Please Pass the Guilt,* 1973.

Selected Collections of Stories and Novellas: *Black Orchids,* 1942; *Trouble in Triplicate,* 1949; *Triple Jeopardy,* 1952; *Three Witnesses,* 1956; *Three for the*

Chair, 1957; *Three at Wolfe's Door*, 1960; *Homicide Trinity*, 1962; *Trio for Blunt Instruments*, 1964; *Death Times Three*, 1985.

Additional Sources

Anderson, David R., *Rex Stout*. New York: Frederick Ungar, 1984. Excellent thematic analysis.

McAleer, John, *Rex Stout: A Biography*. Boston: Little Brown, 1977. Authorized biography.

————, ed. *Royal Decree: Conversations with Rex Stout*. Ashton, MD: Pontes Press, 1983.

David C. Dougherty
Loyola College

WILLIAM STYRON
1925

Publishing History

Styron published his first novel, *Lie Down in Darkness,* in 1951 when he was only 26. He started working on it in 1948 after a bold move from his homely, "very Southern" Virginia to a multi-ethnic, rapidly changing postwar New York. A small legacy from his grandmother gave him relative financial independence and enabled him to take a creative writing course at New School for Social Research. Hiram Haydn, his teacher there, quickly recognized his immense talent and encouraged him to pursue a literary career, although Styron himself never doubted that writing would become his vocation. To his own surprise, Styron completed *Lie Down in Darkness* in just two years, quite a short period for a lengthy first novel written in an elaborate Faulknerian style, intricately structured, and dealing with complex psychological relationships. Ironically, when the book was published by Bobbs-Merrill, Styron was on active duty in the Korean War. Since its publication, *Lie Down in Darkness* has sold 190,000 copies and was translated into eleven languages.

For *The Confessions of Nat Turner,* Styron's first huge critical and commercial success, the public had to wait sixteen long years until 1967. Given the explosive racial tensions of the 1960s the timing, though, for a story of the leader of the only major slave rebellion in U. S. history was perfect. The novel became an instant best seller, selling over 200,000 copies in the first year alone. It occupied first place on the *Publisher's Weekly* list from November 1967 until September 1968 and remained one of the top-ten novels for another half a year. Naturally, it became Book-of-the-Month Club's Main Selection. Since its publication the novel sold two million copies. Its success abroad was equally impressive. It has been translated into thirteen languages.

The idea of a novel about Nat Turner had been on Styron's mind since his early years in New York. After all, Turner's rebellion took place in Southampton County, Virginia, very close to Styron's Tidewater home where he grew up, so he felt it as part of his own cultural heritage. The original *Confessions of Nat Turner,* some twenty pages of text published the year of Nat Turner's execution, was mostly a factual account of what happened and how it happened, but contained very fragmentary information on the man himself. It seemed, therefore, promising material for Styron's imaginative, exploring mind. But Styron, busy working on his novella, *The Long March,* and his least successful novel, *Set This House on Fire,* put his ideas on the projected novel temporarily aside. He returned to Nat Turner with concentrated energy in the early 1960s, strongly supported in his efforts by James Baldwin, the leading contemporary black writer, who spent many months at Styron's house while working on his famous novel, *Another Country.* It was this close association with Baldwin that helped Styron understand black tradition and culture and assured him in his bold plan of narrating the novel from Nat Turner's point of view, a strategy that meant a deeply personal identification of a white writer from the South with a leader of a slave rebellion one hundred thirty years ago. The novel was completed in 1967 after several years of thorough researching. Portions of the novel appeared shortly before its publication in *Harper's* and *Life* magazines.

Sophie's Choice, published in 1979, Styron's only novel since *The Confessions of Nat Turner*, was another instant popular and critical success. The book has already sold over two million copies and remained a hard-cover best seller for almost a year after publication. Its sales went up again in 1982-83 after its successful film adaptation. So far it has been translated into eighteen languages.

It took Styron five years to write *Sophie's Choice,* his longest novel (almost 700 pages), and another five to prepare himself mentally and emotionally for the novel's central subject—the horror of the Holocaust, the methodical extermination of millions of people in the Nazi concentration camps. The origins of the novel can be traced to Styron's formative early years in New York where he met Sophie, a Polish Auschwitz survivor, who thirty years later was to become the heroine of his novel. In the novel, it is Stingo, Styron's autobiographical narrator, whose meeting Sophie establishes the core of the novel. In fact, the answer to the origins of the novel is the novel itself—Styron's personal journey into his past that explains how and why he wrote *Sophie's Choice.*

Critical Reception, Honors, and Popularity

The publication of *Lie Down in Darkness* in 1951 was hailed by most critics as a major literary debut by an artistically mature young writer. For some, it was the best postwar novel marking the beginning of new fiction from the South. Initially, its popularity was moderate, limited to academic circles, but its readership grew steadily in the following years. The critics praised the novel's convincing portrayal of the self-destructive upper-middle-class Virginia family, its original composition, and elaborate Wolfean style. Soon the novel became a popular text in the courses on contemporary fiction. Critical opinion on *Lie Down in Darkness* gradually moved away from depicting Styron's novel in the context of the Southern tradition, towards recognizing its themes as universal and their presentation as strongly influenced by existentialism. *Lie Down in Darkness* was awarded the American Academy of Arts and Letters Prix de Rome in 1952.

Until the publication of *The Confessions of Nat Turner* in 1967, Styron's reputation rested largely on the critically acclaimed first novel. In literary circles, he was often labeled as a writer of great but yet unrealized potential, especially after the poor reception of *Set This House on Fire* by both readers and critics. With the appearance of *The Confessions of Nat Turner,* Styron dispelled all rumors of his artistic frustrations. The novel's immediate success established Styron as a major contemporary novelist in America, the impression reflected in the awards he received—The Pulitzer Prize in 1968 and the Howells Medal of American Academy of Arts and Letters in 1970. The vicious, misguided, and definitely politically motivated attacks on Styron by a group of militant black writers, though aggravating to the author, only increased the sales of the novel.

The tremendous success of *The Confessions of Nat Turner* is easy to justify. First, there was its subject matter: the slave rebellion of 1831, which until Styron's treatment of it was a largely unknown and misinterpreted episode in American history of black/white relations. Secondly, by identifying with Nat Turner and making him a very intimate narrator of his story, Styron succeeded in creating a psychologically convincing evolution of Nat's character, his spiritual and intellectual growth into his destiny. Finally, structurally, by having Nat look back at his life as he awaits his execution, Styron provided an effective dramatic framework for his story. These and other remarkable qualities of *The Confessions of Nat Turner* have ensured it a status of a unique masterpiece of American and world literature.

A deeply personal exploration of the past centering mainly, but not exclusively, on the horrors of the Holocaust explains the success of Styron's latest best seller, *Sophie's Choice*, to many critics his most impressive achievement. Styron's rich, powerful, lyrical style, and his masterful handling of the intricate but dramatically effective narrative structure, have been quickly acknowledged by careful critics. Readers have been especially captivated by the novel's superb development of the three protagonists and their dramatic relationships. *Sophie's Choice* received the American Book Award and was nominated for the National Book Critics Circle Award, both in 1980. Although it may be too early to judge, there is little doubt that *Sophie's Choice* will earn a special place in American literature as a novel of great moral and artistic significance. It certainly holds that place in Styron's career.

Analysis of Selected Titles

SOPHIE'S CHOICE

Sophie's Choice, 1979, novel.

Social Concerns/Themes

Unlike many modern writers, Styron is not afraid to deal with controversial, sensitive issues and the big moral problems of this century. Like traditional storytellers, he believes that serious imaginative fiction rooted in history and the objective world can engage the reader emotionally and intellectually, forcing him to take a decisive moral stand. Then, like a modern writer, he skillfully dresses his content in an intricate, dramatically challenging form. These qualities are embodied in *Sophie's Choice*. It is a novel of many themes, but one overriding moral issue: the inexplicable evil of the Holocaust, the calculated extermination of the Jews, Slavs, and other "inferior races" in the Nazi concentration camps. Styron takes up this subject for at least three reasons. On one hand, as a humanist he feels it is his moral duty and artistic responsibility to confront the Holocaust horror and attempt to comprehend its monstrosity no matter how futile such a task might appear to be. On the other hand, he transports his readers into the reality of the concentration camps to make them witnesses to the indescribable atrocities most of them have never heard nor thought of. Finally, by bringing the experience of the Holocaust so close to the readers' minds, Styron wants to show the carefree American society of yesterday and today how easily civilized, democratic order can slip into collective madness if one surrenders individual freedom to political ideologies, religious doctrines, or racial prejudice.

But *Sophie's Choice,* largely due to the presence of its autobiographical narrator, is not only about the Holocaust. It is also a novel about becoming a writer, of discovering one's own creative voice, of reaching artistic maturity. In addition, *Sophie's Choice* may be read as a novel of sexual initiation, growing up in the sexually stifling 1940s, and becoming a man. In a more serious way, the novel is also about the personal, cultural, and national past of the three characters, their guilt, their small and big lies. In that sense, *Sophie's Choice* is as much about the Holocaust as it is about pre-war and Nazi-occupied Poland, the American South, and the Jewish Diaspora.

Characters

The novel evolves around the lives of three characters: Stingo, a young autobiographical narrator, Sophie Zawistowska, a Polish survivor of Auschwitz, and Nathan Landau, her paranoid Jewish-American lover. Stingo's voice controls the novel. He is the reader's mediator, a sensitive listener to Sophie's horrifying confessions and a witness to Nathan's affection and madness, then a reflecting commentator on the impact of these experiences on his life. Through Stingo, Styron is able not only to establish a tactful distance between himself, readers, and the imcomprehensible evil of Auschwitz, but also to provide the reader with light counterpoints—the accounts of his sexual misfortunes—to balance the emotionally devastating gravity of his subject. Finally, as narrator, Stingo fulfills his most important role: as an intimately involved outsider to the doomed lives of Sophie and Nathan, he is the novel's survivor compelled to tell the story and share its impact on his personality. Ultimately, Stingo is the narrator because only he can give his readers the much-needed element of hope, the emotional recovery from the nightmare of monstrous inhumanity and Sophie's hopelessly shattered life.

Styron convincingly shows how the three characters need one another. Nathan brings Sophie back to life, restores her beauty, and liberates her intellectually, emotionally, and sexually. Through him, she can temporarily forget her tortured past and her awful guilt. She holds on to Nathan's love with desperate passion, total abandon, and complete surrender, because there has been no love in her past: the men in her life had victimized, ignored, and humiliated her. Nathan, on the other hand, needs Sophie to satisfy his vanity and sexual needs. He needs her to control his insanity, to forget his loneliness and his cursed life. She is his creation, his Galatea, a devoted listener to his lies, an admirer of his genius, a passionate, submissive lover. At the same time, Nathan's obsessive fascination with Sophie has to do with her past, her Gentile heritage, with the fact that, unlike millions of others, especially Jews, she survived Auschwitz. His insistent prying into her hopelessly scarred life and his cruel questioning eventually trigger off painful memories reminding her of her guilt and her undeserved survival. Both are doomed: Sophie whose future died in Auschwitz, Nathan whose paranoia cannot be cured.

From the moment he first meets them, Stingo is intrigued by both Sophie and Nathan, as if he sensed how much they would mean in his life. Sophie will give Stingo her horrifying life story that will confront him with ultimate evil and haunt him throughout his life. He will be her intimate confessor, someone who will disburden her of her past and absolve her of her guilt so that her tormented soul can rest in peace. Many years later, Stingo as Styron, will give the readers her story, the story of her impossible "choice" that he promises to write at the end of the novel. But Sophie will give Stingo more than the knowledge of evil and death. She will be his first woman, his first complete sexual experience that will put an end to his prolonged virginity and the anxieties that go with it.

To Stingo, the more experienced and the incredibly erudite Nathan, until Stingo discovers his paranoia and drug addiction, is a model intellectual: witty, confident, aggressive, and winning. Nathan also becomes the first critic of Stingo's literary work—his enthusiastic, sound judgement and strong encouragement will send Stingo/Styron on the road to literary fame. On the other hand, Nathan's mad attacks, recurring with greater frequency and increasing violence, will show Stingo man's insanity, his potential for evil. In Nathan, Stingo will see both Sophie's savior and destroyer and realize why he could never take her away from him.

Of the three, only Stingo survives, strong and mature from the experience of the knowledge of the past Nathan and Sophie passed on to him. Only Stingo could make his choice; Nathan and Sophie were deprived of it.

The novel's many other characters either represent the characters' haunting past, thus helping the reader to understand the protagonists' predicament, or the present, the late 1940s, where they enrich the social landscape of the novel.

Techniques

Despite its length, demanding style, and Stingo's frequent digressive reflections, *Sophie's Choice* is a powerfully dramatic work. Its suspense comes from the complex treatment of time. The novel's drama unfolds gradually as the characters, particularly Sophie, reveal the increasingly truthful and painful experiences of their past. This process culminates in Sophie's story of her terrible "choice." This development is paralled by another in which all three characters slowly reveal their true selves. The dramatic power of *Sophie's Choice* is also a result of Stingo's narrative distance—he relates the events after they had already happened, the strategy that gives the novel its fateful, deterministic quality. Finally, Stingo's narrative mediation distances Styron and the reader from Sophie's Auschwitz experiences, thus enabling the reader to share in Stingo's/Styron's meditation on history and the value of human freedom.

Literary Precedents

The confessional, personal character of the novel's narration puts Styron's work beside similarly narrated novels of Saul Bellow, Philip Roth, or even J.D. Salinger. The difference lies in the seriousness of purpose and the moral, historical scope of Styron's novel. Having a narrator/commentator relating human tragedy as a past event recalls Francis Scott Fitzgerald's Nick Carraway of *The Great Gatsby* or even Ishmael of Melville's *Moby Dick* (the second paragraph of Styron's novel beginning with "Call me Stingo" is a direct reference to Melville). Stylistically, *Sophie's Choice* continues and refines Styron's high-Southern, post-Faulknerian diction so strongly felt in *Lie Down in Darkness,* the novel young Stingo/Styron is writing in *Sophie's Choice.*

Related Titles

Sophie's Choice is so self-reflective that a careful reader easily finds references to Styron's earlier novels. After all, *Sophie's Choice* is about young Styron struggling in New York and writing his first novel. For example, Maria Hunt, whose suicide is related at the beginning of the novel, could have been a prototype of Peyton Loftis of *Lie Down in Darkness.* Similarly, the story of the slave, Artiste, Stingo's painful legacy, could have ultimately motivated Styron to undertake writing *The Confessions of Nat Turner.* Stingo's frequent references to Nat Turner certainly justify such possibility.

Adaptations

A successful film adaptation of Styron's novel directed by Alan Pakula and also entitled *Sophie's Choice,* was released in 1982. A powerful performance by Meryl Streep, playing Sophie, brought her an Oscar for Best Actress in 1983. The film's success added to the popularity of Styron's novel even if it could not possibly address all the thematic scope and narrative complexity of the original.

THE CONFESSIONS OF NAT TURNER

The Confessions of Nat Turner, 1967, novel.

Social Concerns/Themes

Coming from a Tidewater region of Virginia, where Turner's rebellion took place, and from a family that once owned slaves, Styron felt it was his moral responsibility to examine the monstrosity of the slavery system by incarnating himself as Nat Turner. No other white writer has so intimately and convincingly identified himself with a black man's psyche. Styron uses this strategy to present the inhuman system from the victim's point of view, to give his readers a physical sense of growing up as a slave, to take them on a journey to the roots of the black-consciousness movement, the beginning of the long road to racial equality.

Since Nat is the sole narrator of "his" confessions, the novel's main theme is the portrayal of Nat's growth into leadership and the recognition of his mission. His recollections take readers through his early education at Samuel Turner's house, his deepening alienation from both whites and blacks, the realization of his captivity, the maturation of his visionary, Bible-inspired mission to free the slaves through violent rebellion, to the actual slaughter and admission of failure.

Related to the above is another theme—the conflict between man's natural yearning to be free and the system that kills that yearning or takes away his freedom. Many slaves in Nat's confessions have been so conditioned by the system that they subconsciously accept it as the only reality. Others who have recognized their desperate need to be free, and thus their humanity, confront the merciless, institutionalized repressiveness of the system that refuses to see them as human beings. In such dehumanizing conditions, a captive man's only alternative becomes violence. Styron's Nat Turner illustrates this truth through his experiences. His bloody rebellion, justified by his readings of the Prophets, becomes a God-blessed mission of vengeance.

In a more universal sense, Styron's book is obviously not only about Nat Turner and American slavery but about all men held in physical and mental bondage by today's repressive systems.

Characters

Nat Turner, the consciousness and conscience of Styron's novel, is a complex character. His psychological development is shaped by the treatment he receives from his successive white masters. As a young boy, he grows up in a household of a benevolent, liberal Sam Turner, who seems to accept slavery as a necessary, if not convenient, evil. His family recognizes Nat's "unusual" potential. They teach him how to read and write (mostly with the Bible), make him a skillful carpenter, and promise freedom when he reaches twenty-one years of age. This stage of his life marks Nat's alienation from his race as well as a slow realization of his institutionalized exclusion from the world of the whites, who, ironically, molded him in their image. In this racial limbo, Nat painfully recognizes the hypocrisy of the whites and his own terrible isolation. As a result, he withdraws into himself finding that the Bible not only offers him spiritual consolation but provides also a parallel to the suffering of his own people and a method of ending it. Once Turner abandons and betrays him, Nat awakens to the grim reality of his bondage. Treated like a skilled animal, sold and rented like a piece of useful machinery, Nat puts into practice his ideas of liberating slaves through the destruction of the whites. He becomes a preacher of doom.

Through Nat's complex narrative, the reader meets a variety of characters. Among the whites there is the idealistic Samuel Turner, the immoral Eppes, the crude, uneducated Moore, the insensitive Travis, Nat's cynical confessor Gray, the enlightened, disillusioned Judge Cobb, and the innocent Margaret Whitehead. The slaves are equally diversified. On one end of the spectrum are the docile, ignorant ones who turn against their liberator to protect their white masters; on the other, the blood-thirsty, raging killer, Will. In the middle there is Hark, Nat's closest friend to the last hours of his life, chained and beaten, awaiting death in the adjacent cell, the painful evidence of the bondage of his whole race.

Styron does not ignore another important aspect of Nat's personality—his sexuality. With great sensitivity, the novelist shows the reader how Nat manages to control and sublimate his violent sexual urges (directed, given the circumstances of his life, towards white women) through religious discipline and spiritual meditation, so essential to the preparation for his mission.

Although his rebellion fails and his Christian God "betrays" him, Nat is ultimately redeemed through his love for Margaret Whitehead, the only white he killed himself. His relation to Margaret is complex: he hates her for her whiteness but loves her emotionally and sexually. In the wake of the rebellion, she becomes a sacrificial lamb, but later, shortly before his death, the memory of her helps Nat transcend his despair into love. His metaphysical union with her is a fit symbol of hope for equality and love in the world to come.

Techniques

Styron's novel begins at the end; that is, with Nat in the cell just days before his execution. Such narrative strategy allows Styron to focus the reader's interest on why and how Nat Turner became the leader of the slave insurrection. After all, Styron is not interested in the mere retelling of events but in Nat's psychological development, in his reasons for what he did. Styron uses excerpts from the original *Confessions of Nat Turner* to give his story historical credibility, but the overwhelming bulk of the text is Styron's own, imaginative creation.

The complexity of Nat's psychological portrait comes from Styron's almost complete identification with his character and his ability to convey Nat's various personae in appropriate narrative styles. Throughout *The Confessions of Nat Turner* readers see Nat in different roles: a submissive slave, obeying and pleasing his masters; an educated, deeply sensitive human being reflecting on his life and future; an inspired, powerful preacher; a determined leader of the rebellion; or a frustrated, humiliated prisoner contemplating his own failure. His various roles make *The Confessions of Nat Turner* a brilliant mixture of facts, fragmented recollections, dreams, and reflections.

Literary Precedents
The Confessions of Nat Turner is a truly unique work of fiction. Styron took the idea of having the narrator awaiting his trial and execution look back at his life from Albert Camus' *The Stranger.* The novel's tone and narrative method resemble Arthur Koestler's *Darkness at Noon.* Thematically, though, *The Confessions of Nat Turner* has no precedents.

Adaptations
Film rights for the adaptation of the novel were bought by Wolper Pictures in 1968, but the work on the film never began as the producers backed away fearing it would further aggravate the already explosive racial tensions. The cinematic qualities of Styron's novel definitely deserve a sensitive visual representation, but the novel has not yet attracted any well-known director.

LIE DOWN IN DARKNESS
Lie Down in Darkness, 1951, novel.

Social Concerns/Themes
Unlike *The Confessions of Nat Turner* and *Sophie's Choice,* in which the characters are victims of the dehumanizing systems (slavery, Nazism) they tried to fight (Nat Turner) or cheat (Sophie), Styron's first novel deals with a self-induced, hopeless suffering of one upper-middle-class Virginia family. Yet *Lie Down in Darkness,* despite its exclusive focus on one family's spiritual and moral disintegration, is Styron's most pessimistic and depressing novel. It offers no hope, no redemption thus reinforcing the novel's theme: the family's inability to love, to overcome their selfishness, to see beyond their petty but deeply rooted misunderstandings. In a way, the Loftis' emotional immaturity, their crippled lives, illustrate the sources of the larger problems afflicting Milton and Helen's pre-war generation—lack of ideals, isolation, moral stagnation, intolerance, and indifference. Their meaningless social rituals awkwardly cover up their failure to communicate with one another and the outside world. Emotionally infantile, they escape into alcohol, promiscuity, cold self-righteousness, insanity, and suicide, unable to simply reach out for each other. Peyton's suicide gives the novel its tragic dimension, introducing the theme of guilt and parental responsibility.

Characters

Of the three main characters, Milton Loftis, the father of the family, is the central voice of the novel; perhaps because he, unlike Peyton and Helen, truly, though desperately, tries to keep the family together. The reader soon realizes that despite his sensitivity, his strong adoration of Peyton, and his attempts to reach out to his wife, he is rather weak. He does not have enough will power or courage to make a radical decision that could have prevented the family's tragedy. Estranged by his prudish, frigid, and authoritative wife, he seduces Dolly Bonner, an attractive, but submissive and simple-minded, wife of a pathetic real estate agent, and hides his infidelity until confronted by his wife. Even then he is unable to commit himself wholly to one or the other. Although Dolly gives him sexual fulfillment and tries to support him emotionally, Milton hopelessly persists in believing he can save his marriage and give Peyton a normal family. Perhaps he wants Helen because he is depending on her financially, or perhaps he wants to prove to himself and Peyton, despite evidence to the contrary, that they can be one, happy family. At any rate, whatever he does is ineffectual because his actions are too cautious and guarded by his selfishness. He remains in a cage he put himself in. Emotionally trapped, Milton lavishes all his love on his beautiful and bright daughter, Peyton, spoiling her and estranging her from her mother who is morbidly jealous of their relationship. In one way, to Milton, Peyton is the woman he would want Helen to be. In another, he idolizes Peyton, seeing in her the huge potential he once had but failed to realize.

Helen's coldness must have developed under the influence of her domineering, self-righteous father, an Army officer. Milton's unmanly indecisiveness, his failure as a lawyer, his dependence on her, and Peyton's manipulation of him all could have led her to withdraw from him. But Helen's intolerance and obsessive jealousy are not normal. As long as Maudie, their second, but retarded and crippled daughter is alive, Helen possessively turns to her for an emotional outlet, which symbolically reflects her own crippled, abnormal psyche. However, after Maudie's death, which Helen irrationally blames on Peyton and Milton, Helen's behavior becomes clearly pathological. On the one hand, Helen needs Milton if only to show Dolly where he belongs and make him feel guilty for what he did. On the other, she hates him for what he is not. In any case, her motives have nothing to do with love. What Milton fails to recognize, and what makes the novel so deterministically tragic, is that Helen's cruel coldness is incurable.

Caught between Helen's irrational hatred and Milton's excessive devotion is the family's victim, Peyton. Beautiful and intelligent, proud and independent, she serves as the mirror in which her parents could see their real selves. But they never look, especially the intractable Helen. Unlike her father, Peyton gradually builds up the courage to rebel, but when she leaves everything behind—her psychotic mother, a loving but weak father, her whole southern background, and marries a Jewish New York artist, she discovers that her rebellion has turned into a continuous and progressively alienating escape from herself and the curse of her family. To her horror, Peyton realizes how much her personality, her emotional instability, her selfishness and inability to love have been shaped by her "peculiar" upbringing. Her father's irresponsibility and dependence on alcohol and her mother's jealousy and intolerance have now become parts of her own personality. Her suicide must be read then in two ways—as a final desperate rebellion in which by destroying herself she destroys that which she hated but could not negate, and as an act of final surrender to death, an admission of her failure to become her own independent self.

Most of the other characters are largely instrumental or simply decorative. They populate the story, enriching its context, and enhance the personalities of the main characters. Interesting, though, is Styron's portrayal of blacks. Although they serve the white people, their world seems completely independent. Racially separated but united as people, they are the silent witnesses of the white family's troubled life.

Techniques

Like all Styron's novels, *Lie Down in Darkness* has an intricate, dramatically justified narrative structure. Although the point of view is omniscient (except for a forced, experimental second-person opening), Styron cleverly limits it by entering, with smooth, natural transitions, the minds of his principle characters, including those who play a significant role in the life of the Loftis family. Styron's skill allows him to engage the reader quite intimately without forcing the author to identify with any of his characters.

Quite original is Styron's treatment of time. Objectively, the novel's action covers the events of just one day—the day of Peyton's funeral, from the time her remains arrive by train until, after some unexpected misadventures, she is buried. In a sense, then, the novel begins at the end and moves forward through many flash-backs. The funeral provides only a compositional frame while the plot deals with the exploration of the fragments of the past to explain the characters' psyches. Instead, then, of building the climax around the old question of what happened, Styron involves the reader in the equally if not more dramatic how and why it happened.

Literary Precedents

Although its theme is universal rather than regional, both structurally and stylis-tically *Lie Down in Darkness* belongs to the Southern tradition. The novel's ornate, often tiring diction, owes much to Thomas Wolfe. Its use of interior monologue in Peyton's section recalls Faulkner's *The Sound and the Fury*. The novel's composi-tion, on the other hand, is heavily indebted to Faulkner's other novel, *As I Lay Dying*. Critics also pointed out that Milton's predicament and character resemble that of Dick Diver in Scott Fitzgerald's *Tender is the Night*.

Other Titles

The Long March, 1956 (short novel); *Set This House on Fire,* 1960 (novel); *In the Clap Shack,* 1973 (play); *This Quiet Dust,* 1982 (essays).

Additional Sources

Butterworth, Keen, "William Styron" *Dictionary of Literary Biography: American Novelists Since World War II,* vol. 2. Detroit: Gale Research, 1981, pp. 460-475. A very informative, introductory essay on Styron's career and fiction.

Crane, John Kenny, *The Root of All Evil: The Thematic Unity of William Styron's Fiction.* Columbia: University of South Carolina Press, 1984. A sophisticated structural analysis of Styron's themes.

Morris, Robert K., and Malin, Irving, eds. *The Achievement of William Styron.* Athens, GA: University of Georgia Press, 1981. Contains some of the best, most illuminating essays on Styron's work. Excellent bibliography.

Ratner, Marc L., *William Styron.* New York: Twayne, 1972. Covers Styron's literary career and thoroughly discusses his fiction.

Tomasz Warchol
Georgia Southern College

JACQUELINE SUSANN
1918-1974

Publishing History

Jacqueline Susann wanted to be a big star in the 1940s. She had some success on Broadway and in radio as a minor actress but she never made it "big, Big, BIG," as her husband Irving Mansfield put it in his biography of her, *Life With Jackie*. It was frustration caused by her lust for fame that drove her to writing. She was determined to be famous; the medium didn't matter. In 1939 she wrote her first play, *Some Fine Day*, in a week. Her husband told her it sounded like it had been written in a week. She fumed and gave up writing for a while. In 1944 she made revisions of a play called *Firefly* (hastily changed to *The Lady Says Yes* after a fire devastated the Coconut Grove nightclub killing five hundred people the night before *Firefly* opened) in which she had a small part as a maid.

Susann decided she was serious about writing and in 1945 she and her friend Beatrice Cole sat down at their respective typewriters and tapped out a play, *The Temporary Mrs. Smith*. It was loosely based on the escapades of a Russian woman who lived near Susann. The play centered on her attempts to land a rich husband to soothe her financial worries. It was bought, produced, and tried out of town. It was not exactly a success. The women revised it and in late December of 1946 the show opened on Broadway as *Lovely Me*. The reviews were not good. The play closed in February of 1947 after going through two theaters. It closed, Irving Mansfield claims, not through any lack of popularity but because no other theater was available.

Undaunted by the failure of *Lovely Me*, Susann and Cole again collaborated and produced a novel, *Underneath the Pancake*. It dealt, as most of Susann's later novels did, with show biz. It was accepted by an agent. Changes were requested. Changes were made. The novel was still rejected but the agent suggested it might make a good play. The women couldn't face another revision so they turned to radio. Their situation comedy, "There's Always Albert" ran for a while.

The 1950s were not a good time for Susann. She continued her career as an actress, appearing in commercials, on talk shows, game shows, but she was not happy. She was not a star. Susann was an avid reader of science fiction and during this period she wrote a science fiction novel whose alien was based on Yul Brenner, whom she had a crush on. It was not published until five years after her death.

In the early 1960s two things happened. Susann got a poodle and her friends Joyce and Billy Rose went to live in the south of France. She wrote them letters recounting the growth and progress of her new pet, Josephine. When the Roses returned they dropped a fat manilla envelope on her coffee table and told her the letters would make a good book. Susann took six months to compile it. After some trouble with publishers, *Every Night Josephine* came out in November of 1963. It made number nine on *Time*'s non-fiction best seller list and gave Susann the confidence to try her hand at another novel.

When it was published, *Valley of the Dolls* sold more than any American novel in the twentieth century. Susann made more than one million dollars on the book in 1966 and it sold more than ten million copies. She sold the movie rights before the novel hit the bookstores. It stayed on the *New York Times* best seller list for sixty-eight weeks, twenty-eight of them in first place. The phenomenal numbers were the same for her next two books. The movie rights for the *Love Machine* sold for a million and a half dollars. *Delores,* her last book, published posthumously, only reached number nine on the best seller lists, but was number one as a paperback.

Susann had trouble with her publishers. She felt her first publisher, Bernard Geis, was cheating her, so she left him, after a lawsuit, for Simon and Schuster. After her second book was published, she felt there was a conflict of interest since Simon and Schuster also represented her competitors, Harold Robbins and Leon Uris, so she left them for William Morrow. This well reflects her concern for the business end of writing. Part of Susann's success can be accounted for by her relentless publicity tours. Even people who disliked her work acknowledged her show biz savvy. Some claimed she had a positive genius for self-promotion. She understood, in a way no author had before, how to exploit the publishing and advertising machine.

Critical Reception, Honors, and Popularity

Though Susann was occasionally praised for her narrative drive, mostly the love of her fans was matched by the disdain of her critics. Much of the critical establishment greeted each novel with scorn. They were not simply dismissive, they were scathing, sarcastic. Susann and her husband were probably not entirely wrong to think that critics were outraged by her success. Here was a writer many critics considered to be third-rate and a sensationalist at best and she was outselling everyone. The most extreme expression of this vitriol was probably expressed by John Simon, when on a talk show he called her a whore and a bitch and screamed that he "would rather see dogs fornicating than read . . ." her "stuff." Susann quite rightly perceived her standing in the literary world as a battle between "them" the critics, and "us," she and her readers. She did not win awards.

Her critics seem to have been borne out. She is little read today. Her books are difficult to find. When her name is mentioned, scholars chuckle at her achievement. She is considered an interesting explosion in the pan. Jacqueline Susann went to her grave believing she was the equal of Charles Dickens.

Analysis of Selected Titles

VALLEY OF THE DOLLS

Valley of the Dolls, 1966, novel.

Social Concerns/Themes

Jacqueline Susann said that one of the purposes of her novels was to show the average woman that money and fame do not equal happiness. All three of Susann's heroines in this novel want a man, children, respectability. Their careers as high fashion models and highly paid actresses and singers are either a diversion until Mr. Right comes along, or a means of making money until they can settle down, have the kids, lead a rather high-style version of a housewife's life. They all fail.

Jennifer North, after one possessive lesbian affair, two disastrous marriages, and an intervening career as an actress in European art films, finally meets her knight in the form of a senator, but discovers she has breast cancer and kills herself. Neely O'Hara whines throughout the novel that all she really wants is one good man, that her success is hollow without one. But her devouring star's ego destroys both of her marriages. Anne Wells, after a long, lackluster affair finally tricks the man she really loves into marriage, but is paid back with his infidelity when her trickery is discovered. The three main characters are done in by ideas of perfection. Jennifer commits suicide because, after her mastectomy, she will no longer embody an ideal of beauty. She believes her fiancé will not marry her. If Neely could admit that she loves herself and her career more than anyone she would be happier. Anne resorts to deception to trap her own true love. All three are victims of traditional images of women, images of perfection, that they do not realize are unattainable, and given their lives, undesirable. Anne Wells could have her great love, Lyon, had she been willing to move back to her small town. But she was not willing. She had, without realizing it, already rejected one stale image of woman solely as helpmate, in favor of a career, excitement, the city. The one role model they might have had, Helen Lawson, a huge success on Broadway, is seen as something of a failure because she can only get "fags" as escorts. Susann's prose is at its most unbelievable when she writes about love.

It would be tempting and easy to say that Susann simply doesn't believe that a woman with a career and a woman with a family mix. However, the images of the woman who stayed in small towns, and had children and husbands, are even worse: shrill, frigid, bored, grasping. These women are depicted through the characters' mothers. Jennifer's mother only loves money. Anne's mother was frigid and never really loved. Anne's aunt led a boring, undesirable life.

Susann was sometimes criticized for her pessimism but it is finally the most interesting part of her work. She introduced a new bleakness into mass fiction and with it casual drug abuse, frank language, casual sex, and an acknowledgement of the prevalence of homosexuality, which titillated her readers. Susann's first novel did not just flirt with despair as did most popular fiction. She said her work was about how life and loneliness changed people. Everyone is punished simply by virtue of being alive.

Characters

Valley of the Dolls has three main characters: Jennifer North, Neely O'Hara, and

Anne Wells.

Jennifer North is beautiful and talentless, but her beauty is enough to propel her to stardom. Jennifer, however, is not interested in fame; she wants money. She was programmed by her mother to want money, reminded of what a financial drain she was on the family, how it was imperative that she make a good, wealth-producing marriage. Jennifer doesn't really enjoy money. She's restless with it, always buying new clothes and giving them away. She never really amasses any cash. Her pursuit of money leads her to two bad marriages. She's happy only twice, once with her lesbian lover (until Maria becomes possessive) and later with her senator. Jennifer is good. She keeps her husband's mental illness a secret so it doesn't destroy his career and aborts her child when it turns out that the child will inherit its father's disability, again in secret. There's a rootlessness to Jennifer, a lack of focus, direction. In many ways she's the most appealing character in the book. There's an innocence to her, a sweetness as Anne says of her. Jennifer is not very bright.

Neely O'Hara starts out as an uncouth, free-living kid, brought up by her brother on the vaudeville circuit. She dances in his act. Neely is pretty, not beautiful, but she is the most talented performer of her generation. She remains vibrant and appealing until she reaches Hollywood. Once there, she becomes a star/monster. The long hours, with no time for anything but career, drive her to booze and drugs. She develops a colossal, ugly ego. Her insecurity drives her to self-destruction. She tries to kill herself several times and at one point winds up in a sanitarium. But she always comes back. As Lyon says of her: ''It's like a civil war, with her emotions against her talent and physical strength. One side has to give. Something has to be destroyed.''

Anne Wells is the New Englander with breeding, manners. She is compassionate and a devoted friend. She is honest. This woman is too good to be true. Her one flaw is her love for Lyon Burke. She will do anything for him except move back to her small town. As a result she loses him and for the next fifteen years has an unfulfilling affair and becomes rich and famous. When Lyon comes back she deceives him into marrying her. Anne can't stop loving Lyon even after his adultery with her best friend. But by the end of the book she loves him less and realizes one day she won't love him anymore. She starts taking "dolls."

Susann had a sense of depravity but not a sense of evil. None of her characters are wicked. They may end up badly but they start out nice. Lacking that sense of evil may be morally questionable but it gives her characterizations a certain edge missing in most mass fiction. It's strangely Freudian fiction; her characters have their reasons. It is the fiction of victims.

Techniques

Susann tells her story chronologically and from three different third-person points of view: Anne's, Neely's, Jennifer's. The novel begins with a terrible poem announcing its themes. It is then broken up into sections labelled with the names of the heroines. These sections are divided into smaller sections, establishing a time frame such as February, 1948, or simply 1956.

Susann's use of point of view is relatively sophisticated. The characters relate their stories through each others' eyes. This shifting point of view gives insight into the characters perceived and the characters perceiving at the same time. It adds depth. Readers would probably be less disposed to what little liking they have left for Neely at the end of the novel if they only saw her and listened to her from her own strident point of view. Anne's point of view softens Neely. Readers also learn more about secondary characters than they would if only one point of view were used. Tony Polar is more intelligible through Jennifer's perspective.

Though the voices of each section are relatively similar, Susann does try to make each section distinctive. She infuses some of Jennifer's lost quality into the prose of Jennifer sections and it is easy to identify coarse Neely's by the word "Geez." Anne's sections are the most romantic and contain some of the slushier prose.

The novel doesn't really end in the conventional sense for anyone except Jennifer, who's dead. Neely will continue to careen between success and disaster but readers don't know which side of her will finally be the victor in her emotional civil war: whether she will survive like Helen Lawson or destroy herself. Anne says she will eventually not love Lyon, but the question remains, will she become a drug addict and end badly or will she restore herself and eventually leave him? Susann leaves her characters' fates up in the air. Again, Susann is showing her peculiar and perhaps unwitting modernity.

Literary Precedents

Susann's most immediate precedent is probably Harold Robbins. In fact Elliot Fremont-Smith in the *New York Times Book Review* described *Valley of the Dolls* as a book that might have been written "by a slightly bashful fan" of Robbins. But there are older traditions from which Susann is working. One is that tradition which pits the purity of the pastoral life against the corruption of urban living. This idea flourished in the nineteenth century and was one of the hallmarks of Romanticism. Another tradition Susann was working through was that of the romance or love story whose most recent incarnation is "pulp" gothic romances. This is a fiction geared towards women. The protagonists are usually women and the plot centers on lost and found love. Eric Segal, scholar and popular author himself, says that these kinds of stories have existed since early Greek culture.

Yet Susann does not merely continue these traditions: she gives them a modernist spin. Irving Mansfield gives this description of *Valley of the Dolls* in *Life with Jackie:* "In fact, in this book, almost nothing ever works. Success corrupts. Power destroys. Love fades. Marriage breaks up. Money undermines. Health fails. Youth and beauty erode away. Only death and pills prevail." It is this bleak sensibility which transforms the traditions Susann is working out of. The city is still corrupt, but it is also glamorous and stimulating. The country is still pure but it is also stifling. Susann changes the choice to one between corruption and stultification, which is hardly a choice at all.

The same is true of what she does with the love story tradition. The heroines still dream of a knight in shining armor (one of its medieval manifestations) but this time they are destroyed by their longing. The forever-and-always love usually awarded to the heroine after her trials and tribulations is withheld from Susann's characters. It isn't possible in the fictional world she creates.

It is this dark vision which gives Susann another interesting set of literary ancestors, those modernists for whom despair was the only reasonable response in a century they perceived as foul. In a corrupt world there are no possible choices but corrupt ones. The values which sustained people are useless and beside the point. To long and strive for those values is perverse and ultimately destructive since they cannot be attained.

Susann probably did not consciously choose literary antecedents like Samuel Beckett, whose *Waiting for Godot* is considered by many to be the quintessential existential play of the 1950s, but he is there. The Godot her heroines were waiting for was perfect love, the ideal husband, angels for children (Anne is rewarded with at least one of those). Seen from one perspective, Susann's readers had so fully internalized the alienation Beckett's radar had sensed some years before, that what they were in part responding to was her illustration of it in a mass fiction art form. This helps to account for her incredible popularity.

Adaptations

Valley of the Dolls, the movie, is now considered a camp masterpiece by many. It opens with Mr. Vesuvius sideways pumping out pills. The silly costumes and glitzy sets, especially the commercials Anne appears in with their allusions to great art and the Calderesque set Helen Lawson swings around on in her Broadway show belting out her pseudo-show-stopping number, are sublimely bad. They come full circle and become art again. The whole movie has the glamorous look of a third-rate imagination running wild within the confines of its limitations. The dialogue, for which Susann must take some credit, is preposterously self-serious. Susan Hayward as Helen Lawson hams it up. Patty Duke as Neely whoops it up (her final scene in which she screams her own name on a deserted New York street is jaw-dropping in its excess). Barbara Parkins as Anne has two expressions, dewey when she isn't on drugs, and not-dewey when she is. Sharon Tate feigns innocence. It is all as intoxicating as heavy perfume.

Susann was furious when she saw the movie. She felt the subtlety of her characterizations had been trampled upon. After she saw a preview she told the director Mark Robson that she thought the movie was "a piece of shit." The critics agreed. Her public, however, didn't. It grossed over 70 million dollars and set box office records that were not broken until *Butch Cassidy and the Sundance Kid* a year later.

The only people who seemed to understand the great awfulness of the movie were Roger Ebert and Russ Meyer. Ebert wrote *Beyond the Valley of the Dolls.* Meyer directed it. They took the excesses of the original and soared with them, creating for example, a male director, who gets himself up in a kind of bizarre drag for sex, and calls himself superwoman. Susann, unfortunately, couldn't see their achievement. She felt betrayed and thought her good title was being used to sell pornography. The courts agreed with her though Susann never knew. Her suit did not come to trial until after her death and was finally settled for 1.4 million dollars.

Later, *Valley of the Dolls* was made into a CBS television mini-series, with the late Susann's husband as executive producer. It was not well-received.

ONCE IS NOT ENOUGH
Once is not Enough, 1973, novel.

Social Concerns/Themes
Once is not Enough is Jacqueline Susann's most overtly Freudian novel. In *Valley of the Dolls* Neely's mammoth insecurity is a result of her early deprivation of a mother and father but this is only one small facet of the book. In *Once is not Enough,* January Wayne's obsessive love of her father (her mother commits suicide when January is seven), her overblown Electra complex, is the center and soul of this fiction. January is not attracted to men of her own age. Her first encounter is with a steamy Italian and her response is icy, in part because she is young, but mostly because she only loves her father. Later, after her father remarries Dee Granger, to January's extreme disappointment, January tries to fall in love with David Milford. She even makes love with him but it is a horrible experience and she withdraws from men even more. It is not until she meets Tom Colt, a macho writer and a man several years older than her father, that she finally falls in love. She doesn't even mind that his penis is the size of a thumb and that he is mostly impotent. There are several older women with young male lovers in the book, but the attraction isn't as overtly Freudian.

January Wayne, as a result of her father fixation, is a relatively old-fashioned girl. She doesn't go so far as to believe in sex only after marriage, but she does believe that sex should be accompanied by love. None of the other characters feel this combination to be mandatory.

January's values are out of date. Susann's fictional world is the free-swinging world of the 1960s. It is a time of nudity, even fornication on the state. In *Valley of the Dolls* it seemed that the only people who abused drugs were the ones with the fame to need them, and the money to afford them. Drug abuse in *Once is not Enough* is much more democratic. January is displaced in this world because of her traditional values, but this time the displacement is even more extreme. The alienation of Anne, for example, in *Valley of the Dolls,* resulted because she was still encumbered by small town values in a privileged world where they no longer worked. In *Once is not Enough*, the topsy-turvy moral universe of the privileged class has filtered down to the masses. Interestingly, January is the freak. Her values are the result of a major neurosis. Susann does not condemn the other characters for their flexible moral codes; she accepts it as they do. Characters like Linda Riggs, an editor in the novel, may suffer some for their free-wheeling lives, but not as much as January. There is none of the traditional retribution awaiting them at the end of the novel either. They continue. Still, if January were set up as some sort of moral touchstone one might condemn the others, but she isn't. She's simply bewildered. Like nearly all of Susann's major protagonists, January is victimized for buying into the traditional images of women. Linda, the career woman, who may in some small way long for marriage, etc., is not a victim. She survives, shallowly perhaps, but with gusto.

Susann's treatment of homosexuality in this novel is more tolerant than it was in *Valley of the Dolls*. In her first book she freely acknowledged its presence but gay men were still referred to peripherally and derisively as "fags." In *Once is not Enough* one of the main characters, Karla, is an aging, reclusive Garboesque movie star. She is a lesbian. Throughout the novel she has an affair with David Milford and at one point makes the traditional recant that she really wasn't a lesbian after thirty odd years or so of being one. But near the end of the book Karla's female lover, Dee Granger, is redeemed from her frivolous life as a socialite by her love for Karla. Dee decides to leave her husband and lead an honest life.

This novel has the strangest ending of any of Susann's novels: January is carried off by a beautiful alien from another planet. It is quite an unexpected denouement given the realistic texture of the rest of the book. Yet subtly, in her own way, Susann has prepared the reader for it. There is a character, Hugh Robertson, and he is a retired astronaut. During the novel January has several conversations with him about the probability of life on other planets. Hugh tells her that there is probably life similar to humankind, some civilizations more advanced, some less, in the universe. Susann returns again and again to the imagery of the stars (the heavenly variety, not the fan magazine type, though there are plenty of those too). Finally, January repeatedly dreams, with particular intensity after her father's death, of the being who rescues her. Susann nudges the reader toward the ending, taking him through January's experiences with hallucinogens. The reader is not sure the ending is real until the novel is over.

Susann was a science fiction fan and had written her unpublished science fiction novel, *Yargo,* during the 1950s. The creature that saves January sounds suspiciously like the Yargo of her previous book. Susann, who didn't like to waste anything, probably couldn't resist using him. Possibly, it was also the closest she felt she could come to writing a science fiction book given the type of audience she had amassed.

Thematically, it is also an interesting ending. This is not as bleak a book as *Valley of the Dolls*. There is the dark strain. Dee Granger and Mike Wayne die in a plane

explosion just as both have resolved to change their lives for the better. But David
Milford does wind up with Karla. January meets her dream man. True he is an
alien, but nothing is perfect. What is interesting is that January's salvation has to
come from another world. Like the main characters in *Valley of the Dolls,* January's salvation isn't possible in the world as it exists. It isn't so much that January
is too good for this world, as she is too alienated for it.

Characters

Like *Valley of the Dolls, Once is not Enough* is notable for its absence of real
villains. No one is evil. There is plenty of deception but the deceptions are usually
perpetrated in the name of a higher love. No one is with the person he or she loves.
It's like a *No Exit* in a mass fiction art form. Hell is loving other people, all of
whom are unavailable.

Techniques

Once again Jacqueline Susann uses multiple, shifting third-person point-of-view
to tell her story. The story is seen mainly through the eyes of January Wayne, but
also through David Milford's, Dee Granger's, and Karla's eyes. Susann no longer
sets off the changes in narrator under chapters bearing the appropriate character's
name. She will shift for a page or two or as many as she needs to tell her story. The
reader is never in doubt as to who is narrating. There is a confidence to her use of
the technique though she loses something of the little distinctiveness the different
narrators had in *Valley of the Dolls.*

Adaptations

In 1974 *Once is Not Enough* was made into a film. It starred Deborah Raffin as
January, David Jansenn as Tom Colt, Kirk Douglas as Mike Wayne, Alexis Smith
as Dee Granger, and Melina Mecouri as Karla. Brenda Vacarro won a Golden
Globe for her role as Linda Riggs. Susann had a cameo as a T.V. newscaster. She
was like a little Hitchcock, putting in an appearance in all of the movies made of
her books. The film was relatively successful, but created nothing like the furious
ticket-buying for *Valley of the Dolls.* The critics, as usual, were less than kind.

Other Titles

Every Night Josephine, 1963 (non-fiction); *The Love Machine,* 1969 (novel);
Delores, 1976 (novel); *Yargo,* 1979 (novel).

Additional Sources
Irving Mansfield, *Life with Jackie*. New York: Bantam Books, 1983. A biography by Susann's husband.

Wesley Gibson

PAUL THEROUX
1941

Publishing History/Critical Reception, Honors, and Popularity

Paul Theroux prepared for his writing career by garnering as much experience as possible in Europe and the Third World. After graduating from the University of Massachusetts in the early 1960s, he went to the University of Urbino (Italy) as a lecturer in American literature. From there he joined the Peace Corps and taught in schools in Malawi and Uganda for five years. Between 1968 and 1971, he lectured at the University of Singapore, where he set the novel *Saint Jack* (1973). His first noteworthy novel was *Girls at Play* (1969), which had a limited success. *The Family Arsenal* (1971) won him recognition as an author of wit and style, but he did not achieve anything approaching fame until the publication of his account of a fascinating train trip through Europe and Asia, *The Great Railway Bazaar* (1975). This literary gem was followed by another paean to rail travel, from Boston to Argentina, *The Old Patagonian Express* (1979). Sections of these books read like novels, and they support the view that Theroux was collecting images for his fiction while sitting in seedy stations or observing the passengers who regularly pestered him.

No doubt the South American train adventure had something to do with the creation of a novel about a North American's excursion into the wilds of the Honduran jungle. *The Mosquito Coast* (1982), which critics have hailed as his finest work, marries his witty, sardonic vision with a powerful adventure tale and a central character of mythic proportions. The book was selected by the Book-of-the-Month Club and has become an international best seller. As of this date, a movie based on the novel is in production at Warner Brothers; Harrison Ford has the starring role.

Whether Theroux the novelist will surpass Theroux the travel writer is still in doubt. A successful movie may well do for his career what the film *Terms of Endearment* did for the fortunes of Larry McMurtry. Indeed, Theroux appears now to be a hot property for filmmakers; his latest novella *Half Moon Street* (1984) is also being made into a movie. It is unlikely, however, that a writer of such quality and versatility will simply turn to writing scripts for Hollywood. The popularity of *The Mosquito Coast* guarantees that his name will become better known to a larger audience and will no doubt prompt him to publish more fiction in a similar vein.

Analysis of Selected Titles

THE MOSQUITO COAST

The Mosquito Coast, 1982, novel.

Social Concerns

In the 1960s and 1970s, Americans began to question their country's image as the material paradise, "the land of opportunity." That questioning led to the founding of communes and other experimental societies. It also prompted some adventurers to escape the stifling, success-oriented climate of American city life to recover those Thoreauan values of self-reliance and resourcefulness in still untouched regions of the world. The hero of *The Mosquito Coast* is just such a frustrated fellow, who uproots his family from the security of their Massachusetts home and drags them to the Honduran jungle to help him build his own brave new world. Even though the family at first functions smoothly as a unit, the reader soon realizes that Father's missionary spirit has its darker side. In fact, his scorn for the natives' habits, especially their lack of industry in helping him to build an ice-making factory, begins to look more like the working out of America's "manifest destiny" on foreign soil. Father changes into a parody of the ugly American as he attempts to teach the inhabitants the technology needed to make their own ice.

The portrait of oppression suggests as well the consequences of an unharnessed patriarchy. Father's authority goes unquestioned by Mother, who qualifies as a classic enabler, indulging her creative child-husband yet trying to limit the damage his abuse inflicts on her children. The tragic conclusion of the novel signals an escape for Mother and her offspring from Father's control; readers hope that the narrator, 13-year-old son Charlie, can likewise escape the role of all-powerful male that Father tried to impose on him. In the surroundings of the Acre, the children's secret camp in the jungle, Charlie manages to establish a truly cooperative, natural society in which technology and its attendant hierarchy have no place. Though short-lived, this community appears to offer a reasonable alternative to Jeronimo, Father's settlement.

While deftly depicting the flaws in American society, Theroux also demonstrates that missionary zeal—both religious and technological—is a major cause of America's tarnished image in the world. (This view may stem from Theroux's own experience as a Peace Corps teacher in Africa.) The events of *Mosquito Coast* dramatize how the unthinking imposition of these values on native cultures can suppress human impulses and lead to destruction.

Themes

The Mosquito Coast treats many subjects, but its main themes concern the potential destructiveness of the social rebel and of modern technology. The novel's hero Allie Fox rejects the shabby workmanship of America's mass-produced goods, the hedonistic features of its TV-influenced culture, and the self-satisfied pomposity of its religious establishment. Calling America a dead society, he takes his family back to nature, founding a settlement called Jeronimo in the Honduran jungle. Yet he brings with him the engineering know-how to build an ice house for his own pleasure and the benefit of the Mosquito Indians. The ice he produces clearly symbolizes a scientific Eucharist, the means of worshipping the technological god he believes will save them all. When Allie blows up the ice house (called Fat Boy, echoing the name given to America's first atomic bomb), killing three intruders whom he desperately fears, readers realize that this appealing, often hilarious loner has been transformed into a madman like Jim Jones, who destroyed his Jonestown encampment when it too was "visited" by snooping outsiders. What Theroux seems to offer is a parable of the incestuous horror of patriarchy.

Forced to leave his now desecrated paradise, Allie finds that his iron-fisted control over his family is slipping. He seeks to regain it by bullying Charlie and his younger brother Jerry even more fiercely than before. He forces the family to head even further into the heart of the jungle's darkness, an outward sign of his own distorted inner world. When Allie is fatally shot by his alter ego, an evangelist named Reverend Spellgood, the minister believes he is dispatching Communists attempting to take over *his* jungle church grounds. Theroux's ironic turn of plot here underscores the maniacal fervor of the missionary spirit housed in the rebel's personality.

Characters

Allie Fox (his name suggests the tenacious alley cat and the prophetic Allah), idiosyncratic inventor in his mid-30's, wears a Hawaiian shirt and old baseball cap, chomps on a cigar butt, and emphasizes his many assertions with a forefinger cut off at the big knuckle. He holds opinions on everything from the Bible to television commercials, and most of his views contain disturbing kernels of truth. (One thinks of him as an intelligent Archie Bunker.) America has let him down; in his crackling colloquial language, his country is "in gridlock." Allie's favorite declaration is "I'm the last man!", emphasizing his resourcefulness but also ironically prophesying his tragic death. His escape to the Mosquito Coast, taking with him the knowledge of how to make ice—"Ice is civilization"—brings his family in harm's way, even though he believes the adventure will toughen and eventually save them. But as he erects his Jeronimo and the ice house called Fat Boy, it becomes clear that Father has become obsessed with proving his ability to save the natives from all the sapping side-effects of civilization. Obsession leads to madness after he destroys Jeronimo; their comfortable house is replaced by a raft tied to a bending tree. Pushed by a flood and father's willfulness deeper into the jungle, the family begins to rebel against his tyranny. His death comes when vultures rip out his tongue, the object that symbolizes his power to hypnotize and manipulate his listeners.

The novel's plot is narrated by Charlie Fox, Allie's teen-aged son. His devotion to Father is unquestioning as they leave America for Honduras; he actually accepts Allie's declaration that the U.S. is being destroyed. Father tests this loyalty and Charlie's manhood by making him undergo initiation rites that endanger his life. When they arrive in Jeronimo, Charlie serves as Father's agent in controlling the younger children, who balk at the demanding tasks they are asked to perform. Even though Charlie remains loyal, he manages to escape to a small lake at some distance from the family camp. His domain is dubbed the Acre, where he and the other children are free from Father's despotism and can live their own, more playful and creative lives. Charlie proves a much more tolerant and benevolent leader in this world; his laws give his playmates more freedom and responsibility. The Acre becomes a valuable spot later on because it is the locale to which the family escapes after Father detonates Fat Boy and obliterates their camp.

Realizing that Father is now not just a kooky genius but a killer (Charlie is the only one who knows what Father did), Charlie begins to show signs of doubt and mistrust. Urged on by his younger brother, Charlie tries to subdue Father and take over as head of the family. It could be argued in fact that the novel is a kind of *bildungsroman,* tracing the maturing of Charlie into a manhood that is more sensitive than the model Father tried to create for him. It is also possible that Charlie is simply Theroux's narrative voice, providing an ambiguous portrait of a complex central character.

Mother (who is never otherwise named) qualifies as Father's crutch; her unwillingness to question allows him to indulge his every whim. She seems indeed to be Allie's mother, the name by which he regularly addresses her. Yet in spite of her weakness, she also manages to teach the children something about the flora and fauna of the jungle. Where Father lectures, she gently points out; while he mimics and derides those who fail, she encourages them to try again. Given her name and this role, she appears to be Mother Earth, warm and life-giving but unable to stand up to Father's machine-aided power.

The Reverend Spellgood and his family are likewise residents of the Fox clan's jungle world. Readers are meant to regard Spellgood (his name suggesting both "Gospel" and "good spell") as the religious equivalent of Father. Both men burn to save the natives, but Father is an atheist and contemptuous of the proselytizing activities of the Reverend and his ilk. Readers cannot easily embrace the self-assured Spellgood either, since his electronic, state-of-the-art ministry turns out to be little more than an opiate for the naive masses. When he cannot preach in person, for instance, he sends videotapes of his sermons to be played for the assembled Indians. He brings big-business religion to Honduras and deludes himself into thinking that numbers equal converts. That this man of God should be Father's nemesis, believing his victim leads a Communist takeover, is one of the novel's rich and telling ironies.

Among the natives, Mr. Haddy emerges as the most appealing character. He ferries the Fox family to its new home, listening in awe to the magical tales spun by "Fadder" but wondering as well why they chose to come. His charming, take-life-as-it-comes attitude represents a challenge to Allie, who tries to teach him leadership and survival skills. But Mr. Haddy cannot learn because he cannot understand the need; to him Father appears as a god capable of miracles, someone to be worshipped. In return for this devotion, Father manages to wreck Mr. Haddy's boat, his only source of income. As payment Father gives him his watch, a useless item in the timeless world of the jungle. While the Foxes have spelled trouble for Mr. Haddy, he manages to save them from a terrifying flood by bringing Charlie a motor and gasoline to propel their otherwise rudderless raft. In another instance of irony, Mr. Haddy turns out—unknown to Father—to be the family's savior.

Techniques

By using a young first-person narrator, Theroux creates an effective point of view from which to observe Father's character. Readers experience the tension and ambivalence that Charlie feels, and alternately laugh and shudder at Allie's words. Charlie proves a faithful reporter, honest and less critical than the other children. His relationship with Father is psychologically complex, because Charlie both fears and respects him and this lends considerable tension to the story. The sensitivity of Charlie's vision can also be seen in his descriptive powers as he makes the jungle come alive. Readers may feel slightly manipulated, however, because many passages reveal the professional hand of Theroux himself. Charlie also lacks the personality and perspective of such entertaining first-person narrators as Huck Finn or Jack Crabb from Thomas Berger's *Little Big Man.*

Key episodes in *The Mosquito Coast* have Biblical parallels. The levelling of Jeronimo recalls the destruction of Sodom and Gomorrah and Babylon, with the accompanying implication that the settlement and Fat Boy represent unnatural evil. After the family relocates on a primitive raft, they experience a frightening storm and a floodtide that nearly swamps them. Here the parallel with the Flood and Noah's deliverance could have ironic relevance, since Father revives only to lead his family toward greater danger. The final event of the book, with the appearance of vultures on the beach, calls to mind the chapters in Revelation prophesying the Apocalypse. On the simplest level of fable, Father can be seen as receiving just punishment for his Satanic defiance of God and God's representatives. Yet Theroux is too complex a novelist to promote this moralistic reading. The parallels lend instead a mythic quality to plot and character, lifting *The Mosquito Coast* above the class of straightforward adventure tales.

Literary Precedents

The Mosquito Coast belongs to the tradition of the novel of character. Father's speech and behavior rivet the reader's attention, even though Charlie serves as first-person narrator. Theroux traces Charlie's development as the action unfolds— he clearly matures, gains insight—but this change comes as a reaction to Allie's actions. The closest American precedent for this technique is F. Scott Fitzgerald's *The Great Gatsby,* in which the narrator gives a detailed portrait of a complex character whom he both admires and fears. Gatsby's death, like Father's, both haunts and liberates the narrator. A recent popular precedent is James Dickey's

Deliverance, a novel about a Georgia hunter and he-man who convinces three of his less rugged, city-softened friends to take a perilous canoe trip down a beautiful but dangerous river soon to be flooded as part of a dam-building project. The narrator here is a sensitive man who is fascinated by their leader, both drawn to and pulling back from his influence. Dickey suggests, as does Theroux, that life for modern man is a struggle between natural and civilizing influences.

Probably the most important literary precedent for *The Mosquito Coast* is Joseph Conrad's *Heart of Darkness*. Conrad typically places his heroes in situations where the principles they have lived by no longer fit the circumstances in which they find themselves. Either they gain some degree of self-knowledge or they destroy themselves. Kurtz, the central character of *Heart of Darkness*, is a victim of self-destruction. We are told of his nightmarish crimes by a narrator named Marlow, who like Charlie does not understand all that he hears and sees. Theroux of course shapes his novel into a tract about an entire family's adventure (see also *The Swiss Family Robinson*), but like Conrad he does not allow the violent action to obscure his central theme of the irreconcilability of social and individual values. Political and economic questions, especially those related to a "civilized" foreigner out of place in a primitive society that he tries to rule, preoccupy both writers. Though there are important differences in style and content in the two novels, it is hard to believe that Theroux could have written *The Mosquito Coast* without having read Conrad's powerful tale of exploration—of a primitive world and the inner self.

Related Titles

Two other Theroux works offer portraits of heroes in unfamiliar surroundings attempting to survive and prosper. *Saint Jack* (1973) exposes the poverty, vice and political corruption of Singapore as observed by Jack Flowers, an expatriate American with the dubious responsibility of providing prostitutes for visiting business- and servicemen. His dream is to own his own brothel and win fame as a writer. The dream becomes a reality but at a price: he secures the money for the brothel from a man charged with building a rest and recuperation "center" for U.S. troops fighting in Vietnam. But the Army soon closes the place down, and Flowers is cast adrift. He manages to survive, however, believing that he still has "all the time in the world" to regain his dream. Like Father he yearns for something better than his present life; unlike him, he finds a way of accommodating to the society in which he has chosen to live.

In a novella written after *The Mosquito Coast, Half Moon Street* (1984), Theroux portrays an American woman living in London and working for an investment think-tank seeking ways to recycle Arab petrodollars. She wants some adventure in her life and hires on with an escort service, dating interesting but dangerous Arabs with petrodollars to burn. Her adventure turns sour when her life is threatened, but she manages to escape with an enlightened understanding of the workings of high finance and underworld dealings.

Adaptations
Saint Jack was made into a successful film in 1979. Ben Gazzara played Jack Flowers with skill and insight. Peter Bogdanovich directed the movie and caught the seamy flavor of Singapore and the world-weariness of the British colony of expatriates that Theroux so brilliantly caricatures. *The Mosquito Coast* will come to movie theaters in 1986, with Harrison Ford cast in the role of Allie Fox. Peter Weir, the Australian who is known to Americans for his work on *Witness,* is directing *Mosquito Coast.* It is being shot on location. A film version of *Half Moon Street,* starring Sigourney Weaver, is in production in London and will probably appear in late 1986 or early 1987.

Other Titles
Jungle Lovers, 1971 (novel); *The Family Arsenal,* 1971 (novel); *V.S. Naipul,* 1972 (criticism); *The Counsel's File,* 1976 (novel); *The London Embassy,* 1982 (novel); *The Kingdom By The Sea,* 1983 (travel); *Sailing Through China,* 1983 (travel); *Sunrise With Seamonsters,* 1985 (essays and autobiography); *O-Zone,* 1986 (novel).

Additional Sources
Encounter 58 (January 1982): 49. Very positive review of *The Mosquito Coast.* Theroux's best novel yet: "A novel of compelling excellence." The reviewer praises characterization and political message.

Library Journal 98 (July 1973): 2150. Generally negative review of *Saint Jack.* Reviewer cites influence of Joseph Conrad and Graham Greene, believes that the "author's true bent seems . . . for the fragmentary and insignificant."

Library Journal 107 (February 1982): 274. Reviewer calls Theroux's "one of the liveliest voices in fiction today" and sees *The Mosquito Coast* as "a mythic tragedy and a tall tale."

New Republic 186 (February 24, 1982): 40. Positive review of *The Mosquito Coast,* but the reviewer classifies it as a novel for teenagers. He stresses the importance of Charlie Fox as narrator in developing the novel's main theme of conflict between father and son.

New Statesman 85 (April 20, 1973): 591. Negative review of *Saint Jack.* Reviewer believes that "style overshadows content" and that the "narrative competes with dialogue for our attention." Yet he suggests that libraries interested in experimental fiction might want to take a chance on it.

Saturday Review 9 (February 1982): 55-56. Very positive review of *The Mosquito Coast*. Jonathan Raban devotes two pages to the novel, calling it "a marvellously told realistic story." He concentrates on main character Allie Fox, praising Theroux's ability to bring the reader uncomfortably close to "both a god and a madman."

Robert F. Willson, Jr.
University of Missouri
Kansas City

HUNTER S. THOMPSON
1939

Publishing History

Hunter S. Thompson began his career as a sports reporter in Florida. Following a *Time, Inc.* journalism scholarship at Columbia University which "failed to bear fruit," according to the author, he became South American correspondent for the *National Observer* in 1962.

As a free-lance journalist in the mid-1960s, he also contributed articles to *Nation* before his first book, *Hell's Angels,* was published in 1966. The work generated much attention since the author had actually "run" with the notorious motorcycle gang for eighteen months while compiling material for the book, and he had been beaten savagely by several members in a dispute over money.

Thompson then wrote briefly for *Pageant* and *Scanlon's Monthly* before publishing *Fear and Loathing in Las Vegas,* the book that, because of its style, subject matter, and tone, made his name synonymous with scathing satire. By this time Thompson was a regular contributor to *Rolling Stone* where, as National Affairs editor, he covered the 1972 presidential campaign. In 1973, Straight Arrow Press published *Fear and Loathing on The Campaign Trail,* a collection of his campaign reports.

Although Thompson continued to write for *Rolling Stone* throughout the 1970s and early 1980s, his appearances in that publication became infrequent. In 1979, a collection of his shorter journalistic pieces was published in a volume, *The Great Shark Hunt,* that became his best-selling book and which includes examples of his earliest 1960s reportage as well as less conventional gonzo journalism.

In 1983, *The Curse of Lono,* which began as an account of the Hawaii Marathon, was published, and in 1985, Thompson began writing a regular column for the *San Francisco Examiner* on current events and the mass media.

Critical Reception, Honors, and Popularity

As founder and main practitioner of what he calls "gonzo journalism," Thompson has been harshly criticized, along with other New Journalists, for deliberately obliterating the distinctions between fact and fiction. Conservative journalists and academics claim that the heady blend of traditional reporting techniques and utter freedom of invention results in a superficial, morally irresponsible form of "parajournalism" that serves no clear purpose other than the author's self-advertisement.

In describing "gonzo" (a word he chose because he liked the sound of it), Thompson says that he wants to get personally involved in his stories. Objective journalism is a "pompous contradiction in terms." Traditional reportage gets in the way of conveying the "truth" of a story, relying as it does on the perspective of an outsider, far removed from the emotional, psychological complex of the subjects of a story. Thompson, then, places himself and his own extreme reactions at the center of his narratives.

Most commentators, even ones who take a negative view of Thompson's methods, readily admit his books are entertaining, at the very least. His political coverage is widely respected though it is as wildly subjective as his other work. Even political conservatives admire Thompson's tenacity and energy. He was the only journalist to cover the entire 1972 presidential campaign from beginning to end.

Analysis of Selected Titles

FEAR AND LOATHING IN LAS VEGAS
Fear and Loathing in Las Vegas, 1972, new journalism.

Social Concerns/Themes

This work, subtitled "A Savage Journey to The Heart of The American Dream," attacks the tawdry, oppressive manifestation of greed and materialism in the microcosm of Las Vegas. Outrage is the response of the narrator, an outrage that is fueled by a steady ingestion of drugs and alcohol, as though intoxication were the only possible response to the horrors of corruption and ignorance. Horatio Alger is invoked several times, mockingly, and it is Alger's dream of success, distorted in the neon glitter of the casinos, that Thompson explores.

Illegal drugs play a major part in stoking the narrator's shock and horror. A significant implication is that contraband substances are no more harmful or debilitating than the routines of contemporary life that make grostequeries of nearly everyone. The reader is reminded occasionally of events outside Las Vegas which create a "heinous background" for this nightmare, such as the Manson murders, the invasion of Laos, atrocities in Vietnam, and random violence in the cities.

Characters

The first-person narrator, whose alias is Dr. Duke, and his attorney, Dr. Gonzo, another "alias," are the two protagonists of the book. Though it is through Duke's eyes that the horrors unfold, he and Gonzo are almost identical in their misanthropic attitudes and fears.

The drug-induced madness, the attacks of free-floating paranoia and disorientation, and the self-destructive drinking of the characters are all summed up in Thompson's title, which has become a code phrase in his later writing. He uses it in the title of his collection of campaign reports and in various magazine articles. Fear and loathing is the only response, the narrator makes clear, to the insanity within his own drug-addled mind and without, in the world of mad greed. The term marks a black dimension where personal demonology intersects some awful nexus of cultural collapse, political breakdown, and bad karma. The fear and loathing the narrator and his attorney experience is as much for themselves as it is for Las Vegas.

Techniques

Thompson is a master of using dialogue to pace his stories and to involve the reader with the action. The character of his narrator is established early in the book in humorously fractured exchanges with his attorney and with hapless bystanders. Another technique lending immediacy to the narrative is the use of tape transcription—pure dialogue—that reads much like a film script.

Interior monologues also reveal much about the narrator. Since these often take the form of drug delusions or hallucinations, the narrator ostensibly explores a raw consciousness, one driven to the brink of total breakdown, not only by the drugs but by the awful reality of the American dream. As an epigraph to his book, Thompson uses a quotation from Samuel Johnson: "He who makes a beast of himself gets rid of the pain of being a man." It is this pain, exacerbated by the bizarre hucksterism of Las Vegas, that drives the author to his beastly escapades. The marathon, five-day binge he describes results from his "super-sensitivity" as one commentator put it, his awareness of the discrepancy between American ideals and the harsh working out of America's brutal manifest destiny.

This fate, the national fate of delusion and greed exemplified in the Circus-Circus casino, is given shape and a voice in the narrator himself. His mad visions make him one with the frantic "believers" of Las Vegas. What sets him apart is his uncompromising drive to locate an authentic understanding of just what has gone wrong, with himself and with his country.

Thompson is effective in conveying what Tom Wolfe calls the status life of his characters—the complete pattern of behavior by which people reveal their social, cultural, and political identities, real or imagined. With only a few words of dialogue or a simple description, he places his characters firmly in a social class or niche.

Literary Precedents

Much controversy has been generated by the New Journalism of Tom Wolfe, Jimmy Breslin, and Hunter Thompson, in part because traditional journalists believe that the "facts" tend to be tainted by the style with which they are presented, and in part because the New Journalists created a genre of reportage which seems more engaging and interesting than the more objective, drier traditional approach. Part of the criticism levied at the New Journalists was rooted in the fear of returning to the "muckraking" reportage rampant prior to World War II. Unlike muckraking, however, the New Journalists insist on the accuracy of fact and detail—Thompson and Wolfe are both exceptional scholars and researchers—and it is this same insistence on accuracy that led them to present facts within a context rather than as pure information.

It is both interesting and predictable that Thompson and Breslin have sports reporting in their backgrounds. American sports reporters, especially baseball announcers during the radio era, developed descriptive powers and sound effects to bring the game alive for listeners and readers who had to enjoy the sport by osmosis. Wolfe, observing Breslin's ability to use "pop" words to describe action, experimented with the same technique in reporting the news. Following the cue of "Pop Artists" of the 1960s, these New Journalists combined the images and language of the ordinary world with the hard and often cruel facts which molded it.

Novelists have been quick to adapt the spirit of New Journalism to their more traditional form so that an identifiable genre of New Journalist novels has emerged. Some critics have dubbed this genre "faction," reflecting the combination of fiction and fact. Although novelists have always used facts to give credibility to their stories, and even though the historical novel is a well established and enduring form, the "factionalists" are attempting to elevate the reader's awareness that it is not only presence of truth that is important but the relationship among those truths. *Ragtime* by E.L. Doctorow, for example, meticulously presents true facts from the 1930s, ranging from the rise of socialism to Houdini's magical tricks, but it deconstructs the order of information, and in this rearrangement and juxtaposition of nonsequential data creates its themes and messages in a manner that is entirely different from the "realistic" descriptions of cultures and places in novels such as Hemingway's *The Sun Also Rises.*

The New Journalists, then, can be credited with liberating both journalism and modern fiction from some of their traditional bonds. Although what the New Journalists have achieved is not entirely "new" either to reportage or fiction, it is new in that it has become a conscious aesthetic and philosophy for analyzing society.

Related Titles

Three of Thompson's books are closer to the more traditional New Journalism than to the pure gonzo of *Fear and Loathing in Las Vegas.* At least one reviewer has called his fifth book a novel, though the same claim can be made for most of Thompson's work, depending on what elements are stressed.

Fear and Loathing on The Campaign Trail is the closest of his work to conventional journalism, focusing as it does on a subject that is a matter of public record. *Hell's Angels* is also "nonfiction," recording several well-publicized events in the life of motorcycle chieftan Sonny Barger.

Thompson's approach to his material is almost identical in every book whether it's labelled fiction or otherwise. He is suspicious, on edge, and wide awake to nuances of non-verbal communication. He watches people closely, while he hides behind dark aviator glasses. He listens skeptically, all the while plotting escapes, hoaxes, and rearguard actions. Most importantly, he always places himself at the center of the story, confronting and sometimes attacking his subjects, always physically committed to seeing his assignment through regardless of personal cost.

Adaptations

In 1980, a feature film, *Where The Buffalo Roam,* directed by Art Linson, was released. Based on "the legend of Hunter S. Thompson," the film adapted elements from both *Fear and Loathing* books and also incorporated characters and incidents from *The Great Shark Hunt.* With Bill Murray in the lead role, the film depicts Thompson as a clownish psychotic. He is a mumbling outsider who never confronts his subjects openly but lurks in the background. The essence of Thompson's gonzo approach to journalism is lacking in Murray's portrayal. The real protagonist of the movie is Thompson's attorney, played with gusto by Peter Boyle, who moves from one extra-legal enterprise to the next with insouciance.

The movie was released with little fanfare and was roundly panned by the critics.

Additional Sources

Booth, Wayne, "Loathing and Ignorance on the Campaign Trail: 1972," *Columbia Journalism Review* (November 1973): 7-12. Conservative criticism of Thompson's journalistic methods.

Green, James, "Gonzo," *Journal of Popular Culture* (Summer 1975): 204-210. A description of Thompson's unique brand of New Journalism.

Mandell, Arnold J., M.D., "Dr. Hunter S. Thompson and a New Psychiatry," *Psychiatry Digest* 37: 12-17. A discussion of the effects of drugs on Thompson's prose style.

Vonnegut, Kurt, "A Political Disease," *Harpers* (July 1973): 92, 94. A review of Thompson's 1972 campaign coverage.

Wolfe, Tom, *The New Journalism.* New York: Harper and Row, 1973. An anthology containing an excellent introduction by Wolfe defining the New Journalism and awarding Thompson the "Brass Stud Award" for his book on the Hell's Angels. Also includes an excerpt from *Hell's Angels* and a piece on the Kentucky Derby which was later collected in *The Great Shark Hunt.*

Roger Dendinger
Francis Marion College

THOMAS TRYON
1926

Publishing History

Thomas Tryon is a successful movie actor, having played in such films as *Moon Pilot, The Longest Day, The Cardinal, In Harm's Way,* and others. He decided that acting was not sufficiently satisfying and tried writing. His first book, *The Other* (1971), was immediately popular. His subsequent fiction, *Harvest Home* (1973), *Lady* (1974), and a volume containing four long stories about movie stars, *Crowned Heads* (1976), always made it to the best seller lists.

Critical Reception, Honors, and Popularity

The Other is listed in *80 Years of Best Sellers 1895-1975* as having sold 3,594,693 copies. The story also got some favorable reviews as a promising first novel. *Harvest Home,* another foray into the gothic mode, remained on the best seller list for seventeen weeks. Critical reception was not so enthusiastic; *The New York Times Book Review* (July 1, 1973) called it "tedious, pretentious, and mannered," and complained that the symbolism is clumsy, the characters are caricatures, and the dialogue unreal. Nevertheless, *Harvest Home* was a Literary Guild selection.

Library Journal (June 1, 1973) seems to be misleading in its identification of the corn festival in *Harvest Home* as a "medieval mystery play" and the main staple of the tale as "mystery and demonology." Mystery, yes, but "mystery play" suggests a Christian pageant rather than archaic nature worship, originating in pre-Christian times, and "demonology" implies a dedication to evil spirits. Of course, Christianity designated all pre-Christian deities or spirits as demons, except when they could be masked or incorporated into Christianity. The most startling secret ritual of the novel, a sexual one between the Harvest Lord and the Corn Maiden in the fields, was never a part of medieval mystery plays, nor was it, in pagan terms, malevolent in intent. The critic needs to read James Frazer on the subject of Corn Mothers and fertility rituals.

Tryon said that he struggled for fifteen years to avoid being typecast as an actor, and he did not want to be typed as a writer of occult thrillers. *Lady* avoids such gothic techniques, therefore, though it does not entirely desert mystery. *Library Journal* called it Tryon's best, but much overwritten in terms of length. *Christian Science Monitor* (November 13, 1974) comments drily, "It has been Mr. Tryon's habit to create a picture-postcard New England town and then poison it with some nasty supernatural goings on. There's nothing occult in his latest—and nothing very convincing either. Even its chills are lukewarm." *Lady* was on the best seller list for fifteen weeks.

Crowned Heads stayed on the top ten for fourteen weeks, in spite of Paul Gray's witty remark in *Time* (June 28, 1976) that "Weaving fiction around such a monstrously self-mythologizing place as Hollywood is like gilding a plastic lily."

His 1986 work, *All That Glitters,* was a Literary Guild main selection.

Analysis of Selected Titles

THE OTHER

The Other, 1971, novel.

Social Concerns/Themes

The theme of the Double is one of the most fascinating elements of gothic fiction, carrying with it a whole catalogue of literary conventions: the reflected image in the mirror or in water, the identical twin, the changeling, the dead who possess the living, the unfettered subconscious, family madness, the Devil. All these apply to *The Other,* which is a rather vague term for some possibly metaphysical entity which imposes its will on one's consciousness or behavior, a presence never recognized as a part of oneself, though psychologists may call it a projection of forbidden impulses, perhaps the Jungian Shadow.

In medieval literature, the projected source of evil was often the Devil or the witch. Modern gothic novels are somewhat more circumspect, suggesting that devils are probably internal and human, perhaps devices for escaping personal guilt. Nevertheless, since the modern imagination has never given up its fondness for personified evil, the mysterious "Other" lives on in many variations as werewolf or ghost or monster. Here, he is the strangely perverse twin, Holland, who presumably inherited evil, while his brother Niles seems remarkably free of any moral taint.

The author is not really so naive as to suggest that good and evil are neatly divided so that one twin, by some twist of fate, might get all the "morality genes," while the other boy inherits only from Cain. In fact, the demarcation between one twin and the other progressively blurs as the reader gradually realizes that Niles, the "good" one, has so perfected his powers of extra-sensory perception that he can assume his brother's identity and act as Holland might act. He learned from his grandmother Ada a mental game of concentrating on an external object so singlemindedly that he seems to be that object, knowing it intimately from the inside. When Holland falls into a well while hanging his grandmother's cat from the well rope, Niles is so traumatically shocked that he cannot admit his companion's death. The grandmother, fearing that Niles will literally die of grief, encourages him to think of Holland as still alive. She thinks Niles will outgrow this harmless fiction when he becomes strong enough to live without his twin. Instead, the dead Holland becomes a living and acting presence to his brother, doing those things which his gentler twin deplores. Thus, Niles is obsessed and possessed by his potentially cruel and amoral twin, creating one disaster after another.

Tryon is using certain psychological or quasi-scientific ideas, such as the uncanny sensitivity of twins to each other's mental state, the propensity of some children to create imaginary companions, the principle of ESP, to provide plausibility for a gothic tale of demonic possession. The supernatural possibilities are contained in events which might conceivably have some psychological explanation.

Characters

Niles and Holland Perry appear initially as normal thirteen-year-old boys, Niles just a bit more considerate than most, while Holland, apparently the more strong willed of the two, has a streak of malice. The reader suspects, however, that Holland's tendency to mockery may derive from a secret envy of Niles, who is generally more competent in games of skill than Holland and more beloved, perhaps, for his sunnier disposition. No matter what mean pranks Holland is guilty of, however, Niles never violates the code of secrecy between them—even when Holland causes their father's death.

Certain odd facts suggest that Niles is more ambivalent than he first appears. Although he seems subservient to Holland's whims, he possesses a gold ring with the family crest of a peregrine falcon on it, which once belonged to Holland. He carries it, with another mysterious object, eventually revealed as a severed finger, in a tobacco can concealed in his shirt next to his skin, a hiding place shared by a live chameleon. These objects feature in macabre events in the course of the story, as the full complexity of the double personality of the surviving twin comes to light.

There are several minor characters which receive minimal character development: a mysteriously ill mother confined mostly to her room, an obnoxious cousin who jumps into the hay mow where he is impaled on a pitchfork, an aged neighbor woman with a weak heart who may have been helped into the next world by a close encounter with the pet lizard.

The really important character, other than the twins, is the maternal grandmother, Ada Katerina Vedrenya, formerly a Russian peasant, something of a mystic and a wise woman, or perhaps in one sense a mythic queen of the night. She teaches the boys, especially Niles, who is the more apt pupil, to have hypnotic or out-of-body experiences, projecting themselves into a bird or a butterfly, for instance, to know the miracle of flight. It is, for the most part, a joyous game of expanded awareness. When she realizes to what pernicious purposes this ESP is being used, however, she assumes another mythic role, that of the angel of death.

Techniques

Like most gothic novels, *The Other* is replete with symbols and allusions. In one scene, Niles is trying to interest Holland in the constellations, especially the Gemini, those famous brothers of classical myth, Castor and Pollux, models of brotherly love. Though there is no direct mention of the story, students of mythology may remember that the bond of the Gemini extended beyond the death of Castor. When the surviving twin prayed for death, Zeus allowed him to share his life with his brother, both brothers spending every other day in Hades and every other day alive on earth.

Grandmother Ada always wears on her dress a pin shaped like the crescent moon, symbol of the ancient queen of heaven, who, in another phase, was the death goddess. Niles scratches his cheek on the moon pin in the compulsive, despairing embrace of Ada when she realizes the truth about her beloved grandchild.

Christian symbols share the stage with references to Classical and Norse mythology. Niles is entranced by a stained glass window in the church representing the Angel of the Annunciation, which he interprets as a kind and loving make-believe creature whom he fancies as a guardian spirit. When Ada seeks to destroy her grandson, she appears to him first as the winged Angel of the Annunciation, whom he wished most to see at the moment of his death, then changes in his hallucination to the Angel of Death.

Some symbols, though vaguely associated with Christian imagery of evil, such as the lizard, have also a natural relevance to the conditions of the story. A chameleon is the master of disguise, literally changing color to fit the environment. Niles might be called an internal chameleon, changing psyches, but not his outer appearance, since he is already the mirror image of his brother Holland.

Literary Precedents

The theme of two brothers or mysterious doubles as contrasts in temperament or moral nature is literally as old as written literature itself, appearing in the first written story of the hero (c. 2500 BC or earlier) about Gilgamesh, king of Uruk, and his wild companion, Enkidu. Pagan mythologies abound with sets of often opposed brothers: Osiris and his murderous brother Set in ancient Egypt, for instance, or Ahura Mazda, ancient Persian god of light, and his evil twin Ahriman, god of darkness, both born of the androgynous Ur-principle, Zurvan (Time). In the Hebrew-Christian tradition, of course, the first two brothers, Cain and Abel, feature in the first murder story, and have many literary descendents, such as Steinbeck's *East of Eden*.

With the nineteenth century and the popularization of depth psychology, the concept of the unconscious mind contributed a new slant to stories of demonic possession. Mr. Hyde was neither a devil nor a separate person, but the good Dr. Jekyl's suppressed Shadow self. Writers such as Edgar Allen Poe developed a whole repertoire of traditional images and ideas to suggest that a weird and horrifying reality exists just under the surface of everyday life. One of the most successful ploys of such writers is to combine the occult notion of possession with the presumed innocence of children. The history of New England, where children did, in fact, inspire the only real American witchhunt, seems especially fertile ground for such tales. Perhaps the most obvious literary precedent for the demonic possession of children is Henry James's *The Turn of the Screw*. It is no accident that *The Exorcist*, a contemporary novel exceeding even *The Other* in popularity, also deals with a possessed child.

Adaptations

Tryon wrote the screenplay for Otto Preminger's 1972 film version of *The Other* for Twentieth Century Fox.

HARVEST HOME
Harvest Home, 1973, novel.

Social Concerns/Themes

If one were to take *Harvest Home* seriously, one would suggest that it dramatizes an ancient male awe and dread of the Female as a source of love, creativity, and death. The author may have no actual belief that contemporary men still carry that secret fear of female power, though its vestigial presence in many men, in spite of long-standing male domination supported by the Judeo-Christian tradition, may seem clear from a study of history and Freudian psychology. (Try reading the infamous *Malleus Maleficarum*, the Hammer of the Witches, medieval guide to recognize witches, for its amazing superstitious dread of female sexuality.)

The imagination of an archaic farming community in New England, ostensibly Christian, but actually more concerned with the ancient Corn Mother of pagan Europe and Celtic England, is not so fantastic as to be utterly implausible for literary purposes. Certain pagan customs, or at least related superstitions, and the arts of herbal folk medicine, often dominated by women, may still persist among isolated rural communities.

The village Cornwall Combe was presumably settled by people from Cornwall, England, which, according to the novel, had once some racial intermixture with Cretan sailors, long before the Caesars invaded Britain. Ancient Crete, the reader should realize, was the stronghold of the cult of the Mother Goddess as many archaeological artifacts amply attest, goddesses associated with snakes, bees, or water birds. Moreover, Robert Graves and other popular mythologists have maintained that religion was once dominated by a Triple Goddess of Moon, Earth, and Underworld. She was variously represented in different parts of Old Europe and the Middle East and associated, as well, with the Three Fates of Greek mythology and the three Norns of Scandinavian myth who meted out justice under the world tree. Perhaps the best known is Demeter, Grain Mother of ancient Greece, and her daughter Persephone, who was both the Spring Maiden and, in another phase, queen of the dead. The cult of Demeter was a viable religion for two thousand years.

The Great Goddess not only controls the propagation, nurture, and death of all living beings, but also, according to Robert Graves, acts as the poet's Muse, or inspiration of all art. In *Harvest Home,* the protagonist's talent as a painter, long stifled in an urban business setting, blossoms among the bucolic scenes of Cornwall Combe, just as the mental and physical problems of his wife and asthmatic daughter are likewise healed. He finds these benefits have a rather terrible price, however, and require a degree of submission to the female-dominated order that he cannot accept. The Widow Fortune, apparently the high priestess of the Corn Mother, seems to be everyone's nurturing grandmother, but, for Ned Constantine, she turns into what every man fears (according to Freud), the Terrible Castrating Mother.

Characters

Mr. Constantine, would-be artist turned advertising executive, his nervous, run-down wife, Beth, and their chronically-ill daughter Kate exemplify those whom Thoreau described as living lives of quiet desparation. Their flight from New York City to Cornwall Combe partakes of the romantic back-to-the-land movement—conveniently hastened by Ned's losing his job and the pair of them falling in love with an eighteenth century house that needed renovating.

They meet a great many local people who receive somewhat sketchy, but distinctive characterization: a kind neighbor Maggie Dodd and her blind husband, George, who is always listening to recordings of classic books; a traveling peddler who sees too much, talks too much, and suffers a grisly fate; a stalwart, handsome, blond farmer (almost a caricature of the Jolly Green Giant) who is the Harvest Lord, a title held for seven years; a local sexpot named Tamar and her feeble-minded girl-child, a village seeress; an ill-fated young man who rebels against the system; and, of course, the Widow Fortune, local midwife, expert in herbal cures, maker of fine traditional quilts and unique scarecrows, honored elder of the secret Corn Mother ceremonies, attended only by women—except for the Harvest Lord, who with his chosen Corn Maiden, performs the ancient ritual that assures the fertility of the fields.

Techniques

Occasional mystery and gradually mounting suspense combine with local color, folklore, and mythic symbols in this tall tale. The Widow Fortune, with her obviously symbolic name and the scissors that hang at her belt, might be the third Greek Fate who cuts off the thread of life. Most of the folk festivals, ceremonial fires, and pagan fertility rituals will be recognizable to readers of James Frazer's *The Golden Bough.*

Literary Precedents

Actual late survivals of pagan customs in rural England are probably more accurately portrayed in Thomas Hardy's *The Return of the Native.* Certainly ritual bonfires, the ashes of which were sprinkled on the fields, lived on long after the earlier burning of human sacrifices was replaced by the burning of effigies made of straw. In *Harvest Home,* the scarecrows are ritually burned, but Ned discovers to his horror that one bonfire includes a hidden human victim.

Ancient cults of the Mother have received considerable attention from mythologists, anthropologists, psychologists, and also many feminists who take comfort in the former prominence of female deities. For interesting contrasts to Tryon's horror story, one may turn to Robert Graves's *Seven Days in New Crete* (published in America as *Watch the North Wind Rise)* and Marian Zimmer Bradley's *The Mists of Avalon.* The former deals with a utopian reconstruction of the religion of the Mother Goddess in Crete because of the obvious failure of male-dominated Western culture that emphasizes technology and war. The Bradley book deals with the interface between the receding cult of the Mother and the new Christianity in early Britain—the King Arthur legend retold from the point of view of the women involved. Both of these books deal more kindly with a female-dominated religion than Tryon's American gothic. On the other hand, for the theocratic horrors of what might happen if chauvinist males, resentful of recent advances in female power, could impose their will on society, one may read Margaret Atwood's *The Handmaid's Tale.*

Adaptations

Harvest Home was adapted for made-for-TV movie with the aging Bette Davis perfectly cast as the mysterious Widow Fortune.

FEDORA

"Fedora," lead story in *Crowned Heads,* 1976, novella.

Social Concerns/Themes

This work concerns a post-mortem revelation about the mysterious identity of a famous movie star who retained her popularity, beauty, youth and talent for an incredibly long acting career. The story has to do with the masks that veil public personalities, especially those whose business it is to play a role, on stage and off, maintaining romantic fictions that enhance their careers. A line from the French writer Colette appears several times in the story, translated as "Nothing provides as much assurance as a mask." A more serious theme, proposed but not adequately developed, is the unfortunate psychological effects of always playing a fictional role.

Characters
  Barry Detweiller, who "knows everybody," responds to the appeal of a Marion Walker, hostess of a TV talk show, for some new insights into the career of Fedora, who played romantic leads through three generations of movie goers. Neither of these persons receive more than minimal characterization, nor does Fedora herself, although one gets glimpses of her at widely spaced points in her career.

Techniques
  This story, which might have been an in-depth character study, really centers on a publicity trick which Barry manages to reveal with sufficient slowness to sustain the semblance of a plot. There is, for instance, popular talk of a mysterious Dr. Vando, who was supposed to have prolonged Fedora's youthful appearance by some esoteric scientific treatments. This is not science fiction, however; nor is there anything occult about Fedora. She is simply a successful actress, who secretly had a daughter out of wedlock—a daughter who resembled her mother so closely that she was secretly trained to take over her mother's career.
  References to real movie actresses who won Academy Awards in this or that year instead of Fedora and footnotes to books and well-known magazines add verisimilitude to the story.

Literary Precedents
  This is a new angle to the problem of identity among actors. The more usual movie scenario is the suggestion that actors may so immerse themselves in their roles as to lose track of their own psyches, as in the well known scenario in which Ronald Coleman, as an actor, becomes so buried in the Othello role that he tries to murder his wife who is playing Desdemona.

Additional Sources
  New York Times Book Review (July 1, 1973). Unenthusiastic review of *Harvest Home.*

  Philadelphia Inquirer (November 17, 1974). Review of *Lady.*

  Philps, Robert, "Two Small Boys in a Ghostly Glen," *Life* (May 14, 1971). Favorable review of *The Other.*

  Times Pecayune (November 27, 1974). Review of *Lady.*

  "Vacant Possession," *Times Literary Supplement* (October 29, 1971). Review of *The Other.*

Katherine Snipes
Eastern Washington University

ANNE TYLER
1941

Publishing History

Anne Tyler began her writing career as a secondary interest to her work in Russian and her family life. While a student at Duke University, she was encouraged by Reynolds Price, a promising novelist, who referred her to his agent. Beginning with short stories, she published a few and had a novel, she says, turned down everywhere before publishing *If Morning Ever Comes* in 1964 at age twenty-two.

In 1967, writing became Tyler's primary interest, and she now has nine other novels to her credit. *Dinner at the Homesick Restaurant* (1982) and *The Accidental Tourist* (1985) have been best sellers. In 1986, the 1.1 million first printing of the paperback edition *The Accidental Tourist* resulted in the book's reaching number 5 on the paperback best seller list four days after its release.

Critical Reception, Honors, and Popularity

Reviewers have consistently praised Tyler for her sensitive characterization and her eye for descriptive detail. Although generally complimentary, book reviews of her early novels also criticized the lack of plot development, and the reviews were not front-page items. With *Celestial Navigation,* however, Tyler gained the attention of Gail Godwin; and after John Updike highly recommended *Searching for Caleb,* reviews of her work gained prominence. Most critics see *Dinner at the Homesick Restaurant* as a turning point—continuing the treatment of her central themes but offering greater depth and expanded perspectives.

The Accidental Tourist received widespread acclaim. While some reviewers criticized Tyler's limited concern, for family, most were impressed once again with her ability to write believable dialogue, develop characters at once eccentric and ordinary, and select details that precisely depict the setting. Particular attention was called to her lighter touch with humor.

Like any contemporary author, Tyler is still making her literary reputation. Her maturation as a novelist, however, makes it likely that she will be termed one of the best twentieth-century American novelists.

Tyler was nominated for numerous awards in the early 1980s, including the Pulitzer Prize for *Dinner at the Homesick Restaurant.* She has received the *Mademoiselle* award for writing, 1966; the Award for Literature of the American Academy and Institute of Arts and Letters, 1977; and the P. E. N./Faulkner Award for fiction, 1983. In 1986 *The Accidental Tourist* won the National Book Critics Circle Award.

Analysis of Selected Titles

DINNER AT THE HOMESICK RESTAURANT

Dinner at the Homesick Restaurant, 1982, novel.

Social Concerns/Themes

Except insofar as the basic social unit is the family, Anne Tyler is not concerned with social issues so much as issues of human relationships. A preoccupation in many of her novels is the paradoxes of family life, which are the paradoxes of all emotional relationships in microcosm. Nowhere are these more carefully explored than in *Dinner at the Homesick Restaurant*. In this novel of the Tull family, Tyler examines the way people within a family often hurt and harm those they most love, the balance they seek between longing for love and closeness and wanting to break free from constricting family bonds, and the armor they put on to protect themselves from emotional vulnerability. Pearl Tull loves her children, but her rage at having been left to rear them alone makes her screech at and strike them. She does not mind showing her temper, but considers it a source of pride that she has never cried before them. Two of her children, Cody and Jenny, react to her treatment by trying to break away, but they are always drawn back. The other son, Ezra, reacts by trying to bring the family closer together, planning dinners at his Homesick Restaurant that are always interrupted by an argument.

The novel is also about the way people adjust to the hand life deals them. Tyler acknowledges that people are shaped by their past experiences but intimates that dwelling on past injustices stunts one emotionally and is fruitless. Closely allied to this theme is Tyler's recognition that the happy family, the perfect relationship, is a myth. When attaining that mythic perfection becomes life's goal, the inevitable result is dissatisfaction with reality. The discrepancy between the myth and reality is often apparent in the contrast between characters' memories and reality. Pearl, for example, remembers a beach vacation as an idyllic time; in fact, she spent the time fretting about whether the stove at home was off.

Characters

The Tull family of *Dinner at the Homesick Restaurant* has five members. Although he leaves abruptly early in the novel, Beck Tull, the father, is a presence against which the other characters react. Pearl is cold, stiff, and unbending on the surface. But in her memories of her early relationship with Beck, she reveals another side of herself, one that could light up at being courted and warm to her children. Cody is the restless traveling man his father was, but he takes his family everywhere because he knows what it feels like to be left behind. Ezra tries to establish the togetherness the rest of the family secretly longs for but tries to escape. Only Ezra easily accepts people at face value, sees their good qualities and endures their bad ones. Jenny becomes the loving, freewheeling, cheerful mother her mother wanted to be but never could be, especially after Beck left her. Typical of characters in all Tyler novels, these characters have quirks and oddities that make them a bit eccentric and yet they have recognizable bits of ordinariness with which readers identify.

Techniques

Each chapter in *Dinner at the Homesick Restaurant* is, as John Updike noted, as self contained as a short story. All the characters' viewpoints are presented separately, and each chapter focuses on one character. The novel begins with Pearl's thoughts on her deathbed and then moves back and forth from the present to the past, ending with Pearl's funeral. This juxtaposition of past and present and variation of point of view allow Tyler to expose the subjectivity of memories that influence one's life and the complexity of character revealed by those memories. For example, Cody remembers a family outing to try an archery set with anger and resentment, particularly toward his father. Beck Tull's version reveals a creditable motive, of providing family fun, that went awry. Thus Beck's actions are presented from two perspectives, and his character is more fully developed.

Tyler's attention to detail and her ability to use it thematically are evident in this novel. An illustration of this technique is Pearl's describing her sense of her children's fading away from her by telling about the changes in the lights left on for them at night—hall lights for them as children, single lights downstairs when they were older—the fading light outside her bedroom door paralleling their lessening dependence on her.

As several critics have pointed out, the humor in this novel is dark humor. The tricks that Cody plays on Ezra, for instance, are funny but cruel as well.

Literary Precedents

Anne Tyler regards herself as a Southerner and acknowledges Eudora Welty as an important influence. This novel, like other works by her, is Southern in its emphasis on family. Although many of her novels are set in Baltimore, emphasis on region is more obvious in *Searching for Caleb*. *Dinner at the Homesick Restaurant* concerns the way the present can be influenced by past wrongs but does not insist on the inevitability or degree of corruption that one expects in the fiction of Southern writers like Faulkner. One critic has pointed out, however, that the opening scene is reminiscent of the beginning of Faulkner's *As I Lay Dying*.

The treatment of emotional isolation and longing for affection is similar to that of numerous authors who examine similar themes, including Carson McCullers and Sherwood Anderson. The short-story-like chapters in this novel are certainly similar to the vignettes of Anderson's *Winesburg, Ohio*.

Related Titles

While family relationships are an ongoing concern for Tyler, *Dinner at the Homesick Restaurant* is thematically related quite closely to *Searching for Caleb*. In both novels, individuals are caught in a tension between desires for closeness and freedom, and characters who run away from the family somehow never completely escape. Characters in both novels are also similar in the difficulty they have admitting to loving and to needing love.

THE ACCIDENTAL TOURIST

The Accidental Tourist, 1985, novel.

Social Concerns/Themes

In this novel, Anne Tyler pokes serious fun at the narrowness of characters' lives when they resist moving beyond the comfortable boundaries of home—their families or their country. Her protagonist, Macon Leary, therefore learns in the course of the novel that living fully means being open to new and different experiences. Having concentrated on families in previous works, Tyler extends her range here, demonstrating that extending oneself to the world family can open vistas of living not dreamed of.

Another theme that appears in this novel and elsewhere in Tyler's canon is the question of order—how much is necessary for a sense of control over one's life and how much is stultifying because it eliminates spontaneity. Macon, for instance, thinks his ability to order his life enables him to cope well with the inconveniences of travel, his wife's leaving him, and the tragedy of his son's death. In fact, it reduces his ability to share his feelings. In this and other Tyler novels, characters like Muriel Pritchett who rebel against too much order or who thrive on an outwardly chaotic lifestyle are admirable and emotionally freer. In this novel, Macon's life, run according to his "systems" is really a mess; he cannot work or think clearly. It is only when he moves into Muriel's messy but homey apartment that he moves from isolation to openness.

With openness and caring come danger, however. To love puts one in danger of losing. But as Tyler clearly points out, isolation is only imaginary protection. There is no protection from life's vagaries, but with isolation one misses the felicitous ones and must still suffer the disastrous ones. Macon is shattered when his son is senselessly killed in a holdup at the Burger Bonanza; unfortunately, his method of coping is to keep his emotions under tight rein, to act sensibly and carry on, mowing the grass and giving away the boy's things. He avoids commitment to Muriel's son in an effort to avoid the pain of loss again; until he gives in, however, he also misses the love and sense of being needed that the boy can provide.

Characters

The same eccentric, quirky characters that appear in all Tyler's works also appear in this one. From Macon's sister, Rose, who alphabetizes her kitchen, placing allspice next to ant poison, to Muriel, who faces down robbers and Dobermans in her stiletto heels and shiny eyeshadow, the novel is filled with memorable, endearing characters. Even Edward, the dog, has a distinctive personality as he reacts to the disruption in his life with the anger and violence Macon would never consider.

Macon Leary is like his logo, a winged armchair, in that he dreams of traveling but stays put. He writes travel books that tell people how to find home in a foreign environment—that is, how to find the Taco Bell, if there is one, in Mexico City. His systems and energy-saving methods would be laughable if he were not so miserable. Tyler is careful to establish that Macon is not the cold person his outward demeanor leads others to believe he is. His memories of his son, Ethan, reveal deep love and sorrow and show his potential to live more fully.

Muriel Pritchett is a different kind of character for Tyler. She is one of the few female characters in Tyler's works without the notion that she will be provided for. A strong, independent character, her feistiness is admirable. Like Macon imagines himself to be, she is inventive, acknowledging that there is a trick to getting through life. She describes herself as good at spotting a chance—for herself and for Macon. But unlike Macon, her tricks are not intended to help her escape experiencing life.

Macon's wife, Sarah, seems his opposite at first—sociable and happily disorganized. But she leaves Macon because she fears she is becoming like him. Her anger at her son's killer and her growing sense that people are generally evil rather than good distresses her; she fears her experience of things will become, as she says his are, "muffled." Because she is a sympathetic character, the choice Macon must make between her and Muriel demonstrates that every decision has a cost.

Techniques

The dark humor that appears in works like *Celestial Navigation, Searching for Caleb,* and *Dinner at the Homesick Restaurant* is also found in this work. But there is a new hilarity and a lighter touch that demonstrate a development of Tyler's skill with humor.

Consistently praised for her attention to detail, Tyler continues to use the concrete to evoke emotional states. Macon's distress over his wife's leaving is most evident as he reflects on the unlikely things around the house that call up her aura—the kitchen radio tuned to her station, drops of rouge, strands of her hair in the sink. These details create Macon's mood for the reader, and they also establish his sensitivity, thus developing his character.

Literary Precedents
The mixture of humor and pathos and the concentration on the ordinary in this work are also the hallmarks of other contemporary writers like John Cheever. Tyler's characters are more eccentric than Cheever's, but they remain rooted in a reality that separates her narratives from the bizarre tales of a writer like John Irving.

Related Titles
In *The Accidental Tourist,* Tyler once again considers family in conjunction with the longing for order and the danger of physical and emotional isolation. These concerns have appeared in previous novels, but the difference here is that Tyler moves subtly to a statement about the stultifying nature of nationalism as well.

Other Titles
If Morning Ever Comes, 1964 (novel); *The Tin Can Tree,* 1965 (novel); *A Slipping-down Life,* 1970 (novel); *The Clock Winder,* 1972 (novel); *Celestial Navigation,* 1974 (novel); *Searching for Caleb,* 1976 (novel); *Earthly Possessions,* 1977 (novel); *Morgan's Passing,* 1980 (novel).

Additional Sources
Betts, Doris, "The Fiction of Anne Tyler," *The Southern Quarterly* 21 (1983): 23-37. Discusses narrative technique.

Gibson, Mary Ellis, "Family as Fate: The Novels of Anne Tyler," *Southern Literary Journal* 15 (1983): 47-58. Treats narrative structure.

Shelton, Frank W., "The Necessary Balance: Distance and Sympathy in the Novels of Anne Tyler." *The Southern Review* 20 (1984): 851-860. Discusses detachment and sympathy.

Rebecca Kelly
Southern Technical Institute

JOHN UPDIKE
1932

Publishing History

"My novels," Updike says, "are all about the search for useful work." Few authors, however, have found their life's work as early or as steadily as John Updike. He was only eleven years old when first given a subscription to *The New Yorker*. Updike sold his first story to *The New Yorker* in his senior year at Harvard, and he became a staff writer for the magazine after returning from a postgraduate year at Oxford. He left the staff position before long in order to devote full time to his writing, but *The New Yorker* has continued for three decades to publish his stories and reviews. No other contemporary American author has enjoyed such a close relationship with a major journal.

The same steady record is evident in the publishing history of Updike's books. With only a few exceptions, Alfred A. Knopf has published all of his thirty-two volumes. Few authors of contemporary literature have been so prolific, have found success in so many different kinds of writing, or have continued to appeal to popular taste as well as to academic critics. Updike's success does not depend upon one major breakthrough or one kind of best seller, instead his idea of "useful work" is to write a few pages every day, and the volumes of stories, poems, essays, and novels add up to one of the most impressive records in American publishing history.

Critical Reception, Honors, and Popularity

Updike has been treated with media attention throughout his long career, but the popular success of *Couples* in 1968 and *Rabbit is Rich* in 1981 put his face on the cover of *Time* magazine. Given the fact that Updike describes his own fiction as a picture of "normal, everyday life . . . an investigation of the quotidian," it is a nice irony that the American press reports his literary career as news.

Updike's reputation as a short-story writer for *The New Yorker* prepared the way for several laudatory reviews when his first novel, *The Poorhouse Fair,* appeared in 1959, but even Updike's debut as a novelist did not escape the slings and arrows of a few resentful critics. The debate has continued for more than two decades with each new Updike book praised for its faithful rendition of contemporary America and attacked by a few for its cerebral and urbane style. The growing evidence of Updike's achievement does nothing to stop his more persistent detractors, which suggests, perhaps, that the debate reflects a basic difference in sensibility. Updike has made fun of the difference by inventing a character, Henry Bech, whose own fiction is praised by Updike's most relentless critics.

Analysis of Updike's fiction has become a growth industry among scholars and professors of contemporary literature. Several monographs and scores of essays have been devoted to Updike's craftsmanship and a discussion of how his books reflect the aspirations and decadence of modern America. The subjects given the most critical attention have been Updike's moral realism and the precision of his style.

Several honors have come to Updike including a National Book Award for *The Centaur,* a Pulitzer Prize for *Rabbit is Rich,* and election to the American Academy of Arts and Letters.

Analysis of Selected Titles

RABBIT REDUX

Rabbit Redux, 1971, novel. Series: *Rabbit, Run,* 1960; *Rabbit is Rich,* 1981.

Social Concerns

Rabbit Redux is the centerpiece of a trilogy about the adventures of Harry Angstrom. All three novels are concerned with the deterioration of the American dream, but *Rabbit Redux* offers the strongest indictment of a contemporary America in crisis. The novel takes place during the late 1960s when pride in the success of Apollo 11 is set against the anguish of Vietnam. The location is a small city in Pennsylvania where the flaws of an industrial society are evident, and the chances for life are diminishing. The chief character works at a linotype machine for a local newspaper, but the day arrives when his skill is no longer needed, and with little notice his job disappears.

The disintegration of American culture is further described as violence comes to the suburban life of Harry Angstrom. *Rabbit Redux* includes a black militant who cannot forget the chaos of Vietnam, and a young girl who uses drugs and sex to escape the limits of her rich but uncaring family. When both characters move into Angstrom's house, the result is a desperate play of drugs and sex followed by scenes of arson and death. Updike's realistic style exposes the crisis in America after a decade noted for its social revolution, race riots, and television coverage of the war in Vietnam.

Themes

The rival claims of freedom and responsibility are explored in *Rabbit Redux* from several different points of view. After twice deserting his wife in the earlier novel of the series, the title character is now trying to maintain a home in the face of increasing odds. This time his wife experiments with freedom by having an affair with a used car salesman. Harry learns about this at a bar where the television repeatedly shows Apollo 11 blasting off to the moon. Updike thus reveals the emptiness in the life of his chief character at the very moment that America is ready to explore a new world in space.

The drug crazed young girl and the black veteran offer two more examples of the contest between freedom and responsibility. Both characters think of themselves as free from the rules of any conventional society. His experience in Vietnam has convinced the Black that the entire American system is bankrupt. What he offers in its place is a mad vision of himself as a black Messiah. The young girl expects to find love and freedom by rejecting the materialism of her family, but instead she is sexually exploited and left to die in a burning house. Updike shows in *Rabbit Redux* how the quest for freedom can be mad and dangerous when responsibility is exchanged for a limbo of self indulgence and chaos.

Characters

The protagonist of *Rabbit Redux* is a rather passive man in his mid-thirties. No longer does he live up to the nickname "Rabbit" left over from his high school days as a fast moving basketball player. Now he stays home to watch television while his wife and son go their different ways. Circumstances are so beyond his control—a dying mother, a teen-age son, an unfaithful wife, and then a lost job— that the protagonist finds comfort in a stoical and passive retreat. Near the end of the novel he has moved back into his boyhood home and is wearing his old basketball jacket. Lacking any obvious sign of intelligence or passion, Harry Angstrom appears to be a born loser, and some critics have faulted Updike for writing such a long novel about a "quintessential anti-hero." It is true that Harry gives himself a low grade—"As a human being I'm about a C minus."—but he does learn from experiences in the novel. Harry may not travel to the moon and back like the astronauts on his television screen, but he does explore the empty landscape of a broken marriage and the failure of his dreams.

Updike creates two other characters to shock and educate the protagonist. The angry veteran who claims to be a black Jesus is a reflection, however exaggerated, of the decade that fought against racial injustice and the war in Vietnam. The runaway girl is a flower child of the 1960s who masks her self-destructive yearning with shallow idealism. Updike's characters are thus rooted in a particular decade of American history, but their special combination of bitterness and vulnerability transcends time and place.

Techniques

Updike is best known as a novelist of manners. The clarity and precision of his style create the illusion of real characters in a plausible setting. Updike is true to form in *Rabbit Redux*, but he adds another element of craft that is more experimental and original. The novel is united by several references to the flight and landing of Apollo 11. Each chapter begins with a quotation from men in orbit around the earth or the moon. The exploration of space thus becomes a controlling metaphor to describe the way Harry Angstrom is subject to the voids and craters of his experience. The young girl who moves into his house is identified as a "moon child," and Harry learns from her much about the love and madness so long associated with the moon. Updike's experiment with references to space travel and its related metaphors adds a new dimension to his achievement of social realism.

Updike also finds a new way to project the interior monologue of his main character. Harry works at a linotype machine for the newspaper of a small city. He often thinks in terms of newsprint, and Updike exploits this as a stylistic device by including in the text of the novel several of Harry's mistakes at the typesetting machine. The mistakes are direct evidence of the distraction and confusion suffered by the protagonist. Harry feels that the rules for his life are "melting away," and Updike reflects the chaos directly on page after page.

Literary Precedents

Two of Updike's contemporaries published books just before *Rabbit Redux* that respond in different ways to the success of Apollo 11.

Norman Mailer was invited to the NASA facilities in Houston and Cape Kennedy. He interviewed the scientists and astronauts, had dinner with Wernher von Braun, and witnessed the lift-off of Apollo 11. The result is a book, *Of A Fire On The Moon,* that contains some of Mailer's best descriptive writing, but he was too close to the events to be able to turn them into metaphors and images for fiction. Mailer and Updike, however, share a fascination for the language used by the astronauts, and quote several examples of how the men in space are programmed to talk like robots.

Saul Bellow was so inspired by the success of Apollo 11 that he planned to call his next book "The Future of the Moon," but second thoughts relegated that title to a manuscript owned by a comic character in *Mr. Sammler's Planet.* There is a scientist in Bellow's novel who talks rather insanely about the immediate need for establishing colonies on the moon. Updike does not create a comic advocate for the space program to match Bellow's scientist, but in *Rabbit Redux* he does work the language of space exploration into the very texture of the novel.

Related Titles

Updike began the adventures of Harry Angstrom with *Rabbit, Run* in 1960. The protagonist is in his mid-twenties, feels trapped by the responsibility of a young family, and tends to run away each time the pressure mounts. He leaves behind a trail of hurt feelings, bitter accusations, and tragic events. His wife accidentally drowns their new baby after one of Harry's repeated desertions. Although his actions may be selfish and cruel, Harry remains a sympathetic character in so far as his restlessness is marked by a nostalgia for the innocence of lost youth, and his sexual adventures are described as a metaphysical longing.

Ten years later in *Rabbit Redux* the protagonist still has more questions than answers, but he is less apt to run away from his problems. Despite the chaos of the novel, the ending shows a tentative reconciliation of husband and wife. Updike builds upon that for the last book in the trilogy, *Rabbit is Rich,* in 1981. The education of Harry Angstrom continues as he makes love on a bed full of gold coins and discovers the unexpected dividends of wife swapping. The echoes of space travel, however, are only dimly heard. The novel is written in Updike's realistic style, but now it seems limited to probing deeply into the surface of things. The hero enjoys more sex and money than he deserves, but Updike can no longer find what he revealed in *Rabbit Redux*—the violence and fear at the heart of contemporary America.

THE WITCHES OF EASTWICK
The Witches of Eastwick, 1984, novel.

Social Concerns/Themes

Updike explores the frustration of broken marriage by representing three divorced women as contemporary witches. The result is a gothic novel complete with magic spells, totem figures, and a real devil, but the supernatural activity takes place in a small New England town, and the time is the present.

All three divorced characters play at adultery as if it were a casual pastime: "Being a divorcee in a small town is a little like playing Monopoly; eventually you land on all the properties." Updike has long been famous for describing adultery in small town America. *The Witches of Eastwick* is a new treatment of the subject that first landed its author on the cover of *Time* with the success of *Couples* in 1968. Perhaps the women are only playing at adultery, but their circuit of the Monopoly board leaves a trail of broken marriages, sickness, and death. Unable to sustain any love or affection, the witches are ready to destroy other homes and lives. They seek forbidden power or pleasure, and more than anything would like to give themselves to the devil. Updike thus uses the metaphor of witchcraft to explore the jealousy and frustration of his modern characters.

"My books," explains Updike, "are all meant to be moral debates with the reader." *The Witches of Eastwick* is a discussion of evil. The satanic character named Van Horne is invited to deliver a sermon, "This is a Terrible Creation," at the local church. The devil naturally blames an indifferent or incompetent Creator for all pain, cruelty, and evil in the world. Updike's dark comedy, however, implies that evil resides in human nature because the impulse for sexual pleasure and the drive for power are competitive. The jealousy and spite of his divorced characters are not limited to a particular time or place.

Characters

   Each of the main figures in Updike's novel is associated with a different form of artistic expression. One woman gives harmless music lessons in the daylight, but alone with her cello at night she makes contact with a dark world of magic and death. A second woman practices the art of sculpture. She molds figurines out of clay, and sells them to the local boutiques. Her poor attempts at self-expression resemble small totems meant to propitiate the dark spirits. If pins and tacks are stuck into one of her sculptures, however, an innocent victim may experience pain and death. Updike's third witch is a reporter for the local paper in Eastwick. She likes her work because she learns about the secret relationships which link the men and women of Eastwick in a network of envy, guilt, and jealousy. Her art preys upon the hidden evil of the community, and then assumes the form of gossip: spiteful, charming, and deadly.

   The devil in Updike's novel pretends to help the divorced women to improve their music, sculpture, and journalism. In return they are ready to offer him their bodies, but he, of course, is more interested in obtaining their souls. The devil himself is also an art collector, and his gothic mansion is filled with contemporary pieces that are grotesque and violent. Updike uses witchcraft as a metaphor of artistic practice, and the main characters in *The Witches of Eastwick* are all related to the dark roots of artistic power.

Techniques

   Updike's narrative strategy is to mix the natural and the supernatural until the line between them disappears. Fantastic happenings are reported in a matter-of-fact tone. Witchcraft is described as a common activity in a familiar small town setting. Updike's style remains realistic no matter what incredible event is being reported. His language often includes scientific terms mixed together with magic and superstition. Updike knows that contemporary science replaced the formulas of alchemy, and he shrewdly builds the artifice of his novel by playing the history backwards.

   The conventions of gothic fiction are updated in *The Witches of Eastwick,* and the result is often a bizarre comedy. The haunted mansion of the devil is equipped with a cauldron for the witches, but it is a large hot tub with an expensive music system. Updike has fun describing the lifestyle of the devil as a mixture of early Salem and late Southern California.

   The setting for *The Witches of Eastwick* is quite contemporary, but Updike adds depth to his novel by several reminders of the long history of witchcraft in New England. The novel takes place in Rhode Island, where the first outspoken woman in America, Anne Hutchinson, met her death in exile. Nor does Updike let his readers forget about the tragic events that happened farther up the coast at Salem. Nineteen accused witches were hanged on Gallows Hill in the late seventeenth century. Updike may suggest a comic fate for his modern witches; they are married off to absurd new husbands at the end of the novel; but the whispers of bitterness and guilt still echo from Gallows Hill. The result is a contemporary novel that often reverberates with the fears and accusations of history.

Literary Precedents

When asked to give a lecture at the American Academy of Arts and Letters in 1979, Updike decided to talk about Nathaniel Hawthorne. The choice was prophetic because the fiction of Hawthorne, concerned with the history of New England witchcraft and adultery, is the most important precedent for the novel that Updike would write a few years later. Updike referred to *The Scarlet Letter* in his lecture to the American Academy, and surely it was still on his mind when he wrote *The Witches of Eastwick*. Indeed, one of his divorced characters even has an affair with the local minister. The shades of Hester Prynne and Arthur Dimmesdale haunt Updike's novel. Hawthorne thought of his own creation as a romance—"where the Actual and the Imaginary may meet"—and the same double vision is characteristic of Updike's novel. *The Witches of Eastwick* is a blend of realism and the supernatural that Hawthorne would appreciate.

Updike also borrowed some hints about the dark roots of artistic power. Sensuality and art are closely related in *The Scarlet Letter*. Hester Prynne has decorated her badge of guilt and shame with an elaborate embroidery. The women in Updike's novel all turn the frustration of broken marriage into some form of artistic expression. *The Witches of Eastwick* is a study of the power that has fascinated the American imagination from the time of Salem. Updike returns to contemporary literature its dark inheritance: in the tradition of Hawthorne he traces again the common ground of art, adultery, and witchcraft.

Related Titles

For an earlier Updike novel about adultery in a small New England town, a novel with more sex and less witchcraft, a notorious example is *Couples* in 1968. Despite his claim that *Couples* is "about sex as the emergent religion," many of Updike's critics saw the novel as cheap and scandalous. The book remained on the best seller list for almost a year.

For another novel with just four main characters who live for adultery and guilt, a much criticized example is *Marry Me: A Romance* in 1976. The subtitle indicates Updike's debt to Hawthorne. The protagonist of *Marry Me: A Romance* is a hypocrite in the tradition of Arthur Dimmesdale, and the novel explores the mutual desire and guilt of sex and religion.

Couples and *Marry Me: A Romance* break some of the ground for Updike's later romance about witchcraft and adultery, but neither book reaches the sophistication or depth that Updike creates in *The Witches of Eastwick*.

Other Titles

The Poorhouse Fair, 1959 (novel); *The Same Door,* 1959 (short stories); *Rabbit, Run,* 1960 (novel); *Pigeon Feathers,* 1962 (short stories); *The Centaur,* 1963 (novel); *Olinger Stories: A Selection,* 1964 (short stories); *Of the Farm,* 1965 (novel); *Assorted Prose,* 1965 (literary parodies, sketches, and reviews); *The Music School,* 1966 (short stories); *Couples,* 1968 (novel); *Bech: A Book,* 1970 (related stories); *Museums and Women and Other Stories,* 1972 (short stories); *Buchanan Dying,* 1974 (play); *A Month of Sundays,* 1975 (novel); *Marry Me: A Romance,* 1976 (novel); *The Coup,* 1978 (novel); *Too Far To Go,* 1979 (related stories); *Problems and Other Stories,* 1979 (short stories); *Rabbit is Rich,* 1981 (novel); *Bech is Back,* 1982 (related stories); *Hugging the Shore,* 1983 (essays and reviews); *Roger's Version,* 1986 (novel).

Additional Sources

Berryman, Charles, "The Education of Harry Angstrom: Rabbit and the Moon," *The Literary Review* 21, 1 (Fall 1983): 117-126. Analysis of *Rabbit Redux* with special attention to the metaphors of space exploration.

Detweiler, Robert, *John Updike.* Boston: Twayne Publishers, 1972. Critical introduction to the first decade and a half of Updike's fiction.

Greiner, Donald J., *John Updike's Novels.* Athens, OH: Ohio University Press, 1984. Detailed analysis of ten novels and a collection of stories.

Macnaughton, William R., *Critical Essays on John Updike.* Boston: G. K. Hall and Co., 1982. Selected reviews, essays, and a survey of Updike scholarship.

Searles, George J., *The Fiction of Philip Roth and John Updike.* Carbondale and Edwardsville: Southern Illinois University Press, 1985. Comparative study of theme, method, and character in the fiction of Roth and Updike.

Thorburn, David, and Eiland, Howard, *John Updike: A Collection of Critical Essays.* Englewood Cliffs, NJ: Prentice-Hall, 1979. Introduction, chronology, selected bibliography, and twenty-three essays representing different critical approaches to Updike's novels and short stories.

Uphaus, Suzanne Henning, *John Updike.* New York: Frederick Ungar Publishing, 1980. Limited discussion of theme and character included with plot summaries of Updike's novels through the 1970s.

Charles Berryman
University of Southern California

LEON URIS
1924

Publishing History

Leon Uris has been a full-time writer since 1950. Reported to have failed high school English three times, and to have left school before graduating, Uris has been quoted as saying, "It's a good thing English has nothing to do with writing." His first novel, which later became the basis for a film, reflects the experience of his years with the U. S. Marine Corps during the Second World War. Extensive research has been described as the hallmark of a Uris novel. *Exodus* is based on the information gathered from wide reading, extensive travel, multitudinous interviews, and Uris' experiences as a war correspondent in the Sinai. In his acknowledgments at the beginning of *The Haj*, Uris refers to "the years necessary to travel, research, and write a novel such as *The Haj*," in thanking those who helped him with the project. Sales of *Exodus* ran into the millions—over six and a half million copies were in print as of early 1986, at which time the novel had had almost a hundred printings—and *The Haj* became a national best seller.

Critical Reception, Honors, and Popularity

Exodus received a generally more favorable critical reception than *The Haj*. While *Exodus* received praise for its fidelity to history, by the time of the publication of *The Haj*, critics questioned Uris' employment, in a fictional context, of history. *The Haj* became the target of attack, with critics claiming that the work includes historical fact but blurs the boundary between fact and fiction.

Despite reservations about Uris' work expressed by critics, especially since the publication of *The Haj*, Uris remains the author of best-selling work.

Uris received the Daroff Memorial Award in 1959, and a National Institute of Arts and Letters grant in the same year.

Analysis of Selected Titles

EXODUS

Exodus, 1958, novel.

Social Concerns

The social history leading to the foundation of the modern state of Israel is the focus of *Exodus*. The story opens by giving the viewpoint of an American journalist; like this character, the reader becomes an observer of history unfolding. *Exodus* appeared in 1958, only a few years after the Holocaust. Uris spends a significant proportion of the novel describing how the Holocaust effects the lives of his major characters. In the work, children, who are concentration camp survivors detained in a British refugee camp on Cyprus, try to obtain permission to sail to what was then British Palestine, and is now Israel, on a boat named the *Exodus*. References to the Biblical Exodus recur in the novel, and as the children on the *Exodus* wait for permission to sail, an appeal to the British authorities is formulated in Biblical language: "Let my people go." *Exodus* aligns the Biblical Exodus, various historical episodes of anti-Semitism, Eastern European persecution of Jews, and the Nazi attempt to annihilate the Jewish people; these events are presented as the circumstances leading to the mid-twentieth century attempt to create an independent Israel.

Themes

The themes of the novel are generally related to the background and circumstances of Israeli independence: characters behave in the present according to their reactions to the past and their visions of the future. Alienation repeatedly appears: victims of the Nazis manifest levels of alienation ranging from silent agony to madness. Tolerance is another theme which receives extensive treatment. For individuals and communities, tolerance enables harmony and peace, while intolerance breeds division and violence. The subject of freedom is a central concern in *Exodus*; characters seek, with varying degrees of intensity, forms of liberation, and to some extent the novel links personal and political liberation. History itself becomes a theme of the work as Uris includes and provides a context for such events as the United Nations vote on whether or not to partition Palestine.

Exodus touches on the theme of the role of the artist. The novel refers to different writers' reactions toward prejudice. *Exodus* includes references to Shakespeare's *Othello*, Zola's interest in the Dreyfus case, and Tolstoy's objection to anti-Jewish activity. In total, these references imply the historical and fitting concern of the artist with social issues.

The themes of *Exodus* culminate in the question that is the cri-de-coeur of the novel's protagonist, Ari Ben Canaan, who fights for Israeli independence: " 'God! God! Why don't they let us alone! *Why don't they let us live!*' "

Characters

Some of the novel's significant characters are paired, with one character drawing the other of the pair away from a distorting or damaging degree of alienation. The American nurse, Kitty Fremont, if initially "a nice woman who looks at Jews as though she were looking into a cage at a zoo," acquires an affection for Ari that causes her to revise her outlook. Karen Hansen Clement, a young and beautiful survivor of the Holocaust, helps another survivor, Dov Landau—variously described as "a very good artist" and "a real artist"—overcome his isolation in pain and alienation. However, no simple solutions are offered for some of the forms of alienation presented: Nazi violence drives Karen's professor father into insanity, Ari's father and uncle part because they disagree on what are feasible ways of managing besieged Israel's survival, and Ari's friend, David Ben Ami, dies for his attempt to bring relief to the besieged city of Jerusalem.

Techniques

In *Exodus*, Uris presents his characters in terms of historical events that both shape them, and in turn, they themselves influence. For example, Dov Landau learns to survive in the hellish conditions of the besieged Warsaw Ghetto, and German concentration and British refugee camps; later he is willing to take violent action in defiance of the restriction placed on Jewish immigration to British Palestine. Ari's father and Uncle Akiva walk to the Promised Land from an Eastern European ghetto, but while Ari's father defends Israel as a soldier and diplomat, Akiva joins a group that bombs the King David Hotel. Ari, a captain in the British Army who is awarded the Military Cross, and who as a young man was in Germany to help Jews leave just before the outbreak of the Second World War, protests the British refusal to allow the *Exodus* to sail; he declares to the press, " 'I say the same thing to the Foreign Minister that a great man said to another oppressor three thousand years ago—LET MY PEOPLE GO.' " Uris presents his characters in relation to historical events in describing the reasons for an attempt "to resurrect a nation that has been dead for two thousand years."

Literary Precedents

Exodus includes elements of the documentary and historical romance. The novel makes frequent use of historical detail, and careful use of chronology, but also includes elements closer to the world of literary romance; Ari tends to be unswervingly heroic, Kitty unimpeachably selfless and Karen flawlessly fair. Uris himself draws attention to the story of the Biblical Exodus, which in the novel serves as a precedent for the Jewish fight for freedom, although other precedents, such as the siege of Masada, also receive mention. Each section of the novel is prefaced by a Biblical quotation, and although the book of Exodus is the source of only one of these, the Biblical Exodus—which Passover commemorates, and the celebration of Passover is the final scene of the work—is the keynote of the novel.

Adaptations

More than one Uris novel has become the basis for a film. Uris himself wrote the screenplay for the film version of *Battle Cry*, which was directed by Raoul Walsh, released by Warner Brothers, and included in its cast Van Heflin, Tab Hunter, Dorothy Malone, Raymond Massey and Aldo Ray. A 1955 review claims the film exhibits sentiments reminiscent of a "recruiting poster."

Objection to conventionality also appears in a 1959 review of the film *The Angry Hills*. A. I. Bezzerides adapted *The Angry Hills* for the screen; the director was Robert Aldrich, the producer Raymond Stross, and the film a Metro-Goldwyn-Mayer release. Actors appearing in the film include Theodore Bikel, Sebastian Cabot and Robert Mitchum.

Exodus, a United Artists film, was shot on location in Cyprus and Israel. Dalton Trumbo wrote the screenplay; Otto Preminger was director and producer. Ari Ben Canaan is played by Paul Newman, and Kitty Fremont by Eva Marie Saint; the cast also includes Lee J. Cobb, Peter Lawford, Sal Mineo and Ralph Richardson. *Exodus* is well over three hours long. The film was seen as attempting to reflect the inclusivity of the novel, and having a strong emotional impact. *The New York Times* rated the film version of *Exodus* as one of the top ten English language films of 1960: *Exodus* received praise for effective acting, was described as being a "massive drama of the fight to liberate Israel," and was summed up as being, if not flawless, "the best 'blockbuster' of the year."

THE HAJ

The Haj, 1984, novel.

Social Concerns

Two contemporary social issues receive attention in *The Haj*: the apparent ease with which war can be sparked, and social expectations assigned on the basis of an individual's sex. The novel's setting in time is roughly the first half of the twentieth century, the predominant setting in place is the militarily-simmering Middle East, and the social setting is the milieu of the Haj of Tabah, (an Arab village near Jerusalem), and the Haj's family. The Haj, his family and the villagers of Tabah become pawns as various Arab nations and leaders vie for power and attempt to stop Jewish settlement and conquer the state of Israel. Uris presents the Haj and his people as being displaced, exiled and trapped by a variety of causes: political power-broking and a willingness on the part of leaders to wage war contribute to the creation of a refugee population; in addition, circumstances conspire, and the Haj himself makes mistakes that, to a relatively minor degree, contribute to the downfall of himself and his people. Among the forces that eventually work toward harming the Haj and his family are the traditional sex roles in Arab life, and the clash that results when traditional Arabic ways and modern Western approaches confront each other. In Uris' novel, the Haj and the people of Tabah suffer because they are slowly harassed and hemmed in by political manipulation; the Haj himself is further undermined by the traditional sexual stereotyping that, among other things, dictates the compatibility of virility, violence and domination.

Themes

While the destructive nature of war and, to a secondary degree, sexual stereotyping are central themes in *The Haj*, another significant theme involves the imagination. In *The Haj*, fantasy is presented as being dangerous when used for the purpose of escaping reality, and can become a form of madness when the constructive use of the imagination is abandoned. Uris focuses attention on this theme by repeated references, direct and indirect, to *A Thousand and One Nights*. In *The Haj*, imagination is a double-edged sword: used constructively it can spare people from harm and lead to peace between individuals or factions, but fantasy can also be used to lull awareness into latency and deny the plight of oneself or others.

Characters

Much of the novel deals with how the Muktar of Tabah, Haj Ibrahim al Soukori al Wahhabi thinks, behaves and acts during a prolonged time of personal and political crisis. However, the main narrator is Ishmael, the Haj's youngest son, and in telling the story of his father he reveals a great deal about himself. The Haj is a man of keen intelligence, shrewdness, pride and imagination, with a taste for power. Ishmael is like his father, but is less willing to resort to violence, and Ishmael thus moves away from his culture's capacity to yoke together violence and virility. While all the wives and children of the Haj are characterized in some detail, his youngest daughter, Nada, receives extra attention. She is very like the Haj in being independent, in having a natural inclination toward independent thought and action, but like Ishmael in her willingness to move beyond the boundaries determined by tradition. More specifically, of all the children in the family, Ishmael is drawn most to Nada, and what the two have in common is the desire to be free of sexually-determined roles, although Nada has a more pronounced and defined desire to do so than her brother.

Two other characters reflect the novel's concern with politics other than sexual politics. Gideon Asch first comes to the Haj's attention as a spokesman for the kibbutz that is established across the road from Tabah, when he visits the village in order to sue for peace. For political reasons, the two meet discreetly, and out of their meetings evolves a profound but politically illicit friendship. Over the years, Asch is increasingly involved in the political and military life of Israel, while the Haj moves along a parallel but less happy route in the Arab world. In context, the point of the friendship is that it is one between a peace-seeking Arab and a peace-seeking Jew. After his biological brother succumbs to political pressure and betrays him, the Haj acknowledges Gideon as being his true "brother," but this bond is one that the Haj cannot afford to acknowledge in public. A character of importance who emerges into the limelight as the novel draws to a close is Dr. Nuri Mudhil, who is a professor of archaeology. Like the Haj, he refuses to be swept up in the waves of anti-Zionist propaganda to which his milieu is subjected. As a disinterested explorer of the past, seeing archaeological discoveries as more than an income-generating proposition, Mudhil is again like the Haj in being able to see, think and speak in terms ranging beyond his own self-interest. Mudhil is a physical cripple, which both underlines by contrast Mudhil's moral and intellectual strength, and serves as a reminder of his plight, for like that Haj he is a far-seeing man caught in circumstances which are not entirely within his control.

Techniques

The main technical feature of *The Haj* is Ishmael's first-person narration. A Prelude, which describes his father's accession to power, closes with the one-sentence paragraph, "Ibrahim al Soukori was in his mid-twenties and Muktar of Tabah, and he knew the power of the dagger in Arab life." Although Ishmael begins the story proper with a statement of identity—"I am Ishmael"—this statement is placed in the context of a life said to be influenced by "the power of the dagger." The narrator repeats the statement, "I am Ishmael," later in the novel: technically, Ishmael as narrator enables the reader to be privy to the narration of a fairly reliable source, while the narrator's increasing reluctance to declare his identity in the terms of a world dominated by "the power of the dagger" provides a tension that parallels the predicament of the Haj himself.

Another important technique is the use of repetition, which can be associated with the stagnation resulting from the resignation to fate that the Haj laments as the plague of his people. A demonstration of the related hesitancy to be decisive goads the Haj to fury: when Ishmael gives him the automatic answer "Mumkin . . . Perhaps," the Haj retorts, "We live on too much mumkin."

Also of technical interest is the inclusion of set pieces: an Arabic wedding feast, Ishmael and others exploring a cave with the excitement of discovery, conferences at which the Haj voices dissenting opinions. These set pieces tend to be atmospheric holidays from the increasingly sordid circumstances of the Haj and his family.

Literary Precedents

The Haj, in presenting movement in space as a reflection of a search for things material and not, follows the quest pattern found in Homer's *Odyssey.* Like Odysseus, the Haj seeks restoration to his previously-held geographical and political place. Both characters, accustomed to wielding power, are restless in their removal from rule.

Like the Biblical Ishmael, Uris's exiled Ishmael has a mother named Hagar and a father who is a leader (who, if not called Abraham, is named Ibrahim), while references to both the Bible and the Koran occur in *The Haj.* These references, like the quest of the Haj for a return, which has roots in an epic, give the work the air of a spaciousness in scope. The choice of name, Ishmael, is also that of a character in a central work of American literature: Melville's *Moby-Dick.* Melville's work depicts an obsessive quest, includes an encyclopedic range of information, and opens "Call me Ishmael." *The Haj* opens "I am Ishmael." The parallel of the two beginnings is another prompting concerning the scope of *The Haj*. Yet the disparity of the two opening sentences, despite their similarity, is also of interest: Melville's work begins with a command, which in being a little cryptic in context suggests the tentative nature of grasping identity, while Uris' work begins with a clear statement of identity, the apparent authority of which is impaired, if not demolished, by the subsequent narration.

The Haj's inclusion of multiple references to *A Thousand and One Nights* constitutes a generic reminder of storytelling with a definite purpose. Uris's novel, to some extent, displays the conscious storytelling characteristic of twentieth-century fiction. Ishmael addresses the reader directly, throws the reliability of his information open to question, and repeatedly refers to his milieu as being one permeated by propaganda. These elements in *The Haj* tend to underline that the activity of making fiction can have radically different motives, and suggests that there is a definite distinction to be made between the constructive use of the imagination and the escapist or perverse use of fantasy. In short, a number of related elements in *The Haj* imply that the act of storytelling, behind which lies human motivation, has moral implications.

Related Titles

The Haj can be compared to *Exodus* in a number of ways. While *Exodus* celebrates what can be accomplished at fearful human cost, *The Haj* examines the terrible human price extracted by political ambition, racial intolerance and sexual discrimination. Although the two novels share approximately the same historical setting, *Exodus* was written in the post-establishment of the modern state of Israel era, while *The Haj* was written after the establishment of O.P.E.C. and an oil crisis in the industrialized world. At the time of the publication of *Exodus,* world-wide terrorism was not a subject of major news stories, but by the time of the publication of *The Haj* such phenomena as airplane bombings were not unheard of events. The two novels are related in historical background but different in emphasis and angle of approach. A comment appearing early in *The Haj* helps define the common ground as well as the shift in emphasis between the two works. Ishmael reports, in the course of discussing the background of Gideon Asch, "most Jews in nineteenth-century Europe remained locked into a repetitive cycle of anguish." *Exodus* presents the Jewish people as freeing themselves from the relentless persecution, culminating in the Holocaust, that caused a "cycle of anguish"; *The Haj* presents the Haj and his people as betrayed into the anguish of exile and its attendant miseries by an intolerance for what the Haj himself comes to acknowledge privately—his brotherhood with Gideon.

Other Titles

Battle Cry, 1953 (novel); *The Angry Hills,* 1955 (novel); *Exodus Revisited,* 1959 (also published as *In the Steps of Exodus*) (photo-essay); *Mila 18,* 1961 (novel); *Armageddon,* 1963 (novel); *Topaz,* 1967 (novel); *QB VII,* 1970 (novel); *Ireland, a Terrible Beauty: The Story of Ireland Today,* with Jill Uris, 1975; *Trinity,* 1976 (novel); *Jerusalem: Song of Songs,* with Jill Uris, 1981 (portrait of Jerusalem).

Additional Sources

Crowther, Bosley, Review of the film *Exodus, The New York Times* (16 December 1960): 44. A detailed review that reflects the reception of *Exodus* at the time it appeared.

Gilroy, Harry, "The Founding of the New Israel," *The New York Times Book Review* (12 October 1958): 32. A review of *Exodus* that takes exception to Uris's use of historical fact in fiction.

Hunter, Evan, "Palestine in Black and White," *The New York Times Book Review* (22 April 1984): 7. A review that reflects the hostile reception with which some critics have greeted *The Haj.*

Joy Kuropatwa
Bresica College, Canada

GUY VANDERHAEGHE
1951

Publishing History

A full-time writing career was something that Guy Vanderhaeghe pursued only after having worked as a teacher, archivist, and researcher. Originally from Esterhazy, Saskatchewan, Vanderhaeghe published numerous stories in magazines and anthologies, winning in 1980 *Canadian Fiction Magazine's* annual contributor's prize for short fiction, and having his story "Reunion" included in *Best American Short Stories*. He amazed the literary world in 1982 by winning the Canadian Governor General's Award for fiction with his very first collection, *Man Descending: Selected Stories*. Alice Munro, in the very front rank of short story writers, attested: "These stories are wonderful: I thought I'd 'sample' them, and I've read them all with that astonished gratitude you feel when you meet a real writer." Other established Canadian authors such as Rudy Wiebe, Jack Hodgins, Richard Wright, and Robert Kroetsch hailed Vanderhaeghe's unmistakable talent.

His subsequent collection, *The Trouble With Heroes*, did not win quite the same plaudits, but was, nevertheless, evidence of his prowess with imagery and dark comedy. The next year, *My Present Age*, a novel, proved that Vanderhaeghe was no flash-in-the-pan, but an accomplished craftsman who could go the distance in fiction. This novel was a Book-of-the-Month Club Selection, and easily established Vanderhaeghe's gifts for dialogue, humour, and psychological insight.

Critical Reception, Honors, and Popularity

Man Descending sent shivers of delight and joy through the literary community. Critics crowed that Vanderhaeghe's ascent was well worth tracking, and saw him as a possible successor to Alice Munro, Margaret Atwood, or Clark Blaise for the top rungs of the literary ladder. Called masterful, perceptive, witty, and poignant, the stories were praised for their technical virtuosity and stylistic variety. Critics noted the remarkable way in which the stories celebrated the individuality of ordinary people, and praised the author's unobtrusive wisdom—his deft depiction of human frailty and hope. One critic wrote: ". . . they are frightening and funny, and painful, and pleasant as the world itself. And, ironically, they provide us, as all good literature should, with a new vision of that world, and perhaps some armour against it."

Vanderhaeghe's novel, though highly praised in some quarters, did not receive the same plaudits. *My Present Age* was seen to be an energetic, superbly organized book with many outrageous moments of a bittersweet flavor. Its dark sense of "the tragicomic tangle of modern life" was delicately conveyed by deft prose and sharp dialogue, but some critics complained that the swaggering, bullying narrative style swamped the book. The protagonist was felt to be a verbose boor with a remarkable propensity for clichés. His greatest shortcoming was his portentous exaggeration of characters around him into oversimplified grotesques. Vanderhaeghe's talent did shine in many splendid moments, and some critics were certainly impressed by the novel's irony and satire, but it was left to *The Trouble With Heroes* to restake Vanderhaeghe's claims on the territory of short fiction.

Analysis of Selected Titles

MAN DESCENDING

Man Descending, 1982, short story collection.

Social Concerns

This is a collection of twelve superbly crafted stories about males at various stages of life, but the settings for the fiction are vividly rendered and provide telling evidence of the modern age that breeds regret, impotent rage, comic exasperation, and bittersweet inertia. Human wisdom in these stories is not necessarily linked to urban sophistication, for in "The Watcher," a marvelous story about a young boy's initiation into a world of adult conflict and treachery, an old hard-talking, quick-witted grandmother on a farm shows her skill with the ways of the world. Her daughter's lover, a sadistic bully from the city with supercilious contempt for rural life, is given a tough lesson in justice and treachery.

Family relationships are sharply etched in this book, with their span of love, resentment, teasing cruelty, and vanity. Vanderhaeghe explores with perfect poise the stifling enclosures for his characters, allowing us to probe the family background of his suffering protagonists. In "Cages," a deeply touching story about an adolescent's changing perception of his father, Vanderhaeghe creates a suffocating mood at once congruent with the father's occupation as a miner and with the young narrator's sense of psychological constriction. The boy's impulses towards bitterness are checked by an underlying sympathy and love for the father—somewhat reminiscent of another young narrator's elegiac love for his paranoid father in "What I Learned From Caesar."

The widest social reach in this collection is shown in "The Expatriates' Party," where a middle-aged widower discovers in expatriation (his own and that of others) a metaphor for the anxiety-neurosis of our times. Marked and marred by restlessness, his journey to England for a reunion with his married son becomes a painful journey into his own self.

Perhaps the most powerful sector of social concern is that of marriage, for it is here that domestic trial and tribulation are read as a symptom of a much broader ethos. When things fall apart and the center does not hold, chaos—both comic and serious—takes hold, and suffering in various modes becomes a vivid graph of society's descent into perplexity, inertia, or proliferating folly. The final story,

"Sam, Soren, and Ed" is clearly about a marriage on the rocks, and although its wild, dark comedy is abundantly entertaining, there is a sense of topsy-turvy moral standards. The narrator is betrayed by a former close friend, once a hairy radical activist, but now blunted by affluence. The narrator, a writer-*manqué*, feels dissociated from what he does—a malady of the modern age. It is to Vanderhaeghe's great credit that gloom and doom are turned into startling black comedy which mirrors a confusing age.

Themes/Characters/Literary Precedents

Although most often about victims—people caged by their limited imaginations, personal problems, and paranoid feelings—Vanderhaeghe's stories are suffused with sympathy or compassion for the vulnerable. The existential gloom is somewhat dispelled by a wry humour in the major characters, whose perceptions of reality, although occasionally whacky, unhinged, or eccentric, are rather tempered by simple urges for love, security, and acknowledgment.

If pessimism is viewed as a prelude to a new world—why write if there is no hope?—then one would certainly be justified to call *Man Descending* a pessimistic book. It is filled with stories about fear, guilt, anxiety, the loss of control, mental unhingement, and life in descent. Yet the insights are so humanely wrought, the balance of pain and laughter so skillfully maintained, that there are cracks of light, glimmers of faith and grace amid the gathering gloom.

Family problems are only the start of much larger existential conflicts. In "The Watcher," young Charlie victimized by a bad chest since childhood, suffers greater psychological afflictions on his grandmother's farm when he has to choose between loyalty to her hard pattern of living, and a stranger's aggressive, bullying stratagems to take control of everything. The boy's naiveté about his essential role as a voyeur generates much humor, but the real subject is not so much the boy's amazing experiences as a watcher, but of his widening awareness of his own struggle to liberate himself from the "grip of ignorance" and the spheres of weakness.

Families frequently become dangerous cages of emotional turmoil and personality conflicts (as in "Reunion") or of great fears (as in "How The Story Ends"), but the worst cage of all is that sense of life as a suffocating, parasitical pattern ("Cages"). In "Reunion" the young boy at the center of a vicious family quarrel is confused by the internecine upheaval. The teasing toughness of one side of the family and the reciprocations of the other generate an unpleasant tartness, which is quite unusual in Vanderhaeghe's literary universe. This is not a book of unrelieved gloom. In "Cages," where the boy-narrator's father is a miner, the images of descent, mining, and elevator cars are of crucial significance to the sense of a close, choking feeling about life. This is a touching story about a father's slipping from his sense of high courage, and of the narrator's dawning realization of what family love means.

Vanderhaeghe graphs the loss of psychological control. In "The Expatriates'

Party," Joe, the middle-aged widower who goes to England to be reunited with his married son, allows his personal recriminations to get the better of him. Wishing to punish his son, he presents him with a photograph of his mother's embalmed body. This moment is epiphanic in more ways than one, for, in addition to showing Ed's callous irrationality, it reveals an underlying motif. The world for Ed has changed so radically since his wife's painful death from cancer, that he does not recognize the England of the present, his own son beneath the ersatz Anglophilinism, or his own boundary of emotional breakdown. Something bothers him about his son and his friends. Something bothers him about modern England. Something bothers him about expatriates in general. And it is only at the end that he discovers that he himself might be the ultimate expatriate. Had he been lost for thirty years, "an expatriate wandering"? Had those hot clamors of his schoolteaching days been exile? Was he a harder man than he himself had imagined? Was he nothing but "a drunkard who kicked at strangers in the streets, a man who punished his son by giving him pictures of his dead mother?"

"The Expatriates' Party" ends with a piece of truth that becomes the acid test of every adult character in Vanderhaeghe's fiction: how to learn the trick or knack of survival. The final two stories in the collection present the process and part of the results of this test.

"Man Descending" and "Sam, Soren, and Ed" share the same protagonist—a rather obese, enervated married man with adolescent behavior patterns. Continually criticized by his wife, for being lazy, immature, and unimaginative, he is fired from his job but lies about his future prospects, knowing full well that he is in descent: "I know now that I have begun the inevitable descent, the leisurely glissade which will finally topple me at the bottom of my own graph. A man descending is propelled by inertia; the only initiative left him is whether or not he decides to enjoy the passing scene."

The action of this story occurs at a New Year's Eve party, where Ed's attempts to kill time compound his woes. He gets involved in a political argument that sours the mood of the guests against him. His inebriation pushes him into picking a quarrel with his wife's lover. The result is a knockdown and a battering for him, and a subdued but remorseful ending.

The same Ed is at the core of the final story—only this time he is in a classic voyeur's stationing—a park bench on a weekday. His impulse to be a passive observer of the passing scene yields a momentary peacefulness until personal reality breaks into this lulling tranquility when he spots his own wife jogging in the park. This releases a flood of autobiographical revelations about the state of their union and respective psyches, and the general tone of the story is established.

This short story is a prelude to *My Present Age.* Two of the most entertaining characters from the novel make their first appearance here: Benny, the bourgeois lawyer who handles divorce proceedings for Ed's wife, Victoria; and Victoria herself, a rather righteous, sexy, determined woman. But the two most important abstract influences in this story—and again they anticipate their own magnifications in the novel—are Kierkegaard and Sam Waters (the "Soren" and "Sam" of the title)—the former being the gloomy philosophic touchstone for Ed; the latter being the projection for Ed's wish-fulfillment fantasies. Where Kierkegaard's journals breed Ed's pessimistic world-view, Sam Waters, the Western hero in Ed's own creative writing, is a remedy for the modern age's malaise. However, by the end of this story, Ed confesses that Kierkegaard is slowly supplanting Sam Waters as his guide through life's pitfalls. He proposes to finish his Sam Waters book and chooses an epigraph from Kierkegaard. This quotation is also his apology to his former wife and his admission that she was right all along, because it admits to the various excuses and evasions that have their being between a person's understanding and his act of willing.

The amazing thing about the Ed stories is not simply the brilliant control of the prose, but the remarkable way in which Vanderhaeghe takes stock characters—the sensuous wife, the aggrieved husband, the cuckold, the Western hero—and explores the tangle of modern life.

Techniques

Often the significance of a story hinges on a single image or a powerful twist in the action. In "The Watcher," the image that crystallizes the final irony is that of an Oriental statue. The boy puts the academic bully in mind of *Padma-sambhava*, the Hindu idol with close-set eyes that suggest concentration and intense inner vision. Ironically, it is the boy who, after witnessing every sordid incident in the story, makes the final decision to side with his grandmother against Thompson, and passes in the process from pastoral innocence to a rather risky adventure in the lower regions of experience.

In "Cages" the title is most expressive of the psychological mood of a story that moves from occupational discomfort to emotional and mental entrapment. The miner's cage and occupation become stark analogies for the young narrator's descent into his father's mind and heart.

Vanderhaeghe's technique is emblematic rather than symbolic, for the images are precise and their context concretely rendered. There is no impulsion towards airy, abstract generalizations, for the images appear to grow naturally out of the stories—as in "Dancing Bear," for instance, where the title expresses the paradox of a dangerous, persecuted animal which is as much a victim as a killer. This bear is a perfect analogy for the central character, an old, incapacitated man whose perfervid imagination causes him to burst with pent-up frustration.

The wonder of Vanderhaeghe's writing consists in the suspenseful mixture of terror and comedy. Although the vision of the present and the future is generally gloomy, Vanderhaeghe always leaves the reader with some protection against the spreading dark.

MY PRESENT AGE
My Present Age, 1984, novel.

Social Concerns

An epigraph from Soren Kierkegaard encapsulates the social and philosophic tenor of the novel: "But the present generation, wearied by its chimerical efforts, relapses into complete indolence." This is an age of fragmented families—the narrator's parents have retired to a mobile-home park near Brownsville, Texas. His estranged wife, Victoria, having walked out months ago, leaves Ed in a postlapsarian phase—something he wryly calls "that *paradis perdu*" when he feels a victim of "the Great Persecution" by an irascible old neighbour and the thudding banalities of the Beast of the radio hotline who continually berates the unemployed protagonist for sloth.

"We're all becoming what we really are," Ed contends, and offers us as evidence Sadler, "the ultimate Simplifier." Once a big-time campus radical urging Luddite atrocities on computer centers, and now a wild-eyed prophet for the Independent Pre-Millennial Church of God's First Chosen, Sadler shows us the vulgarizing power of trendiness.

Ed's story is that of a struggle against those social forces that conspire against man—especially the weaker of men who cannot struggle except by excuses and evasions.

Themes/Characters

A black comedy about a man whose frustrations and crises often explode into lurid fantasies, *My Present Age* provides a sharp portrait of a modern loser. Tormented by the failure of his marriage, stigmatized by an irascible, prying neighbour, Ed is trapped by the repetitive rituals of a banal existence. His unceasing diet of Cocoa Puffs is a perfect expression of his own essential softness as a person. Made obese by his junk food and laziness, he is a perennial adolescent in his exasperation and wish-fulfillment fantasies. His ex-wife, Victoria, is everything he is not: "assured, idealistic, ungrubby." When asked by her what he intends to do with his life, he replies: "Simplify it," but his compulsive chatter and chronic inability to cope with frustrations stamp him as the modern century's man of *Angst*. His anger, hurt, and neurosis lead to some near-demented acts of retaliation against his antagonists.

The one sustaining strength in his life is his imagination which, although translated into grotesque scenarios of absurdly incredible heroism, swaddles him in an illusion of victory over awesome odds. A boy-man who identifies with boyhood heroes, Huck Finn, D'Artagnan, Chingachgook, he dreams of revenge against his foes, and projects his deepest urges in his fictional creation, Sam Waters, a laconic, cold-eyed, fantastically potent western hero. This "lie" in his fictional world mirrors the "lies" in his real life. He pretends to be more important than he really is, impersonating a type of writer who has made *The Paris Review.* Deficient in his own literary productivity, he plagiarizes from other writers and dares to lecture on creative writing.

He knows himself as "a bad risk, a man on the margin, a doubtful character." His vulnerable personality is assailed all to easily by the forces of establishmentarian law and authority. Unable to convince his ex-wife to return to him, he spies on her and attempts to track her down. Unable to activate his own frequently inert will, he is liberal in judging others. Considered by some as being "terminally narcissistic," he is actually helplessly dependent on the sympathy of others, and would like to use his ex-wife as a psychological crutch.

Reduced by his own paranoia into being a grotesque victim, he bids goodbye to his world of enemies, ex-lovers, and former friends, in the hope of embracing a simpler life.

Techniques/Literary Precedents

In the black comedy tradition of J. D. Salinger, Ken Kesey, and Robert Kroetsch, *My Present Age* manages to take clichéd neurotic characters and exploit their foibles and fancies for the reader's satiric entertainment. This is a novel that has the pulse of modern times, and although its protagonist is eccentric, even demented at times, he is really an anti-hero and should not, therefore, be taken as an altogether reliable mirror of reality.

In the hands of a less skillful writer, the characters and plot of this book would have turned into soap-opera, but Vanderhaeghe knows how to turn boors and fools into entertainment.

The structure incorporates the standard conflict between reality and fantasy, as Vanderhaeghe shows us a man with several complexes seeking refuge in flights of literary imagination, and thereby acquiring yet another problem—that of unfulfilled revenge. Much of the comedy is derived not only from the quirks and kinks of modern life—the platitudinous radio hotline-host, the creepy neighbor, the adulterous yet righteous wife, the former radical socialist turned affluent apologist for law and order, the *soi-disant* ex-convict with aspirations for literary fame—but from the expansions and contractions of the protagonist's will as well. Ed's obesity is, perhaps, a symptom of his overweighted pull towards earth and the spheres of gluttony, sloth, lies, and anguish. His literary creation, Sam Waters, offers only momentary transcendence from life's problems. Ed's usual movement is downward—a gravitation towards inertia, laziness, dreaming, and complaining. The supreme irony is that of the voyeur observing his own inaction and frustration—perfectly aware of the very things that hold him down as a victim, yet unable to stir his will sufficiently to break out of narcissistic folly.

Other Titles
The Trouble With Heroes, 1983, short story collection.

Additional Sources
Vanderhaeghe, Guy, "Influences," *Canadian Literature* (Spring 1984): 323-328. An article in which Vanderhaeghe cites literary influences from boyhood on his writing, and suggests the root of his "traditional" interest in plot and story.

Keith Garebian

GORE VIDAL
1925

Publishing History

Gore Vidal (born Eugene Luther Vidal, Jr.) published his first novel when he was just nineteen and has been publishing major works only a year or so apart ever since. Prolific and versatile, Gore Vidal has maintained a remarkably consistent standard of excellence in his large body of work.

Critical Reception, Honors, and Popularity

Vidal's first two novels were well received by the critics; however, his third, *The City and the Pillar,* caused a considerable scandal when it was published because of the daringly frank treatment of homosexuality. Although the book was a best seller for many weeks, Vidal came to be regarded both by the public and by the critics as a celebrity first and a writer only secondarily. Notoriety has been the curse of Vidal's career. Whenever the critics are about to take him seriously as a writer, he publishes another controversial work. Although Vidal is sometimes dismissed by highbrow critics as a minor, though prolific, popular writer, his work always has important social and political implications. In his novels with modern settings, Vidal's ear for contemporary idiom is so perfect and his understanding of the latest fads and obsessions so sure that he is always readable and often, in addition, an incisive critic of modern lifestyles. In particular, his stylistic experiments in such works as *The Judgment of Paris, Myra Breckinridge, Two Sisters,* and *Myron* indicate both by their virtues and by their failings that when he controls his art he has the stylistic powers of a major craftsman. His works are almost always well plotted, and the style is both interesting for its own sake and appropriate to the subject. His weakness is characterization, for in his serious works many of the characters seem to share his psychological tastes, and in his satirical works the characters expound the same incisive views on sex and politics that Vidal reveals as his own in his essays. Nevertheless, in *Myra Breckinridge* he has created a mythic character symbolizing a unique element of the contemporary American experience. Vidal's very popularity may have denied him some of the serious critical attention he deserves, yet he consciously writes for popular taste. In fact, he is that rare phenomenon, a contemporary writer of distinction who both courts and reaches a mass audience.

Analysis of Selected Titles

MYRA BRECKINRIDGE
Myra Breckinridge, 1968, novel; *Myron,* 1974, novel.

Social Concerns

Myra Breckinridge marked Vidal's return to the public eye at the center of a major controversy. This novel, delineating some rather fantastic consequences of a sex change operation, scandalized some readers, but it allowed Vidal to paint a strongly satirical portrait of American society. Myra shows, on the one hand, that the ideals of the American way of life are identical to those of the B movies of the 1940s and 1950s and, on the other, that all power is in some ultimate sense sexual power.

Themes

Myra Breckinridge seeks to make readers rethink all sexual stereotypes. Just when the crazed feminist has shown the ultimate absurdity of the new theory of woman, the reader discovers that Myra is, after all, a transsexual (fiction's first transsexual heroine) and thus in her very nature a parody of womanhood, yet the satire does not stop here, for a terrible accident destroys the effects of the surgery, and Myra is turned willy-nilly back into a man. Myra/Myron illustrates twice over in a very concrete fashion the difficulty of the contemporary struggle to acknowledge the essential androgyny of humankind. For Vidal, every man seems to envy the freedom and creative power of woman. Myra is the consequence, and she is a neat satirical twist on the folk wisdom that today's is a patriarchal society. Traditional male power represented by Buck Loner is easily outwitted by Myra's legal machinations; traditional couples like Rusty and Mary-Ann are torn apart and transformed; and yet the plot so cleverly integrates these changes that they seem inevitable. The theme clearly emerges that American society is already on the brink of androgyny.

Characters

Myra is the bitch goddess she proclaims herself to be, a symbolic embodiment of the new woman, larger than life and twice as deadly. The fact that she is a transsexual only makes her symbolic power the stronger because she can be seen to have chosen womanhood. Other characters include Letitia Van Allen, yesterday's nymphomaniac, a self-directed woman but one living in the past and only fooling herself that she is using men, and Buck Loner, the ineffectual remnant of male supremacy. Rusty and Mary-Ann represent the misguided values of the past thoughtlessly perpetuated by the younger generation. Myra puts a stop to this. She abuses Rusty with a dildo, turning him first into a sadist (Letitia Van Allen winds up in a full body cast) and then into a homosexual, and she seduces Mary-Ann into a lesbian affair. Of course, when Myra turns back into Myron this relationship metamorphoses into precisely the conventional sort of thing Myra has been at war against. Inside every Myron, Vidal seems to say, there is a Myra fighting to get out, but it is a difficult struggle, and few will make it. Of course, none of these characters have any depth, but that very fact makes them perfectly effective for the book's satiric purpose.

Techniques

Myra Breckinridge uses alternating first-person narrators (one as if transcribed from unedited tape recordings) to provide its exposé of the superficiality of contemporary sexual mores. This method works very well in withholding the book's secrets for disclosure at the right moments. Myra's diary gives full insight into her overripe vision of reality, and Buck Loner's tape recordings provide an appropriate leavening of the mundane and help keep the reader from taking Myra too seriously.

Literary Precedents

Henry James's experiments with multiple narrators in works like *The Princess Casamassima* and *The Golden Bowl* are behind Vidal's use of alternating narrators. James's experiments, in turn, have behind them a long tradition including works like Emily Brontë's *Wuthering Heights* and earlier epistolary novels, for example the anonymous *Lazarillo de Tormes, La Princesse de Clèves (The Princess of Cleves)* by Madame de La Fayette, *Les Liaisons dangereuses (Dangerous Love Affairs)* by P.-A.-F. Choderlos de Laclos, and *Clarissa* by Samuel Richardson. In his use of transcripts of unedited tape recordings for one of the narrative voices, Vidal also owes something to the documentary novel illustrated by the John Dos Pasos work *U.S.A.* and Bel Kaufman's *Up The Down Staircase*. This technique substitutes for a straightforward narrative a gathering together without authorial comment of materials from which the reader pieces together a story. Discussing Vidal's picture of the decadence of the world, more than one reviewer compared *Myra Breckinridge* to *Les Liaisons dangereuses,* and there are other precedents in the *Justine* of the Marquis de Sade and the *Satyricon* of Petronius. Both the deft plotting of the novel and the satiric voice owe a great deal to the Evelyn Waugh of *Black Mischief* and *Scoop*.

Related Titles

In *Myron* the theme that all power is sexual power is carried even further than it is in *Myra Breckinridge* as Myra shows that saving the MGM movie studio and ending the world population crisis are in some sense the same problem: all she need do is emasculate all the movie extras (just as she was once emasculated) and substitute her own drag queen hyperreality for Maria Montez in the 1948 movie "Siren of Babylon," for which express purpose she has been transported back to the past through the magical time lapse of television commercials. The levels of reality in this book are complicated to describe, but not difficult to follow in context. Additional complications are provided by the narrator's schizophrenia, with sometimes the cautious Myron in control and sometimes the wild Myra. *Myron* uses film-making effectively as a metaphor for time travel to contrast the present unfavorably to the past; the book is also highly successful in manipulating euphemisms to mock Nixon-decade Supreme Court justices and others who want to use community standards to determine what is obscene. But even with all these stylistic pyrotechnics and a raunchy sexuality, the book was neither a critical nor a popular success. Perhaps in part because of changing standards of taste, although appearing only six years after *Myra Breckinridge*, *Myron* was not even a *succès de scandale*.

Adaptations

Michael Sarne directed a movie version of *Myra Breckinridge* that was released in 1970. This was damned by the critics and not particularly popular despite extensive pre-release publicity. Although Vidal is a successful and effective screenwriter himself, his work has seldom been transferred to film effectively. The one exception is his own adaptation of his play *The Best Man*. The worst travesty is the Jerry Lewis movie made from *Visit to a Small Planet*. The movie version of *Myra Breckinridge* falls somewhere in between. The casting and acting are excellent (although unusual and much criticized at the time), and many of the individual scenes are effectively recreated. The problem is a screenplay that makes no sense, and the reason for this seems to have been the decision to lure Mae West out of retirement to play Letitia Van Allen. While she has exactly the right style for the role, she rewrote parts of the script and refused to do other parts while insisting on top billing. The movie that was released is an abbreviated version of what could be shot around these demands. Myra is played by Raquel Welch, bringing an effective larger-than-life intensity to the part her own plastic surgery had destined her to play. The film critic Rex Reed was the unlikely choice to play Myron, but his cool detachment is right for the part. Other members of the cast include John Huston as Buck Loner, John Carradine as the doctor, Roger Herren as Rusty, and Farrah Fawcett as Mary-Ann. Old film clips are effectively intercut to underscore the satire.

BURR

Washington, D.C., 1967, novel; *Burr*, 1973, novel; *1876*, 1976, novel; *Lincoln*, 1984, novel.

Social Concerns

Burr illustrates Vidal's dark view of American history. He feels that the Founding Fathers have been mythologized and glamorized in a way that blinds Americans to the nature of their political institutions. He shows that human failings can influence the destiny of nations despite even the best of political institutions.

Themes

The character of Aaron Burr is, of course, a vehicle for expressing Vidal's revisionist view of American history, but Vidal is also interested in rehabilitating Burr's reputation for its own sake and at the expense of the reputations of some of his contemporaries. The historical record in some places supports and nowhere contradicts Vidal's theory that Burr was the victim of Hamilton's jealousy and the scapegoat for a temporary setback to Jefferson's imperial designs on the West. The plot concerns a conspiracy by the enemies of Martin Van Buren to discredit him as a presidential candidate by establishing that he is the illegitimate son of the aging Burr. His law clerk Charles Schuyler is in the pay of these enemies, and the book unfolds as Schuyler learns the story of Burr's life first hand. The intrigue fails, and Van Buren is able to succeed to the presidency when Schuyler discovers that he is himself the illegitimate son of Burr.

Characters

As Vidal presents him, Aaron Burr is both more clear-sighted and less devious than any of his contemporaries. He is an engaging and interesting character, more honest and straightforward in going after what he wants than anyone around him. Charles Schuyler, one of the few entirely fictional characters in the book, is neither engaging nor straightforward, but he is useful to Vidal in bringing closure to the plot and in manipulating the effective point of view. More interesting to most readers and far more controversial are the many minor portraits of the Founding Fathers. Alexander Hamilton appears as a paranoid and vindictive social climber, George Washington as inarticulate and a bad military strategist but one with a knack for taking advantage of every available opportunity, and Jefferson as a hypocritical demagogue. The last portrait is Vidal's most controversial, but he makes it entirely plausible in the context of the book.

Techniques

In a first-person narrative Schuyler tells of his association with Burr and reveals his growing understanding and affection. He reports Burr's view of the momentous events of his life from the perspective of his old age. Interspersed are excerpts from Burr's diary that are shared with Schuyler from time to time. This technique allows Vidal to maintain suspense and affords him numerous opportunities to comment from a number of different perspectives on everything from Burr's one-vote loss of the presidential election of 1800 and his trial for treason after the Louisiana Affair to the byways of Jefferson's sex life and the rise of Jacksonian democracy. This technique also allows Vidal to circumvent the direct recreation of important historical scenes like the duel with Alexander Hamilton. Avoiding the dangers of implausibility inherent in a more conventional narrative reconstruction, Vidal has Burr reënact the duel for his clerk. If anything fails to ring true, the reader may ascribe this to the filter of Schuyler's narrative, the haze of an old man's memory, or the inevitable distortions of a reënactment. The one element of Vidal's technique in this book that elicited serious complaints from some critics is his language. He struck a compromise between the language of the Age of Reason and more accessible language. The vocabulary is not anachronistic, yet some reviewers felt that the syntax was—and of course the ideas often illustrate Vidal's special insights into the workings of American political institutions. This must remain a fairly petty complaint in light of the achievement of the book as a whole, and indeed it is hard to imagine a more effective way of suggesting the language of the past without risking obscurity.

Literary Precedents

Burr is a biographical novel; that is, it represents the branch of historical fiction that presents real personages from history as central characters rather than merely as peripheral characters, as in the more familiar genre of the historical novel. The author is obliged to adhere to the known facts concerning external events but is free to invent probable minor characters and to develop the psychology of the main characters in any way that is not logically inconsistent with the facts of history. *The Fifth Queen* by Ford Maddox Ford is the ancestor of the modern biographical novel, but the form is fairly popular among readers of today's Gothic novels. Jean Plaidy, Anya Seton, and M. M. Kaye are familiar contemporary writers of the biographical novel. In another sense, however, the history of the biographical novel is much older. Ancient historians and biographers like Herodotus and Plutarch used much the same technique and even invented probable speeches to put into the mouths of historical figures. The growth of modern historical scholarship limited the biographer's permission to shape the facts of history to make political points and provide aesthetic closure. In retrospect, Izaak Walton's *Lives* of seventeenth-century divines, Samuel Johnson's *Lives of the Poets* and James Boswell's *Life of Johnson* are fiction of the biographical novel genre. The documentary novel provides the precedent for the point of view used in *Burr.*

Related Titles

Burr is the volume in Vidal's American political tetralogy describing the earliest events in American political history. In historical order the other volumes are *Lincoln, 1876,* and *Washington, D.C.* While *1876* was planned as a sequel to *Burr* and while *Lincoln* completes a sequence of analysis of American political institutions, each volume (despite some continuity in the few invented characters) is an independent work, and Vidal seems not to have begun with a plan for a series of novels. All four works indicate a detailed knowledge of history and show an impressive ability to make the names of the past come alive in the present. Together the American novels provide a particularly incisive critique of American political institutions. Vidal has also written historical and biographical novels on classical and medieval subjects.

THE CITY AND THE PILLAR
The City and the Pillar, 1948, novel; *The City and the Pillar Revised,* 1968, novel.

Social Concerns
Although Vidal's two earlier novels had homosexual characters, *The City and the Pillar* was the first major mainstream novel to present a full realistic picture of homosexuality in America. In light of the standards of the day, the book was shocking to many, but despite a certain self-conscious sensationalizing, Vidal managed to demonstrate a compassion and first-hand knowledge of the subject that other readers found compelling. One of the things that most outraged readers of conventional sensibility was the fact that the hero was so normal: flamboyant homosexuality was then more acceptable than the idea that homosexuals might be able to circulate among ordinary people undetected. The book's success changed the extent to which homosexuality and all sexual matters could be discussed in work written for a mass audience.

Themes
The City and the Pillar is the story of a man who never outgrows the homoerotic longings of his first schoolboy crush. Bernard Dick has pointed out how neatly the book extrapolates the recursive themes of American literature seen in Cooper, Melville, and Twain, including the boyhood idyll, the mysterious call of the sea, the quest for the unattainable, and the taming of the frontier—in this case a cultural frontier. More specifically, the book is on the surface the familiar tale from the romance tradition of a search for something that is not really there at all. It is not so much that Bob fails to reciprocate Jim's feelings when the two finally meet again, nor even that he has neglected to pursue a parallel quest (although Jim has always thought of Bob as a twin who must inevitably be sharing his feelings). The fact is that Bob has genuinely forgotten the boyhood idyll and its moment of forbidden erotic pleasure. It never meant anything special to him. This discovery is what causes Jim to turn on him so viciously (in a different way in each version of the book).

Characters
The hero of this novel, Jim Willard, is accurately enough described as a "dumb bunny" by one of the characters in *Two Sisters.* He is an incarnation of a certain brand of typically American innocence—a descendant of Billy Budd and Huck Finn and a slightly older brother to Holden Caulfield. Vidal has shrewdly exploited the effect of placing this traditional character in a milieu never before revealed in mainstream fiction, and he has made Jim a sympathetic character by the slowness with which he comes to act on the feelings that he has had from the time of his

junior year in high school, when the book begins. Bob Ford, his love object, is an idea rather than a developed character, but the way he overlooks the implications of boyhood sexual experimentation while drifting into a conventional adulthood is realistically presented. Ronald Shaw is a closeted movie star who keeps Jim for a while. Paul Sullivan is a bitter, second-rate novelist with whom Jim also has an affair. These portraits are not well rounded, but like Vidal's portrait of Jim they are important for the suggestion they carry that homosexuals can escape detection— even when they are conspicuous public figures. Through Sullivan, Jim meets Maria Verlaine, an exotic, sympathetic woman. Although he tries, Jim is unable to consummate an affair with her.

Techniques

The City and the Pillar is written in the same terse Hemingwayesque prose as Vidal's first two novels. This fact may have contributed to the scandal caused by the appearance of the work because many readers of the time felt the style to be uncomfortably inconsistent with the subject. On the other hand, the novel is written from a third-person restricted point of view with the focal character usually Jim. This fact led other readers to misapprehend the work as autobiography. Vidal's prose always carries a conviction of deep interest in his subject no matter what it is. While he has disavowed the naïve autobiographical interpretation of this work and all of his works (he is not an untutored tennis bum, and he was never kept by another man), it is sometimes difficult to distinguish his personal life from his professional persona. In *Two Sisters* he has the character bearing his name claim to make up everything in his novels and to copy nothing from life, but this statement occurs in what must be, of course, the most suspect of contexts.

Literary Precedents

At this point in Vidal's career, the main influence on his style is clearly Ernest Hemingway. Not only the terse prose but the artless, almost plotless, narrative structure also owes much to Hemingway in a novel like *The Sun Also Rises*. Only the melodramatic ending (either version of it) seems to suggest other antecedents. James M. Cain or hard-boiled detective fiction like Raymond Chandler's might have been an influence here. While there is no precedent for discussion of this particular subject in mainstream fiction, there are many instances in literary history of authors expanding the range of subject matter available for literature. Gustave Flaubert's *Madame Bovary* is a case in point. It was damned as obscene yet went on to become a best seller for its day and is now recognized as a literary classic at least in part because of the originality of its presentation of sexual longing in a woman. Generically, *The City and the Pillar* belongs to the class of the *Bildungsroman,* or novel of growing up.

Related Titles

The sympathetic portrait of homosexuality in the first version of the book was not at all explicit. By 1968, however, public sensibility had changed so much—at least in part because of Vidal's work—that he found this early work of his to be conventionally melodramatic. As a result, he published *The City and the Pillar Revised*. The style and narrative remain substantially the same, but the ending is altered. Again Jim finds Bob, but he no longer murders him; this time he rapes him. This change is inimitable Vidal; while the ending is still melodramatic, it is both far more likely and far more threatening to readers unacquainted with the homosexual subculture. As a result, Vidal scandalized and disturbed a whole new generation of readers and made them see homosexuality as part of the real world. He did this, of course, without sentimentalizing, in fact while brutally rejecting a sentimental view of Jim's unrequited love.

TWO SISTERS

Two Sisters: A Novel in the Form of a Memoir, 1970, novel.

Social Concerns

Vidal uses himself as one of the main narrators of this unusual book and shows himself finding the artistic and moral freedom in Europe that is denied to him in convention-bound America. The book is also a kind of potpourri of such fashionable modern sexual practices as incest, autoerotic asphyxia, troilism, pederasty, and nymphomania. It takes such a genial, casual view of these practices that it immediately identifies itself as peculiarly modern in outlook, making the point that the time has passed to view such things with anything more than ennui.

Themes

Two Sisters is a series of permutations on the theme that one cannot recapture the lost loves of youth because they were not the loves one thought them to be. The plot, especially in light of the complicated technique, is ever so slight, but the numerous pieces of material for a plot (including additional autobiographical elements in Eric's screenplay) are brought together in the last few pages of the book as the character Vidal learns almost inadvertently that he is not, after all, the father of Erika's child. The son Vidal had lacked the courage to acknowledge is revealed as the fruit of Eric's incestuous liaison with his sister. The tenuous thread tying Vidal to an unseen and unacknowledged replication of himself snaps, and no connection remains between him and either the Erika or the Eric of twenty years earlier.

Characters

The main narrative is in the form of musings on the passing scene by a character named Gore Vidal. Despite this persona's disclaimer that "he" invents everything in "his" novels, Vidal uses the persona not only to express his own views on life and art but also to make a number of daring personal revelations about his sex life. Interesting minor characters who pass through this portion of the work include Marietta Donegal, largely a caricature of Anaïs Nin, and Fryer Andrews, to some extent a caricature of Norman Mailer. Vidal deftly diffuses possible accusations of defamation of character in the traditional way of the author of a *roman à clef* by including a number of references to Nin and Mailer under their own names.

In the sections of the novel presented as excerpts from the twenty-year-old diary of Eric Van Damm, the illusive Eric is himself the main character, but the novel's chief weakness is the characterization of Eric. Vidal the character (or V. as Eric calls him) is in the process of discovering that the great (unrequited) love of his life was not the person he thought he was. The trouble is that Vidal the author has made Eric into very much the Vidal of twenty years earlier and left the book with more witty satire but less variety of characterization than most readers need and expect, but *Two Sisters* is the triumph of style over characterization, so this is a minor quibble. The other major character in the passages from Eric's diary is a fly-by-night film producer named Murray Morris who has aesthetic and sexual tastes that suggest a caricature of Louis B. Mayer. Drifting through these two narrative portions of the book (the Vidal and Eric first-person narrations) is the character of Eric's twin sister Erika, a genuinely illusive portrait of an archetypal lost love of another sort.

Among the characters in a sceenplay written by Eric at the same time as his diary and included in its entirety are Helena, widow of the Emperor of Persia, and her sister Artemisa, wife of the King of Caria. These are in some sense satirical portraits of Jacqueline Lee Bouvier Kennedy Onassis and her sister Princess Radizwell, who are step-sisters to the author Vidal's half-sister N. A. Steers. The relationship of Helena and Artemisa to their half-brother Herostratus also provides analogies for Eric's relationship to Erika, the relationship to Helena representing the incestuous feelings and the relationship to Artemisa representing the alienation. The character of the enuch Bogoas in the screenplay provides a further layering since the character Vidal recognized this as a caricature of Murray Morris. The screenplay also includes a wealthy but social-climbing Egyptian merchant named Achoris who is at some level a satiric portrait of Aristotle Onassis. This labyrinth of *roman à clef* naturally leaves little room for fully rounded character development, but the virtues of the book lie elsewhere.

Techniques

Two Sisters is, in fact, Vidal's most successful *tour de force* in the radical use of point of view. In this work of the first rank, Vidal proves himself to be a dazzling and audacious ventriloquist. Built around an unproduced screenplay from the 1940s, *Two Sisters* combines alternating past and present first-person narrators with very different perspectives on the nature of this work.

Literary Precedents

Unlike more traditional autobiographical novels (for example, *David Copperfield* by Charles Dickens or *The Naked and The Dead* by Norman Mailer)—works in which an author reshapes the materials of his own life to give them form and closure—and in distinction from the biographical novel (described above under *Burr*), the sort of autobiographical novel Vidal is writing in *Two Sisters* fuses fact and invention by remaining true to the psychology of the author while inventing a fictional world for him to observe. In classic illustrations of this point of view, like *The Moon and Sixpence* and *The Razor's Edge* by W. Somerset Maugham or *The Berlin Stories* by Christopher Isherwood, the narrator participates only intermittently in the action. By encouraging the reader to confuse the third-person observer narrator with the author as a real person, works in this mode carry a greater sense of conviction than works using other sorts of first-person narrators. The point of view of *Two Sisters* also owes something to the documentary novel and to the *roman à clef* as practiced by such contemporary writers as Harold Robbins and Jacqueline Susann and also seen in *The Moon and Sixpence* and *The Sun Also Rises* and various novels of Evelyn Waugh.

Related Titles

In *The Season of Comfort* Vidal made his first significant stylistic experiments—involving elaborate but not completely successful use of stream of consciousness and including a chapter in which two characters are followed simultaneously on facing pages. *Messiah* is an earlier use by Vidal of the pseudomemoir, the most congenial mode for his style—strong on wit and weak on character development. *Messiah* is an intense work describing a religious visionary with the satanic plan of seducing the world into mass suicide. *The Judgment of Paris* is another earlier stylistic experiment, this one combining (as Ray Lewis White has pointed out) the all-dialogue technique of Thomas Love Peacock and I. Compton-Burnett with the direct address to the reader familiar from Anthony Trollope and Henry Fielding.

Other Titles

Williwaw, 1946 (novel); *In a Yellow Wood*, 1947 (novel); *The Season of Comfort*, 1949 (novel); *Dark Green, Bright Red*, 1950, revised 1968 (novel); *A Search for the King*, 1950 (novel); *The Judgment of Paris*, 1952 (novel); *Death in the Fifth Position*, 1952 (mystery written under the pseudonym Edgar Box); *Death Before Bedtime*, 1953 (mystery written under the pseudonym Edgar Box); *Death Likes It*

1422 Gore Vidal

Hot, 1954 (mystery written under the pseudonym Edgar Box); *Messiah,* 1954, revised 1965 (novel); *Visit to a Small Planet,* 1955 (television play, published 1956, produced in revised form on Broadway 1957, filmed from a screenplay disowned by Vidal 1960); *The Catered Affair,* 1956 (film script adapted from a play by Paddy Chayefsky); *A Thirsty Evil,* 1956 (short stories); *I Accuse!,* 1958 (film script); *The Scapegoat,* 1959 (film script adapted from a novel by Daphne Du Maurier); *Suddenly Last Summer,* 1960 (film script adapted from a play by Tennessee Williams); *The Best Man,* 1960 (play, filmed from Vidal's own screenplay 1964); *Rocking the Boat,* 1962 (essays); *Julian,* 1964 (novel); *Romulus,* 1966 (play in free translation from Friedrich Dürrenmatt); *Weekend,* 1968 (play); *Sex, Death, and Money,* 1968 (essays); *Reflections Upon a Sinking Ship,* 1969 (essays); *Homage to Daniel Shays,* 1972; *An Evening with Richard Nixon,* 1972 (play for which then President Nixon was given tongue-in-cheek credit as co-author); *Matters of Fact and Fiction,* 1977 (essays); *Kalki,* 1978 (novel); *Caligula,* 1979 (film script disowned by Vidal); *Creation,* 1980 (novel); *The Second American Revolution,* 1982 (essays; a somewhat different collection was published in England as *Pink Triangle and Yellow Star*); *Duluth,* 1983 (novel); *Dress Gray,* 1986 (script for television miniseries from a novel by Lucien Truscott, IV); *Vidal in Venice,* 1986 (travel book; also a television special narrated by Vidal).

Additional Sources

Aldridge, John W., *After the Lost Generation: A Critical Study of Writers of Two Wars.* New York: McGraw-Hill, 1951. Thorough readings explaining the failures of some of the minor works.

Barber, Michael, "Crusader against Cant," *Books and Bookmen* (May 1974): 65-69. Presentation of Vidal's truth telling as the bane of his political ambitions.

Berryman, Charles, "Satire in Gore Vidal's *Kalki,*" *Critique: Studies in Modern Fiction* 22,2 (1980): 88-96. Review article seeing Vidal as an incisive prophet of doom.

Dick, Bernard F., *The Apostate Angel: A Critical Study of Gore Vidal.* New York: Random House, 1974. Intelligent discussion of mythic themes.

Kiernan, Robert F., *Gore Vidal.* New York: Ungar, 1982. Most comprehensive study, relating even minor works to Vidal's career as a whole.

White, Ray Lewis, *Gore Vidal.* Boston: Twayne, 1968. Sensitive reading of the earlier novels.

Edmund Miller
Long Island University
C. W. Post Campus

KURT VONNEGUT
1922

Publishing History

Kurt Vonnegut began writing for the *Cornell Daily Sun* as an undergraduate, and he continued to work as a reporter while studying anthropology at the University of Chicago after World War II. After taking a job in the public relations department at General Electric, Vonnegut began to publish stories in *Colliers* and *The Saturday Evening Post*. In 1950 this success encouraged him to quit his job with G.E. and to move to Barnstable, Cape Cod where he supported himself by publishing stories in science fiction magazines such as *Galaxy* and *Fantasy*.

Because of Vonnegut's reputation as a commercial science fiction writer, his first novels—*Player Piano* (1952), *The Sirens of Titan* (1959), and *Mother Night* (1962)—were published as paperbacks with lurid covers that misrepresented the novels and discouraged serious critical attention. The hardcover editions of *Cat's Cradle* (1963) and *God Bless You, Mr. Rosewater* (1965) were a significant improvement, although they sold only a few thousand copies. In 1966-1967 all of his novels were reissued in paperback, and Vonnegut began to develop a substantial underground following, particularly among college students. But it was the publication of *Slaughterhouse-Five* (1969) by Boston independent publisher Seymour Lawrence that changed Vonnegut's career. The novel's great popularity and broad critical acclaim focused new attention on his earlier work, and soon *The Sirens of Titan* had sold over 200,000 copies. From that point on anything with Vonnegut's name was virtually guaranteed success.

When he published the play *Happy Birthday, Wanda June* (1971), Vonnegut stated that he was "through with novels," and he withheld *Breakfast of Champions* from publication. But he returned to the genre that had brought him his greatest success by releasing the novel in 1973 with an initial printing of 100,000 copies. He has since continued to publish novels as well as collections of autobiography, opinion, and nonfiction.

Critical Reception, Honors, and Popularity

Slaughterhouse-Five was a critical and personal breakthrough for Vonnegut, yet the extravagant praise afforded the novel has sometimes been turned against the author when his subsequent books have been dismissed as "cute" and "thin" in comparison. Many critics continue to praise Vonnegut as a "masterly stylist," a jazz improviser in prose, and an author who has reinvented the America novel, but others complain of his "coy rhetorical trickiness," oversimplification, and sentimentality. One reviewer of *Galapagos* (1985) maintains that Vonnegut's "complacent detachment and sentimental cynicism have been fossilized for years." Another suggests that "Vonnegut's recent work has seemed fatigued, marred by sloppy writing." None of this, however, has diminished his continued popularity with the reading public, for each new offering has been an immediate best seller.

Vonnegut received a Guggenheim Fellowship in 1967 and a literature award from the National Institute of Arts and Letters in 1970. In 1974 he was awarded an honorary LHD by Indiana University, and in 1975 he was named a vice-president of the National Institute of Arts and Letters.

Analysis of Selected Titles

SLAUGHTERHOUSE-FIVE
Slaughterhouse-Five or the Children's Crusade, 1969, novel.

Social Concerns
Vonnegut was a prisoner of war in Dresden on February 13, 1945 when the city, a cultural center of no military value, was destroyed by Allied incendiary bombs, and in *Slaughterhouse-Five* Vonnegut, who was born on Armistice Day 1922, focuses on the particularly human madness of war. He consciously wanted to avoid writing a novel that glamorized the brutality of war, so as his subtitle suggests, he portrays wars as fought by young and uncomprehending innocents. He is equally appalled by a technology that can destroy 135,000 people in two hours, and the absence of an adequate moral response to such destruction.

The novel, which was published as America was escalating its involvement in Southeast Asia and nightly newscasts were filled with body counts and bloody footage from the field, makes explicit and implicit references to Vietnam. This was also a time of widespread experimentation with mind-altering drugs. Thus, the novel's mixture of fantasy and anti-war philosophy made the book particularly relevant and popular.

Themes
Slaughterhouse-Five describes man's inhumanity to man, and the mass destruction of Dresden by Allied forces serves as Vonnegut's primary example. Although a humanist at heart, Vonnegut repeatedly demonstrates the human aptitude for cruelty, and he shows how technology magnifies this cruelty beyond human control.

At a deeper level the novel explores the moral vacuum in which contemporary human life exists. Vonnegut's outrage over Dresden was as much a result of the lack of attention given to this event as it was to the bloodshed, but there are no villains in Vonnegut's novels, and he fully recognizes the ambiguous connection between agent and victim. Thus, in one of the novel's many biblical allusions he sympathizes with Lot's wife who looks back at the destruction she is escaping before being turned to stone.

Slaughterhouse-Five, which is about Vonnegut's effort to tell his story as much as it is about Billy Pilgrim, explores the ambiguous nature of communication, a recurrent theme in his work. In *Mother Night* Howard Campbell's Nazi propaganda broadcasts are also strategically coded messages to the Allies, messages that even he does not understand. In the end it is uncertain whether his strategic assistance to the Allies has outweighed the moral support his broadcasts gave the Nazi regime. Accordingly, Vonnegut approached the narration of his war experiences cautiously, fearful that by retelling his adventures he would inadvertently glamorize war. The result is a mix of historical and fantastic perspectives that discourages suspension of disbelief.

Finally, the novel explores the irreconcilable conflict between free will and determinism. Billy Pilgrim's motto—"God grant me the serenity to accept the things I cannot change, courage to change the things I can, and wisdom always to tell the difference"—is undercut by the narrator's comment that "among the things Billy Pilgrim could not change were the past, the present, and the future." The book accepts the logic of Tralfamadorian determinism, but it is nevertheless clear that Vonnegut cannot excuse the fire-bombing of Dresden as fated, and although Billy Pilgrim escapes into the Tralfamadorian belief that the perpetual existence of all moments of time eliminates the negation of death, he still finds himself at times inexplicably shedding tears.

Characters

As though to emphasize his vision of the life-denying nature of most modern existence, Vonnegut abandons the mimetic effort to develop character through motivation and causality. He explains that "there are almost no characters in this story, and almost no dramatic confrontations, because most of the people in it are so sick and so much the listless playthings of enormous forces."

Slaughterhouse-Five was Vonnegut's conscious leap toward a more personally revealing fiction. However, he directly presents himself as the spokesman only in the opening and closing chapters. Inside this autobiographical framework, the protagonist is Billy Pilgrim. Born in Vonnegut's version of Schenectady, New York (Ilium) in the year of Vonnegut's birth (1922), Billy also experiences the fire bombing of Dresden as a prisoner-of-war. He later marries Valencia Merble, becomes a successful optometrist, and fathers two children, including a Green-Beret son. Billy has been described as one of Vonnegut's "crucifieds," a passive, suffering character who fights brutality by shutting it out of his mind.

Slaughterhouse-Five is a self-conscious novel, and Vonnegut tries to insure that his readers will remember that it is only a novel. He emphasizes the artificial nature of his book by populating it with characters from his earlier work: Eliot Rosewater, Kilgore Trout, Howard Campbell, the Rumfoords, and the Tralfamadorians.

Techniques

On the title page Vonnegut says that *Slaughterhouse-Five* is written in the "telegraphic schizophrenic manner" of the Tralfamadorians, a self-deprecating, but fairly accurate description of the author's nontraditional approach. Actually, *Slaughterhouse-Five* was the first broadly popular work to completely abandon traditional restrictions of linear time and fixed space. Billy Pilgram's time travel is paralleled by Vonnegut's free movement through narrative time, mixing descriptions of historic Dresden and his personal wartime experiences with Tralfamadorian fantasy and bits from his earlier fiction to create fragments of meaning. Similarly, Vonnegut uses stream of consciousness to portray Billy's difficulty in fully adopting the Tralfamadorian objectivity toward the Dresden bombing and to underscore the inexplicable interrelatedness of experience.

Literary Precedents

Slaughterhouse-Five's numerous references to other books emphasize the multiplicity of Vonnegut's vision. The books, actual and fictional, that become part of *Slaughterhouse-Five* range from documentary studies such as *The Bombing of Dresden* and *The Execution of Private Slovik* through realistic portrayals such as Stephen Crane's *Red Badge of Courage* to Kilgore Trout's fantastic *Maniacs in the Fourth Dimension*. The stylistic conflict between these books echoes the novel's examination of fact, fancy, and the place of art in society.

The protagonist's name suggests a connection with Bunyan's allegory, *The Pilgrim's Progress,* and like Bunyan's Christian, Billy is exposed to the evils of the world. Unlike Christian, however, Billy is not supported by the vision of a Celestial City at the end of his journey; instead he envisions the moment of his own death.

Related Titles

Just as Vonnegut mixes history and fantasy in *Slaughterhouse-Five,* he combines his new material with characters and references to his earlier fiction. The city of Ilium was the setting for *Player Piano* (1952); the Tralfamadorians were the central focus of *The Sirens of Titan* (1959); Howard Campbell was the protagonist of *Mother Night* (1961); and Eliot Rosewater and Kilgore Trout return from *God Bless You, Mr. Rosewater* (1965).

The apocalyptic nature of *Slaughterhouse-Five* is echoed in many of Vonnegut's other works: In *Mother Night* Howard Campbell defends the holocaust; in *Cat's Cradle* the earth is destroyed by Dr. Hoenniker's ice-nine; in *Deadeye Dick* (1982) the citizens of Midland City are inadvertently killed by a neutron bomb; and *Galapagos* (1985) is narrated from a distant future long after man has been all but wiped out by an AIDS-like virus.

Adaptations

The film version of *Slaughterhouse-Five,* directed by George Roy Hill, starring Valerie Perrine, Michael Sacks, and Ron Leibman, with a screenplay by Stephen Geller, was released by Universal in 1972. The film won a special jury prize at the 1972 Cannes Film Festival.

BREAKFAST OF CHAMPIONS

Breakfast of Champions, 1973, novel.

Social Concerns

Breakfast of Champions is set in an America stripped of physical and spiritual beauty. Before setting out on the darkly humorous journey to the heartland that takes him past various scenes of ecological and human destruction, Kilgore Trout cries out, "I have no culture, no humane harmony in my brains. I can't live without a culture anymore." But when he arrives in Midland City, where anti-personnel bombs and body bags are manufactured, he is confronted by a garish array of fast-food restaurants and neon-lit motels divided by a vile stream called Sugar Creek.

The interspersed historical notes, which rewrite American history as a tale of racist sea pirates, place these observations in a larger context, reminding the reader of the dark and paradoxical nature of American capitalism. The contradiction between the ideal of American independence and the actual carceral experience of Vonnegut's Americans is symbolized by Thomas Jefferson's ownership of slaves. In summary, the book reminds its readers of the continuing bloodshed in Vietnam, addresses Americans' increased concern over the ecological destruction of the planet, satirically explores the vacuity of American culture, questions the benefits of capitalism, and suggests that racism is central to the structure of American society.

Themes

One important theme explored in *Breakfast of Champions* is the proper role of the artist, a particularly difficult question in a society so adept at transforming art into commodity and so immersed in the consoling fantasies supplied by Washington, Wall Street, and Hollywood. By writing a self-conscious, anti-novel Vonnegut hopes to prevent his readers from trying to "live like people invented in story books." It is a reworking of a favorite Vonnegut theme, explicitly stated in the preface that was added to the 1966 reissue of *Mother Night:* "We are what we pretend to be, so we must be careful about what we pretend to be."

In *Breakfast of Champions* Dwayne Hoover, the man of property, is set against Kilgore Trout, the man of vision, and at the center of their confrontation is the question of free will. Near the end of *Breakfast of Champions* Hoover reads Trout's *Now It Can Be Told* which tells him that he is the only creature in the universe with free will and that other people are only robots. This message seems to confirm the alienation Hoover has experienced and encourages a psychotic binge of violence that leaves both of the principal characters physically and spiritually damaged.

Yet in *Breakfast of Champions* there is some hope for melioration. Although experiential evidence indicates that life is mechanistic, intuition suggests, in the words of the minimalist painter Rabo Karbekian, that there is an "unwavering and pure" "immaterial core" in people, the " 'I am' to which all messages are sent." In this sense, *Breakfast of Champions* is Vonnegut's attempt to define a new humanism, a world in which "we are healthy only to the extent that our ideas are humane."

The difficulty of true communication is repeatedly emphasized in the novel, as the author portrays trite conversations and failed efforts to express the truth. In one absurd example, Vonnegut records the bodily measurements of all the main characters, but the language used in Midland City is an equally meaningless amalgamation of clichés and ritualistic responses. Before he goes mad, Dwayne Hoover starts repeating the last words spoken to him, but the citizens of Midland City do not notice the change. The book shows that faulty communication can be dangerous, too. After Hoover's rampage "it shook up Trout to realize that even *he* could bring evil into the world—in the form of bad ideas." Yet, when Trout sees "What is the purpose of life?" scrawled on a men's room wall, he immediately answers, "to be the eyes and ears and conscience of the Creator of the Universe, you fool."

Characters

The characters in *Breakfast of Champions* are puppets, and Vonnegut makes sure that his reader is aware of their artificiality. Like Robbe-Grillet, Vonnegut believes that the novel of character is dead, so *Breakfast of Champions* is filled with cartoon figures who can be adequately described with a single identifying phrase, but Vonnegut also fears that actual human beings are little more than robots leading determined existences. This depressing view of character is tempered in the novel by the minimalist painter Rabo Karabekian. In defense of his abstract painting *The Temptation of Saint Anthony,* Karabekian passionately argues that "our awareness is all that is alive and maybe sacred in any of us. Everything else about us is dead machinery."

In *God Bless You Mr. Rosewater* Kilgore Trout was the pathetic science fiction hack, a vision of what Vonnegut had feared he might become. In *Breakfast of Champions* he is a visionary who accepts the invitation to appear at the Midland City Arts Festival in order to confront Americans' romantic notions of art with his own experience of frustration and failure.

Dwayne Hoover, the "hero of this book" is a businessman whose wife has killed herself with Drano, whose lover is scarred by the death of her husband in Vietnam, and whose son is a homosexual. Until he reads Trout's "explanation," Hoover, despite having followed the path of success, leads a life of mystifying loneliness and despair.

Techniques

Written after a brief-lived rejection of prose, the novel is a conscious effort to break away from the successful formulas of his earlier writing. Vonnegut openly addresses himself in the role of creator "on a par with the Creator of the Universe," and with a Prospero-like gesture releases the characters from his earlier fiction. He also talks freely of his own personal experiences, including his mother's suicide and his relationship with his psychiatrist.

The result is a colloquial anti-novel, a further break from the confines of realistic fiction. Vonnegut undercuts suspense by revealing his plot in the first few chapters. In one of his numerous authorial intrusions, Vonnegut states that his purpose is to bring "chaos to order," to undercut his readers' comfortable expectations. Vonnegut freely ranges in time from 1492 forward into the future, saying that life is like an endless polymer without beginning or end. He stylistically emphasizes this notion of continuity by beginning many of his sentences with the word "And." In another rebellion against the order of realistic fiction, he makes no effort to dish out moral justice; the good and the evil suffer equally.

Other technical experiments in *Breakfast for Champions* derive from pop art. Vonnegut's felt-tip-pen illustrations reduce experience to its inexorable essence while parodying Americans' tendency to accept simplistic, commercial versions of reality. Their crudeness mocks a culture that rewards efficiency more than truth, as did the original hardcover edition of the novel, which was packaged to resemble a box of cereal.

Literary Precedents

Perhaps the most important literary precedent is *The Tempest*, Shakespeare's symbolic exploration of the role of the artist. Like Shakespeare, Vonnegut explores the ambiguous connection between the real and the invented, questions the authority of the artist, and considers the paradox of freedom. Like Prospero, he frees his literary thralls at the novel's end although he cannot grant them the happiness and immortality they want.

Related Titles

Although Vonnegut frees his characters in *Breakfast of Champions,* several are recalled in later books: In the Prologue to *Jailbird* (1976), Vonnegut announces that "Kilgore Trout is back again. He could not make it on the outside"; *Deadeye Dick* (1982) is set in Midland City in the years prior to Kilgore Trout's disastrous visit and describes many of the same characters; the ghost of Leon Trotsky Trout, the son of Kilgore Trout, narrates *Galapagos* (1985) from a distant future long after humanity has extinguished itself.

CAT'S CRADLE

Cat's Cradle, 1963, novel.

Social Concerns

Cat's Cradle, published in the wake of the Cold War weapons buildup and the tensions of the Cuban missile crisis, focuses on man's ability to destroy life on earth. The narrator sets out to write a book, *The Day the Earth Ended*, about the Hiroshima bombing, but soon his background research into Dr. Felix Hoenikker, one of the creators of the atomic bomb, and his family, shifts the focus of the story to the new apocalypse brought on by his discovery of ice-nine, a substance that causes any water it contacts to freeze at 114 degrees Fahrenheit.

Themes

In *Cat's Cradle* Vonnegut brought together themes from his first three novels: the threat of technology from *Player Piano*, the question of free will from *The Sirens of Titan*, and the problem of communication from *Mother Night*.

The overriding theme of *Cat's Cradle* is the narrator's warning that if technological advancement continues without a concurrent growth in ethical awareness, annihilation of the human race is a real possibility. This, of course, parallels the biblical story of Jonah who so vividly prophesies the destruction of Ninevah that the city repents and is spared by God. As in other books, Vonnegut shows that intellect harbors the temptation to rule over life, death, and nature, and he hopes that his novel will have the cautionary effect of Jonah's prophecy.

The confrontation between technology and morality is represented in the book by the two primary settings: Ilium, New York is the city of science, a world of materialistic absolutism in which scientists create in a moral vacuum; San Lorenzo is an island of belief, a tyrannic and hopelessly impoverished island nation in which the religion of Bokononism has been created to provide "dynamic tension" that will distract the people from the oppression and material suffering that mark their lives.

The book also shows how lies can overcome truth. Bokononism's purpose is to "provide people with better and better lies," lies that will keep them from seeing the Hobbesian truth, that "life was as short and brutish and mean as ever." This view justifies fiction and art, yet Vonnegut cannot easily resolve the "cruel paradox of Bokononist thought, the heartbreaking necessity of lying about reality, and the heartbreaking impossibility of lying about it." The uncertainty of truth is emphasized in the biblical parallel, for when God spared Ninevah he made Jonah's prophecy a lie.

Characters

John, the novel's narrator, opens by echoing *Moby-Dick* with the line, "Call me Jonah," an allusion that connects him with the biblical story of rebellion and suffering as well as with Melville's Ishmael, a prophet tempered by affliction. Like Melville's narrator, John's function is to observe, and he remains after the apocalpyse to tell the tale.

Other characters in the novel exhibit various forms of deception. Dr. Hoenikker epitomizes self-deceived intellect untempered by human feelings. His misshapen children (the amoral Franklin, the horse-faced giantess Angela, and the dwarf Newt) are love-starved indications of his disinterest in humans. Dr. Asa Breed is a spokesman for the spirit-crushing marriage between science and industry that transforms truth into commodity. Papa Monzano, San Lorenzo's brutal dictator, threaten Bokononists with torture and death, but secretly works with Bokonon, a cynical American named Lionel Boyd Johnson who established his phony religion as a means of controlling the people.

Techniques

Some critics have dismissed *Cat's Cradle* as a thin summation of the three books preceding it, but technically the novel marks some significant changes for Vonnegut. The fragmentary effect of 127 chapters, short units of prose often structured as three-line jokes, marked the beginning of Vonnegut's subsequent method.

It is also a book marked by irony. The book is cautionary, even prophetic, but it also makes fun of prophets. In keeping with its warning to beware of the ascendency of lies, the novel ends with the statement the "Nothing in this book is true."

Literary Precedents

Most obviously, *Cat's Cradle* uses the *Book of Jonah* and *Moby-Dick*. This levianthic motif is broadened by references to Hobbes and in descriptions of the landscape—the highest mountain in San Lorenzo looks like a "blue whale." Some critics have compared the novel to prophetic works such as Blake's *Marriage of Heaven and Hell* and Swift's *Tale of a Tub*, and others have concentrated on its place in the tradition of dystopian literature. However, *Cat's Cradle* is also a mock-apocalyptic novel that reacts to the popularity of books such as *Seven Days in May* and *On the Beach*.

Other Titles

Player Piano, 1952 (novel); *The Sirens of Titan*, 1959 (novel); *Mother Night*, 1961 (novel); *Canary in a Cat House*, 1961 (stories); *God Bless You, Mr. Rosewater*, 1965 (novel); *Welcome to the Monkey House*, 1968 (stories); *Wampeters, Foma and Granfalloons*, 1974 (nonfiction collection); *Slapstick*, 1974 (novel); *Jailbird*,

1976 (novel); *Palm Sunday,* 1981 (autobiographical collage); *Deadeye Dick,* 1982 (novel); *Galapagos,* 1985 (novel).

Additional Sources

Giannone, Richard, *Vonnegut: A Preface to His Novels.* Port Washington, NY: Kennikat Press, 1977. Analyzes Vonnegut's novels, concentrating on his development as an artist.

Goldsmith, David H., *Kurt Vonnegut: Fantasies of Fire and Ice.* Bowling Green, OH: Bowling Green University Popular Press, 1972. Apocalypse in Vonnegut's writing.

Klinkowitz, Jerome, *Vonnegut.* London: Methuen, 1982. Surveys nine of Vonnegut's novels, emphasizing his relationship to American culture.

Klinkowitz, Jerome, and Somer, John, eds. *The Vonnegut Statement.* New York: Delacorte, 1973. Collection of essays written to explain Vonnegut's popularity.

Lundquist, James, *Kurt Vonnegut.* New York: Frederick Ungar, 1977. Argues for essential Midwestern quality of Vonnegut's work.

Reed, Peter J., *Kurt Vonnegut, Jr.* New York: Warner Paperback Library, 1972. Biography and analysis of novels through *Slaughterhouse-Five.*

Schatt, Stanley, *Kurt Vonnegut, Jr.* Boston: Twayne, 1976. Outlines the concurrent development of Vonnegut's style and epistemology.

Tanner, Tony, "The Uncertain Messenger," *City of Words.* New York: Harper & Row, 1971, pp. 181-201. Examines the ambiguity and uncertainty of communication in Vonnegut's first five novels.

Carl Brucker
Arkansas Tech University

ALICE WALKER
1944

Publishing History

Considering the enormous critical and popular success of her novel *The Color Purple,* one may be surprised to learn that Alice Malsenior Walker began her literary career as a poet. While an undergraduate at Sarah Lawrence College in 1964, Walker began writing poems with great intensity after a traumatic abortion. Each morning Walker would slide copies of the previous night's poems under the door of her professor, the renowned poet Muriel Rukeyser (1913-1980), who showed them to her personal literary agent. In turn, he gave them to Hiram Haydn, an editor at Harcourt Brace Jovanovich, who accepted the poems for publication. The volume, entitled *Once,* appeared in 1968, and Walker's career was launched. Despite her activities in the Civil Rights Movement in the 1960s, a short-lived marriage to a white attorney, the birth of their daughter Rebecca, and periodic stints as a college professor and lecturer, Walker has proved to be an unusually prolific and versatile writer, producing poems, short stories, essays, and novels. In recent years, however, she has turned her attention more towards long fiction: *The Third Life of Grange Copeland* (1970) and *Meridian* (1976) achieved only moderate commercial success, although they helped maintain Walker's high status in Black literary circles and attracted the interest of a few white commentators. But as a result of the success of *The Color Purple,* written in less than one year in a California town that resembled Walker's native Georgia, she is now known and respected by a large white readership both here and abroad, and her popularity has been extended even further with the enormous success of the novel's 1985 movie version. *The Color Purple* sold almost 60,000 copies in hard-cover when it was first published by Harcourt Brace Jovanovich in 1982, remaining on the *New York Times* best seller list for over 25 weeks. Paperback editions (Washington Square Press, Pocket Books) have sold approximately four million copies, and the novel has been translated into French, Italian, Dutch, Swedish, Danish, Norwegian, German, Spanish, Portuguese, Finnish, Hebrew, and Japanese. The continued success of *The Color Purple* in the four years since its publication tends to substantiate *Newsweek*'s 1982 appraisal that it is "of permanent importance" in American literature.

Critical Reception, Honors, and Popularity

For almost twenty years, Alice Walker has received national recognition for her achievements. Her collection of poems entitled *Revolutionary Petunias* (1973) won the Lillian Smith Award of the Southern Regional Council for 1974 and was nominated for a National Book Award. Walker's first collection of short stories, *In Love and Trouble* (1973), received the 1974 Richard and Hinda Rosenthal Award from the American Institute of Arts and Letters, and her essay entitled "Beyond the Peacock: The Reconstruction of Flannery O'Connor" won the 1976 Front Page Award for Best Magazine Criticism from the Newswomen's Club of New York. By far, however, *The Color Purple* is her most honored work, having received the two most prestigious literary awards in the United States: the Pulitzer Prize for Fiction and the American Book Award (1983). Walker also has been the recipient of various fellowships and grants, including a Merrill Fellowship for writing (1966), two National Endowment for the Humanities grants (1969, 1979), a Radcliffe Institute Fellowship (1971-73), and a Guggenheim Fellowship (1978). She also holds an honorary doctorate in literature from Russell Sage College.

Despite these honors and grants, Walker's critical reception has been mixed. As noted above, she has enjoyed considerable status in Black literary circles, but—at least until the appearance of *The Color Purple*—white commentators have generally been more tepid in their response to her work. Walker's novel *The Third Life of Grange Copeland,* for example, has been chided repeatedly for poor character development, an over-reliance on clichés and platitudes, and a superficial handling of important themes. Walker's second collection of short stories, *You Can't Keep A Good Woman Down* (1981), has been criticized for her tendency to present Black women as so sympathetic, so beyond reproach, as to strain credulity. In large measure, these difficulties seem to have been resolved in *The Color Purple,* and from the moment of publication it has been widely praised by both Black and white critics. However, as Black commentator Trudier Harris points out in the *Black American Literature Forum,* the virtual "canonization" of the novel may be not only unwarranted but also symptomatic of two dubious trends. First, the almost universally hyperbolic praise lavished on *The Color Purple* by Black women may in part reflect their fear of "betraying" one of their number by pointing out distortions or inaccuracies in Walker's presentation of Black life in the rural South. At the same time, white readers' passion for the book may suggest that they are "spectator readers" who regard the incest, lesbianism, and violence of *The Color Purple* as titillating confirmation of derogatory racial stereotypes. Harris's reservations are well-taken, for there are indeed various problems with the novel's conception and execution. Several of these problems will be discussed below.

Predictably, the warm reception accorded *The Color Purple* has renewed interest in Walker's earlier writings. The novels and short story collections are now available in attractive paperback editions, and are selling briskly. However, *The Color Purple* is still regarded as Walker's masterpiece, and at this point in time it seems likely that her long-term literary reputation will rest on that novel.

Analysis of Selected Titles

THE COLOR PURPLE

The Color Purple, 1982, novel.

Social Concerns

In tracing the life of one woman, Celie, from the early 1900s to the mid-1940s, *The Color Purple* reveals the harsh emotional, social, and economic difficulties facing Blacks (especially women) in the rural South during the first half of the twentieth century. Just as important, it traces how these difficulties can be at least partly resolved by hard work, faith (in oneself, if not in God), and education. As these remarks suggest, the novel veers dangerously close to the platitudes which marred Walker's earlier writings, but the incisiveness with which she presents her material tends to rescue it from sentimentality.

Particularly striking is her uncompromising treatment of Black males early in the novel. Both Celie's stepfather Alphonso (usually called simply "he") and her husband Albert ("Mr.") are vicious, amoral men who regard their wives and daughters as ignorant live-in maids and sex objects. As Walker points out, though, their mistreatment of women reflects Black men's sense of impotence in a white-dominated society and, concomitantly, the inheritance of social practices: Albert's son Harpo tries to beat his wife Sofia because that is how Albert treated his own wives. More than this, as the series of letters from Celie's sister Nettie, an African missionary, reveal, the systematic mistreatment of women is common among the Olinka tribe: abuse is in part an African phenomenon unrelated to white oppression in America. On the topic of violence, then, *The Color Purple* is an illuminating document which approaches this social concern from a variety of angles.

Closely aligned with this is Walker's probing of the dynamics of sexual behavior. *The Color Purple* opens with 14-year-old Celie being raped by her "Pa," and Walker's rendering of how fornication appears to an ill-informed little girl is unforgettable. Equally powerful is the callousness with which Pa takes Celie's two babies away from her, and then arranges to have her married to a neighbor his own age (a cow is included to sweeten the deal: after all, Celie "ain't fresh . . . She spoiled. Twice.") It will be 200 pages before Celie learns that "Pa" is not her biological father, but nonetheless the apparent incest which opens *The Color Purple* sets the aura of sexual laxity which permeates the novel. In light of this, it is surprising that Celie's lesbian relationship with her husband's lover, Shug Avery, is quite touching. Primarily because Celie herself seems so innocent about sexual matters (Shug repeatedly calls her a virgin) and so in need of the acceptance which Shug amply provides, the lesbian relationship is one of the few examples of genuine love in the novel. Indeed, the lack of love in society—and the importance of accepting it, in whatever form it appears—are twin concerns to which Walker returns time and again.

Likewise, Walker is deeply concerned with the status of religion in modern American society. Approximately half the novel consists of Celie's confiding letters to God, whom she envisions as "some stout white man work at the bank." But when she finds out the truth about her family—that her biological father was lynched, that her mother was insane, that "Pa not pa"—her conclusion is that God is not omnipotent: "You must be sleep." From that point on, her letters are addressed to her sister Nettie, with whom she maintains a correspondence for 30 years despite the fact that neither knows if the other is alive. Sisterly love, rather than organized religion, can be one's "faith," the element which enables one to overcome the worst circumstances and to endure. But as Shug points out, even sisters are not necessary for faith: "God is inside you and inside everybody else," and to find God all one need do is "lay back and just admire stuff. Be happy. Have a good time." Walker herself identifies this attitude as "animism," a legacy of the African past; students of Transcendentalism will recognize it as the Emersonian "Oversoul"; but whatever one labels it, Walker does recognize the need for some sort of faith in modern society.

Interestingly, one social concern which Walker does not probe in *The Color Purple* is Black/white relations. Except for brief glimpses of a redneck prison warden and a rather dubious lady missionary, there are no whites in this novel. Their omission suggests the insularity of rural Black life, but it may also help explain why *The Color Purple* is so popular among white readers: Walker has studiously rendered it non-offensive to them.

Themes

As may be surmised from the discussion of social concerns, while Walker writes of the sources (and possible modes of resolution) of Black violence, the paucity of love, and the loss of faith, she also addresses more specific themes which are related to these concerns.

First, she probes the whole issue of personal identity. Celie's last name is never given; Pa's true identity is not revealed until late in the book; Albert remains the anonymous "Mr." until he develops into a secure, caring man; and Celie's children, raised as virtual Africans, do not even realize they were adopted until they reach adulthood. The deliberate confusion which Walker generates points to the tenuousness of personal identity in a world where little girls are forced to marry strangers, where men derive their sense of virility from sexual abuse and violence, and where work is a harsh, hopeless activity necessary purely for physical survival. For Walker, a major step in the achievement of personal identity is the emergence and nurturing of one's creativity. In Alice Walker's own life, it was her ancestors' quilts and her mother's gardens which served as outlets for creativity and enabled them to leave their marks on an otherwise hostile world. In *The Color Purple*, it is not until she receives Shug's support in establishing "Folkspants Unlimited" that Celie finds her own identity as a successful designer and manufacturer of pants. But creativity is not the only source of personal identity: the brutal Mr. is humanized into "Albert" when he openly accepts the fact that he loves to sew, a "womanish" activity. The degree to which Albert's transformation is credible is a moot point: Walker simply is arguing that one must reject sex-role stereotyping in one's quest for identity.

A less obvious theme is the need to assume responsibility for one's actions. For example, although Black men's violence against women can be understood in terms of sociology, economics, or whatever, it cannot be excused on those grounds. Celie is scarred for life, emotionally and physically (the second rape-induced pregnancy left her barren), by her stepfather Alphonso's sexual abuse, while the high-spirited Sofia's attack on the mayor results in an 11¹/₂-year prison sentence that turns her innocent children into virtual strangers. In short, isolated personal acts can hurt oneself and others, and the "bad" characters (such as Alphonso) either die or are converted to goodness by the end of the novel. In Walker's fictional world, people are punished or rewarded for their actions: *The Color Purple* is an insistently moral book, its violence and sexuality notwithstanding.

More subtle is one of the most important themes of the novel: the need to look to the future. This is not to say that Walker denies the importance of one's ethnic, racial, or familial past; in fact, in her essay "In Search of Our Mother's Gardens," she confirms her belief that one's heritage is to be recovered and revered. But Walker perceives an orientation towards the past as counterproductive. Celie becomes a secure, attractive woman precisely because she is willing to embark on a new relationship (with Shug), move to Memphis, and begin a pantmaking business; even her former husband Albert literally does not recognize Celie when she returns to town. Likewise, Nettie—who could have been just one more sexual victim of Alphonso—becomes an articulate, happily-married missionary in Africa. Granted, sometimes these transformations strain credulity (Walker relies heavily on coincidence for the development of character and plot), but in general she points to courage, education (formal or otherwise), and faith in the future as the keys to happiness.

Clearly Walker's themes tend to be platitudinous, and too often she has the articulate Nettie state them outright (e.g., ". . . unbelief is a terrible thing. And so is the hurt we cause others unknowingly"). But the themes nevertheless are timeless and universal, and Walker injects them with new life by virtue of her frequently memorable characters and imaginative techniques.

Characters

The protagonist of *The Color Purple* is Celie, a woman whose life is traced over a 30-year period, from the age of 14 on a poor sharecropper's farm to success as a middle-aged pants manufacturer. More than half of the novel consists of her letters, addressed first to God and then to her missionary sister Nettie. The epistolary (letter-writing) format guarantees that readers see the story entirely from Celie's point of view, and it affords them the opportunity to trace her growth from ignorant child, to abused and despairing wife, to lesbian lover, to independent and self-assured businesswoman. The reader tends to sympathize with Celie, who is based on Walker's great-grandmother, a slave raped by her owner when she was 12 years old. And perhaps part of the power of the presentation of Celie is due to the fact that another prototype for her was Alice Walker herself: having been blinded in one eye with a BB gun at age 8 and raised on a poor Georgia farm, Walker felt she was ugly as a child: "I felt old, and because I was unpleasant to look at, filled with shame." As Celie's self-image improves dramatically in the course of the novel, she never resorts to physical or verbal aggression and she never indulges in self-pity. Even so, there are serious problems with her characterization. As Trudier Harris points out, Celie's growth "is frequently incredible and inconsistent;" a more blunt commentator, Maria K. Mootry-Ikerionwu, believes that Celie "comes across as a bit stupid and elemental." True, Walker is trying to make the point that Celie's unfortunate situation is largely the result of her stultifying environment, but Nettie, the product of the same environment, seems vastly more intelligent and assertive than Celie. This discrepancy is partly the result of Nettie's escape from that milieu at an early age and it is magnified by the differences in the sisters' speech (Black folk dialect *versus* standard English); but there still seems to be some justice in Mootry-Ikerionwu's remark that "after 200 pages the reader suspects [Celie is] a case of arrested mental development."

A deeper, more memorable character is Shug Avery. With her mannish directness and low-cut dresses, Shug (short for "Sugar") comes across as a tough but tender bisexual with a special passion for weak, physically attractive men. Immune to guilt, she fully enjoys the material goods and sexual favors which her musical ability and unorthodox attitudes have brought her, and of all the characters in *The Color Purple* she seems to be the most physically whole. Some parts of her characterization do seem untenable, however. How can she be so loving with Celie, but so callous about her illegitimate children? And how are readers to respond to a woman who enters into sexual liaisons with no thought for the feelings of anyone else? Challenging sex-role stereotyping is one thing; amorality is quite another. Shug is a more interesting character than Celie, but she is also more problematic.

The least successful major character in *The Color Purple* is Nettie. Although it is clear that her growth into a missionary is meant to parallel and illuminate Celie's growth into a successful designer and manufacturer, the fact is that Nettie is too remote from Celie—intellectually, experientially, and geographically—to have any sort of relevance for her. Worse, she means nothing to the reader. Her letters from Africa, which constitute almost half the novel, reveal little about her except for an unappealing pedantry: the reader tires quickly of her lectures on European colonialism in Africa and the condition of British teeth, and even her religious faith seems cloying and naive at times. Far from being an enriching "foil" character for Celie, Nettie is simply a "flat" one.

The plethora of other characters in *The Color Purple* also suffer from varying degrees of flatness. Celie's daughter-in-law Sofia seemed to have potential as a fascinating character early in the novel, but after her prison term she seems pallid. The various male characters barely come to life; and although that is understandable for a book written by someone whose admitted career-long interest is Black women, it becomes a problem when Walker attempts to drive home her identity theme by transforming Mr. from a sex-crazed brute to a tender-hearted seamstress.

This is worse than unconvincing; it is ludicrous. The flurry of characters who suddenly emerge at the end of *The Color Purple* (e.g., Henrietta, Miss Eleanor Jane) transparently exist for the sole purpose of conveying particular themes. Although Walker's handling of characterization is said to be better in this novel than in her previous two efforts, it is still not a strong element of her fictional art.

Techniques

Barbara Christian points out that Alice Walker writes in a way that is "organically spare rather than elaborate, ascetic rather than lush," and in fact the letters which constitute the book (especially Celie's early letters to God) rarely fill a page. The literal physical barrenness of the book reflects the painful limitations of Celie's life and, perhaps, her fear of expressing herself—a manifestation of low self-esteem. It is an imaginative technique, but in so short a book it provides too limited a canvas on which the author can work. In the case of *The Color Purple,* the physical limitations are partly responsible for the many underdeveloped characters. On a more practical level, it is difficult for the reader to accept the notion that 30 years pass when the book itself consists of approximately 250 partly blank pages. Fictional time demands an appropriately weighty text.

And yet Walker tries to have those letters—to God, to Nettie, to Celie—convey the entire story. The epistolary format is not new (Samuel Richardson utilized it in his 1740 novel *Pamela*), but it is quite unusual for Black literature, and critics have had mixed reactions to Walker's handling of it. Peter S. Prescott in *Newsweek* found the parallel Celie/Nettie correspondence "deeply moving;" Frank W. Shelton believes that Celie's writing to God is a way simply for her to assert that "she is still alive"; and Mel Watkins in the *New York Times Book Review* finds Nettie's letters "lackluster and intrusive." What seems less debatable, however, is that the shift from (a) Celie writing to God to (b) Celie and Nettie writing each other effectively splits *The Color Purple* in half. Some readers find this technique to be brilliant; others find it jarring.

Part of what makes the split so blatant is the striking shift in language. *The Color Purple* has been much praised for Walker's utilization of Black folk speech, and Gloria Steinem is especially impressed that "there are no self-conscious apostrophes and contractions to assure us that the writer, of course, really knows what the proper spelling and grammar should be." The rural, idiomatic speech used by Celie contrasts dramatically with the standard English used by Nettie, and it illustrates graphically how a change in environment can affect something as fundamental as language.

Whereas most commentators are impressed with Walker's handling of dialect, there is more debate over the conclusion of the novel. *The Color Purple* features Walker's first "happy ending," and as much as the Fourth of July family reunion delights Peter S. Prescott in *Newsweek,* it appalls most other critics, who regard it as shamelessly contrived and sentimental. Perhaps, however, Trudier Harris is correct in characterizing *The Color Purple* as a type of fairy tale, complete with an ugly duckling and a nasty stepfather, which requires a happy ending to maintain the fairy tale formula. On a less abstract level, the ending can be defended as emotionally satisfying: two people who have struggled and suffered as much as Celie and Nettie deserve to be reunited. It would counter everything Walker has presented for over 200 pages if those German mines had indeed sunk Nettie's ship off Gibraltar.

Literary Precedents

As noted above, the epistolary format owes much to the example of English novelist Samuel Richardson. Further, as various critics have pointed out, it is their letters and diaries which have enabled contemporary historians to reconstruct the private lives of women before the late nineteenth century when, for the first time, the literary marketplace became receptive to "female scribblers." These most intimate of literary genres are thus often identified as the forté of women, and in particular of women who, like Celie, have no other outlets for their emotions and creativity.

Walker's focus on rural Southern Blacks may well show her indebtedness to the example of William Faulkner (e.g., *Light in August, Go Down, Moses),* although she has indicated that a more important Southern influence on her work is the fiction of Flannery O'Connor. It should be noted, however, that O'Connor exhibits little interest in racial matters, and that her strong Roman Catholic orientation is quite antithetical to Walker's "animism."

Walker's deepest literary interest is in such Black writers as Jean Toomer *(Cane,* 1923) and Zora Neale Hurston *(Their Eyes Were Watching God,* 1937). Hurston is credited with being an early recorder of rural Black speech, and it seems likely that Walker was influenced by Hurston's example. There also is some indication that Langston Hughes' folk philosopher "Jesse B. Semple" is evident in Celie's passive satisfaction in being alive. In short, despite Walker's widely-acknowledged love of Russian novelists, the Brontës, and Kate Chopin, most of the literary precedents for *The Color Purple* would appear to be found in Black literature.

Related Titles

Most of the social concerns and themes of *The Color Purple* are also evident in Walker's two earlier novels, *The Third Life of Grange Copeland* and *Meridian,* although the three books are not part of a sequence or otherwise related. *The Third Life* traces the history of the Copelands, a poor rural Black family, from 1920 to the Civil Rights Movement of the 1960s. As with *The Color Purple,* Walker posits the fortunes of the Copeland family (and in particular of the patriarchal Grange) as emblematic of the Black experience in the United States for that 40-year period. Walker's second novel *Meridian,* generally felt to be the best book to emerge from the Civil Rights Movement, is a more ambitious work which features a non-chronological format and a poetic, almost impressionistic style. Both books have been criticized, however, for excessive violence, uneven characterization, and blatant, pretentious symbolism.

Adaptations

Warner Brothers purchased the movie rights of *The Color Purple* for $350,000; filming began in June of 1985, and the film was released at Christmas. It proved to be an enormous box office success, but it was criticized heavily for the banal and sentimental treatment of some of its most powerful issues and scenes. David Ansen of *Newsweek*, for example, said that it was like "watching the first Disney movie about incest." Part of the blame went to the Dutch screenwriter, Menno Meyjes, but for the most part critics held director Steven Spielberg responsible for creating a beautiful but superficial "white man's version" of *The Color Purple*.

Other Titles

Once, 1968 (poems); *The Third Life of Grange Copeland*, 1970 (novel); *In Love and Trouble*, 1973 (short stories); *Langston Hughes: American Poet*, 1973 (biography for children); *Revolutionary Petunias*, 1973 (poems); *Meridian*, 1976 (novel); *Good Night, Willie Lee, I'll See You in the Morning*, 1979 (poems); *I Love Myself When I am Laughing . . . and then Again When I Am Looking Mean and Impressive: A Zora Neale Hurston Reader*, 1979 [editor]; *You Can't Keep a Good Woman Down*, 1981 (short stories); *In Search of Our Mothers' Gardens: Womanist Prose*, 1983 (essays); *Horses Make a Landscape Look More Beautiful*, 1984 (poems).

Additional Sources

Anello, Ray and Abramson, Pamela, "Characters in Search of a Book," *Newsweek* (June 21, 1982): 67.

Ansen, David, "We Shall Overcome," *Newsweek* (December 30, 1985): 59-60. Review of the movie version of *The Color Purple*.

Brewer, Krista, "Writing to Survive: An Interview with Alice Walker," *Southern Exposure* 9 (Summer 1981): 12-15.

Callahan, John F., "The Higher Ground of Alice Walker," *New Republic* (September 14, 1974): 21-22. Review of *In Love and Trouble*.

Christian, Barbara, "Alice Walker: The Black Woman Artist as Wayward," *Black Feminist Criticism: Perspectives on Black Women Writers*. New York: Pergamon Press, 1985, pp. 81-101; reprinted from Mari Evans, *Black Women Writers* [see below], pp. 457-477.

————, "No More Buried Lives: The Theme of Lesbianism in Audre Lorde's *Zami*, Gloria Naylor's *The Women of Brewster Place*, Ntozake Shange's *Sassafras, Cypress, and Indigo*, and Alice Walker's *The Color Purple*," *Black Feminist Criticism*, pp. 187-204.

Corliss, Richard, "The Three Faces of Steve," *Time* (December 23, 1985): 78. Review of the film version of *The Color Purple*.

Current Biography Yearbook: 1984, pp. 430-433.

Davis, Thadious M., "Alice Walker," *The Dictionary of Literary Biography: Volume 6: American Novelists Since World War II, Second Series*. 1980, pp. 350-358.

————, "Alice Walker's Celebration of Self in Southern Generations," *Southern Quarterly* 21 (Summer 1983): 39-53; (Reprinted in Peggy Whitman Prenshaw, ed. *Women Writers of the Contemporary South*, Jackson: University Press of Mississippi, 1984.)

Erickson, Peter, " 'Cast Out Alone/To Heal/and Re-create Ourselves': Family-Based Identity in the Work of Alice Walker," *College Language Association Journal* 23 (September 1979): 71-94.

Evans, Mari, ed., *Black Women Writers (1950-1980): A Critical Evaluation*. Garden City, NY: Anchor Press/Doubleday, 1984.

Gaston, Karen C., "Women in the Lives of Grange Copeland," *College Language Association Journal* 24 (March 1981): 276-286.

Harris, Trudier, "From Victimization to Free Enterprise: Alice Walker's *The Color Purple*," *Studies in American Fiction* 14 (Spring 1986): 1-17.

————, "On *The Color Purple*, Stereotypes, and Silence," *Black American Literature Forum* 18 (Winter 1984): 155-161.

Howard, Lillie P., "Alice Walker," *American Women Writers*, New York: Frederick Ungar, 1982, pp. 313-315.

McDowell, Deborah E., "The Self in Bloom: Alice Walker's *Meridian*," *College Language Association Journal* 24 (March 1981): 262-275.

McGowan, Martha J., "Atonement and Release in Alice Walker's *Meridian*," *Critique* 23 (1981): 25-36.

Mootry-Ikerionwu, Maria K., *College Language Association Journal* 27 (March 1984): 345-348. Review of *The Color Purple*.

O'Brien, John, ed., *Interviews with Black Writers*. New York: Liveright, 1973, pp. 185-211.

Parker-Smith, Bettye J., "Alice Walker's Women: In Search of Some Peace of Mind," *Black Women Writers*, Mari Evans, ed., New York, Doubleday, 1984. pp. 478-93.

Prescott, Peter S., "A Long Road to Liberation," Newsweek (June 21, 1982): 67-68. Review of *The Color Purple*.

Schorer, Mark, "Novels and Nothingness," *American Scholar* 40 (Winter, 1970-1971): 168, 170, 172, 174. Review of *The Third Life of Grange Copeland*.

Shelton, Frank W., "Alienation and Integration in Alice Walker's *The Color Purple*," *College Language Association Journal* 28 (June 1985): 382-392.

Steinem, Gloria, "Do You Know This Woman? She Knows You: A Profile of Alice Walker," *Ms.* 10 (June 1982): 36-37, 89-94.

Walker, Alice, "In Search of Our Mothers' Gardens: The Creativity of Black Women in the South," *Ms.* 2 (May 1974): 64-70, 105.

_____, *"One* Child of One's Own: A Meaningful Digression within the Work(s)," *The Writer on Her Work.* New York: W. W. Norton, 1980, pp. 121-140.

_____, "Saving the Life That is Your Own: The Importance of Models in the Artist's Life," *The Third Woman: Minority Women Writers of the United States.* Boston: Houghton Mifflin, 1980, pp. 151-158.

_____, "Writing *The Color Purple*," *Black Women Writers*, pp. 453-456; rpt. from Walker's *In Search of Our Mothers' Gardens*.

Washington, Mary Helen, "An Essay on Alice Walker," *Sturdy Black Bridges: Visions of Black Women in Literature.* Garden City, NY: Anchor Press, 1979, pp. 133-149.

_____, "Her Mother's Gifts," *Ms.,* 10 (June 1982): 38.

Watkins, Mel, "Some Letters Went to God," *New York Times Book Review* (July 25, 1982): 7.

Alice Hall Petry
Rhode Island School of Design
Providence

IRVING WALLACE
1916

Publishing History

Irving Wallace began his freelance writing career in the 1930s. At 15 he sold his first article for five dollars; at 18 he sold his first short story for twelve dollars. In the next twenty-five years Wallace sold over 500 articles and stories to America's leading periodicals. In the early 1950s Wallace started writing screenplays and by 1958 he had twelve filmed scripts to his credit.

Wallace abandoned journalism for commercial publishing in the mid-1950s when he undertook three volumes of popular biography for Alfred Knopf. Three years later he turned from screenwriting to fiction writing. Though his first novel was unremarkable, his second and third novels (*The Chapman Report* and *The Prize*) were best sellers. Henceforth Wallace's name on a title page guaranteed a hefty publisher's advance and huge sales. Since his first book Wallace has averaged about a volume a year. By 1986 his books had sold over 200 million copies around the world.

In the 1970s Wallace's vocation became a family business. He has coauthored several books with his son David, his daughter Amy, and his wife Sylvia.

Critical Reception, Honors, and Popularity

Though immensely popular with readers, Wallace's novels have not generally impressed reviewers. Most critics deny Wallace literary merit; they attribute his success to a breezy journalistic style, formulaic plots, and always titillating, sometimes tasteless subject matter. Literary critics see in Wallace's books the worst aspect of bestsellerism: pandering to the lowest common denominator of public taste in order to increase sales.

Wallace defends himself by pointing out nobody writes *not* to make money. As Samuel Johnson succinctly phrased the matter, "None but a blockhead ever wrote except for money." Wallace asserts that he gives readers good value for their money. His stories make readers ask "What happens next?"; they use topical plots; and they blend interesting facts with suspenseful fiction.

Wallace has won several literary awards, primarily for selling a lot of books, but also for bringing contemporary problems to a wide audience. His novel *The Man* (1964), about a black politician who becomes President, won awards from the State of California, the George Washington Carver Institute and *Bestseller* magazine. His extraordinary sales record was recognized by the Popular Culture Association award in 1974 and the Venice Rosa d'Oro award in 1975.

While literary critics ignore Wallace's fiction, scholars of popular culture are increasingly attracted to the novels. They are less inclined to judgments about literary quality and more attentive to the ways in which his books captivate and hold an audience. Wallace's novels are profitably read as barometers of the hopes, anxieties, and interests of contemporary American society.

Analysis of Selected Titles

THE PRIZE
The Prize, 1962, novel.

Social Concerns

The Prize is a long, complex novel about six Nobel laureates assembling in Stockholm for the awards ceremony. Through their stories Wallace meshes four issues of Americans in the early 1960s: the Technological Revolution, the Sexual Revolution, the Holocaust, and the Cold War.

The five scientists among Wallace's Nobel Prize winners are on the cutting edge of experimentation. Wallace attributes to them discoveries in heart transplant techniques, sperm preservation, and solar energy that within a decade became realities. Wallace's anticipation of these developments makes the novel seem, as the clichéd blurb puts it, "as exciting as today's headlines."

The sixth laureate, a writer, discovers the Sexual Revolution in Stockholm. In 1962 Sweden was Americans' metonymy for sexual liberation and sophistication. In Sweden nudity is casual, pre-marital sex routine, and out-of-wedlock birth without stigma. The American novelist accepts Swedish sensuality as a positive alternative to native puritanism.

Even as Wallace teases his readers with scientific and sexual novelty, he reminds them of worrisome political realities. Two laureates have mysterious roots in the Holocaust, the unending nightmare of Nazi Germany's attempt to liquidate the Jews. One laureate is also the object of a Cold War intrigue: his ingenious research and present fame tempt East German agents to arrange his defection, by lure or by force.

Themes

Though capitalizing on four social concerns, Wallace pays most attention to the Sexual Revolution. The others are handled perfunctorily. The social impact of the technological discoveries are ignored. The East German agents threatening one prize winner are stereotypical "heavies" and easily thwarted. The Holocaust victims, mentally and psychologically scarred, readily earn the readers' sympathy but offer no insights into this historical tragedy.

The personal and social implications of the Sexual Revolution are thoroughly explored. The novel dramatizes the healthiness and the healing power of sensuality. Open sexuality heals the emotional and psychological wounds of various characters. Adultery restores *élan* to the dulled marriage of two French biologists; friendly fornication frees the novelist from guilt and alcoholism. Romantic wooing erases the scars of sexual abuse from a concentration camp survivor's psyche.

The sexual theme predominates because Wallace pays more attention to the private lives than to the professional activities of his characters. He attends so much to their jealousies, lusts, anxieties, and fantasies that readers may wonder how such luminaries ever found time for scientific research or artistic creation.

Characters

The Prize tells four stories involving seven protagonists. The dynamic in each story is a different human failing or fault. John Garrett, the medical researcher is bitterly jealous of his co-recipient Carlos Farelli. Denise Marceau, the biologist, avenges herself against her husband Claude for his infidelity. Andrew Craig, the novelist, is mired in guilt-ridden alcoholism over his wife's death. Having built rockets for the Nazis, Max Stratman the engineer assuages his conscience by experimenting with solar energy and raising his orphaned niece Emily.

All these protagonists are developed in one sense. Wallace gives each of them complete histories: parents, lovers, childhood, careers. There are also numerous minor characters who are briefly sketched, with just enough detail to fill the stereotype: the exposé-hungry journalist, the ruthless Communist agent, the sensuous Swedish actress.

Though Wallace tries to develop all seven protagonists equally, his heart is obviously with two: Denise Marceau and Andrew Craig. He takes the reader deeper inside the minds and hearts of these characters than into the others. Marceau is a clever, self-reliant, and likeable heroine, a plain woman who turns *femme fatale* to save her marriage. Craig the writer is the real hero to Wallace the author. He has the most adventures and undergoes the fullest transformation of any protagonist. Though in terrible physical, mental, and emotional condition as the novel opens, Craig quickly recovers to enjoy seduction by a Swedish nymph, to repudiate his sycophantic sister-in-law, to outwit Communist agents, and to win the love of Emily Stratman. As in other Wallace novels, the writer character is the real hero.

Techniques

The Prize is an excellent example of Wallace's formula for a best seller. The author alternately tells several stories, bringing one to a suspenseful point before turning to another. Wallace probably brings this technique to fiction from his experience as a playwright. As the novel progresses, the plot lines intersect and begin affecting each other. The conclusion brings all the characters together, like buses from different routes arriving at a central station.

Another technique that keeps reader interest is the steady flow of actual information about Stockholm and the Nobel Prizes. The novel is set in a real place that the author renders accurately and in detail. The author likewise puts his character through the actual rites of a Nobel Prize ceremony. Punctuating the fictional episodes are factual accounts of Alfred Nobel, previous prize winners, and political pressures affecting the judges.

Literary Precedents

The Prize is the kind of fiction called a "summer novel" or a "beach book." Its length, topicality, varied plots, and numerous moments of suspense fill a reader's leisure hours with diverting but not difficult material. It is a book easy to pick up, put down, and pick up again.

Such novels have an ancient lineage. Knightly romances of the seventeenth century ran to hundreds of thousands of words to divert aristocrats in their inactive hours. Eighteenth-century Gothic novels, lengthy tales of terror spun over several volumes, sent ladies and gentlemen to the lending library almost daily. In the nineteenth century "triple deckers" (i.e., three-volume novels) depicted getting married and keeping an inheritance as a complex and time-consuming chore for fictional characters and readers alike.

In short, Wallace writes the sort of fiction that has been the staple of popular audiences for almost three centuries.

Related Titles

Wallace has never written a sequel to one of his novels. Each fiction has a different urgent topic, a different far-away locale, and a different subject for "behind-the-scenes" information.

The Prize exemplifies a group of Wallace's novels that may be called "exotic melodramas." It was followed by *The Word* (1972), *The Pigeon Project* (1979), *The Almighty* (1982), and *The Seventh Secret* (1986). Each exotic melodrama places a cast of globe-trotting, beautiful people in a scenic locale (Zurich, Venice, Berlin) where all are swept up in intrigue. *The Word* recounts the intrigue surrounding a new, unorthodox translation of the Bible which challenges Christ's divinity. *The Pigeon Project* describes the East-West battle for a scientist's discovery that lengthens life to 150 years. *The Almighty* tells how the son of a media mogul battles to keep and expand his father's empire. *The Seventh Secret* has a researcher stumble upon evidence that Hitler did not die in a Berlin bunker.

These novels take the ordinary reader into unfamiliar worlds of public relations, publishing, and historiography; the subjects provide topical urgency, invite speculation about fascinating but improbable hypotheses, and offer a wealth of insider information. It is Wallace's formula for a "good read."

Adaptations

The Prize was made into a motion picture in 1963. Directed by Mark Robson, it starred Paul Newman, Edward G. Robinson, and Elke Sommer. The film was a commercial success, although most critics gave it only two-and-a-half stars: not bad, but nothing unusually good either.

The movie, departing from the novel in significant ways, increases the comedy and the adventure of the story. Andrew Craig is no longer alcoholic, guilt-ridden or suffering from writer's block; instead he is the adventuresome author of pseudonymous detective fiction who discovers and exposes the East German plot to kidnap Max Stratman. In the film the East Germans successfully plant a double for Stratman who makes propaganda speeches against the United States until Craig's derring-do exposes the situation.

THE FAN CLUB

The Fan Club, 1975, novel.

Social Concerns

In America in the 1960s, the assassinations of John F. Kennedy, Robert Kennedy, and Martin Luther King seemed to make murder an extension of politics by other means. Hostage-taking in the early 1970s became the terrorists' weapon for achieving publicity and escaping pursuit: at the Munich Olympics (1972), for instance, Israeli athletes were kidnapped. Anyone became a possible target for a radical with a cause or a criminal with a plan. In February 1974 newspaper heiress Patty Hearst was kidnapped by an undergound group calling itself the Symbionese Liberation Army, an act which made clear how vulnerable even a celebrity was to assassination or abduction. Her fate was still unknown two months later when *The Fan Club* was published. The novel describes how four men kidnap the reigning sex goddess of Hollywood. Once again Wallace chose as his central plot a situation as timely as the day's headlines.

Themes

Initial reviewers found *The Fan Club* preposterous as well as tasteless. They objected to a plot in which four sexually-frustrated males abduct a film star in the hope that she will act out their erotic fantasies. When she objects, they rape and brutalize her. Hoping to weaken or divide them, she decides to cooperate. Satiated with sex, the kidnappers then demand a ransom for Sharon's return. Their plans foiled by Sharon's cleverness, three of her captors are killed as the police move in.

As sensational as the plot is, Wallace explores several serious dimensions of sexuality. The four captors are presented as a cross-section of American males whose sexual psychology is the product of popular media. The novel shows a powerful male sexual drive overriding other emotions like love, greed, ambition, and pride. The novel also explores male assumptions about female sexuality, assumptions proved wrong or exploded by the self-reliant actress.

Characters

Sharon's abductors are an unattractive quartet, contrasting pairs of sexually immature males. Adam Malone (who has the idea to kidnap Sharon) fantasizes about movie stars but is unable to consummate a relationship with a real woman. His opposite is Kyle Shively (a Vietnam veteran guilty of murdering civilians) who receives sexual thrills by degrading women. Howard Yost (an insurance salesman bored with job and wife) craves the excitement of novelty. Leo Brunner (an accountant too timid to be bored with career or marriage) is Yost's opposite: suffering from reduced libido, he feigns the lust his companions expect.

The Fan Club offers no male character whose sex life is under control or in balance. A Wallace novel usually features a male protagonist who moves from sexual dysfunction to sexual fulfillment, but in this book only Adam temporarily approaches normalcy. Sharon's sensual skills enable Adam to consummate his passion, but after Sharon's escape, Adam returns to the world of fantasy and contemplates creating a new fan club in honor of another starlet.

At first Sharon is no more attractive a personality than her captors. All her life Sharon manipulated men by her beauty. Ironically she is kidnapped just when she has decided to stop using her physical beauty as a tool. Rich and famous enough to secure independence, Sharon contemplates for the first time a mature relationship with a man. She proves a resourceful captive, gifted intellectually as well as physically. Ingeniously she uses a code to guide police to the hideout; coldbloodedly she herself executes Shively, the most ruthless of her attackers.

Techniques

The first half of *The Fan Club* is like *The Prize*, interweaving four stories. The reader follows the formation of the club as sexual disappointments gradually lead the men into conspiracy. The next quarter of the novel concentrates in clinical detail on Sharon's repeated ravishment at the isolated cabin. The last quarter of the novel flashes between Hollywood where Sharon's rescuers search for clues and the cabin where the abductors' harmony quickly breaks down.

Wallace attempts one narrative variation: parts of the novel are told through "Adam Malone's Notebook." Written in the first person, the notebook takes the reader inside Adam's fantastic, disturbed mind. These passages are chilling juxtapositions of logical thoughts and bizarre fantasies. Unfortunately they are underused, brief and randomly placed.

The Fan Club, like all Wallace novels, benefits from the author's attention to setting and to detail. Carefully the novelist follows the abductors' plan to kidnap

Sharon off the street, and just as closely follows police efforts to track Sharon and her captors.

Related Titles

The Fan Club is the fifth Wallace novel with sex as its explicit subject matter. It presents a grimmer picture of the state of American sexual union than do the previous novels, but at the same time it is the logical completion of them.

The Sins of Philip Fleming (1959) tells of the protagonist's impotency with a woman he desires to make his mistress. *The Chapman Report* (1960) records the impact that the arrival of a sex research team has upon the lives of several suburbanites. *The Three Sirens* (1963) contrasts the promiscuity of South Sea Islanders with the puritanism of American anthropologists who study the tribe. *The Seven Minutes* (1969) depicts the obscenity trial of an erotic novel allegedly responsible for a rape. These novels depict modern Americans, male and female alike, caught in a sexual contradiction: naturally spurred by desire towards a variety of partners but weighted down with the guilt at the prospect of sex without love. The lucky characters in each book seize a moment of pure passion before settling into a monogamous relationship of sex-with-love.

The Fan Club is grimmer than the other sexual melodramas because no character wins both pure passion and eternal love. At the same time the novel logically concludes the earlier books by bringing together all the sexual frustrations and dysfunctions studied piecemeal in the previous novels. *The Fan Club* seems to rebut the other four novels by showing that really there is no resolution to the sexual contradiction between individual sexual desires and the social injunction to call them love.

Adaptations

Columbia Pictures bought the movie rights to *The Fan Club*. Despite several starts, no production has gotten very far. Someone seems to realize that Wallace's sensational story has the potential to outrage much of its potential audience.

THE SECOND LADY

The Second Lady, 1980, novel.

Social Concerns

The Second Lady tells of the successful plot by Soviet intelligence to substitute a look-alike agent for the wife of the President of the United States. The novel is remarkable for not only making a First Lady the protagonist but also depicting her sexual activity. Such a sensational story line became possible partly because Americans had grown used to a succession of colorful first ladies in the 1960s and 1970s. (Jacqueline Kennedy, Lady Bird Johnson, Patricia Nixon, Betty Ford, and Rosalynn Carter were younger, more fashionable, and more activist than their predecessors, dowager-like Eleanor Roosevelt, Bess Truman, and Mamie Eisenhower.) The story line was also possible because American readers have grown accustomed to gossip about the sex lives of celebrities.

The plot also shows that Americans have not tired of tales of the Cold War. Stories of Soviet deceit and duplicity in the hidden war to subvert America remain the stock in trade of the popular novelist.

Themes

An implicit assumption of *The Second Lady* is that politically powerful people experience the same passions as ordinary citizens. While this assertion is comforting in one sense, it is frightening in another: a president worried about his sexual dysfunction may not make wise decisions at a Summit Conference. *The Second Lady,* however, never convinces its readers of its political reality; any resemblance between the novel and the real world, readers realize with a sigh of relief, is purely coincidental.

The explicit theme of *The Second Lady* is a feminist one. A woman is better off looking after herself than relying on anyone. The two protagonists, the First Lady and the Second Lady, illustrate the need for self-reliance. The First Lady, held captive in Moscow, deduces that help will come neither from unsuspecting Americans or seemingly friendly Russians. The Second Lady deduces that she must save herself because of Soviet plans to execute her when the masquerade is done. Although one of the ladies fails in her effort to survive, both are resourceful fighters for their lives.

Characters

Billie Bradford is the First Lady abducted and replaced by the imposter. Young, attractive, passive, Billie makes a lovely First Lady who performs her political duties for the benefit of her husband's career. Like Sharon Fields in *The Fan Club,* she reluctantly uses sex in the effort to save herself.

Vera Vavilova is the Russian actress who impersonates Billie effectively. Though Wallace never makes clear why Vera willingly undergoes the plastic surgery and rigorous training needed to become Billie's double, she seems wonderfully human in several scenes where she must improvise or be exposed.

Billie and Vera are the two convincing characters in the novel. The rest are contrived or stock pieces. Alex Razin is a Russian KGB agent; half-American, half-Russian, his liking for Billie and his love for Vera allow him sometimes to facilitate the plot, sometimes to impede it. Gary Parker is the American counterpart to Razin. Parker, ghost writer of Billie's autobiography, is the first to suspect that the First Lady is not who she seems. The plot unfolds with the help of other cardboard figures: a good guy American president, as careful about his wife's orgasms as America's freedom; Ivan Petrov, the ruthless KGB officer who conceives the plot; a lot of attractive Americans who work for world peace; a lot of surly Russians who work against it.

Techniques
The Second Lady is noteworthy for one surprising ploy. Wallace uses Frank Stockton's famous "Lady-or-the-Tiger" device to conclude the novel. When a Russian agent ambushes Vera, Billie, and Alex, Razin and one of the women are killed. The survivor proclaims herself Billie Bradford, but is she really? Perhaps it is Vera who prefers illusion to a fatal homecoming. Perhaps it is Billie who wants to keep secret her experience in Moscow. No character in the novel can tell. The novelist could, but won't.

Related Titles
The Second Lady is Wallace's fourth political melodrama. *The Man* (1964) reflected the contemporary debate about the Civil Rights movement and the future of black Americans in the political process. The novel tells how a black man becomes President through accident, coincidence, and the chain of succession. *The Plot* (1967) takes up the theme of detente and political assassination; it records the efforts of a disgraced American diplomat to expose a plot by right-wing Soviet generals to murder a liberal Russian premier at a summit conference. *The R Document* (1976) refurbishes the Watergate scandal of the Nixon presidency with an Orwellian fear of Big Brother: a brave politician uncovers a plot by FBI agents to take over the government and subvert the Constitution.

These three political melodramas are lengthier than *The Second Lady,* more loosely plotted, and without a strong, interesting, or likeable protagonist. Thematically the novels do not form a pattern. Wallace does not seem to have arrived at any vision of the American political system. The only continuity in the four books is an admiration for occasional individuality, initiative, and self-reliance among public servants.

Other Titles
The Fabulous Originals, 1955 (biography); *The Square Pegs,* 1957 (biography); *The Fabulous Showman,* 1959 (biography); *The Twenty-Seventh Wife,* 1961 (biography); *The Sunday Gentleman,* 1965 (biography); *The Nympho and Other Maniacs,* 1971 (biography); *The People's Almanac,* with David Wallenchinsky, 1975; *The Book of Lists,* with Amy Wallace and David Wallenchinsky, 1977; *The Two,* with Amy Wallace, 1978 (biography); *The People's Almanac 2,* with Amy Wallace

and David Wallenchinsky, 1978; *The Book of Lists 2,* with David Wallenchinsky, 1980; *The Book of Predictions,* with David Wallenchinsky, 1980; *The People's Almanac 3,* with Amy Wallace and David Wallenchinsky, 1981; *The Intimate Sex Lives of Famous People,* with Amy Wallace, Sylvia Wallace, and David Wallenchinsky, 1981 (group biography); *Significa,* with Amy Wallace and David Wallenchinsky, 1983.

Additional Sources

Cawelti, John G., *Adventure, Mystery and Romance.* Chicago: University Chicago Press, 1976, pp. 284-295. Interprets Wallace's novels as formula fictions and "social melodramas."

Leverence, John, *Irving Wallace, A Writer's Profile.* Bowling Green, OH: The Popular Press, 1974. An informal study that offers much anecdotal information about Wallace and his books, several interviews with Wallace, and numerous photographs.

Mazurkiewicz, Margaret, "Irving Wallace," *Contemporary Authors: New Revision Series.* Detroit: Gale Research, 1981, I, pp. 687-689. Provides a thorough bibliography and a brief critical overview of the literary merit of Wallace's novels.

Wallace, Irving, *The Writing of One Novel.* New York: Simon and Schuster, 1968. Wallace offers insights into his methods and interests as he recounts the writing of *The Prize.*

Robert M. Otten
Indiana University-Purdue University
Fort Wayne

JOSEPH WAMBAUGH
1937

Publishing History

In 1967, Joseph Wambaugh, a former Marine, was a Los Angeles policeman who went to school at night, doing graduate work in English literature. He kept a record of his experiences and wrote two short stories in the little spare time he had. These stories were rejected without comment by every magazine he submitted them to with the exception of *The Atlantic*. *The Atlantic* did not accept them, but it did bring them to the attention of a former editor, Edward Weeks. Weeks found them interesting and suggested Wambaugh write a novel. He did, producing one thousand words a day after work. The novel was accepted for publication but Wambaugh was in trouble with his bosses at the police department for not getting permission to publish. In addition, he had lost the money paid him in advance in an unsuccessful business venture. At this low point in his life, the novel, *The New Centurions*, was chosen as a Book of the Month Club selection and went on to be a great success, appearing on the best seller list for nearly seven months in 1971.

Critical Reception, Honors, and Popularity

Critics praised Wambaugh's crack story telling, and his tough, realistic dialogue. They note that not only do his novels contain a great deal of exciting action, but also that his graphic, visceral writing illuminates the souls of his characters. The novels also contain scenes of hilarious but sometimes brutal humor which some critics appreciate and some do not. All his books have been best sellers. The early books, *The New Centurions*, *The Blue Knight*, *The Choir Boys* and *The Onion Field* have won the most critical praise. Although Wambaugh has not won any literary awards, his novels have sold well over 15 million copies world-wide and have been translated into nearly all the major languages.

Analysis of Selected Titles

THE NEW CENTURIONS

The New Centurions, 1971, novel.

Social Concerns

When Wambaugh was in graduate school during the late 1960s, he could not discuss his police work with his fellow students because they considered policemen "pigs." This book is an attempt to explain the difficulty of police work and to demonstrate the day to day heroism of the police officer to the ordinary citizen.

The New Centurions follows three men, whose backgrounds vary, as they learn how to be police officers. The novel begins as they train at the police academy and experience the insecurities and fears of their first five years of service. During this time, they marry, divorce, become fathers. They mature, discovering strengths they did not know they had and they take on the values of policemen. These young men must cope with horrific social conditions, not only in ghetto neighborhoods, with their muggers, prostitutes, pimps and juvenile gangs but in "good" neighborhoods too, where neurotics, drug addicts, sexual perverts and child abusers create chaos. Wambaugh sees a society sliding into a pathologically selfish hedonism where the police must compromise their own honor and endanger their own lives to trap criminals whom the courts will not punish, or others, homosexuals, for example, whom the courts should not punish. At that point in time the police also had to cope with the Black Power movement and the hostility of the Black Moslems. Worse than this, according to Wambaugh, is the white, liberal guilt and condescension which refuses to consider Blacks as responsible for their own actions and therefore denies them manhood. This must result in social breakdown and Wambaugh ends his novel with the Watts riots, demonstrating how fragile the social order really is and how crucial it is to maintain law and order.

Themes

Wambaugh's major theme has to do with the difficulties involved in being a police officer in what he has called "The Big Sewer," the modern city. Society recognizes the physical dangers policemen face, but does not recognize the emotional dangers which are far greater. The urban police officer is under constant emotional strain, knowing he can be killed at any moment, yet, paradoxically, he is often bored as he patrols the same streets, arresting the same criminals, seeing the courts release them almost immediately. His marriage often ends in divorce; he often succumbs to alcoholism, even suicide. Surrounded as he is by inhumanity, it is a terrible struggle for him to maintain his own humanity. He is sworn to protect the community but the community makes it almost impossible for him to do so because of ludicrous rules for obtaining evidence, incompetent supervision and general hostility. The worst of it is, no one except another police officer has any notion of how difficult his job is, or cares. The police officer holds society together at great personal cost, according to Wambaugh, but no one respects him for this.

Characters

In *The New Centurions,* Wambaugh takes his heroes from different walks of life. Serge is a Chicano who wants to forget his ancestry but cannot. Gus is a small gentle man who hates himself because he thinks he is a coward. Roy considers himself an intellectual, but finds that the people he despises, other policemen, members of minority groups, even his wife, are at least as smart as he is.

Also memorable are the older cops, his heroes' mentors, especially Kilvinsky, a genuine philosopher who understands the world but because of the demands of his job cannot cope with other emotional demands. He loses his wife, after losing his child, and ends up alone. All the young policemen learn and grow. Serge outgrows sexual promiscuity, finds a wife and learns to accept his heritage. Gus learns to accept himself. Roy unexpectedly finds his true love. Each of them typifies the fate of the policeman, yet each is an individual.

The female characters tend to be less highly developed. Mariana, with whom Serge falls in love, is exactly what he needs. Vicki, who is married to Gus, is fat and helpless, one more heavy burden for him to carry and resent. Roy's wife sees through him and leaves him, but he falls in love with Laura Hunt, who is black— even though he has begun to hate blacks. If these men find solace at home, they may survive the trauma of their profession.

Wambaugh also peoples this novel with rebellious college students, juvenile gang members, winos and prostitutes who are seen as symptoms of society's disintegration.

Techniques

This is a procedural novel; that is, a novel in which police work as it is actually carried out provides the basis for the action. The novel's plot moves quickly and excitingly. The policemen train together, do their job in various Los Angeles neighborhoods and are reunited during the Watts riots. Crimes are committed; the police officers face danger. But when they are off-duty, these young men fall in love. Life is unpredictable and shocking, often brutal, yet the novels seems plausible and authentic, securely based on Wambaugh's own police work. The dialogue is funny and again seems totally genuine. Wambaugh has an ear for police lingo and also for the speech of the ghetto. Both are sometimes scatological, but tremendously expressive and often hilarious. Wambaugh's descriptions are graphic, too graphic for some readers. He shows the reader the bruised babies and the cop's guts on the sidewalk; the reader smells the public toilets and the winos.

Literary Precedents

The techniques Wambaugh uses can be traced to Daniel Defoe (1660-1731) who wrote with great realism about crime and the city. Jonathan Swift (1667-1745) too, was a master of graphic, even scatological description. Charles Dickens' (1812-1870) novels often concerned crimes committed in an urban setting and described grotesque characters living in hideous slums. Wambaugh's novels are also similar to the writings of Theodore Dreiser (1871-1945) who wrote about crime and the seamier side of the American city with great realism in *An American Tragedy*, and James T. Farrell, (1904-1979) a contemporary writer, who dissected the slums on the South Side of Chicago in his 1930's Studs Lonigan trilogy. Wambaugh is in the tradition of those novelists who write realistically about the sordid side of city life and those who must cope with it.

Related Titles

Although Wambaugh's major theme, the difficult necessity of policework and the toll it takes on police officers, remains the same from work to work, his novels have evolved. In *The Blue Knight* (1972), the reader accompanies Bumper Morgan on his rounds during what are supposed to be his last three days of duty before retirement. He is an excellent police officer, but the system, and the city, seem intent on breaking him. Like all heroes, he is rough with evildoers and kind to the weak. Unlike the stereotypical hero, he is lonely even though a wonderful woman loves him; he suffers from nightmares and dyspepsia, feels displaced and can only find solace in drink.

The Choirboys (1975) focuses on the work of an assorted group of officers reminiscent of those in *The New Centurions*. Although this novel stresses the absurd side of police work, the efforts of those officers, some young, some nearing retirement, to overcome the excruciating emotional pain of their profession leads to tragedy.

Adaptations

Joseph Wambaugh's work has been adapted for television and for film. *The Blue Knight,* starring William Holden, appeared on NBC in 1973 as a four part miniseries. It received good reviews and Wambaugh himself was pleased with it. During 1975, it ran as a weekly show on CBS.

The Choirboys was made into a film by Universal Studios in 1977. Wambaugh was furious with the director, Robert Alrich, and the producers, Lorimar Productions, for changing the tragic ending to a happier one. He won his suit against them for one million dollars as well as the right to have his name removed from the screenplay.

THE BLACK MARBLE
The Black Marble, 1978, novel.

Social Concerns/Themes

Wambaugh is still primarily concerned with the emotional cost of being a policeman, but he widens his focus in this novel to include the loneliness of a socially well-connected but discarded wife and the world of championship show dogs.

Characters

The policeman, Andrei Mikhailovich Valnikov, is a product of his Russian heritage although he was born and bred in Los Angeles. He drinks Russian vodka, listens to Russian music, and dreams of Russian scenery. He is also an absent-minded alcoholic whose former partner, Charlie Lightfoot, committed suicide and whose present partner, Natalie Zimmerman, thinks he is insane. He is, however, a very capable detective who sympathizes with the lonely losers of this world because he recognizes a bond with them.

Madeline Dills Whitfield is one of those unfortunates. She was born rich but her divorce and her mother's illness have used up her trust fund. She is now middle aged, and alone. Her only friend is her Schnauzer, Vicki. When Vicki is stolen and held for a ransom she does not have the money to pay, her only hope is Valnikov.

He does help her, but he falls in love with Natalie, the one sane, organized and well-adjusted character in the novel. To her great surprise, she reciprocates, saving Valnikov's sanity and possibly his life.

Philo Skinner, the villain, is yet another loser. He has been beaten by bullies as a child, beaten up by rednecks in the army. His one moment of triumph occurs when he vanquishes Valnikov in a fight, and almost gets away from him, except that he slips on a pile of dog feces and is nearly torn to pieces by an attack animal.

Techniques

This novel is structured differently from Wambaugh's earlier works. Here he focuses on one detective's case, making this more a mystery novel than a procedural novel. The cast of characters is more varied too, as the reader is introduced to the country club set, and the dog show world as well as to policemen, their families and their friends. The comedy in this novel is broader and more physical than in the earlier novels; it is often close to slapstick.

Literary Precedents

The Black Marble is in the tradition of the mystery novel, where by a combination of skill, luck and guile, the hero-detective solves the case. This genre originated in England with Wilkie Collins' *The Woman in White* (1860) and *The Moonstone* (1868). It was continued in Sir Arthur Conan Doyle's novels and short stories about the adventures of Sherlock Holmes. Wambaugh's emphasis on the ugliness of the urban scene is also close to that of Louis-Ferdinand Celine, the French author of *Journey to the End of Night* (1932) and *Death on the Installment Plan* (1936).

Related Titles

Wambaugh's recent novels, such as *The Glitter Dome* (1981), *The Delta Star* (1983), and *The Secrets of Harry Bright* (1985) are also set in Wambaugh's new, wider world. The reader is shown that the upper classes: Hollywood producers in *The Glitter Dome,* scientists in *The Delta Star,* and Palm Springs millionaires in *The Secrets of Harry Bright* are as corrupt, crime-ridden, lonely and vulnerable as anyone else. Wambaugh's pictures of these worlds as they impinge on the consciousness of the lower middle class policeman is very effective.

His heroes are getting older in these books. They are excellent detectives but their jobs have taken their toll, turning them into emotional invalids. Sidney Blackpool in *The Secrets of Harry Bright* and Mario Villalobos, in *The Delta Star,* like Andrei Mikhailovich Valnikov in *The Black Marble,* are alcoholics, but excellent detectives nonetheless. Even when they are redeemed by love and work and manage to salvage their lives, their innate goodness is highly vulnerable to the assaults of a vicious world. Wambaugh's most recent hero, Sidney Blackpool in *The Secrets of Harry Bright,* is a bereaved father who is asked by another bereaved father to solve the murder of the latter's son. The psychological cost to the detective is nearly unbearable.

From *The Choirboys* on, Wambaugh's female characters become more differentiated and memorable. His policewomen are at least as capable as their male partners and far less emotionally vulnerable. His crime victims are often lonely women who bravely manage to survive.

Wambaugh has also written factual crime books. *The Onion Field* (1978) is a thorough dissection of an actual crime, the murder of a police officer. Wambaugh recreates the experiences of the victims, analyzes the background and motivation of the perpetrators, and lays out all the circumstances of the investigation and the trial, which was the longest criminal proceding in California history. He demonstrates that the police, particularly the murdered officer's partner, suffered far more than the murderers. In the tradition of Truman Capote's *In Cold Blood,* this book is as exciting as a novel, but much more dismaying as a picture of society.

In another non-fiction work, *Lines and Shadows,* (1984) Wambaugh tells the true story of a police unit formed to fight crime directed against illegal aliens in San Diego. It is a much less ambitious book than *The Onion Field,* but like all his work to date, also describes the pressures of police work on the police officers involved.

Adaptations

The Onion Field, starring John Savage and James Woods, was released by Avco-Embassy Pictures in 1979 and received excellent reviews as did *The Black Marble* which was released by Avco-Embassy in 1980. It starred Robert Foxworth and Paula Prentiss.

In 1985, *The Glitter Dome* was made into a film for cable television, directed by Stuart Margolin and starring James Garner, John Lighgow, Margot Kidder and

Colleen Dewhurst. That film adhered to the plot lines of the novel, and succeeded in clarifying a few of the more complicated plot twists. Wambaugh's characterizations lose some of their individuality in the film, however, and too much of his humor is lost.

Additional Sources

Reviews of *The Delta Star* (1982) were mixed. George Stade in the *New York Times Book Review* (20 March 1983): 12 noted its "formal elegance" and found it "great fun to read" while David Kusnet in the *New Republic* (4 April 1983): 36 found it "disappointing."

The Glitter Dome (1981) was reviewed enthusiastically and lengthily in the *New York Times Book Review* by Evan Hunter (28 June 1981): 3. The *New Yorker* (31 August 1981): 108 was less enthusiastic; the reviewer did not appreciate Wambaugh's humor.

Lines and Shadows (1984) was reviewed fairly favorably by Gerry Clark in *Best Sellers* (April, 1984): 32. Elmore Leonard wrote a more enthusiastic review for the *New York Times Book Review* (5 February 1984): 12.

The Secrets of Harry Bright (1985), Joseph Wambaugh's most recent novel, has been reviewed in the *Wall Street Journal* (22 November 1985): 28 and in *Time* (28 October 1985) as well as in the *New York Times Book Review* (6 October 1985): 11.

"Wambaugh, Joseph (Aloysius)," *Current Biography* (1980), pp. 418-21, supplies the facts about Wambaugh's life and summarizes the critical reaction to his work until 1980.

Barbara Horwitz
Long Island University
C.W. Post Center

MORRIS WEST
1916

Publishing History

Morris West was born in Melbourne, Australia, in 1916. Educated by the Christian Brothers, he spent twelve years with the Order before leaving without taking vows. No doubt his lifelong interest in theological and philosophical issues stems from that experience. After service with Army Intelligence in World War II, West began a career in literature as a member of a translation firm. His first published book, *Children of the Sun* (1957), is a study of the children of the Italian slums. In 1958, West took a job as a correspondent for the English paper, the *Daily Mail;* in the next year, he published the first of several novels that would bring him both popular and critical acclaim: *The Devil's Advocate.* Since then, he has written consistently about topical issues of international concern and perennial issues of morality and philosophy, weaving these larger concerns into novels that move swiftly and contain significant action to hold the interest of the reader of popular fiction. *The Devil's Advocate* and *The Shoes of the Fisherman* sold over two million copies.

Critical Reception, Honors, and Popularity

West ranks with the more popular novelists of this century in terms of copies sold and adaptations. His success with more highbrow literary critics has been mixed. Some of his earlier works, especially novels such as *The Devil's Advocate* and *The Shoes of the Fisherman* (1963) were both popular and critical successes. Novels published during the 1970s, however, were generally considered shallow in substance—attempts to capitalize on current world events, with heavy-handed doses of philosophy and theology tossed in to give the book an aura of respectability that would set it apart from the mere pot-boiler.

Several of West's novels have been adapted for the stage, and *The Shoes of the Fisherman* was adapted for the screen as well, with Anthony Quinn playing the lead. West's books have been translated into 27 languages, and almost every new novel has appeared on best seller lists in America and abroad. The University of California at Santa Clara and Mercy College in New York have awarded West honorary doctorates. He has been elected a Fellow of the Royal Society of Literature and the World Academy of Arts and Sciences, and has received the Dag Hammarskjöld Award (Grand Collier au Mérite) for his achievements.

Analysis of Selected Titles

THE NAVIGATOR

The Navigator, 1976, novel.

Social Concerns

As he does in many of his novels, West uses the adventures of his characters in *The Navigator* to explore the ramifications of important social issues. In this novel, the questions surrounding discoveries in anthropology and archaeology, especially those dealing with comparative societies, form the basis for that investigation. Through techniques of plotting, West creates a cosmopolitan cast of characters, then has them marooned on a deserted island where they are free to try their hands at a variety of social arrangements, testing out the validity of traditional and innovative practices of living together as a group. In this way, West exposes both the weaknesses and the strengths of primitive and contemporary social orders, suggesting that much of the old is still valid, requiring only minor modification to be useful in today's terror-filled world. Through his examination of changing and changeable social orders, West reveals the unchanging nature of man.

Themes

Underlying the fast-paced plot of this novel is West's continuing concern with the nature of the good society. The roles of leader and follower, governor and governed, are examined in detail through conversation and episode. Additionally, West spends considerable time exploring the tensions in human relationships brought on by radical changes in environment: the issue of "nature" vs. "nurture" in developing human character comes under West's literary microscope for careful scrutiny. Men and women who, by accident of birth or through hard work and manipulation in Western society have risen to the top of the social ladder, suddenly find themselves displaced by those whose inner strength permits them to cope better with the primitive conditions of the far-away Pacific island. Stripped of society's long-standing conventions, these men and women discover the real strengths of human character as they work to establish a new order for themselves.

Characters

West's cast of characters is international in scope. The dozen men and women who comprise the ship's crew hail from all points of the globe. The hero, Gunnar Thorkild, is a mixture of Scandanavian explorer and Polynesian native, an East-West melting pot who symbolizes in himself the amalgamation of philosophies, and the tensions of different world-views that West places in conflict on the far-away island where most of the action takes place. Because West wishes to emphasize the variety of nationalities which make up the party of castaways on the Island of the Navigators, many of the characters are little more than stereotypes; the "villains" are especially shallow. Nevertheless, West does manage a highly successful presentation of Thorkild, whose constant struggle to maintain social order on the island, establish a harmonious political climate, and satisfy the needs of this disparate band provides the central interest of the book.

Techniques

The Navigator is, at first reading, an adventure novel. From the opening pages, characters encounter a series of crises and disasters: careers challenged, finances strained, love relationships forged and torn apart, shipwrecks, hurricanes, births and deaths. Simultaneously, West explores important contemporary social and moral issues through the extensive dialogue in which his characters engage. This group of castaways talks out almost every problem, from ways to erect shelters to the difference in philosophies between American financial magnates and Polynesian islanders. Because the cast of characters is international, West is able to use conversation, argument, and group debate to highlight the strengths and shortcomings of Western civilization.

Literary Precedents

The Navigator has much in common with other West novels: its international cast of characters, its focus on the impact of one man on society as a whole, its heavy dose of philosophy and theology running beneath the surface of the adventure story. However, the novel also has literary forebears in the pantheon of travel literature, both fictional and nonfictional. Like *Robinson Crusoe,* it examines the ways in which man can bring order to the wilds. Like Captain Cooks' *Voyages* and Thor Heyerdahl's true-life narratives of his adventures in the Pacific, it presents vivid accounts of life in that region. More significant, however, is the novel's ties to the tradition of Utopian literature, works which examine the problems of founding and maintaining the perfect society.

THE SHOES OF THE FISHERMAN
The Shoes of the Fisherman, 1963, novel.

Social Concerns/Themes

On one level, this novel provides an inside look at the hierarchy of one of the world's most extensive and powerful social bodies, the Roman Catholic Church. The extent to which seemingly religious decisions are made for political reasons provides an eye-opening view of modern organized religion and its relationship to society as a whole.

The Shoes of the Fisherman is also the story of the effect one good man can have on the world around him. The concerted efforts of one willing to abandon the status quo can, in West's view, make a difference both within organizations and in the lives of individuals touched by this dedicated individual.

Finally, the novel also presents a vision of the world of the 1960s from an unusual perspective. The problems of the world superpowers appear in a different light when viewed from within the walls of the Vatican; the apparent hopelessness of deteriorating world conditions is contrasted with the spirit of optimism that the pope displays, and his willingness to take personal risks offers a slim hope for improvement in international relationships. West suggests that the pope in his novel may serve as a model for leaders of other groups to follow in confronting the problems of living in the nuclear age.

Characters

The Shoes of the Fisherman is dominated by the central figure, Kiril Lakota, the first Russian pope. A man of genuine goodness who has suffered much in the real world before assuming his position as head of the church, his struggle to make genuine Christian principles work in the world about him provides the main interest for this tale. Kiril's efforts, Christ-like in both intent and simplicity, somehow touch all of the other characters whose stories are told in the pages of this novel. West is careful to weave the lives of all these characters into an encompassing pattern that extends even beyond their direct contact with Kiril. Through these interlocking separate stories West creates a microcosm of the world itself, a place of constant contacts that shape both individual and social destinies.

PROTEUS

Proteus, 1979, novel.

Social Concerns/Themes

West's subject in this novel is the effect of government-sponsored terrorism and repression. The central questions that the hero of this fast-paced tale must continually ask himself are: How far will men in power go to protect the sovereignty of their country and their own interests? When is one justified in retaliating, and how far can such retaliation be carried, against governments which resort to violence to silence dissent? A succession of orchestrated atrocities committed against the family of business magnate John Spada lead him to adopt his own extreme means for dealing with this crisis. West introduces the central issues by creating a hero already involved as head of Proteus, an international organization committed to helping those who are victims of inhumane treatment at the hands of supposedly responsible governments. The novel displays the futility of dealing with repressive governments; while small victories are possible, it is apparently no more than a utopian dream to believe that repression practiced by those empowered to run countries can be totally eradicated. The portrait of a world hopelessly in the grips of such men is chilling, and West suggests no hope for improvement.

Characters

The tragedy of the Proteus organization, one consisting of good men from all around the world committed to helping those who cannot help themselves, is crystallized in the personal tragedy of the hero of this novel, John Spada. Presented initially as a larger-than-life figure similar to those in other popular novels who can overcome any impossible obstacle, John Spada gradually crumbles under the weight of the task he is forced to undertake. West's use of a figure who is far above the norm in political and financial circles heightens the tragedy by magnifying the helplessness of individuals to deal with organized efforts at repression. Other characters in the novel promote moderation—which is actually the same thing as capitulation. Spada refuses to give in without a fight, and not until the end of the novel, when he has orchestrated a plan to blackmail the world into releasing political prisoners, does he finally realize the impossibility of his task. When the nations of the world refuse even then to give in, he is faced with initiating mass destruction or admitting defeat. At that point he affirms what nations cannot: the importance of the individual human life. Rather than launch biological warfare, he commits suicide. Ironically, by taking his own life, Spada asserts the value he places on life itself.

Related Titles

The Salamander (1973) and *Harlequin* (1974) are predecessors of *Proteus* in West's continuing exploration of international political and social issues. Like *Proteus*, these novels deal with global issues. *The Salamander* deals with political crisis in a country teetering on the brink of chaos, being tugged to Left and Right by extremists who seek to gain from the fall of the present regime. *Harlequin* examines the new phenomenon of computer-directed criminal activity, and explores the perennial theme of justifiable violence. These novels, too, are populated with characters whose lives are far from ordinary, and whose actions can change the course of history for millions. Beneath the finely developed plots, both novels deal with questions of values in societies that seem to be moving progressively farther from humanistic and Christian principles of individual and social action.

Other Titles

Moon in My Pocket, 1945 (novel) [*pseud.* Julian Morris]; *Kundu,* 1957 (novel); *The Crooked Road,* 1957 (novel), published in Britain as *The Big Story; Children of the Shadows,* 1957 (nonfiction), in Britain *Children of the Sun; Backlash,* 1958 (novel), in Britain *The Second Victory; Gallows in the Sand,* 1958 (novel); *McCreary Moves In,* 1958 (novel) [*pseud.* Michael East], republished as *The Concubine,* 1966; *The Devil's Advocate,* 1959 (novel); *The Naked Country,* 1960 (novel) [*pseud.* Michael East]; *Daughters of Silence,* 1960 (novel); *Daughters of Silence,* 1961 (play); *The Ambassador,* 1965 (novel); *The Tower of Babel,* 1968 (novel); *The*

Heretic, 1970 (play); *Scandal in the Assembly: The Matrimonial Laws and Tribunes of the Roman Catholic Church*, 1970 (nonfiction); *The Summer of the Red Wolf*, 1971 (novel); *The Salamander*, 1973 (novel); *Harlequin*, 1974 (novel); *The Clowns of God*, 1981 (novel); *The World is Made of Glass*, 1983 (novel); *Cassidy*, 1986 (novel).

Additional Sources

Contemporary Literary Criticism, Vol. 6. Detroit: Gale Research, 1976, pp. 563-565. Provides excerpts of reviews of several novels: *Summer of the Red Wolf*, *The Salamander*, *Harlequin*. Brief assessments of West's techniques and talent.

Contemporary Literary Criticism, Vol. 33. Detroit: Gale Research, 1985, pp. 427-435. Brief sketch of West's publishing career, and critical commentaries excerpted from reviews of *The Devil's Advocate*, *Daughters of Silence*, *The Navigator*, *Proteus*, *The Clowns of God*, and *The World is Made of Glass*.

Contemporary Novelists. ed. James Vinson. New York: St. Martin's Press, pp. 684-685. Biography, bibliography, brief assessment of West's literary career.

Laurence W. Mazzeno
U. S. Naval Academy

DONALD WESTLAKE
1933

Publishing History

Donald Westlake began writing short stories when he was eleven years old, and by his early twenties his work was appearing in a number of mystery and science-fiction publications. His first novel, *The Mercenaries,* was published in 1961, and was followed by four other books exemplifying the hard-boiled brand of mystery fiction. He continued to develop this aspect of his literary persona in the series of paperback originals written under the pseudonym "Richard Stark," which began with *The Hunter* (also known as *Point Blank!*) in 1962 and had reached twenty titles by the time the last of them appeared in 1974. In 1965 Westlake's *The Fugitive Pigeon* inaugurated a radical change in mood with a humorous tale of a callow hero and some incompetent villains, and since that time most of the books published under his own name have mined a similarly comic vein. *Kahawa* (1982) and *High Adventure* (1985), large-scale thrillers in the Ludlum-Follet manner, may signal another major shift, although Westlake has at the same time continued to write such typically humorous novels as *A Likely Story* (1984) and *Good Behavior* (1986).

In addition to the tough-as-nails thrillers written as "Richard Stark," Westlake has used several other pseudonyms in touching upon a variety of fictional bases. As "Tucker Coe" he has penned an unusual series of novels about a guilt-ridden ex-cop; as "Curt Clark" he has published one science-fiction novel and a number of short stories; and as "Timothy Culver" he has written a spies-versus-spies opus. Although his work seldom appears on best seller lists, its ready marketability and thorough professionalism ensure that whatever he writes will find an eager publisher.

Critical Reception, Honors, and Popularity

Westlake's penchant for a comic approach to crime fiction and the fact that much of his work has been published pseudonymously have both worked against his being taken seriously by the more influential critics. His work is often lauded for its entertainment value, but is seldom treated as a noteworthy or important contribution to the genre. His pseudonymous writing as "Richard Stark" and "Tucker Coe" has gained an underground following among fans of the hard-boiled idiom, and it may well be these books which posterity considers his most significant achievement.

Westlake's 1967 Edgar for *God Save the Mark,* awarded by the Mystery Writers of America, symbolizes the high esteem in which he is held by his colleagues. His books are often dedicated to other authors in the field, an expression of professional respect which is often reciprocated, and his name can be expected to turn up in any discussion of underrated writers. Despite this, he has not as yet achieved the degree of commercial success accorded many of his peers, although his work sells steadily and has often been used as the basis for motion-picture productions. It is probably most accurate to view Donald Westlake as the consummate professional, extremely good at what he does but lacking that air of singular intensity which distinguishes the exciting writer from the merely entertaining one.

Analysis of Selected Titles

GOD SAVE THE MARK

God Save the Mark, 1967, novel.

Social Concerns/Themes

It is all too easy to treat *God Save the Mark*'s story of a tainted inheritance and its pursuit by a variety of greedy schemers as pure entertainment with no evident social concerns. The protagonist, Fred Fitch, is an introverted bachelor whose inability to avoid confident tricksters is used as both a running gag and the explanation for his failures in human relationships. It is precisely Fitch's difficulties in distinguishing between deceivers and truth-tellers, however, that determines his—and since the book is narrated in the first person, also the reader's—perception of society: it is seen as an essentially unregulated confusion of conflicting claims, where appearances are seldom an accurate reflection of reality and the most surprising event is for someone to turn out to be exactly what they say they are.

Although Westlake's comic novels continually mitigate this somewhat dystopian vision with amusing incidents and a generally light touch, there is no doubt that he is offering a serious analysis of contemporary American society. In the series of books published as "Richard Stark," this is presented in a brutally direct and even shocking manner; in the titles Westlake writes under his own name, humor and whimsy soften his nonetheless bleak view of people's capacity for living together. In *God Save the Mark,* Fred Fitch can never be sure of the authenticity of those attempting to influence his behavior. The police, when they are not laughably incompetent, may well be in cahoots with the bad guys; respected social institutions turn out to be fronts for organized crime; and Fitch's relatives, when they deign to notice his existence at all, have only a mercenary interest in his well-being.

Westlake does, however, offer a partial remedy for this general absence of social cohesion. The process of making friendships, of understanding, accepting and coming to love the peculiarities of a particular individual, does hold out the hope of establishing a meaningful relationship. In *God Save the Mark* this occurs when Fitch comes to know and trust the girlfriend of the policeman assigned to his case, which leads him to put his life in her hands with gratifying results. Although superficial social relationships may not permit one to have faith in others, a commitment to mutual communication can result in the kind of interpersonal bonds that help to hold off the anarchy which is never far below the surface of Westlake's work.

Characters

Fred Fitch, the protagonist of *God Save the Mark,* is typical of the anti-heroes who narrate Westlake's humorous fiction. Reclusive by nature, he has found an occupation—in his case, that of freelance researcher—which requires the minimum of contact with others. As a consequence, his reactions to characters such as his late uncle's mistress, a stripper whose brassy exterior masks a heart with at least traces of gold, are much stronger and sharper than they would be if he were an experienced man of the world. The reader feels that Fitch is discovering new people rather than simply being introduced to them for the first time, and this adds a great deal of zest to his story.

In comparison to the exotic characters Westlake delights in inventing for his narrator's enlightenment, Fitch's persona is a *tabula rasa* when the plot gets underway. But as the pace of events quickens, Fitch is forced to define himself against the various extreme forms of behavior he encounters, and by the end of the book he has a good idea of the sort of person he wants to be. Readers see his character in the process of formation, and this both adds to their empathy with him and gives the book an element of moral choice one does not expect to find in a humorous thriller. Although Westlake does not write "novels of character" in the sense in which the psychological realist understands the phrase, he does deal with many of the same issues by constructing his characters from the ground up rather than introducing them at a given point in their development, and the results are often extremely affecting.

Techniques

God Save the Mark is an excellent example of Westlake's adroitness with the first-person narrative. By restricting the reader's knowledge to that of the protagonist's, he builds suspense, increases the sense of identification with Fitch and keeps his authorial eye focussed upon the significant events of the plot. The one major disadvantage of this approach is that Fitch has to actually encounter everyone and everything of importance in the book, and in less practiced hands this might seem unbearably manipulative; but as Westlake handles it, Fitch's increasingly frenetic activity is believably motivated by unfolding plot developments and never seems forced or based upon gratuitous coincidence. Westlake's skill at plotting is often commented upon by reviewers, and in *God Save the Mark* it can be observed at the service of a first-person mystery narrative fully worthy of the technique's Hammett-Chandler origins.

Literary Precedents

The idea of a humorous thriller is to some extent a contradiction in terms, and there are few successful examples of the integration of comedy with suspense. Books such as Dashiell Hammett's *The Thin Man* (1934) and Richard Powell's *Lay That Pistol Down* (1945) utilized highly stylized upper-class settings as a means of distancing the impact of violence upon their somewhat fey heroes, but this cannot be done for the sort of average-guy protagonist Westlake presents in novels such as *God Save the Mark*. Fred Fitch probably has more in common with characters such as Cervantes' *Don Quixote* and Hasek's *The Good Soldier Svejk*, who also bring invincible ignorance to their struggles with a world shot through with corruption and deceit. Basically, however, Westlake's humorous thrillers are not part of any well-established literary genre, this being attested to by both the surprised enthusiasm with which they were greeted and the fact that they have spawned no evident imitations.

THE HUNTER (a.k.a. POINT BLANK!)

The Hunter, 1961 novel (reissued as *Point Blank!*, 1967). Sequels: *The Man With the Getaway Face*, 1963 (novel, reissued as *The Steel Hit*, 1971); *The Outfit*, 1963 (novel); *The Mourner*, 1963 (novel); *The Score*, 1964 (novel, reissued as *Killtown*, 1971); *The Jugger*, 1965 (novel); *The Seventh*, 1966 (novel, reissued as *The Split*, 1969); *The Handle*, 1966 (novel, reissued as *Run Lethal*, 1972); *The Rare Coin Score*, 1967 (novel); *The Damsel*, 1967 (novel); *The Green Eagle Score*, 1967 (novel); *The Black Ice Score*, 1968 (novel); *The Dame*, 1969 (novel); *The Sour Lemon Score*, 1969 (novel); *The Blackbird*, 1969 (novel); *Deadly Edge*, 1971 (novel); *Slayground*, 1971 (novel); *Lemons Never Lie*, 1971 (novel); *Plunder Squad*, 1972 (novel); *Butcher's Moon*, 1974 (novel).

Social Concerns/Themes

This novel and several others about the exploits of an armed-robbery specialist were reissued under the series title "The Violent World of Parker," which sets exactly the right tone for a discussion of their distinctive attributes. Parker's world isn't merely *characterized* by violence, it is *founded* upon violence: to an extent seldom found in even the hardest-boiled thrillers, it is the willingness as well as the ability to kill that separates the quick from the dead in these volumes.

In *The Hunter*, violence is used to force Parker's loving wife to attempt to murder her husband, which establishes the relative priorities of force and sentiment for the remainder of the series. Subsequent books often place Parker in situations where love or trust is a tempting possibility, but his memory of his wife's treachery is always invoked as a warning against emotional involvement. There is usually a double-cross or a sell-out in the offing where Parker is concerned, and it is only his profound awareness of human fallibility that ensures his continued survival.

As was noted in the previous discussion of *God Save the Mark,* Westlake has little faith in either the integrity or the competence of established social institutions. In the comic entertainments written under his own name, this is played for laughs; in the Parker novels written as "Richard Stark," it is presented with a brutal directness that both shocks and fascinates the reader. If Parker wants something, he takes it; if he wants to change an organization's policy, as is the case in *The Hunter,* he kills so many of their personnel that it becomes imperative for them to meet his demands. It is almost as if Westlake were indulging the manic and depressive poles of a split personality, with Donald Westlake writing as the bemused cynic and "Richard Stark" writing as the paranoid pessimist. Whether or not this is a conscious division of labor on Westlake's part, one can't help but speculate that these two very different aspects of his literary work reflect his ambivalence regarding the prospects of a society in which selfish motives predominate over altruistic ones.

Characters
Parker is the epitome of the hero as pure will, whose Nietzsche-an drive to exert power cannot be stopped by merely human forces. His mastery of the violent arts is, however, complemented by a thorough knowledge of how the world really works, and it is this that differentiates him from most of the heroes of hard-boiled fiction. A character such as Mickey Spillane's Mike Hammer simply wades into a situation and keeps punching and shooting until the bad guys are vanquished; and even Raymond Chandler's much more intellectually-inclined Philip Marlowe sees himself as a gadfly who stirs up trouble without necessarily being able to control the consequences. Parker, on the other hand, knows the right buttons to push and the right people to threaten in order to achieve the desired result, which may help to explain why this series of novels has earned both respectful critical attention and substantial mass-market sales.

Techniques
The Parker books are "no frills" thrillers, tightly and economically told with the bare minimum of descriptive scene-setting. If this has been in a sense required by the more than a-book-a-year pace with which they have been produced (while Westlake has at the same time been very active under his own and other names), it is also a perfectly appropriate and highly satisfying method of narration: since Parker's interests in people and places evaporate when he has achieved what he wants, there's no reason for either him or readers to dwell upon the transitory phenomena of day-to-day existence. In reducing the hard-boiled thriller to its essential elements, Westlake's Parker novels offer a bracing dash of stimulant to a readership all too often sapped down by purplishly-overwritten prose and tedious psychological speculation.

Literary Precedents
Although Parker is a compellingly individualized example of the thriller hero, he is clearly a product of the *Black Mask*-Hammett-Chandler line of hardboiled detectives. Parker is of course on the other side of the law, but like the typical "private dick," he is well aware of the fine and easily crossable line that separates the good guys from the bad guys; and Parker also shares the conviction that stirring up action produces far better results than does armchair detection. Parker's aversion to sentimental feeling, which is carried to a point dangerously near self-parody in later novels in the series, is the final link in a chain which firmly conects him to such archetypal hard-boiled heroes as Sam Spade and Philip Marlowe.

KAHAWA
Kahawa, 1982, novel.

Social Concerns/Themes
Kahawa is a much longer and more complex novel than anything Westlake has previously published, and it does touch upon general social issues and broad themes in ways new to his work. Although the basic situation is one of some not-entirely-good guys trying to rip off some definitely-bad guys by stealing the Ugandan coffee crop, Westlake places his large cast of characters in a social context that demands their attention and concern. It is the Uganda of Idi Amin that they are going to rob, and in describing the realities of this totalitarian society Westlake paints a horrifying picture of gratuitous brutality and the systematic suppression of dissent. The muddled, more-or-less democratic society of Kenya with which it is contrasted is certainly not a utopia, but it is clearly preferable to the Ugandan model: unlike the novels that precede it, *Kahawa* does make an argument for one kind of social system as opposed to another, even though this preference is expressed in relative rather than absolute terms—Kenya is seen as less bad rather than intrinsically superior.

Thematically, *Kahawa* continues and to some extent expands upon Westlake's humorous thrillers in its conception of personal friendship as a partial solution to the inadequacy of social institutions. The relationships between his characters involve a high degree of mutual trust, which they for the most part succeed in preserving; although sexual fidelity may not survive a temporarily attractive alternative, keeping one's commitment to another's personal safety is of paramount and universally-acknowledged importance. *Kahawa* presents readers with a story in which a large cast of characters is able to carry through a complicated plan because of their respect for and liking of one another, and in this it seems both a realistic picture of social cohesion at work and a welcome upward leap in complexity for Westlake's literary creations.

Characters

Kahawa also represents something of a change for Westlake in its use of multiple points of view. Where he has previously given one well-defined character per book, *Kahawa* features a much larger number of *dramatis personae* who are sketched with dextrous economy before being sucked into the whirlwind of events. The resulting group portrait succeeds, through variety and contrast, in highlighting the human components of this broad canvas of action and adventure, as Westlake demonstrates that he can construct a wide range of credible characters when the nature of his material requires it.

Techniques

Plotting has always been one of Westlake's strengths, and in *Kahawa* he gets a chance to keep several narrative lines in simultaneous motion. He accomplishes this with such apparent ease that one would think he had been turning out novels on this scale for years, and one is again reminded of the thorough professionalism with which he approaches his various literary projects. Having already mastered the techniques of the humorous thriller and the hard-boiled mystery novel, with *Kahawa* Westlake proves that he can also write an action-packed adventure story that seems perfect for wide-screen treatment. Although it would be foolhardy to attempt to forecast the future course of his development as a writer, one can predict that Donald Westlake's work will continue to attract a large readership by offering it a varied feast of well-prepared entertainments.

Literary Precedents

Kahawa is a large-scale adventure opus of the sort Robert Ludlum and Ken Follett have made popular. Like them, it features a large cast of characters, a complicated plot and a leavening of fiction with historical fact, and the commercial success of the genre is presumably a good part of the reason why Westlake has begun to work in it. As observed previously, however, Westlake usually adds something distinctive to whatever he undertakes, and in this case he has injected complex ethical and social issues into a type of novel that more typically exhibits straightforwardly conventional attitudes. *Kahawa* is just as exciting as anything by Ludlum or Follett, but its sophisticated treatment of its thematic elements makes it a much more satisfying example of the adult entertainment.

Other Titles

As Donald Westlake: *The Mercenaries*, 1960 (novel, reissued as *The Smashers*, 1962); *Killing Time*, 1961 (novel, reissued as *The Operators*, 1964); *361*, 1962 (novel); *Killy*, 1963 (novel); *Pity Him Afterwards*, 1964 (novel); *The Fugitive Pigeon*, 1965 (novel); *The Busy Body*, 1966 (novel); *The Spy in the Ointment*, 1966 (novel); *Philip*, 1967 (juvenile); *The Curious Facts Preceding My Execution and Other Fictions*, 1968 (short stories); *Who Stole Sassi Manoon?*, 1969 (novel); *Up Your Banners*, 1969 (novel); *The Hot Rock*, 1970 (novel); *Adios, Scheherazade*, 1970 (novel); *I Gave at the Office*, 1971 (novel); *Bank Shot*, 1972 (novel); *Under an English Heaven*, 1972 (belles lettres); *Cops and Robbers*, 1972 (novel); with Brian Garfield, *Gangway*, 1973 (novel); *Help I Am Being Held Prisoner*, 1974 (novel); *Jimmy the Kid*, 1974 (novel); *Two Much!*, 1975 (novel); *Brothers Keepers*, 1975 (novel); *Dancing Aztecs*, 1976 (novel); *Enough*, 1977 (novel); *A New York Dance*, 1979 (novel); *Castle in the Air*, 1980 (novel); *Why Me*, 1981 (novel); *Nobody's Perfect*, 1981 (novel); *A Likely Story*, 1984 (novel); *High Adventure*, 1985 (novel); *Levine*, 1985 (short stories); *Good Behavior*, 1986 (novel).

As Tucker Coe: *Kinds of Love, Kinds of Death*, 1966 (novel); *Murder Among Children*, 1968 (novel); *Wax Apple*, 1970 (novel); *A Jade in Aries*, 1971 (novel); *Don't Lie to Me*, 1972 (novel). As Curt Clark: *Anarchos*, 1967 (novel). As Timothy Culver: *Ex Officio*, 1970 (novel).

Additional Sources

Adams, Abby, "Living with a Mystery Writer," *Murder Ink: The Mystery Reader's Companion*. Ed., Dilys Winn. New York: Workman, 1977, pp. 76-78. An amusing and insightful account of what it is like to live with Westlake and his various pseudonyms.

Clute, John, "Donald E. Westlake," *The Science Fiction Encyclopedia*. Ed., Peter Nichols, et al. New York: Dolphin Books (Doubleday), 1979, p. 651. The best source for information about Westlake's science-fiction writings.

Nevins, Francis M., "Donald E. Westlake," *Twentieth Century Crime and Mystery Writers*. Ed., John M. Reilly. New York: St. Martin's, 1980, pp. 1463-1467. Includes an exhaustive bibliography as well as a general critical discussion.

Pavett, Mike, "Crooks and Cops," *Crime Writers*. Ed., H.R.F. Keating. London: British Broadcasting Corporation, 1978, pp. 118-119. A brief discussion of Westlake and "Richard Stark," with a photograph of Westlake and stills from the films *Point Blank* and *Bank Shot*.

Penzler, Otto, "Donald E. Westlake," *Encyclopedia of Murder and Detection*. Ed., Chris Steinbrunner, Otto Penzler, Marvin Lachman, Charles Shibuk. New York: McGraw-Hill, 1976, pp. 417-418. A useful general reference entry that is particularly good on film adaptations of Westlake's books.

Ruehlmann, William, *Saint With a Gun: The Unlawful American Private Eye*. New York: New York University Press, 1974, pp. 12-14. A discussion of the serious aspects of Westlake's comic novel *Cops and Robbers*.

Westlake, Donald E., "Hearing Voices in My Head," *Murder Ink: The Mystery Reader's Companion.* Ed., Dilys Winn. New York: Workman, 1977, pp. 7-11. An imaginary dialogue between Westlake and several of his pseudonyms that is probably the best single introduction to his work.

Paul Stuewe

TOM WOLFE
1931

Publishing History

Wolfe began publishing magazine articles for *New York* (then the Sunday supplement to the New York *Herald Tribune*) in the early 1960s after receiving a Ph.D. in American Studies from Yale University. Many of his articles first appeared in *New York, Esquire* or *Rolling Stone;* he has served as a contributing editor to all three publications. Throughout his writing career, which began in traditional journalism, the status of his books as fiction has always been dubious. After the enormous success of *The Electric Kool-Aid Acid Test,* which follows Ken Kesey's journey from the West Coast to New York City and in doing so defines the characteristics of a generation, Wolfe created a cult following of his own. Traditional journalists did not approve of his reporting methods, and the labels "New Journalism" or "non-fiction novel" were often applied to his work. His reportage typically includes conventional novelistic devices in developing character, narrating action, and describing setting. Several of his books are collections of essays that earlier appeared in various magazines. His only work identified as a novel, *The Bonfire of the Vanities,* was serialized in *Rolling Stone* between July 1984 and July 1985.

Critical Reception, Honors, and Popularity

In 1965 *New York* ran a two-part article by Wolfe about *The New Yorker* entitled "Tiny Mummies! The True Story of the Ruler of 43rd Street's Land of the Walking Dead." Shortly thereafter, Wolfe, and his fellow writers of New Journalism, were attacked in the *Columbia Journalism Review* and *The New York Review of Books.* Dwight Macdonald condemned Wolfe and others for "parajournalism."

Critical response to his work has over the past two decades remained sharply divided between those who praise, often extravagantly, Wolfe's stylistic genius, lively reportage, and careful research and others who condemn him for working in a "bastard form," sensationalism, and unconventional use of language, punctuation, and syntax.

Wolfe's works have sold extremely well, especially in paperback. Many of his titles have remained in print for well over a decade after their initial publication. His irreverence has offended many reviewers and critics, especially in *The Painted Word* and *From Bauhaus to Our House,* which deal with American painting and architecture since 1945. In both cases Wolfe refutes the vehement attacks of art critics and art historians by arguing that these books are social histories rather than aesthetic theories or judgments. In general, the more popular the publication reviewing Wolfe's books, the more enthusiastic its reception.

His most impressive awards came in 1980 for *The Right Stuff:* The American

Book Award for general non-fiction; the Columbia Journalism award; and the Harold D. Vursell award from the American Academy and Institute of Arts and Letters.

Analysis of Selected Titles

THE RIGHT STUFF

The Right Stuff, 1980, reportage. A four-part article on the U.S. astronauts first appeared in *Rolling Stone* in 1973, six years before the publication of *The Right Stuff* as a separate volume. Although the work is largely factual and based on seven years of meticulous research and interviews, Wolfe takes many of the liberties accorded novelists: he changes the names of four figures; he often describes a character's state of mind and thoughts; he records long stretches of dialogue as direct quotation.

Social Concerns

As in all his works, Wolfe shows how the events chronicled were presented to and perceived by the American public. Chuck Yeager, the undisputed hero of the book, was relegated to obscurity when tight security was clamped on his breaking the sound barrier. The Mercury 7 astronauts, on the other hand, were made available to the media as stellar examples of "single combat warriors" who could win the Cold War. Presented to the media and, therefore, the American public like debutantes at a society ball, they were celebrated and feted before actually going into space. Ironically, after Wolfe's book and the film based upon it, Yeager himself became a celebrity. Rediscovered nearly three decades after his most impressive accomplishments, Yeager wrote a best-selling autobiography and starred in a number of television commercials.

Wolfe shows that media coverage or the lack of it shaped public opinion. One of the clearest examples concerns Yeager's invitation to the American premiere of a British film *Breaking the Sound Barrier.* Made more than five years after Yeager had been the first to fly at Mach 1, the film depicts Geoffrey de Havilland exceeding the speed of sound "by *reversing the controls* at the critical moment during a power dive." Surprised as Yeager was by this fiction, he is stunned when the Secretary of the Air Force asks him if that is what he did to break the sound barrier.

Themes

The Right Stuff deals with the American astronauts and test pilots who, from the late 1940s to the mid 1960s, conquered the sound barrier and space. The book's attention is divided between the test pilots like Chuck Yeager, who repeatedly set new air speed and altitude records flying experimental aircraft, and the Mercury 7 astronauts who went into space first in sub-orbital and later orbital missions. Throughout the work, Wolfe places these events in a well-defined social and political context. The drama of the Cold War, from the late 1940s through the Cuban missile crisis and the Vietnam War, is a clearly drawn background. But the focus always falls upon individuals for whom the race against the Russians is a matter of life and death, pride or humiliation, "the right stuff" or failure.

Characters
Many of the "characters" in *The Right Stuff* were actual participants in the programs Wolfe describes; most of them were alive at the time of publication. The book is largely about the heroism of men with the right stuff—that combination of bravery, pride, skill, luck, and health—epitomized by Chuck Yeager. Yeager is a compendium of American virtues: fearless, dedicated, cool, self-possessed, and unpretentious. Wolfe depicts Yeager as a self-made man who rose from humble origins without a college education to the top of a highly competitive system, a great ziggurat of prestige among test pilots.

The Mercury 7 astronauts, on the other hand, had not ascended to Yeager's heights, but were packaged for the American public by press conferences, exclusives in *Life* magazine, and extensive media coverage. To men like Yeager, the astronauts were "spam in a can"—men who did not pilot an aircraft but merely rode in one.

Much of *The Right Stuff* dwells, however, on how the astronauts demanded some control over the capsule and asserted their humanity and individuality. They insisted, for example, on a window. They were not the trained chimps that NASA officials sometimes might have preferred. They repeatedly demonstrated that they had "the right stuff."

The Right Stuff portrays these pilots and astronauts as code heroes who embody the American ideal.

Techniques
Often identified as a writer of "New Journalism," Wolfe relies upon exhaustive research and interviews to recreate events. He is part social historian, part novelist, and part wide-eyed spectator. *The Right Stuff* reports momentous events through a very human perspective—often that of the wife of a test pilot or astronaut.

As elsewhere, Wolfe is a great phrasemaker. Like the phrase "the Me Decade," "the right stuff" has entered common parlance. The book is filled with similar epithets and catch phrases: "Flying & Drinking and Drinking & Driving"; "Booming and zooming"; "stretching the envelop."

In *The New Journalism,* Wolfe himself describes four techniques that distinguish his work from traditional "beige" journalism: First, "scene-by-scene construction . . . resorting as little as possible to sheer historical narrative"; second, the frequent use of realistic dialogue, usually taken from taped interviews and detailed notes; third, the author's presentation of himself in the third-person and the use of shifting perspectives that easily flow from omniscience to stream-of-consciousness to third-person narration; finally, and most importantly, the symbolic use of realistic detail drawn from precise and immediate observation.

Literary Precedents

Wolfe's originality in both style and subject is probably his most acclaimed feature. His subjects are American cultural phenomena—ranging from relatively isolated ones like Ken Kesey's Merry Pranksters or the world of customized cars to ones that become national obsessions like the Space Race. Wolfe invariably places these phenomena in a cultural context. His characters' language, clothing, homes, vocations, and avocations become emblematic of their social standing, political convictions, and moral values.

In *The New Journalism* Wolfe offers a cogent account of the development of his style. He argues that by the mid-twentieth century novelists had all but abandoned realism, which Wolfe sees as the most enduring and effective method for dealing with experience.

Wolfe also provides a list of "Not Half-Bad Candidates" of literary precedents for the New Journalism. They include Boswell's diaries, Dickens' *Sketches by Boz*, Henry Mayhew's *London Labour and the London Poor*, Twain's *Innocents Abroad*, Chekhov's *A Journey to Sakhalin*, Stephen Crane's vignettes of the New York Bowery, John Reed's *Ten Days that Shook the World*, Orwell's *Down and Out in London and Paris*, and several works since the 1930s.

Among contemporary authors, the strongest comparisons are with nonfiction novelists such as Truman Capote, Gay Talese, and Norman Mailer and new journalists like Joan Didion, Hunter S. Thompson, and Terry Southern.

Adaptations

The Right Stuff was released as a motion picture in 1983 starring Sam Shepard as Chuck Yeager, Ed Harris as John Glenn, and Scott Glenn as Alan Shepard, and directed by Philip Kaufmann. The film did only moderately well at the box office, but won four Academy Awards: Best Original Score, Best Editing, Best Sound, and Best Sound Effects Editing.

THE BONFIRE OF THE VANITIES

The Bonfire of the Vanities, 1984-1985, serialized novel. Serialized in *Rolling Stone*, this novel was not reviewed because it has not been published as a separate volume.

Social Concerns

As in *The Right Stuff* and other works, *The Bonfire of the Vanities* deals with the power of the media to shape public opinion through the presentation of events. Killian, Sherman McCoy's lawyer, refers to the handling of his case as a "media circus." Demonstrations reported on the evening news have the appearance of spontaneity, but are in fact carefully staged. Even the District Attorney's Office in the Bronx is described as publicity hungry. In every instance, especially that of Peter Fallow, a British reporter for *City Lights,* the media are manipulated yet remain oblivious or indifferent to that fact.

The Bonfire of the Vanities also scrutinizes the American legal institution. Specifically, the novel looks at the question of inequality before the law. With some disturbing similarities to the prosecution of Bernard Goetz, the case of Sherman McCoy shows that the law is not blind and especially not color blind.

Above all *The Bonfire of the Vanities* deals with class—upper, middle, and lower. Wolfe's novel is filled with detailed descriptions of architecture, interior decoration, clothing, and food. McCoy's study, where he takes police investigators to avoid the $150,000 living room decor, is furnished with expensive bookcases that do not escape the police officers' attention. Characters are identified, first, by ethnic or religious origins and racial epithets. The novel begins with the words "Yo, Goldberg!" the anti-Semetic taunt of a black audience to the Jewish mayor of New York City. More importantly, Wolfe identifies the income of virtually every character from a court reporter in the Bronx to international business tycoons. The reader knows how much Judy McCoy's shoes cost, the value of the Lum B. Lee armoires, and the price of lunch at a chic Manhattan restaurant.

Themes

The Bonfire of the Vanities deals with a successful New York writer, Sherman McCoy, "the Great Observer." McCoy and his wife, Judy, travel in the best social circles, own two entire floors of a prestigious Park Avenue apartment building, and have all the material comforts money can buy. McCoy's affair with the wife of an extremely wealthy businessman, Maria Ruskin, has been discovered by Judy. When McCoy attempts to break off with Maria while driving in from Kennedy Airport, he becomes so involved that he misses the Manhattan turn-off from the Tri-Borough Bridge. McCoy and Maria find themselves lost at night in a dangerous section of the South Bronx. McCoy inadvertently hits a young black man with his 380SL Mercedes. Maria, even more panicked than McCoy, flees the scene of the accident. McCoy is ticketed by the police; the victim, Henry Lamb, is taken to the hospital. A witness to the accident reports what she has seen to her churchman, the Reverend Bacon, a black neighborhood organizer and power-broker. Bacon decries the incident as Park Avenue justice and orchestrates street demonstrations and a media campaign against McCoy.

McCoy's wealth offers no protection from the indignities and terror of arraignment. Brought in wearing handcuffs, he must first run the gauntlet of the media. Harassed by vile epithets, McCoy spends several hours being fingerprinted and photographed before he appears before a judge.

The pace of the novel is entirely disrupted by its hasty conclusion. Charges against McCoy are dismissed, but not before "the Great Observer" has been more deeply involved in the legal system than he ever hoped to be.

Techniques

The techniques employed in Wolfe's only novel are no different from those of his other works. A wealth of realistic detail, convincing dialogue, and a rapidly shifting narrative stance are effectively used in *The Bonfire of the Vanities* just as they are in his other works.

Wolfe's interest in language is especially evident in *The Bonfire of the Vanities*. He devotes his considerable talents to exploring the varieties of non-standard American English. Dialect, accent, jargon, affectation, and even technical means all distort language, sometimes beyond comprehension. Balkan cab drivers respond to an unintelligible jibberish issuing from their radios. Lawyers in the Bronx D.A.'s office habitually and deliberately avoid subject/verb agreement. The profanities hailed upon lawyers and judges by a van-load of defendants are as realistic as they are hilarious.

Related Titles

Some sections of *The Bonfire of the Vanities* borrow heavily and even directly on Wolfe's previous works. Judy McCoy's futile attempt to enter into conversation at a posh dinner party is directly taken from "The Invisible Wife" in *In Our Time* (1980).

Other Titles

The Kandy-Kolored Tangerine-Flaked Streamline Baby, 1965 (essays); *The Pump House Gang*, 1968 (essays); *The Electric Kool-Aid Acid Test*, 1968 (journalism); *Radical Chic and Mau-Mauing the Flak Catchers*, 1970 (essays); *The New Journalism*, 1973 (anthology with essays by Wolfe); *The Painted Word*, 1975 (non-fiction); *Mauve Gloves & Madmen, Clutter & Vine*, 1976 (essays); *Bauhaus to Our House*, 1981 (non-fiction), *The Purple Decades: A Reader*, 1982 (essays).

Additional Sources

Hollowell, John, *Fact and Fiction: The New Journalism and the Nonfiction Novel*. Chapel Hill: University of North Carolina Press, 1977. Includes a chapter on Wolfe's *The Electric Kool-Aid Acid Test.*

Johnson, Michael L., *The New Journalism: The Underground Press, the Artists of Nonfiction and Changes in the Established Media.* Lawrence: University Press of Kansas, 1971. Examines New Journalism by tracing its origins in the underground press in the 1960s.

Joan F. Dean
University of Missouri
Kansas City

HERMAN WOUK
1915

Publishing History

Herman Wouk came to his career as a writer of long, serious novels in a most unusual fashion. After graduating from Columbia University, Wouk worked for several years as a writer for the famous comedian Fred Allen, turning out one-liners and short programs. After the outbreak of World War II, he turned to writing radio programs to support the war effort. Eventually he joined the Navy, and while in service turned to writing novels. His first publications were only moderately successful, but when, at the beginning of the 1950s, he turned to the war as a subject for his fiction, he discovered the *metier* that would provide him commercial success and critical acclaim.

Critical Reception, Honors, and Popularity

The publication of *The Caine Mutiny* in 1951 brought Wouk the kind of acclaim afforded few novelists in recent decades. The novel was immediately popular, topping best seller lists for weeks and running through several editions and paperback issues. Since its publication, *The Caine Mutiny* has not been out of print. Other Wouk novels have been similarly successful on commercial markets, but none has yet received the critical acclaim of this novel of men at sea in World War II. Adaptations of several of Wouk's works have helped promote the novels themselves, and characters from *The Caine Mutiny,* and more recently those from *Winds of War* and *War and Remembrance,* have become familiar to millions of Americans. *The Caine Mutiny* won for Wouk the Pulitzer Prize in 1951, and the Columbia Medal for Literary Excellence the following year.

Analysis of Selected Titles

THE CAINE MUTINY

The Caine Mutiny, 1951, novel.

Social Concerns

The Caine Mutiny is the first of Wouk's novels in which he explores the social phenomenon for which he has gained fame: the impact of World War II on the lives of Americans. In this novel, Wouk concentrates primarily on the effects of the conflict on those called to fight in it: the professional navy men who have been preparing for war during the years of peace, and the thousands of Americans whose normal lives are interrupted when they are forced to don uniforms in the service of

1483

their country. Through his cast of characters from various walks of life, Wouk explores the peculiar attitude of Americans toward World War II and toward warfare itself: this hoι.ible aberration in human behavior is something with which Americans have a love/hate relationship, glorying in its successes while simultaneously cursing the necessity of engaging in such slaughter. Wouk also explores the attitudes the American populace has toward military service and toward those who have dedicated their lives to careers in the armed forces during peacetime. Essentially conservative in his viewpoint on the subject, Wouk has great praise for these professionals, even though there is, as he illustrates so vividly, always the danger that individuals like Captain Queeg may be harbored and even promoted in a bureaucracy.

Themes

In addition to exploring topical issues about the Second World War, Wouk delves into several enduring human problems in *The Caine Mutiny*. Questions dealing with the War are played out as parts of the saga of Willie Keith's maturation; in the larger sense, the novel is a *Bildungsroman*, the story of a young man growing up and finding himself and his place in the world. Keith's involvement in the various conflicts between Queeg and the crew provides a central point of interest for readers. The plot of the novel, as E. M. Forster defines plot (the arrangement of incidents to show cause and effect), centers on Keith's progress from green officer candidate to his ascendancy as the last captain of the *Caine*.

The novel also explores the larger issue of man's responsibility for his fellow man. The actions of the *Caine*'s officers to counter the blunders of their captain are presented as moral dilemmas representative of those which all men face: when can one violate the social order to prevent disaster or promote the common good? What responsibility does the individual have for such actions, especially if these actions are open to question? Finally, *The Caine Mutiny* is a psychological study of men in conflict, an examination of the effects of heightened stress on social groups. In this respect, the ship becomes a microcosm of the world itself, and the struggles of the officers and crew of the *Caine* become a metaphor for the larger conflicts in which all societies find themselves from time to time.

Characters

Occasionally, a novelist is able to introduce a character that becomes a part of his country's "folklore"; Wouk has done so with Lieutenant Commander Philip Queeg. Millions of Americans who have never read *The Caine Mutiny* know of the tyrannical, paranoid skipper of the *Caine,* rolling a pair of steel ball bearings between his fingers as he becomes more nervous and frightened of the responsibility thrust upon him by the nature of his command. Queeg, the only career Navy man on the *Caine,* sees himself as a man alone against a hostile universe: his ship is aging, his officers and crew plot against him, those higher up the bureaucratic chain have no sympathy for his problems.

The Caine Mutiny's other major characters all serve in some way as foils for Queeg. Executive Officer Steve Maryk and Gunnery Officer Tom Keefer, both reservists called to duty because of the War, struggle to make sense of Queeg's erratic behavior; Maryk finally finds himself forced to relieve the captain to save the ship. The only character who shows significant development in the novel, however, is Willie Keith. He joins the *Caine* as a raw ensign from a rich family in which everything was given to him, growing in experience during the course of the ship's adventures and eventually coming to some understanding of the nature of global warfare and of the men of vastly different backgrounds forced to join together as a fighting force. Like the wedding guest in Coleridge's "Ancient Mariner," Keith leaves the ship at the end of the novel "a sadder but wiser man," bettered by his experiences and ready to face the challenges of life as a responsible adult.

Techniques

While Wouk concentrates on individual episodes to explore the character of the ship's captain and the reactions of those trying to cope with Queeg's apparently psychotic behavior, his use of point-of-view contributes subtly yet significantly to the novel's effectiveness. The reader is allowed to see events from the perspective of almost every character in the story—except Queeg. Hence, one can never be sure of the captain's real motives. Virtually everything Queeg says or does can be interpreted as evidence of abnormal behavior—by those who wish to make a case for insanity or unfitness for command. As the story progresses, however, it becomes equally apparent that there is a shadow of doubt about such interpretations. Thus Wouk is able to set up a tension in the reader between emotional reaction and logical response: the reader feels, as the officers of the ship do, that Queeg is insane, yet nothing Queeg does is technically outside his authority as commander, and every one of his actions can be explained as an attempt to preserve discipline or safety aboard ship. That tension makes *The Caine Mutiny* appealing to readers years after the book has disappeared from the best seller lists.

Literary Precedents

The Caine Mutiny is often compared with other important novels that emerged from World War II, especially James Jones' *From Here to Eternity* and Norman Mailer's *The Naked and the Dead*. Unlike these novelists, however, Wouk treats the military profession sympathetically. Wouk's novel also shares in the tradition of sea literature that stretches back through such twentieth-century classics as the *Mutiny on the Bounty* trilogy to the sea tales of Joseph Conrad (especially *The Nigger of the Narcissus)* and Herman Melville.

Adaptations

One of the major reasons for the enduring popularity of Wouk's story of the *Caine* was its adaptation as a movie. With legendary actor Humphrey Bogart playing the role of Philip Queeg, *The Caine Mutiny* was an immediate box-office success, and it continues to be shown on both network and local television. The stage version of the book, cut down to concentrate on the court-martial scenes, was a Broadway hit in 1953, and it continues to live in revivals, with such noted actors as Charlton Heston having played the lead.

WAR AND REMEMBRANCE

War and Remembrance, 1978, novel, 2 vols. A sequel to *The Winds of War,* 1971.

Social Concerns/Themes

Wouk's two-volume story of World War II, dubbed by the author a "historical romance," uses fictional characters to show the impact of the global conflict on Americans of various walks of life. Wouk traces the wartime career of Captain Victor "Pug" Henry, a career navy officer, and of Henry's family. Through the Henrys and their associates, Wouk is able to take a close look at the way war forces families to cope with death, separation, divorce, and constant trials. Additionally, Wouk explores the impact of the holocaust on the victims as they are pursued throughout Europe and carted off to the concentration camps to be gassed and cremated. The length of the work and Wouk's narrative technique also allow him to offer a view of the War from the Germans' perspective, and to introduce real-life figures to speculate on their motives for acting as they did to influence the course of the conflict.

Characters

War and Remembrance contains nearly a dozen major characters. Though Wouk concentrates on Pug Henry's career and his relationship with his wife Rhoda and the woman he loves, Pam Tudsbury, the stories of his sons Warren and Byron and their wives Janice and Natalie are also significant. Natalie, a young Jewish girl caught in Italy with her uncle, serves as the vehicle for Wouk's exploration of the phenomenon of the holocaust. Even within the generic limitations of romance, Wouk is able to achieve a surprising degree of character development with his major characters. Though most act predictably, Wouk's narrative skill makes the reader sympathize with them and become concerned for their fates.

Techniques

Wouk uses a complex method of narration in this romance to achieve a breadth of coverage of what is certainly an imposing topic. He alternates third-person narrative with first-person accounts of various characters, entries from fictional journals, even fictional memoirs of a German general "edited" by Pug Henry in the years after the war. Wouk makes it clear in editorial apparatus that he is not attempting to present a faithful picture of history as much as he is trying to bring to life the flavor of the period. Thus some of his characters not only meet real-life figures, but actually influence the course of historical events. Such a technique may disturb the historical purist, but it adds greatly to the drama that Wouk unfolds in *War and Remembrance;* within the context of the novel it is both believable and acceptable.

Related Titles

The volumes of *War and Remembrance* are a continuation of the story Wouk begins in *The Winds of War* (1971). Indeed, much of the exposition that allows the reader to make sense of the various major plot lines of *War and Remembrance* is provided in the earlier novel. Thematically, these volumes are also closely allied to *The Caine Mutiny.* Wouk is consistent over the decades in touting the virtues of the career military officer, the capability and adaptability of the non-careerist under pressure, and the courage of Americans when faced with adversity.

INSIDE, OUTSIDE
Inside, Outside, 1985, novel.

Social Concerns/Themes

Those who know Wouk only from his "navy" novels will discover from *Inside, Outside* that he is not limited in the scope of his imagination. This highly autobiographical novel deals with the increasingly popular subject of "growing up Jewish," relating the struggles of the hero, Israel David Goodkind, as he comes to grips with life in cosmopolitan America. A *Bildungsroman,* the novel focuses on the crises of a youth faced with conflicts brought on by family and peer pressures, the pain and ecstasy of early loves, the dilemma of career choices. These are seen retrospectively by the older Goodkind, who is now counselor to President Nixon and is engaged in helping to solve world crises, including the 1973 Arab-Israeli War.

Characters

While maintaining a central interest on David Goodkind, Wouk introduces a series of characters who serve as types: the Jewish mother doting over her son; the Jewish father, good-hearted toward all in his family but demanding of his offspring; the second-generation Jewish-American young men and women struggling to reconcile their heritage with the demands of American society; the cast of characters that make up the Jewish community in which the hero lives, and the dozens of "outsiders" with whom he comes in contact as he grows up and moves away from the protection of his Jewish home. Less interested in developing characters than in capturing them as they appeared to him when growing up, Wouk provides a wide-angle snapshot of men and women who inhabited New York in the decades before World War II.

Techniques

Wouk's narrative technique in *Inside, Outside* is largely first-person reminiscence, mostly by Goodkind himself. Goodkind's story of his days as a youngster in New York City are balanced by vignettes of his present-day work as counselor to the president. In that capacity, he deals directly with the "outside" world, and the balance with the "inside" world of the Jewish community in which he was raised provides a tension that is pleasing in its dramatic contrast. Through the detailed accounts that Goodkind provides, Wouk is able to offer the reader a kind of compendium of Jewish life in America.

Other Titles

Aurora Dawn, 1947 (novel); *City Boy*, 1948 (novel); *Traitor*, 1949 (play); *Slattery's Hurricane*, with Richard Murphy, 1949 (screenplay); *Confidentially Connie*, with Max Schulman, 1953 (screenplay); *The Caine Mutiny Court-Martial*, 1953 (play); *Marjorie Morningstar*, 1955 (novel); *Slattery's Hurricane*, 1956 (novel); *Nature's Way*, 1957 (play); *This is My God*, 1959 (nonfiction); *Youngblood Hawke*, 1962 (novel); *Don't Stop the Carnival*, 1965 (novel); *The Winds of War*, 1971 (novel); *The Winds of War*, 1983 (television screenplay).

Additional Sources

Bolton, Richard R., " 'The Winds of War' and Wouk's Wish for the World," *Midwest Quarterly*, XVI, iv (Summer 1975): 389-408.

Contemporary Literary Criticism, Vol. 1. Detroit: Gale Research, 1973, pp. 375-377. Brief assessments from reviews of *The Caine Mutiny* and *Marjorie Morningstar*.

Contemporary Literary Criticism, Vol. 9. Detroit: Gale Research, 1982, pp. 579-583. Excerpts from reviews of various novels provide a general assessment of individual works and of Wouk's stature in the profession.

Critical Survey of Long Fiction. Englewood Cliffs, NJ: Salem Press, 1983, vol. VII, pp. 2961-2973. Brief biography, plot summary and critical assessment of selected novels.

Dictionary of Literary Biography, Yearbook 1982. Detroit: Gale Research, 1983, pp. 383-388. Biography and brief review of Wouk's career through the publication of *War and Remembrance.*

Geismar, Maxwell, *American Moderns, From Rebellion to Conformity.* New York: Hill & Wang, 1958, pp. 38-45. Discusses Wouk as a modern critic of American society and culture.

Laurence W. Mazzeno
U.S. Naval Academy

CHELSEA QUINN YARBRO
1942

Publishing History

Chelsea Quinn Yarbro (whose fans refer to her as Quinn Yarbro) began writing in the mid-1960s, but began writing on a steady and regular basis, she says, in 1975. Since then she has produced a formidable number of novels and short stories, usually of a mixed genre type, that feature most prominently among them the vampire series that catalogues the long life of the Count St.-Germain. This series, originally projected as a trilogy, has run to its fifth and final volume; the life is capped off by a collection of four short stories entitled *The Saint-Germain Chronicles*. In addition, Yarbro has produced several non-vampiric historical/fantasy/occult novels, three modern novels of the horror/supernatural type, two apocalyptic novels, two modern detective stories, two young adult novels set in the distant past, and two spiritualist works that purport to be the transcripts of a spirit's messages transmitted through a Ouija board. This wide-ranging and prolific author has been both praised and reviled by her critics for every aspect of her work. Her various works have been translated into French, Spanish, Italian and German, and her readership seems well established.

Critical Reception, Honors, and Popularity

Yarbro's eclectic tendencies have been noted by nearly every reviewer; the results have been mixed. While some, from the beginning, were impressed by the innovativeness of her making a historical novel, for example, into a vampire novel, and then making the vampire the hero, others complained that the idea did not yield an interesting story, and that the author really had little to say. One critic called her *Ariosto* "extremely demanding reading" for its complexity of plot, while another found *The Godforsaken,* a werewolf novel, "dull" and its 393 pages of Poe-like evocation of mood "too much for the reader to bear." Similar vacillations in critical reputation have been typical, suggesting an uneven level of dedication to excellence.

A self-proclaimed atheist, Yarbro's "fairly pronounced antipathy to the Catholic Church" and simultaneous "equally pronounced sympathy for the Church's more 'liberated' opponents, pagan or otherwise," has put off some readers, and so has her devotion to spiritualism and to other subconscious modes of communication. Her two books of messages from the spirit Michael have been panned as "unconvincing" and lacking in profundity, and her first detective novel was panned for allowing the Ojibwa detective to solve the case using his "racial subconscious" mind, a device which led Newgate Callendar in the *New York Times Book Review* to come within a hair of calling Yarbro a racist. While she has stated, in an interview in the English publication *Foundations,* that she doesn't believe in vampires or werewolves although she writes about them, she does appear to believe in some form of life after death and the ability of the living to communicate with the dead if they (or a medium) have the talent.

While Yarbro's books always get reviewed in the trade journals like *Kirkus Reviews* or *Library Journal*, there are no critical articles in the scholarly journals. The science fiction and fantasy specialist publications offer the same sort of mixed reviews as the mainstream journals do, although occasionally somewhat more outspokenly.

Yarbro has won one award, the Mystery Writers of America scroll in 1973 for "The Ghosts at Iron River."

Analysis of Selected Titles

HOTEL TRANSYLVANIA: A NOVEL OF FORBIDDEN LOVE

Hotel Transylvania, 1978, novel. Sequels: *The Palace*, 1979; *Blood Games: A Novel of Historical Horror*, 1980; *The Path of the Eclipse*, 1981; *Tempting Fate*, 1982; *The Saint-Germain Chronicles*, 1983, collection of four stories.

Social Concerns

The picture of society in Yarbro's work is clearly summarized in this most popular of her works, the vampire series, featuring the elegant and learned Count Ragoczy Saint-Germain. Here, the human beings, and especially the males among them, are the cause of the bloodshed and suffering throughout the novel, and by extension, since the series ranges, in order of publication, through Renaissance Florence, Nero's Rome, Jenghiz Khan's China, and Nazi Germany, with other stops added in each of the novels, they are the cause of suffering through all of history and on every continent. Compared to the slaughters that have been perpetrated by human beings, the vampires of the earth seem almost harmless, and that is in fact the situation in these works. The Count, who has put his many centuries to good use academically, is more intelligent and sensitive than ninety per cent of the "normal" people he meets. There are always oppressed (or endangered) women who are in need of someone strong to rescue them from their (male) enemies. This is not always possible, but whether Saint-Germain fails or not (he usually does not), he manages to fall in love with the woman as a rule, and this love is reciprocated. Occasionally the woman becomes, as in the flagship novel and in *Blood Games,* a vampire herself as a favor from the Count, so that she may remain devoted to him forever, even as he leaves to travel about with his ghoulish valet, Roger. In *Hotel Transylvania* the damsel in distress is one Madelaine de Montalia, who is sought after eagerly by a group of Satanists led by the evil Baron Clotaire de Saint Sebastien because her father, in the waywardness of his youth, had promised his first-born child to the devil-worshippers, and they have never forgotten. Their intent is to make her the subject of a ghastly and painful sacrifice to Satan. Enter Saint-Germain, who loves and saves Madelaine at great risk to himself, permitting her to join the ranks of vampirism as a reward for her devotion.

Themes

The inhumanity of man to man (but especially, it seems, to woman) is dominant throughout the series. The way in which the point is made is for the author to describe in gruesome detail the depredations that have been visited upon the helpless and their defenders over all the centuries of what is referred to as civilization. Some reviewers have complained about the extent of the violence here and in other novels, and find the characters that Yarbro seems to consider typical in every age to be actually unbelievable. Since the historical background of her novels seems to be an element which the author especially values, one assumes that the atrocities are all documented rather than the product of one over-active imagination.

Love is present in every novel in which Saint-Germain appears, and so, in one way or another, is sex. The Count is inconvenienced by sexual impotency, but he is considerate enough of the women whom he loves and from whom he usually obtains his modest wineglassful of blood every few days to guarantee them sexual gratification through his considerable manual and oral skills. This woman-centered sexuality, combined with humanitarian concern for the oppressed, makes Saint-Germain, scholar and scientist, not to mention handsome and rich, easily the most desirable male in the novel, mutant though he be.

Characters

Saint-Germain is good to the extent that he has almost nothing with which to revile himself after four thousand years of life. He never kills, he fights for truth and justice, and he fights evil human males, usually in hand-to-hand combat, in order to right the wrongs they have inflicted or wish to inflict. He has been referred to by critics as the Robin Hood of vampires and the Prince Charming of the darker arts. No one has yet referred to him as the Lone Vampire and his faithful companion, but the comparison is tempting. Some readers find this revisionist vampire novel form to be fascinating; others won't even pick it up, on the grounds that the vampire element has become sanitized to the point that there is no longer any horror or sense of lurking threat, and that the vampire level of self-acceptance is too high even to admit a sense of tragedy or an adequate sense of isolation. It is altogether inappropriate to imagine a need to drive a stake through Saint-Germain's tender heart, although one could easily conceive of a group of misled and narrow-minded human beings dedicated to just that end.

The evil opposition, is correspondingly, without redeeming qualities. One reviewer complained that Saint Sebastien, for example, was so extreme a villain that the author "apparently felt she had to scrape the floor of a charnel house" to find someone bad enough to put up against a vampire as hero. Evil, however, is in the eyes of the beholder. An sf reviewer, less thin-skinned, found the Baron an example of "stark reality." "He is one of those homicidal maniacs who [sic] we have become so familiar with today. Think of the Manson, or Texas mass murders, or the British moor murders in which children were tortured to death and their cries tape-recorded."

The women are, for those who appear in the works of a "non-dogmatic feminist," as Yarbro called herself in a 1977 *Berkeley Barb* interview, rather passive and helpless, with notable exceptions such as the valiant Warlord T'en Chih-yu in *The Path of the Eclipse.* The non-dogmatic form of feminism which Yarbro espouses appears to include an acute awareness of the actual helplessness (and thus passivity) of women throughout the eras in history which she treats, and thus leads to an emphasis on their roles as victims. The redoubtable woman, as an exception in history, is also in short supply in her historical novels. The author has defended the right to use unflattering portraits of women "if a female twit happens to be necessary to the plotline," which means that the dogmatic feminists are probably distressed at her, though none has reviewed her works and said as much.

Techniques/Literary Precedents

The Saint-Germain series, like any vampire novel, ultimately is traceable to Bram Stoker's *Dracula,* but beyond that there is little here that will seem familiar to devotees of the traditional vampire-as-child-of-Satan-bloodthirsty-killer stories, or even to those who have come to appreciate the more recent vampire stories in which the vampires are intensely aware of their isolation and loneliness, and sometimes even fear that they will eventually be damned for their inevitable murders of their victims. While an occasional nod is given to Saint-Germain's world-weariness and other common vampire traits like a fear of running water and a need to sleep on his native soil, the emphasis in these novels is definitely action on the field and in the bedroom, combined with political intrigue and lengthy descriptions of gore. Further, because Saint-Germain never stalks a prey with whom the reader identifies (although the evil antagonist may), suspense is held to a minimum. One reviewer, in fact, insisted that the sequels were really "prequels" since they all covered an era earlier in time than the original novel (he wrote the year before *Tempting Fate* was published), and that it hurt suspense for the reader to know that Saint-Germain would survive his various crises in some way or another.

Yarbro loves to use letters in her novels. In *Hotel Transylvania* this epistolary technique is successful, with the letters helping to move the plot forward. In the more recent of the series, however, they become too lengthy and cumbersome, and begin to impede the forward momentum of the work. Reviewers have complained about the later novels as they did not about *Hotel,* and by the fourth novel one was already commenting, "this series has run out of steam," in part because of the slow movement of events. It appears that the fifth novel, *Tempting Fate,* is the last of the series.

FALSE DAWN

"False Dawn," short story, in *Strange Bedfellows*, ed. Thomas Scortia (expanded to novel length in 1978).

Social Concerns/Characters

This widely reviewed novel, which appeared the same year as the first Saint-Germain novel, is both bleak and poorly constructed. The bleakness comes from the fact that this is a post-holocaust novel that offers no hope for the future; the weakness in construction owes its existence to the author's expansion of the story into a full length work.

In this work, Doomsday has come, but readers are not certain how, except that pollution is extreme and plants and animals have both adapted to it in bizarre ways long since. The Ponderosa pines are red now, and deadly water spiders that resemble scorpions bunch together wherever there is water; their sting brings a swift, painful death. Danger is everywhere people are found, virtually, for groups of indeterminate size range the California setting of this novel and possibly elsewhere, all viciously mean men on motorcycles who owe their inspiration to the Mongols, it would seem. Paul Walker complained in *Galaxy* that it seems at first that there is an army, but in the end only a handful are fought off by the two central characters, both of whom are mutants, but why or how readers do not know.

Thea, a young woman born in 1986, is now about twenty-six years old. She was made a mutant by someone, possibly a consenting parent, in an attempt to create various types of mutants ("mutes" in the novel) who might survive more successfully than ordinary human beings in the post-holocaust world. But Thea has a nictitating membrane in her eye (vestigial in most people) which is of dubious value. More to the point is the ability she and her male savior-sidekick Evan share to regenerate tissue and apparently, at least in the forty-six-year-old Evan's case, to regenerate bone, too; he loses an entire arm to the Pirates, but it grows right back. They spend the nearly 200 pages of the novel trekking around the ruined Western mountains trying to find a safe home, but instead the homicidal maniacs that seem to abound in every era in Yarbro's work do everything they can to destroy the two. Besides the Pirates, there are cannibals and fanatical monks who persecute the pair. Gretchen Rix, writing in *Science Fiction Review*, found the "gimmicky villains" the one flaw of the novel, but others have a longer list.

Themes

Man's inhumanity to man is allowed full reign here, since no law enforcement agency exists. In a 1980 symposium on post-holocaust literature, Yarbro warned feminists away from the idea that a holocaust, "even a mini-holocaust," would be a welcome way to start with a clean slate and begin to establish female equality. Once anything like that occurs, she declared, history shows that "any small rights that you may have had for anyone but the physically strongest are gone, kaput, zowie. You do not see them again. If you want to be reduced to a state of chattel again . . . the best thing you can do is to get yourself a holocaust, even a small one. You're going to find out how it feels to earn your bread on your back." Thea is spared that fate, but she is raped once, quite brutally, and the scar that remains is a major block to her acceptance of Evan's love for her.

Man's stupidity is the cause, in some way that is left vague, of the pollution and radioactivity of the planet. Yarbro's lack of confidence in the human race is evident in the fact that no hope whatever is offered. The hope implied in a dawn is here inevitably and always false. This hopelessness and cynicism is best for those who are embittered anyway, and love gloomy affirmations of their bias.

Techniques

John Clute, writing in the *Magazine of Fantasy and Science Fiction,* was very critical of Yarbro's decision to expand this story into a novel. In the short story, he noted, the rape of Thea and the rape of the land "model each other effectively," but the effect is lost when the novel drags out for many more pages, episodic in nature and "shambling."

Related Titles

The Time of the Fourth Horseman, (1976), is an apocalyptic novel concerning the Modest-Proposal-style decision of some Doctors at The Top to kill off the excess population by using placebos for one third of all the vaccinations for diphtheria and typhoid and such illnesses. Of course epidemics rage and the diseases mutate into unstoppable forms. Horrors dominate. Spider Robinson, in *Galaxy,* charged the author with appealing to one's paranoia—"You're *supposed* to walk away from it horrified and afraid and ashamed to be human and frustrated to despair at your helplessness before the Great Conspiracy of Evil Ones In Power, and I say phooey."

Other Titles

Historical Fiction: *Ariosto Furioso, A Romance for An Alternate Renaissance,* 1980 (novel); *The Godforsaken,* 1983 (novel); *A Mortal Glamour,* 1985 (novel); *To the High Redoubt,* 1985 (novel).

Modern Occult or Science Fiction: *Dead and Buried,* 1980 (novelization of screenplay by Ronald Shusset and Dan O'Bannon); *Sins of Omission,* 1980 (novel);

Hyacinths, 1983 (novel); *Nomads,* 1984 (novelization of a screenplay by John McTiernan).

Detective: *Ogilvie, Tallant, and Moon,* 1976 (novel); *Music When Sweet Voices Die,* 1979 (novel). These both feature Charlie Spotted Moon, Ojibwa lawyer.

Spiritualist: *Messages from Michael,* 1979 (transcripts of Ouija board messages from a spirit contacted through a medium Yarbro has known and attended seances with for nine years previous to the publication of this book). *More Messages from Michael,* 1986.

Young Adult/Historical Fiction: *Locadio's Apprentice,* 1984 (novel); *Four Horses for Tishtry,* 1985 (novel).

Short Story Collections: *Cautionary Tales,* 1978 (stories); *Signs and Portents,* 1984 (stories).

Drama—Children: "The Little-girl Dragon of Alabaster-on-Fenwick" 1973 (satiric fairytale play).

Music: *Save Me A Place by the Rail,* year unknown but pre-1977 (on opera). "Stabat Mater" "Sayre Cycle" "Alpha and Omega" "Cinque Ritratti" "Nightpiece for Chamber Orchestra"

Other: "Wonder Woman," *Berkeley Barb,* June 10-16, 1977 (interview); "No Such Thing as Tearing Down just a Little," *Janus,* Winter 1980 (panel participant); "Songs Sweet and Haunting," *Foundation,* Spring 1985 (interview); "Imaginary Homework," *Writer,* February 1986.

Additional Sources

Clute, John, "Books," *The Magazine of Fantasy and Science Fiction,* 56, 1 (January 1979): 45-52. A review article on *False Dawn* which concentrates on the problem of changing a short story into the first chapter of a novel. Comments on Yarbro's intent while questioning the artistic value of changing the relationship of every word and image when she alters the work from an integral whole to an introductory section. Clute finds the plot too episodic, a charge that has been directed at a number of Yarbro's works.

Rix, Gretchen, Review of *False Dawn, Science Fiction Review,* 8, 1 (January-February 1979): 47. Points out that the novel *False Dawn* is an expansion of a short story first found in *Strange Bedfellows,* edited by T.N. Scortia. Rix comments that the run of Thea and Evan is the whole story, and that the plot relies upon "gimmicky villains" who turn on the two. This is the major flaw in the novel. The work is not a novel of characterization, but a "graphic, fast, violent and tragic look at a futile journey."

Shwartz, Susan M., Review of the Saint-Germaine series, *Washington Post Book World* (March 28, 1982). Schwartz discusses the Saint-Germaine series, saying that they broke every canon of the "classic 1950's" science fiction by combining genres and breaking taboos. The result is a product that is difficult to categorize but exciting to read. The central character in particular has an "almost tragic dignity."

Winter, Douglas E., *Shadowings: The Reader's Guide to Horror Fiction: 1981-1982*, Starmont Series in Literary Criticism, vol. I. San Bernardino, CA: The Borgo Press, 1984. This is a collection of short essays, some by Winter and reprinted from *Fantasy Newsletter,* of which he is the Interviews Editor. In an introductory essay he ranks Yarbro's vampire novels as "the best" and "certainly the most romantic" of the genre. In a forum of interviews on "Horror and the Limits of Violence" that included Yarbro and six other authors, she commented that it was the appropriateness of and necessity for the violence that was the real point, and not its degree. When it is used to reveal character, as with Norman Bates in *Psycho,* or is intrinsic to the plot, as with the blinding in *Oedipus Rex,* it is vital to the work. For this reason, the artist, not the censor, should decide what type or degree of violence belongs in a given work.

Kay Kinsella Rout
Michigan State University

FRANK G. YERBY
1916

Publishing History

Yerby showed early signs of creativity at Paine College, Augusta, where he started writing poetry and short stories, which appeared in little magazines such as *Chard*, *Challenge*, and *Arts Quarterly*. James Weldon Johnson, the famous black writer, encouraged Yerby to continue his literary efforts after seeing some of his early pieces. Another positive influence was his mentor, Emma C. W. Grey, a Paine faculty member, in collaboration with whom he wrote "March On," an historical commemoration of Paine's fiftieth anniversary and a history of black America. Yerby began by publishing protest stories in the 1930s and early 1940s, achieving first national recognition with "Health Card," a short story which won the O. Henry Memorial Award for a first published story in 1944. In fact, his initial recognition came through several stories of social protest, the most prominent being "My Brother Went to College," "White Magnolias," and "The Homecoming," all dealing with the plight of the Negro in America. As is the case with most writers, Yerby's attempts to make headway in the literary field were not smoothly successful. So disheartened was he by the rejection of his first novel, submitted for competition to *Red Book Magazine*, that he supposedly burned the manuscript.

From there he turned his attention to popular historical fiction, a mode he has been following ever since. This change in direction also reflected Yerby's desire to escape the trap of racially conscious fiction and in practical terms, because he himself felt the pangs of everyday racism, particularly in the South, and in America in general, he did not wish to relive these experiences in his fiction. This also explains Yerby's decision to live permanently in Spain. Yerby is not the first black author to write novels with historical bent. Lorenzo D. Jackson, Paul L. Dunbar, W. E. DuBois, Arna Bontemps have all used historical facts in their works, but Yerby avoids overt racial propaganda in his novels. Instead, he utilizes the vernacular of popular historical fiction and writes predominantly about white people (with blacks as props or minor characters as "good Negroes"), for mainly white audiences. There is a continuing debate as to whether his works contain an underlying concern with the question of race. Although his early work was critically acclaimed amongst black intellectuals, he was later excoriated for abandoning direct black themes. He was charged as being a 'homo economicus,' i.e., writing "immoral trash" simply to make money. But in some sense, the "raceless" novels are the prototype of society he would like America to be. Those critics who believe such a concern is present, point to the fact that there is a continuing thematic link between his early protest stories, written in the vein of Richard Wright, and *The Foxes of Harrow*, his first novel, published in 1946. *The Foxes of Harrow* was an immediate overwhelming success, followed by more than twenty-five such works, each selling over a million copies. Yerby's works have been selected by various book clubs, among them the Literary Guild, Dollar Book Club, the Fiction Book Club and Book of the Month Club.

Critical Reception, Honors, and Popularity

According to Russell B. Nye, *The Unembarrassed Muse*, Yerby ranks as one of the five most popular writers of the second half of the twentieth century. He is the first black writer to ever experience such financial and popular success. In the South, interest in Yerby runs as high as in William Faulkner, Margaret Mitchell and Tennessee Williams. His work has consistently figured on the best seller lists (more than eight times), with combined total sales of all his novels both in hard cover and paperback exceeding fifty million copies. It has been translated into fourteen languages. In 1986 *The Foxes of Harrow* was reprinted by Delacorte; to date it has sold over three million copies, while *Vixens* and *Pride's Castle* have also each sold over three million. Yerby's success as a popular fiction writer is attributed to the magic formula and philosophy of art which he fashioned for himself and of which he made constant use. His self-avowed intention is "to instruct, to entertain and to set straight readers' historical perspective" because historical themes dealing with Negro history, the Civil War South and the Reconstruction Era have been distorted. At the same time, Yerby avoids racially conscious writing since he is neither a sociologist nor a preacher. Instead, "the novelist must try to write with a universality of appeal so that it hits all segments of the people."

As far as the critics are concerned, while some praise him for his prolific output, others condemn him for his prolixity, his "superficial research, freshman grammar, comic-book characterization, melodramatic plotting, escapism, perpetuation of stereotypes and betrayal of his Negritude." However, Yerby's latest novels have been praised for his accurate historical research. Yerby's answers to the critics' charge of spurious historical material is that he himself rejects the label "historical" since his editors remove "ninety-nine and ninety-nine one-hundredths" percent of the historical material. Of all Yerby's novels, *The Dahomean* is the only one which deals with a black African historic figure, but the critics have found its pace sluggish and have faulted it for "excessive anthropological detail," but overall, others have found this to be his best work, with "great sympathy, seriousness and control." His latest works, showing promise of maturity, deal with themes related to the universal condition and experience of humanity. Some critics are of the opinion that his future works will truly represent the man and his philosophy.

Yerby's creative efforts have been acknowledged by academic institutions in the form of an Honorary Doctorate Degree from Paine College in 1977.

Analysis of Selected Titles

THE FOXES OF HARROW
The Foxes of Harrow, 1946, novel. Sequel: *The Vixens*, 1947, novel.

Social Concerns/Themes

The Foxes of Harrow, like most of Yerby's novels, concerns itself with specific Southern social issues. Most prominent among these is the importance of social position, which, because of the influence of the aristocratic mentality, must be attained by the protagonist, regardless of personal cost, by fair means or foul. This particular aspect of Southern life takes its roots from the background of the Southern world, in which gentlemen's duels, gallant deeds and lovely ladies tend to predominate. In addition, the decay of Southern social manorial patterns is strongly delineated. In this respect, Yerby is repudiating the notion of the Southern aristocracy, its so-called heroism, its ancestry, chivalry and its sterling character. Stephen Fox, the protagonist of *The Foxes of Harrow* personifies the hollow, unsavory character of the aristocrat of the South.

The Foxes of Harrow historically covers the years 1825 to 1865. The rakish Stephen Fox is a twenty-one-year-old illegitimate Irish immigrant to Philadelphia who treads the road from rags to riches and back to rags again when Harrow, his Southern plantation, falls on hard times. Naked ambition prompts him at the age of twenty-five to go South where he is befriended by Andre Le Blanc, a French Creole, and by other aristocrats. Fox's ambition is to join the ranks of the local aristocracy, thereby realizing his version of the American Dream. As an outsider, Fox holds no respect for Creole culture. He disapproves of the Creole-black relationships, except in the context of slavery, which he fully exploits to make his fortune. Thus the confidence man/swindler begins his imperial designs. Through connivance and chicanery he marries Odalie Arceneaux, daughter of a Creole aristocrat and acquires two huge plantations replete with slaves. His ill-begotten gains give him entrance to the New Orleans aristocracy. At the peak of his fortune, he has become one of the wealthiest of the Southern plantation owners. However, his marriage proves disastrous and he must seek solace in the arms of Desiree, a New Orleans quadroon. Personal tragedy and unhappiness mar Fox's life and despite his huge wealth, happiness eludes him. His social acceptance has cost him dearly. Thus Yerby debunks the myth of the superiority of the Southern aristocracy.

Prominent themes in *The Foxes of Harrow* are to be found throughout Yerby's canon: the protagonist, an outsider of low birth and shady character, makes his money through exploitation of slaves. In spite of his riches and power, he is hated and attains no permanent happiness or wealth. Thus, the theme of alienation figures strongly. Fox's wife, Odalie, dies alienated and unloved.

Frank Yerby has been known for his political stand as far as overtly racist issues are concerned, but in *The Foxes of Harrow*, as in *Floodtide*, Yerby touches a very sensitive social nerve in the South. The issue of slavery is very much evident in this novel. As an outsider, Stephen Fox does not fully understand that complex institution from which he reaps his profits. He tends to condemn the illicit relationship between the aristocrats and the slaves, but although many would not admit it, this illicit relationship is a centuries-old part of the fabric of Southern life. Stephen Fox would very much like to defy an entrenched Southern law forbidding literacy of slaves. He allows Inchcliff, one of his slaves, not only to read but to borrow books from Fox's personal library. He would have sanctioned the manumission of his slaves if a Georgian law had not prohibited this action until the master's death. Fox's attitude stands in direct contrast to that of his own son, Etienne, a confirmed racist.

Another pertinent social concern that Yerby addresses is the action of genuine and false aristocracy and respectability. While Stephen Fox's disreputable background buys his way into New Orleans aristocracy, the captured African princess, La Belle Sauvage, is ironically his slave. Even though infidelity, swindling and cheating are universal traits, all contribute to the picture of the nature of life in this sanctimonious Southern society. Again, the hypocrisy of Southerners, aristocracy included, is a recurring concern in the works of many contemporary Southern writers such as Flannery O'Connor.

Characters

The Yerbian costume-fiction formula—first introduced in 1946 with *The Foxes of Harrow*—reappears in virtually all subsequent twenty-six novels. As far as characterization is concerned, a handsome blonde or red-haired protagonist, usually an outcast by choice or circumstances, always figures as the Yerby hero or heroine. Of course, a villainous antagonist opposes this central figure. The third constant element in terms of characterization consists of the loyal companion, who understands and assists the protagonist. A bevy of beauties, male or female, depending on the gender of the protagonist, possessing a variety of attributes, are in love with the protagonist. Plebian figures, usually blacks or poor whites, slaves or serfs, oppressed by society, complete the standard cast of characters.

Generally, Yerby wants a mutually cordial relationship between major and minor characters. Though his popularity stems from the manipulation of his plot and the treatment of subject matter of his costume novels in their settings, Yerby has created some very memorable and unique characters in his works. Most of these characters (major and minor) naturally follow his formulaic stipulations. Hugh Gloster sums up the qualities of a typical Yerby hero/heroine: the hero is usually bold, handsome, rakish, honorable, willful. Then, in contrast is a frigid, respectable wife, or a torrid, anything but respectable, mistress.

In addition to the protagonist, other memorable characters populate Yerby's novels. They are drawn from a wide cross-section of the American ethnic population, thus giving the "melting-pot" concept a real literary meaning. Interestingly, most of these characters have fanciful names, Fancy, Inch, etc., with dynamic and vigorous personalities. In the novels, whites generally are depicted as irresponsible, villainous, malicious people, while blacks are portrayed as "idealized victims of a savage White-dominated caste system." While the blacks are idealized dreamers, strangers and serfs in the white man's world, their role is that of victim rather than partaker. An obvious exception to this is in *Judas, My Brother* where a black chieftain of a Dahomean Empire is autocratic, and malevolent. What Yerby here indicates is that a human being, regardless of color, can be either benevolent or wicked and even blacks in power have no guarantee of saintliness.

The characters in *The Foxes of Harrow, The Vixens, Floodtide, A Woman Called Fancy* and *McKenzie's Hundred* should be examined in the light of Yerby's own costume formula already defined above. Yerby may be the "Prince of Pulpsters," interested in sexy romances, but most readers would agree that Stephen Fox is an omnipotent, omniscient figure. Judged by the formulaic pattern for a Yerbyian protagonist, Stephen Fox fits perfectly into his slot. He is diabolical, wild, deceitful, a ladies' man, a true manipulator of people. In fact, the critic Nathan Rothman describes him as a reincarnation, in one body, of Lucifer, D'Artagnan, Frank Merriwell and Superman. This is quite a combination indeed. No wonder that Stephen Fox becomes the tycoon of New Orleans society. Such a cunning character can never lose. He had the best of everything—women, slaves, plantations—but in typical Yerby fashion these brought him no happiness.

Even the portrayals of ladies of Creole society, the quadroons, and the blacks, who play minor roles in the story, are just as alive as the leading characters. In *The Foxes of Harrow* these minor figures are not cardboard stereotypes as some critics believe. Some are vital ladies, gentlemen, mistresses, monarchs of all they survey. Many of the blacks are people with dignity and honor. Usually black characters in American letters (and perhaps in American life) are traditionally condemned to play second fiddle, to do only menial tasks in accordance with their assigned role in life: domestics, laborers, handymen or even carriers of water and perpetrators of foul deeds; in other words, what Fanon refers to as "the wretched of the earth." In *The Foxes of Harrow* and many of the other Yerby novels, Yerby tried to change the negative image of the American black. Whether or not they suffer slavery or lynchings, the black characters' humanity is never sacrificed. Milton Hughes explains Yerby's philosophy in the delineation of black characters in his novels when he says that: "Yerby insists, rightly so, on presenting the Negro as an unusual person of stature and dignity, in some cases, despite the shackles of slavery. He is keen on giving the psychology behind the rejection of Black people."

The portraiture of the character Inch, Etienne's Negro servant, in *The Foxes of Harrow* is a clear example of Yerby's pro-black stance in characterization. Inch is outstanding as a character and as a scholar-politician. Being book-oriented from the start, he learned to read by using Stephen Fox's library. The autodidactic Inch became one of the leading Negro politicians of the Reconstruction Era despite the activities of such hate groups as the KKK. In the delineation of Inch in *The Foxes of*

Harrow Yerby attempts to raise the position of the Negro who had traditionally occupied the lowest layer in the social strata but again he did not create a superman figure, in contrast to the white protagonist, Stephen Fox. The aristocracy and dubious origin of the gentry stands in sharp contrast to the nobility of birth of several of the Negro slaves. At the same time, Yerby skillfully explodes the myth of the true nobility of Southern aristocracy: the values which created the rise of Stephen Fox from rags to riches are a direct criticism of the legend of Southern gentility. A dishonest gambler and entrepreneur, he marries into the Arcenaux family for position and power. Thus he begets Etienne to establish a lineage, and in the fashion of a typical Yerby hero, seduces Desiree (a quadroon) and creates a very complex interrelationship between himself and his women, ultimately leading to his downfall.

In sharp contrast to his father, the white racist Etienne Fox appears in a very bad light. While Stephen still subscribes to the Southern ideas of the moral and mental inferiority of the Negro, he perceives the Negroes as human beings, even if they are slaves. He is kind to them and is comparatively liberal in his political ideas. He is critical of Southern attitudes, including even the practice of slavery. But to sympathize with the slaves is one thing; to go against this cherished institution is another. For this reason, Stephen cannot contravene Southern law and manumit his slaves while he is still alive. He also shows a genuine concern and doubts whether premature freedom for Negroes will do them any good: "Perhaps it would be only the greatest unkindness to free the Negro—he would be helpless without a kindly, guiding hand." In contrast to his son, Stephen Fox is more of an enlightened gentleman and Southern slave owner.

Another set of contrasting characters in *The Foxes of Harrow* consists of Etienne and of Inch, the slave, who grew up together on Harrow. The contrast between these two is fully explored in *The Vixens*, a sequel to *The Foxes of Harrow*. Inch is of noble birth, being the son of LaBelle Sauvage, an African princess sold into slavery. Her fighting spirit is inherited by her son, Inch, who also inherits his grandparents' love of freedom. Inch creates for himself the opportunity to study law at the University of Paris (perhaps the Sorbonne?) and his letters home to Harrow are far superior to those of Etienne, who is also away from Harrow, in France. Upon his return from Paris, Inch, having seen the benefits of personal freedom, yearns greatly to set himself free. He bitterly complains to Caleen that he cannot "belong to Etienne like his horse, . . ." He wants his freedom as an individual human being and to be responsible for his own destiny. Upon Caleen's death due to the yellow fever plague, Inch escapes to Boston. There he meets Frederick Douglass, Wendell Phillips, Theodore Parker and Thomas Wentworth Higginson. Unfortunately, he is recaptured and taken back South as Etienne's slave. At the end of the Civil War, Inch becomes a very important politician and the Police Commissioner, assuming the name Cyrus M. Inchcliff. Yerby has reversed traditional roles, with subordinates becoming masters. True aristocracy thus reasserts itself. Even in death Etienne and Inch are contrasted, with Inch dying as a true hero while Etienne dies ignominiously as president of one of the hated white supremacy groups. The downfall of the protagonist and the glorificaiion of the subordinate character have been described amongst scenes of lust and passion, scandal, and decadence. Immorality has helped to seal the fate of the Foxes. While Stephen Fox was flagrantly violating all laws of Southern ethics, and while Etienne even rapes Desiree, his father's former mistress, Cecilia Fox, Etienne's wife, conducts an affair at the hospital with her physician, Dr. Shane. Such a mixture of romance and serious historical drama make Yerby's readers yearn for more such soap opera-like episodes, and ensure continuing popular success.

There are not many woman protagonists in the novels. Most prominent are Fancy in *A Woman Called Fancy* and Rose Ann McKenzie, the first-class spy in *McKenzie's Hundred*. They both conform to the typical Yerbian protagonist's formula.

Techniques

The Yerbian technique follows the very accepted conventional tradition used by the most popular writers in American letters. Yerby's popularity can partially be explained by his manipulation of subject matter in which he explores the themes of everyday life seen from an historical and contemporary perspective. More importantly, he dwells on the sexual fantasies of most ordinary people and tries to captivate the essence of the concrete daily course of love with its romance and taboos. Taking into consideration his avowed aim as a novelist in teaching and entertaining, Yerby succeeds in doing this by using parody and melodrama, satire and irony to bring forth his message. In this way, Yerby illustrates the follies of humankind, to show man as a romantic being and to debunk social and spiritual institutions, and to condemn war. Yerby uses the picaresque or episodic tradition, as represented in *Tom Jones*, *Moll Flanders*, and *Joseph Andrews*, which affords him the opportunity to rapidly shift both scenes and themes from one place to the other and from one historical epoch to another.

The portrayal of the picaro is also part of Yerby's technique, a mode specifically learned from the European model. The portrayal of the Yerbian protagonist also follows a specific pattern and all the protagonists throughout the novels, from *The Foxes of Harrow* to *McKenzie's Hundred*, follow this pattern consistently. Yerby himself has said he wishes to undertake the writing of serious novels on serious themes. Whether this new trend will depart from the magic Yerbian formula is still to be seen.

The protagonist is the chief link in the series of adventures in the plot, and part of the plot includes the corruption of a young person by a deceitful world in either a contemporary everyday setting or in an historical milieu. Part of the plot often touches on accepted values which the characters either accept or reject conditionally.

The ingredients of the popular Yerbian hero are always connected with an individual of low birth and disreputable background, a protagonist who attempts to eke out a respectable living for himself through all sorts of dubious means: begging, deception or petty theft. The protagonists most often have suspicious views concerning romance, love and marriage; more specifically, they see love and marriage as sorts of snares, but use them as a ladder to climb to higher social standing.

Another technique Yerby employs is the idea of the anti-hero, a readily identifiable individual, usually a character with no social standing let loose upon respectable society. By fair or foul means, the individual wins a place for himself, influences events and manipulates people. This particular notion runs through all Yerby's novels, from the first to the latest. Interestingly, the concept of the hero in literature changes as the centuries go by. In Greek and Roman literature, the heroes were god men; in medieval times men of God, in the Renaissance universal men, in the nineteenth century gentlemen and in the twentieth century the hero has been reduced to the anti-hero. Stephen Fox of *The Foxes of Harrow* embodies all the characteristics of the modern concept of the hero in American literature.

Characterization cuts across the melting-pot. Again, what the characters try to do reflects generally on the foibles of humanity. Even though the essence of the story might be limited to a parochial study of a particular group, the overall effect is an illustration of the foibles of humanity in a particular situation.

One interesting technique that Yerby employs in most of his novels is that of authorial commentary, or intrusions. Often, where Yerby has very strong views on a particular point, he projects his loud thinking into the text and addresses the reader directly. He does this in the novels dealing with the South where he tries to debunk the cultural barreness, widespread illiteracy, hollow aristocratic values, political corruption, slavery, and racism.

This love of commentary often leads to flamboyant rhetoric and bombastic style. The use of foreign words and phrases, italicized and capitalized letters abounds in Yerby's novels. This adds to the exotic flavor of the text.

Literary Precedents

Yerby's *The Foxes of Harrow* is usually compared with Margaret Mitchell's best seller, *Gone with the Wind*. Both are historical Southern novels, using the Civil War as the background, and both have similar characterization and events. In terms of technique, both employ a touch of satire. *Gone with the Wind* has a Southern belle, Scarlett O'Hara, as protagonist, who· struggles to maintain the ancestral home against overwhelming odds after the defeat of the South. Of course, Yerby's protagonist in *The Foxes of Harrow* is an Irish immigrant of dubious character, obviously not a true aristocrat. Like Stephen Fox, Scarlett O'Hara and Rhett Butler must struggle to overcome adversity in order to be accepted amongst aristocratic society. Both Fox and Butler are dishonest, alienated from society, although Fox's alienation stems from his plebian origins and Rhett Butler has been disinherited by his family in Charleston. But Rhett Butler rejects the aristocratic privileges which Stephen Fox craves. Both characters, however, are critical of Southern values and mores, and both tend to hold very unpopular political views. Though Rhett Butler reluctantly fights in the Civil War, Stephen Fox is against the secession of the South. At the end of the war, Butler leaves the South, while Stephen realizes that the old Southern aristocratic values and way of life are forever doomed.

Tyler Meredith, the protagonist of Yerby's *Captain Rebel*, can also be compared with the figure of Rhett Butler. Both attended military academies, with Butler being booted out of West Point, and both accumulated their wealth as illegal blockade-runners. Like Stephen Fox, Meredith becomes a liberal after the war and refuses to join the racist organization, called the New Orleans' White Man's Protective Association. Instead, filled with remorse, he builds a school for black children in honor of a Negro slave, Fred Peters, whom he had injured years before.

Related Titles

The major themes and social concerns throughout Yerby's writing, from the early short stories to *McKenzie's Hundred*, deal with issues of romance and the warfare of the sexes, the Civil War and Reconstruction, racism, inferiority, slavery, religion (evil, man's relationship with God, man against himself), poor whites, and the decaying Southern aristocracy. Other themes include life in ancient Greece, free will versus fate, societal alienation, illegitimacy, and the problems of human beings irrespective of race, color or religion.

Racism and slave trade are recurring themes. Since *The Foxes of Harrow* is set in the era of the Civil War, Yerby mentions especially the massacre of Negroes at Fort Pillow, while further debunking the image of the fearless, heroic, Confederate fighter. However, it is the novel *Floodtide* (1950) that devoted itself to a full examination of this theme.

While in *The Vixens* Yerby refers to the racist activities of the various hate groups of New Orleans, the KKK, the Knights of the White Camellia (a particularly cruel and powerful organization), who surface to perpetrate atrocities against the minority groups, in *Floodtide*, he deals concretely with the source of the slave trade in Africa and its attendant cruelties. A further ironic note in *Floodtide* concerns two black slaves arguing about their respective costs and the importance of their masters, until Brutus, another Negro, points out the folly of their attitude. The protagonist of *Floodtide*, Guy Falks, is a notorious slave trader residing in Africa. He despises even the local chief and refuses to shake his hand because "in Mississippi, Sir, we don't shake hands with niggers." In the novel *Benton's Row* (1954), Yerby describes the pogrom against the Negro soldiers after the Civil War.

Other themes and social concerns include infidelity and Caribbean piracy in *The Golden Hawk*, and in *Pride's Castle* (1949) railroad and labor problems in New York in the 1890s, Cuban revolution, pre-Civil War Georgia, secession politics, political corruption, Yerbian romance and intrigue (complete with duels, illicit love and brutal assaults), and miscegenation (as in *A Woman Called Fancy*). Lynching concludes the list of Yerbian themes. In *The Serpent and the Staff*, a white mob attempts to lynch the black man Mose Johnson, when he performs a tracheotomy on a white child stricken with diptheria. Unused to such medical procedures, the whites misunderstand Johnson's motives. Subsequently, black killings in the area proliferate. Where all these related themes seem to meet is in the portrayal of Stephen Fox (in *Foxes of Harrow*) and Tom Benton (in *Benton's Row*). *Benton's Row*, set in nineteenth-century Louisiana, depicts the adventures of Tom Benton, who escapes a Texas posse. In typical Yerbian fashion, the rakish Benton seduces and dispossesses the minister's wife, driving her husband to suicide. He makes religion his business, fakes confession in public at the Protracted Meeting for the Salvation of Sinners and is eventually accepted into respectable society through an act of mercy. Like Stephen Fox, he becomes very wealthy, a plantation owner, gets away with murder and conducts numerous illicit affairs. At a ripe old age, he dies, still amassing illegal wealth. Wade Benton, an even more thorough rogue, his son, succeeds him. Wade becomes the local leader of the Knights of the White Camellias. Thus Yerby depicts another opportunist, a ruthless, frivolous, immoral, dishonorable anti-hero, like Stephen Fox, in *The Foxes of Harrow*. Both men sire renegade, racist sons and both men end up lamenting their lot as alienated, unhappy outcasts.

In the words of Tom Benton, "I was a stranger and alone in my house that I built. I wandered, an alien guest across the sweep of the fields I had stolen, bought, acquired. I belong to no time and to no people. I believe in my superiority." In the same vein, Stephen Fox commiserates with himself in the following words, "I have a house, the greatest in the state, in which I am hated. I have a son, but he is strange and wild towards me. I have much wealth, but no happiness." Thus, both Tom Benton and Stephen Fox have sons who hated and despised their parents.

Judas My Brother: The Story of the Thirteenth Disciple is one of the most significant works in the Yerbian canon. It raises several themes and social issues connected with a very touchy subject, affecting man as a religious being, man as homo sapiens. It concerns the issue of religion in general and the doctrine of Christianity in particular. The theme here expounded is the origins of Christianity and Christian myths. According to one critic, these are the most important Yerbian themes. In some ways, the novel also charts the course of Christianity and can then be seen as a documentary history of the religion. Scaap, touching on the controversial theme of the novel, believes that Yerby wrote *Judas My Brother* "in a rage; it is an attack upon blind faith, in some ways an indictment of Jesus, in some ways a justification of Judas."

Adaptations

Yerby's novels have been adapted for the screen with great popular success. *The Foxes of Harrow*, 1947 Fox Studios; *The Golden Hawk*, 1952 Columbia Pictures. *Pride's Castle* was adapted as a TV presentation.

Other Titles

The Golden Hawk, 1948 (novel); *Pride's Castle*, 1949 (novel); *The Saracen Blade*, 1952 (novel); *The Devil's Laughter*, 1953 (novel); *Bride of Liberty*, 1954 (novel); *The Treasure of Pleasant Valley*, 1955 (novel); *Captain Rebel*, 1956 (novel); *Fairoaks*, 1957 (novel); *The Serpent and the Staff*, 1958 (novel); *Jarrett's Jade*, 1959 (novel); *Gillian*, 1960 (novel); *The Garfield Honor*, 1961 (novel); *Griffin's Way*, 1962 (novel); *The Old Gods Laugh: A Modern Romance*, 1964 (novel); *An Odor of Sanctity*, 1965 (novel); *Goat Song: A Novel of Ancient Greece*, 1967 (novel); *Speak Now*, 1969 (novel); *The Dahomean*, 1971, published in London as *Dahomey* (novel); *The Girl from Storyville: A Victorian Novel*, 1972 (novel); *The Voyage Unplanned*, 1974 (novel); *Tobias and the Angel*, 1974 (novel); *A Rose for Ana Maria*, 1976 (novel); *Hail the Conquering Hero*, 1977 (novel); *A Darkness at Ingraham's Crest*, 1979 (novel).

Additional Sources

Bone, Robert, *The Negro Novel in America*. New Haven, CT: Yale University Press, 1965. An historical and critical study of the fiction of black American authors.

Cash, Wilbur J., *The Mind of the South*. New York: Knopf, 1941. A background study of the South—its people, its history, cultures and institutions.

Fishwick, Marshall, *The Hero: American Style*. New York: McKay, 1969. Explores the concept of the hero in American literature.

Gloster, Hugh M., "The Significance of Frank Yerby," *Crisis*, 55 (1948): 12-13. Yerby's role and importance as a black author.

Hill, James Lee, "Anti-heroic Perspectives: The Life and Works of Frank Yerby." Ph.D. Dissertation, University of Iowa, 1976. A general survey of Yerby's works in relation to the hero.

Hill, Werdna, Jr., "Behind the Magnolia Mask: Frank Yerby as Critic of the South." M.A. Thesis, Auburn University, 1973. A critique of Yerby's novels and short stories dealing with racial issues in the South. Attests and documents that Yerby is not a "raceless novelist" as most critics believe.

Leisy, Ernest, *The American Historical Novel*. Norman, OK: University of Oklahoma Press, 1950. A general survey of the American historical novelist.

Nye, Russell B., *The Unembarrassed Muse*. New York: Dial Press, 1970. An historical survey of major forms of popular arts (including literature) in America, in their socio-cultural milieu.

Rothe, Ann, "Frank Yerby," *Current Biography*. New York: Wilson, 1947. A biographical sketch of Frank Yerby. Emphasis on his early life and works.

Turner, Darwin T., "Frank Yerby as Debunker," *Massachusetts Review* (Summer 1968): 569-577. A thematic study of Yerby's novels dealing with his refutation of Caucasian racial superiority and other prevalent myths.

"The Negro Novelist and the South," *Southern Humanities Review*, 1 (1967): 21-29. The South as a theme and setting for black authors, including Yerby.

K. Amoabeng
C. Lasker
State University of New York
at Stony Brook

ROGER ZELAZNY
1937

Publishing History

Roger Zelazny published his first stories, "Passion Play" and "Horseman", in 1962. But it was the publication of "A Rose for Ecclesiastes" in the July, 1963 issue of *The Magazine of Fantasy and Science Fiction* that captured critical and popular attention. In the first few years of his career he sold short stories at an astonishing rate for such a small market, occasionally using the pseudonym Harrison Denmark to disguise the frequency of his contributions to a particular magazine. In 1966 he began publishing novels as well, and since 1969, when he quit the Social Security Administration to write full time, he has concentrated more on novels than on short fiction. He has now published more than twenty novels and six collections of his shorter pieces. In 1985 he published *The Trumps of Doom,* first in a trilogy that will apparently follow-up on one of his biggest successes, the five "Amber" novels.

Critical Reception, Honors, and Popularity

Zelazny enjoyed one of the most spectacular debuts of any American science fiction and fantasy writer. Within a very few years of his first publication he was being hailed by critics, fans, and fellow writers as one of the best writers in his field—one of a handful who were breathing new life into science fiction. Advocates of a literature which had yet to win serious critical respect proudly pointed to Zelazny—singling out his style for special praise. His stories were poetic, witty, filled with learned allusions, studded with odd but apt metaphors and dialogue that recalled Jacobean blank verse in one sentence and East Village slang in the next. Critics and reviewers were also fascinated with his frequently brilliant adaptations of mythic stories and characters. While some critics grumbled (and continue to grumble) that Zelazny simply stole and rewrote tales from classical and eastern mythology, other critics have defended Zelazny, arguing that he uses those myths as an effective way of grappling with timeless human concerns—mortality, mutability, and the possibility of human enlightenment.

Zelazny has often been identified as a member of the "New Wave," a group of science fiction writers in the 1960's and early 1970's who were perceived as rebelling against the traditional themes and techniques of science fiction. While there was not, in fact, any coherent literary movement, nor any absolute break with earlier science fiction, the label "New Wave," used cautiously, has some critical value, for it does help to identify concerns and techniques common to a number of writers, including J. G. Ballard, Samuel R. Delany, Harlan Ellison, and Zelazny. They brought to science fiction a new artistic self-consciousness; an awareness of the literary mainstream; a willingness to experiment with style, structure, and subject matter; a concern with precision of language rather than scientific accuracy; and a tendency to explore human consciousness—often through myth, symbol, and archetype—rather than outer space. Zelazny has shared most of these characteristics throughout his career, and he has been among the most popular and influential of these writers.

Given the intensity of the early praise, it is not too surprising that Zelazny's star has dimmed somewhat in the last few years. Critics and reviewers occasionally compare his recent work unfavorably with his earlier stories. Others suggest that he has started to repeat himself, or that the pressure of being a full-time writer has led him to rush novels into print without sufficient thought or revision. A few critics have suggested that his style conceals a lack of substance or even that his poetic prose is frequently strained or overdone. Nevertheless, he remains a popular and respected writer, one who may well have many more years of productive work. But it is fair to say that both his popularity and his critical reputation are to a great extent confined to the science fiction and fantasy field. He has yet to win much recognition outside that considerable but limited world.

Zelazny is among the most honored of American science fiction writers. The Science Fiction Writers of America have awarded him three Nebulas—for the novellas "He Who Shapes," 1965 (in a tie with Brian Aldiss's "The Saliva Tree") and "Home is the Hangman," 1975, and for the novelette "The Doors of His Face, The Lamps of His Mouth," 1965. Readers have voted him three Hugo awards (Science Fiction Achievement Awards) for the novels . . . *And Call Me Conrad*, 1966 (in a tie with Frank Herbert's *Dune*), and *Lord of Light*, 1968, and for the novella "Home Is the Hangman," 1976. Zelazny has also won the French Science Fiction Award, the Prix Apollo, for *Isle of the Dead*, 1972, and he has been nominated many other times for Hugos and Nebulas. His work has been translated into the major European languages and into Japanese.

Analysis of Selected Titles

LORD OF LIGHT
Lord of Light, 1967, novel.

Social Concerns
At first glance, *Lord of Light* might seem a novel devoid of any social concern. Certainly it lacks the themes readers usually associate with science fiction—awful warnings about technology run amok, over-population, nuclear war, or ecological disaster. Its premise suggests highly imaginative escapist fare. In the remote future a ship filled with colonists from earth reaches a distant planet. The crew, armed with remarkably advanced technology, has conquered the natives and established itself as a virtually immortal ruling elite, lording it over classes of servants, peas-

ants, and artisans descended from the original colonists. To strengthen their hold over the masses, the former crew members have used their technological skills to assume godlike powers and personas, drawn from Hindu mythology. They become "gods" and rule over a populace denied education, technology, and freedom. One of the "gods" rebels against this static, hierarchical society, and the readers are treated to a spectacular war of the gods.

Yet even such a plot summary begins to suggest the levels of social concern. The novel is about a rebellion against a stagnant, repressive society, about an attempt to liberate people from the chains of ignorance and superstition imposed on them by arrogant leaders. The setting is indeed exotic, but a novel of revolution doubtless struck a chord in many readers—especially during the 1960s. The "gods" want to maintain the status quo; the hero, Sam, and a few friends want everyone to have the benefits of all the knowledge and technology available. Given the nature of this conflict, Zelazny's use of Hindu mythology is no mere gimmick, for Hinduism, with its intricate rituals and rigid caste system, is precisely the kind of system he sees as sterile and oppressive. The novel even reenacts the historical conflict between Hinduism and Buddhism, for Sam briefly assumes the persona of the Buddha to attack the ruling class and stir up the people. From this perspective, then, the novel argues the need to overthrow entrenched authoritarian rule in order to liberate a society.

Themes

Zelazny suggests, both here and in many other stories and novels, that personal enlightenment is the necessary prelude to political or social liberation. Typically his protagonists are confronted with challenges which, successfully met, lead to some kind of enlightenment or spiritual/emotional growth. Those characters who fail the test usually face death, sometimes physical but more often spiritual. Connected with this movement towards enlightenment is the notion of immortality. A large number of Zelazny's protagonists enjoy immortality—whether as a supernatural given or as the result of technology. Immortality allows for some interesting plot developments, but for Zelazny it is primarily a metaphor for the human need for growth and fullness of experience. The characters' long lives give them the chance to play a variety of roles, to experience all that life has to offer. And this richness of experience, the knowledge of many lives, becomes the source of enlightenment. Such is the case for Sam.

But enlightenment is not just a private affair. Whatever form it takes in Zelazny's fiction—the attainment of spiritual and psychic wholeness, the awareness of one's shared humanity, or simply the recognition of the responsibility that accompanies power—enlightenment is followed by action in the social sphere. For Sam it is the recognition of how his former crewmates have abused their power that provokes his determination to liberate the people from bondage—a determination that leads him to wage two bloody wars. In *Lord of Light,* as in many other works by Zelazny, the land is sick and must be restored, often through the destruction of the old order. Often the healing of the land is achieved only at a terrible cost; Sam dies and is brought back to life only by a former enemy. And then to win his final battle he must cause the deaths of many of his former friends and destroy much that is beautiful before his world is free to grow naturally.

Characters

Zelazny's protagonists are almost always extraordinarily gifted individuals. In addition to immortality they enjoy unusual intellectual, physical or psychic powers and a measure of socio-political power or wealth. Sam for instance is one of the "First," an original crewman, a warrior who helped conquer the energy creatures native to the planet. He is, by right and invitation, one of the "gods" entitled to rule over the rest of humanity, but he rejects that role. Indeed Sam can be best described in mythic terms. He is, like so many of Zelazny's heroes, a Promethean figure, one of the immortals who renounces his privileged position in order to steal for humanity the power of the gods. And like Prometheus he is punished and imprisoned (before his final victory) for his rebellion. Sam is also a Protean figure. He plays a variety of roles—warrior, general, preacher, assassin, lover, mystic. The multiplicity of his roles is suggested by the many names and epithets attached to him: Siddhartha, Lord Kalkin, Binder of Demons, Lord of Light, Mahasamatman; and his sardonic self-awareness, his refusal to be overwhelmed by his own legend, is typified by his preferred name. He drops the Maha-and the -atman and calls himself Sam.

Indeed what distinguishes Sam from both his allies and his enemies among the gods is the level of self-knowledge he has attained. While his antagonists like Kali and Brahma are obsessed with the roles they play, with submerging their humanity in their supposed divinity, Sam maintains a rueful sense of self. When he impersonates the Buddha, he is the only one not taken in by his own act, the only one to recognize that a disciple named Sugata, an assassin once sent to kill him, has truly reached a Buddha-like state of enlightenment and sacrificed his life for Sam.

Techniques

The plot of *Lord of Light* follows a pattern critics have shown to be typical of Zelazny. The novel opens in the middle of its action, with a disoriented hero (Sam brought back from a kind of death) groping to find his way. As Sam prepares to renew his rebellion, he reviews the past that led him to this juncture. Thus the reader begins poised on the brink of some great action, is kept in suspense while the background is filled in, and finally experiences the climax. This proves a good method of grabbing the reader's attention, building the suspense, and gracefully handling the necessary exposition.

It has already been suggested that Zelazny's adaptation of the Hindu pantheon for his fictional purposes is quite suitable for the novel's attack on static, lifeless societies. It should be noted, moreover, that Zelazny adapts the Hindu mythos very freely—changing characters and emphases to suit the needs of the novel. The god Yama, for instance, plays a more important role in the novel (as Sam's former antagonist who becomes his staunchest ally) than he actually does in the Hindu pantheon.

Literary Precedents

Zelazny gives every indication of being an omnivorous reader, and *Lord of Light* is at times a very literary novel. His style owes much to the Elizabethan and Jacobean dramatists he studied in graduate school, and to the metaphysical and symbolist poets. In addition Zelazny is well versed in mythologies from around the world—including Hindu writings of course, but also the myths of "the dying god" gathered by Sir James Frazer in the *Golden Bough*—and in Jungian psychology. A science fiction novel comparable in its imaginative use of myth and in its witty, allusive, poetic style is Samuel R. Delany's *The Einstein Intersection,* 1967. But it is doubtful, given the publication dates, that there is any influence beyond a shared set of literary concerns.

THE CHRONICLES OF AMBER

Nine Princes in Amber, 1970, novel; *The Guns of Avalon,* 1972, novel; *The Sign of the Unicorn,* 1975, novel; *The Hand of Oberon,* 1976, novel; *The Courts of Chaos,* 1978, novel.

Social Concerns

The surface of the Amber novels suggests just another sword and sorcery epic—battles, intrigues, and magic set in some fantastic landscape—an unoriginal work redeemed, to some extent, by Zelazny's wit and gift for characterization. A closer reading, however, reveals a more thoughtful work in which spectacle is actually subordinated to concept and character development.

Amber is, for its inhabitants, the only real world—the source of an infinite number of "Shadows," worlds (including the earth) which reflect some aspect of Amber and have their own histories and mythologies. The rulers of Amber can manipulate these "Shadows," traveling from one to another and even creating new ones, but ultimately all these "Shadows" depend on Amber for their very being.

Or so it seems. The crux of the five novels is the growing recognition on the part of the princes and princesses of Amber that Amber is not the "real" world at all—that it is merely an offshoot of Chaos, created by their ancestor, a rebel lord of Chaos. In fact Amber and the whole universe as they know it is imperiled by a growing imbalance between the forces of Chaos (which seeks to resume its ancient sovereignty) and the forces of Amber. What Zelazny has done is to take the old myths of the creation of the world out of primeval chaos and cast them in a modern form.

Amber represents "form" or "order" or "pattern"—indeed it was formed by the creation of a "Pattern" in the midst of Chaos, a Pattern that is inscribed in the genes of all of the Lords of Amber. For Zelazny the Universe (and any microcosm of the Universe—a society or an individual) must maintain a dynamic balance between form and chaos (or law and freedom); one must never overwhelm the other. It is important not to equate form with goodness nor chaos with evil, for then one would desire the total victory of form over chaos, which Zelazny believes would be as destructive as the absolute triumph of chaos. An excess of form would result in the kind of static, repressive, lifeless society against which Sam rebels in *Lord of Light*. Zelazny's is a philosophy that celebrates balance and creative tension and rejects final answers and absolutes.

Themes

In many respects the Amber novels represent a more detailed and elaborate exploration of the themes embodied in *Lord of Light*. Corwin, the protagonist, and his siblings are immortals (at least they do not die of natural causes; though incredibly tough, they are not immune to violent death), but their long lives and extraordinary powers have bred in them an arrogance and capriciousness which make them an amoral, manipulative elite. The disappearance and presumed death of their father Oberon has touched off a vicious battle for the succession between rival factions of the family—a display of intrigue, betrayal, and counterplots that recalls the Borgia family at its most Machiavellian. Yet within this drift to moral anarchy, a counterforce begins to emerge, as some of the siblings, notably Corwin and his brother Random, begin a slow growth to maturity (one of the novel's ironies is that it seems to take immortals a long time to grow up). Their ambitions, jealousies, and lust for vengeance gradually give way to a sense of duty. Amber ceases to be a prize to be fought over and becomes instead a place of beauty and order to be preserved even at the cost of one's life.

The novel's plot, which at first appears to be a tale of ambition and revenge, gradually reveals itself to be a quest to heal a wounded land. The primal Pattern, which created Amber and upon which Amber's continued existence depends, has been damaged by Corwin's brother Brand, who has shed the blood of a kinsman on the Pattern to disrupt it. The break in the Pattern is growing, threatening the very existence of Amber. At this point Corwin renounces his desire for the throne and seeks to restore the Pattern. It is not he who in fact will restore it, but his willingness to sacrifice his life in the attempt suggests how much he has grown and does aid in the restoration of the land.

Characters

One of the strengths of the Amber novels is the way in which Zelazny individualizes the members of the royal family of Amber. They are recognizably members of the same family, united by blood and mutual distrust, yet each is very much a unique individual, responding to the crises of the story in distinct ways. Corwin, the narrator and focus of the reader's attention, is in many respects the prototypical Zelazny hero—tough, resourceful, gifted with a sardonic wit and a cynical veneer that covers a growing sense of compassion and duty. Like many of Zelazny's heroes, he has been shocked out of complacency into growth (by spending centuries as an exile, deprived of his memory, on our earth). He no longer kills gratuitously; he no longer denies the reality and the value of other lives. Corwin's growth is slow—often others are more aware than he of a change in his behavior—but the very slowness of his development makes his final enlightenment more plausible. Corwin's moral maturation is paralleled by (and is perhaps one cause of) a similar growth in at least some of his siblings. And, as in *Lord of Light,* the enlightenment of the individual precedes and makes possible the restoration of society.

But the novels do not conclude in a sentimental reconciliation of the whole family. That would be too neat, too orderly an ending for Zelazny, who prefers, after all, a balance between form and chaos, not some final, unchanging answer that precludes the possibility of new developments. Corwin does come to a new understanding of his relations, but some die without reconciliation, and others, including the mother of his son, remain estranged. And at least one character, Brand, dies unrepentant and unredeemed. Brand is the evil genius of the story (significantly he is described with images that tend to recall Satan and his name may be intended to suggest the fires of hell). Brand seeks power; he seeks to dominate the world and impose his own image upon it. To rule, he is willing to kill his family and even destroy Amber itself—so that he can literally recreate it in his own image by establishing a new Pattern. Brand is Corwin's opposite, what Corwin might have become had he not been shocked into growth. In fact Brand stands in opposition to all of Zelazny's Promethean heroes. Like them he would steal the power of the gods, but he would do so only for his own gratification. Unlike Corwin he does not and cannot grow, and thus he is doomed to sterility and defeat.

Techniques

The five Amber novels comprise, in one sense, a single mystery story. The first book opens with Corwin awakening in a hospital on earth, unable to remember his past, and the initial action recounts his attempt to regain that past. Once his memory is restored, the novels are concerned with Corwin's attempt to solve a series of mysteries: who ordered his disappearance and the numerous attempts on his life; what caused the disappearance of Oberon; what threatens Amber; what is Amber's real place in the universe? Corwin is as much detective as he is quest hero.

Like a good detective Corwin listens to conflicting stories and tries to piece together a coherent, truthful version of events. And as critics have observed, the novels' emphasis is not on swashbuckling action but on the telling of tales. Nearly all of Corwin's relatives have a story to tell; each has a piece of the puzzle Corwin is trying to solve. Thus he must weigh all of the rival stories—including Brand's—with all of their omissions and biases before he can learn the truth. And the five novels themselves are revealed, in the end, to be the story Corwin tells to the son he never knew, as they meet on the brink of Chaos.

Literary Precedents

While Zelazny does not borrow a whole mythos for the Amber stories, as he did in *Lord of Light*, his eclectic borrowings from a whole range of mythic and literary sources add much to the richness and moral weight of the five books. Critics have observed, for instance, that Zelazny draws heavily on the Grail legends—which in essence tell of a quest to heal a broken land—and from the vegetation myths underlying those legends. Zelazny makes considerable use of the symbols associated with the Grail, especially as they have been incorporated into the Tarot. Indeed the princes and princesses of Amber are all portrayed on Tarot like cards which provide them with a magical means of communication and travel.

The novels' allusiveness frequently enlarges the reader's response to characters or situations. The King of Amber, for instance, is Oberon, the name of the King of Faerie in medieval legend (and *A Midsummer Night's Dream*) and the suggestiveness of the name reveals much about Oberon's character—mysterious, powerful, manipulative—and much about his family and his world. In a key scene, Corwin is linked with the Jester or Fool of the Tarot deck. The Fool is linked with the cycle of life, death/chaos, and resurrection; and with the journey through experience to Wisdom. All of this has clear resonance for the character of Corwin. One need not recognize all the allusions to enjoy the Amber novels, but the greater the reader's familiarity with myth and literary tradition, the greater his appreciation of the story is apt to be.

Zelazny's Amber series is one of the few recent fantasies to betray little or no debt to Tolkien's *The Lord of The Rings*. Unlike Tolkien and his imitators, Zelazny seems uninterested in creating an imaginary world complete with history, mythology, languages, vividly realized geography, fauna, and flora. As critics have observed, Zelazny's worlds tend to be little more than stage sets. There are some dazzling special effects, some lovely descriptions, but for the most part Zelazny tells the reader no more about the socio-economic realities of Amber than he absolutely needs. Again one might see the influence of Jacobean drama—vivid characterization, heightened action and language in a deliberately stylized and artificial setting.

Related Titles

In *The Trumps of Doom* (1985), Zelazny resumes the story of Amber in the next generation, initiating the conflict between the sons of Corwin and Brand. Like the five books that make up the original Amber series, *The Trumps of Doom* is not really a novel by itself, but the first installment of a novel in several parts.

Other Titles (selected)

. . . *And Call Me Conrad*, 1966 (novel); *Isle of the Dead*, 1967 (novel); *Damnation Alley*, 1969 (novel); *The Doors of His Face, The Lamps of His Mouth*, 1971 (collection); *Today We Choose Faces*, 1973 (novel); *Bridge of Ashes*, 1976 (novel); *Doorways in the Sand*, 1976 (novel); *My Name is Legion*, 1976 (collection); *Road Marks*, 1979 (novel); *The Last Defender of Camelot*, 1980 (collection); *Eye of Cat*, 1982 (novel).

Additional Sources

Barbour, Douglas, "Roger Zelazny," *Supernatural Fiction Writers: Fantasy and Horror*, E. F. Bleiler, ed. New York: Scribners, 1985, Vol. II, pp. 1113-1119. Brief but stimulating critical comments.

Delany, Samuel R., "Faust and Archimedes," *The Jewel-Hinged Jaw: Notes of the Language of Science Fiction*, New York: Berkley, 1977. A perceptive and laudatory essay by a fellow writer, typical of the early response to Zelazny.

Sanders, Joe, "Zelazny: Unfinished Business," *Voices for the Future: Essays on Major Science Fiction Writers*, Vol. 2, Thomas Clareson, ed. Bowling Green, OH: Popular Press, 1979, pp. 180-196. Emphasizes Zelazny's concern with human growth and freedom and his preference for open ended resolutions. Sanders has also published *Roger Zelazny: A Primary and Secondary Bibliography*, Boston: G. K. Hall, 1980.

Yoke, Carl B., *The Reader's Guide to Roger Zelazny*, West Linn, OR: Starmont House, 1979. Yoke is a close friend of Zelazny, and in this study and a number of essays he provides a thorough, though at times uncritical, introduction to Zelazny's themes and techniques.

Kevin P. Mulcahy
Rutgers University

APPENDIX I:
TITLES GROUPED BY SOCIAL ISSUES AND THEMES

Academia/Education
Annunciation, The (Ellen Gilchrist)
Conjure Wife (Fritz Leiber)
Death in a Tenured Position (Amanda
  Cross)
Godwulf Manuscript, The (Robert B.
  Parker)
Have Spacesuit—Will Travel (Robert
  A. Heinlein)
No Word from Winifred (Amanda
  Cross)
Professor of Desire, The (Philip Roth)
White Noise (Don DeLillo)

Adolescence
Are You There God? It's Me,
  Margaret. (Judy Blume)
Bluest Eye, The (Toni Morrison)
Catcher in the Rye, The (J.D.
  Salinger)
Endless Love (Scott Spencer)
Forever (Judy Blume)
Heart is a Lonely Hunter, The
  (Carson McCullers)
In the Land of Dreamy Dreams (Ellen
  Gilchrist)
It's OK If You Don't Love Me
  (Norma Klein)
Lake Wobegon Days (Garrison
  Keillor)
Less Than Zero (Bret Easton Ellis)
Member of the Wedding, The (Carson
  McCullers)
Ordinary People (Judith Guest)
Peyton Place (Grace Metalious)
Unsuitable Job for a Woman, An
  (P.D. James)
Victory Over Japan (Ellen Gilchrist)

Alienation/Loneliness
Accidental Tourist, The (Anne Tyler)
Attachments (Judith Rossner)
August (Judith Rossner)
Ballad of the Sad Cafe, The (Carson
  McCullers)
Bats Fly at Dusk (Erle Stanley
  Gardner)
Big Enchilada, The (L.A. Morse)
Breast, The (Philip Roth)
Bright Lights, Big City (Jay
  McInerney)
Burning House, The (Ann Beattie)
Cathedral (Raymond Carver)
Children of Light (Robert Stone)
City and the Pillar, The (Gore Vidal)
Clan of the Cave Bear, The (Jean M.
  Auel)
Confessions of Nat Turner, The
  (William Styron)
Dog Soldiers (Robert Stone)
Eight Million Ways to Die (Lawrence
  Block)
Exodus (Leon Uris)
Eye of the Needle (Ken Follett)
Fan Man, The (William Kotzwinkle)
Flag for Sunrise, A (Robert Stone)
Foreign Affairs (Alison Lurie)
Foxes of Harrow, The (Frank G.
  Yerby)
Heart is a Lonely Hunter, The
  (Carson McCullers)
Interview with the Vampire (Anne
  Rice)
Job's Year (Joseph Hansen)
Looking for Mr. Goodbar (Judith
  Rossner)
Man with a Load of Mischief (Martha
  Grimes)

Member of the Wedding, The (Carson McCullers)
Midnight Cowboy (James Leo Herlihy)
Once is not Enough (Jacqueline Susann)
Painted Bird, The (Jerzy Kosinski)
Stories of John Cheever, The
Thief Who Couldn't Sleep, The (Lawrence Block)
To Kill a Mockingbird (Harper Lee)
Tropic of Capricorn (Henry Miller)
Vampire Tapestry, The (Suzy McKee Charnas)
Vida (Marge Piercy)
Wapshot Chronicle, The (John Cheever)
What We Talk About When We Talk About Love (Raymond Carver)
World of the Ptaavs (Larry Niven)

Art/Artists
Agony and the Ecstasy, The (Irving Stone)
Blue Movie (Terry Southern)
Breakfast of Champions (Kurt Vonnegut)
Children of Light (Robert Stone)
Dorothea Dreams (Suzy McKee Charnas)
Exodus (Leon Uris)
Great Jones Street (Don DeLillo)
Grendel (John Gardner)
Haj, The (Leon Uris)
Lady Oracle (Margaret Atwood)
Lake Wobegon Days (Garrison Keillor)
Lust for Life (Irving Stone)
Mistral's Daughter (Judith Krantz)
My Name is Asher Lev (Chaim Potok)
On Wings of Song (Thomas Disch)

Riders of the Purple Wage (Philip José Farmer)
Sophie's Choice (William Styron)
Tropic of Cancer (Henry Miller)
Witches of Eastwick, The (John Updike)

Black Concerns
Another Country (James Baldwin)
Bluest Eye, The (Toni Morrison)
Color Purple, The (Alice Walker)
Confessions of Nat Turner, The (William Styron)
Cotton Comes to Harlem (Chester Himes)
Foxes of Harrow, The (Frank G. Yerby)
Go Tell It on the Mountain (James Baldwin)
I Know Why the Caged Bird Sings (Maya Angelou)
If Beale Street Could Talk (James Baldwin)
Invisible Man (Ralph Waldo Ellison)
Pink Toes (Chester Himes)
Roots (Alex Haley)
Song of Solomon (Toni Morrison)
Sula (Toni Morrison)
Tar Baby (Toni Morrison)
To Kill a Mockingbird (Harper Lee)

Class Conflict
Bonfire of the Vanities, The (Tom Wolfe)
Cannibals and Missionaries (Mary McCarthy)
Collector, The (John Fowles)
Doomsters, The (Ross Macdonald)
Foxes of Harrow, The (Frank G. Yerby)
In the Best Families (Rex Stout)
King Rat (James Clavell)
Love Story (Erich Segal)
No Adam in Eden (Grace Metalious)

Peyton Place (Grace Metalious)
Scapegoat, The (Mary Lee Settle)
Sleeping Beauty (Ross Macdonald)
Tight White Collar (Grace Metalious)

Coming-of-Age
Are You There God? It's Me,
　Margaret. (Judy Blume)
By Love Possessed (James Gould
　Cozzens)
Caine Mutiny, The (Herman Wouk)
Catcher in the Rye, The (J.D.
　Salinger)
Chilly Scenes of Winter (Ann Beattie)
Color Purple, The (Alice Walker)
Deliverance (James Dickey)
Finishing School, The (Gail Godwin)
Forgotten Beasts of Eld (Patricia
　McKillip)
Have Spacesuit—Will Travel (Robert
　A. Heinlein)
Inside, Outside (Herman Wouk)
Love Story (Erich Segal)
Member of the Wedding, The (Carson
　McCullers)
Midnight Cowboy (James Leo
　Herlihy)
Old Ramon (Jack Schaefer)
Peyton Place (Grace Metalious)
Portnoy's Complaint (Philip Roth)
Ransom (Jay McInerney)
Season of the Witch, The (James Leo
　Herlihy)
Stories of John Cheever, The
Temple of Gold, The (William
　Goldman)
To Kill a Mockingbird (Harper Lee)
Tree Grows in Brooklyn, A (Betty
　Smith)
Wapshot Chronicle, The (John
　Cheever)
Wizard of Earthsea, A (Ursula K.
　Le Guin)

Corruption
Blue City, The (Ross Macdonald)
Burglar Who Studied Spinoza, The
　(Lawrence Block)
Centennial (James Michener)
Cotton Comes to Harlem (Chester
　Himes)
Eight Million Ways to Die (Lawrence
　Block)
Farewell, My Lovely (Raymond
　Chandler)
God Save the Mark (Donald
　Westlake)
Hunter, The (Donald Westlake)
Last of the Wine, The (Mary Renault)
Lonely Silver Rain, The (John D.
　MacDonald)
Magic Christian, The (Terry
　Southern)
Manchurian Candidate, The (Richard
　Condon)
Night Work (Joseph Hansen)
Pink Toes (Chester Himes)
Private Practice of Michael Shane,
　The (Brett Halliday)
Prizzi's Honor (Richard Condon)
Proteus (Morris West)
Running Dog (Don DeLillo)
Spartacus (Howard Melvin Fast)
Stone for Danny Fisher, A (Harold
　Robbins)
Taste for Violence, A (Brett Halliday)
Waking the Dead (Scott Spencer)

Counterculture
Another Roadside Attraction (Tom
　Robbins)
Candy (Terry Southern)
Confederate General from Big Sur
　(Richard Brautigan)
Dharma Bums (Jack Kerouac)
Fan Man, The (William Kotzwinkle)
Great Jones Street (Don DeLillo)
Kinflicks (Lisa Alther)

On the Road (Jack Kerouac)
Season of the Witch, The (James Leo
  Herlihy)

Crime

Big Sleep, The (Raymond Chandler)
Case of the Grinning Gorilla, The
  (Erle Stanley Gardner)
Cotton Comes to Harlem (Chester
  Himes)
Demolished Man, The (Alfred Bester)
Double Indemnity (James M. Cain)
Eight Million Ways to Die (Lawrence
  Block)
Fan Club, The (Irving Wallace)
French Powder Mystery, The (Ellery
  Queen)
Friends of Eddie Coyle, The (George
  V. Higgins)
Godfather, The (Mario Puzo)
Godwulf Manuscript, The (Robert B.
  Parker)
In the Best Families (Rex Stout)
Lonely Silver Rain, The (John D.
  MacDonald)
New Centurions, The (Joseph
  Wambaugh)
Peyton Place (Grace Metalious)
Pyx, The (John Buell)

Death

Antagonists, The (Ernest K. Gann)
Book of Lights, The (Chaim Potok)
Children of Light (Robert Stone)
Falconer (John Cheever)
High and the Mighty, The (Ernest K.
  Gann)
Job's Year (Joseph Hansen)
Love Story (Erich Segal)
No Adam in Eden (Grace Metalious)
Ordinary People (Judith Guest)
Side Effects (Woody Allen)
Sophie's Choice (William Styron)
Stories of John Cheever, The

Unsuitable Job for a Woman, An
  (P.D. James)
Wapshot Chronicle, The (John
  Cheever)

Drug/Alcohol Abuse

Big Sleep, The (Raymond Chandler)
Black Marble, The (Joseph
  Wambaugh)
Burning (Diane Johnson)
Children of Light (Robert Stone)
Confederate General from Big Sur
  (Richard Brautigan)
Death Claims (Joseph Hansen)
Dog Soldiers (Robert Stone)
Fan Man, The (William Kotzwinkle)
Fear and Loathing in Las Vegas
  (Hunter S. Thompson)
Flag for Sunrise, A (Robert Stone)
Flow my Tears, The Policeman Said
  (Philip K. Dick)
French Powder Mystery, The (Ellery
  Queen)
Great Jones Street (Don DeLillo)
Less Than Zero (Bret Easton Ellis)
Lonely Silver Rain, The (John D.
  MacDonald)
Love Medicine (Louise Erdrich)
Martian Time-Slip (Philip K. Dick)
No Adam in Eden (Grace Metalious)
October Light (John Gardner)
Once is not Enough (Jacqueline
  Susann)
Valley of the Dolls (Jacqueline
  Susann)

Environmental/Ecological Concerns

Airport (Arthur Hailey)
Bellefleur (Joyce Carol Oates)
Centennial (James Michener)
Deliverance (James Dickey)
Demon Breed, The (James H.
  Schmitz)

Dragonflight (Anne McCaffrey)
Dune (Frank Herbert)
Gods Themselves, The (Isaac
    Asimov)
In the Ocean of Light (Gregory
    Benford)
Jaws (Peter Benchley)
Mickelsson's Ghosts (John Gardner)
Night Work (Joseph Hansen)
Old Dick, The (L.A. Morse)
Pale Gray for Guilt (John D.
    MacDonald)
Ring of Endless Light, A (Madeleine
    L'Engle)
Sleeping Beauty (Ross Macdonald)
Surfacing (Margaret Atwood)
Tales of the South Pacific (James
    Michener)
Watership Down (Richard Adams)
White Noise (Don DeLillo)
Wizard of Earthsea, A (Ursula K.
    Le Guin)

Existentialism
Breast, The (Philip Roth)
Fixer, The (Bernard Malamud)
Invisible Man (Ralph Waldo Ellison)
My Present Age (Guy Vanderhaeghe)
Neighbors (Thomas Berger)
On the Road (Jack Kerouac)
Rockabilly (Harlan Ellison)
Side Effects (Woody Allen)

Family Relationships
Are You There God? It's Me,
    Margaret. (Judy Blume)
Bellefleur (Joyce Carol Oates)
Big Sleep, The (Raymond Chandler)
Blue City, The (Ross Macdonald)
Changes (Danielle Steel)
Cider House Rules, The (John Irving)
Compromising Positions (Susan
    Isaacs)
Davita's Harp (Chaim Potok)

Death of an Expert Witness (P.D.
    James)
Dinner at the Homesick Restaurant
    (Anne Tyler)
Doomsters, The (Ross Macdonald)
Evergreen (Belva Plain)
Family Album (Danielle Steel)
Fer-de-Lance (Rex Stout)
Fire from Heaven (Mary Renault)
Godfather, The (Mario Puzo)
Godwulf Manuscript, The (Robert B.
    Parker)
Immigrants, The (Howard Melvin
    Fast)
Innocent Blood (P.D. James)
Ironweed (William Kennedy)
It's OK If You Don't Love Me
    (Norma Klein)
King Must Die, The (Mary Renault)
Lake Wobegon Days (Garrison
    Keillor)
Lie Down in Darkness (William
    Styron)
Looking for Mr. Goodbar (Judith
    Rossner)
Love Story (Erich Segal)
Man Descending (Guy Vanderhaeghe)
Man, Woman and Child (Erich Segal)
Mom, the Wolf Man and Me (Norma
    Klein)
My Name is Asher Lev (Chaim
    Potok)
Once is not Enough (Jacqueline
    Susann)
Ordinary People (Judith Guest)
Other, The (Thomas Tryon)
Peyton Place (Grace Metalious)
Portnoy's Complaint (Philip Roth)
Rabbit Redux (John Updike)
Ring of Endless Light, A (Madeleine
    L'Engle)
Roots (Alex Haley)
Shining, The (Stephen King)

Sleeping Beauty (Ross Macdonald)
Something Happened (Joseph Heller)
Stories of John Cheever, The
Surfacing (Margaret Atwood)
Tales of a Fourth Grade Nothing
(Judy Blume)
Terms of Endearment (Larry
McMurtry)
them (Joyce Carol Oates)
Thief Who Couldn't Sleep, The
(Lawrence Block)
Thorn Birds, The (Colleen
McCullough)
Tree Grows in Brooklyn, A (Betty
Smith)
Wapshot Chronicle, The (John
Cheever)
War Between the Tates, The (Alison
Lurie)
White Noise (Don DeLillo)
Women's Room, The (Marilyn
French)
World According to Garp, The (John
Irving)
Wrinkle in Time, A (Madeleine
L'Engle)

Feminism/Women's Concerns
Annunciation, The (Ellen Gilchrist)
Attachments (Judith Rossner)
Bellefleur (Joyce Carol Oates)
Book of Common Prayer, A (Joan
Didion)
Cities of the Interior (Anais Nin)
Clan of the Cave Bear, The (Jean M.
Auel)
Close Relations (Susan Isaacs)
Color Purple, The (Alice Walker)
Compromising Positions (Susan
Isaacs)
Davita's Harp (Chaim Potok)
Death in a Tenured Position (Amanda
Cross)
Democracy (Joan Didion)

Dorothea Dreams (Suzy McKee
Charnas)
Edible Woman, The (Margaret
Atwood)
Faded Sun, The (C.J. Cherryh)
Fanny (Erica Jong)
Fear of Flying (Erica Jong)
Female Man, The (Joanna Russ)
Final Payments (Mary Gordon)
Full Circle (Danielle Steel)
Harvest Home (Thomas Tryon)
High Cost of Living, The (Marge
Piercy)
Hollywood Wives (Jackie Collins)
Hotel Transylvania (Chelsea Quinn
Yarbro)
In the Land of Dreamy Dreams (Ellen
Gilchrist)
Kinflicks (Lisa Alther)
Lady Oracle (Margaret Atwood)
Mary, Queen of Scots (Antonia
Fraser)
Mists of Avalon, The (Marion
Zimmer Bradley)
Mom, the Wolf Man and Me (Norma
Klein)
Mother and Two Daughters, A (Gail
Godwin)
Murder Against the Grain (Emma
Lathen)
Myra Breckinridge (Gore Vidal)
No Word from Winifred (Amanda
Cross)
October Light (John Gardner)
Other Women (Lisa Alther)
Picnic on Paradise (Joanna Russ)
Play It As It Lays (Joan Didion)
Pride of the Chanur, The (C.J.
Cherryh)
Royal Charles (Antonia Fraser)
Rubyfruit Jungle (Rita Mae Brown)
Shadow Knows, The (Diane Johnson)

Ship Who Sang, The (Anne
McCaffrey)
Superior Women (Alice Adams)
Surfacing (Margaret Atwood)
them (Joyce Carol Oates)
Thendara House (Marion Zimmer
Bradley)
Thorn Birds, The (Colleen
McCullough)
Valley of the Dolls (Jacqueline
Susann)
Vampire Tapestry, The (Suzy McKee
Charnas)
Victory Over Japan (Ellen Gilchrist)
Vida (Marge Piercy)
Walk to the End of the World (Suzy
McKee Charnas)
When It Changed (Joanna Russ)
Women's Room, The (Marilyn
French)
World According to Garp, The (John
Irving)

Freedom (The Nature of)
Another Roadside Attraction (Tom
Robbins)
Antagonists, The (Ernest K. Gann)
Collector, The (John Fowles)
Confessions of Nat Turner, The
(William Styron)
Even Cowgirls Get the Blues (Tom
Robbins)
Exodus (Leon Uris)
Fahrenheit 451 (Ray Bradbury)
Fixer, The (Bernard Malamud)
French Lieutenant's Woman, The
(John Fowles)
Jonathan Livingston Seagull (Richard
Bach)
Magus, The (John Fowles)
Painted Bird, The (Jerzy Kosinski)
Queen of Air and Darkness, The
(Poul Anderson)
Rabbit Redux (John Updike)

Spartacus (Howard Melvin Fast)
Still Life with Woodpecker (Tom
Robbins)
Thief Who Couldn't Sleep, The
(Lawrence Block)
World of the Ptaavs (Larry Niven)

Friendship
Animal Farm (George Orwell)
Attachments (Judith Rossner)
August (Judith Rossner)
Chosen, The (Chaim Potok)
Compromising Positions (Susan
Isaacs)
Fafrhd and the Grey Mouser Stories,
The (Fritz Leiber)
God Save the Mark (Donald
Westlake)
Kahawa (Donald Westlake)
Left Hand of Darkness, The (Ursula
K. Le Guin)
Sula (Toni Morrison)
Superior Women (Alice Adams)
Thief Who Couldn't Sleep, The
(Lawrence Block)

Government/Politics
Animal Farm (George Orwell)
Blood Tie (Mary Lee Settle)
Blue City, The (Ross Macdonald)
Burr (Gore Vidal)
Chronicles of Amber, The (Roger
Zelazny)
Cotton Comes to Harlem (Chester
Himes)
Davita's Harp (Chaim Potok)
Dragonflight (Anne McCaffrey)
Family Affair, A (Rex Stout)
Farewell, My Lovely (Raymond
Chandler)
Forgotten Beasts of Eld (Patricia
McKillip)
Good as Gold (Joseph Heller)
Kahawa (Donald Westlake)

King Must Die, The (Mary Renault)
Last of the Wine, The (Mary Renault)
Left Hand of Darkness, The (Ursula
  K. Le Guin)
Little Drummer Girl, The (John le
  Carré)
Man in the High Castle, The (Philip
  K. Dick)
Mary, Queen of Scots (Antonia
  Fraser)
Pink Toes (Chester Himes)
Pyx, The (John Buell)
Royal Charles (Antonia Fraser)
Shardik (Richard Adams)
Taste for Violence, A (Brett Halliday)
Waking the Dead (Scott Spencer)
Watership Down (Richard Adams)
Whipping Star (Frank Herbert)
Wizard of Earthsea, A (Ursula K.
  Le Guin)

Greed/Materialism

Banker (Dick Francis)
Bats Fly at Dusk (Erle Stanley
  Gardner)
Breakfast of Champions (Kurt
  Vonnegut)
Bushwhacked Piano, The (Thomas
  McGuane)
Complete Stories of Flannery
  O'Connor, The
Death Shall Overcome (Emma
  Lathen)
Double Indemnity (James M. Cain)
Fear and Loathing in Las Vegas
  (Hunter S. Thompson)
Godwulf Manuscript, The (Robert B.
  Parker)
I'll Take Manhatten (Judith Krantz)
Last Woman in his Life, The (Ellery
  Queen)
Magic Christian, The (Terry
  Southern)
Mosquito Court, The (Paul Theroux)

Murder Against the Grain (Emma
  Lathen)
Natural, The (Bernard Malamud)
Nightwork (Joseph Hansen)
Pale Gray for Guilt (John D.
  MacDonald)
Play It as It Lays (Joan Didion)
Postman Always Rings Twice, The
  (James M. Cain)
Private Practice of Michael Shane,
  The (Brett Halliday)
Proof (Dick Francis)
Rockabilly (Harlan Ellison)
Sleeping Beauty (Ross Macdonald)
Some Buried Caesar (Rex Stout)
Stories of Bernard Malamud
Trout Fishing in America (Richard
  Brautigan)
Whip Hand (Dick Francis)

Hollywood

Blue Movie (Terry Southern)
Carpetbaggers, The (Harold Robbins)
Family Album (Danielle Steel)
Fedora (Thomas Tryon)
Hollywood Wives (Jackie Collins)
Tinsel (William Goldman)
Valley of the Dolls (Jacqueline
  Susann)

Homosexuality/Lesbianism

Another Country (James Baldwin)
August (Judith Rossner)
City and the Pillar, The (Gore Vidal)
Class Reunion (Rona Jaffe)
Color Purple, The (Alice Walker)
Death Claims (Joseph Hansen)
Falconer (John Cheever)
Family Album (Danielle Steel)
Fire from Heaven (Mary Renault)
Group, The (Mary McCarthy)
High Cost of Living, The (Marge
  Piercy)
Hotel New Hampshire (John Irving)

Job's Year (Joseph Hansen)
Last of the Wine, The (Mary Renault)
Last Woman in his Life, The (Ellery Queen)
Myra Breckinridge (Gore Vidal)
Once is not Enough (Jacqueline Susann)
Other Women (Lisa Alther)
Rubyfruit Jungle (Rita Mae Brown)
Stories of John Cheever, The
Sudden Death (Rita Mae Brown)
Tight White Collar (Grace Metalious)
Two Sisters (Gore Vidal)
Valley of the Dolls (Jacqueline Susann)

Individualism
Avatar, The (Poul Anderson)
Bloody Sunrise (Mickey Spillane)
Bodysnatchers, The (Jack Finney)
Deliverance (James Dickey)
Dune (Frank Herbert)
Go Tell It on the Mountain (James Baldwin)
Have Spacesuit—Will Travel (Robert Heinlein)
Hombre (Elmore Leonard)
I, the Jury (Mickey Spillane)
In the Best Families (Rex Stout)
Jonathan Livingston Seagull (Richard Bach)
Monte Walsh (Jack Schaefer)
Rubyfruit Jungle (Rita Mae Brown)
Shane (Jack Schaefer)
Sometimes a Great Notion (Ken Kesey)
Thief Who Couldn't Sleep, The (Lawrence Block)
Time and Again (Jack Finney)
Time Enough for Love (Robert A. Heinlein)
Trader to the Stars (Poul Anderson)
Tropic of Cancer (Henry Miller)

Individuals vs. Oppressive Society/Government
All the Myriad Ways (Larry Niven)
Another Country (James Baldwin)
Bellefleur (Joyce Carol Oates)
Camber of Culdi (Katherine Kurtz)
Catch-22 (Joseph Heller)
Catcher in the Rye, The (J.D. Salinger)
Downbelow Station (C.J. Cherryh)
Fahrenheit 451 (Ray Bradbury)
Forgotten Beasts of Eld (Patricia McKillip)
Gorky Park (Martin Cruz Smith)
Heritage of Hastur, The (Marion Zimmer Bradley)
High Cost of Living, The (Marge Piercy)
Man Descending (Guy Vanderhaeghe)
Memos from Purgatory (Harlan Ellison)
My Present Age (Guy Vanderhaeghe)
Nineteen Eighty-Four (George Orwell)
Ninety-Two in the Shade (Thomas McGuane)
One Flew Over the Cuckoo's Nest (Ken Kesey)
Painted Bird, The (Jerzy Kosinski)
"Repent, Harlequin" Said the Ticktockman (Harlan Ellison)
Riddley Walker (Russell Hoban)
Rumble (Harlan Ellison)
Steps (Jerzy Kosinski)
Stories of John Cheever, The
Vida (Marge Piercy)
Wapshot Chronicle, The (John Cheever)
Whipping Star (Frank Herbert)

Intercultural Conflict/Relationships
At Play in the Fields of the Lord (Peter Matthiessen)

Book of Common Prayer, A (Joan
  Didion)
Centennial (James Michener)
Death Shall Overcome (Emma
  Lathen)
Doomsters, The (Ross Macdonald)
Faded Sun, The (C.J. Cherryh)
Far Tortuga (Peter Matthiessen)
Foreign Affairs (Alison Lurie)
Hawaii (James Michener)
Hotel New Hampshire, The (John
  Irving)
Immigrants, The (Howard Melvin
  Fast)
In the Ocean of Light (Gregory
  Benford)
Key to Rebecca, The (Ken Follett)
King Rat (James Clavell)
Little Big Man (Thomas Berger)
Love Medicine (Louise Erdrich)
Martian Chronicles, The (Ray
  Bradbury)
Mists of Avalon, The (Marion
  Zimmer Bradley)
Mocassin Telegraph, The (W.P.
  Kinsella)
Moon Flash (Patricia McKillip)
My Brother Michael (Mary Stewart)
Navigator, The (Morris West)
Nightwing (Martin Cruz Smith)
No Adam in Eden (Grace Metalious)
Ragtime (E.L. Doctorow)
Shogun (James Clavell)
Surfacing (Margaret Atwood)
Tales of the South Pacific (James
  Michener)
Tar Baby (Toni Morrison)
Thendara House (Marion Zimmer
  Bradley)
Wind Over Wisconsin (August
  Derleth)
World of the Ptaavs (Larry Niven)

International Politics/Relationships

Bodysnatchers, The (Jack Finney)
Cannibals and Missionaries (Mary
  McCarthy)
Captains and the Kings (Taylor
  Caldwell)
Democracy (Joan Didion)
Gorky Park (Martin Cruz Smith)
Holcroft Covenant, The (Robert
  Ludlum)
Hunt for Red October, The (Thomas
  L. Clancy, Jr.)
Key to Rebecca, The (Ken Follett)
King Rat (James Clavell)
Little Drummer Girl, The (John
  le Carré)
Murder Against the Grain (Emma
  Lathen)
On Wings of Eagles (Ken Follett)
Prize, The (Irving Wallace)
Right Stuff, The (Tom Wolfe)
Saving the Queen (William F.
  Buckley)
Second Lady, The (Irving Wallace)
Shoes of the Fisherman, The (Morris
  West)
Spy Who Came in from the Cold,
  The (John le Carré)
Tinker Tailor, Soldier, Spy (John
  le Carré)

Jewish Concerns

Antagonists, The (Ernest K. Gann)
Book of Lights, The (Chaim Potok)
Breast, The (Philip Roth)
Chosen, The (Chaim Potok)
Close Relations (Susan Isaacs)
Davita's Harp (Chaim Potok)
Evergreen (Belva Plain)
Exodus (Leon Uris)
Fear of Flying (Erica Jong)
Fixer, The (Bernard Malamud)
Good as Gold (Joseph Heller)

Inside, Outside (Herman Wouk)
My Name is Asher Lev (Chaim
   Potok)
Portnoy's Complaint (Philip Roth)
Professor of Desire, The (Philip Roth)
Side Effects (Woody Allen)

Justice
Bloody Sunrise (Mickey Spillane)
Bonfire of the Vanities, The (Tom
   Wolfe)
Case of the Grinning Gorilla, The
   (Erle Stanley Gardner)
Demolished Man, The (Alfred Bester)
Eight Million Ways to Die (Lawrence
   Block)
Fer-de-Lance (Rex Stout)
Fixer, The (Bernard Malamud)
Godfather, The (Mario Puzo)
I, the Jury (Mickey Spillane)
If Beale Street Could Talk (James
   Baldwin)
In the Best Families (Rex Stout)
Lord of Light (Roger Zelazny)
Man with a Load of Mischief, The
   (Martha Grimes)
Shrewsdale Exit, The (John Buell)
Some Buried Caesar (Rex Stout)
Thinner (Stephen King)
True Grit (Charles Portis)

Law Enforcement
Burglar Who Studied Spinoza, The
   (Lawrence Block)
Case of the Grinning Gorilla, The
   (Erle Stanley Gardner)
Fer-de-Lance (Rex Stout)
Friends of Eddie Coyle, The (George
   V. Higgins)
Godwulf Manuscript, The (Robert B.
   Parker)
I, the Jury (Mickey Spillane)
Lonely Silver Rain, The (John D.
   MacDonald)

Love
All Creatures Great and Small (James
   Herriot)
Ballad of the Sad Cafe, The (Carson
   McCullers)
Bellefleur (Joyce Carol Oates)
Bluest Eye, The (Toni Morrison)
Businessman, The (Thomas Disch)
Children of Light (Robert Stone)
Crossings (Danielle Steel)
Falconer (John Cheever)
Finishing School, The (Gail Godwin)
Grendel (John Gardner)
High Cost of Living, The (Marge
   Piercy)
If Beale Street Could Talk (James
   Baldwin)
Looking for Mr. Goodbar (Judith
   Rossner)
Love Story (Erich Segal)
Loving (Danielle Steel)
Man, Woman and Child (Erich Segal)
Mistral's Daughter (Judith Krantz)
Nineteen Eighty-Four (George
   Orwell)
October Light (John Gardner)
Pale Gray for Guilt (John D.
   MacDonald)
Peyton Place (Grace Metalious)
Princess Daisy (Judith Krantz)
Severed Wasp, A (Madeleine L'Engle)
Sophie's Choice (William Styron)
Still Life with Woodpecker (Tom
   Robbins)
Stories of Bernard Malamud
Stories of John Cheever, The
Thorn Birds, The (Colleen
   McCullough)
Tim (Colleen McCullough)
Time Enough for Love (Robert A.
   Heinlein)
Wapshot Chronicle, The (John
   Cheever)

Man vs. Nature

All Creatures Great and Small (James
  Herriot)
Centennial (James Michener)
Clan of the Cave Bear (Jean M. Auel)
Deliverance (James Dickey)
False Dawn (Chelsea Quinn Yarbro)
Jaws (Peter Benchley)
Little Big Man (Thomas Berger)
Mosquito Court, The (Paul Theroux)
Nightwing (Martin Cruz Smith)
Sometimes a Great Notion (Ken
  Kesey)
Surfacing (Margaret Atwood)

Marriage

Best of Everything, The (Rona Jaffe)
Burning (Diane Johnson)
Changes (Danielle Steel)
Class Reunion (Rona Jaffe)
Fear of Flying (Erica Jong)
In the Land of Dreamy Dreams (Ellen
  Gilchrist)
Love Story (Erich Segal)
Man Descending (Guy Vanderhaeghe)
Rabbit Redux (John Updike)
Shadow Knows, The (Diane Johnson)
Terms of Endearment (Larry
  McMurtry)
Tomorrow Will Be Better (Betty
  Smith)
Valley of the Dolls (Jacqueline
  Susann)
Victory Over Japan (Ellen Gilchrist)
War Between the Tates, The (Alison
  Lurie)
Women's Room, The (Marilyn
  French)

Mental Illness/Psychiatry

Assassins, The (Joyce Carol Oates)
August (Judith Rossner)
Deadly Visions (Brett Halliday)
Dispatches (Michael Herr)

In the Last Analysis (Amanda Cross)
Lust for Life (Irving Stone)
One Flew Over the Cuckoo's Nest
  (Ken Kesey)
Ordinary People (Judith Guest)
Other Women (Lisa Alther)
Shining, The (Stephen King)
Tim (Colleen McCullough)

Past (The Significance of the)

Bodysnatchers, The (Jack Finney)
Carpetbaggers, The (Harold Robbins)
Chilly Scenes of Winter (Ann Beattie)
Dinner at the Homesick Restaurant
  (Anne Tyler)
Doomsters, The (Ross Macdonald)
LaBrava (Elmore Leonard)
Lonesome Dove (Larry McMurtry)
Lonesome Places (August Derleth)
Martian Chronicles, The (Ray
  Bradbury)
Murderer is a Fox, The (Ellery
  Queen)
My Name is Asher Lev (Chaim
  Potok)
Sleeping Beauty (Ross Macdonald)
Something Wicked This Way Comes
  (Ray Bradbury)
Sophie's Choice (William Styron)
Tar Baby (Toni Morrison)
Waking the Dead (Scott Spencer)

Political/Social Protest

Animal Farm (George Orwell)
Aquitaine Progression, The (Robert
  Ludlum)
At Play in the Fields of the Lord
  (Peter Matthiessen)
Blood Tie (Mary Lee Settle)
Dispossessed, The (Ursula K.
  Le Guin)
Endless Love (Scott Spencer)
Even Cowgirls Get the Blues (Tom
  Robbins)

Flow my Tears, The Policeman Said
(Philip K. Dick)
God Save the Mark (Donald
Westlake)
Hollow Hills, The (Mary Stewart)
Lord of Light (Roger Zelazny)
Lovers, The (Philip José Farmer)
Nineteen Eighty-Four (George
Orwell)
Spartacus (Howard Melvin Fast)
Still Life with Woodpecker (Tom
Robbins)
Sunlight Dialogues, The (John
Gardner)
Vida (Marge Piercy)

Racism

Bloody Sunrise (Mickey Spillane)
Centennial (James Michener)
Complete Stories of Flannery
O'Connor, The
Confessions of Nat Turner, The
(William Styron)
Cotton Comes to Harlem (Chester
Himes)
Guard of Honor (James Gould
Cozzens)
I, the Jury (Mickey Spillane)
Invisible Man (Ralph Waldo Ellison)
New Centurions, The (Joseph
Wambaugh)
One Flew Over the Cuckoo's Nest
(Ken Kesey)
Ragtime (E.L. Doctorow)
Tales of the South Pacific (James
Michener)
To Kill a Mockingbird (Harper Lee)

Religion

Agony and the Ecstasy, The (Irving
Stone)
Another Roadside Attraction (Tom
Robbins)
Are You There God? It's Me,
Margaret. (Judy Blume)

At Play in the Fields of the Lord
(Peter Matthiessen)
Businessman, The (Thomas Disch)
Candy (Terry Southern)
Canticle for Leibowitz, A (Walter M.
Miller, Jr.)
Cat's Cradle (Kurt Vonnegut)
Complete Stories of Flannery
O'Connor, The
Confessions of Nat Turner, The
(William Styron)
Davita's Harp (Chaim Potok)
Dear and Glorious Physician (Taylor
Caldwell)
Death Claims (Joseph Hansen)
Dharma Bums (Jack Kerouac)
Dune (Frank Herbert)
Even Cowgirls Get the Blues (Tom
Robbins)
Exorcist, The (William Peter Blatty)
Fanny (Erica Jong)
Far Tortuga (Peter Matthiessen)
Go Tell It on the Mountain (James
Baldwin)
Harvest Home (Thomas Tryon)
Hawaii (James Michener)
Hotel Transylvania (Chelsea Quinn
Yarbro)
Jonathan Livingston Seagull (Richard
Bach)
Lake Wobegon Days (Garrison
Keillor)
Love Medicine (Louise Erdrich)
Man in the High Castle, The (Philip
K. Dick)
Mickelsson's Ghosts (John Gardner)
Mists of Avalon, The (Marion
Zimmer Bradley)
Mosquito Court, The (Paul Theroux)
One More Sunday (John D.
MacDonald)
Origin, The (Irving Stone)
Pyx, The (John Buell)

Riverworld Series, The (Philip José
  Farmer)
Shoes of the Fisherman, The (Morris
  West)
Shogun (James Clavell)
Stranger in a Strange Land (Robert
  A. Heinlein)
Thorn Birds, The (Colleen
  McCullough)
Thy Brother's Wife (Andrew Greeley)
Violent Bear It Away, The (Flannery
  O'Connor)
Wise Blood (Flannery O'Connor)

Revenge

Carpetbaggers, The (Harold Robbins)
Glitz (Elmore Leonard)
I Have No Mouth and I Must Scream
  (Harlan Ellison)
Innocent Blood (P.D. James)
Painted Bird, The (Jerzy Kosinski)
Rumble (Harlan Ellison)
Shrewsdale Exit, The (John Buell)
Stars My Destination, The (Alfred
  Bester)
Steps (Jerzy Kosinski)
True Grit (Charles Portis)

Sexual Politics

And Chaos Died (Joanna Russ)
Best of Everything, The (Rona Jaffe)
Edible Woman, The (Margaret
  Atwood)
Female Man, The (Joanna Russ)
Full Circle (Danielle Steel)
Hollywood Wives (Jackie Collins)
Lady Oracle (Margaret Atwood)
Myra Breckinridge (Gore Vidal)
One Flew Over the Cuckoo's Nest
  (Ken Kesey)
Princess Daisy (Judith Krantz)
Reinhart's Women (Thomas Berger)

Sexuality

Another Country (James Baldwin)

August (Judith Rossner)
Bellefleur (Joyce Carol Oates)
Businessman, The (Thomas Disch)
Candy (Terry Southern)
Carpetbaggers, The (Harold Robbins)
Class Reunion (Rona Jaffe)
Close Relations (Susan Isaacs)
Color Purple, The (Alice Walker)
Confederate General from Big Sur
  (Richard Brautigan)
Death of an Expert Witness (P.D.
  James)
Double Indemnity (James M. Cain)
Endless Love (Scott Spencer)
Family Album (Danielle Steel)
Fan Club, The (Irving Wallace)
Fear of Flying (Erica Jong)
Female Man, The (Joanna Russ)
Forever (Judy Blume)
It's OK If You Don't Love Me
  (Norma Klein)
Kinflicks (Lisa Alther)
King Must Die, The (Mary Renault)
Less Than Zero (Bret Easton Ellis)
Looking for Mr. Goodbar (Judith
  Rossner)
Lovers, The (Philip José Farmer)
Loving (Danielle Steel)
Man, Woman and Child (Erich Segal)
Midnight Cowboy (James Leo
  Herlihy)
Myra Breckinridge (Gore Vidal)
No Adam in Eden (Grace Metalious)
Once is not Enough (Jacqueline
  Susann)
One More Sunday (John D.
  MacDonald)
Peyton Place (Grace Metalious)
Pink Toes (Chester Himes)
Portnoy's Complaint (Philip Roth)
Postman Always Rings Twice, The
  (James M. Cain)
Prize, The (Irving Wallace)

Professor of Desire, The (Philip Roth)
Riverworld Series, The (Philip José
   Farmer)
Side Effects (Woody Allen)
Sophie's Choice (William Styron)
Stranger in a Strange Land (Robert
   A. Heinlein)
Thy Brother's Wife (Andrew Greeley)
Tight White Collar (Grace Metalious)
Time Enough for Love (Robert A.
   Heinlein)
Tropic of Cancer (Henry Miller)
Witches of Eastwick, The (John
   Updike)

Sports
Endzone (Don DeLillo)
Fan's Notes, A (Frederick Exley)
Iowa Baseball Confederacy, The
   (W.P. Kinsella)
Natural, The (Bernard Malamud)
Shoeless Joe (W.P. Kinsella)
Sudden Death (Rita Mae Brown)

Supernatural Phenomena/Powers
Camber of Culdi (Katherine Kurtz)
Conjure Wife (Fritz Leiber)
Demolished Man, The (Alfred Bester)
Exorcist, The (William Peter Blatty)
Fanny (Erica Jong)
Fafrhd and the Grey Mouser Stories,
   The (Fritz Leiber)
Harvest Home (Thomas Tryon)
Heritage of Hastur (Marion Zimmer
   Bradley)
Hotel Transylvania (Chelsea Quinn
   Yarbro)
Hollow Hills, The (Mary Stewart)
Lonesome Places (August Derleth)
Other, The (Thomas Tryon)
Shining, The (Stephen King)
Stars My Destination, The (Alfred
   Bester)
Universe Against Her, The (James H.
   Schmitz)

Vampire Tapestry, The (Suzy McKee
   Charnas)
Witches of Karres, The (James H.
   Schmitz)

Technology
Book of Lights, The (Chaim Potok)
Camber of Culdi (Katherine Kurtz)
Canticle for Leibowitz, A (Walter M.
   Miller, Jr.)
Cat's Cradle (Kurt Vonnegut)
Downbelow Station (C.J. Cherryh)
Dragon in the Sea, The (Frank
   Herbert)
Foundation Trilogy, The (Isaac
   Asimov)
Genocides, The (Thomas Disch)
Heritage of Hastur, The (Marion
   Zimmer Bradley)
I Have No Mouth and I Must Scream
   (Harlan Ellison)
I, Robot (Isaac Asimov)
Little Big Man (Thomas Berger)
Mosquito Court, The (Paul Theroux)
Nightwing (Martin Cruz Smith)
Pet Sematary (Stephen King)
"Repent, Harlequin" Said the
   Tocktockman (Harlan Ellison)
Ringworld (Larry Niven)
Riverworld Series, The (Philip José
   Farmer)
Spartacus (Howard Melvin Fast)
Surfacing (Margaret Atwood)
Timescape (Gregory Benford)
World of the Ptaavs (Larry Niven)

Urban Life
Blue City, The (Ross Macdonald)
Eight Million Ways to Die (Lawrence
   Block)
Ironweed (William Kennedy)
Memos from Purgatory (Harlan
   Ellison)
New Centurions, The (Joseph
   Wambaugh)

Old Dick, The (L.A. Morse)
Rumble (Harlan Ellison)
Time and Again (Jack Finney)
Tree Grows in Brooklyn, A (Betty Smith)
World's Fair (E.L. Doctorow)

Violence

Adrift Just Off the Islets of Langerhans (Harlan Ellison)
Assassins, The (Joyce Carol Oates)
Blue City, The (Ross Macdonald)
Book of Common Prayer, A (Joan Didion)
Confessions of Nat Turner, The (William Styron)
Dog Soldiers (Robert Stone)
Eight Million Ways to Die (Lawrence Block)
Falconer (John Cheever)
Female Man, The (Joanna Russ)
Flag for Sunrise, A (Robert Stone)
Friends of Eddie Coyle, The (George V. Higgins)
Grendel (John Gardner)
Hunter, The (Donald Westlake)
Little Drummer Girl, The (John le Carré)
Lonely Silver Rain, The (John D. MacDonald)
Shrewsdale Exit, The (John Buell)
Stories of John Cheever, The
them (Joyce Carol Oates)

War/The Military

Antagonists, The (Ernest K. Gann)
Big Time, The (Fritz Leiber)
Caine Mutiny, The (Herman Wouk)

Catch-22 (Joseph Heller)
Chosen, The (Chaim Potok)
Crossings (Danielle Steel)
Davita's Harp (Chaim Potok)
Deadly Visions (Brett Halliday)
Demon Breed, The (James H. Schmitz)
Dog Soldiers (Robert Stone)
Dragon in the Sea, The (Frank Herbert)
Dune (Frank Herbert)
Endzone (Don DeLillo)
Eye of the Needle (Ken Follett)
Flag for Sunrise, A (Robert Stone)
From Here to Eternity (James Jones)
Guard of Honor (James Gould Cozzens)
Haj, The (Leon Uris)
Hunt for Red October, The (Thomas L. Clancy, Jr.)
King Rat (James Clavell)
Left Hand of Darkness, The (Ursula K. Le Guin)
Little Big Man (Thomas Berger)
Marathon Man (William Goldman)
Painted Bird, The (Jerzy Kosinski)
Prize, The (Irving Wallace)
Riverworld Series, The (Philip José Farmer)
Slaughterhouse-Five (Kurt Vonnegut)
Sophie's Choice (William Styron)
Tales of the South Pacific (James Michener)
War Between the Tates, The (Alison Lurie)
War and Remembrance (Herman Wouk)

APPENDIX II:
SOCIAL ISSUES AND THEMES GROUPED BY TITLES

Accidental Tourist, The (Anne Tyler)
interpersonal relationships
nationalism

Adrift Just Off the Islets of Langerhans (Harlan Ellison)
importance of self-knowledge
violence

Agony and the Ecstasy, The (Irving Stone)
artist's "Everyman"
religion

Airport (Arthur Hailey)
noise pollution
workings of an airport

All Creatures Great and Small (James Herriot)
animals
birth
death
disease
morality
love
rural life

All the Myriad Ways (Larry Niven)
dangers of bureaucracy
importance of the individual

And Chaos Died (Joanna Russ)
alien encounters
consciousness
mental telepathy
sexual roles

Animal Farm (George Orwell)
disillusionment
friendship and comradeship

illusion and reality
revolution
social injustice
victimization

Annunciation, The (Ellen Gilchrist)
academic community
women's issues

Another Country (James Baldwin)
dehumanizing influence of Western culture
homosexuality
sexuality
social oppression of blacks

Another Roadside Attraction (Tom Robbins)
personal freedom
religion
social action

Antagonists, The (Ernest K. Gann)
death
freedom
Judaeo/Roman history
war

Aquitane Progression, The (Robert Ludlum)
espionage
political protest

Are You There God? It's Me, Margaret. (Judy Blume)
adjustment to new surroundings
coming-of-age
family
menstruation
religion

1535

Assassins, The (Joyce Carol Oates)
guilt
insanity
power
violence

At Play in the Fields of the Lord (Peter Matthiessen)
Christian missionaries
cultural relativity
imperialism
minority rights
political activism
primitive civilization

Attachments (Judith Rossner)
friendship between women
loneliness
need for women to have independent
   and meaningful lives

August (Judith Rossner)
friendship between women
homosexuality/lesbianism
loneliness/need for love
psychoanalysis
sexuality

Avatar, The (Poul Anderson)
extraterrestrial life
free enterprise
the nature of and the search for
   happiness
statism

Ballad of the Sad Cafe, The (Carson McCullers)
isolation
unrequited love

Banker (Dick Francis)
ambition
greed
social climbing

Bats Fly at Dusk (Erle Stanley Gardner)
American Dream
disguises
greed
hard-boiled detective
loneliness

Bellefleur (Joyce Carol Oates)
egocentric
environmental concerns
familial relations
love and sex
power
society vs. the individual
women's status

Best of Everything, The (Rona Jaffe)
career
marriage
sexual politics

Big Enchilada, The (Larry Alan Morse)
detective fiction conventions
exploitation
isolation of individual who resists
   being used

Big Sleep, The (Raymond Chandler)
alcoholism
family
organized crime
romantic quest
wealth

Big Time, The (Fritz Leiber)
militarism
pacifism

Black Marble, The (Joseph Wambaugh)
alcoholism
show dogs

Blood Tie (Mary Lee Settle)
CIA
democracy
dissidents
domination of society by bosses
Turkey

Bloody Sunrise (Mickey Spillane)
democracy/communism
individualism
law/justice
racism
sexism

Blue City, The (Ross Macdonald)
parent/child relationships
political corruption
urban underworld
violence

Blue Movie (Terry Southern)
art/aesthetics (feigned devotion of directors and producers to)
Hollywood
pornography

Bluest Eye, The (Toni Morrison)
black, adolescent, underprivileged Americans
inadequate love

Bodysnatchers, The (Jack Finney)
Cold War
extraterrestrial life
individualism
nostalgia

Bonfire of the Vanities, The (Tom Wolfe)
American legal establishment
class conflict
power of the media

Book of Common Prayer, A (Joan Didion)
sisterhood as a counterforce to international violence

Book of Lights, The (Chaim Potok)
cultural conflict
dangers of technology
death
Jewish vs. Far Eastern values
guilt
meaning vs. meaningless

Breakfast of Champions (Kurt Vonnegut)
artist's role in society
commercialism
difficulty of true communication
free will vs. determinism

Breast, The (Philip Roth)
alienation
existentialism
Jewish society
metamorphosis

Bright Lights, Big City (Jay McInerney)
drug-related humor
drugs
social alienation

Burglar Who Studied Spinoza, The (Lawrence Block)
caper books
corruption of the police
professionalism

Burning (Diane Johnson)
California lifestyles
child welfare system
marriage
psychiatry

Burning House, The (Ann Beattie)
dislocation
identity crisis
modern anxiety
narcissism

Burr (Gore Vidal)
historical myths
political power

Bushwhacked Piano, The (Thomas McGuane)
anti-social behavior
consumerism
corporate ethics

Businessman, The (Thomas Disch)
afterlife
Christianity
dreams
imagination
love
nature of evil
sex

By Love Possessed (James Gould Cozzens)
duty
reason
upper-class values

Caine Mutiny, The (Herman Wouk)
bildungsroman
limits of individual responsibility
World War II

Camber of Culdi (Katherine Kurtz)
fantasy as an antidote to problems of modern world
price of social responsibility

Candy (Terry Southern)
bohemian life

communes
free love
group therapy
sexual deviation
liberalism
oriental cults
pop psychology
pornography
satire of the 1960s
tourism

Cannibals and Missionaries
class conflict
terrorism

Canticle for Leibowitz, A (Walter M. Miller, Jr.)
morality
nuclear power
religion
science and technology
scientific ethics

Captains and the Kings (Taylor Caldwell)
international cabal of bankers
Irish immigration to the US
Irishmen

Carpetbaggers, The (Harold Robbins)
entrepreneurship
Hollywood decadence
rape
revenge
sexual language
significance of the past

Case of the Grinning Gorilla, The (Erle Stanley Gardner)
altered states of consciousness
American legal system
criminality
justice
law
underdog

Cat's Cradle (Kurt Vonnegut)
difficulty of communication
free will vs. determinism
messianic religion
threat of technology

Catch-22 (Joseph Heller)
absurdity of the military bureaucracy
individuals' battle against destructive
    systems
war

Catcher in the Rye, The (J.D. Salinger)
alienation
conflict between society and the
    individual
Time as the destroyer

Cathedral (Raymond Carver)
anxiety
growth
hope
suffering
survival

Centennial (James Michener)
American Indians' plight
American west
environmental concerns
genocide
racism
relationship between man and nature

Changes (Danielle Steel)
family relationships
fear of change
marriage

Children of Light (Robert Stone)
addiction
alienation
art and artists
death
drugs
love and infatuation

Chilly Scenes of Winter (Ann Beattie)
1960s generation
coming-of-age
nostalgia for the past
separation and loss

Chosen, The (Chaim Potok)
dangers of assimilation
friendship
human soul
Jewish experience in America
war

Chronicles of Amber, The (Roger Zelazny)
immortality
personal growth

Cider House Rules, The (John Irving)
abortion
adoption
family life

Cities of the Interior (Anais Nin)
female sensibility
nature of reality
quest for self

City and the Pillar, The (Gore Vidal)
alienation
homosexuality
lost illusions

Clan of the Cave Bear, The (Jean M. Auel)
alienation
cooperation
feminism
survivalist movement

Class Reunion (Rona Jaffe)
homosexuality
lifestyles

marriage
sexuality

Close Relations (Susan Isaacs)
feminism
sexuality

Collector, The (John Fowles)
conflict between social classes
freedom of choice
misuse of power

Color Purple, The (Alice Walker)
black women
civil rights movement
identity
women's movement

Complete Stories of Flannery O'Connor, The
centrality of Christ in one's life
convergence upon the Omega point
greed
materialism
moral values
racism
respectability
social responsibility

Compromising Positions (Susan Isaacs)
family
female autonomy and self-realization
friendship
indictment of the American dream

Confederate General from Big Sur (Richard Brautigan)
casual sex
counterculture
drugs

Confessions of Nat Turner, The (William Styron)
Christianity and slavery
dilemmas of leadership

freedom
man's isolation
slavery in America
sources of racism
violence as despair

Conjure Wife (Fritz Leiber)
academia
university life
university politics
witchcraft

Cotton Comes to Harlem (Chester Himes)
black concerns
crime
futility and absurdity
political corruption
racism

Crossings (Danielle Steel)
conflicting loyalties
tragic nature of love
World War II

Davita's Harp (Chaim Potok)
Christianity
economic exploitation
family relationships
fascism
Great Depression
Judaism
Marxism
women's roles
World War II

Deadly Visions (Brett Halliday)
child abuse
effects of war on society
mistreatment of the mentally ill

Dear and Glorious Physician (Taylor Caldwell)
fundamentalist Christianity
parallels between ancient and modern worlds

Death Claims (Joseph Hansen)
drugs
homosexuality
religion

Death of an Expert Witness (P.D. James)
broken home
jealousy
quest for personal identity
sexual fears and needs

Death Shall Overcome (Emma Lathen)
greed
high finance
race relations

Death in a Tenured Position (Amanda Cross)
academia
feminism
gender roles

Deliverance (James Dickey)
coming of age
ecology
individualism/self-reliance

Democracy (Joan Didion)
national/international intrigue as a
    threat to society
women's concerns

Demolished Man, The (Alfred Bester)
business ethics
crime and punishment
extrasensory perception
human and cultural evolution
maturation
nature of reality
psychological motivations

Demon Breed, The (James H. Schmitz)
ecology

importance of creativity
war

Dharma Bums (Jack Kerouac)
Buddhism/spiritual quest
rebellion/nonconformity

Dinner at the Homesick Restaurant (Anne Tyler)
family
influence of the past
interpersonal relationships

Dispatches (Michael Herr)
blindness of military leadership
madness inflicting those in combat
war

Dispossessed, The (Ursula K. Le Guin)
anarchy
capitalism vs. socialism
temporal theory in physics
utopianism

Dog Soldiers (Robert Stone)
alienation
disillusionment
drugs
violence
war

Doomsters, The (Ross Macdonald)
class system
economic exploitation
family saga
minorities
past

Dorothea Dreams (Suzy McKee Charnas)
art
artist's debt to society
feminism

Double Indemnity (James M. Cain)
greed
guilt
sexuality

Downbelow Station (C.J. Cherryh)
bureaucratic stifling of initiative
impact of technology on the future
political neutrality

Dragon in the Sea, The (Frank Herbert)
technology
war

Dragonflight (Anne McCaffrey)
change vs. tradition
community
ecology
leadership

Dune (Frank Herbert)
ecology
individualism
religion
war

Edible Woman, The (Margaret Atwood)
female quest for identity and
  psychological independence
sexual politics and the heterosexual
  power struggle

Eight Millions Ways to Die (Lawrence Block)
ability of people to change
alienation
corruption
crime
justice
professionalism
urban disintegration
violence

Endless Love (Scott Spencer)
1960s social awareness vs. 1930s
  social activism
adolescent sexual conflict
destructive potential of physical
  passion
obsessive behavior

Endzone (Don DeLillo)
football
militarism
Nazi and nuclear holocaust

Even Cowgirls Get the Blues (Tom Robbins)
personal freedom
religion
social action

Evergreen (Belva Plain)
family saga
Jewish experience

Exodus (Leon Uris)
alienation
freedom
holocaust
Israeli independence
role of the artist
toleration

Exorcist, The (William Peter Blatty)
nature of personal identity
religion
supernatural occurrences

Eye of the Needle (Ken Follett)
patriotism
social isolation

Faded Sun, The (C.J. Cherryh)
absolute power exercised by female
evil
human suffering
intercultural cooperation

Fafhrd and the Grey Mouser Stories, The (Fritz Leiber)
friendship
male companionship
sword & sorcery

Fahrenheit 451 (Ray Bradbury)
censorship
dystopia
intellectual freedom
literacy

Falconer (John Cheever)
addiction
death
homosexuality
human degradation
incarceration
love
redemption
violence

False Dawn (Chelsea Quinn Yarbro)
holocaust
inhumanity of man
rape
survival in wilderness

Family Affair, A (Rex Stout)
ethical responsibility
Watergate

Family Album (Danielle Steel)
family relationships
Hollywood
homosexuality
promiscuity vs. monogamy

Fan Club, The (Irving Wallace)
American sexual mores
kidnapping

Fan Man, The (William Kotzwinkle)
alienation
contemporary bohemia

counterculture
drug use and abuse
self-discovery

Fan's Notes, A (Frederick Exley)
American Dream
fame
sports
success/failure

Fanny (Erica Jong)
childbirth
feminism
prostitution
witchcraft/women's religion

Far Tortuga (Peter Matthiesson)
cultural myth
cultural relativity
primitive cultures
Zen Buddhism

Farewell, My Lovely (Raymond Chandler)
corrupt government
hypocrisy
romantic quest
wealth

Fear of Flying (Erica Jong)
feminism
Jewish identity
marriage
sexuality

Fear and Loathing in Las Vegas (Hunter S. Thompson)
drugs
materialism
social criticism

Fedora (Thomas Tryon)
Hollywood publicity gimmicks
masking of famous personalities

Female Man, The (Joanna Russ)
gender roles
male dominance

violence and sexuality
women's liberation

Fer-de-Lance (Rex Stout)
artificial (created) world
failure of the legal system
familial responsibility
poetic vs. official justice

Final Payments (Mary Gordon)
charity
feminism
guilt

Finishing School, The (Gail Godwin)
coming-of-age
idealized love
nonconformity

Fire from Heaven (Mary Renault)
bisexuality
decline of Greek city-states and rise of Macedon
father-son power struggle

Fixer, The (Bernard Malamud)
anti-semitism
existentialism
human freedom
justice and law

Flag for Sunrise, A (Robert Stone)
alienation
disillusionment
drugs
human degradation
revolution
third world
violence
war

Flow My Tears, The Policeman Said (Philip K. Dick)
drug use and abuse

nature of reality as a social construct
political unrest of the 1970s

Foreign Affairs (Alison Lurie)
growing old
romance
self-deception

Forever (Judy Blume)
infatuation
teenage romance
teenage sexual activity

Forgotten Beasts of Eld (Patricia McKillip)
growing-up
individual vs. society
political conflict

Foundation Trilogy, The (Isaac Asimov)
free will and determinism
social planning
technology

Foxes of Harrow, The (Frank G. Yerby)
alienation
exploitation
false vs. genuine aristocracy
flaws of Southern society
slavery

French Lieutenant's Woman, The (John Fowles)
freedom to choose
quest for individual freedom
quest for self-knowledge
Victorian England

French Powder Mystery, The (Ellery Queen)
1920s narcotics trade
social order and disorder

Friends of Eddie Coyle, The (George V. Higgins)
crime

law enforcement
violence

From Here to Eternity (James Jones)
American masculinity in the context
  of war
human suffering
peacetime Army life
war

Full Circle (Danielle Steel)
complexities of male-female
  relationships
women's changing role in society

Genocides, The (Thomas Disch)
advanced technology
alien invasions
end of the world
insignificance of humanity

Glitz (Elmore Leonard)
ambition
good vs. evil
revenge

Go Tell It on the Mountain (James Baldwin)
individuality vs. conformity
oppression of blacks
religion

God Save the Mark (Donald Westlake)
anarchy
corruption of social institutions
friendship
selfishness

Godfather, The (Mario Puzo)
crime
family relationships
justice
Mafia
paternalism

Gods Themselves, The (Isaac Asimov)
environmental and scientific concerns
optimistic view of man

Godwulf Manuscript, The (Robert B. Parker)
dissolution of family relationships
law enforcement
materialism
organized crime
problems in academia

Good as Gold (Joseph Heller)
Jewish heritage in an anti-Semitic
  society
satire of American government

Gorky Park (Martin Cruz Smith)
conformity
individual vs. society
quality of life in the Soviet Union

Great Jones Street (Don DeLillo)
artist's public role
communal living
drugs
relationship between public persona
  and the "self"
rock music

Grendel (John Gardner)
art and love as creations of order
random vs. ordered universe
violence in a meaningless universe

Group, The (Mary McCarthy)
homosexuality
marriage
sexual politics
urban life

Guard of Honor (James Gould Cozzens)
acting within the possible
crises of confidence

Haj, The (Leon Uris)
Middle East
role of the artist
sexual stereotyping
war

Harvest Home (Thomas Tryon)
female dominance
mother cults
pagan rituals

Have Spacesuit—Will Travel (Robert A. Heinlein)
education
growing-up
humanity
individualism

Hawaii (James Michener)
Christian evangelism
importance of exploration
interracial love and marriage
religion

Heart is a Lonely Hunter, The (Carson McCullers)
alienation
lack of communication

Heritage of Hastur (Marion Zimmer Bradley)
personal growth
psychic powers
repressive authority
technology

High Cost of Living, The (Marge Piercy)
feminism
hypocrisy
individual vs. society
lesbianism
nature of honor
nature of love

High and the Mighty, The (Ernest K. Gann)
American society
aviation
courage
death

Holcroft Covenant, The (Robert Ludlum)
espionage
political protest

Hollow Hills, The (Mary Stewart)
destiny
free will
psychic powers
social upheaval and change

Hollywood Wives (Jackie Collins)
Hollywood/show business world
liberated women
sexual politics

Hombre (Elmore Leonard)
good vs. evil
purgation of evil in society

Hotel New Hampshire, The (John Irving)
homosexuality
incest
race relations
rape

Hotel Transylvania (Chelsea Quinn Yarbro)
life in 18th century France
rights of women
satanism
vampire as hero

Hunt for Red October, The (Thomas L. Clancy, Jr.)
betrayal
military

political conflicts between Soviet
  Union and U.S.
technology

Hunter, The (Donald Westlake)
corruption of social institutions
paranoia
the superman
violence

I Have No Mouth and I Must Scream (Harlan Ellison)
dangers of technology
vengeance
violent nature of man

I, the Jury (Mickey Spillane)
democracy
individualism
law/justice
racism
sexism
silent majority

I Know Why the Caged Bird Sings (Maya Angelou)
black concerns
search for identity
triumph over obstacles

I, Robot (Isaac Asimov)
prejudice and reason
social planning
technology

I'll Take Manhatten (Judith Krantz)
celebration of self-indulgence
destructiveness of envy

If Beale Street Could Talk (James Baldwin)
legal system
love as a humanizing power
oppression of blacks
religious hypocrisy

Immigrants, The (Howard Melvin Fast)
ethnicity
family relationships
industrial capitalism

In the Best Families (Rex Stout)
justice and social class
organized crime
persistence in the face of defeat
personal integrity and vigilantism

In the Land of Dreamy Dreams (Ellen Gilchrist)
female adolescence
women's issues

In the Last Analysis (Amanda Cross)
integrity
professional ethics
psychiatry

In the Ocean of Light (Gregory Benford)
ecology
human contact with aliens
importance of the space program

Innocent Blood (P.D. James)
adoption
family relationships
quest for personal identity
revenge

Inside, Outside (Herman Wouk)
American Jews
bildungsroman

Interview with the Vampire (Ann Rice)
alienation
immortality
lost innocence
societal ambivalence about crime and
  victimization
vampire

Invisible Man (Ralph Waldo Ellison)
black nationalism
existentialism
naturalism
race relations
segregation/integration

Iowa Baseball Confederacy, The (W.P. Kinsella)
baseball as an American heritage
social change

Ironweed (William Kennedy)
depression era Albany
father/son relationships
urban transient community

It's OK If You Don't Love Me (Norma Klein)
female sexuality
single-parent families
teenage sexuality

Jaws (Peter Benchley)
ecology
human behavior en masse
sharks

Job's Year (Joseph Hansen)
death
homosexuality
personal and societal loneliness

Jonathan Livingston Seagull (Richard Bach)
Christian Science
freedom
immortality
individualism
mysticism
perfection

Kahawa (Donald Westlake)
cooperation
friendship

relative superiority of democracy
totalitarianism

Key to Rebecca, The (Ken Follett)
British colonialism
Egyptian history

Kinflicks (Lisa Alther)
1960s generation
feminism
self-discovery
sex roles

King Must Die, The (Mary Renault)
conflict between patriarchy and
  matriarchy
kingship/the king's worthiness and
  hybris
Oedipal conflict

King Rat (James Clavell)
Asian vs. European culture
class hatred in Britain
ethics

LaBrava (Elmore Leonard)
decadence
living in the past

Lady Oracle (Margaret Atwood)
dynamics of popular cultural
female quest for identity vs.
  fragmenting cultural expectations
satire of contemporary literary
  scene/celebrity-making
sexual politics and the heterosexual
  power struggle

Lake Wobegon Days (Garrison Keillor)
adolescent rebellion
community
family
midwestern culture

nostalgia
puritanism
religion
small town life
value of art

Last of the Wine, The (Mary Renault)

ambivalence of homosexual
  relationships
nature of democracy
power and corruption in charismatic
  leadership

Last Woman in His Life, The (Ellery Queen)

homosexuality
materialism/greed

Left Hand of Darkness, The (Ursula K. Le Guin)

friendship
gender roles in society
political behavior
war and aggression

Less Than Zero (Bret Easton Ellis)

affluent youth
alienation of the young
boredom
casual sex
drugs
failures of communication

Lie Down in Darkness (William Styron)

failure of communication in human
  relationships
family (moral and spiritual
  disintegration of the American
  middle class)
guilt and parental responsibility
man's emotional immaturity

Little Big Man (Thomas Berger)

American Indians
genocide
moral and religious hypocrisy
spirituality
technology vs. nature
war

Little Drummer Girl, The (John le Carré)

democracy/totalitarianism
Israeli-Palestinian conflict
terrorism

Lonely Silver Rain, The (John D. MacDonald)

corruption
drug trafficking
ineffectuality of law enforcement
organized crime
violence

Lonesome Dove (Larry McMurtry)

juxtaposition of past and present
loss and change
myth of the American west
relationships between men and
  women

Lonesome Places (August Derleth)

childhood innocence
psychic residue
supernatural restitution

Looking for Mr. Goodbar (Judith Rossner)

lack of self-esteem
loneliness in modern society
need for love
singles lifestyle

Lord of Light (Roger Zelazny)

immortality

personal growth
revolution
social justice

Love Story (Erich Segal)
coming-of-age
death
father-child relationships
marriage
nature of love
relationships between social classes

Love Medicine (Louise Erdrich)
alcoholism
native Americans
poverty
religion

Lovers, The (Philip José Farmer)
political repression
sexual repression
sexuality

Loving (Danielle Steel)
importance of self-knowledge
sexual relationships

Lust for Life (Irving Stone)
epilepsy
mental illness
relationship between art and life

Magic Christian, The (Terry Southern)
corrupting nature of the almighty
   dollar
materialism

Magus, The (John Fowles)
masques and unmasking
quest for freedom and self-knowledge
search for self

Man Descending (Guy Vanderhaeghe)
contemporary moral standards
family relationships

innocence
journey into the self
marriage and domestic trials
pessimism
social victims

Man in the High Castle, The (Philip K. Dick)
fascism/totalitarianism
nature of reality as a social construct
Taoism

Man with a Load of Mischief, The (Martha Grimes)
alienation
justice
social responsibility

Man, Woman and Child (Erich Segal)
casual sex
family relationships
loyalty
natural childbirth

Manchurian Candidate, The (Richard Condon)
American society's human nature
malleability of psychological
   possession
paranoia
post-war America's corruption

Marathon Man (William Goldman)
espionage
evil
Nazism

Martian Chronicles, The (Ray Bradbury)
dangers of technology
nostalgia for the past
pacificism
race relations
reality vs. illusion

Martian Time-Slip (Philip K. Dick)
capitalism as an exploitative system
drug use and abuse
nature of reality as a social construct

Mary, Queen of Scots (Antonia Fraser)
life of a female monarch
political atmosphere in the 16th century

Member of the Wedding, The (Carson McCullers)
adolescent loneliness
coming-of-age

Memos from Purgatory (Harlan Ellison)
social institutions as oppressors
street gangs

Mickelsson's Ghosts (John Gardner)
apathy and responsibility
ethics and everyday life
religious fanaticism
toxic and nuclear wastes

Midnight Cowboy (James Leo Herlihy)
alienation
coming-of-age
sexual exploitation

Mistral's Daughter (Judith Krantz)
modeling world
nature of true love
world of the artist

Mists of Avalon, The (Marion Zimmer Bradley)
cultural change/conflict
intuition
mysticism
religion/spirituality
woman-centered powers

Mocassin Telegraph, The (W.P. Kinsella)
man's ability to cope with change
social change
social ramifications of Indian reservation life

Mom, the Wolf Man and Me (Norma Klein)
feminism
single-parent families

Monte Walsh (Jack Schaefer)
individualism vs. domestication

Moon Flash (Patricia McKillip)
cultural conflict
lost-race motif
primitive societies

Mosquito Court, The (Paul Theroux)
civilization vs. nature
dangers of messianic impulse
dangers of technology
materialism as an American value

Mother and Two Daughters, A (Gail Godwin)
family relationships
nonconformity
women's roles

Murder Against the Grain (Emma Lathen)
bureaucracy
greed
US-Soviet relations
women in the workplace

Murderer is a Fox, The (Ellery Queen)
small town society
war experiences

My Brother Michael (Mary Stewart)
personal discovery
positivity
post-war world
social involvement

My Name is Asher Lev (Chaim Potok)
artist's role in community
father-son conflict
Jewish community
role of the past
self-realization

My Present Age (Guy Vanderhaeghe)
black comedy
existential fragmentation
imagination and reality
paranoia
social forces against the individual
vulnerability

Myra Breckinridge (Gore Vidal)
androgeny
decadence
gender roles
sexual stereotypes
transsexuality
women's roles

Natural, The (Bernard Malamud)
American dream
materialism
questing
ritual sacrifice
sports

Navigator, The (Morris West)
cultural conflict
utopian society
Western culture

Neighbors (Thomas Berger)
social relationships

New Centurions, The (Joseph Wambaugh)
crime
poverty
racial conflict
urban decay

Night Work (Joseph Hansen)
corporate corruption
toxic waste

Nightwing (Martin Cruz Smith)
Indian vs. white society
magic vs. technology
man in nature
man in society

Nineteen Eighty-Four (George Orwell)
illusion and reality
individual against society
love and infatuation
political oppression
revolution
social injustice

Ninety-Two in the Shade (Thomas McGuane)
cultural decline
individual vs. society
personal honor, courage

No Adam in Eden (Grace Metalious)
alcoholism
class system
death
French Canadians
immigrants
money
sexual hypocrisy

No Future for Luana (August Derleth)
evil women
serpent in Eden

No Word From Winifred (Amanda Cross)
academia
feminism
gender roles

October Light (John Gardner)
drug culture
loss of public values
love and the unlocking of the heart
role of women in society

Old Dick, The (Larry Alan Morse)
detective fiction conventions
irrationality of modern life
society's treatment of the elderly

Old Ramon (Jack Schaefer)
initiation into adulthood

On the Road (Jack Kerouac)
existentialism
hedonism
rebellion/nonconformity

On Wings of Eagles (Ken Follett)
Iranian hostage crisis (1979)
US foreign rescue missions
US-Iranian politics

On Wings of Song (Thomas Disch)
aesthetics
creativity
false appearances
racism

Once is not Enough (Jacqueline Susann)
alienation
drugs
family
homosexuality
sexuality

One Flew Over the Cuckoo's Nest (Ken Kesey)
criticism of psychiatric treatments
criticism of racism
power struggle between the sexes
protest against a monolithic system
    that threatens the individual

One More Sunday (John D. MacDonald)
hypocrisy
sexuality
spirituality
weaknesses of fundamentalist religion

Ordinary People (Judith Guest)
adolescence
depression
family
perfectionism
psychiatry
suicide

Origin, The (Irving Stone)
Darwinism
role of science

Other, The (Thomas Tryon)
Cain and Abel theme
the double
psychological shadow

Other Women (Lisa Alther)
lesbianism
psychoanalysis
self-discovery
sex roles

Painted Bird, The (Jerzy Kosinski)
alienation
freedom
individual and society
oppression
power

society as oppressive and evil
survival of the self
vengeance
victimization

Pale Gray for Guilt (John D. MacDonald)
ecology
evils of American commerce
importance of love

Pet Sematary (Stephen King)
forbidden knowledge
moral responsibility
nature of evil

Peyton Place (Grace Metalious)
adolescence
adultery
bildungsroman
child abuse
class system
crime
life in the 1950s
love
sexual hypocrisy

Picnic on Paradise (Joanna Russ)
male chauvinism
patriarchy
social decay
women's roles

Pink Toes (Chester Himes)
black and white relations
civil rights movement
political corruption
sexuality

Play It As It Lays (Joan Didion)
failure of love and concern for others
opportunism in America
women's studies

Portnoy's Complaint (Philip Roth)
bildungsroman
Jewish middle-class morality
mother-son relationships
sexuality

Postman Always Rings Twice, The (James M. Cain)
accident
chance
cheating
deception
fortuity
fraud

Pride of the Chanur, The (C.J. Cherryh)
growing old
male instability
sexual role-reversal

Princess Daisy (Judith Krantz)
importance of self-acceptance
nature of true love
self-knowledge
sexual politics

Private Practice of Michael Shane, The (Brett Halliday)
corrupt American society
greed
personal and professional loyalty

Prize, The (Irving Wallace)
Cold War
holocaust
sexual revolution

Prizzi's Honor (Richard Condon)
American society's crime
human nature
malleability of corruption
self-delusion

Professor of Desire, The (Philip Roth)
academia
erotic ambition vs. intellectual
  devotion
Jewish stereotypes

Proof (Dick Francis)
greed
selfishness
selflessness

Proteus (Morris West)
corrupt government
government-sponsored terrorism
individual's responsibility to fight

Pyx, The (John Buell)
complexity of evil
crime
evil grace
goodness
underground religion (Black Mass)

Queen of Air and Darkness, The (Poul Anderson)
freedom
human nature
mythologizing
subconscious mind

Rabbit Redux (John Updike)
failure of the American dream
freedom vs. responsibility
social violence
space exploration

Ragtime (E.L. Doctorow)
early 20th century American history
immigrant's success
racial prejudice
social and political changes

Ransom (Jay McInerney)
bildungsroman/male rites of passage
exile
expatriatism

Reinhart's Women (Thomas Berger)
male-female relationships
mutability of fate
social change

"Repent, Harlequin" Said the Ticktockman (Harlan Ellison)
dehumanizing forces in society
individual vs. society
nonconformity

Riddlemaster of Eld (Patricia McKillip)
ambiguity of power
futility of war
growing-up
identity crisis

Riddley Walker (Russell Hoban)
ethical dimensions of power
individual vs. authority
man's relationship to knowledge
man's relationship to language
nuclear holocaust

Riders of the Purple Wage (Philip José Farmer)
artist's role in society

Right Stuff, The (Tom Wolfe)
American astronauts and test pilots
Cold War
power of the media

Ring of Endless Light, A (Madeleine L'Engle)
implications of pollution
importance of the family
interconnectedness of all human
  beings

Ringworld (Larry Niven)
importance of technology
space exploration

Riverworld Series, The (Philip José Farmer)
religious faith
scientific and social progress
sexuality
warfare

Rockabilly (Harlan Ellison)
absurdity of popular fiction
existential isolation
media manipulation
rock music
selfishness of Americans

Roots (Alex Haley)
black family life
black history
quest for identity

Royal Charles (Antonia Fraser)
political atmosphere of 17th century
roles of women

Rubyfruit Jungle (Rita Mae Brown)
feminism
individualism
lesbianism
rags to riches

Rumble (Harlan Ellison)
revenge
society as oppressor
streetlife

Running Dog (Don DeLillo)
corruption
pornography
survivalism
terrorism

Saving the Queen (William F. Buckley)
communist threat
national security

Scapegoat, The (Mary Lee Settle)
Appalachia
democracy
domination of society by bosses
labor/management relations
social classes

Season of the Witch, The (James Leo Herlihy)
1960s social upheaval
coming-of-age
weaknesses of countercultures

Second Lady, The (Irving Wallace)
Cold War
feminism

Severed Wasp, A (Madeleine L'Engle)
centrality of love in human existence
need for social commitment

Shadow Knows, The (Diane Johnson)
appearance vs. reality
divorce
feminism
race relations

Shane (Jack Schaefer)
individualism vs. domestication
social evolution

Shardik (Richard Adams)
child abuse
failure of an empire

Shining, The (Stephen King)
family relationships
madness
nature of evil
paranormal phenomena

Ship Who Sang, The (Anne McCaffrey)
romance in science fiction
women in science fiction

Shoeless Joe (W.P. Kinsella)
baseball as an American heritage
social change

Shoes of the Fisherman, The (Morris West)
East-West political conflicts
man's impact on society
role of religion in modern society

Shogun (James Clavell)
Asian vs. European cultures
political power
religious clashes

Shrewsdale Exit, The (John Buell)
built-in traps of society's system
justice
murder
retribution
victim theme

Side Effects (Woody Allen)
death
existentialism
illusion vs. reality
Jewish hero
sex/lust

Slaughterhouse-Five (Kurt Vonnegut)
free will vs. determinism
war

Sleeping Beauty (Ross Macdonald)
class system
economic exploitation
environment
family saga
past

Some Buried Caesar (Rex Stout)
greed/materialism/competition
means vs. ends
poetic vs. official justice

Something Happened (Joseph Heller)
dehumanization caused by business world
satire of middle-class American family

Something Wicked This Way Comes (Ray Bradbury)
childhood
importance of imagination
nostalgia for the past

Sometimes a Great Notion (Ken Kesey)
human suffering and the need for brotherhood
individualists' battle against the union
man vs. nature

Song of Solomon (Toni Morrison)
black heritage
collective dreams
ethnocentricism

Sophie's Choice (William Styron)
death
evil of Nazism
growth of the artist
love
man's potential for evil
past as a source of guilt, destruction and knowledge
repression of the individual
sexual initiation

Spartacus (Howard Melvin Fast)
corruption
freedom vs. slavery
imperialism

rebellion
self-sacrifice
technology

Spy Who Came in from the Cold, The (John le Carré)
German East-West tensions
moral ambiguity in modern society
post-war malaise

Stars My Destination, The (Alfred Bester)
betrayal
business ethics
exploitation
human and cultural evolution
maturation
nature of reality
revenge
social responsibility
telepathy
teleportation
time travel

Steps (Jerzy Kosinski)
depersonalization in society
domination
individual and society
oppression
power
self-definition/self-discovery
society as oppressive and evil
survival of the self
vengeance
victimization

Still Life with Woodpecker (Tom Robbins)
personal freedom
romantic love
social action

Stone for Danny Fisher, A (Harold Robbins)
black marketeering
blackmailing

depression of 1929
lower-middle-class values
poverty
welfare cheating

Stories of Bernard Malamud
compassion/human responsibility
greed
intense human relationships
losers
love

Stories of John Cheever, The
alienation
death
family
father-child relationships
homosexuality
human degradation
individual against society
initiation into maturity
love and infatuation
redemption
violence

Stranger in a Strange Land (Robert A. Heinlein)
messiahs
morality
religion
sexuality

Sudden Death (Rita Mae Brown)
lesbianism
tennis
women's athletics

Sula (Toni Morrison)
black concerns
sisterhood

Sunlight Dialogues, The (John Gardner)
irrationality
order and anarchy
the weight of tradition

Superior Women (Alice Adams)
feminist concerns
honorable behavior
importance of friendship
women's roles in society

Surfacing (Margaret Atwood)
Canadian nationalism/reaction against
    US cultural colonization
dehumanizing effects of
    technological/consumer society
estrangement within the contemporary
    family
female quest for identity
human violation of the natural world

**Tales of a Fourth Grade Nothing
(Judy Blume)**
adjustments to new surroundings
family
honesty to one's self and others
sibling rivalry

**Tales of the South Pacific (James
Michener)**
cultural conflict
ecology
racism
war

Tar Baby (Toni Morrison)
importance of understanding
    heredity/history
racial/social divisiveness

**Taste for Violence, A (Brett
Halliday)**
corruption in American business
labor injustices
political corruption

**Temple of Gold, The (William
Goldman)**
coming-of-age

**Terms of Endearment (Larry
McMurtry)**
failure of marriage as a workable
    institution
mother-daughter relationship

them (Joyce Carol Oates)
familial relations
malaise of modern life
social and economic inequality
violence
women's status

**Thendara House (Marion
Zimmer Bradley)**
culture conflicts
feminism
male-female relationships
patriarchy

**Thief Who Couldn't Sleep, The
(Lawrence Block)**
alienation
family
freedom
friendship
individualism

Thinner (Stephen King)
moral responsibility
nature of justice

**Thorn Birds, The (Colleen
McCullough)**
family life
love vs. duty
religious life
role of the mother

**Thy Brother's Wife (Andrew
Greeley)**
celibacy and the priesthood
Irish Catholics
Kennedy era
sex and Catholicism

Tight White Collar (Grace Metalious)
adultery
class system
homosexuality
money
New England life
sexual hypocrisy
small town life

Tim (Colleen McCullough)
mental retardation
nature of love

Time and Again (Jack Finney)
community
individualism
time-travel
urban blight

Time Enough for Love (Robert A. Heinlein)
individualism
love
meaning of life
sexuality

Timescape (Gregory Benford)
dangers and benefits of technology
scientists at work
time

Tinker, Tailor, Soldier, Spy (John le Carré)
ambiguous loyalties
infidelity
Soviet-West European relations

Tinsel (William Goldman)
Hollywood
nature of success

To Kill a Mockingbird (Harper Lee)
American South
black concerns
civil rights

compassion/empathy
growing up
loneliness
racial prejudice
social injustice

Tomorrow Will Be Better (Betty Smith)
freedom from lower middle class bonds
sterility of workingmen's lives

Trader to the Stars (Poul Anderson)
entrepreneurship
free enterprise
free trade
space travelers as frontiersmen

Tree Grows in Brooklyn, A (Betty Smith)
bildungsroman
desolation of urban poverty
family unit/Freudian romance

Tropic of Cancer (Henry Miller)
creativity and sustenance of artistic consciousness
freedom of expression
individual liberty

Tropic of Capricorn (Henry Miller)
alienation from conventional life pattern
alienation and fragmentation of the self

Trout Fishing in America (Richard Brautigan)
capital punishment
materialism
poverty

True Grit (Charles Portis)
justice
revenge

self-reliance
trustworthiness

Two Sisters (Gore Vidal)
decadence
expatriate experience
homosexuality
lost illusions

Universe Against Her, The (James H. Schmitz)
conformity vs. nonconformity
telepathy

Unsuitable Job for a Woman, An (P.D. James)
juvenile problems
suicide

Valley of the Dolls (Jacqueline Susann)
drug abuse
fame
Hollywood
homosexuality
marriage

Vampire Tapestry, The (Suzy McKee Charnas)
alienation
feminism
vampires

Victory Over Japan (Ellen Gilchrist)
female adolescence
women's issues

Vida (Marge Piercy)
alienation
government as oppressor
rebellion in the 1960s
social change
women's roles in politics and society

Violent Bear It Away, The (Flannery O'Connor)
atheistic humanism/moral relativism
concern for salvation
fate
role of the preacher

Waking the Dead (Scott Spencer)
honest vs. corrupt politics
obsessive memory
political idealism

Walk to the End of the World (Suzy McKee Charnas)
dystopia
post-atomic war society
radical feminism

Wapshot Chronicle, The (John Cheever)
alienation
death
family
father-child relationships
individual against society
initiation into maturity
love and infatuation

War Between the Tates, The (Alison Lurie)
1960s
children
marriage
self-deception
Vietnam War

War and Remembrance (Herman Wouk)
holocaust
World War II

Watership Down (Richard Adams)
community

ecology
government

What We Talk About When We Talk About Love (Raymond Carver)
alienation
helplessness
loneliness
suffering

When It Changed (Joanna Russ)
altered consciousness
patriarchy
women's roles

Whip Hand (Dick Francis)
good vs. evil
greed
purgation of evils in society

Whipping Star (Frank Herbert)
individual vs. society
powerful leaders

White Noise (Don DeLillo)
absurdity of contemporary academia
breakdown of communication
family relationships
pollution

Wind Over Wisconsin (August Derleth)
native American decline
regionalism
Wisconsin social history

Wise Blood (Flannery O'Connor)
acceptance of Christ
evangelism
false religion
integrity
religious quest
role of the prophet

Witches of Eastwick, The (John Updike)
adultery
artistic expression
contemporary witchcraft
gothic comedy

Witches of Karres, The (James H. Schmitz)
extrasensory powers
magic
search for identity

Wizard of Earthsea, A (Ursula K. Le Guin)
ecology
growing up
importance of names
uses and abuses of power

Women's Room, The (Marilyn French)
feminism
marriage
motherhood
rape

World According to Garp, The (John Irving)
feminism
gender roles
single parenthood
transsexuality

World of the Ptaavs (Larry Niven)
alienism of universe
basis of ethics
colonization/slavery
importance of freedom
technology

World's Fair (E.L. Doctorow)
1939 World's Fair in New York

America in the 1930s
childhood memories
Great Depression

Wrinkle in Time, A (Madeleine L'Engle)
effect of conformity on the individual
impact of courageous individuals
importance of the family

APPENDIX III:
CONTENTS BY GENRE

Adventure
Anderson, Poul
Auel, Jean M.
Benchley, Peter
Block, Lawrence
Buckley, William F.
Buell, John
Clancy, Thomas L., Jr.
Clavell, James
Dickey, James
Follett, Ken
Gann, Ernest K.
Gardner, Erle Stanley
Goldman, William
Hoban, Russell
Kosinski, Jerzy
Kotzwinkle, William
Leonard, Elmore
McInerney, Jay
Morse, Larry Alan
Portis, Charles
Robbins, Harold
Schaefer, Jack
Smith, Martin Cruz
Stone, Robert
Theroux, Paul
Wambaugh, Joseph
West, Morris
Westlake, Donald
Wouk, Herman

Detective/Mystery
Anderson, Poul
Block, Lawrence
Buell, John
Chandler, Raymond
Cross, Amanda
Derleth, August
Francis, Dick
Gardner, Erle Stanley
Grimes, Martha

Halliday, Brett
Hansen, Joseph
Himes, Chester
Isaacs, Susan
James, P.D.
Lathen, Emma
Leonard, Elmore
MacDonald, John D.
Macdonald, Ross
Morse, Larry Alan
Parker, Robert B.
Queen, Ellery
Spillane, Mickey
Stout, Rex
Wambaugh, Joseph

Experimental
Brautigan, Richard
Ellis, Bret Easton
Kerouac, Jack
Nin, Anais
Thompson, Hunter
Wolfe, Tom

Fantasy
Adams, Richard
Anderson, Poul
Bach, Richard
Berger, Thomas
Blatty, William Peter
Bradbury, Ray
Bradley, Marion Zimmer
Charnas, Suzy McKee
Derleth, August
Ellison, Harlan
Farmer, Philip José
Finney, Jack
Hoban, Russell
King, Stephen
Kinsella, W.P.
Kotzwinkle, William

Kurtz, Katherine
L'Engle, Madeleine
Le Guin, Ursula K.
Leiber, Fritz
McKillip, Patricia
Miller, Henry
Rice, Anne
Russ, Joanna
Schmitz, James H.
Smith, Martin Cruz
Stewart, Mary
Tryon, Thomas
Yarbro, Chelsea Quinn
Zelazny, Roger

Historical

Buckley, William F.
Caldwell, Taylor
Clavell, James
Derleth, August
Doctorow, E.L.
Fast, Howard Melvin
Follett, Ken
Fowles, John
Fraser, Antonia
Gann, Ernest K.
Greeley, Andrew
Haley, Alex
Herr, Michael
Malamud, Bernard
McMurtry, Larry
Michener, James
Oates, Joyce Carol
Renault, Mary
Schaefer, Jack
Settle, Mary Lee
Stewart, Mary
Stone, Irving
Styron, William
Uris, Leon
Vidal, Gore
Wouk, Herman
Yarbro, Chelsea Quinn
Yerby, Frank

Humor

Allen, Woody
Berger, Thomas
Blume, Judy
Brautigan, Richard
Cross, Amanda
DeLillo, Don
Herriot, James
Irving, John
Keillor, Garrison
Kesey, Ken
Kotzwinkle, William
Lurie, Alison
McGuane, Thomas
McInerney, Jay
Miller, Henry
Morse, Larry Alan
Portis, Charles
Robbins, Tom
Roth, Philip
Salinger, J.D.
Southern, Terry
Theroux, Paul
Tyler, Anne
Vanderhaeghe, Guy
Vonnegut, Kurt
Wambaugh, Joseph
Westlake, Donald

Mainstream

Adams, Alice
Alther, Lisa
Angelou, Maya
Atwood, Margaret
Bach, Richard
Baldwin, James
Beattie, Ann
Berger, Thomas
Blume, Judy
Brown, Rita Mae
Buell, John
Cain, James M.
Carver, Raymond
Cheever, John

Clavell, James
Collins, Jackie
Condon, Richard
Cozzens, James Gould
Dickey, James
Didion, Joan
Doctorow, E.L.
Ellison, Ralph Waldo
Erdrich, Louise
Exley, Frederick
French, Marilyn
Gann, Ernest K.
Gardner, John
Gilchrist, Ellen
Godwin, Gail
Goldman, William
Gordon, Mary
Greeley, Andrew
Guest, Judith
Hailey, Arthur
Harper, (Nelle) Lee
Herlihy, James Leo
Herriot, James
Higgins, George V.
Irving, John
Isaacs, Susan
Jaffe, Rona
Johnson, Diane
Jones, James
Jong, Erica
Kennedy, William
Kesey, Ken
Kinsella, W.P.
Klein, Norma
Lurie, Alison
Malamud, Bernard
Matthiessen, Peter
McCarthy, Mary
McCullers, Carson
McCullough, Colleen
McGuane, Thomas
McMurtry, Larry
Metalious, Grace

Morrison, Toni
O'Connor, Flannery
Orwell, George
Piercy, Marge
Portis, Charles
Potok, Chaim
Puzo, Mario
Robbins, Harold
Rossner, Judith
Roth, Philip
Salinger, J.D.
Settle, Mary Lee
Smith, Betty
Spencer, Scott
Stone, Irving
Stone, Robert
Styron, William
Susann, Jacqueline
Tryon, Thomas
Tyler, Anne
Updike, John
Vanderhaeghe, Guy
Vidal, Gore
Walker, Alice
Wallace, Irving
Wambaugh, Joseph
West, Morris
Wouk, Herman
Yerby, Frank

Romance
Fowles, John
Jaffe, Rona
Kotzwinkle, William
Krantz, Judith
McCullough, Colleen
McKillip, Patricia
Miller, Henry
Oates, Joyce Carol
Plain, Belva
Puzo, Mario
Segal, Erich
Steel, Danielle

Stewart, Mary
Styron, William
Yarbro, Chelsea Quinn

Satire

Cheever, John
DeLillo, Don
Disch, Thomas, M.
Heller, Joseph
McInerney, Jay
Orwell, George
Roth, Philip
Southern, Terry
Theroux, Paul
Vanderhaeghe, Guy
Vidal, Gore
Vonnegut, Kurt

Science Fiction

Anderson, Poul
Asimov, Isaac
Benford, Gregory
Bester, Alfred
Bradbury, Ray
Bradley, Marion Zimmer
Charnas, Suzy McKee
Cherryh, C.J.
Dick, Philip K.
Disch, Thomas M.
Ellison, Harlan

Farmer, Philip José
Finney, Jack
Heinlein, Robert A.
Herbert, Frank
Hoban, Russell
Kotzwinkle, William
L'Engle, Madeleine
Le Guin, Ursula K.
Leiber, Fritz
McCaffrey, Anne
Miller, Walter M., Jr.
Niven, Larry
Russ, Joanna
Schmitz, James H.
Vonnegut, Kurt
Yarbro, Chelsea Quinn
Zelazny, Roger

Spy/Thriller

Block, Lawrence
Buckley, William F.
Clancy, Thomas L., Jr.
Follett, Ken
Goldman, William
le Carré, John
Ludlum, Robert
Smith, Martin Cruz
Westlake, Donald

INDEX